A Pirate's Tale

for

Ronnie Hulley

Welcome aboard, matey
Bon voyage. Aargh!!

Gertjan

March 06, 2009

Gertjan Zwiggelaar

apiratestale.com

PublishAmerica
Baltimore

PublishAmerica has allowed this work to remain exactly as the author intended, verbatim, without editorial input.

ISBN: 1-60563-960-5
PUBLISHED BY PUBLISHAMERICA, LLLP
www.publishamerica.com
Baltimore

Printed in the United States of America

Dedicated to my Father and Mother
For all they have done for me.
Without them this
book would not be here.

Foreword

A few years ago, my son Michael and I were looking in a computer store for a new game to play. We found a copy of *Patrician II* by the wonderful British game maker, Ascaron, and distributed by Strategy First. This game quickly became a favorite of both father and son. Eventually, as we played, the idea came to me to write a pirate novel entertaining some of the ideas presented by the game. Albeit the game is set in the 15th Century, during the Hansiatic League, my story bridges two centuries, the 18th and 19th, and takes place in a different part of the world. However, lots of ideas regarding how pirates might have plied their sweet trade came from the game, hence I thank the makers of *Patrician* for the inspiration which led up to this book.

Piracy has been a phenomenon I have been long interested in. People who have nothing often covet that which the rich possess. Albeit people are taught to be content with their lot, it is not an easy thing to see people living off the backs of others; indeed some of those wealthy people, the aristocracies and business leaders, literally beat their fellow creatures into submission through all manner of spurious laws and regulations governing the behavior of those who are not members of the elite. Against that sort of oppression, piracy is perhaps the only option to get back what is rightfully belonging to everyone; that being the planet's wealth. Indeed, if one believes that God is in us and we are in God, and that God is All Abundance, then abundance is our right. Piracy is a way of establishing that right, through force, if necessary.

When the king steals it is called, *taxation*. When we steal from him it is called, *theft*. When the king murders hundreds of thousands of innocent people it is called, *war*. When we do it, it is *mass murder*. When the state abducts people and sticks them in cells it is called, *justice*. When ordinary people do it, it is called, *kidnapping*. And so on. Piracy, like guerilla warfare, or underground warfare, occurs in places where people are oppressed by some crown, or other oppressor, and seek to get their own back. Piracy, in light of the arbitrary poverty imposed by the elite on the majority of humanity, is a reasonable response, I think. Until everyone shares in the abundance the universe provides, there will always be pirates.

Special thanks to my daughter, Carey Annbrie for helping with preliminary editing. Her finely tuned reading revealed some errors which I was able to correct before sending the manuscript. Thanks to my son, Michael, for pointing out a few things, here and there, as well. Thanks to my daughter, Tereigh Danielle, for encouragement and continued faith in her dad. Thanks to Karen Hillier for help with my French.

Thanks also go out to the excellent staff of PublishAmerica for helping to bring this book to fruition. Jim Schruefer and Catherine Martin for having enough faith in my work to acquire the manuscript for publication. Thanks to Jeannette Gartrell for her assistance with pre-production. And a big thank you to Jaime Polychrones who helped with the final text editing. Thank you, PublishAmerica, for making a dream come true.

Chapter One

Rain.

I should have expected it. It was March. What else can you expect in Halifax in March? Rain or snow. And more rain or snow. That is what I should have expected. I saw the clouds. Oh, well, c'est la vie. I got wet.

Was it worth it? I certainly think it was worth it. Whether you think so, well, it is your prerogative what you think. Me, I got wet that rainy day in Halifax in order to get to the jail, before the authorities hanged the man whose story came to involve me in more ways than I ever imagined. If I had run back to my rooming house, to get my rain slicker, I might not have had the chance to interview him. Where pirates are concerned the authorities could sometimes act very quickly. I was only recently appraised of his capture and jailing while enjoying a pint with my friends, Stacey and Stuart. In spite of the clouds, I did not think they threatened rain when I left my rooming house.

The pirate was facing a hanging at the harbour entrance. That is what Stuart told me. When Stuart mentioned the condemned man's name I immediately excused myself. There was just no way I was going to miss interviewing Captain William Bartleby, the notorious pirate. He apparently plundered and sank seven English merchantmen in the Caribbean, in one year alone. He was the most feared pirate on the Seven Seas, so the stories went. I wanted to hear the man's story for myself because I am a writer, and pirates interested me.

So, I slurped down the rest of my pint; I wasn't going to waste a good pint of bitters, and rushed off into the rain, without an umbrella, without my rain slicker, to the jail to interview the man whose story I am about to tell you. However, before I do, let me fill you in on what happened when I got to the jail. That part is also of interest. I mean, it is not easy getting into jail when you haven't done anything except write articles for the Morning Post.

The last time I tried to interview a pirate I was told to, 'Piss off.'

This was by the pirate.

He was hanged that very afternoon.

I watched him swing. I did not feel any sympathy for him. Maybe he shouldn't have told me to, 'Piss off.' I guess I am sensitive that way. It runs in the family. My mother didn't like it when my father said it, either.

Anyway, when I got to the jail, quite dripping wet; my boots muddy, the guards laughed at me when I tried to explain that I had come to interview William Bartleby, the famous pirate.

'Whadda ya wan a inerfew dat pirate fer? He don deserve a inerfew. He's a bloody pirate, fer Chrys sake,' said the one guard, a short, pudgy man, with a bulbous nose and fat lips.

The other guard looked nervously about. Then he looked at his colleague and told him that he had better watch his blaspheming or he could end up in trouble.

The blasphemer didn't seem to care too much about his blaspheming, shrugging his shoulders.

I repeated my request to be allowed to interview Captain Bartleby.

The guards looked at me with smirks on their faces.

I had to ask them once more, this time with the price of two pints of ale in my hand.

The blasphemer looked around, to see if anyone was watching. When he ascertained no one was, he took the coin and smiled at his partner.

The two guards stood aside and let me enter the building. I noticed that they were already licking their lips, as they looked forward to the pints after work.

Inside the jail, as I well knew from previous visits, was the entrance lobby, on the left of which stood a table; behind which sat, Corporal McFee.

The corporal eyed me as I stepped into the lobby. His face was in its usual ugly scowl mode. Sometimes I wondered if perhaps Corporal McFee had been hit with an ugly stick and his face was permanently disfigured into a scowl. I can't remember ever not seeing his face screwed up thusly.

'You here to interview the pirate?' he sneered.

'I'm not here to interview you, McFee,' I replied.

'It's going to cost you. Pirate stories don't come cheap,' he said.

'This is a public gaol. How can you continue to get away with charging newspaper reporters to interview prisoners?' I glared at McFee, who remained unmoved, as usual. And, just as per usual, I never knew when to shut up, when it came to dealing with Corporal McFee. 'It is one of the ways prisoners have an opportunity to be heard by the community,' I told him.

Corporal McFee laughed. 'Pirates don't need to be heard. They're the scum of the sea. This one is the collective scum of all the seas. He don't deserve an interview.'

I am sure my shoulders must have sagged, as I felt in my pocket for the few coins I had with me. McFee's prices were always considerably higher than any of the other officials in the jail. It was just my luck to find him on duty that day.

I didn't want to argue with the man and paid him with the thropence I had been saving for an other occasion. I sighed as I gave them to him, but it had no effect. McFee could have cared less what my plans for the coins were. He greedily put the coins into his purse and jingled it in front of me. Obviously he had already been carrying on a steady trade, that day, in his favorite hobby, coin collecting.

McFee sneered at me and called a guard. He told the man to take me to the pirate's cell.

On the way the guard also tried to extract a coin from me, however I managed to deflect him by telling the guard I had no more coins left; the corporal and the entrance guards having taken the lot. The guard accepted my answer without an argument. He just sighed. He probably had come to accept the fact that most of the fleecing was done up front. He being a guard inside the jail, was on the bottom of the receiving line.

It was a grim situation for a mere jail guard in Halifax in this, so called, 'enlightened century.'

A bit of extortion was necessary just to make ends meet. The guard probably had a missus and some kids, I reckoned. However, I didn't know him. I didn't care. Jail guards are not my favorite people. Whether he made any extra money, or not, was not my concern. All that I was concerned with, regarding the guard, was that he not get any of my money. I had paid enough. The skinflint, who owned the paper, wouldn't reimburse me anyway. Sometimes a writer has to pay for his research, it is the way it is. There is no free lunch. I just wanted to avoid paying more than I had to.

So, anyway, the guard took me down into the lowest level of the jail; into what one would call, the dungeon; a dank, dark, cold place. I never liked going down there. It gave me the creeps. I prayed I would never end up down there. It was not a fit place for a human being.

Whether anyone was ever tortured there, that I couldn't say. However, judging from the appearance of the place, and the faces of some of the jailers, I would say there was a distinct possibility.

So, I asked the guard, point blank, whether anyone had been tortured down there.

He just grunted, like they all did when I asked any of the guards about it. I guess the authorities didn't want people to know about it and just pretended it didn't happen. That was my suspicion.

When we arrived at the pirate's cell I was quite surprised to see him standing, waiting for my arrival. (He must have heard our footsteps). All of the other pirates I had interviewed had remained lying down on the cot against the far wall. The gentlemanly courtesy, of standing to greet a guest, was lost on most pirates.

I was further surprised by his appearance. Instead of a greasy, long haired, ear ringed, peg-legged, and hook handed pirate captain, with an eye patch, I found a tall, handsome, well groomed, bearded gentleman with both of his legs and hands intact; one of which was extended through the bars of his cage to welcome me.

'Company at last,' he said, a big grin on his face.

The guard told the pirate to stick his hand back into the cell or he would chop it off with his short sword.

The pirate told the guard what to do with his short sword in a most peculiar and quite humorous fashion.

Even the guard found it funny and repeated the phrase. Then he said that he would have to try it on Corporal McFee.

I warned the guard he had better not, if he knew what was good for him.

The guard just shrugged his shoulders and sauntered off, repeating the pirate's suggestion regarding what could be done with the short sword. The joke warmed me to William Bartleby right away. I like a pirate with a sense of humor.

'Peter Mann,' I said, extending my hand.

The pirate took my hand and we exchanged a warm handshake. 'Call me, Bill,' he said.

The pirate's hand was strong, and somewhat larger than my own. I had the distinct feeling that if he had wanted to, he could have crushed every bone of my right hand with an effortless squeeze. I got the impression that William Bartleby was incredibly strong. He certainly was stronger than this quill pusher, there was no doubt about that.

I have only shaken the hand of one other pirate, and I remember his hand being small, wet, and lacking any conviction or strength. Perhaps the fact he was about to be hanged, might have had something to do with it. But, to my way of thinking, there is no excuse for a limp, wet handed handshake. Well, actually it was to my father's way of thinking. He drilled the idea into me. I guess it stuck. My dad had been a sergeant in the Royal Marines. 'A firm handshake is the mark of a man,' he had said, on more than one occasion. Bill's handshake would have impressed my old man.

'You're all wet,' is the next thing he said to me.

'Yes, it's raining,' I replied, for want of something better to say.

'Why didn't you wear your rain slicker?' he asked puzzled, like an old friend wondering if you're daft or not.

I explained that I had gone for a pint with friends, not far from where I lived. I told him I had planned to stay drinking with my friends and had not really thought about rain, when I had stepped out.

'You're mad to go out without a rain slicker in Halifax, in March,' he said.

'The winter's nearly over,' I countered.

'It's only March,' he replied.

'It didn't rain yesterday,' I said.

'It was a fluke,' laughed the pirate as he stepped over to his cot. 'It was a bloody fluke. You know it always rains or snows here at this time of year.'

I nodded my head. 'Yeah, I know. I guess I was just being optimistic. I don't like winter and want it to go away. When it didn't rain yesterday, I was hoping spring was here. So, I went out in this sweater and these corduroy trousers, with my heavy hose. As you can see, my hat is large enough to keep most of the rain off.'

Bill looked at my hat and laughed. 'You call that a hat?'

I looked at my hat and shrugged my shoulders.

'I had a hat, with a brim which was much better than an umbrella. It totally protected me, like a roof. It was red velvet, with a gold braid and a magnificent peacock feather from Madagascar. I plucked it out of the bird myself.' Bill smiled, a glint in his eye. 'He was most indignant for my removing it,' he chuckled. 'His indignation did not last long. We ate him shortly there after. Tough old bird, though. Cookie did his best to cook the cock, but it was to no avail. We should have grabbed the hen. I understand a peahen is probably much more tender'. William looked at me and grinned lasciviously. 'Like all things female, eh, Peter?' he said.

William stared into space for a moment and sighed. 'I miss my little senorita in Hispaniola. Now there is a tender little woman for you. Skin like creamy chocolate. Hair like black coal, with eyes to match, except that hers are on fire.'

I watched as Bill paused to reflect upon his lady in New Spain. It gave me a chance to look the man over.

William Bartleby was tall, well over six feet, and lanky. His hair was cut short and his face was probably, normally, clean shaven, except there in jail. He already had a couple of week's growth, or so. His hair was blond. He was wearing green velvet breeches, with torn, dirty hose and black shoes. His white shirt was torn and dirty. It looked like he had been manhandled by the guards. I commented on my observation and he told me that his shirt was torn when he tried to resist a soldier in Lunenburg.

I asked him if he had any objection to me interviewing him. He replied that he would be honored. So, I looked around for something to sit on. I noticed one of the cell doors, several cells down the corridor, was open. I stepped over to it and peered into the little room. Lucky for me, there was a small, three legged stool inside. I picked it up and carried it back to the captain's cell and set it down beside the bars. Then I plunked myself on the stool and faced the pirate, who was lying on the cot.

'So, who in the blue blazes are you, anyway, Peter Mann? Do I know you? Do you know me? What brings you here? Are you here to gawk at a condemned man? You're not a priest in disguise are you? I mean if you are…by Gawd I will tell you to piss off right now'. Bill rolled onto his side and regarded me intensely. 'You're not one of those new protestant lay preachers, are you? I know some of them dress differently than most men of the cloth. Why didn't you bring your rain slicker? Doesn't it bother you to be wet like that?

William's questions came lightning fast. He shot them out at me like gun fire.

I told him that I was a writer for the Morning Post and that I was interested in pirates and their stories, and so was the newspaper, I lied.

Bill eyed me suspiciously.

I further told him about my plans for a book about pirates and told Bill some names of pirates whom I had interviewed before they were hanged; Bony Jane, John Racker, and Bartholomew Robson.

Bill knew one of the pirates personally. He was sad to hear the woman had been hanged. Then he asked me again why I didn't go home to pick up my rain slicker; reminding me I could catch my death, being wet like that in a cold, dank place like the dungeon.

I told Bill that I had come in a hurry, fearing that he would be hanged before I had a chance to see him.

Bill laughed when I expressed fear he would be hanged right away.

'They haven't hung me, so far. Why, they've had me for near a month. Held me in Lunenburg up till a few days ago, when they finally brought me here.' Bill looked about his cell. 'Definitely this place is far worse. I didn't mind the Lunenburg cell.' He smiled broadly and chuckled, 'They're not about to hang me yet. Chances are they will take me back to London and try me there. They sent word of my capture to London two days after I arrived in gaol. Even though Halifax is a busy port, and my body hanging from the gibbet is a good warning to lots of sailors, you have to remember, I am not an ordinary privateer. I am Captain William Bartleby. I am not some smuck pirate. The King will be very interested in seeing me personally hanging from a gibbet at Wapping. They only brought me here three days ago, as I said. That is why I look as good as I do. If I am any judge of character, I fully expect to be maltreated by the scum in this gaol.' He gestured in the direction where the guards were. 'But, they can't kill me here. So, until they arrange for my transfer, I think I will be dependent on this gaol's hospitality, meagre as it is. So, I fully expect to live for some weeks, or possibly months here in Halifax.'

I was glad to hear the news of his having to accept Halifax's hospitality for a while. It gave me the opportunity of doing a thorough job interviewing an important pirate. I could go home and fetch my notebook, quills and ink. The opportunity of a lifetime presented itself to me. The opportunity to interview so important a pirate as William Bartleby, was something not to be missed. I told him that, seeing as how he was not going to be hanged until he was brought to London, I would have time to go home, get dried off, put on my rain gear and bring my notebook etcetera. I also told him I would bring some food and wine.

Bill was pleased to hear that I was interested in his story, and that I would see to his needs, in a better fashion than he could expect from the jail. We shook hands and I hurried out of the place to fetch my stuff.

On the way out, Corporal McFee reminded me that it would cost money to get back in.

I told him he should be the one behind bars.

McFee didn't like that. He shouted behind my back that the price of entry had just doubled.

When I got home I was drenched and cold. I immediately got out of my wet clothes and dried off with my big, warm towel. However, since I had been drenched, I was still cold inside. Fortunately Missus Findlay had hot water on the stove in the kitchen. She made me a hot cocoa with cream and sugar. This was not only very warming, but also very delicious. Missus Findlay was always so nice to me; like a mother, really. I was grateful for her and never complained about the room and board she charged, it being slightly higher than elsewhere.

When I was sufficiently warmed up I obtained a loaf of rye bread, a hunk of cheese, some green onions, and a bottle of wine, to take to the pirate. I gathered up enough food and wine to enable me to spend as many hours with the pirate, as time would allow. I was so convinced that the pirate's tale would be of great interest, that I was certain I would get hungry at some point in his telling. Perhaps there might be enough in his tale alone, to form the contents of a book. A man of William Bartleby's stature doesn't get there without an interesting story line unfolding along the way. In my opinion, at the time, his story would make a good book.

Anyway, I gathered up everything into my leather bag. I also remembered to take some coins from my stash behind my book case. I quickly left the rooming house and hurried in the direction of the jail.

The streets were muddy from the rain. As horses clopped past, I had to be careful not to be splashed by their hooves pounding into a puddle, or from the wheels of the conveyance which followed. There was no sense in getting my dry clothes wet and muddy. I didn't have many changes of clothing. Missus Findlay only did laundry once a week. And it cost extra.

When I returned to the jail, I was nice and dry under my umbrella and rain slicker.

The guards were surprised to see me.

'Whada ya wan, dis time?' asked the blasphemer.

I told him I had come to interview Captain Bartleby.

The guards looked at each other and burst out laughing.

The other guard told me that Corporal McFee had ordered no more visitations for the rest of the day. If I wanted to talk with the pirate, I would have to come back tomorrow.

I wasn't surprised to hear the news. McFee had done it before. He was probably up to something with the prisoners, which he didn't want visitors to see. I was not surprised. People of his race seemed to be like that, it seemed. I had met some others like him, and they were schemers and thieves, as well. I get the distinct impression it is in their blood. Needless to say, I did not leave the food. I knew it would never get past the guards and corporal McFee.

So I had to go back to my lodgings and give up on William Bartleby that day. It was unfortunate because the following day would be Sunday. I was committed to helping with the church picnic. The day after would be Monday and I had to work most of the day. Whether I would have much time after work depended on the discretion of the jailer in charge. If it was McFee, I was out of luck.

Whether I could interview the pirate during the work day entirely depended on the editor. To get his permission always took some doing. He hated pirates. Although, I did feel somewhat confident that a pirate, like William Bartleby, would attract Mister Burnett's attention.

I was wrong.

When I approached Mister Burnett with the idea of giving me time to interview William Bartleby he said he wasn't interested. He felt the paper had been giving too many columns to pirate's tales and that the press was giving the pirates much too much attention. Since we only printed two pages per day, there were too many other things which needed to be printed, like advertisements and announcements.

I reminded him that people liked reading about pirates. Whenever there was a pirate to be hanged, the paper's stories about him were eagerly read.

Mister Burnett shrugged his shoulders and told me that if I was interested in the pirate, I had to interview him on my own time, not the newspaper's. Then he sent me off to interview some old ladies who were planning to hold a bake sale.

Being a junior reporter had its drawbacks. I just prayed Mister Burnett didn't assign William Bartleby to another reporter.

After I finished work, that Monday, I ran home and gathered up another load of food and another bottle of wine, along with my notebook, quills, and ink.

It was five o'clock when I again stood before the guards. There were two other guards standing in front of the guard houses. When I requested entrance into the jail I was surprised to be let in right away, without charge.

'You look surprised,' sneered Corporal McFee, as I stepped into the lobby.

'I didn't expect to get in so easily,' I told him.

McFee laughed. 'I have issued orders that the guards are, under no circumstances, to extort money from prisoners and visitors.'

I stared at McFee and raised an eyebrow.

McFee laughed. 'That way, any extortion that goes on in this gaol, is under my direct supervision and control.' McFee laughed louder, and jingled the bag of money on his desk. Then he leaned forward and eyed me coldly. 'If you breathe one word of this in the newspaper, I promise you this, you would live just long enough to regret it.'

I stared at McFee for a moment, but realized it would not do me any good to argue. I asked him how much a visit with the pirate was going to cost me.

The price had gone up, but I had come prepared. The money which I would have had to pay the guards, plus McFee's charges, was now incorporated into one fee, the equivalent of five pints of ale. I handed McFee the coins he wanted. Then I walked off with a guard who looked a whole lot like a bull mastiff.

When I arrived in the dungeon, Captain Bartleby was standing, as before. He smiled when he was able to see my face in the light of the torch the dog faced guard was holding.

'Back, at last. It is good to see you, Peter. I was wondering if you would come back to see me. The guards here aren't exactly company for a learned man, like myself. They haven't got much to grunt about, do they?' Bill directed his voice towards the guard, who was lighting the torch on the wall. He continued in a sweet voice, 'You canine visaged cretin, your cranium couldn't contain a grain of rice, could it?'

The guard grunted, not understanding what the pirate was talking about. He shuffled off, back to the guard station, leaving me alone with the pirate.

First thing we did was exchange a warm handshake and pleasantries about seeing each other, and that sort of social stuff. Then I handed him the food, for which he was immensely grateful. I found the three legged stool, and then he and I shared the food and wine, as he began his tale; the one I am about to tell you.

I am writing this tale in the first person, in order to attempt to convey to you, as close as possible, what Captain William Bartleby told me, and what I experienced since meeting him on that fateful day in March, 1775.

Chapter Two

I began life as a baby,' laughed Captain Bartleby.

I looked at him and saw the merriment in his eyes. 'Doesn't everyone?' I replied.

'Of course, that is the point,' he said. 'We all start out the same way. What makes me so different from you, for example?'

'I wasn't born in London,' I replied.

'Neither was I,' he retorted. 'I was born in Liverpool. I was born into poverty November 21, 1736. My mum had eight kids. I was the oldest. My father was a chimney sweep. They did the best they could, but life was hard. What more can I say about that? The one thing which saved us was the fact that my mum could read. She taught us kids to read and to write. If it wasn't for her, there would not have been books in the house, besides the Bible.'

William bit off a piece of bread and chewed it thoughtfully for a moment, as I wrote in my shorthand what he had said to me. When I lifted my head, signifying I was done, he continued.

'When I was eight, things changed for me and determined the course of the rest of my life. My vocation was thrust upon me, out of the blue, when I wasn't expecting it. My father is the one who informed me. He simply told me, one day, while we were having our meagre dinner of leek soup, with bits of pork scrapings, and my mother's rye bread. 'Son,' he said, 'You are old enough to go out and work. I've found you a place with the merchant Stevenson, in Manchester. He needs a boy to help around his shop. We leave in the morning.'

That is all he said.

Next morning I had to say good bye to my mum and my brothers and sisters. I was very shook up. Imagine, being torn from your family at eight years of age.

Anyway, we left the next morning, and before I knew it, I was in a strange city and in the employ of Mister Stevenson, who turned out to be a kind, but stern master. He was a seller of spices, rich cloth, unusual trinkets, jewels, jewelry, gold, silver, and all sorts of other exotic things; food stuffs I had never seen before. How my father ever managed to get me into the employment of Mister Stevenson, is something he never told me. To this day I don't know. Perhaps he cleaned his chimney one time. It is one of the mysteries in my life.'

At this point I remember the pirate drank a long sip of wine and sat still for a while, pondering his past. I was writing like mad. My fingers were becoming quite stained from ink, already. I tend to do that, whenever I am writing. I get ink all over my hands, it seems. I wish there was some other sort of dispenser of ink, than a quill. Perhaps ink should be put in a tube, or something. I don't know. I'm sure someone will invent something, eventually.

When Captain Bartleby had thought for a while, he continued his story.

'My work at Mister Stevenson's shop consisted, at first, of sweeping floors, dusting, helping people carry things out of the shop to their carriages, cleaning windows, unloading packing crates… That was always exciting. I loved it when new packing crates came in, which was usually after Mister Stevenson had been away for two months or more. He usually traveled in the winter months. He didn't like to stay in Manchester during the winter. It was too cold for his tastes. That is what he told me.

Missus Stevenson was a cruel witch of a woman, who used to beat me with a belt for missing spots on the windows, or for forgetting some little thing, or other. I tried to tell Mister Stevenson about it, but he never believed that his wife was capable of such behavior. She was so sweet and loving to her own son; a spoiled, vindictive little demon, who got me into lots of trouble with his mother. One time she shut me up under the stairs for a week, with only bread and water. I still have scars from where she beat me. The ill treatment was probably good for me because it toughened me up and prepared me for what eventually came my way, thanks to my father sending me to Mister Stevenson. I've forgiven him long ago, but it sure cost me a lot of blood.'

I cringed at the thought of young William being beaten blue by a cruel matron. Compared to what Bill had experienced as a child, my childhood was a heavenly affair. I commented on this. He just sighed and nodded his head as he replied that I was fortunate, and should always thank God for having been given good and loving parents, who could afford to keep me. I agreed with him as we both reflected, for a moment, on our parents. Mine were dead. He had no idea where his parents were.

It was at this point I calculated his age, which turned out to be thirty eight; a full thirteen years, and a whole lifetime older than me. I reflected on that and he smiled. 'Aye a whole lifetime...,' he said. Then suddenly he asked me if I had ever killed a man.

Of course I had never killed a man, at that point in my life. It had never even crossed my mind, to kill somebody.

When he heard my answer, he nodded. 'Indeed, we're a whole lifetime apart, you and me. I have no idea how many men I have killed. Probably a couple of dozen, at least. And then a few hundred more, I suppose, during raids on the ships of England.'

I asked him why he had such a hatred for England.

His eyes became fire as he stared at me, lifting his shirt.

'Because of these!' He said it with such vehemence that it surprised me, however, looking at the numerous scars on his body, I could understand why he would be angry. The scars of lashings are never a pretty sight. He had quite a number of them.

I asked him how long he had been in the employ of Mister Stevenson.

'Until I was twelve. That is when my circumstances changed again, in a drastic fashion. Those circumstances resulted in the scars on my back.

You see, as I grew older, I began to grow a very good relationship with Mister Stevenson. When he was home, I was not beaten by his witch. Mister Stevenson liked me.

When I was eleven, he took me along on one of his winter trips, on board his merchantman, which he and his partner, Mister Thurgood, owned. The ship was called, *Venture*. It was on this trip that I learned how Mister Stevenson acquired the things he sold in his shop. Mister Stevenson was a pirate during the winter months; in the Caribbean or Mediterranean Seas. He plundered indiscriminately, any merchantmen that he could find. When he and his men were lucky, the take was very lucrative. Mister Stevenson and Thurgood had a knack for picking the right ships.'

I asked Bill how Mister Stevenson managed to get away with piracy for so long.

'He changed the name of his ship each time, when he was out at sea; out of sight of anyone. It was then that he hoisted the Jolly Roger. I learned a lot from him. Of course, at the time, I was not really interested in becoming a pirate. I was just a little kid. I was only eleven, for goodness sake.'

I noted the pirate's lack of blasphemy. That was unusual in a pirate, I thought. But, then, what do I know. I have only interviewed ten pirates in total. One out of ten who doesn't blaspheme, in my limited experience, is not enough to establish a statistic. When I commented on it, he replied that it is a sin to take the Lord's name in vain and simply left it at that. It was a given as far as he was concerned.

'So, anyway,' he continued, 'There I was, eleven years old, on a pirate ship, floating about in the Caribbean. I had no idea that is what I would be doing, when we set out. Unfortunately, Misters Stevenson and Thurgood had no idea that they would run into an English man o' war during that particular winter's trip. We were lucky the man o' war didn't sink us. We were in shark infested waters at the time. The English navy captured us and took us, and our cargo, on board. Then they scuttled Mister Stevenson's ship.

We were all put in shackles in the forecastle. They whipped a few of us during the trip to England. They hung five pirates in front of the ship's company and us. The captain figured that England would understand that a few pirates would have been killed in the process of capture. The bodies were used for shark trolling. The navy officers found that to be a marvelous sport. One of Mister Thurgood's sons was left to hang in a fore yard arm, as a trophy. I noticed that it made Mister Thurgood very sad, every time he was allowed up on deck for air and exercise, under the watchful eyes of the Royal Marines.'

I commented on the fact that my father had been a Royal Marine.

Bartleby frowned and said he was sorry to hear it, but that he wouldn't hold it against me as he continued with his story.

'When we got back to London, we were all tried for piracy. Everyone was hung, but me. The judge took pity on me because of my circumstances and age.

So, I was sentenced to impressment into the Royal Navy and was assigned to the ship from hell on my twelfth birthday. His Majesty's Ship, *Pluto*, under the command of Captain Jamison. That was my first ship. It was just my luck that the captain was a tyrant. How he ever came to represent the British Navy was beyond me. I was later to find that he was a saint compared to Diablo himself, Captain Blight, under whom I served for two years, prior to becoming a pirate at the tender age of nineteen.'

At this point Bill took a long drink from the bottle. It was obvious to me that his experience in the navy had been a very unpleasant time.

'I hated the navy,' is how he put it.

I can't say I blamed him, judging from the scars. They were an ugly map of roads and canals; a testament to state inflicted inhumanity. He saw me wince when I looked at them.

'You never seen anything like it, have you?' he said.

'I have seen a pirate flogged, but I've never seen the end results,' I answered. 'I think flogging is barbarous,' I added.

'Aye, barbarous,' he spat. 'Here we are in the 18th Century and we still flog people like the ancient Romans did. We think we are so civilized.' He shook his head sadly. 'We are not as civilized as we think. People are still being burned at the stake, in some remote corners. Maybe, as we speak, some poor woman is being burned for having special knowledge about herbs and mushrooms. Maybe she has a black cat.'

Bill began to pace.

'I knew a young woman, when I was about twenty four or five. She was beautiful. Long blond hair, down to her waist. Big blue eyes, with the voice of an angel. She lived in Scotland; in Edinburgh.

Anyway, she was so like an angel, in every way. Her mother had taught

23

her about the healing arts. Eventually this angel became very good at healing. Lots of people came to her and received great benefit from their visits.

Karen attracted the attention of certain clergy members, who were friends with the heads of the medical establishment. Eventually they trumped up charges of witchcraft against her. They had her stripped naked. Then they horribly tortured her with thumb and toe screws!'

Bill stared at me; his voice breaking. 'Those twisted bastards tortured her on three separate occasions. Of course she confessed to every leading question they put to her. Wouldn't you, under the circumstances? Think of it. The last digits of her toes and fingers were crushed. She couldn't use her hands properly anymore, after the first time. They let her alone for a month and then did it again. After the second time she couldn't walk anymore. When they were done, a third time, some months later, she was completely crippled.'

Bill's eyes were wild, like a hunted animal. He grabbed for the bottle and took a long drink before continuing with his story.

'A couple of more months went by, in which she lived in extreme pain, and suffered horribly. They finally came to get her and burned her alive. They burned that lovely girl, one afternoon, on the commons outside of the city.'

I noticed, in the dim light of the torch, the pirate had tears in his eyes. His voice wavered, as he continued the story. Hardened as he might have become, as a pirate, he was obviously a sympathetic man. The witch burning incident had affected him in a powerful way. He had to pause for some time to collect himself. Then he came over and took another long sip from the bottle. I watched him as he went back to sit on the edge of the cot, his head in his hands. I believe that moment was probably the saddest in the pirate's tale.

It took Bill quite a while before he spoke again.

I have a way of doing that. I bring things out of people. I guess that is why I am a reporter. People tell me things. Sometimes the things they tell me dredge up all sorts of sordid memories. It is not the first time I have seen someone shook up over something they were telling me.

When Bill was sufficiently recovered, I had caught up with the writing, so it worked out very well, his pausing like that. Were I was concerned; as the person who had to write it all down, that is, when a story teller pauses to reflect, or whatever, that is something which we quill pushers appreciate. It is not easy writing everything down as people speak. Especially because we have to keep dipping our quills in an ink bottle. And, we have to keep those feathers sharpened. It is such a nuisance. Someone really ought to invent some sort of a tube filled with ink, with a metal nib, which stays sharp. I can't imagine why someone hasn't done it yet. I for one would buy such a pen.

'Have you ever seen anyone burned alive, Peter?' he said, just like that; startling me.

Of course I had to answer in the negative, and I am glad for that.

'She couldn't stop screaming. That is probably what I remember the most. Her screaming and screaming, as the flames first burned the skin off her legs and began to work on the bones. She was tied with chains to the stake, so that she could barely move. Even so, she writhed against the constraints of the chains, as she screamed and screamed; her face contorted into a horrible mask of excruciating pain; shrieking at the top of her lungs, until she couldn't scream anymore, on account of the smoke and the flames. The last I saw of her, before the pyre went up with an explosion of flame, when her fats dripped into the fire, was of her screaming, contorted face looking at me. It is something I shall never forget. It is the most horrific thing I have ever seen.'

A long pause followed. Neither one of us could say anything more for a long while. As I reflected on the image Bill had presented, I nearly vomited. Thinking of the girl, screaming in the flames, was something I hoped to never see in real life. I did not know what to say. The image Bill had related was horrific. The thought burned into my mind and stayed for a long while. After what seemed a long time of quiet, during which I wrote like mad, trying to capture the words, I finally asked, 'Was this girl related to you?'

'No. I just knew her. She healed some wounds. I had been in a skirmish with a naval officer, at a pub in Edinburgh. I never trusted physicians. I have always gone to healing women whenever I have had cuts and whatever. Karen's sister, who healed me, when I was very sick for a few weeks, some time later, was also burned at the stake. She apparently caused the flame of a candle to move. The fact that she had a black cat exacerbated the charges. Fortunately I was not in Edinburgh when they burned her. I heard about it some years later. It is a great tragedy of our times.'

William stepped over to the bars and reached for the wine bottle. It was at this point that a guard came stomping into the cell block.

'Pull your hand back into the cell!' he demanded. 'Or I will chop your hand off with this short sword.' He pulled the sword from its scabbard and wielded it menacingly.

Bill laughed. 'You guards and your short swords. You think those are swords? They're merely table cutlery. Compared to the sword I wielded, your so called sword is but a tooth pick.' Bill looked at the guard and gestured as if he was holding a big sword in his hand. 'Now, that was a sword. It could slice a man in half, from head to groin. D'you ever see a man sliced thusly?' Bill stared menacingly at the guard.

The man faltered in his bravado. He stood back and announced, 'Corporal McFee said it is time for you to leave.' He returned the little sword to its scabbard.

'What do you mean, it is time to leave? I just got here,' I replied.

'Corporal's orders.' The guard crossed his arms over his chest.

'I paid good money to come here,' I pleaded.

The guard just stood there and waited; his arms crossed over his chest.

I could see there was no dissuading the grunt. So, I made sure all of the food was inside the pirate's cell. The only thing we couldn't get through the bars of the cage was the wine bottle. Captain Bartleby drank most of it down, before the guard grabbed the bottle from his hand.

I knew there was no way I could have stopped the burly guard. He was built like a rhinoceros. His nose was upturned, which gave him a piggish look. The guard was definitely not one of his mother's most beautiful creations. I felt sorry for the poor brute. Life for the good looking was definitely easier, it seemed. Except for Captain Bartleby, of course. He was handsome, of that there was no doubt. But life had taken a turn for the worse, as far as he was concerned. There he was, in prison; facing a hanging in front of the King. I was certain there would be a lot of fashionable ladies present to watch such a handsome pirate meet the end of his rope.

The guard prodded me to leave.

I sighed and bid good bye to William Bartleby. Then I accompanied the grunt back to the lobby, where Corporal McFee had several other guests assembled.

'Why do I have to leave?' I asked. 'I've only been here an hour. I paid you the price of five pints.'

'Five pints? He charged me the equivalent of seven pints,' said a man to my right.

'You were here since two o'clock, Murphy, so quit your complaining,' McFee shot back.

Then, just to get under McFee's skin, I added, 'And besides, why do we have to pay you money to visit in a public gaol?'

The other people obviously felt the same way and immediately asked the same question.

McFee was taken off guard, but he covered himself admirably, I have to give the old bastard that. He was no mean pin head. His reply was that the money, the state spent on the prison, was not enough to ensure that the prisoners were adequately fed, clothed, and given blankets. 'The moneys, graciously given and thankfully received, are well used, believe me,' he said in his oily voice.

I'd heard it all before, of course. McFee knew it because he kept eyeing me, to see if I would say anything. But, I wanted to get home and review my notes. So, I just let it go and waited patiently for McFee to finish his lies, before he let us out.

When I stepped outside, it was drizzling. The temperature had dropped considerably. I felt chilled immediately and rushed home, like any poor creature would do, seeking warmth. Heat. Comfort.

Images of the screaming girl haunted my thoughts as I hurried through the rainy mist, a righteous indignation burning in the pit of my stomach as the screaming became louder, and the contorted face of the burning girl began to etch itself into my brain. As I rushed towards my rooming house, I began to wish I had not heard that story. Perhaps interviewing the pirate might prove to be too harrowing for me? Maybe the tale of the girl was not the worst of stories to come? Maybe William Bartleby had more horrific tales to tell? Little did I suspect that I would eventually experience pirate horror, first hand.

I resolved to harden myself, as best I could. If I was going to continue to interview a famous pirate, who has lived ten times the lives I had lived, I had better brace myself. Certainly the story of the burning girl is a tragedy. It is one of the tragedies of our times, and of those past. It is up to us reporters to write about the tragedies and draw the peoples' attention to them, so that they may be appraised of the situations, and protect themselves accordingly, by forming opinions and resolutions, to not step on the same paths to perdition. It is the great and noble mandate of we news paper reporters. Hence, I vowed to write dispassionately about the burning girl and not let it bother me any more.

However, try as I might, even now, years later, as I reflect on this Pirate's Tale, the story of the burning girl still haunts me to this day. I guess the idea of burning girls is so repugnant to me, the thought is difficult to erase.

Anyway, when I got home, around seven that evening, Missus Findlay had a pot of hot water on the stove. She fixed me a cup of hot cocoa, which I took up stairs to my room. Fortunately, Missus Findlay had put some coal into the little stove, so my room was toasty warm when I stepped in. Missus Findlay looked after me so well. She was worth every shilling I paid her. Missus Findlay was a lot like my mother. I had a great appreciation for that woman.

After I had drunk the hot cocoa I felt a whole lot better. I changed into my pajamas and put on my dressing gown. Then I lit a candle on the table beside my bed, and began to transcribe the notes I had made, all the while wondering what manner of harrowing tale the pirate would tell me the next time I saw him.

Chapter Three

Next morning I woke up early.

For some reason I woke up fresh and ready for action at six a.m. Normally I sleep until seven. I don't have to be at the office until eight. When it is dreary outside, one normally feels less inclined to get up early. However, I woke up with a fire and energy which was raring to go. I couldn't wait to return to the jail and continue my interview with the pirate.

As I ate a quick breakfast of oatmeal and hemp porridge I thought about telling Mister Burnett about yesterday's interview. Persistence is what gets a junior reporter into the upper ranks of journalism, I reasoned. I vowed to be persistent and approach Mister Burnett again.

When I did, later that morning, Mister Burnett again expressed his disinterest. This time he was a little less emphatic about it, though. I remember sensing a hesitation when I told him the story of the burning girl. However, he shrugged his shoulders and said that stories like that were sensationalistic and were not in the best interests of the general public's Christian sensibilities.

I reminded him that the burning was done by Christians, but that just made him angry. So I left it alone and accepted his assignment to cover the Tuesday cattle market.

Whoopee! The cattle market. He gave me the cattle market to cover, instead of paying me to spend days with William Bartleby, whose tale could be the story of the year. Sometimes I think Mister Burnett had no vision. But, it was his newspaper, and he paid my wages, I had to do what he assigned, or seek employment elsewhere.

The cattle market that day was not much different from cattle markets any other day. Farmers sold: bulls, cats, chickens, cows, dogs, ducks, geese, horses, oxen, pigs, and sheep. Everywhere one went there was the smell of excrement and urine. I found going to the cattle market always a smelly affair. It was not my favorite assignment. I remember that day a farmer selling a prize cow, with a massive udder, for over a hundred florins. The udder is what impressed me. The poor cow was in great discomfort because nobody would milk her. She was so full, the veins of the udder were sticking out, and milk was leaking from her teats. She mooed so plaintively, it was quite sad, actually.

Anyway, just as I did on Monday, I rushed home and changed my clothes, grabbed some food and a bottle of wine, and rushed off to the jail.

When I got there I found the guards standing in front of one of the guard houses, talking.

'Hey, aren't you supposed to be standing at your posts?' I asked them, deliberately trying to be a smart ass.

The two guards looked at me as if I was something odiferous one of them had picked up on the bottom of his boot.

I detested their insolence. They were only a few years older than me. The guard on the left, a grunt named Kurt, managed to growl an answer to the effect that Corporal McFee was not on duty that day, so that it did not matter if they were having a talk. Nobody was escaping from the prison through the front door, he added.

When I reminded him that people, who shouldn't get in, might sneak into the prison through the front door; to help someone escape, they laughed and dismissed me, as if one of them had tossed something detestable into the street.

I vowed, then and there, that I would give those two guards bad press, if I actually did write a book about the pirate. I am sure Kurt and his partner, the grunt with the elephantine ears, will not appreciate my words. It certainly will not impress any girls, that's for sure. If they read my words, those two morons will never get a date in Halifax again.

I picked up my dignity and stepped into the lobby.

Instead of Corporal McFee sneering at me, there was a new face sitting behind the desk. This face had a smile on it. Behind the smiling man stood two guards, one on each side. They were also smiling. I found it quite peculiar.

When I requested to be allowed to interview William Bartleby, the men cleared their throats and looked everywhere but at me. When I repeated the request they stared at me and jingled coins in their purses. I just played dumb and asked again to be allowed to interview the pirate.

This time the man at the desk spoke about the need for donations to feed the prisoners. He waxed quite eloquent regarding the prices of commodities and the impending shortages. He spoke about the price of grain having gone up and that chickens and beef were in short supply.

When I told him I had been to the cattle market, and did not see a short supply of either creature, he reminded me that they were collecting to cover future shortages; that he and his two colleagues, just like Corporal McFee had always done, collected fees to make certain the prisoners would never do without.

I laughed and threw some coins on the table. I reminded them that I had no delusions as to where the money was going. Then I asked them where McFee was; receiving an answer which surprised me, and shocked me at the same time.

Apparently, Corporal McFee had been run through with a sword, outside the Hanover Boar Public House. A friend of a prisoner, who McFee had mistreated, had done the deed. The swordsman was brought in, that afternoon.

At that point in this history, McFee, unfortunately, was expected to live.

The man who did the deed probably would not. That was my guess. Attempted murder of a public official, like Corporal McFee, would bring a hanging for sure. Even if McFee deserved it, the law was not about justice.

When I arrived at Bill's cell I found him waiting, as usual, with his hand outstretched. This time the guard didn't say anything and lit the torch on the wall. The tiny window, high up in Bartleby's cell, did not provide much light, it being quite dreary outside.

After Bill and I had exchanged pleasantries, I handed him the food. The first thing he did was eat a piece of bread. He was quite ravenous.

'Isn't the food up to your usual standards here?' I asked him.

Bill grunted and smiled. I could tell that meant, the food in jail was not very good, or plentiful. It was pretty much what I expected. Jails are not inns.

When Bill had eaten some bread and a piece of the roast beef I had brought, he began to feel more like talking. He drank some wine and went to sit on his cot.

I had sat down on my little stool, which the guards had left where I last used it. Since there was no one else in the lowest level of the jail, they did not need it for anyone else. I took out my writing stuff and Bill cleared his throat.

'I have no idea how long they'll let me be here today, so we had better get started, as soon as possible,' I told him.

Bill nodded. 'One of the gaolers told me he figured the ship, advising of my capture, should be nearing England by now. I think it's a bit fast, to my way of reckoning. At this time of year, it is not easy sailing. The Atlantic gets rough in March.' Bill smiled. 'I think we will have lots of time to talk over the coming weeks.'

I looked at Bill for a moment and frowned. 'I don't know if my money will hold out that long. I need to get as much information as I can. My visits here are already beginning to cost me.'

Bill smiled. 'Oh,' he said, 'I don't think you need to worry about that.'

'Oh? Do you propose to talk to Mister Burnett and have him raise my salary?'

'Trust me, Peter. If you are sincere about wanting to tell my tale, money will not be an object for long.'

'Do you think Mister Burnett is going to give me a raise?'

Bill did not answer. He winked at me and gestured that he was ready to begin his tale.

I wondered about his cryptic words, regarding money, as I opened my note book and took the writing implements from my bag.

When I was ready, he began to talk.

'As I told you, I was impressed into the Royal Navy at the age of

32

twelve. It was my birthday, when I was walked up the gangplank of His Majesty's Ship, *Pluto* and met Captain Jamison. He was a tall, lanky man, with a gaunt face and cold blue eyes, which stared a hole right through me. I was just twelve years old. You can imagine that he scared the bejeebies out of me. I visibly trembled when I was brought before him.

'What are you trembling for, boy?' he demanded in a stern voice.

I nearly peed in my breeches. I told him that he presented a frightening demeanor to a young boy.

The captain said that it was good, that I was frightened. He said that way I would do as I was told.

I assured him I would obey his orders. I was twelve years old for heaven's sake.

At first my tasks, on board the *Pluto*, were helping in the officer's quarters. I had to sweep floors, and polish brass, and that sort of thing. Sometimes I had to help with serving dinner. I liked that best because I got to eat some of the leftovers. The officers always ate better than the rest of the men on board. I was what you would call, the cabin boy.

However, for one of the officers, Second Lieutenant Wolfman, I was more than a cabin boy.' Bill stared at me and grimaced. 'I know this is an unpalatable tale, but if I am to get my story out, I must tell it like it was.'

I asked him what he meant, being naive in those matters.

He continued in an uneasy voice. 'Well, you see, being a twelve year old cabin boy on a navy ship, which is out at sea for months at a time, some men, who have trouble controlling their animal urges, seek out certain comforts, which ought to be enjoyed with women, not with those of the same sex; especially not this twelve year old boy. But, I learned fast, and understood what the second lieutenant was up to.

The first few times that he tried to corner me, I managed to get away. Then, I had to go out of my way to avoid him. I tried telling the captain about it, but he just laughed uneasily, and told me to keep my mouth shut. I remember his words were something like, 'Such behavior is not becoming of a British Navy Officer, and would most certainly not be practiced by such a gentleman.' What I was misconstruing, according to the captain, were merely the second lieutenant's attempts at being friendly. 'He means nothing by it,' were his words.

Some time later, after my third month on board, Second Lieutenant Wolfman found me alone in the sail room, taking an inventory for Petty Officer Pettigrew. I didn't even have time to yell or anything. The second lieutenant clasped his hand on my mouth, and being as how he was much bigger and stronger than me, proceeded to bugger me, right there in the sail room. There was nothing I could do except to vow that I would get my revenge.

When he was done, he stumbled off and left me with a severe pain in my rectum. It was awful. I could barely walk, afterwards, I was in so much pain. Anyway, I finished the inventory, as best I could, and managed to find my way back to Petty Officer Pettigrew. When he asked me why I was walking strangely, I told him the story of what had happened.

The petty officer was quite flabbergasted and he promised to talk with Captain Jamison. However, it was to no avail. The captain told Pettigrew that I was trying to stir up trouble for the second lieutenant because I had something against him. If I brought it up again, he would have me flogged for trying to stir up trouble for a British officer and a gentleman.

Some days later, Second Lieutenant Wolfman cornered me in the galley store room. He scolded me for telling Pettigrew and laid a beating on me, leaving me with welts all over my body. He literally beat me black and blue. Then he buggered me again and left me lying in a heap, in the galley store room.

Cookie found me there, an hour later, when he returned from his card game in the officers' mess. When he asked me what had happened, I told him about Wolfman. Cookie told me that Wolfman and the captain were peculiar friends and that I should be careful about reporting it.

However, when the captain saw me, later that day, he asked me what had happened to me. I told him the truth about Wolfman. This was in front of Wolfman and the first mate. The captain became very angry with me and accused me of trying to stir up trouble for a ship's officer and ordered me to be flogged ten strokes. Ten strokes! Imagine, I was twelve years old!

So, the captain ordered me on deck and in front of the ship's company had me stripped bare and tied face down on the webbing of the midship hatch. Then he ordered me lashed ten strokes with a cat of nine tails. That is the equivalent of ninety strokes! I was twelve years old for God's sake. My back, buttocks and legs were cut and bleeding. Then, to make the pain worse, they washed the blood off with buckets of sea water. It was then and there that I decided to kill both the second lieutenant and the captain.

It took me months to heal. Every day, for weeks, my back hurt like hell. I could barely move. And yet they made me perform my chores. The one saving grace was that Wolfman left me alone and gave me time to plan my revenge. Wolfman didn't know what he was up against, I assured myself.

As time went on, I eventually had my thirteenth birthday on board ship, off the coast of Jamaica. I had grown wise in the ways of the ship and did my utmost to keep the suspicions of the captain and the second lieutenant off me. After my lashing, I think the captain must have spoken with Wolfman because he never bothered me again. However, I did not forget what he had done to me.

One day, when I was serving in the galley, I managed to steal one of cookie's knives. It was a real sharp one, about twelve inches long. I hid it in my trousers and slipped out of the galley, unobserved. Since a day before I had pretended to have a stiff leg, my walking out with a stiff leg did not draw attention from cookie. Since it wasn't one of his best knives, Cookie wouldn't miss it, I thought.

Once I had the knife, I carefully hid it under the tarp, which covered the yawl, sitting in the centre of the main deck, between the fore and main masts.

Some days later, when I learned that the second lieutenant had drawn the two a.m. watch, my plan was ready to put into effect.

That night, I went to my hammock, as usual, but I worked at staying awake, going over the plan in my head. I went over it and over it. After the first bell, I carefully climbed out of my hammock and quietly snuck up on deck. I couldn't see any one from my observation spot behind the fore hatch.

When I saw that the coast was clear, I climbed under the tarp of the yawl and found my knife.

Then I waited.

When two bells sounded, I was ready. Eventually, Wolfman would walk by the yawl on his watch. Then I would have him, I thought. After he had passed, I would climb out of the boat and sneak up behind him.

When Wolfman was standing by the fore rail, admiring the bow waves, I snuck up behind him. I jumped up on a coil of rope, next to which he was standing, and managed to slice the bastard right across the throat. He tried to yell, but since I had sliced his trachea, he couldn't make any sounds. Then I jammed the knife as hard as I could, right through his left kidney. Wolfman began to thrash around, but I knew he couldn't do anything and would be dead in minutes. I watched him collapse in a bloody pool on the deck. Fortunately, I wasn't too badly spattered, and managed to wash the blood off, before returning to my hammock.

They found him, stiff as a post, when the watch changed at six a.m. The knife was still sticking in his kidney. The disgusting child molester had soiled his trousers. It was a most sorry sight when the captain came out of his cabin and stood over the body. I heard about it from some sailors who had been summoned on deck.

Captain Jamison, ruling out suicide, vowed to find the perpetrator. When he made his vow, I was still happily sleeping in my cozy hammock. He had no idea that a thirteen year old kid could do such a thing.

I didn't either.

The captain's suspicions lay with the second mate, who had some peculiar traits, as well. However, since the knife clearly came from the galley, it being a kitchen knife, and not a sailor's knife, the captain charged Cookie with the death of the second lieutenant.

Cookie, of course, protested his innocence, but it was to no avail. The knife was a kitchen knife, so it had to be Cookie, in the captain's opinion. It could not possibly have been an officer.

'Officers don't murder other officers. That just is not done in the Royal Navy,' pontificated the captain as he sentenced Cookie to his fate.

A couple of marines strung old Cookie up from a fore yardarm and then, when he was good and dead, they tossed his body into the sea. Justice came swiftly in the navy. There was no denying that. It helped keep the sailors in line. The officers were scared to death of the sailors and did what ever it took to, 'Keep Order'. It was a lot like it was in the old Roman Empire, where the Romans were scared to death of their slaves; cruel punishments being regularly inflicted to terrorize the slaves into submission. The legal system favored the wealthy then, just as now.

When the captain showed up dead, one morning, a few weeks later, the officers really exhibited some bizarre behavior. I mean, I had never expected they would react the way they did. It became a dark chapter in the logbook of, *H.M.S. Pluto.*'

I asked Bill if he had killed the captain, as well.

He paused for a moment and smiled slyly. 'For having me flogged. That's why I killed him. Any man who flogs a twelve year old kid, doesn't deserve to live.' He drank some wine, then returned to the cot and lay down. He put his hands behind his head and continued his tale.

'I did it during the night. Unbeknownst to the captain, I had stolen one of the extra keys to his cabin, which he kept in a key cabinet, on the wall by his bunk. I stole it when he was trying to have a bowel movement. He had three keys to the Great Cabin. One he always carried on a key chain, with some other keys. He rarely looked at the keys in the cabinet. Anyway, one night I simply snuck into his cabin and slit his throat wide open. Then, for good measure, I stabbed him through the heart. I made sure he was dead, before leaving the cabin.

When they found him the next morning, the knife was no where to be found; I had thrown it overboard, through the window of the captain's cabin. I left the window open to make it look like the culprit might have come through there. Then I carefully closed the cabin door and locked it. I threw the key overboard, as well. Returning to my hammock, one of my bunk mates opened his eyes and asked where I was. I told him I had gone to the head and quickly went back to sleep.

The officers didn't find the captain until a couple of days later. No one had bothered crashing in the door of the Great Cabin. They just assumed the old man was ill and confined to his bunk. He was confined to his bunk alright, but not because of illness. He was confined because of rigor mortis.'

Bill laughed uproariously and repeated the phrase, 'He was confined to his bunk because of rigor mortis.' Bill seemed to find that particularly funny.

'D'you ever see a dead body, Peter? Did you ever see a body, where rigor mortis has set in?'

I told him that I had seen a dead body, once. It was the body of a man who had been eaten by a bear. 'I had to write a report about it for the newspaper. It was very gruesome. I don't suppose a stabbed body is quite so bad as one which has been chewed by a bear.'

'Aye, bears,' he said, 'Not being a landlubber, I haven't had any experience with bears, except to see one baited in Belgium. Bears are dangerous animals, alright. I wouldn't want to be caught by one.'

I gave Bill a few more details concerning the bear story, which made him shiver; the results of the bear attack having been quite horrible. The man's head was never found.

'Have you ever seen a white shark?' asked Bill, suddenly. 'Now there is a dangerous animal for you. I've seen a white shark bite a man in half. Bit him clean through the middle, he did. An amazing sight.' Bill grimaced. 'I avoid sharks.'

'You have seen a lot of death, by the sounds of it,' I said.

'Not so much. However, having served in the Royal Navy, and having been a pirate for twenty years, I have seen more deaths than you have, that's for sure. Some of them were more brutal than your bear story. Ever see anyone blown to pieces?'

Bill shook his head sadly. He got up from the cot and walked over for a sip of wine. When he had drunk his fill he handed the bottle to me. I took a sip and set the bottle on the ground, where he could easily grab it.

'I am getting ahead of myself,' said Bill, when he had returned to the cot. 'I was never even suspected of the murder of Captain Jamison. The navy did suspect the second mate, however, based on the testimony of the first mate and several other sailors, who swore that the second mate had something queer going on between the captain and Second Lieutenant Wolfman. The fact that Wolfman was dead, and now Captain Jamison, made it abundantly clear to the court, the second mate had to be guilty.

So, in spite of the many protestations of innocence, on the part of the second mate, they hung him. The law is such a strange thing. There is no justice in hanging an innocent man. However, I am glad it wasn't me they hung.'

I asked Bill if he wasn't concerned to admit those murders to me, considering I was a newspaper reporter. He figured it didn't matter, because he was a dead man anyway, and he wanted his story told. The fact that I expressed an interest, by returning to visit him, indicated I was serious, so he figured I was his only chance. His full story would not come out in court. He would only be asked specific questions there, mostly requiring only yes or no answers. Bill figured that his story was worth more than that. I guess I was the lucky newspaper man.

'So, anyway, there I was, still on the *Pluto,* now under a new master. This time he was a fair, and approachable man. Captain Stoddard was the epitome of a navy officer and a gentleman. He treated the sailors fairly and with respect. I never saw him issue orders for cruel punishment, not like Captain Jamison, who had two sailors keel hauled during the time I served with him. Keel hauling is a horror you don't wish on your most hated enemies. D'you know what that is, Peter?'

I had heard the term, once before, but was not entirely certain.

Bill began to pace. 'Keel hauling is a punishment Jamison inflicted on poor Ted Norton and Jake Pillard. It was when we were off the coast of Cuba, searching for pirates. Ted and Jake had the balls to sneak overboard and cavort in Havana, when we were at anchor in the harbour. Jamison had canceled all shore leave. The captain assumed Jake and Ted had spoken with people, who could have given information to pirates. It was all nonsense, of course. Jake and Ted only went into the city to cavort with a couple of girls they knew there. If I had been older, like them, I probably would have gone, as well. Cavorting with women sure beats the heck out of being cooped up with three hundred men in a smelly wooden ship.

Jake and Ted's hands, and feet were bound. Then a long rope, which had been run out under the ship from bow to stern was tied to Jake's feet. Sailors were made to throw him off the bow and he was dragged under the water from bow to stern, his yielding flesh subjected to thousands of razor cuts from the barnacles. When they hauled him back up, he was bleeding from head to foot, and barely alive. The ship's doctor immediately attended to the poor bastard. It is a wonder he lived.

Ted was not so lucky. When they hauled him up, there were only pieces left. Jake's blood must have attracted the sharks. They must have found the poor wretch a tasty treat. Ted was a good man. His only sin was, he wanted to see his girl friend in Havana.

Bill leaned against the bars and watched me writing for a moment, before continueing. 'It was another good reason to kill Jamison. Jamison was one of those despicable human beings, who deserved killing.' Bill smiled. 'Vengeance is mine sayeth the Lord.' It says that in the Bible. 'Vengeance is mine.' Of course God can't do it alone. He needs agents to carry out his vengeance.' Bill pointed at his chest. 'I was such an agent. Jamison was diabolical. I am convinced he was in league with the dark forces.' Bill walked away from the bars and lay down on the cot.

'Do you believe in the dark forces, Peter?' Bill stared at me from the cot. The whites of his eyes stood out in the dim light. 'Do you believe in Diablo? Do you believe in Beelzebub and the Devil? What about Lucifer and Satan? Do you think they are real, Peter? Or are they just some myths an ancient writer thought to include in the Bible, to scare us silly?'

The questions surprised me, coming from a pirate. They made me pause as I thought about his questions and came to the conclusion that I wasn't sure whether I believed in the Devil or not. Did believing in God preclude believing in the Devil? Is it possible for God to exist, but the Devil to be a fabrication? Maybe it was all a fabrication of the priests to keep us in line with our heads bowed down. I had a feeling about God existing, but the dark forces...I suppose it made sense, considering the inhuman cruelties which Bill had spoken of earlier.

Or, perhaps the so called dark forces are merely the manifestations of the depths of depravity humans can fall into. After all, we have free choice. There would not be much of a choice if there was not a dark side and a light side. If it was all light, then there would be no choice. The choice is necessary to sort us out. It is how God could see what we are made of. If we choose the good, then we get in, if we choose the dark, then we do not get in. Something like that, that is what I believed in, at the time. I never could quite buy the traditional Christian line. However, I did not let too many people know that. There were always people around who did not like people believing differently than they.

William liked what I had to say and remained quite serious. He replied that he believed Lucifer and Satan were real. 'They're just as real as the

Creator is real,' he said. 'But, I don't believe any of the traditional Christian messages concerning them. The Bible is a political document which that vile, disgusting monarch, King James had commissioned, so as to legitimize the concept of divinely appointed kings. It is a giant lie. God only appointed one king, ever. He alone is my sovereign. Hence, I serve no man. Read Saint Matthew, chapter 23. You will see what Jesus said about who your master is.'

Bill came over to the bars and reached for the wine bottle. He took a long sip and smacked his lips. 'Hmmmm, that is good wine,' he said. 'It sure beats the slop they serve in here.'

'They serve wine in here?' I asked naively.

'No, not wine. Some sort of flavored water. I'm not sure what's in it. Maybe it's rust. Whatever it is, It's not pure water, that's for sure, and tastes even worse. This wine is a nice change from what I've been drinking.' Bill took another long sip and shook the bottle, to feel how much was left. Then he handed the bottle to me. 'There is still some wine left, do you want it?'

I turned it down and let him have it. I figured he probably needed it more than I did.

Bill took a deep breath and then continued his narrative.

'Anyway, getting back to Captain Stoddard. Now there was a captain for you. A real officer and a gentleman. I learned a lot from him. How to treat people. How to be a leader and have people respect you, and follow your orders willingly. I sailed with him until I was sixteen years old. Unfortunately, he was shot through the eye in a skirmish with a French ship. The bullet lodged in his brain and he died a few days later. There really was nothing the doctor could have done for him. It was a great loss to us sailors on the *Pluto*. We all liked the old man and gave him a real hero's send off.'

Bill paused and thought for a moment.

When he continued, his voice was a bit softer. I think he missed Captain Stoddard.

'He was a real officer and a gentleman. A great loss for the navy.

The man who replaced him was something none of us had ever experienced before. I think this new captain was Lucifer himself. Captain

Blight was the name Lucifer had chosen to call himself. Ezekiel Malachai Blight. He was appropriately named because he was a blight; a blight in the navy, a blight amongst men. Captain Blight was the most cruelly malevolent monster disguised as a human being that I have ever come across, except for Golden Jim, but I'll tell you about him later. We're talking about Captain Blight. He made Captain Jamison appear like a country parson in comparison. I knew right from the beginning that I would have to kill him too.

Right from the beginning we knew that a very dark power was now reigning from the quarterdeck. We were only a few days out of London, bound for Kingston, when a minor skirmish broke out amongst some deck hands. One of the men had taken the other man's favorite sponge. They were merely squabbling over the sponge, when one of them pushed the other man, who tripped over a pail of soapy water, spilling the soapy water all over the deck. When one of the officers stepped down to quell the argument, he slipped on the soapy water and fell. The captain saw the entire episode from the quarterdeck and immediately ordered the two sailors clapped in irons and tied to the foremast, one on each side, facing each other. Their shirts were ordered stripped off.

So they were left on bread and water for two weeks, through two storms and a merciless sun.

The rest of the sailors were made to scrub the deck non stop for the rest of the day with the water that had spilled. Eventually, there was no water and the sailors were merely dry cleaning the decks.

Fortunately for me, I worked in the galley by this time, and attended to the officers' mess. I only heard about the scrubbing incident and daily saw the effect the punishment was having on the two sailors. After two weeks their backs were blistered from the sun and the wind. When the sailors were finally released, they couldn't walk and had to be helped to their hammocks. The lesson was not lost on the rest of the sailors. No body raised their voices any more. Fights were avoided, at all costs.

The next time Blight showed his evil hand was when a sailor was caught stealing a bottle of rum from the galley stores. Unfortunately, I didn't catch the thief, or I would have let him go. Our new boatswain caught him, instead. This officer saw Blight as a hero, and was anxious to be noticed by the captain. He turned the thief in. It was a fatal decision for the boatswain, as far as I was concerned, because I happened to like the thief. I totally understood why he tried to steal the rum. Life was not easy onboard a Royal Navy ship in the 18th Century. Liam Clancy was not a bad man. He and his mess mates liked to drink a bit more rum, to make life tolerable on board ship.

Anyway, after what amounted to a kangaroo court, Captain Blight ordered that Liam be forced to drink rum until he nearly burst, and then to be lashed three hundred strokes. Three hundred strokes for stealing a bottle of rum! Three hundred strokes with that horrible, flesh ripping instrument. It was madness.

At this point, dear reader, I just want to further acquaint you with the instrument known as the, *cat of nine tails*, just so you understand exactly what the implications were for poor Liam Clancy. In the Royal Navy, and other navies as well, the instrument was sometimes made by the very sailor, who was to be punished with said instrument. In those cases, it consisted of a three foot piece of unraveled hemp rope, making nine strands, at the ends of which the hapless sailor would tie knots. The other end would be wrapped with felt, to make a good handle.

Some ships had permanent cats made of leather. These were the most lethal instruments, especially if the knotted strands were left to soak in salt water for a day and then dried in the sun, making the strands like razor blades, imbedded with salt. Needless to say, you can well imagine what that would do to a man's back, when administered by an unfeeling brute.

Liam was strapped to a chair, on deck, in front of the entire crew. Then a funnel was forced into his mouth and rum poured down his throat. Two full bottles of rum were poured down poor Liam's gullet. All the while Captain Blight harangued the crew with a monologue regarding Divine Vengeance being administered to a wrong doer, 'A despicable, vile thief, who would taste the Lord's wrath,' and so on.

When the rum had been administered, two marines tied the poor chap around the mainmast, making sure to stretch him good and tight. We could see the man was already extremely drunk because he kept sinking in the knees. Or, perhaps it was lack of courage. Facing three hundred strokes of the cat, which by the way, the captain had ordered to be soaked in salt water from the time he came on board, was something any man would falter at receiving. Because the cat, having been soaked in salt water, and left to harden in the sun, as I said, had hard, salt encrusted strands, which cut like razor blades. How any man could possibly wield such a thing against the flesh of an other is something I can never understand.

The sergeant at arms was the first to administer the lethal instrument. After fifty strokes Liam's back was raw meat and the knobs of his backbones were exposed. He had long passed out and the sergeant at arms was tired. When he looked up at the captain, the captain signaled that the punishment was three hundred strokes.

Several friends of the man pleaded with the captain for clemency, but the captain was hardened and signaled for the whipping to continue.

The next seventy strokes were administered by a marine corporal, another one of those people who takes pleasure in an other's pain.

After about thirty strokes, there was nowhere else on the man's back to whip, it having been reduced to a bleeding, pulverized mess of chopped meat. The corporal indicated this to the captain.

So, what did that inhuman creature do? He ordered Liam's trousers pulled off and his legs and buttocks whipped. Just like what happened to me, when I was twelve, except that I only got ten strokes altogether, but they did cover my whole backside, including my legs and buttocks.'

Bill took a drink and then continued his story.

'By the time Liam had received the three hundred strokes, his shoes were slopping full of blood. He had long ago passed on to His Maker and could have cared less. I bet he was dead by the two hundredth stroke. The entire ordeal made me sick to my stomach and strengthened my resolve to visit the Lord's vengeance on Blight, at the earliest opportunity.

And, if I had an opportunity, I vowed I would do the marine, as well. I could tell he was enjoying the beating.

The sergeant at arms was just doing his duty, so I wouldn't bother with him. His heart was not into it, you could tell that. He actually was a fairly decent fellow; a career navy man.'

Bill collected his thoughts for a moment and then continued with his story.

'I hatched my plan after listening to some of my sailor friends talk about Saint Dominigue and the practice of voodoo. They talked about drugs and poisons which were available in Saint Dominigue and nowhere else, as far as they knew, although one did admit to some interesting experiences with the bark off an African tree which had been given to him by a Bantu.'

Bill smiled wickedly, a glint in his eye, as he related how he resolved to poison Lucifer. However, the immediate problem he had was that he was not in Saint Dominigue, and had no access to voodoo poison.

'Since I looked after the officers' mess,' he chuckled, 'I got to know the doctor, who was an intelligent, well educated man. I liked the way he talked, and over time became quite friendly with him. He even invited me into his cabin, from time to time, to talk about all kinds of things. He lent me books to read, and over the period of a year, or more, the doctor and I became good friends.

One night I engaged him in a discussion regarding the voodoo poison I had heard the men talk about. The doctor, whose name was Matthew McTavish, had a great interest in native medicines, which included strange drugs and poisons. He quite casually mentioned that he had poisons with him, in his medicine chest, which were quite lethal, if administered in high enough doses. He showed them to me and explained the dosages for various poisons he had. In small amounts, the drugs were useful in treating various maladies, however, in bigger doses, he had poisons which would kill a man, most assuredly. They would surely kill Lucifer himself, I figured.

As it turned out, the doctor was no great appreciator of Captain Blight, either. He also found the captain to be a vile, and evil man. His treatment of the crew, and even his attitude, regarding the officers, was not in keeping with the traditions of the Royal Navy, he felt.

However, I had learned at an early age, because of my involvement with Mister Stevenson's spoiled brat, not to trust too easily and keep one's plans to oneself. This I did. I had no plan to involve Doctor McTavish in my plot to murder Captain Blight. Because I believe some people deserve killing, I had no qualms about doing the old man in by myself. I always focused on the fact that I was doing the Lord's work.

One night, when I was visiting the doctor, I had brought a small bottle of rum with me, which we drank fairly quickly, there not being but half a pint. Then, when the doctor had to go to the head, I took some of the poisons from his medicine chest and poured them into the empty rum bottle. Because the bottle was dark, you couldn't see any liquid in it, but the doctor had seen me empty it into our cups. When he returned from the head I was sitting where I was before, and the supposedly empty rum bottle, sat on the table in the same location. The doctor suspected nothing when I told him I had to go, and in getting up, taking my rum bottle with me.'

Bill smiled and gestured with his right hand, it was time for a drink. He got off the cot. I handed the bottle to him and he took another long drink. He dried his mouth on his sleeve and remained standing beside the bars of his cage.

'As I told you, I worked in the officer's mess, so it was relatively easy to pour the poisons into the captain's drink, and here and there in his food. I had no idea how fast the mixture of poisons would react. I hoped they would not act too quickly. Having a man die over dinner is not a very polite thing to have happen in the company of gentlemen, as some of these officers were. They weren't all bad.

Blight was the monster and the boatswain was a monster in the making. However, to be fair, most of the officers were actually gentlemen, who did not really agree with Blight, either. I often overheard them arguing with Blight over the treatment of the crew. Blight was not liked by his officers, or his crew. He was setting himself up for a mutiny. However, I saved him from that disgrace. I saved everyone a lot of trouble.

Dinner began with a prayer from the vicar. He had taken a verse from an old prayer book. I remember it had something to do with salvation from the wrath of the Norsemen. I thought it quite appropriate because I am sure that I have Norse in me.

Anyway, my wrath was about to strike the captain. However, much to my surprise, he ate the entire meal, and drank his glass of wine without noticing a thing. He even commented that the wine tasted really good. After dinner he told me to compliment the cook on a job well done. My eyes must have been quite bugged out as I watched the old bastard light up a Cuban cigar.

However, as I began clearing the dishes from the table, I noticed that the captain's speech was changing. It was the first indication that something was beginning to work. When I had cleared the table, and the officers were enjoying their brandies and cigars, I noticed that the captain had gotten up. He wandered around the cabin, looking at things, as if he had never seen them before. Eventually, he began to examine things very closely, much like a very young child might do. As he examined things, he muttered about something.

When any of the officers asked the captain what he was saying, the old tyrant yelled at them, and complained that nobody ever listened to him. It was most peculiar.

Then all of a sudden the captain flew into a rage and ordered everyone out of the cabin. He even grabbed a pistol and discharged it; the bullet barely missing the first mate and lodging in the lintel of the door.

Since I saw it all developing, I was out of the door before anyone else.

The first mate managed to swing the door shut before another shot was fired from the captain's other pistol. No one had any idea he kept them loaded. The first mate had the good sense to hold the door closed as we listened to the captain raging inside the cabin. We could hear things crashing and the captain yelling and screaming. No one, not even the doctor, had any idea what was wrong.

Then, all of a sudden, there was dead silence. Not a sound could be heard from behind the door. The Great Cabin was still as a tomb.

The officers, who were all gathered in the gang way, whispered to each other. They were trying to encourage one of them to enter the cabin and see what the captain had done. When no one volunteered, I said I would go.

I carefully opened the door and peered inside.

The cabin was a mess. The table had been upturned. Maps were thrown about. The captain's closet was emptied and his clothes were scattered hither and thither. In the middle of it all stood the captain, still as a post. He was staring straight up, but obviously not seeing, because he didn't move when I entered the cabin.

I said, 'How you feeling, Captain Blight?'

Captain Blight remained still. Not even his eyes were moving, although they were wide open and staring. When I touched him, he didn't react. When I touched his hand, it was cold as ice. I remember shivering after I touched him.

When the officers had entered the cabin, the doctor had them lay the captain on his bunk. Then he examined the old bastard and pronounced him dead. The captain was dead as a plank. The doctor looked at me, but I kept a straight face and acted as if I was as ignorant of the event as anyone else there. Then the doctor pronounced that the captain had suffered a heart attack and severe stroke. Everyone heaved a sigh of relief. Mine was probably the loudest.'

Bill laughed and looked down at what I was writing as he continued. 'The old man died of a heart attack! No one suspected it was poison. I got away with ridding the earth of Lucifer himself. Not one of his minions suspected me. Not even the boatswain, who fell overboard a week later, under unusual circumstances.' Bill laughed even louder. 'It was a complete mystery how the boatswain went missing.' Bill looked at me with a mischievous smile on his face. 'But, these things happen at sea,' he chuckled.

'Oh, yes,' he continued, 'I forgot to tell you. The captain was buried at sea with full military honours. The event was duly recorded in the log book by the first mate and signed by the doctor. Case closed.

As for the boatswain, he was just one of those accidents that happen when a knot is not tied properly and a block comes swinging from a yardarm. It is most unfortunate, but these things happen on a ship. Some people die on a navy ship, that's life. Some deserve it.'

Bill smiled and watched as I wrote down the last of the words he had just spoken. 'You can actually understand what all of those scribbles mean?'

I told him it was my own personal shorthand. If he looked closely he could make out words.

As he was examining my notes, a guard came into the cell block, carrying a torch. He had come to inform me that visiting time was over.

I was glad the guard had come. I looked at Bill and thanked him for the day's story. I told him it held me spell bound and that his stories would most certainly be included in a book, if his tale was to come to such. We shook hands and then I followed the guard, leaving the food behind, but taking the empty wine bottle with me.

I was glad to leave. Although I am fascinated by pirates, some of the stories they told made me quite ill. Bill's stories were certainly up there with the best of them, albeit, his stories were better told, by a more eloquent speaker. Most pirates I met, so far, had been fairly illiterate, poor speakers of the King's English.

When I left the jail I decided to stop at the Hanover Boar Pub, just to see the place where McFee was run through. I thought perhaps I might find someone who saw the incident. Besides, even if I met no one, I needed a toddy and some roast pork. The dungeon had given me the chills. Captain Bartleby's stories of murder did not help matters. The casual manner in which he told of such horrific cruelties, and the way he sought revenge for them, made me realize that I was interviewing a cold blooded killer. However, I had to agree, Bill killed people who were not good people. Killing them was probably a good thing, I suppose. However, for a person to take that upon themselves…?

I pondered those questions as I entered the pub and sat down at an empty table. I ordered a hot rum toddy.

Moments later, my friends, Stacey and Stuart, walked through the door. They sauntered to my table with big grins on their faces. We shook hands and began talking almost at once, each of us excited to share the day's news.

Stacey began with an accounting of his day on the MacGain farm, which, at that time of the year, consisted of repairing equipment, in readiness for the planting season to come. He complained about the poor work ethic of his assistant, some man named Sam. Apparently Stacey could work circles around Sam, but because Sam was the son of Mister MacGain's sister, Stacey had to tolerate him. The situation did not sit well with Stacey and he made no bones about letting me know about it, even though I did not have the slightest interest in the state of affairs at the MacGain potato farm.

Stuart described his day at the ship building yards, where he worked as an assistant ship designer. His day was pleasantly spent working on the design for a new type of schooner to be built in Lunenburg. Apparently it was to have a racing deck and three masts with fore and aft rigging, carrying a massive amount of sail for the size of ship, it being only 112 feet in length.

Sailing was not something I had much interest in, then.

Eventually, we got around to me, when Stuart asked if I had managed to get an interview with the pirate. I nodded and eagerly told them a couple of Bill's stories. My friends listened to every word. Pirate stories interested them, as well.

After telling them some of Bill's stories, my curiosity got the better of me and I asked my friends whether they knew anything about Corporal McFee's sword fight., which, as it so happened, was witnessed by both friends, Stacey quickly filling me in on the details.

'It was a magnificent fight,' began Stacey. 'McFee had come in for a pint with two other men.'

'Judging from their clothes,' interjected Stuart, 'They were government officials. They probably had something to do with the prison system.'

'Anyway,' continued Stacey, eager to tell the story, 'After they had sat down and were served their drinks, a tall man approached McFee's table, pretending to be drunk. I had never seen him before.'

'Neither had I,' commented Stuart. 'I noticed he was wearing a sword at his side.'

'Anyway,' interjected Stacey, glaring at Stuart; not wanting to be interrupted. 'The tall man approached McFee's table and bumped McFee, just as he was about to take a drink, causing some of McFee's drink to spill.' Stacey's eyes sparkled as he became more animated, telling his story. 'McFee took great offense over that and stood up, demanding an apology from the drunk.' Stacey grinned, 'So, what do you suppose McFee done?'

I shrugged my shoulders, 'I don't know, what did he do?' I asked.

Stacey laughed as he revealed what the drunk had told McFee, 'To piss off!'

Stuart, who was equally anxious to contribute to the story, continued the telling. 'So, McFee drew his sword and challenged the drunk to a fight.'

Stacey glared at Stuart.

Stuart cleared his throat and took a drink from his pewter stein, as Stacey went on with the story.

'The drunk agreed and went outside with McFee, where he thoroughly out fought the corporal. The tall man was only pretending to be drunk, to lure McFee into the fight.' Stacey burst out laughing. 'The drunk had us all fooled!'

Stuart finished the tale, a big grin on his face. 'McFee, thinking he was dealing with a drunk, found himself run through.'

At the time of my friends' telling, dear reader, it was doubtful if McFee would live. There is no doubt now, when I am writing this book. McFee died from his wound, two weeks later. It was not much of a loss, to my way of thinking. I never liked Corporal McFee.

Anyway, after drinking a toddy more than I should have, I stumbled home. The air was chilly and damp, making the boards of the sidewalk, slippery. When I crossed the street, mud stuck to the bottom of my boots. Halifax would eventually get cobblestones, like London, for example.

When I returned to my rooming house, my bladder was so full that I had no choice. I had to pass water against the oak tree in the front yard. I felt like a horse as my urine came out in buckets. I had no idea a human bladder could hold so much liquid. When the water eventually stopped, I managed to find my way into the house without making too much noise. I didn't want to wake Missus Findlay. She didn't like it when I came in late. But, at that point, I really didn't care what she thought. She could go take a flying leap, for all I cared.

Even though I was trying to be careful, it inevitably happened, I knocked something over, or I banged a wall. This time I tripped over a fold in the rug and fell against a candle stand, knocking it over.

The clatter woke, not only Missus Findlay, but old Mister Morgan, and Betsy, the maid, as well. They were not pleased about being woken up and let me know this in no uncertain terms.

I apologized profusely of course, knowing I would not hear the end of it, for some days to come. I climbed into bed and fell into a deep but troubled sleep, full of whippings and murder; not the sort of subject matter to instill comfort and rest.

It's the price one pays for being a pirate reporter.

Chapter Four

Next morning I woke up slightly disoriented, not having slept very well. My head was throbbing. Throughout the night I was woken up by the sound of a cat of nine tails striking a man's back. The whistle of the leather strands, and the screams of the hapless sailor, mercilessly beaten by an unfeeling marine, made sleep nigh on impossible. It was especially impossible when the hapless sailor turned out to be me.

I managed a quick shave that morning, thanks to Missus Findlay having hot water ready on the stove. She scolded me for making noise when I came home late. I told her again that I was sorry, and left it at that.

After breakfast I hurried to the newspaper office and approached Mister Burnett, once again. Perhaps, if I told him some of yesterday's tale, he might reconsider, I reasoned. He might allow me to interview the pirate on company time.

However, as before, it was to no avail. Mister Burnett's mind was closed. He refused to budge and perfunctorily gave me two assignments for the day. The first required me to visit the local churches, to get information pertaining to the sermons for that coming Sunday.

The second assignment was to interview a lady who had come from Holland with a tulip. Apparently she wanted to start a tulip club.

I sighed as I walked away from Mister Burnett's office. A tulip club was the farthest thing from my mind that morning. I had enough trouble getting myself to work. Interviewing a tulip lady was not exactly something which energized me. My heart was not with tulips, or any other flowers, for that matter. I was interested in William Bartleby. Having spent a few hours with him made me want to hear more and more.

Bill's stories were becoming a drug. The whole day that I spent gathering sermon information, and the hour spent talking with the tulip lady, my mind was focused on the pirate. I could hardly wait for the five o'clock bell, to hear more.

When the bell finally rang, I had already written up the sermon information and had made a start on the story pertaining to the tulip club. Mister Burnett stopped by my desk, just before I left the office, and examined what I had written. He sniffed his approval and dropped the articles on my desk.

'So you really think this pirate is worth interviewing?' he asked, just as I was about to step out of the door.

Of course I told him in more detail how I felt. If I could spend more time with the man, I would be able to write some very good stories for the paper. I told Mister Burnett how well the pirate spoke, and how interesting he was.

Mister Burnett listened attentively, but he still did not give me the assignment. I was afraid that he was planning to give it to Jones, a senior reporter, who had been with the Post for two years, already. I began to doubt myself and thought that perhaps I should not have told Mister Burnett about William Bartleby. If Jones got to do the interview it would have choked my chicken.

I ran home and gathered up my stuff, including food and wine. I was beginning to realize, the interview with the pirate was beginning to cost me money. That was already the third bottle of wine going onto my tab at Missus Findlay's. I thought perhaps Bill might have some money and he could help defray expenses. I didn't know. I was just a poor, junior reporter. I didn't have much money. It had to come from somewhere. I remembered Bill saying I wouldn't have to worry about money. People always say that; especially those who have money. I often fantasized about finding a treasure chest. I wouldn't have to work for the Morning Post, ever again. I could actually do what I really wanted to do. Interview pirates and write books about them.

When I got to the jail, the guards waved me through the gate. As I stepped into the lobby I immediately noticed there was a new official sitting at the desk.

He smiled and politely asked me for a contribution to the 'Prisoners' Welfare Fund.'

'So that is what you call it now? The Prisoners' Welfare Fund?' I asked him.

The new official, whose name was Sergeant Fish, seemed an agreeable fellow, who explained that the jail had a new governor, whose goal was reform. Apparently the new man in charge did not support private coin collecting. All moneys collected from visitors were to be legitimately used for the prisoners' well being.

Of course I expressed support, but, when Sergeant Fish informed me of the new price of admission, I hesitated for a moment, because the price had gone up steeply. It was going to cost me six pence each time. There was no weekly rate. When I protested, Sergeant Fish smiled and crossed his arms on his chest.

'Pay, or leave,' is all he said.

I had no choice. I laid the coins on the table.

When I arrived in the dungeon, I found Captain Bartleby lying on his cot. He appeared to be sleeping. I gently rattled the door of the cage, hoping he would wake up. I did not want to forfeit the price of admission by leaving without an interview.

The pirate breathed a big sigh and then stirred on the cot. He opened his eyes and stared uncomprehendingly at me for a moment, then he smiled and sat up.

'It is you, Peter? Please excuse me. I must have fallen asleep.' Bill rubbed his eyes. 'I am getting lethargic here. No exercise and poor food is beginning to have an effect on me.' When he stood up, he stretched luxuriously and farted mightily, for which he apologized, grinning. Then, as he walked towards the bars, 'I've been here two weeks already. I can't say the place has improved any, since I came here, except for your visits, of course.' Bill stepped over to where I was standing and gave me his usual warm handshake. 'It is good to see you,' he said.

I handed him the food I had brought, for which he thanked me profusely.

What little I brought everyday obviously helped improve his diet. The wine helped, as well, I'm sure.

As Bill ate a piece of roast duck, left over from dinner the night before, he asked me how I liked the story he told me the other day.

I told him that I found some of the story a bit unsettling, however, I assured him that I could handle it. I added that it mattered not to me if the truth is unpalatable at times. 'Such is the nature of truth,' I told him. 'It isn't always pretty.'

My answer obviously satisfied the pirate because he grunted approvingly over a mouthful of roasted duck.

While Bill was eating, I prepared my quills, set out my ink pot, and looked over my notes from the previous days. Bill watched me intently. He obviously enjoyed the serious, journalistic attention I was giving him. When a person writes down another's story, it must be a good feeling. People like being taken seriously by a journalist. Even if he is only a junior reporter. Even the tulip lady was all proud that I had come especially to interview her. She even introduced me to her old mother as, 'The journalist from the Morning Post,' as if I was some highly important person. It made me feel good, I must admit. I like it when people think I am important. They like it when I think they're important. I guess we all want to feel that way; that someone cares enough to listen to our story.

When Bill had finished eating, he drank a hearty sip of wine, to wash it all down, and then he lay on his cot, with his hands behind his head. He looked at me and I nodded that he could begin. I had to remind him where he had left off. It only took him a few seconds to gather his thoughts. He began the day's tale with gusto.

'So, there I was, sixteen years old with four murders under my belt. Good murders. The kind of murders which made me feel glad to be alive. I had rid the world of four monsters. It was something to be proud of.' Bill smiled and chuckled. 'Four villains were sent to their just rewards. It made me feel like I was God's private henchman. I was the archangel, Michael, wreaking the Lord's vengeance. It was an important role I had chosen for myself. I began wondering who would be next. Everywhere I looked I saw candidates. Who the Lord would present next was always a constant question in my mind.

I did not have to wait long for the Lord to show me whom He next intended for a journey to Hell. The Lord actually seemed to have quite a list prepared for me. I met the next candidate three months after Captain Blight had his heart attack, although it took almost five months to effect that person's removal from the ranks of the living.

Murder is not something you want to rush. Every aspect of the plan must be in place, to avoid detection. It isn't much good to the Lord if his henchman is caught and executed. Finding good henchmen is not an easy task for the Lord.

Anyway, the new candidate was the marine corporal I told you about yesterday. The one who helped to beat Liam Clancy to death. He was a lot trickier to do because he was a marine, and he was always in the company of other marines. I tended to avoid them, as did most of the sailors on board. The marines were the police force, and nobody likes police. Isn't that right, Peter?'

He had to repeat the question because I was concentrating on my writing.

'Isn't that right, Peter? Nobody likes the police,' he said again.

I thought about the question for a moment and then answered that I thought he was wrong. Lots of people like police because they keep the order, I told him. They investigate murders and bring murderers to justice.

'But, think about it for a moment, Peter. Police pry into people's private affairs. Some murders are justified. As we have already seen, some people deserve killing, because they are such monstrous scum. Can the police make the distinction? Can a so called, court of justice? I don't believe there is justice in the courts. They are courts of law. They are sparring rings for learned barristers, who argue over the trivialities, not justice. The police are the agents of the courts, and the courts are the collection agencies of the Crown, which manufactures laws to make work for the lawyers and the judges, and makes criminals of many decent human beings. I have little use for police. If it wasn't for the criminal activities of the Crown, we wouldn't need so many police, if any at all.'

'What about keeping the peace?' I asked. 'When people lose their wits in a pub, for example. When they break out into a drunken brawl and start to break things. Don't we need police for that?'

Bill looked at me and smiled. 'How often does that happen?'

'It happens,' I replied.

'So, for the few times something like that happens, or somebody good is murdered, perhaps you need a few detective types and a couple of burly meat heads for enforcement, but that is about it. I think we have way too many police and soldiers. Why do we need so many soldiers? Because of kings who want to go to war, that is why. I hate everything to do with all of that. Everything to do with government has to do with less freedom for the rest of us. I guess you can say that is about as good a statement for why a person becomes a pirate in the first place. Freedom.'

I looked up from my notes, when he said that, and asked him if police and soldiers weren't needed to prevent people from stealing their stuff. As for instance in his case. He was a pirate and he stole from merchants, as did Misters Stevenson and Thurgood. They were hanged for their crimes.

Bill stepped over to the bars and reached for the wine bottle, all the while looking at me and smirking. He took a long sip and wiped his lips. Then he handed the bottle to me.

I took a small drink. I was still feeling after effects, that many hours later, from the pints I had drunk the night before. I didn't need more alcohol. What I did need was water and that I had not brought with me. I was very hesitant to drink the jail water, so had to content myself with small sips of the wine. It didn't help my thirst.

'You see, Peter, the question of theft is an interesting one. When the king does it, it is called, *taxation*. When I commit theft, it is, *piracy*. When the king kills people it is done in the name of national security. When I do it, I am a murderer. When the king kills people, he usually kills good ones. When I killed people, I usually killed bad ones. When the king believes that he is next to God, or indeed, sometimes he thinks he is God, then the problem for us becomes ever worse, because the God who our Christian kings model themselves after is, Yahweh, the God of Thunder; the diabolical god of Deuteronomy. And that sets up a world view which results in official plunder, torture, and death for the rest of us. When there are kings there is no peace and I must needs be a pirate. I take back from the king that which he has stolen from us. My shipmates and I share the swag evenly, according to our stations, according to our code. Everyone benefits from our combined efforts. No one is forced into anything. Our code is about honour and trust.

Many of my shipmates have families whom they support. Most of them are very generous with whatever money comes their way. Bar wenches do very well by the single men.

Of course, we don't always have money at our disposal. We have to barter lots of the things we obtain from the merchantmen we rob. Those ships don't always carry treasure and such like. Sure there will be money on the ship. I mean, the sailors and officers generally have some of their money with them. And there is money for the ship, to buy supplies and such like. But usually it doesn't amount to a great deal. Most of the ships I have plundered have contained general merchandise; cloth, cotton, wool, sheep, goats, beans, pickled beef and pork, that sort of thing. One ship had a piano forte that it was bringing to the colonies in New England. I remember a ship carrying twenty camels, bound for Florida. We gave that ship back to the owners, so they could take the camels. I didn't have the heart to sink the ship with those incredible animals on board. We took everything else, except some food and water for the animals and crew.

Actually, come to think of it, we didn't kill a lot of people, or sink many ships, really. Most people didn't put up much of a fight. Remember, we were robbing merchantmen, not navy vessels. Sometimes people even joined us, seeking a life of adventure on the high seas. I mean, being a pirate is a pretty good life; if you're not caught that is.'

Bill frowned and waited a moment for me to catch up again. While he waited, he took another drink from the bottle. When I looked up, he continued.

'Piracy could be a quick death, as well, don't get me wrong. Such is life. There are no guarantees, so you might as well have some excitement and say you have lived when you die, instead of looking back to a life of mediocrity. I don't care if they hang me, Peter. At least I have lived a life.' Bill smiled. 'What do you say to that, my young friend?'

What could I say? Everything he said sounded good to me. At twenty five I felt unfulfilled. I didn't particularly feel like I was really alive as a junior reporter in Halifax. Everything the pirate had said made good sense. He made piracy sound highly attractive to me. Perhaps there lay the freedom I sought in my heart of hearts. Maybe that is why I was so interested in pirates. Maybe secretly I was wanting to be a pirate and lived vicariously in their stories. Bill was beginning to open my eyes to something.

'You haven't answered me,' said Bill, snapping me out of my ruminations. 'You haven't told me what you think about what I just said.'

I told him that he made it all sound so reasonable to be a pirate. He almost made it sound like it was a moral obligation.

Bill laughed at that. 'A moral obligation,' he said. 'I like that, Peter.' He laughed louder and then grabbed a hearty drink from the wine bottle. 'You have a way with words, my young friend. I think you are going to write a splendid book. Too bad I'll probably be dead by the time you publish it. It's unfortunate that I won't be able to read what you said about me.' Bill watched me writing for a moment and then added, 'I hope you won't paint me in too bad a light, Peter. I am not a bad man, really.'

I assured him I would be fair.

He looked at me for a moment longer and then set the wine bottle on the ground and began to pace back and forth as he continued his tale.

'I was talking about getting revenge on the marine corporal, before I digressed. You want to know how I got the corporal, don't you?'

I confessed that I was curious, of course. 'Murdering a marine corporal must have been quite a feat,' I said.

'It's an interesting story,' he replied. 'It wasn't easy. It never was easy, but this job was especially not easy. As I said, the corporal was a marine, who stayed in the company of marines. I rarely saw him without other marines around. The only time I reckoned he was alone was when he used the head. Of course, I wasn't watching him so closely to know when he would go there. I mean, I had duties to perform on board. I wasn't about to be lashed for a breach of duty, or some foolish thing like that. I kept my wits about me, I did.

Anyway, I figured that the best way for me to find the corporal on the head was to ensure that he use it frequently. A laxative is what I needed for the corporal.' Bill waggled his right index finger at me. 'Having a doctor friend is very useful for those sorts of circumstances.' Bill smiled wickedly.

'So, I complained to the doctor that I was constipated and asked if he had anything for that. As it turned out he did have something; some sort of mushroom. Of course, when the doctor was not looking, I availed myself of enough mushrooms to ensure the corporal's regular visitations to the marines' head, near the fo'c's'le.

I administered the laxative into the corporal's food, when it was my turn to serve the marines in their mess, a few weeks later. The corporal never saw me put the powder into his soup, which he ate with gusto. Marines always eat with gusto, like ravenous dogs. I didn't like marines.

After dinner was done, and my coworker and I had finished cleaning up, I went to my hammock and fetched a loaded pistol, which I had stolen from the armory, right under the quartermaster's nose. I also grabbed a heavy duffle bag, which I had stuffed with cotton I had stolen from the number two gun deck. Then I sauntered off to the fo'c's'le and waited behind some barrels for the corporal. He arrived shortly after me and looked somewhat the worse for wear, and a little green around the gills. He groaned as he entered the cubicle. Nobody was around, and I had made certain that nobody had seen me, either.

As soon as I felt enough courage, I quickly entered the cubicle, placed the heavy duffle bag over his head and shot point blank into it, muffling the sound of the discharge sufficiently that no one would have heard it. The corporal crumpled right there on the seat of the marines' head. Blood was soaking into the duffle bag, so I left it on his head, and just as quickly as I had come, left the place. Moments later I appeared on deck by way of the midship hatch. When no one was looking, I threw the pistol overboard.

The dead corporal was found a couple of hours later, when a marine began to grow suspicious, as to why the head was being tied up so long. He decided to look in and found the corporal to be recently deceased. The death caused quite a stir amongst the marines, as you can well imagine. It certainly affected their behavior towards the sailors from then on. I distinctly detected an increased respect on the part of the marines.

Of course there was an investigation. However, since they could not find a gun, and had nothing else to go on, the captain could not identify a culprit.

Of course, a young, sixteen year old galley hand was not even close to making the list of suspects. I felt pretty good about that. I had rid the ship of a detestable demon. I never told anybody.'

Bill paused for a moment and looked at me with a serious expression.

'That is the first rule you must always follow, Peter. If you kill somebody, don't tell. It is only for you and God to know. Also, make sure you kill someone who deserves killing. That way you won't be haunted by a bad conscience. Killing is not for the faint of heart. Even the most hardened killers sometimes do have a conscience. Killing a good person is something you want to avoid. You never kill a woman or a child, either. You only kill bad men. That's it. Plain and simple. I tried to stick to that agenda pretty much throughout my career. Hence, I am not plagued with a guilty conscience. I only killed bad men.'

Bill leaned against the bars and regarded me as I wrote what he had said. The pirate pointed to what I was writing and asked me if I was sure I could understand what I was scribbling.

I assured him I could understand the scribbles and read back what he had just said.

'Amazing. I must learn how to do that. Perhaps you can teach me, Peter,' he said, craning his neck to see more clearly what was on the page of my note book.

'Please continue,' I said, when I had caught up to where he left off.

Bill cleared his throat and began pacing as he continued his tale.

'On my seventeenth birthday I was transferred to a new ship. His Majesty's ship, *Buckingham*. It was a 70 gun ship of the line, commanded by the Honorable Temple West, Rear Admiral of the Red. It was decided, by him, that it was high time I served time aloft. Hence, I was sent to crew in the yards. I became very miserable. I much preferred working in the galley and the officers' mess. But, so be it. I did the best I could. It gave me an other perspective on the vile nature of King George and his navy.

In the spring of 1755, the *Buckingham* was accompanied by a 60 gunner, the *Dreadnought*, when we came upon three small French boats heading to

Calais. Since that bastard George III has issued commands to fire on French ships, those hapless French sailors had no idea the English king had unofficially declared war on France.

The Frenchmen never had a chance. The two British ships opened fire and sank them.

A few French sailors were left scrambling in the water, but we were commanded to leave them. I'll never forget their plaintiff cries for help. I felt very ashamed of my government. It became another one of the reasons I declared a personal war on English shipping, and that demon, George III. He officially declared war on France the following year. Then everybody knew. Those poor French sailors didn't even know why we fired on them. Some British naval officers were cold hearted bastards, for the most part. It's why I never had much of a problem with killing them, whenever we caught them.'

Suddenly, out of the blue, he mentioned Corporal McFee. He had heard about the sword fight and wondered if I knew whether the miscreant would live or not. Bill didn't like McFee, either.

'He deserves whatever he got. According to one of the guards, who is capable of speaking coherent English, McFee made life hard on most of the prisoners that came in here. I was lucky, I guess. They apparently are under orders not to molest me. King Georgie wants me intact, so he can watch me squirm. He'll probably have me hanged and then broken, or some other disgusting torture. Maybe he'll have me drawn and quartered. I think he really dislikes me, Peter.'

Bill laughed. It was abundantly clear he had no respect for the King.

I was indifferent. King George didn't bother me. He was in England and I was in Halifax.

'You know, Peter, King George has stirred up a lot of trouble in the American colonies. I've heard some interesting discussions when I was in Boston, and some of the other ports. The people of the American colonies are not happy with the British Crown, that is abundantly clear. As you probably know, they have had some scuffles already, at Boston. I have even heard talk of a revolution. The common people are prepared to fight the British, if they are pushed any longer. I think we are in for some interesting times, my young friend. It might be a good time to be a reporter. Who knows, maybe your editor will send you there to cover the war.'

What war?' I asked him. 'Surely you don't think the colonies are going to war with England, do you?' At that time I had no idea what was brewing in the south. I had very little contact with American colonists. For all I knew, they were content with growing cotton and breeding slaves.

Bill said he didn't hope that war would come, 'Because in wars there are always innocent people killed.' However, he hoped that if war came, the colonists would, 'Whip George's arse.'

The way Bill said it made me laugh. I was still laughing when the guard came to tell me it was time to leave.

I said good bye to Bill and thanked him for the day's stories.

He smiled and shook my hand warmly.

I could tell that we were becoming friends.

When I stepped outside it was raining. I put up my umbrella and hurried home on the muddy street. The gray stone buildings of the jail complex looked ominous in the gray mist. A few windows, in the houses I passed, had candles burning already. Not many people were in the street, most having gone inside for their dinner. I was hungry and thirsty, but I had no desire to detour into a public house and decided, instead, to head straight home.

When I returned to Missus Findlay's rooming house she was pleased to see me arrive at a decent hour, and after helping me to remove my wet rain slicker, guided me to the dining room, where a delicious hot meal was set out and waiting. The old folks were already seated, and Betsy was serving soup from the large tureen.

Missus Findlay was particularly attentive to me throughout the meal.

I found out the reason, half way through dinner. She was looking for a partner for bridge and hoped I would comply. Since I felt it to be a social obligation, I agreed, and spent the rest of the evening playing cards with old Mister Morgan, Betsy, and Missus Findlay. Fortunately, Missus Findlay had put out the brandy. Hence, the evening was pleasantly spent with a glow in my cheeks as I told them, a pirate's tale.

Chapter Five

The following morning I didn't even bother asking Mister Burnett about interviewing William Bartleby. I just took my assignments from him without a word. He looked puzzled, but didn't say anything.

The assignments were the same old boring crap that he always gave me. First I had to interview an old lady who was organizing a women's auxiliary for the Presbyterian Church. Then I had to interview three chaps who wanted to set up a volunteer fire brigade. My final assignment was to interview somebody whose horse had run away. I don't know, but I had the distinct impression Mister Burnett did not really want too much excitement in his news paper. Perhaps he was a jelly fish?

After work I had to stay over time, to help clean the press. I was tired, but it was my job. So, I helped clean the press; a messy business I detested. However, we all took turns helping the press man, Mister Carrot, pronounced Carro. We finished the job around six thirty.

When I finally got home, I didn't feel overly motivated to go to the dungeon, however, I forced myself to go. I had no idea how much longer Bill would be in the jail. I had to take the opportunity to get as much out of him as I could. So, I gathered up food, a bottle of ale, my writing stuff, and set off for the jail, a twenty minute walk from where I lived.

The guards were used to me by now, and since the payment policies had changed, I was no longer being fleeced along the way. It was a very pleasant change. I figured I had spent at least four or five shillings already, interviewing pirates. Alas, most of the money was misspent, because the majority of pirates didn't have much to say. William Bartleby was an exception. He was worth the money I paid; every last penny.

Bill was standing, awaiting my arrival. He had a big grin on his face. He was obviously happy to see me. He gave me a warm handshake and suddenly pulled me close to the bars; giving me a hug. I immediately felt glad I had forced myself to come for the visit. It felt good to be appreciated. He asked how my day had been.

I told him about my boring assignments that day.

He laughed.

I told him that I thought interviewing a famous pirate beat the hell out of interviewing old ladies.

William laughed and told me that I shouldn't sell old ladies short. He said he knew some old ladies, 'Who may have had snow on their roofs, but had plenty of fire in their hearths.'

I wasn't sure what he meant, but I laughed along with him, just to be polite.

Bill looked at my leather bag.

I could tell that he was hungry. This time I had brought left over turkey and ham, with a potato salad. Missus Findlay had made the salad especially for him. When I told Bill about her doing that, he was very touched and grateful. He told me profusely to thank Missus Findlay, and after tasting it, how delicious it was.

We eagerly dug in; I was famished also. We ate, barely exchanging words, other than to say how good everything tasted. We were done in about ten minutes.

When we were finished eating, we drank some ale and toasted our new friendship. Then I got out my writing stuff and he took up his story telling position on the cot, hands behind his head.

When I was ready, he began.

'So, as I was telling you yesterday, I had been transferred to the *Buckingham;* the 70 gun flag ship of a rear admiral. Well, as I told you, the rear admiral was no saintly human being, although he was called the, *Honorable* Temple West, I thought him most dishonorable for gunning down those French vessels, as I told you. It deepened my hatred for the British navy and the Crown. There is no honour in subterfuge. At least we pirates run up a Jolly Roger. We let everyone know what we are. The governments of the world hide their thievery behind colorful flags and pretty ribbons.

Anyway, the *Buckingham* was a bigger ship than the *Pluto*. There were more men on board. Invariably someone rubs one the wrong way. There was such a person on the *Buckingham*. His name was Boatswain's Mate, Clarence McNairn.

McNairn was a sneaky bastard, who was always trying to ferret out trouble. He would report a man for swearing, even if something heavy had fallen on the man's foot, for example. McNairn would have turned in his own mother if she'd done something, he thought was against the rules. And believe you me, the British navy has a lot of rules about all kinds of things. People are whipped on a regular basis in the navy for the slightest infractions. And that is regulation flogging, according to the book.' Bill emphasized the point by pointing his right index finger at me. 'Flogging by the book, Peter. Imagine that.'

I just shook my head and continued writing, mumbling what Bill had just said.

Bill, seeing that I was concentrating on writing his words down, lay back on the cot and continued his tale.

'McNairn loved to see people whipped. In fact, because he was a boatswain's mate, he got to do a good lot of it. He seemed to like it, and laid it on, as hard as he could, according to regulations. The stuff Blight was pulling, that was beyond regulations. That is why he had to be killed. If I had relied on a court martial, it could have taken months, and even then, there was no guarantee a man like Blight would have gotten a noose, like he deserved. I merely saved everyone a lot of trouble. Right, Peter?'

I nodded and grunted something, I don't remember what. I was writing like mad, trying to keep up.

Bill noticed that I was having trouble keeping up and slowed down his speech a little.

'Anyway, there I was on the *Buckingham*, when we went to war with France. We were hit amidships and lost twenty sailors. A close friend of mine amongst them. Unfortunately, the boatswain's mate was not one of them.

Because we were a flag ship, we were helped to escape the melee and managed to make it back to Woolwich. The *Buckingham* had sustained substantial damage and needed a month in dry dock. We were all given shore leave.

It would have been a good time if it hadn't been for Boatswain's Mate, Clarence McNairn, who watched us like a hawk. Everywhere I went, he seemed to be there. The Crown and Anchor, The Bloated Pig, The Demon's Maw, it didn't matter. There was nowhere we could go to have some drinks and fun, McNairn was everywhere.

So, there was only one thing we could do. We had to get rid of him. My friends agreed. So, we hatched a plot to get him drunk. It wasn't hard to persuade him. McNairn liked his rum and we pretended to be nice to him; like we were not annoyed to see him at the Blue Rhinoceros, one afternoon, when we thought we had found the pub he had not visited.

And yet, there he was.

We had agreed that if we saw McNairn we would act pleased to see him and invite him to have a drink with us.

So he did. He liked his rum, as I told you, especially if others were buying.

Gradually, cup by cup, we got him totally pissed drunk. He could barely stand, but we managed to convince him to come outside with us, which he did. Then we led him to a dark area of the docks and dumped him in the sea.

McNairn wasn't missed until roll call the next morning. They found him later, washed up on shore; an obvious case of a drunk falling off the docks. It wasn't the first time that had happened in Woolwich. I'm sure it has happened here, in Halifax. What do you think, Peter?'

Bill stepped from his cot and took a drink from the bottle I had brought. It was ale, this time. Wine was beginning to cost me too much. When he asked, I mentioned that I was actually quite poor. The newspaper did not pay me very much, so that he would have to be content with ale, from then on.

He immediately told me again that there was nothing to worry about. And this time he told me why.

'I have a buried treasure, Peter, my lad. What I always advised my colleagues was to stash gold and silver, here and there, where ever we regularly made port. I have done that for years. I have a stash in Halifax. It is why I came here, in the first place. I came up to grab my Halifax treasure.' Bill's tone became more enthusiastic and persuasive. 'There is more than enough to pay for food and wine. There might even be some left over to help me escape.'

Bill had slipped the word, 'escape' into the conversation so subtly, I almost missed it. However, since I am a reporter, I have learned to listen with both of my ears.

'Help you escape?' I said, looking over my shoulder, to see if any guards were within earshot.

'Yes, help me to get out of this place. I have easily enough money in that stash to buy a disguise and hire a ship. You could help me, Peter. Just think of it. You could help me carry on my struggle against the English.'

I reminded him that he was English.

His reply was that he was ashamed to be English and had taken on an international citizenship. The English, as far as he was concerned, were one of the most predatory races on Earth. He therefore felt no allegiance to any country; only the world.

I couldn't comment because I did not have much experience with other peoples and was not aware of the rapaciousness of the English in particular.

'What do you say, Peter? Will you help me? Will you help me escape?'

I looked at the pirate for a long time and thought about the things he had said over the last few days. I had to admit he did have good reasons for his hatred against the English. However, I did remind him that the French had equally tortuous discipline in their navy, and that other navies probably did, as well.

He agreed, but, he being English, should only involve himself with a struggle against his own government, he said. It was up to the French, or the Spanish, or any other nation's people to solve their own problems with oppressive governments. 'However, judging from what most people have said about France,' he continued, 'It is a very progressive country. They have the highest minimum wages in Europe.'

I knew Bill was telling the truth because I interviewed a French man, who was setting up a bakery in Halifax. I doubted if people had much reason to complain in France, is what he told me.

Bill agreed and stressed it was all the more reason to fight against the English Crown, because it was oppressive, not progressive.

I told Bill that his talk was treason. If I helped him to escape, I could be charged with treason! I didn't like what I heard was done to people who committed treason against the British Crown. To be drawn and quartered was not my plan for my demise. When it comes, I want it to be painless, and preferably in my sleep. 'An easy transition from one life to the next,' I said.

'Aye, but Peter, think of it. You could not only help me to escape. You and I could team up and we could go to sea on a ship. I know where many of my friends are. We could round them up and we could go pirating on the Seven Seas. Then you would have a first hand experience with pirating. Wouldn't that make a much better book? I can fill you in about my life along the way, plus you would get some first hand experience on the bounding main. I could teach you to sail. Just think of it. We can float about in southern waters, enjoying the sun, roasting a turtle on the beach, drinking good wine and rum. Maybe, if we're lucky, we find some nice girlfriends in a port somewhere...

Peter, it is the best life there is! It is true freedom. You would be amongst friends who love you and would die for you. We have a lot of laughs, we pirates. I think we're way more free than some of those, privateers. Those cowards still want protection from the king, by asking him for permission to steal from the merchants of other countries. It is such a scam. I have no respect for those kind of pirates, and would rob from them, as well. And that goes for the privateers of any country.'

I reminded Bill that many privateers were simply people who were willing to use their private ships to help their king or queen protect the land from invaders.

'Those are the other kind of privateers, for which I do have some regard. If they are protecting their country. But many use that as a smoke screen to hide behind, while they plunder merchant ships belonging to those countries with which their king has an issue.' Bill drank from the ale bottle and stared at the wall behind me for a moment. Then he looked directly at me, reached out through the bars, and touched my right shoulder. He pleaded with me to help him.

'Before telling you about my treasure, I had to be sure about you, Peter. I think you can help me; and it would be really worth your while. There is a lot of money in that treasure of mine.'

Treasure. So it was as I suspected. There actually was no reason for me to be worried about money. Perhaps my dreams had come true. I looked at Bill.

He looked back at me with pleading eyes. 'Please help me, Peter,' he said.

I did not have the heart to say no, he looked so wretched at that moment. However, I told him I would think about it. I told him the idea of committing treason was not something I took lightly. The consequences were severe, if I was caught. Plus, I didn't think I could do it alone.

He sternly advised me not to involve anyone. 'Loose lips sink ships,' he said meaningfully. 'Remember that.'

I assured him I would keep my mouth shut.

'Are you coming to see me tomorrow?' he asked.

I told him that Friday, after work, was when the staff went out for a pint, together. It was important to me, because it was the only opportunity I might have to spend some time with a particular girl whom I liked. She would be at the pub on Friday.

Bill totally agreed that it was important to see the girl. 'Besides, why would you want to come and see a pirate in gaol, when you can see a pretty girl in the pub. I don't blame you one bit.'

I assured him that on Saturday I would have a good part of the day to speak with him and would give him my answer then.

Bill nodded and smiled. Then he leaned closer to me and looked over to see if the guard was coming yet. When he was sure that we were alone, he told me where his treasure was hidden.

I wrote the details carefully in my notebook and repeated them to him.

Bill sighed. 'Oh, Peter, I surely pray to God that you do not betray me, and that you will help me. There is more than enough money there, and I would surely give you what is left, if only you buy me a ship, new clothes, and some food and water, and help me to get out of here. I don't want to be made a bloody spectacle in front of King George and his despicable sycophants, and their blood crazed minions. It is not a fit way for a man like me to go out of this world.' He held on to my arm and I could feel him pleading through his grip.

I assured him that I would not betray him and would think about his proposals. I reminded him that my life was at stake, as well.

'Aye, that is true,' he agreed. 'I have to remember that you have something of a life here. And there is the girl. Girls do have a way of keeping a man home based. However, Peter, you have to realize, girls are everywhere. Beautiful girls. Sweet, delicious girls, who know how to love a man. I have met them in every port I have been. It is how God has made girls. They are creatures who love. Where there are women, there is love, and house plants.'

I laughed when he added, 'house plants' to the equation. It was such a simple observation, but it was so true. Women loved to nurture plants. They usually liked, plants, cats, and little dogs, children, and cooking good food for everybody. Missus Findlay was like that. My mother was like that, God rest her soul.

I asked Bill, if I was to buy a ship, what kind of vessel he would want.

He described a sloop. 'That would suit our purpose very well. Two men can sail her. She is small, quick, and not easily seen until close up. She'll hold ten or more men and weapons. A couple of small cannons, say four pounders, for punching in below the water line, when we're close up. Muskets, crossbows, and swords, those are all the weapons we need.' Bill thought for a moment and then added, 'A sloop is what I need. I think you will find more than the price of a new sloop in my stash. However, you don't have to buy a new one, because there might not be one for sale. And to order a new one made, there is no time. I need to get out of here as soon as possible. The sooner the better.'

I asked Bill how I would go about avoiding suspicion, buying an entire sloop with cash.

He told me to pretend that I was an agent for a buyer who wished to remain anonymous. That his affairs were his own and nobody else's. 'If the seller wants the cash, he'll sell the vessel,' he said knowingly.

I asked how I would know if it was a good boat, or not.

Bill shook his head. 'You don't know anything about sailing vessels, do you?'

'Not really,' I told him.

'Alright. The first thing you have to learn is the difference between a ship and a boat. To my way of thinking, a boat is an open vessel you row, perhaps sometimes a sail is added, as in a yawl. In the case of the vessel I want you to buy, it will be a ship. It must have closed quarters and sails, preferably lots of sails. But not so many that we can't handle her. Therefore, I suggest you buy a sloop.

What you need to do first, is go into the ship and tap the hull with a small hammer and check for rot. It would be a good idea if you can get into the water and check the hull from the outside, as well. Check all of the rigging, to see if the ropes are in good order and not frayed and tattered looking. Check all of the hardware to see that it is fastened and in proper working order. Look over the mast and check the sails. You will know if the sails are rotten, or not. You will know if the ship is up to my requirements. And, besides, depending on whom you buy the ship from, you can tell by talking with the owner. Not all ship dealers are unscrupulous. In fact, most are very respectable and would not send you out in a leaking ship. Life is dependent on a sturdy ship when you are out at sea.'

Buying a sloop. I was beginning to commit myself to buying a sloop. Even if I only went that far, wouldn't I be suspect, I asked. Halifax is not such a big town. Surely, when the pirate was missed from the jail, the mystery purchase of a sloop would certainly direct attention to me. Under torture, I could easily see myself confessing the whole thing. If I bought the sloop, I would have to buy the entire package. There would be no remaining in Halifax for me. When Missus Findlay figured out that I was gone, the connection between me and the escaped pirate would be pretty obvious. Remaining in Halifax, after helping Bill to escape, would get me executed for sure, I told him.

Bill agreed that it was a dangerous request. 'It is a big favour to ask,' he said. 'I shall forever be in your debt, Peter. Trust me, I shall make it up to you a hundred fold.'

'I will think about it,' I told him.

Bill took another drink of ale and went to sit on his cot. I could see that he was going into deep thoughts concerning his revelations; probably about giving me the details regarding his treasure. He had only known me a few hours. I am sure, because of my hesitations, he was having second thoughts.

I assured him that I would not betray him, just as the guard entered the cell block. I gathered my things into my leather bag and set the remainder of our meal on the stool, leaving the bottle where it was. I don't think the guard noticed it.

It wasn't raining when I walked home. The streets were still muddy, and chewed up from the horses and wagons. It made walking home a slow going affair. As I approached the fish monger's shop, I could smell the day's catch heavy on the air. I hoped we would not eat fish for supper.

When I got home, I had supper with Missus Findlay and Betsy, in the kitchen. The others had already eaten. Missus Findlay had served them and waited for me. As it turned out, she had made a delicious fish chowder, which totally changed my opinion about eating fish that day. She and Betsy were such good cooks.

Missus Findlay was curious about my visit with the pirate. Since I had told her about him over bridge, the other day, she seemed to be very interested. I guess it goes to show you that everyone likes a pirate story. Even Betsy was listening intently, as I told them the tale of Bill and Captain Blight.

After supper I went to my room and had a short nap, after which I assembled my notes and looked them over. I had trouble focusing. I kept thinking about Bill's request. It was an incredible opportunity for adventure. However, it could be a horrendous end to a young, upwardly mobile, junior reporter from the Morning Post.

I fantasized that maybe, if I remained in Halifax, I might even marry Virginia Spencer, the girl whom I hoped to meet in the pub on Friday. She and I had talked about a permanent relationship. I was head over heals in love with her, and I think she with me, as well. Whenever I thought of her, all thoughts of risking my life evaporated like a dissipating cloud. Why would I risk being drawn and quartered, when I could be making love to

Virginia? It made the choice pretty clear, when I put it in that perspective. I mean, what would you do under the circumstances? Would you stay in your dreary life to have the girl, or would you take the risk and live an adventurous life, however short it might be? Those are momentous questions. My heart was sorely troubled over it. I knew sleep would be an issue, if I didn't come to some sort of conclusion.

As I sat there in my room, I realized it was the wrong place for me to be. I needed to go to a pub. Fortunately, the Boar's Snout was only two blocks away. I decided to go there. Before stepping out, I checked out of the window. It was raining again. I made certain to bring my umbrella and rain slicker.

When I got to the pub, it was about eight thirty. There were quite a number of people enjoying drinks around small, round tables. Three young women were sitting with two gentlemen, by the fire. I didn't take close notice of them, at first.

When I had obtained a pint of dark ale, on account it was raining and cold, I sat down at an empty table and glanced over at the three young women by the fire. As I became more accustomed to the light in the pub, I noticed that one of the young women was non other than, Virginia, the girl I was hoping to see on Friday.

Of course I stepped over to her and said hello. She appeared very happy to see me, which encouraged me considerably. She introduced the two gentlemen as her father and uncle, and the two other young women, as her sister and cousin. It was a most fortuitous occasion for me. They invited me to join them. Hence, I came to pass several pleasant hours in conversation with these new friends.

As it turned out, Virginia's father, whose name was, Edward Spencer, was the owner of the shipping company, Spencer & Spencer, where Virginia worked as a clerk. She never told me that her family was wealthy. I guess she wanted to make certain that I loved her for her, and not her father's money.

Virginia's uncle, her father's brother, was the partner, who apparently knew a lot about ship building. Of course, somewhere along in the conversation I steered it towards ships, and how to purchase one. 'A sloop for instance,' I ventured. 'How much would such a vessel cost?' I asked.

Uncle Thomas was full of information. I even learned where I could find a sloop for sale, and he would even help me look it over. Nobody questioned whether I had the money or not. Being as how these folks were rich, they just assumed I was too. I was pleased to be thought so.

When we bid each other good night, I had a private moment with Virginia and told her how I had been looking forward, for over a week, to see her on Friday, at the staff get together. She agreed it was nice to see me too and gave me a kiss on the cheek, before she climbed into her father's coach. They offered me a ride home, but since I only lived a short distance away, I told them I wanted to walk. I had my umbrella, I said.

I lied about liking to walk in the rain. I just didn't want them to see the massive erection I had bulging in my pants, after Virginia kissed me on the cheek. Smelling her up close like that, always did something to my blood pressure.

I wanted her.

As I walked home, thoughts of Virginia and me flooded my brain, only to be smashed by thoughts of me being drawn on a rack. It was not a pretty sight. I much preferred looking at Virginia. I didn't want to look at both. My mind had a hard time trying to focus on her and to dismiss the other.

By the time I got into bed, I had resolved to take Virginia with me. I would clear it with Bill and take her with us. Maybe she would love to come roving on the Seven Seas? She had an adventurous spirit. It certainly wouldn't hurt to have her along. She could cook. She might like that. To cook for pirates on a ship. No harm in asking, I thought, as I blew out my candle and pulled the covers over me. Maybe Virginia might even like to learn to sail. I could envision her, standing at the helm, wind filling the sails, gulls, and waves all around, in the warm sunshine, on a glorious day. Virginia looked radiant as she held the wheel with strength and assurance, her long brown hair flying behind her. The vision was the beginning of a dream. She was so alluring.

As I lay back into my warm bed, and tried to sleep, all sorts of images flickered behind my eyes. Beautiful scenes of Virginia and I would be quickly disolved by images of Bill and I on the deck of a ship in the midst of a battle, or scenes of people dangling from gibbets in the harbour, then back to scenes of Virginia and I, living in bliss. I guess my mind was sorting through my options and trying to make sense of things.

Chapter Six

I couldn't wait for morning to get me where I needed to be; awake and in the world of reality. All night I had dreamt of Virginia, and a pirate's treasure. I dreamt of me as a pirate captain, with Virginia at my side. I liked that dream. But then, just as quickly the dream was of me being drawn and quartered. Whenever I got to that part I would wake up. That part is gruesome and I didn't like that dream, not at all. Maybe I have a pessimistic streak. I don't know. Whatever.

When I jumped out of bed I couldn't wait to get to the office. I had decided, in the time that I cleaned my teeth and got dressed, that I would take the afternoon off work, if it wasn't too busy, which it usually wasn't on a Friday. Then I would follow the directions Bill had given me and locate his treasure, if it even existed. Even though I liked the pirate, and everything, he was still a pirate. I wasn't sure if any pirate could be trusted.

When I got to the office, the first thing I did was see Mister Burnett and ask him if I could take the afternoon off. He asked me why and I said, I was looking for pirate's treasure. He laughed and thought I was joking. Then he told me to finish my articles from yesterday's interviews, and then I could go. He reminded me it was on my own time. I told him that it did not matter. I was looking for pirate's treasure. He found that very funny, the fact that I repeated it like that. I won some points with Mister Burnett. Little did he know, I really wasn't joking.

After completing the last article, about the man whose horse had run away, I literally ran home. I couldn't wait to begin the search for Bill's treasure. Hopefully, I would find it before pub time. I couldn't wait to see the living treasure, about whom I had passionate dreams all night. Just thinking of her made my pocket snake stir in its sack.

Missus Findlay wasn't expecting me, but she made me some lunch anyway, to take with me on my excursion. I explained to her that I had to go into the country, on an assignment. That is as far as I went with her. If I had said to her what I told Mister Burnett, she would have believed me and probably wanted to come along. She was a spry old duck for her age.

I got my umbrella, just in case, and my rain slicker, because you never know, and of course my leather bag, with my note book, quills and ink pot. I put the bread and roast beef, Missus Findlay had given me, in the bag, along with a bottle of water. Then I set off, west of town, towards the big forest, where the road bends and heads south. It was about four and a half miles, he had told me.

The air was chilly. There was a breeze coming off the ocean, which sent chills deep into my bones. Gulls were screeching in the air above me. Fortunately, the road was beginning to dry, making the walking somewhat easier, and not so slippery.

After walking about twenty minutes, I was plenty warmed up, so that the cold didn't bother me anymore. I stopped to check my notebook, in order to make sure I was heading in the right direction. My notes said, 'On the main road, west of town, there is a large oak tree to the left, by the bend where the road turns south.' Judging from the traffic, I was on the main road, alright. People on horseback, and on wagons, or carriages were coming and going every eight minutes, or so. I hoped that I would have some privacy when I got to where I had to go.

When I got to the bend in the road, as Bill had described, I stopped and drank some water. I had been walking for about forty minutes and couldn't see the town in the distance. I checked my notebook again. I had to look for a large, square rock, covered with green moss and orange lichen, at the base of a large oak tree. It was supposed to be off the road, about fifty yards to the left.

Sure enough, there they were, the rock and the tree. They were beautifully situated away from the road, and out of view behind shrubbery and some willows.

Bill told me to look around the base of the oak tree and I should see a bronze spike driven into a large root, facing the rock.

Sure enough, there was the bronze spike, just as he said. It had been covered up with some moss, so that it was not visible to anyone, unless they were specifically directed to look there. If I jiggled the spike it was supposed to pull out a big plug which had been cut from the tree root, like the lid of a small box. Inside I was to find a key. Which I promptly did.

Then I was to count off twelve paces to the immediate right of the key's little hideout. There I was supposed to find a large flat stone lying on the ground. I was to lift that stone and under it I would find a box which could be unlocked with the key.

When I found the flat stone and tried to lift it; it was as far as I got with the treasure hunt. The stone was too heavy. I couldn't lift it.

So, there I was, four miles away from Halifax, with a stone I couldn't lift. I knew I should have gotten help.

I sat down and had another drink of water. I didn't feel like eating. I was in a quandary. I couldn't ask anyone passing on the road. Imagine asking someone on the road, 'Excuse me, could you help me please. I need to lift a stone off a chest of pirate treasure.' First of all people would think I was daft. And secondly, if they helped, they would want a share, and blabber about it all over town.

I had to realize a solution involving only me.

As I sat there I was staring at a rock, about the size of my leather bag, lying on the ground in front of me. Nearby lay a goodly piece of oak branch, which had fallen from the tree. It looked like a pretty solid piece of wood.

I left my bag where it sat and dragged the rock towards the flat stone and then, using the oak branch for a lever, lifted the slab out of the way.

The branch moved the slab about twelve inches. It was enough for me to look inside the hole.

Sure enough, there was a small chest in the hole.

Wasting no more time, I placed my lever under the stone, in a better position this time, and slid the stone completely away from the hole, totally enabling the removal of the chest.

When I attempted to remove the chest, however, I couldn't lift it. The chest was too heavy. It was too darned heavy! Can you imagine? After all that, the box was too heavy to lift out of the hole.

So, there was nothing for me to do but open the box inside the hole and take some of the heavy stuff out. I had no idea what I would find in there, but, whatever it was, it was too heavy.

With a fast beating heart I unlocked the box and lifted the lid.

What I saw, sat me back with surprise. The pirate had been correct. The box was filled with gold and silver coins; rijksdaalders, florins, pieces of eight, doubloons, sovereigns, there were even some old Greek and Roman coins. An amazing pile of coins to be sure. It was no wonder that the box was heavy.

There was no way that I could take the contents home in my leather bag. However, I could take some of it, in several trips. Eventually I would have it all at home. Thus, I took out some handfuls of coins and put them into my bag, until it was heavy on my shoulders. Then, I carefully closed the box and locked it, putting the key snugly into a small pocket in my waistcoat. I struggled with the stone and managed to restore it pretty much like it was before. I wasn't worried. The chance of someone walking off the road and sliding that stone aside, was pretty slim.

The moment I had that thought, someone stepped from behind the shrubbery, intent on relieving himself. He must have come from the road and needed to take care of nature's call. He had his trousers down and was beginning to squat when he saw me. I pretended not to see him and walked away in the other direction. I didn't look back. I never like to watch someone having a bowel movement.

After walking back to the road, circumventing the pooping man, I made it home in record time.

By the time I got up to my room, my shoulders were sore from the weight of the gold coins in my bag. When I set the bag on my bed and opened it, I was quite ecstatic, as you can well imagine. Here alone, in one haul, I had enough gold to live happily ever after. There were at least five more loads like that left in the box. It certainly would buy food and wine for a long, long time, and then some. Bill could afford to buy at least five sloops with what was in the box, I figured. But, then, I did not know how the gold coins would translate into a ship. That I would have to figure out. I was only guessing, there were so many coins.

The assortment of gold coins wasn't exactly the usual method of financial transaction in Halifax. The variety of coins shouted pirate treasure to me, as it probably would do to anyone else. How to legitimize the treasure became the question of the day. Perhaps I could claim that I inherited some of my great uncle's coin collection. It was a singular problem, which would take some fancy figuring to solve. Perhaps Virginia's father might be able to help. As I thought of Virginia's father, it suddenly dawned on me, she was going to be at the pub. I didn't want to miss her. I had no idea what time it was, but I knew I had to hurry.

I quickly stashed the coins in the bottom drawer of my dresser and changed my clothes. I put on my good, going out clothes, and carefully combed my hair and brushed my teeth. I grabbed three gold coins from the drawer. If anyone was to ask where I got them, I figured I could say they came from my rich uncle.

When I arrived at the pub it was five o'clock. It was the perfect time to be there. People were finishing their day's work and stopping for a pint. The gang from the newspaper would be arriving. I was able to secure a table before the major crowd got there.

I managed to find a table in the nick of time. I was so glad I had been able to secure the table, because it impressed Virginia. She said so, when she sat down next to me, moments after I had arrived. She touched my arm and smiled. I had to be careful I didn't upset the table with; he who doesn't listen to my commands and rises to what ever occasion he bloody well pleases. I couldn't believe the effect the woman had on me. My boner certainly confirmed the fact my body liked her.

Virginia told me she had come a little early, hoping I would be there early as well. She wanted to sit beside me. She told me that she loved me.

I thought I had died and gone to heaven. I could only stare into her incredibly beautiful eyes. I hung on every word she said. The sound of her voice was like angels singing. Her breath was expensive perfume. Her teeth were pearls. Her skin like the finest cream. Her hair a cascade of brown. I breathed her in. I adored her. She was my angel.

Eventually, the rest of the gang arrived and broke the euphoria I was feeling, but only for a moment, as we said hello to the arrivals. Of course I did not stand up, which in our younger crowd, was not unacceptable behavior. Had they brought their elders, then that would have been a different story. I would have projected something more of myself than would be considered appropriate, under the circumstances.

When everyone was seated, I turned my attention totally on Virginia. I couldn't get enough of her. We talked and talked. She laughed when I said something funny. She threw her head back and exposed her exquisite neck. I wanted to bite that neck. I wanted to nibble on her ears. I wanted to sniff her hair in my face. I wanted to immerse myself in her, she was so wonderful. I wanted her forever. Virginia totally captivated me that night. I was her slave.

I know you are thinking, 'Poor guy, totally ruled by his dick.' Let me assure you, it's not completely so. I was also following my heart, and my mind. My heart was saying to me that she was the girl I would marry in a flash, and my mind was saying, I like talking with her, because she listens and she has interesting conversation herself. She is intelligent. I like that best of all in anybody.

So, we hit it off. Virginia and I were obviously interested in each other.

By the time she and I had each consumed three pints of ale, we were both grinning from ear to ear and decided to take a walk outside, to get some air.

Outside, Virginia took my hand and we walked, pleasantly plastered, under a cloudy sky. It was on that walk that I told her about Bill and his request to help him escape.

I told her it was important that she keep, what I told her, entirely to herself. I also asked her if she was interested in meeting the pirate in the jail. To my great joy she immediately said that she would love to meet him. That she wasn't at all scared to go into the dungeon. In fact she was looking forward to it. I loved her spirited enthusiasm.

I didn't tell Virginia about the treasure, not yet, anyway. I thought I would wait to see what Bill thought of her. Who knows, maybe she might be interested in an adventure. She was, after all, not exactly your average woman. Virginia had spirit and a mind of her own. It was what I loved most about her. It was her spirit. She laughed a lot. The sound was like heaven's symphony. I adored her.

When we returned to the pub, most of the newspaper group had left. A couple of diehards, the guys who man the press, were still at it. They were probably on their sixth pints and leaning into the wind at precarious angles. Virginia and I decided to leave.

I walked her home, which was only five blocks from where I lived. She lived with her parents in a big, brick house with a magnificent verandah and a porch. She was obviously well to do, that was for certain. But, I didn't care. I loved her. I did not care how much money her parents had. Besides, I now had a fortune in my dresser. One gold coin paid for two complete rounds for everybody, and I still got change. Buying the rounds really impressed Virginia. She liked my generosity.

It was about eleven o'clock when I kissed her.

And she kissed me back. I will always remember how she kissed me back. That kiss is forever memorable. The sensation was like having fireworks go off in side. I was convinced the top of my head was going to come off and my crotch explode.

I was transported in a celestial fog. Her lips, her tongue, her teeth, her breath, her heaving bosom…I knew she was a prize and I aimed to do my best to keep her. I knew that I would adore her for the rest of her days.

And I did. As far as I was concerned, the sun rose and set on Virginia for the rest of her life.

We arranged to see each other the next day.

When I walked home, I felt like I was walking on air. I don't know if my feet were touching the ground, or not. I had the distinct impression my feet did not touch the ground and I became slightly paranoid that someone would see me walking on air. It was a totally euphoric experience. I must have literally floated into Missus Findlay's rooming house. I have no recollection of my touching the stairs, or getting undressed, or anything. I have no idea how I got into bed.

I do remember I had to sleep on my side.

Next morning I woke at ten. I had slept in, but it didn't matter, it was Saturday. It was my bath day. Missus Findlay had hot water on the stove, waiting for me. We filled the tub in my room and I had a glorious bath, all the while thinking of my angel, only a few blocks away. I could hardly wait to see her; to touch her hand.

After brunch I walked briskly to Virginia's house, some gold coins in my pocket and my bag over my shoulder. Although it was cloudy, it did not threaten rain. I brought my umbrella, just the same. I had also brought some shepherd's pie and wine for Bill. The pie was still warm, and hopefully, if Virginia would not take too long, the pie would still be warm when it arrived at the jail.

When I got to Virginia's house she was already waiting for me, a huge grin on her pretty face. I couldn't help but grin back. I nearly split my face. It was so fine to see her again. She kissed me when she greeted me. Then she did something I was not expecting, or was ready for. She called her parents out to meet me.

Mister Spencer knew me already, of course, but Virginia's mother had only heard about me. According to her she heard quite a lot about me, and assured me it was all very good.

I was very glad to hear that, and looked at Virginia, who was blushing.

After exchanging some pleasantries, we excused ourselves and headed off to the jail to meet Bill. We didn't tell Virginia's parents where we were going. They probably wouldn't have approved.

We walked holding hands; I floating on air. I had no idea she and I would be able to express our feelings quite so quickly and comfortably. In our silly society, it usually took a long time before a man was allowed to be with his girl, alone. The fact we were both twenty five years old probably had a lot to do with it. We weren't exactly children anymore. Plus, Virginia obviously had very open minded parents and were probably hoping their oldest daughter would find a man. They probably couldn't understand why she was still single at her age. I couldn't either. She was such a prize. I asked Virginia about that.

She said she hadn't met the right man, until she met me.

My cheeks must have glowed when she said that. I nearly burst some buttons on my shirt. Those words were the most beautiful words I had ever heard in my life. I was the right man for Virginia Spencer. I felt so grateful and quietly thanked God for my good fortune. I kissed her and hugged her for a long time, right there, in front of the jail, in full view of the two smirking guards. I didn't care. To hell with propriety. We were in love!

The guards were the same pair of grunts I met on an earlier day. One of them was the blasphemer about whom I told you. He scratched his groin and stared at Virginia. 'That's quite a show you put on there,' he grunted lasciviously.

I told him to watch his mouth or I would have him reported. I told him that his insolence was uncalled for, and rude. He had made Virginia blush. I felt like giving the man a poke in the nose, but thought better of it. The guards had halberds. I had my wits, that was it.

We passed by the guards and entered the lobby. I didn't recognize the man behind the desk. He looked like one of those tin soldiers they sell in the toy shop; just a bit too perfect. There was not one hair out of alignment. His upturned mustaches were waxed and had needle sharp points. His little beard was impeccably trimmed. His uniform, unlike McFee's, was pressed and his brass buttons were highly polished.

The man stood up when he saw Virginia. He was obviously a gentleman.

I introduced ourselves and he gave me a firm, friendly handshake.

The dapper soldier kissed Virginia's hand and clicked his heels. He told us his name was Sergeant Hans von Hollern. He was born at Herrenhausen, 'The birth place of George II.' Hans made quite a point of stressing the latter fact.

I pretended to be impressed.

Since talking with Bill for a few hours, I already was feeling less inclined towards the monarchy. I was beginning to understand that kings were not good for our collective well being.

When the sergeant had finished his introduction he informed me that the prison was in need of new uniforms for the guards. He had taken it upon himself to collect donations from visitors. He assured us the fund raising scheme had been cleared with the superintendent.

I asked Hans if he had worked out a price schedule.

This he had, in fact, done. He produced it from the desk, and proudly held it out to me.

What I saw was a very carefully drawn price list, with columns and headings.

For men, the price was three pence. For a woman it was two pence. A child up to the age of six was free of charge. Children from six to twelve were a half penny. Children over twelve and under eighteen were one and a half pence.

It was quite an achievement; an official chart listing the various prices the jail was charging for various ranks of human beings. At least the price was now fixed and we wouldn't see the fluctuations according to the whim of the official in charge. Now that the post had been upgraded, everything seemed official and correct. Eventually, nobody could question the fees anymore.

I still thought it wrong to charge for visitations, however.

A grunt led Virginia and I down into the lowest level of the jail. Virginia found the air to be foul and covered her delicate nose with her handkerchief.

I reminded the guard that perhaps the place could stand a cleaning.

His reply was that I was welcome to do it, if it bothered me.

I wasn't surprised to hear his answer.

Bill was standing, as usual, when we arrived. He was surprised to see Virginia and attempted to straighten out his clothes and hair.

When I introduced her, he took her hand tenderly and kissed it.

'Peter has spoken of you. He never mentioned how beautiful you are. You certainly bring rays of sunshine into this dreary place,' he said sincerely.

Bill had a way with words. I could see that Virginia was immediately charmed by the pirate.

I set my bag down and pulled out the shepherd's pie and a fork. I handed the pie to Bill through the bars. He thanked me profusely. The pie was still a little bit warm, I think. He ate it right away. I don't think he had breakfast that morning. If he did, it was, either, very meagre, or it was a while ago.

I cleaned the seat of the little stool for Virginia to sit on. Then produced a bottle of good ale and a bottle of wine. I figured, why not feed Bill with some of his money. There was more than enough money to fill his entire cell with food and wine and still there would be enough for years to come. It was a good stash I told him.

He looked at me with surprise on his face. Then he looked at Virginia and raised an eyebrow.

I shook my head to indicate she didn't know anything. I told Bill I wanted him to meet Virginia before we discussed any more plans.

Bill reminded me that his days might be numbered, so there was not much time.

This part Virginia clued into. She burst right out and said it. Not that any guards could have heard, down the hall, but it was enthusiastic and surprised both Bill and I.

'We should help you get out of here,' she volunteered. 'We can't let you be hanged. Peter has told me so much about you. I totally agree with your point of view and want to help you,' she said.

I couldn't believe my ears. Virginia was willing to help spring the pirate. She was quite a woman, that one. I explained to her that if we were caught, we would face severe punishments, even breaking on the wheel, or some such horror.

Virginia didn't blink an eye. 'Then we'll just have to escape together. I never liked living in Halifax. Life is boring here. I want adventure, Peter! I want to get out of town. Maybe this is the way it will come about. By helping Bill escape. What do you think?'

Neither Bill, nor I, could believe our ears. It took us a moment for Virginia's words to sink in. Women like Virginia were not common. She was a woman with a spirit for adventure. Most women seemed to be very conservative Christians, who walked in constant fear of the Lord. I didn't get the impression my girl was one to look over her shoulder much.

When Bill felt sure of her sincerity, he told me that I might as well tell Virginia about the treasure.

I showed him a gold coin.

Bill smiled broadly. 'Was it as I said?'

I told him that the treasure was more than I could carry and that I had taken about a fifth of it, stashing it in my dresser.

Virginia asked to see the coin, which she examined closely. It happened to be an old Roman coin. She found it a fascinating object, turning it over and over. 'Makes me wonder how many hands, over the centuries, have handled this coin,' she mused.

'Judging from how worn it is, I'd say lots of people have handled it,' said Bill, turning the coin over in his hand.

When Virginia examined the coin closer she announced that it showed a profile of the emperor Nero and a woman by the name of Poppaea, whom she assumed was his wife. 'See, you can read their names, if you look closely,' she said, pointing to the inscription.

In the dim light of the dungeon, I had trouble reading the worn coin.

Bill couldn't make out the inscription, either.

Virginia asked if there were more coins, such as the one we were examining.

Both William and I assured her there were plenty more where that coin came from.

The information delighted Virginia, who obviously had an interest in old coins.

Bill told her she could keep the coin, as a memento of her visit.

Virginia thanked Bill and again reiterated her desire to help the pirate escape. She said she hoped we would let her in on our plan. Virginia explained how she could be of service by cooking for us, for example.

Bill and I exchanged a glance and happily agreed to include her.

We decided, then and there, to join company and effect an escape from Halifax, for all three of us.

Thus we began to plan in earnest, me taking notes when necessary.

Virginia was an excellent contributor. She had a lively, and quick thinking mind. Her ideas were welcome additions to our own.

When visiting time was over, we had spent four hours in the jail. It had been enough to cement a solid plan which was quite fail safe, but would take some days to effect. We told Bill that we would not visit on Sunday, but would use the day to fetch the rest of the treasure.

Bill agreed that it was a good plan.

When we left the jail, we walked briskly home. Fortunately there was no rain and the sun was even beginning to show its face through the clouds. We were both happy for that. Perhaps we would see the end of winter soon.

Virginia asked if I wanted to stay for supper at her house, but I told her I felt dirty from such a long visit in the jail, and that I didn't feel comfortable. She smiled and said she understood. We parted company with a long kiss and a promise to fetch the treasure, first thing after lunch on Sunday.

On the way home I worked through the plan in my head.

The first thing we had to do was to obtain a sloop and provisions. Virginia said that she would explain to her uncle that I needed to obtain a vessel in Halifax and get her ready for an uncle of mine, who was arriving in a few days from Liverpool. The money could be explained by saying my uncle had it shipped ahead. Once we had the sloop, we would get Bill out of jail.

Our plan was most ingenious, and very risky. However, nothing ventured, nothing gained, is something I always said to myself, in situations like that.

Next morning, I went to church with Missus Findlay and Betsy. I saw Virginia, but she was sitting with her parents. All we could do was make a little eye contact, every now and then.

The morning's sermon, I remember, had something to do with rendering unto Caesar that which is Caesar's. I remember thinking that, if Caesar was the government, I already had some ideas regarding the rendering unto Caesar bit. As far as I was concerned, Caesar had it coming, the old bastard.

After lunch I met Virginia in front of her house. Her mother came out on the porch to say hello to me, which was nice. It showed that she was interested in getting to know me. She asked me where we were going.

I told her we were going for a walk in the countryside.

Mrs. Spencer smiled and wished us a pleasant afternoon.

When we had said goodbye to Virginia's mother, we walked quickly out of town and arrived at the bend in the road within less than an hour. Virginia was a good walker, with strong legs. I had to work hard to keep up with her.

Because it was Sunday, there was hardly any traffic on the road. The day was calm and still, like a Sunday ought to be.

We walked straight to the flat stone, where she helped me lever it out of the way with the oak branch. Then we lifted the box out of the hole and I let her open the chest with the key.

Virginia's eyes nearly popped out of her head when she opened the lid and beheld the glorious pile of gold and silver coins gleaming in the sunlight. She eagerly reached into the box and let the coins run through her fingers. The shiny disks rang with a glorious clinking sound, as she let them drop into the box.

'There is enough to buy a cathedral in here!' she exclaimed.

I told her that a cathedral wouldn't float very well, and that we had better buy a sloop with the money.

She found that very funny and laughed.

I loved listening to her laugh. It was infectious. Soon she had me laughing as well, as we proceeded to unload the coins into my bag, but only as many as I could carry comfortably on my shoulders. Unfortunately, we had forgotten to bring a second bag to carry coins in, so I put the bag over Virginia's shoulders and I carried the box. It was still heavy, but manageable. On the way back we stopped several times to set the coins down and take a break. We spent the time kissing and fondling each other behind some shrubbery, or trees, along the route.

When we returned to Halifax, we took the coins straight to my rooming house. Fortunately Missus Findlay was out, so I was able to bring Virginia up to my room.

It was the first time I ever had a girl up to my room at Missus Findlay's. I felt somewhat awkward. Here she was in the room of a junior reporter. Virginia Spencer, who was used to living in a large house with servants.

She looked around the room and admired the two paintings on my walls. They belonged to the house, but I treated them as if they were mine. Having lived in Missus Findlay's establishment for two and a half years, I had grown accustomed to the accoutrements. A few things were mine, the large candle stand by my reading chair was mine. I also owned some fine books, which I had sitting in a small book case, which I also owned. It was made of oak, and sturdy like the tree itself.

The book shelf is where Virginia gravitated for a moment, as I began to pour the coins onto my bed. At the sound of the clinking coins, she came right over and ran her hands through them, letting the disks slip through her fingers. Then she took a coin out of the pile and examined it.

'It looks like it might be Greek,' she said. She pointed at the letters on the coin. 'Those are Greek letters,' she said. 'This coin must be very old.'

I took the coin from her hand and examined it. 'It is all Greek to me,' I said. 'I can't understand a thing it says.'

Virginia smiled as she took the coin from my hand. 'It's Greek to me too. I think it says, *Alexander*, something. The rest of the letters are quite worn off. This coin has also seen many hands over the centuries.' She let it fall as she picked up another coin. It was a silver Rijksdaalder from Holland. It was a fairly new coin, the date 1756, clearly visible. Virginia remarked that it was the year that the Seven Year War, between England and France, began.

I reminded her that it was England who declared the war. I was beginning to develop a dislike for England, from my talks with Bill. He was having a very profound effect on my thinking. Helping him to escape, indeed, escaping myself, and perhaps becoming a pirate, that might be what lay in store for me. The more I spoke with Bill, the more I began to think it was the right thing to do.

When we had finished looking at the coins, we carefully stashed them in the drawers of my dresser, under my clothes; silver coins in a separate drawer from the gold, of which there was the most. I noticed Virginia checking out my underwear as she placed a handful of coins under them. I pretended I didn't notice and brought an other handful of coins over. She carefully laid my clothes over the coins.

The next thing I remember is that she led me to my bed and pushed me down on it, and then lunged herself upon me. She smothered me in kisses and began to caress my inner thighs. Eventually, she was moving her hand over the mighty bulge I could not restrain. Her kisses became ever more passionate. Our tongues were exploring, as my hand was moving under her dress when we heard the door bang closed downstairs. Missus Findlay was home.

We stopped kissing for a moment and listened to the sounds downstairs. Virginia asked if Missus Findlay was likely to come up to my room.

I assured her that she would not likely come up. The only problem we faced was how I would have to sneak Virginia out of the house, so that Missus Findlay wouldn't know there had been a girl in my room. As long as we were quiet, she wouldn't suspect anything. My room was my private place. However, just to be sure, I locked the door before returning to my angel on the bed.

Before I knew it, our clothes were off and we proceeded to enjoy each other in the only way a man and woman can.

Virginia was delightful in every way. I was totally thrilled with her. Our love making was hot and passionate. However, we had to be careful and controlled, lest the bed began to make too much noise. Even as it was, the springs squeaked. At one point, the head board banged against the wall, which necessitated a momentary disentanglement, so that we could move the bed away from the wall.

For good measure, we pulled the rug from my sitting area, and put it under the bed. Perhaps it would soften the noise of the bed on the floor, we reasoned. It probably did, because I never heard anything from Missus Findlay about Virginia having been in my room.

When the bed was in place, we went back to our love making. And such it was. The most delicious, satisfying love making, the like of which I wanted always, for ever and ever, amen. What joy, I felt. It is hard to explain, but it resulted in a bond that could never be severed, as far as I was concerned. I still love her to this day and never forget her.

Anyway, at some point later in the day, when we were both exhausted and lying in bed, napping, someone knocked on my door.

We both woke up instantly.

'Who is it?' I asked.

It turned out to be old Mister Morgan.

Just a minute, I shouted, as I motioned for Virginia to gather up her clothes and hide in the wardrobe. As she quickly rushed about gathering up her clothes, I watched her, while I put on my dressing gown. Seeing her naked like that, gathering up her clothes, made my unruly organ stand up again, in order that he could have a good look, as well. It was a most inconvenient time for him to stand up and take notice.

There was nothing for me to do but grab a book to hold in front of my groin. When I saw that Virginia was safely stowed in the wardrobe, I opened the door a crack and peered out at old Mister Morgan.

What is it? I asked.

He had come to inform me that Missus Findlay would have supper ready in fifteen minutes.

I thanked him for the information and apologized for taking so long to answer the door. I told him I wasn't feeling well and would not be coming down for supper.

He didn't suspect a thing and shuffled off.

I relocked the door and retrieved my angel from the wardrobe. She pushed me into my easy chair and we made love in it, looking out of the window into the deserted street below.

When we were done, we sat together for a long time, holding each other, not saying a word. Just having my body touching hers was enough. I was in heaven, snuggled in her arms, breathing her scent. I don't know how long we stayed cuddled like that in my easy chair, but at some point, after what might have been a half an hour, or more, a knock came on the door. We had to make haste, Virginia again hiding in the wardrobe. I put on my dressing gown and answered the door.

This time it was Betsy, with a meal Missus Findlay had sent up,

'Missus Findlay sent this up for you. Seeing as how you is sick,' she said.

Before fully opening the door, I checked to see that Virginia was safely hiding in the wardrobe. Seeing that all was well, I opened the door and accepted the plate from Betsy, apologizing for taking so long to come to the door.

Betsy said she understood and quickly left, not bothering to ask what was wrong with me; just accepting the fact that people get sick in Halifax.

I retrieved Virginia from the wardrobe and kissed her while fondling her right breast. Her nipple was hard and felt so good between my fingers, I could have stood there for ever, however, we needed to figure out a way to get Virginia out of the house, without anyone noticing. The boarders and Missus Findlay would all be in the dining room, so I figured it would be possible to take Virginia out through the front door.

I watched my angel put her clothes back on but asked her to leave her bloomers, which she gladly did. I sniffed them luxuriously.

Virginia giggled when she saw me do that.

When we had finished dressing, I carefully opened the door and peeked out. Nobody was in the hall, so we slowly, quietly, stepped down the stairs, trying our utmost to miss the creaky stairs. I hit one, but it didn't seem to raise anyone's attention. They were probably all chatting, like usual. I was certain the entire household was at table; Missus Findlay, Mister Morgan, Jake, the gardener, Mister Gardener, and old Missus Beardsley, who was deaf as a brick. The others would be talking quite loud so that she could hear and take part in the conversation. We could hear them as we came down the stairs.

We managed to make it out of the house, without anyone noticing, and walked to Virginia's house. On the way she assured me that she would speak with her uncle about a sloop. Apparently, he was coming over for Sunday dinner, and would probably be there already. In her family they usually ate Sunday dinner at seven.

It took us a while to take leave of each other. It was with much affection and promises for the future. She invited me to come and see her Monday, after seven o'clock. Hopefully, she would have an answer regarding the ship, by then. I asked if I could see her at lunch time; that waiting until seven would be an eternity.

She laughed and told me I had to be patient.

I promised that I would try and gave her a final kiss before she went inside.

Virginia blew me a kiss before entering the house.

I stood in a rapture for a few moments before floating home on a cloud of happiness. I could smell her on me. It made me want her all the more. I couldn't believe my luck.

When I returned to the boarding house, I slowly, carefully opened the door and listened. I could hear that everyone was still at dinner. I could hear Mister Gardener's booming voice pontificating about some subject or other, of no interest to me. His subjects usually didn't interest me. He was a bank clerk. I never trusted bankers.

I snuck upstairs and returned to my room as quiet as a mouse. I closed the door and locked it. Then opening one of the drawers of my dresser, I peered under my shirts. A pile of gold coins glinted back at me. Enough gold to buy two houses like Virginia's, in one drawer alone. I had four drawers in my dresser. Surely there was enough to buy a sloop and provisions, I thought.

When I had satisfied my desire to look at the gold, I sat down in my easy chair and peered out of the window. I was already missing Virginia and my stomach was growling because I had not eaten yet. Fortunately, the food which Betsy had brought up, was still a little warm, so I ate contentedly sitting in my easy chair, the one Virginia had warmed up so joyfully. I thought of her as I slowly chewed a piece of delicious chicken.

I also thought of William Bartleby, and our crazy plan to bust him from jail. It was a terribly risky venture. We were staking our lives on it. In Germany pirates were decapitated. I shivered when I thought of it. I hoped an excellent book would come from the adventure. At least I would have that.

After drinking a small cup of rum, I was feeling tired and decided to have a nap. Virginia had worn me out. It was a good feeling. It wasn't long until I was asleep and dreaming of my girl; her scent on my fingers.

Chapter Seven

I woke up very early on Monday morning. I guessed it was six a.m. It was still dark outside. Maybe it was the clouds. I wasn't sure. At any rate, I was wide awake and needed to empty my bladder, which I took care of immediately. I was thankful for the extra large chamber pot which Missus Findlay provided with the room. When I was done, I checked my clock to see what time it was. It was five o'clock. I had slept right through yesterday evening, and never ate anything more, except for the small meal Betsy had delivered. Needless to say, I was ravenous. I had no choice but to sneak down to the kitchen and obtain some food. Everyone in the house was still sleeping, so I had to be very quiet. I had long ago learned how to be quiet, when I am sober. It was only when I had too many pints that I had to worry about making noise.

In the kitchen I found a loaf of bread and a block of cheese. I cut some pieces from each and quickly took the food, with a tankard of water, back to my room. It was dark, as I told you. I more or less had to feel my way back to the stairs. I didn't see Missus Findlay's cat, Jennifer, lying on the rug by the stairs.

I stepped on her.

Jennifer's immediate response was to squeal and run away at top speed. The resultant effect was that I dropped the bread and cheese. Fortunately, they only fell on a step, and in my books the thirty second rule enables one to pick up dropped food within thirty seconds and it is still alright to eat it. I retrieved the food and quietly walked up the stairs, at the top of which I met old Missus Beardsley. She was standing on the landing with a candelabra in her right hand. When she saw me she sighed with relief. She told me she thought there was a burglar when she heard the cat alarm. I assured her it was only me and walked her back to her room.

When I was safely back in my room I lit some candles and drank a large sip of water. Then I ate the bread and cheese with great appetite, all the while thinking of Virginia. My entire body was wanting to be with her. She had seriously gotten under my skin. It was a good feeling. I hoped that feeling would always be there when I was with her.

After completing my simple breakfast I decided I might as well get dressed, since there was no way I could go back to sleep. So, I dressed and decided to go for a morning walk past Virginia's house. Perhaps she was up, as well. Maybe she could not sleep, I hoped.

But, I was wrong. No one was up in Virginia's house at six a.m.

I decided I would find a hot cocoa and fried eggs at a restaurant which opened at six, just three blocks from Virginia's house. I was still hungry.

The restaurant was called, The Leaping Frog Victual Emporium. The proprietor obviously had a sense of humor. I had never eaten there before.

Breakfast came slowly, but it was worth the wait. If you find yourself in Halifax, I recommend the place. Of course if you are reading these pages, in some other century, it is highly possible the Leaping Frog Victual Emporium might not be there anymore. Nothing lasts for ever. Especially when kings make wars and destroy things all the time.

I mentioned this idea to an old timer who was sitting at a table next to mine. He agreed heartily with what I had expressed. But, he cautioned me not to say things like that too loudly in the wrong places. It could get me into trouble.

I thought about what the old timer had said. He was right, of course. I shouldn't be shooting my mouth off. Especially not since I was going to spring a pirate from jail.

As I sat there ruminating over my breakfast it occurred to me that there really wasn't any need for me to go to work. There was so much money, in the drawers of my dresser, I could quit ten times over and still have lots of money to last me to the end of my days. I didn't really like working for the news paper, all that much. Especially not since I wasn't getting any juicy assignments. Just little old ladies with tulips, it seemed.

Virginia didn't need to work anymore, either. Although her father might grow suspicious if his daughter quit work, he wouldn't know if I quit my job. Not unless Virginia told him, and I would tell her not to say anything, of course. We would act as if nothing was different, except I would have more time to put things together. The sooner we had a ship and provisions, the sooner we could be out of Halifax.

After breakfast I headed straight for the newspaper office. It was seven thirty and I knew that Mister Burnett would be there. He was always a half hour early. 'It gave him time to relax into the job,' is how he put it to me.

When I entered his office he was surprised to see me so early. I told him I had come early in order to talk with him before the other workers got there. Then I told him I had come into an inheritance. I wanted it to remain a secret, because I didn't want to be hounded by people. I told Mister Burnett that there was just enough money to buy me a year, in which to write my pirate book.

He said he understood and added that I could have my job back, anytime.

I thanked him and we shook hands. He said that he would have my salary ready by Friday and I could pick it up. He wished me good luck and I quickly left his office and nearly ran out of the building, I was so excited. I couldn't wait to tell Bill of my decision. I guess seeing all that gold probably had something to do with it. I mean, if that was only one of a number of stashes, that meant Bill was a rich man. Perhaps we could all retire on an island somewhere. We wouldn't have to pirate. We could live free. No worries. It was a happy thought which made me smile. With so much money, all kinds of opportunities presented themselves.

It was eight thirty when I arrived at the docks. I immediately set about looking and talking with people, to see if a sloop was for sale somewhere. I wouldn't be able to visit Bill until after one o'clock, anyway. So, I figured I might as well set to work. There really wasn't much time to waste. Bill could be transferred at any time.

The first person I spoke with was an old salt who was sitting on a barrel outside a fisherman's gear shoppe. Floats and nets were set outside. Nearby another old salt was mending a net. He was smoking a small clay pipe. The tobacco smelled nice.

I asked the old salt on the barrel if he knew of any boats for sale.

'Whad're yer lookin' fer?' he asked in a hoarse voice.

I told him I was looking for a sloop.

'Whada ya wan er fer?' he asked, looking at me suspiciously. 'Ya don look like a sailor man,' he added.

I told him that I was shopping for a rich uncle who was coming from England.

The old jack tar sniffed and continued his work. He didn't ask any more questions. He didn't answer mine, either. I guessed the old sailor didn't know of any sloops for sale.

I thanked the wrinkled sailor for his time.

He grunted an answer.

I didn't hear what it was.

The other sailor was more friendly. However, he didn't know of any ships for sale, no ketches, yawls, or sloops.

As I wandered along the docks I noticed a shop with a sign proclaiming they were sellers of sailing vessels. I decided, if I was going to buy a ship, I might as well go to a person who sold them, instead of asking sailors. So, I stepped inside the office of Mister Arnold, the boat seller. He was sitting behind a desk, looking at drawings. Another man was standing beside him, also looking at the drawings. The standing man was the first to look up and acknowledge me.

I told him I was looking for a sloop to buy.

At that point Mister Arnold looked up from the drawing and eyed me suspiciously.

'You want to buy a sloop? Why a sloop? You don't look like a sailor,' he said.

I told him the story about my uncle and said that he needed a ship fairly quickly, and did not have time to have one built. It had to be sea worthy, I told him.

'How will you pay for such a sloop?' asked the standing man.

'Gold,' I said.

That had the desired effect. Gold speaks volumes.

'So, your uncle is wanting a sloop, is he? I have a lovely sloop. She is a great sloop. Wouldn't you say, she's a good sloop, Donald?' asked Mister Arnold.

The standing man agreed the sloop was worth looking at.

Then Mister Arnold told me what the ship would cost, which was more than I would have earned in all my life as a junior reporter for the Morning Post.

I told him money was not a problem.

'Well then, let's go have a look at her,' said Mister Arnold, getting up from his chair and walking over to me. He indicated the door and the three of us went to look at the sloop, which was tied up along a jetty, not far from the shop.

'Her name is, Molly Brown,' said Mister Arnold as we approached the ship.

'Molly Brown?' I asked him. 'What kind of name is that for a ship?'

'Not the ship,' chuckled Mister Arnold. 'The widder who owns her. Her husband owned Julius Brown & Associates. His widder doesn't want to keep the sloop. They used it to travel to the Caribbean in the winter. The old man died last summer. That little sloop has been for sale all that time.'

I asked him why nobody wanted to buy her.

Mister Arnold replied that the market was depressed.

As we approached, I could tell that the sloop was freshly painted and her mast was good and straight. I could tell that the shrouds and stays looked in perfect condition, compared to an obviously neglected vessel lying nearby. From where I stood I could tell there was a distinct difference between the sloop and the tattered, worn looking ship; whose ropes were worn and frayed. The sloop's ropes looked brand new in comparison.

We stepped on board via a gang plank already in place. It was the first time I had ever been on a sloop. As far as I could tell it looked like the ship we needed. It was a manageable size, 42 feet long from stem to stern. At its widest it was about twelve feet. All of the wood and brass was polished. The teak deck was so clean, you could have eaten off it. On the rear deck was the helm. A low cabin sat amidships, and a long bowsprit stuck out of the front. The mast was very tall with a long boom which hung out over the transom. The ship could obviously carry a large main sail and sizable jib. Even though I had little experience with ships, I knew a few things. I could tell that Molly Brown's sloop was a very nice sail boat.

Mister Arnold opened the hatch to access the cabins below deck. The main cabin was down a small ladder with six steps. The cabin contained a large table with a horseshoe bench against the wall and thus surrounding the table on three sides. Five portholes, on either side of the cabin, which was above deck, lit up the room beautifully. All the wood was highly polished and of various types. The table was of mahogany, the floor was teak, cabinets were of assorted woods, inlaid to create beautiful accents of cherry, pine, and walnut. Against the front bulkhead stood a small pot bellied stove; the smoke stack poking through a sealed hole in the roof of the cabin.

The sleeping quarters were gained through a hatch at the front of the cabin, and down another six steps. A narrow gang way ran between two separate cabins, each containing double beds. The cabins were beautifully appointed, as was the rest of the sloop. Extra sails and ropes were stored in cabinets in the crew's quarters in the fo'c'sle. More sleeping space and storage was available directly under the rear deck. The ship was clean and smelled of fresh paint, wood, and varnish. Everything looked ship shape to me.

I asked Mister Arnold if I could bring in an independent inspector to have a look over the vessel.

Mister Arnold agreed that it would not be a problem. 'Who ever you send will tell you that this is one of the finest sloops ever to sail from this port.'

I resolved to speak with Virginia, as soon as possible, to get her uncle to have a look at Molly Brown's sloop. We could even pay him consultancy fees, I figured.

After completely touring the sloop, I thanked Mister Arnold and his colleague. Then I set off for Spencer & Spencer, to see if I could speak with Virginia and her uncle. Fortunately, it was possible and Virginia and I were able to spend a little bit of private time together behind some bales of hemp, in the warehouse, behind the offices.

We kissed and kissed and hugged and hugged. It was so sweet.

When we figured we had been gone long enough, under pretense of her showing me around, we walked nonchalantly back to the office. Virginia took me to her uncle's office and he greeted me warmly. I told him I would not waste his time and got straight to the point. I told him I knew he knew of a sloop for sale. But, I told him about Molly Brown's sloop and asked him if he knew of that ship.

As it turned out, Mister Spencer knew her well. He also knew that Molly Brown was asking too much for it, but that it was an excellent ship, in first rate condition.

I asked him what the difference was, between the sloop he knew of, and the sloop which Molly Brown was selling.

As it turned out there was a big difference. Molly Brown's sloop was like new, the other needed work. Molly Brown's was first class, the other vessel, third class.

'Of course, it is quite a lot more money, Molly Brown's sloop,' said Virginia's uncle. 'I don't know how much money your uncle has.'

I assured him that my uncle was very wealthy, which satisfied Mister Spencer, who nodded his head and reiterated that Molly's sloop was a good buy, even at the price she was asking. When he had finished speaking, I thanked him for his time and we shook hands. He told me I was welcome anytime.

Virginia led me out of the office and we walked back to the warehouse. There was no one there because it was lunch time and the workers were having their victuals. The empty warehouse gave us an opportunity to discuss the next step of the plan. Now that I had found a sailing vessel, as if God put it there, we had to obtain provisions next.

'We have to buy it first. And we should let Bill know about the sloop. There is no sense in provisioning her until we are nearly ready to leave. It is best to get fresh,' said Virginia.

'There are some things we could buy. The dry goods, for example. The more we are ready, the less there will have to be done when it is time to leave.'

Virginia agreed that was a good idea.

'And, besides, it will be fun to go shopping,' I said. 'We can buy some sailor clothes…'

'That's a great idea, Peter. Let's go shopping for sailor clothes,' agreed Virginia enthusiastically.

And so we spent a wonderful couple of hours trying on sailor clothing, eventually settling on the clothes we felt to be most practical. We also bought a similar outfit for Bill; long underwear, woolen socks, boots, woolen breeches, a warm shirt, a woolen turtle neck sweater, a short jacket, and rain gear. The total cost of the three outfits came to four and one half ounces of gold, which I paid with three doubloons, a Louis d'or, and some smaller pieces. The merchant weighed the coins on a scale and tested them for gold content, which was excellent. Satisfied the sale was complete, we shook hands and left the shop, carrying our bundles of clothes under our arms. We hailed a carriage and brought the clothes to the sloop.

Virginia was totally thrilled with the ship. She appreciated how beautifully appointed it was.

'I would have no problem sailing in this ship,' she said. 'It is beautiful!'

When we climbed below, to see the two private cabins, Virginia made certain to test each bed, to see which one would be most suitable for us; if you get my drift. We settled on the starboard cabin; the bed being somewhat more comfortable, since we fell asleep on it, cuddled in each other's arms.

Sometime in the middle of the afternoon, we woke up ravenously hungry. We quickly dressed and walked to an inn nearby and bought a delicious lunch, with several pints of ale; enough to put color in our cheeks. During the entire time we laughed and laughed about the silliest of things. Virginia and I were madly in love.

When lunch was done, I paid with a small gold coin, and got ten English shillings back in change. I tested the coins, to see if they rang silver. I wasn't going to accept debased silver in exchange for good gold. I was beginning to feel like a rich man. I had never had so much money to spend. Eating expensive lunches and drinking ale in the afternoon was not something I was used to. I was beginning to like it.

As it turned out, the shillings were good silver and I accepted them.

Then we floated off to obtain a bag full of gold from my dresser, with which to buy the sloop and provisions, laughing most of the way. Virginia was so much fun to be with. I was already madly in love with her by this time. I couldn't get enough of her. She was a drug; an unbelievable drug, which made me forget everything else.

When we got near Missus Findlay's, I thought it best if Virginia waited outside, for expediency sake. If Virginia was to come in, then there would be all kinds of introductions and questions. Neither she, nor I wanted to waste any time. We wanted to get on with shopping.

I quickly ran upstairs to my room and unlocked the door. It didn't take me long to grab my bag and fill it with a drawer full of coins, making the bag very heavy on my shoulder. I totally forgot to sort through the coins. I was anxious to get going.

I locked my door and headed down the stairs, at the bottom of which stood Missus Findlay.

'It looks like you're packing a pretty heavy bag there, Mister Mann,' she observed.

I had to think quickly. I told her I just made the bag look heavy because my shoulder was sore, that the bag was actually quite light, and only contained my notebooks and ink and such. Then I told her I had to get going to an assignment and didn't have time to visit.

Sometimes Missus Findlay was kind of nosy and I had to put her off, if I didn't want her knowing things. She was a lot like my mother, that way. I found it annoying, but what can you do? I didn't feel like moving, and besides, she was a good cook. It is hard to find that in a rooming house. Most of the others, in which I have lived, well, actually, the two others in which I have lived, the food was not as good as Missus Findlay's and Betsy's cooking. Unless you went out to a good restaurant. But, that gets expensive, eating out all the time. Although, I could now well afford it. I felt like a millionaire, as I walked out of the house towards Virginia, waiting down the block. She had found a cat to converse with. She was content.

'What took you so long?' was the first thing she asked me.

'I wasn't gone long,' I told her.

She told me, anytime I was gone from her was too long.

My heart melted. I was so grateful for her saying that. I gave her a big hug and kissed her well on the mouth. Her lips felt so good on mine. I could have kissed her for hours, but, we had shopping to do. We could always find places along our shopping route, to share a fondle and a kiss; a grope and an earlobe feast, that sort of thing.

I couldn't help it. I also saw Virginia as a food thing. I loved to nibble on her and taste her skin. Her ears were very sensitive. She liked me playing with her ears. Especially when I nibbled on her lobes, or ran my tongue around inside her ear. I could feel her entire body trembling when I did that.

Anyway, I am getting off the topic of the shopping trip. It was a memorable affair.

We first went straight to Mister Arnold's and asked him the price of the sloop.

He told us the price was ten pounds of gold.

I had at least ten pounds of gold in the bag, I reckoned, with a smattering of silver coins which we had missed, but I figured, since Virginia's uncle had said the price was excessive, I would bargain with Mister Arnold.

I told Mister Arnold I thought his price was excessive and offered him five pounds.

'Five pounds?!' exclaimed Mister Arnold. 'Did you hear that, Donald? Did you hear that? He said, five pounds!' Mister Arnold's nose began to change color. 'You might as well have offered me two pounds; it's that ridiculous. Why, five pounds wouldn't even pay for the hull, let alone the rigging! Five pounds!?' Mister Arnold stroked his chin and paced back and forth behind his desk. Then he looked up and said, emphatically, 'Nine and a half, and that is the bottom line. If I take any less, I would be going into the poor house.'

I eyed Mister Arnold. Then I glanced at Virginia and winked at her. She smiled and then looked at Mister Arnold, as seriously as I was. There was no sense in paying more gold than we had to. Virginia and I were being good stewards; the gold not being ours to squander. 'Alright, Mister Arnold,' I said calmly, 'I will give you seven pounds, but that is it. My uncle informed me I was not to spend a doubloon more. If seven pounds of gold is not sufficient, then I will have to take my business elsewhere.' I looked at Donald and locked eyes with him. 'I'm sure there are other ships for sale in Halifax harbour.'

Mister Arnold stared at me. His nose twitched. He eyed me steadily and pursed his lips. 'Alright, nine pounds of gold and that is it, not an ounce less.'

I stroked my chin and eyed Mister Arnold, setting my heavy bag down on his desk. 'I will pay you eight pounds of gold, but really, Mister Arnold, don't you feel a little guilty? I mean, surely eight pounds should more than do it?'

Mister Arnold looked at Donald and threw up his hands. 'What am I supposed to do? Donald, what am I supposed to do? Eight pounds he offers me for a sloop easily worth twice the price. It is a luxury sloop. A rich people's sloop. Not some third class tub like that pile of timber floating nearby. Surely you must see that? Molly Brown's sloop is easily worth sixteen pounds, and here I offer it to you for a cut rate price, nine pounds.'

I figured I had Mister Arnold down to where I wanted him and offered him eight and a half pounds of gold for the ship, which he reluctantly accepted.

'Alright, eight and a half pounds of gold,' agreed Mister Arnold. 'I am going in the poor house. But you seem like nice people. Alright, eight and a half pounds it is. And, of course, there are the extra fees; taxes, paper work; that sort of thing. That shouldn't amount to more than another five ounces, or so.'

'We agreed on eight and a half pounds, Mister Arnold. Not an ounce more. You can't add charges after an agreed upon price.'

Mister Arnold stared at me and then at Donald. 'Eight and a half pounds. I am going into the poor house.' Mister Arnold sighed. 'Donald, please bring the scales.'

Donald stepped into another room and returned with an excellent set of scales upon which we weighed eight and one half pounds of gold.

As I was dumping handfuls of gold from my bag into the pan, Virginia picked the odd piece of silver out of the growing pile on the scale, dropping the silver ones into a dish which Donald had provided for her.

Every once in a while she would pick out a special coin, a Greek, or Roman coin, or some other ancient coin which was mixed in amongst the many crusadoes, ducats, doubloons, guineas, Louis d'ors, pieces of eight, and pesos…

As we were thusly engaged, I demanded that the ship be certified ship shape and that all sails, ropes, tackle, etcetera be inspected and replaced, if found to be wanting.

Mister Arnold agreed and we shook hands.

When the scale tipped we stopped putting coins into the pan. I had to take three coins back to balance the scale.

'That's an interesting coin collection you have there, my young friend,' said Mister Arnold insinuatingly.

I told him it came from my uncle, the European banker.

Virginia acknowledged the lie by stating that my uncle was a very rich banker and liked to deal in gold and silver coins.

The two of us corroborating each other seemed to satisfy Mister Arnold. He quickly filled out the bill of sale without an other word, except to say that Molly Brown would be glad to see the sloop sold, at last. We shook hands, once again, and left the shop, pleased to have made an excellent purchase. We couldn't wait to tell Bill. But first I had to show the sloop to Virginia, once more. We took a little longer than we intended, having to stop and try the beds again, to see which one would really be the better suited for us, if you get my drift.

When we finally arrived at the jail the guards demanded to look into my bag, it obviously being quite full. I had to be careful lest they see the coins. So, I just took things out of the bag for them to look at. Thinking it prudent to prevent them from looking any further, I pulled a thropence from my pocket and handed it to the blasphemer, who happened to be on duty again, that day. He gladly took the coin and winked at his partner. Then they let us through the gate and we stepped into the lobby, depositing a coin in the box, which had been set up for the purpose. The German sergeant smiled at us as we walked past his desk. A guard immediately took us down to see Bill and then left right away.

Our pirate was overjoyed to see us. We had obviously been missed.

We gave Bill a bottle of ale, which he drank thirstily, wiping his mouth on his sleeve as we excitedly told him of the purchase of the sloop.

'You bought a sloop?!' he exclaimed. 'You actually bought one?'

Virginia and I nodded happily.

'You are actually going to do it? You are actually going to help me get out of here?'

'Yes, we have decided,' I replied. 'We figured we might as well get the ball rolling, and bought the sloop before coming over here.'

'That is marvelous! You have actually bought a sloop. Tell me about her.'

Which is exactly what we did; each of us adding details to what the other had described. The more we spoke about the sloop, the more Bill smiled, trusting we had made an excellent purchase.

We began discussing in earnest how we would effect the escape and to set a definite date. In the middle of the conversation, Bill suddenly remarked, 'I surely could use a bath. Is there any way you can use some of the money to have a tub of clean, soapy water brought down here? And some towels. I am becoming quite disgusted with myself.'

Virginia smiled and looked at me.

'I will talk with the gaoler,' I said. 'I'm sure we can persuade him with some of these coins.'

Bill smiled. 'Money talks.'

I guess, now that a fine young woman was coming to visit him, he needed to address his body odours. I had been much too polite to mention them. However, I was glad he asked for the bath. Bill was becoming offensive.

The next day Bill was able to wash and put on a clean set of new clothes, which Virginia and I had bought for him in town. Bill thanked us profusely for helping him. 'A bath and clean clothes sure do make a difference,' he said gratefully.

The following day we were able to bring a barber down to the dungeon, to clean up Bill's hair and beard. When the barber was done, Bill appeared as a new man. 'Thanks to you,' he said, 'Life is bearable in this hole.'

Some days later, Virginia and I arrived a little later than usual. Bill was anxiously pacing in his cell when we arrived. He was in a very agitated state and expressed his sincere gratitude that we showed up.

'What's wrong?' asked Virginia.

'The ship is only two days away,' he replied anxiously.

'What ship?' I asked, not comprehending.

'The ship, to take me back to London,' hissed Bill. 'The ship is two days from port. I received word this morning.' Bill looked nervously at me. 'There is no more time to wait for the right moment. We have to move. I have to get out of here.'

'Well, at least we have the sloop already. We've made it comfortable in the mean time,' I said. 'All we need to do is provision her.'

'There is no time to waste, Peter. You have to go grocery shopping. I can't stay in here any longer.'

Virginia and I agreed to attend to the provisioning right away. 'Maybe we'll be able to get you out of here tonight, or tomorrow,' I said, encouragingly. 'We'll do our best,' I assured him.

'It is all I can hope for,' answered Bill. 'Please hurry.'

So hurry we did.

Virginia and I rushed from the jail and immediately hailed a carriage to take us to the place where most ships obtained their stores, Spencer & Spencer. The huge warehouse general store had its own wagons to deliver to the ships at dock side. Shopping there was very convenient and it kept the money in the family, so to speak. Besides, we were suddenly in a hurry and did not have time to shop around.

The place was busy because there were sixteen new ships in port.

When it was our turn to be served, we ordered: five barrels of water, a couple of kegs of rum, a barrel of ale, two kegs of pickled herrings, two kegs of salted pork, two of beef, and one of mutton. We bought a bag of garlic, two of onions, a bag of leeks, two of potatoes, a small bag of peppers, a box of salt, a large bag of sugar, a twenty pound bag of coffee, a box of tea, a twenty pound bag of lemons, the same of oranges, and apples, a twenty pound bag of rice, and a fifty pound bag of flour. We figured what we had chosen would keep us fed reasonably well for a while. Neither Virginia and I had any idea how long we would be at sea before we could make land and buy more provisions.

When we had paid for the groceries, we gave the clerk directions where the goods were to be brought. He said he knew the ship and had been an admirer of her, ever since Molly Brown had it docked there.

I felt good about the purchase of the sloop even more.

After grocery shopping, we went to a hardware emporium and bought some pots and pans, some utensils, plates, cups, etcetera. The clerk, who handled the transaction, assured us the stuff would be delivered on board the sloop, so we wouldn't have to worry about things getting wet outside, in case it rained.

When we were finished our shopping it was three o'clock. It was time to visit our friend in jail. Hence, we stopped at the grocery store and bought a couple of bottles of good wine and three of fine ale. Then we bought a block of camembert, a couple of loaves of good bread, some green onions, and a pot of olives. We walked hand in hand to the jail; happy to be alive.

When we told Bill the good news regarding the supplies, he was very relieved. The only thing that we had to concern ourselves with was to get Bill out of the jail without the guards suspecting anything. We had already planned it out, but we didn't think we would have to act so soon. There was no time to waste. We would have to effect the rescue, that day.

Fortunately, we still had a couple of hours before the guards would tell us to leave. There were lots of other people visiting their loved ones in the jail's upper levels. Generally, they all liked to prolong their visits, so that usually a small crowd would gather in the lobby as people left the prison. The fact there were lots of people visiting played greatly in our favour.

The plan was for Virginia to go home and fetch; petticoats, a dress, a coat, and bonnet, which Bill would put on. Virginia was to bring these clothes in a bag on top of which would be some more food. If the guards asked, she would tell them it was food for the prisoners. She also took some coins to pay off the guards, if necessary. Then, after a warm kiss, she ran off.

I handed the food to Bill, through the bars. Bill was pleased to see wine and ale. I opened an ale for him and he took it gratefully, drinking a hearty sip.

'We need to make it look like I am sleeping on the cot. What can we stuff under the blanket?' he asked, scratching his head.

I told him that I could bring something from home, but for me to leave, just after Virginia, and then for both of us to return right away, would make things appear suspicious.

Bill agreed. I could see he was nervous; anxious to get out of the jail. He told me that he had a very bad feeling that the ship might get to Halifax early. 'You never know, the winds might have been favorable. Sometimes the passage can take two or three days less, even so much as a week.'

I could sense the worry in his voice. I couldn't blame him. I would be worried too, in his shoes. Then it hit me again. By helping him, I too would be in his shoes, as it were. So would Virginia. We would, all three, be wanted persons.

I told Bill that.

His reply was that it was not too late to back out. He wouldn't think any differently about me. He realized what we were doing was very risky. He told me that he was very grateful for all that I had done for him, up until then.

I assured him that Virginia and I had discussed our decision at some length. I assured him that Virginia was totally desirous of going through with it. She wanted the adventure even more than I did.

'You're a fortunate man,' he said sincerely. 'Women like her are very rare. Make sure you treat her right and she'll stay with you. If she does, you will be a happy man every day.'

Of course I agreed with him. Virginia was my everything. I was already missing her, just sitting there in the jail waiting for her to return with the dress.

The problem we were still faced with was how to make it look like Bill was sleeping on the cot.

Suddenly I had an idea. I ran over to the open cell and grabbed the meagre mattress off the cot, laying the blanket neatly over the bed frame. In the dim light it was nigh on impossible to tell whether the mattress was missing. I brought the mattress to Bill's cell and we squeezed it between the bars. With some pushing and tugging we managed to get the thing into the cell and Bill set about contorting it into something resembling a body on the cot. After covering the bent up mattress with the blanket, in the dim light, a grunt wouldn't know it wasn't the pirate. The only object left was how to unlock the door of the cell. It was up to me to try and steal the key from the guard.

The original plan was to poison the guards with a sleeping potion in a bottle of wine. However, we didn't have any poison. But, we did have wine and ale.

'Instead of us drinking it, maybe we should give it to the guards,' I suggested.

'Why waste good wine and ale on those grunts? All that you need to do is smack one on the head with that stool,' said Bill nonchalantly. 'Hopefully he is the one with the key. I never noticed if the grunt, who brings you down here, is carrying keys.

I thought that hitting a grunt on the head was a bit messy. 'Besides, they usually wear helmets,' I noted. 'What if I don't knock him out right away?'

Bill agreed I had a point there. 'If only I had stashed some poison in the chest. I should remember to do that next time. Poison comes in handy at times. You never know when you're going to need it,' he said.

I saw his point and agreed we should have thought of poison. Or even a sleeping potion. But, then, we didn't know we were going to bust him out that day. The fact that the agenda had been hurried up made things very stressful all of a sudden. We still had to get the rest of the gold from the rooming house. I had to grab some of my stuff, which I didn't just want to leave there. My books. My notebooks. My good quills and ink refill. Some of my clothes…

I mentioned all of this to Bill.

He said it shouldn't be a problem. 'We would have until midnight to get going. The tide would be available around that time, he reckoned. The grunts wouldn't know if I was gone unless they attempted to wake me. So far, they have only come in twice to empty my bucket. They don't overwork themselves with regard to me. Pirates don't merit good service in here.'

Bill looked back at the effigy on the cot. In the dim light you couldn't tell if there was someone sleeping on the cot, or not. He seemed suddenly more at ease. I guess he could foresee his successful escape.

I complimented him on a job well done and then could not think of anything more to say. There was a long, awkward pause as I assessed the situation.

'We don't need to do anything until Virginia gets back,' he said. 'I might as well continue the tale I was telling you.

I stared at Bill for a moment. 'Continue the tale you were telling me? Now? When we are about to break you out of gaol?'

'Nothing better to do, Peter. We have to do something while we wait for Virginia to come back. No sense in pacing back and forth worrying. It will keep us calm.'

Bill had a good point there. I sighed and looked nervously down the corridor. Then I sat down on the little stool and Bill sat down on the edge of the cot as he began telling me another tale from his collection of fantastic memories.

'Remember I told you I was transferred to the *Buckingham*, commanded by his lordship the pompous Temple West, the rear admiral? Remember?'

I nodded as I prepared my notebook and quill.

'That bastard had five ships, at one time, flying French flags off the coast of Guyana. Then, whenever French ships would sail close by, thinking they were safe amongst French ships, he would suddenly switch flags to Union Jacks and attack the hapless French ships. It was a rotten subterfuge, which I totally disagreed with and did so vocally on more than one occasion.

Eventually, I was overheard by a mean spirited boatswain, who happened to be passing by, when I was pontificating about the bastard with my mess mates. That pig reported me to the captain who had me lashed for questioning navy policy. The boatswain did the honours and he gave it to me good and hard. Thirty strokes! For telling the truth and calling them murderers.

Of course they had no idea who they were messing with. I did not take such punishment lightly. Even if it would take me years, I would eventually get even with those who ordered the punishment and, of course, the boatswain who turned me in and who administered the cat.

The boatswain was the first to meet his Maker, that cruel bastard was the King of Demons. Oh, he enjoyed hitting me. It is where most of the scars on my back came from. He scarred me for life and I had no mercy on him when the time came. I was not the only one whom he scarred like that, so I was truly doing the Lord's work when I did him in.'

I asked Bill how long it took, from the time he was flogged.

'It took a good month to heal the wounds. I watched the boatswain the whole time. He knew I was watching him. I noted every move, every routine. He knew it and tried to vary his routines. But, he was a creature of habit and couldn't avoid going to the head at a certain time, every day. He didn't know that I knew this. He always went to the officer's head at two in the afternoon. It was a time when the deck officers would be on deck and the others were in their mess, usually playing cards.

The head was a distance away from the mess and there wasn't likely a line up. So, it was a simple deed. I smashed his skull with a five pound cannon ball. He didn't even have time to react, since he was leaning forward, looking at his feet and grunting. I gave him a good wollop. His head caved in. I didn't have time to check if he was dead. But, I firmly believed he was gone to hell.

I took the cannon ball back to the pile it came from, after wiping the blood off with a cloth, which I let fly out through an open gun port. No one had seen me come, or go. It was two months to the day from the lashing.'

I asked him how they found the boatswain.

'It wasn't until the next officer had to go to the head, when he couldn't hold it any longer, he must have rattled on the door. I imagine he would have seen blood seeping from under the door and then he would have opened it and found him.

An investigation was launched immediately, but they had nothing to go on.

The flustered officers buried the boatswain at sea, two days later, with full military honours.

Because so many men had been flogged by the boatswain, it became an impossible task to figure out who might have killed him. There were a lot of men who had reason to hate him. They all had ample reason to kill him. All of these men were called in to answer questions. The inquiry took ten days. I was questioned on the tenth day, being one of the last who was flogged by the deceased.

I simply told them that I was wrong to question official decisions of the navy and that I deserved to be punished. The boatswain was only doing his job, I said.

My humble and sincerely spoken statement, accepting my punishment, satisfied the officers and they let me go. By the time the inquiry ended, there were at least a dozen men who could have done it. Those men would have to be tortured in London, in an official court martial. The officers did not have time for that and would have to attend to it when we returned to port. So, the ship returned back to normal; all of the sailors were overjoyed the boatswain had been removed. I told no one that it had been my privilege to carry out the Lord's work.'

'You did the Lord's work?' said the voice of an angel as she approached us, with a grunt lumbering behind. Virginia had returned, carrying a bag laden with food, as was obvious. Behind her was the family maid, Marianne. She also had a bag with her, but it was not apparent what was in it.

The grunt lit the torch on the wall and waddled back to the guard station down the hall.

When the grunt was well out of earshot, Virginia introduced Marianne.

I could tell that Bill was immediately taken by her. Marianne was a very attractive, thirty year old woman. She seemed to be attracted to the pirate, as well.

'I told Marianne of our plans. She wants to come along. She hates Halifax and wants to come on an adventure with us,' said Virginia enthusiastically. 'We hired a carriage. That is how we got back so quickly.'

I reminded the girls that this was no Sunday school picnic we were organizing. We were going to help a condemned prisoner escape. Our act would be considered treason. We could face hanging, or worse.

Both girls said they knew what the risks were. They didn't care. They felt their lives were boring in Halifax. They felt this was their only opportunity to really live for once in their lives.

'Or die young,' I said.

They told me to stop being a pessimist and to think positively. Then they proceeded to open Marianne's bag which contained, petticoats, a dress, a cape, and bonnet. They stuffed the clothes between the bars of the cage.

Bill examined the clothes and checked them against his body, to see if they would fit. It looked like they would, so he quickly put them on, petticoats first.

I couldn't help but laugh when I saw him.

The girls told me to be quiet, or I would alert the guards.

Then Virginia did something which forever endeared me to her. That smart woman pulled out a large vial of white powder. 'Sleeping powder for the guards,' she said, smiling happily.

Our problems were solved!

Virginia poured the powder into a bottle of good wine. When she was done, she pushed the cork back and walked to the guard's station. Virginia returned empty handed, moments later, with a big grin on her face. 'I bet they'll be asleep in ten minutes, or less.' She giggled.

I melted in a puddle of adoration.

Ten minutes later Virginia fetched the jailer's keys. There were twelve keys on a large, steel ring. When she tried the fifth key, it worked. Willemina was out of his cage. Looking every inch a lady.

I had a hard time trying not to laugh, as I beheld the pirate in woman's clothing.

We placed the bag of food in the cell, next to the cot, making it look like the pirate had eaten and fallen asleep, his hamper by his side.

Quietly locking the door, we took an other look into the cell. When we were satisfied that everything looked just as if Bill had fallen asleep, we hurried out of the cell block.

Virginia returned the keys to where she found them. Then the four of us left the building without a hitch. Nobody suspected a thing as we mixed with the other men and women leaving the jail.

Bill managed to hide his face with the collar of the cape and the bonnet. He looked hilarious, if you knew it was him under the disguise. To anyone else, he looked like just another one of the numerous women who were visiting in the jail.

Once outside, we took two carriages. Virginia and I rode briskly to my rooming house, while Marianne and Bill hurried to the sloop.

By the time Virginia and I arrived at our sloop, with the rest of the gold and silver, and some of my stuff, Bill had changed out of the women's clothes. He and Marianne had also nearly finished stowing the supplies. Fortunately, the delivery men had placed the barrels in the hold. The kegs we could handle ourselves and within a half an hour we had the ship properly loaded with our provisions. Then we set about lashing everything firmly in the hold, where Bill made sure to balance things and properly tie them down.

By the time the provisions were stored, it was starting to get dark. Bill quickly set about teaching us how to hoist sails and otherwise prepare the sloop for departure on the midnight tide.

When the tide came, we were ready. Neither Marianne, nor Virginia thought about the Spencer family; wondering where the two young women might be. Virginia explained that she had written a letter to her parents, telling them that she was leaving and wouldn't be back. She had said nothing about the ship, me, or Bill. They probably had read the letter, by then. She had placed it on her mother's dresser.

I breathed a sigh of relief. It was best to keep as many strands untied, as possible, where her parents were concerned. It would be better if we were not connected with the miraculous escape of William Bartleby. I preferred people to believe Virginia and I had eloped, and Marianne just quit and left.

When the tide was such that we could sail, we were extremely lucky there was a breeze to enable us to do so. I untied the ropes holding the sloop to the jetty. Then we lit the lamps, hoisted the sails, and slipped out of Halifax harbour, unbeknownst to anybody; as quietly as a dream.

* * *

Bill knew the waters of Halifax harbour like the back of his hand, so we were able to make good time, without having to rely on a pilot.

The girls were excited as two giddy children. They happily explored the ship, laughing and giggling about their new circumstances.

After sailing for an hour, we finally felt secure enough to toast our adventure by opening a bottle of wine, which we drank together under the stars, our sloop bearing south, south east, and heading for the adventure of our lives.

None of us had the slightest idea what lay in store for us. Had I foreseen some of what I eventually experienced, I might have had second thoughts. But, such is life. We make decisions and suffer the consequences. At least I can say that I had an adventurous life, when it comes my time for departure from this earthly coil.

The air was brisk; it only being late March. Clouds filled the sky. Fortunately, it was not raining, and the sea was relatively calm, which was most fortunate, according to Bill. Quite often the Atlantic put up much more opposition at that time of year. We were grateful for the calmness of the ocean and felt that perhaps a certain amount of Divine intervention was at play; helping His henchman escape a premature death.

When the women showed signs of fatigue, Bill and I told them to go sleep. We assured them everything was fine, and that eventually, we would take turns and sleep also.

Virginia and Marianne readily agreed it was best that they sleep, and sauntered off to find their beds in the cabins below.

Bill and I stayed at the helm. He showed me how to steer the sloop and what to watch for; how to keep her on course. After a couple more hours, he told me to go sleep, as well. He said he would wake me in two hours and then I could relieve him, so he could sleep.

I gratefully accepted his offer and stepped down the ladder, making my way to the cabin in which Virginia was fast asleep. I took off my heavy sweater, my shoes, and corduroy breeches. Then I curled up next to my angel and quickly fell asleep, as well.

Thusly, we spent the first night on the sloop.

By morning we were a hundred miles from Halifax, headed for Virgineola.

There were no regrets.

Chapter Eight

Morning found me at the helm.

A glorious sunrise was coming over the horizon. I felt really good and glad to be alive. The sea was calm, and the air, cool and invigorating. The others were still asleep. I was already looking forward to seeing the love of my life and let my thoughts drift towards her.

Virginia must have felt my thoughts because within a few minutes she came to join me at the helm, now dressed in the clothes we had bought for the journey. She looked absolutely marvelous, her long brown hair in a thick braid down her back. The sailor's clothes looked good on her. She kissed me sweetly and asked how I was feeling.

I told her I was happy to see her and that made all the difference in the world. If I was tired, I was not so, anymore. Virginia invigorated me. She was glad I was pleased with her. She put her arm around me and we shared a kiss. Then we stood together for a long time, silently looking out at the majesty of the sunrise greeting us.

An hour later, Marianne came up on deck. She still looked a little bit sleepy. Her dress billowed in the breeze. She had braided her long hair, as well. For the first time I really noticed what a lovely woman she was.

Marianne was tall and slim, with a perfectly proportioned bust in relation to every other part. Although it was difficult to tell, exactly, in her dress, but the way the breeze pushed the cloth against her body, I could tell, she was beautifully put together. Looking at those two women I had the distinct impression God smiled when he made them.

'We're going to have to get you some proper sailor's clothes, Marianne,' said Bill, as he came up out of the cabin below.

All three of us chorused, 'Good morning, Captain!' as he stepped on deck, each of us saluting like regular sailors.

Bill grinned from ear to ear. 'Captain,' he said. He paused for a moment. 'I haven't heard that said to me for nearly two months. It sounds good to my ears.' He surveyed his crew and asked how we were all doing.

All three of us chorused that we were fine. We were happy to be on the adventure.

He asked if any of us felt sea sick.

Virginia told him that she and Marianne had been on ships before. They had been on several cruises with the family.

As for me, I had never been on a ship, but felt no ill effects. Not everyone gets seasickness, apparently. From what Bill described, I was thankful not to have it. Apparently, seasickness is quite a horrible experience.

Bill looked up the mast and at the transom. He noticed that we were not flying a flag. He thought it a good idea to see if there was a flag on board. 'One can not be too careful in these revolutionary times. Now that there is daylight, why don't you girls go and look through all of the cupboards in the cabin and below, who knows, you might find suitable clothes for Marianne, as well as a flag.'

The girls agreed it was a good idea and began their search.

Me, I was suddenly tired and turned the helm over to Bill. I went below and found my bed and fell quickly asleep. I have no idea how long I slept, but, when I woke, my nostrils immediately filled with the delicious smells of cooked food. My stomach told me it was hungry. That is probably why I woke up, in the first place.

When I arrived in the main cabin, the girls were cooking a marvelous, thick soup. The delicious aroma filled our ship and made life even more wonderful.

Marianne had managed to find some baggy corduroy trousers and a turtle neck sweater. She and Marianne looked like girl men. I liked to see them dressed that way.

Bill found the clothes we bought, well chosen and very well fitting. We had sized him up appropriately.

I noticed an English flag was flying from the stern.

'English?' I asked. 'I thought we hated the English?'

'We do,' replied Bill, grinning. 'However, in these waters, it is best to fly an English flag. It will keep them away from us.'

When the soup was ready, Bill tied the wheel and we sat down to dinner. Virginia spoke the grace, giving thanks for our safe exit from Halifax, and asking for safe and prosperous voyages to come. We all said, 'Amen' together, in good friendship and harmony. Then we ate a soup, which had to have been the best soup I ever ate in my life. The girls had obviously learned cooking from a chef.

Virginia's family retained a professional cook, who came to their home, three times per week, to cook dinner. Marianne and Virginia had an interest in cooking and learned a lot from the chef. It was obvious they learned well. The warm food made us feel good and invigorated.

Laughter, I remember, was the sound we mostly made around the table that evening. Marianne proved to be excellent company, as well. The four of us made a good team.

During the days we spent at sea, en route to Virgineola, Bill taught the girls, and me, to sail. We learned about using the sextant for navigation. We learned about reading charts and how to tell directions by the stars. By the time we made port at Virgineola, the girls and I were becoming adept sailors.

We arrived in Virgineola around eleven in the morning, twelve days after leaving Halifax.

The first thing we did, after docking, was to empty the head and prepare the ship for a stay in port for a couple of days. Bill wanted to see if he could locate some friends and try and buy some weapons. We wouldn't be able to do much piracy without weapons and assistance from men who knew how to use them. A few more hands on deck would also help sail the vessel better. According to Bill, we were lucky we had not run into a storm on the way to Virgineola. Apparently, with only the four of us, we would have been hard pressed to sail our sloop in a storm.

When we felt our sloop was sufficiently secure, Bill and the girls went shopping for water, fresh fruits and vegetables, and some appropriate

clothing for a sunnier climate. Virgineola was already quite warm in early
April. Our heavy clothes were becoming uncomfortable.

While the others went shopping, I stayed with the ship, for security
reasons. I wanted to write about our voyage in my notebook, anyway.

Bill told me not to let anyone on board.

'People are friendly, but there are a lot of rogues about,' he said.

I assured him I would be on my guard.

By mid day, the girls returned, followed by a wagon loaded with
supplies. They were each wearing white cotton trousers and loose,
flowing shirts, tied with a colorful sash. On their feet were sandals. They
had each bought a large straw hat. If I had been a painter, I would have
painted them just as they appeared, in their new, manly clothing, and the
wagon of supplies in the background. The sight was something I will
always remember; those beautiful women in their white cotton outfits.

Two porters helped us stow the supplies on board. We had only
emptied one barrel of water, so we gave them the empty barrel and took
on three more full barrels. I paid them for their trouble and they smiled
broadly, thanking me profusely for my generosity. I guess I must have
given them more than they normally got. I think it was a couple of English
shillings.

The girls were happy in their new clothes and immediately set about
preparing some food for brunch. I was ravenous and grabbed a big orange
from the bag, Virginia had hung up in the galley. It was a succulent fruit,
full of juice.

Bill returned an hour later. We had saved food for him, but he had
already eaten at an inn, not far from the harbour. He was carrying a
bundle, which he quickly brought into the cabin and set on the table.
When he unwrapped it we discovered, three cutlasses, and a musket.
'We'll have to find lead and powder for the gun,' he said. 'I'm sure we'll
find that here, as well. I also found an old friend. He's an experienced
pirate. His name is George Malling. He knows where some members of
my former crew are. He'll be sailing with us to Jamaica. I imagine you'll
see him tomorrow. He still has some ends to tie up here. I told him we
would leave in the afternoon.'

The thought of a stranger coming on board our little ship troubled the girls a little bit. They were beginning to feel possessive of the sloop, as if it was their little getaway cruise ship. I don't think they had an inkling regarding our plans for a little bit of piracy, in the near future. Although we had lots of money, the thrill of the chase was the inspiration. And, of course, to further Bill's cause, to wreak havoc on the English. Through his many diatribes, he had managed to convince all of us regarding the morality of his fight against England, and its German King, George the third.

By that time, Bill and Marianne had begun a closer friendship. So, when Virginia and I suggested we do some shopping for appropriate clothing for me, they elected to stay on board. I suspected something from the way Bill and Marianne were looking at each other. It is my guess that while we went shopping, they were up to something completely different.

When Virginia and I returned to the ship, around five in the afternoon, the water in the harbour was calm like glass, yet our vessel seemed to be moving, as if it was rocked by waves. We laughed because we knew for sure, right then, that Bill and Marianne were getting to know each other better.

Virginia and I sat on the dock, our legs dangling over the edge, waiting for the sloop to stop rocking. We didn't think it was polite to interrupt their frolic. So, we talked about her family and our future together, to pass the time. She told me that she was beginning to miss her parents and siblings. As for our being together; she told me she loved me, and was glad we were together, on the adventure of a lifetime.

That is all I needed to hear. I told her I loved her too and couldn't imagine life without her.

When the sloop had finished rocking, we stepped on board, and made certain to make enough noise to let Bill and Marianne know that we were back.

Moments later they appeared in the cabin and regarded us carefully, to ascertain if we knew anything. At that point their new found love was still a secret. Of course, Virginia and I did not let on that we knew anything.

Next morning, George Malling arrived on board. He was a big, tall man, well over two hundred and fifty pounds, with long hair over his shoulders. He wore mustaches and a van Dyke beard on his chin. He wore a long, brown leather coat and a three cornered hat. He had brought a well stuffed duffel bag.

Marianne showed him to the crew's quarters, where he proceeded to set himself up in one of the six bunks available.

The two couples, each had our own cabins, amidships. Virginia had decorated ours with a colorful blanket on the double bed, and decorated curtains made from scarves she had attached over the portholes. She made the place cozy for us. It was our little love nest. Marianne had done similar things in the cabin she now shared with Bill. Women love decorating, I think.

George turned out to be a likable fellow, full of humor, and interesting information about; fish, life, and sailing. He had brought another sword and two pistols. He had also brought a small keg of gun powder, a box of lead, and a ball mold.

We left port at two in the afternoon, on April 7 th, headed for Jamaica.

During our voyage, George taught the girls and me, how to make balls from the lead, which became our pastime for the next seventeen days. By the time we made port in Kingston, we had a formidable pile of ammunition.

The two women had made it a competition for themselves, to perform sailing tasks as proficient as the men. By the time we made port in Kingston, the two women could climb rigging, change and set sails, man the helm, read a sextant and charts; all the tasks a sailor needed to know how to perform, they had learned to do.

'The next thing we are going to teach the three of you,' said Bill, when we had tied up the sloop and made her fast. 'We are going to teach you how to fight with swords.'

Marianne and Virginia, of course, found that an excellent idea. They were beginning to see themselves as pirates, already; enamored of what they thought was their uniqueness. I think the two of them were becoming legends in their own minds. I found it quite funny. So did Bill and George.

We stayed in Kingston for three days, taking on more supplies and gathering up men. Bill had located five more friends; Adam, Carl, Moby,

Nick, and Zeke, who came on board with their duffel bags and weapons. We also managed to acquire a five pounder, which we attached to the starboard gunwale. One of the new men managed to obtain twenty, five pound cannon balls, and another keg of powder, wadding, and fuses. Things were beginning to look as if we would be pirating soon. I was beginning to look forward to that part of our adventure; to actually overtake a ship and plunder it. That was something I had only heard about.

The women trained hard, every day, at their sword fighting. One of the new men, Robert Forley, was an expert swordsman and a capable teacher. I watched in great amusement as Virginia pinned Marianne with a deft maneuver, using a sabre Frank Buttons had brought with him.

Now that we were ten on board, food preparations were taking on larger proportions, which necessitated some larger pots. These were obtained in quick order from the local market. With the new, larger pots, dinners became more complex and varied. All of the men were grateful to the girls for their excellent work on the company's gastronomy. Everyday, at least one of the men would bring our women a little gift, while we were in port, to show their appreciation. Marianne and Virginia liked the attention and did their utmost to provide excellent fare. We were very lucky.

Of course, Bill and I were even more lucky, because we got lucky every night, as well. Our women made certain to keep their men smiling.

As the days lingered, Virginia and Marianne regularly visited the markets and brought back all manner of beautiful blankets, shawls, and jewelry; big hooped earrings, and multiple bands of silver on their arms. Bill gave them plenty of money to amuse themselves with, so they had a lot of fun making the sloop a cozy affair inside and dressing themselves in marvelous clothing.

So far, none of the men had dared make a pass at the girls, because they were a respectful group, who did not mess with an other man's woman. It was the pirate's code, as far as these men were concerned. Bill and I had nothing to worry about.

When we had completed our preparations in Kingston, we sailed for Grand Cayman, where more of Bill's cronies were hiding. We needed at least twenty men on board our sloop, William figured, in order to effect a successful raid on a merchantman, which could have anywhere from ten to thirty sailors on board. Bill was not about to take chances being outnumbered.

En route, Virginia began work on our battle flag, which she modeled after the navy battle flag of the Knights Templar, adding a slight modification. Virginia had planned it out very carefully on a piece of black hemp cloth measuring one by two yards. Her design placed a white skull above a crossed sword and a femur bone. Everyone loved the idea, because it was a different take on the traditional pirates' flags, which showed two crossed femurs, or two crossed swords, but never one of each. It clearly showed that if anyone messed with us, one ended up dead with the slash of a sword. As it turned out, it was mostly bluff. We never actually killed that many people. But, I am getting ahead of myself.

We made Grand Cayman, three days later.

Bill, George, and Robert went ashore to locate their friends and possibly more weapons and ammunition, while the rest of us stayed on board. Virginia and Marianne worked on the flag. Frank and Andy sharpened their cutlasses. Marvin prepared powder horns, while Justin fished.

Me, I worked on my notes for this book. Even though I was now part of a pirate crew, I was still a writer, engaged in compiling this tale. Keeping good notes was imperative. It was so easy to forget details.

After three hours, or so, Bill returned with George and Robert, plus ten more people, three of whom were women. When they all came on board with their stuff, Marianne and Virginia came out to welcome them. I noticed that when they saw the three new women, they seemed a bit apprehensive. I guess they didn't like to share their preeminence with the men. It was apparent that our first crew members were quite fond of Marianne and Virginia. I guess our girls didn't want to share that with three other women. I had no idea women were so territorial.

When our new companions had stored their stuff on board, it became apparent that we would need some more food supplies. These were quickly obtained and stowed below, as were three more barrels of water, four more kegs of gun powder, three of rum, two of wine, six of ale, and a keg of pickled turtles.

The new arrivals had brought plenty more weapons for us. Twelve pistols, five muskets, and nine swords of various descriptions. They also managed to bring another five pounder on board, which was fastened on the port side forward gunwale. We now had two five pounders, which could be pointed straight ahead, or out to each side. They could also be quickly moved to either side of the ship, in order to have two guns pointing from port or starboard, as the occasion dictated.

Our new arrivals had also brought hammocks, which were distributed about the ship's hold, and in the forward bunk room. Some people decided they would sleep on deck, the weather being warm and pleasant in the Caribbean; so much nicer than Halifax, which I missed not at all. It didn't appear that Marianne and Virginia missed it either. Virginia hardly spoke of her family, now that we had been away for a month already.

The girls quickly became friends with the new women and forgot their initial reticence. Maria, Tanya, and Wendy, were mulattos. They had beautiful brown skin and long, dark black hair. They wore colorful scarves on their heads and wore lots of gold jewelry. Altogether, I would say five of the most beautiful women on earth were members of our pirate crew.

The seven new men were named; Douglas, Gerry, Colin, Neil, Leonard, Russell, and Wapoo, a native South American, who was more white than Indian. He was an expert in making poisons, which he used to tip the darts he shot through a long blow tube. While still in port, in Grand Cayman, he demonstrated his proficiency by shooting a seagull as it soared over our ship. The gull landed smack dab in the middle of the cabin roof. We all witnessed it and applauded Wapoo, which made him grin from ear to ear. I knew he would be of invaluable assistance in our upcoming adventures.

We left Grand Cayman on Wednesday, April 25th. The plan was for us to find a secret cove, somewhere, far from ports, to use as our staging place for raids throughout the area. We would build some huts and stash our supplies, in order to lighten the ship as much as possible, to facilitate chases. (A key to successful raiding was a fast ship).

The cove we were seeking lay in the Caicos Islands, the perfect location to cover shipping coming from Hispaniola, Jamaica, and the Island of Cuba. Ships from many nations plied those waters.

We found what we wanted after six days at sea. It was a deep water cove, accessible through a narrow coral channel, which could only be navigated by pulling our sloop behind the long boat, which had to be rowed by six men. There was no way we could sail our sloop into the cove. Hence, it was a well protected location.

The cove itself was plenty deep, so our ship floated just fine in the middle, where we dropped her anchors and made her fast.

We used the boat to ferry ourselves and supplies ashore to a perfectly white sandy beach, behind which were glorious palm trees. Perhaps we would find coconut palms and assorted other edible plants, we hoped. Wapoo assured us the place was full of food, including a great variety of delicious fish, crustaceans, and sea turtles. Looking at the place, I would say we landed in heaven.

After all the supplies had been ferried ashore, we set to work building shelters. As it turned out, most of the men were very handy and capable carpenters. Within three weeks we had built six very nice little houses on stilts, with thatched roofs, covered with banana leaves. One of the houses was used to store our supplies. Another became our cooking and eating house, when it rained. The other four houses became the domiciles of the three new couples; Maria and Neil, Tanya and Gerry, and Russell and Wendy. Douglas, Colin, Leonard and Wapoo shared the sixth house. There were spectacular views of the cove from every hut. Bill, Marianne, Virginia, and I kept our cabins on board ship.

When we were well set up, we began discussing our raiding plans in serious detail. Marianne and Virginia had completed sewing our Jolly Roger, so we were ready to show our colors and collectively, could not wait to begin. We would leave the next morning, if the winds were favorable.

The ship was loaded with water and food for seven days. We also took along a keg of rum, to give us a little extra courage, if we needed it. We left our pirates' cove early on Monday, May 22nd, and headed West North West in hopes of spying sails on the horizon. We flew the English Union Jack; our new Jolly Roger at the ready. A constant watch was placed in the crow's nest. We each took turns on the hour. Those not on watch, prepared weapons. The men made sure that everything was in perfect condition. They even fired each cannon to see that they worked. The bang they produced was quite deafening; the balls landing at least six hundred yards away, with loud splashes.

We cruised all day but never spied one sail, but our own. Bill explained it was the way it usually went. Cruising for sails, could take days, and days. The ocean was very large. It might even happen that we would not catch any ship before having to return to our cove for fresh supplies.

During the day we passed the time practicing fencing, or playing dice, or cards. After dinner we would all partake of some rum, wine, or ale, what ever suited our pleasure, and sang songs around a little brazier we set up on deck.

On the fifth day, we were running out of supplies and had to return to our cove for restocking. When we returned, Wendy and Neil, who had stayed behind to guard our stuff, had already stored fifty coconuts and managed to catch twenty good sized snappers, which they had drying on a rack they had built nearby. When we came into the cove, they were standing on the beach waving at us. It actually felt like we were coming home.

That night we had a big party on the beach. We drank copious amounts of alcohol and sang at the top of our lungs, easily outdoing the screaming monkeys, who inhabited the trees on the other side of the cove.

Next morning everyone slept late. No one was in a hurry to do anything. No one felt like cooking, so we just snacked on fruit and coconuts throughout the day, as we dealt with our hangovers, as best we could. I found myself drinking copious amounts of water, which was not a problem, considering that Neil and Wendy had found a fresh water spring not far from the huts.

When we had rested for a couple of days, during which we explored the island we were on, it was time to set out, once again. This time Gerry and Tanya stayed behind. We again outfitted the sloop for seven days and set out in search of prey.

This time it was not so long in coming. Virginia was the first to sight sails on the third day out. She shouted from the crow's nest, 'Sail ho!' Just like a real professional sailor. I was so proud of her. A finer woman I couldn't find, even if I sailed the Seven Seas.

Immediately everyone ran forward to look. 'Three points off the starboard bow!' shouted Virginia.

Bill pointed the spyglass and confirmed the presence of an English merchantman about two miles ahead and headed East, North East. Then he set a course which would intercept the ship. How long it would take was anyone's guess, at first. We couldn't figure out how fast the merchantman was sailing. However, it became quickly apparent that we were gaining on her. We hoped it was because she was heavy with cargo and hence, low in the water.

When we were about a quarter of a mile from the merchantman, Bill ordered the hoisting of our new flag.

As George flew our colors, we all toasted the flag with a cup of rum and prayed for success in our upcoming venture.

The merchantman must have seen us hoist the black flag, because she suddenly corrected her direction and unfurled more sails, hoping to outrun us.

Unfortunately for them, it was to no avail. The heavily laden merchantman was no match for our swiftly flying sloop. By mid afternoon we had caught up to the merchantman and let go a shot across her bows.

Alas, the English would not stop, so we put a shot into her hull, just above the waterline. The merchantman still did not heave to.

That called for another shot, carefully placed. This shot blasted quite a hole, it having struck an area where worms had obviously done some prior sabotage on our behalf. The hole was just above the water line. Water shipped in when a wave bumped against the ship.

This time the captain of the merchantman ordered the sails luffed and brought the ship to. With muskets loaded and pointing at the merchantman, eight of us climbed into the boat and rowed to the English ship. The boarding party consisted of; George, Robert, Frank, Andy, Marvin, Justin, Leonard, and Russell.

William and I watched as George climbed up the side of the merchantman.

Suddenly a shot rang out and George fell back into the water. Whether he had been killed was not immediately apparent in the melee which followed.

The boarding party shot their muskets and we placed two more five pound balls into the merchantman. This time we shot at some rigging, which fell to the deck, with a clatter.

Then horror befell us, as the English shot at our sloop with an eight pounder mounted on the poop. None of us had seen the cannon and we were surprised to hear its loud report. Fortunately, the man handling the cannon was not a very good shot. His ball passed neatly through our luffed mainsail.

However, there was no time to waste and we placed a five pound ball neatly into the poop of the merchantman, blowing the eight pounder and the gunner to kingdom come. It was unfortunate that the merchantman's crew was belligerent, because we didn't like killing. We were only interested in plundering.

A musket shot rang out from the merchantman. This time a ball came our way, hitting Wapoo in the shoulder. He fell to the deck, a big bleeding hole darkening his shirt.

This time Bill lost patience. He aimed the five pounder and shot in the direction the ball had come. He blasted a hole through the merchantman's gunwale, sending wooden splinters, like shrapnel. We heard a scream. Obviously the splinters had caught someone.

Meanwhile, the boarding party managed to climb onto the deck of the ship. We heard several more shots, and then it was quiet. Moments later George waved to us from the water indicating he was not dead and all was well. The ball had merely grazed his shoulder. Justin rowed the boat to pick him up from the water and then rowed back to the sloop, to fetch the rest of us, so that we could explore the merchantman to see what we could use.

When Bill stepped on board, the captain of the English ship recognized him.

'William Bartleby,' he said. 'I thought you were dead.'

Bill laughed. 'As you can see, Mister Williams, I am very much alive and am here to relieve you of your gold, silver, and cargo which we can use for our purposes.'

'What do you plan to do with us?' asked the captain.

'We will let you sail this tub back to England. I'm sure you can patch those little holes we put into your hull, after we lighten her and she rises in the water.'

Mister Williams heaved a sigh of relief.

Bill requested the manifest, to ascertain what cargo was being carried back to England. The second mate fetched it, forthwith, upon orders from Mister Williams.

While Bill read the manifest over with George; Leonard and Russell rounded up the crew and had them gather in a group, near the forward hatch. They kept their muskets pointed at the ten sailors.

The rest of us explored the ship and plundered what took our fancy.

In the hold we found barrels of Jamaican rum, pickled turtles, salted fish, bales of cotton, bags of coffee, lumber, coconuts, assorted bags of fruits, sweet potatoes, five goats, two cows, twenty chickens, and a large box full of golden objects from Maracaibo, obviously the work of native craftsmen.

With the help of the merchant sailors, we lightened the ship of its rum and food stuffs, including the animals, as well as the box with the golden objects. We had also found some charts which would be of use, as well as the gold watches of those who had them, including the captain, Mister Williams.

When we were done unloading the ship, we gave the crew the option of joining us in piracy, or they could sail back to England, with a nearly empty ship. It was their choice. None of the sailors elected to join us, so we wished them all the best and returned to our ship. The sun had set by the time we were done.

We watched the merchantman's lamp disappear into the night, as we sailed home, to our well hidden cove, happily sampling the rum we had captured; all the while singing our pirate songs at the top of our lungs. Of course, we replaced our battle flag with the English Jack, because we were incapable of carrying out another raid, and did not intend one for some time after returning to our hidden cove.

We arrived at the entrance to our anchorage the next morning.

The rest of the day was spent unloading our cargo.

That night we had a massive celebration party, in which we consumed even more rum than the last time, dancing and singing around a monstrous bonfire on the beach.

I was beginning to really enjoy being a pirate.

So was Virginia.

As for Wapoo, he needed a painful operation to remove the lead from his shoulder. Colin was able to effect the surgery with a sharp knife. Wapoo never uttered so much as a groan, as Colin dug around in his shoulder. When the operation was over, Colin soaked Wapoo's shoulder with rum, and then bandaged the wound tightly with white cotton. He was expected to make a full recovery.

So ended our first successful pirating adventure.

Chapter Nine

After three weeks of pleasant living on our little island, we were getting bored and wanted another adventure. Bill, the undisputed captain, suggested we make a few changes to our ship, before we went out. He figured that the merchantman had probably reached port and reported our activities. Bill reasoned that the name of our sloop was probably on report, and that within a month, or so, we could expect that ships would be looking for us.

Hence, in a well rummed evening around the fire, we came up with the new name for our ship. We changed her name from, *Bluerose*, to, *Phoenix*. Most of Bill's friends figured that the gang was like a phoenix, gaining new life out of the fires of a past defeat. We drank a mighty toast to the new name and sang a rousing song of tribute to our newly named ship.

Next day, Colin and Russell removed the letters forming the name, *Bluerose*. They also removed, *Halifax*, which was printed in smaller letters below. We had decided to change the port of origin to, *Heaven's Cove*. The work of repainting the names took two days. By the third day we were ready, our main sail neatly mended by Marianne.

We took on provisions and set out on our second adventure. This time we decided to look for gold. The only way to do that was to sail to San Juan, where we would have to do some espionage and find out what ships were carrying what to where. This time the women elected to stay behind. We made sure they were well armed. We had no doubts that they knew how to use the tools of our trade. I pitied any man who had the misfortune of crossing them when they were armed like that.

Anyway, we sailed for San Juan Bautista de Puerto Rico, making port in six days. We were slowed down by a squall, something I had yet to experience. It was quite frightening, at one point, when a huge wave came over the bows. I stayed the entire time with Bill and George, who stood at the helm. The entire time, Bill explained what they were doing; furthering my education in the art of sailing.

The sails had been reduced to a storm jib. All hands had made certain that all cargo was firmly secured in the hold and then took refuge in their bunks or hammocks in the forecastle.

I prayed that Virginia was alright at home, and that the squall did not affect her and the other women. I reasoned that the cove provided a good shelter, and the huts were solidly constructed, so there really was no need for concern.

Bill told me not to worry. 'They're strong, and resourceful women,' he added. 'Besides, Peter, this little squall is nothing. Don't worry, this ship will more than handle it.'

And, so it was. We came through the squall, just fine. Even though I had a bout of sea sickness, there was nothing to worry about. Our *Phoenix* was a stoutly built ship. Bill complimented me on buying it. Then, for the first time, he asked me what I had paid for her.

I told him eight and a half pounds of gold.

He thought about that for a moment and then congratulated me on an excellent buy. 'This ship is worth every ounce of gold you paid for her.' Then he laughed. 'And, besides, we'll find way more than eight pounds of gold on this trip. I have a good feeling about that.'

When we made port, flying our Spanish flag, we immediately dropped anchors in the harbour, and secured our ship. Then we ferried ourselves ashore, leaving two men on board to guard the sloop.

On shore we were met by an official demanding to know who we were.

We told him that William was a merchant and that I was the captain of the *Phoenix*. We had come to San Juan to seek mercantile opportunities.

The official seemed pleased and directed us to his office, to fill out some official forms.

Bill told him that we would fill in forms, after we had taken on ale, and victuals. 'We are hungry men and tired of cooking for ourselves. Where is the best restaurant you have?' Bill invited the official to join us, but he declined and suggested we come to see him after lunch. We offered to do so, but of course, we had no intention of actually doing so. As far as we were concerned, all officials could go to hell, and the world would be the better for it.

We followed the directions the official had given us and arrived in front of a busy establishment, some distance from our ship, near the centre of town. Senora Gonzales' Cantina was obviously the place the locals liked to frequent, because, although it was mid afternoon, there were quite a number of people there.

We managed to find tables to sit at, in groups of two, three, four and six. Bill, George, and I sat together at a table by the window.

I looked out at the street and watched two urchins pick the pocket of a well dressed gentleman, who was walking with a fine lady on his arm. I couldn't help but smile, as the resourceful urchins distracted the couple, while one snuck up behind, neatly slipping the man's purse from under his coat. Children had to do what they could to survive; many of them were probably orphans, I reckoned. They could have been the offspring of injured sailors, missing arms or legs, unable to find gainful employment. Who knows?

As we thus sat in a moment of silence, wondering what the topic of discussion was going to be, it occurred to me that I had never asked Bill, how he came to be captured and brought to Halifax. We had talked about all kinds of other things. How exactly he got to be in Halifax, I had mostly taken for granted.

Bill smiled sadly. 'Do you remember that huge storm, a month, or so before you came to the gaol?'

I had to think about the question for a moment. Halifax was far from my mind.

'Shipwreck. It was as simple as that. I was shipwrecked off Sable Island. We were blown off course and ended up on the rocks. I nearly drowned. Fortunately, I was rescued by some fishermen, who brought me to Lunenburg, where I was arrested and put in gaol. I was sailing with a skeleton crew, and lost five good friends. I was coming to Halifax to fetch my treasure. I was the only survivor. It is darn good for me that you worked in Halifax, Peter. I am thankful everyday for you springing me from that place. I would most surely have been drawn and quartered in London.'

I replied that we had better be careful, we might still be caught.

Bill and George both agreed it was prudent to speak quietly. One never knew who was listening. Where our business was concerned, 'Loose lips sank ships.'

After we had eaten and drank our fill of ale, or wine, rum, or whatever else my new companions drank, we stepped outside into the sunshine and discussed the next course of events. We were to go out in twos, and one group of three, to the various drinking establishments, where sailors, belonging to the ships in the harbour, were spending their money. Drunken sailors tend to talk. We were hoping information, regarding the ships' cargoes, would be easily obtained by engaging sailors in conversations and plying them with ale.

To that end, Bill handed everyone some coins from the bag he was carrying. He gave everyone enough money to buy at least fifteen pints each. Of course, one pint each for us, and numerous pints for the sailors we were talking to.

Everyone agreed it would be fun to conduct the espionage.

And so it was that, Bill, George, and I, came to a seedy back street tavern called, El Cresta de Gallo. Three sailors were sitting at a table in the street. Large tankards of ale were sitting in front of them. We could tell that they were already a couple of sheets to the wind and would be pliable.

We sat down at an empty table next to them and ordered a round of ales for ourselves. Gradually, as we began to sip our ales, we got into conversation with the sailors, who spoke only Spanish. Fortunately, Bill and George could speak Spanish fairly well, translating back to me.

They began by asking innocuous questions; the usual things, like what port the sailors were from? What was the name of their ship. How was their passing? How did they like San Juan? That sort of thing.

These particular jack tars came from a Spanish merchant ship named, *Prospero*. She sailed out of Barcelona and had come from San Fernando.

However, try as we might, they would not reveal what it was that they were carrying.

We grew suspicious and knew we might be on to something. However, we did not reveal our intentions or interest in their cargo and carried on the conversation about all manner of things nautical and otherwise. We bought them a round of drinks. They thanked us profusely.

Eventually, we were all seated together. Then we bought the Spanish sailors an other round of drinks, for which they were even more grateful. Soon we were their best friends in the whole world.

After five more rounds, the sailors were leaning into the wind at a precarious angle. I was afraid one of them was going to slip from his chair. We, of course, had kept our consumption to a minimum, because we were working.

When the sailors were good and drunk, Bill and George plied them with questions about their cargo. This time the information came out. The *Prospero* was carrying gold and silver art works of the Mayan culture. The treasures had been uncovered in some tombs in Belize and were bought by their employer, a very rich Barcelonan merchant named, Carlos de Riez, Castagramba. They were taking shore leave in preparation for the voyage to Barcelona.

Bill asked them nonchalantly if they were armed, considering they were carrying such a valuable cargo.

A sailor named Pedro volunteered that they were quite well armed with muskets and swords. He said it had to be thus, because there were fifteen chests full of gold and silver objects, and precious stones; lots of precious stones. Pedro had personally helped to stow the chests in the hold. One of the chests had a broken lock and he was able to look inside. What he described made us all the more interested and desirous of the immediate removal of said treasure to our island cove. We resolved, speaking in English, to effect the rescue of the treasure as soon as possible.

Bill asked them how many sailors formed the crew. He nearly laughed with delight when the sailor answered that there were fifteen crew members plus the captain and first mate. Apparently, the owner thought that a merchant ship, with an inordinate number of sailors on board, would attract the wrong kind of attention. Of course Bill and George heartily agreed.

The sailors were not concerned about the small number of men on the ship, because they would be sailing in a convoy, anyway. There were other ships which were armed.

When we had heard enough we said good bye to the three drunken sailors and sauntered back to the *Phoenix*. We had heard what we needed to hear. Our treasure ship was in port. We decided to sail her away, while the crew was in town.

When the others finally returned, in various stages of sobriety, we sat on deck and held a war council. We discovered that we had all spoken with sailors from the *Prospero*.

From the reports we discovered that most of the crew was accounted for in town.

In our business, one had to act fast when the circumstances presented themselves. The circumstances presented themselves very clearly, right then and there. We decided to steal the treasure, by sailing the ship right out from under the Spaniards' noses.

The plan unfolded as follows:

Four of us would sail the *Phoenix*, and the rest would sail the *Prospero*.

When night had fallen, we loaded up our boat, me included, and rowed under cover of darkness to the Spanish merchantman. We had come equipped with pistols and cutlasses.

Meanwhile, Russell, Colin, and Justin maneuvered the sloop to a position nearer the merchantman and the harbour entrance, where they waited to see what would accrue on the *Prospero*, and how the winds would play in our favour.

We rowed the boat up to the merchantman and quietly climbed on board.

There was no one on deck. We could see a light in the Master's cabin. Bill and George went there, while the others began preparing the ship for sailing.

The only persons on board were the captain and first mate.

Moments later, Bill and George led the two Spaniards out of the cabin. The two gentlemen looked most indignant and vociferously demanded to know the meaning of the outrage.

Bill simply asked them if they would prefer to live, or if they would prefer to die.

Of course both gentlemen chose to live and we graciously let them have our boat. We gave them some money for their lodgings in San Juan, for which they thanked us. We watched them row back to shore, as we began to sail the merchantman out of the harbour, led by our trusty *Phoenix*, winds favoring us.

When we returned to our island, some days later, we found that the merchantman would just barely fit through the narrow channel. We actually had to break off some coral, in places, to avoid damaging the hull. Gradually we brought her into the cove and dropped her anchors. The *Phoenix* was already anchored in the cove, having arrived the day before.

Our little family was happily jumping up and down on the beach, as we clambered into the merchantman's longboat.

The moment I stepped on shore, Virginia flew into my arms and smothered me with kisses. I saw Marianne do the same to Bill, as did the other women to their men. I felt sad for those men who had no women to greet them. I could see them watching us, with envy in their eyes. I sensed potential trouble. I made it an item for discussion and would bring it up at our next council meeting. We needed to have more women join our gang.

When we felt like emptying the *Prospero*, a couple of days later, we hauled the fifteen chests of Mayan gold and silver, plus lots of barrels of provisions, onto our beach and proceeded to examine the Mayan items, one by one, setting them reverentially on blankets we had laid on the sand.

Hundreds of magnificent masks, statuettes of grotesque gods, and jewelry, lots of jewelry; ear rings, ear disks, pectorals, bracelets, anklets, all of the finest gold and silver, plus lots of jade, rubies, and turquoise came to light from the wooden chests. Altogether it was a magnificent hoard of priceless treasures. The success of our raid was the perfect excuse for a huge bonfire party on the beach, which we proceeded to put together, forthwith.

At the bonfire the goods were divided up amongst the members of the gang, Bill receiving a quarter and the rest going to us. There was more than enough and everyone went back to their respective quarters with enough gold, silver and precious stones to purchase many years of easy living on the main land. Fortunately, for the Mayan treasures, we were all too amazed by them to melt them down and kept them as decorations in our various quarters.

Speaking of our quarters, we now had eight huts and a large meeting/dining hall, where we could retire in case of inclement weather. We built it during the time we relaxed, after our first success. No more than two persons shared a hut. Eventually, as we took a break after our Mayan treasure haul, we built private huts for each of the single men. Our hideout was beginning to resemble a small hamlet, with thirteen huts and the large meeting hall.

We even began to cultivate some ground in hope of obtaining seeds for potatoes, onions, leeks, cabbages, tomatoes... The women were hoping to develop a large garden, and had us all digging and scraping ground, to prepare for planting. When that would be was anyone's guess. We had no seeds, but it gave us something else to do, besides playing cards, walking around the island, playing cricket on the beach, cleaning the ships, or sunning in our hammocks.

Speaking of ships, we careened the Spanish merchantman a few days later and breamed her well. She was encrusted with barnacles and assorted other marine growth, which slowed her progress considerably. Others scraped the old name off the merchantman and painted her new name, *Abundance*, on the transom. We painted, *Heaven's Cove*, underneath.

One day, at a council meeting, it was determined that we would build a tall outlook tower at the entrance to the cove, on a small promontory, which rose a hundred feet above the coral. It became an amazing project, as it unfolded. We cut trees and prepared a base. Eventually, after twelve days, we had a thirty five foot high tower, from which we could see for a long distance out to sea. It was decided we would keep the tower manned every day, and a schedule was worked out. We all felt, even though the cove was quite secret, one could never be too safe. By then there were people out looking for us, for sure.

Everybody contributed four hours every three days, or so, manning the watch tower. It was during this time that I took up smoking a pipe. I found it relaxing to sit in the tower and smoke my pipe as I drifted into the clouds. Sitting in the tower never became an onerous chore for anybody and we all gladly kept watch. I loved sitting up there and watching the ocean, and the birds, which called the island home. Even the monkeys were curious about the tower, and they would look at me from the trees. Eventually, I managed to get one to come over to the tower with enticements of food. The little creature became a regular visitor, after a while; eagerly accepting bits of food from whoever sat up there. We decided to call him, Alex.

Sometimes we would form little groups and rehearse pantomimes and skits with which we entertained each other, when we were gathered together in the evenings. Some days we would improvise an entire court procedure, which was lots of fun. One time I had the opportunity of playing the learned judge and we pretended to try Andrew for piracy. I particularly remember that court case, because Andy took it so seriously, it nearly resulted in cracked heads. Because it was so singular an enactment, I will give you, dear reader, some more details regarding that incredible day on the beach.

Wapoo, some days previously, had discovered a fungus growing on our island which had very interesting effects when ingested, he said. Wapoo had cautioned those of us, who were interested in experiencing the effects of eating the mushroom, what he termed a, 'wonder of nature,' should do so with caution, because too much could result in undesirable side effects. Hence, he carefully measured out little amounts, which he deemed sufficient to effect the desired results. Of course none of us, who ate of the fungus, knew what would happen to us, but we trusted our friend.

Andy and I, along with several others had prepared to stage a mock trial that afternoon. After ingesting the fungus, we went about our business of preparing for the trial, which, as time passed, became a very realistic event for us. We began to believe that I was actually a learned judge, George a learned prosecutor, William a barrister, learned in the law acting for the defense, and so on. Eventually, Colin and Russell rushed out and grabbed Andy, putting him in irons, which we had found on board ship.

Andy wildly protested his innocence, beginning to believe we were really trying him, and the whole thing was real. I believe that Andy actually saw himself facing the noose we had strung up over the limb of a tree, nearby.

The people watching, who did not know we had ingested the fungus, were becoming concerned, as the afternoon proceeded, that perhaps the mock court was becoming too real, as Andy tearfully pleaded for his life in front of me, seated on the 'throne,' a large chair from the Great Cabin of our merchantman.

Then, after I had pronounced the sentence, 'That ye be taken from this place to the place of execution, where ye will be hanged by the neck until ye are dead. May God have mercy on your miserable soul.' Andy jumped up and screamed that he was not about to go down without a fight. He grabbed Colin and threw him against Russell, in an attempt to flee. Unfortunately, the irons on his ankles prevented him from running away, but he tried with all of his might, an expression of supreme fear on his face. It was all we could do to convince him that the whole thing was, but a pantomime, he was so frightened.

The rest of us, who performed the mock court, suddenly saw the whole thing as a hilarious farce and we laughed and laughed and laughed, until our bellies were sore and the tears streamed from our eyes. Eventually, Andy also saw the joke and laughed even louder at his foolishness in thinking we were actually going to hang him.

While we danced about, bent over laughing, our bellies and jaws becoming sore from the exertions, Marianne and Virginia looked at us strangely, then shaking their heads, thinking we had gone mad, left the beach to attend to the evening meal, leaving us to our delirium.

The following day, I was not sure whether to thank Wapoo, or curse him for introducing the fungus to us. However, I must admit, the experience was one to remember, and in the right circumstances might prove beneficial. However, I was not prepared to eat the fungus again in a long time, my jaws and belly were still sore the next day. We also stopped playing, 'court room' for a long time after that, thinking we did not need to scare each other with the hang man's noose.

When we had been gone from Halifax for six and a half months, or so, (we had become quite unaware of the passing of time, because I didn't write in my journal every day; there were so many distractions). Virginia and I became pregnant. It was quite by accident. We had been so careful, but there we were. Virginia's menstruation had stopped and her belly was swelling. When we announced our news, everyone in the gang was overjoyed.

After the announcement we noticed a distinct difference in everyone's treatment of Virginia. She became the queen and everyone went out of their way to make sure that she was comfortable and taken care of. As time went on, the baby we had made became everyone's baby. It was a comforting thought for both of us to know, our child would have many aunts and uncles, who would love her or him.

I think Virginia had been pregnant for thirty five days, when it was decided it had become necessary to sail to Port au Prince, which was relatively close by, in order to obtain fresh supplies. We hoped that perhaps a 'supply ship' might be available, en route, and we wouldn't have to sail all the way to the Port. However, be that as it may, our ship was supplied with enough gold and silver to purchase supplies, if necessary.

Since Virginia and I were pregnant, I was strictly forbidden to come along, because everyone felt my place was with her. Virginia protested a little bit on my behalf, saying she wasn't due for eight months, but it didn't matter. I was to stay home with the women.

To be perfectly honest, I didn't mind staying behind, and only pretended to be bothered about not going on a pirate adventure to Port au Prince. Staying home gave me time to work on my book, and to have even more privacy with my lovely partner, and the mother of my child. I made sure to ask Bill to fetch me a big bottle of ink and some new quills, and lots of paper. I also asked him to bring back some beautiful silver for Virginia.

Bill said he would see to it. Then we hugged and gave each other a warm handshake. Bill and I had become best friends. I would miss him while he was gone.

And then they were off, leaving me with five lovely women, on a beautiful island in the West Indies. Life couldn't have been better.

Spending time with five beautiful women was interesting and fun. The girls were good company and took really good care of me, with regards to food and conversation. Sometimes, not because we were bored of their company, Virginia and I had to get away by ourselves. Sitting around five women chatting about women's things, would necessitate a change for me, from time to time. I would take Virginia away at some point every day. Sometimes we would go to the tower, where we would spend a good part of the day, playing with the monkeys, and each other. Fortunately, the tower was built good and sturdy. I'm sure the other women knew what we were up to, because they were always giggling when we came down to eat.

While the others were off to Port au Prince, we decided to have a look in the merchantman to see if we could do something interesting with it, to surprise our friends when they returned. So, one sunny morning we rowed out to the ship and climbed aboard. Virginia had never really looked her over before. I knew the ship pretty well, considering I sailed back with her from San Juan.

As we roamed about the ship, I gradually steered her into the Master's cabin and onto the Master's bed, where I proceeded to slowly remove her clothes and make love with her.

And such love making it was. Virginia was my dream. She was so responsive, so willing, so totally giving of herself, that I went into her, as if to Heaven. Virginia felt so good inside and out. Her scent drove me ever further into a passion from which I never wanted to escape. I loved Virginia and she loved me. We were so happy together. It was as if God Himself had put us together. Heaven was right there on earth.

I am sure we must have set the huge ship rocking, because when we returned from our exploration, the other women were giggling.

Marianne asked me, 'How was she?' pretending to mean the ship, but of course meaning her friend.

I laughed when Virginia told her, 'She was incredible,' and then she laughingly added, 'Uh huh, uh huh' in such a way that it made us all burst out laughing.

On another day the women and I practiced shooting pistols and muskets. We set up targets in the trees and learned to shoot quite well. Virginia and Marianne became especially adept and managed to hit their targets most of the time, with pistols at fifty yards, and with muskets at two hundred. I was very impressed with their natural affinity for the sport. The other women were not quite as good, but good enough to pose a threat to an attacker.

We also practiced the hand to hand combat techniques which Colin, who was well versed in the martial arts, had taught us, some weeks before. It was great fun wrestling with those beautiful women and having them falling all over me in the sand, struggling with all of their might. Often times I was hard pressed to assert myself, because these were not soft, weak girls, but strong and courageous women. Tanya, in particular, was the toughest to beat. In fact, I think she and I were equal in strength.

Sometimes, having these women wrestling with me, feeling their firm breasts pressing against me, smelling their hair in my face, feeling their pubic mound against my thighs as we rolled in the sand, gave me quite a hard on. I couldn't help it. He has a mind of his own.

When Virginia saw that I had quite a tilt in my kilt, so to speak, she forbade me from wrestling with the girls, anymore. It was just as well. I suppose it wasn't healthy for our relationship. Virginia clearly made me see her point when we were alone.

'What's the big idea getting a hard on with Tanya?' she demanded. 'It was practically pushing through your breeches! I'm sure they all saw it.' Then she got very emotional on me, claiming my boner with Tanya was because I didn't want her anymore, claiming it was because I thought she was becoming fat and ugly.

Of course I had to explain that my unit has a mind of its own, and I am not responsible for my hard ons, especially not when he is so curious when a woman is rubbing her breasts on my chest, etcetera. I promised to never wrestle with the girls again, and told her for at least an hour, how beautiful she was becoming, as I rubbed her belly and kissed her, and spoke to our little baby. Eventually, we made love and all was well again.

The others returned after twenty days. I saw the sails of the *Phoenix* on the horizon, one after noon, when I was sitting in the tower. I shouted the good news of their return to the women. An hour later, our friends were back in the cove with; good, and bad news, provisions, and seedlings for the garden.

I noticed that the forward, port gunwale had a big hole in it, and the sails were perforated with holes. I pointed that out to the girls.

'What happened?!' shouted Marianne from shore.

Bill waved and then clambered into the row boat, followed by Colin and six others. They rowed ashore and Bill jumped out of the boat. Colin rowed back to the sloop and fetched the others.

'We are lucky to be alive,' said Bill sadly. Then he bowed his head. 'Justin is dead,' he said. 'Shot through the eye. I saw the back of his head explode, as the slug passed through him. He died on the spot.'

'What spot?' asked Virginia.

'The deck of the *Phoenix*, as we were trying to get away from the wrong merchantman.'

'What do you mean, 'the wrong merchantman?' asked Marianne.

'The wrong one to pick on. This one was armed and dangerous. We misjudged her. We're lucky we got away. They must be carrying something very precious. I'd love to know what it is. Flying, Dutch colors.'

'Those Netherlanders are a tough lot,' said George. 'We generally don't mess with them, but we came upon her shortly after leaving Port au Prince. She was very low in the water and plowing waves. We had no idea this ship was so well armed. When we hoisted our flag, and shot across her bows, she let us believe she was stopping for us, by luffing her sails. Then, as we came close enough to put a plank across, she suddenly opened fire with seven five pound swivel guns they suddenly mounted on the gunwales. We never saw the little cannons until we were up close and the sailors had picked them up and mounted them. The moment they opened fire, so did we, with our muskets.

They also had muskets and began shooting at us. Fortunately, there was a wind, and we managed to set our sails and get away. Justin was shot just as we passed the bow of the merchantman. He was taking aim at a sailor on the forecastle. I guess the sailor got him first. We buried him at sea and the Dutchies continued on their way. We could still see her sails some hours later, slowly passing over the horizon, headed for Holland, I suppose, those sneaky bastards.'

'It sounds like we should thank God that only one of you was killed,' said Marianne vehemently to Bill. 'Maybe we should consider that we have lots of gold and silver, why do we need to take chances on getting more?'

Bill looked at her and then at me. 'We want to make sure there is lots for us, for the rest of our lives. Don't you want to live like this, forever?' Bill gestured towards the houses. 'Maybe all we need to do is find one more loaded ship, and we'll be done.' He looked at Marianne with puppy dog eyes. 'I know you worry about me,' he added and then gave her a big hug.

Marianne's love overcame her anger. She gave Bill a huge kiss, happy it wasn't he who was killed.

Then everyone pitched in and we unloaded our ship.

When the pots of seedlings came on shore, the women were ecstatic. I had never seen human beings go crazy over a bunch of little plants. They immediately set off with them, giggling and laughing, to begin their garden, while we men continued hauling swag ashore; kegs of ale, rum, and wine. Kegs of dried beef and pork. Bags of: alligator pears, prickly pears, mangoes, melons, papa apples, papayas, oranges, bananas, onions, cocoa, cocoa nuts, plantains, guavases,...they had brought seedlings of each of the afore mentioned, except oranges. The variety of plants is probably the reason the women were so ecstatic. A great variety of fresh fruits and vegetables would ensure everyone's good health in the colony.

Each man, with a woman in Heaven's Cove, brought her back a little gift, a new sash, some jewelry, combs, that sort of thing.

Bill brought Marianne a beautiful silver ring with a very unusual design on it and a sapphire in the middle. The ring fit perfectly and everyone admired it. Bill had good taste. He had also brought a superlative armband and earrings for Virginia. As I said, Bill had very good taste. The jewelry looked fantastic.

Everyone was happy to be home.

Judging from the condition of the ship and sails, it was a harrowing voyage. Everyone who made it home felt lucky to be alive.

When night fell, we held a bonfire in honour of Justin. We each spoke some words about him. 'He was a kind and loyal friend.' 'Justin was a friendly man.' 'Justin had a wonderful smile and a special light in his eyes.'

'He was very knowledgeable about edible fish,' 'Justin was special and would be missed,' were some of the comments I remember. It was a melancholy evening, during which everyone of us contemplated their mortality. Gradually, as the fire died out, people drifted off to their huts.

That night, Virginia and I slept in the tower. However, it was an unpleasant night, as we woke up several times thinking of Justin. He would be missed.

Next day everyone was still mourning the loss of their friend.

Eventually, the pain left us and life returned back to normal on our little island. Cheer returned and smiles were again the order of the day. Once again, our island home was such a happy place to be. Our life as pirates could not be better. We were living a dream.

Chapter Ten

A week later, we began the task of repainting the *Abundance*. The men had brought the necessary paint from Port au Prince. First we spent many days scraping the old paint off. This was a difficult task, but we made sure to intersperse our work with a little rum and a jig or two on the deck. We tried to have fun when we could. It made light work and kept everyone in a good mood.

Except for Leonard, I often saw him slacking off and skulking about, trying to avoid work. He seemed to have taken a shining to Maria and kept following her around, much to her annoyance. She must have mentioned it to her husband, because I saw Neil confront Leonard on the deck of the ship. I was painting a railing when Neil confronted Leonard about his bothering Maria.

Of course, Leonard denied everything and skulked off.

I asked Bill about him, sometime later, when I had a chance to talk with him alone.

Bill told me he had always had doubts about Leonard, but because Leonard was Gerry's brother, he had to take him along. Gerry, who was an expert in munitions, was an important member of the team. He wouldn't have come if Leonard had stayed behind. 'So, we will put up with him, for the time being,' said Bill. 'If he steps out of line with Maria, I'm sure Neil will take care of it. Leonard has to face the fact that Neil is very fast with a knife and wouldn't be afraid to use it on Leonard, if Leonard laid a hand on Maria. I think Leonard knows this. Neil warned him. I'm sure it will be enough.'

Leonard did leave Maria alone. Neil's warning obviously had an effect.

Next I saw Leonard bothering Tanya, one evening around the fire. He was pretending to be drunk. As he stumbled past her, he pretended to trip over a rock. As he fell, he grabbed one of her breasts.

It was a big mistake because she just up and punched him on the side of his head.

Leonard fell backward and Tanya fell on him with a vicious pummeling. We all found it very funny and figured Leonard had it coming. When Tanya was done, she sat down and had another drink of rum. 'Arrrrr, that felt good,' she said. We laughed all the louder. But not Leonard, he took some days to heal from his mistake.

After three weeks of steady work, the *Abundance* had a new coat of dark blue paint on the hull and bright yellow railings. We had painted the masts yellow and blue, in alternating rings, a yard wide.

The women had stained the sails yellow and then painted blue stripes on them.

When our new ship was done, she looked like a true party ship, like no ship on the seas. It was time to take her for a maiden voyage.

Alas, storm season hit us and we were confined to quarters for two months, during which powerful winds blew the banana leaves off some of our huts. During a particularly fierce episode, we were actually quite concerned our huts would blow away. However, we had built them in amongst the trees, and the cove being on the lee side of the island, made the storms bearable.

The merchantman had come with several barrels of candles, so we had plenty of light and managed to pass the time telling stories, singing songs, reading, playing cards, and fixing the sails of the *Phoenix*. I spent a good amount of time on my book, sorting notes and interviewing the members of our gang, who seemed to enjoy being asked questions by a reporter.

Virginia's belly was swelling beautifully. She was no longer suffering morning illness and steadily felt better and better. Her breasts were swelling, as well. I must admit, I liked that too. Not that I felt her breasts were not big enough, they certainly were. But, they were definitely getting bigger. I often complimented her on how she glowed, and how pleased I was with her. She was a treasure. I was a lucky man.

When the storm season passed, we felt confident we could take the *Abundance* out for a cruise. We carefully stashed our Mayan treasures deep in the forest, packed plenty of money in bags, provisioned the ship with food and weapons, just to be sure, and clambered on board. Bill and George had rigged up a boatswain's chair and carefully hoisted Virginia on board, much to everyone's delight.

Virginia loved the attention.

When everyone, but the rowers, were on board, we pulled up the anchors, and were pulled out through the coral channel. Ever so carefully, so as not to scratch the new paint job, of which we were all very proud. We couldn't wait to see the sails unfurled.

After the rowers had climbed on board, the long boat was hauled up and lashed on deck. Then the sails were ceremoniously unfurled with a mighty toast of Jamaican rum. The women had done a magnificent job; the sails looked absolutely stunning. Altogether we were quite the colorful company on our colorful ship

All of us were dressed in brightly coloured scarves, loose fitting shirts with sashes, loose cotton trousers and sandals. Many of us had earrings in our ears and wore shawls or wide brimmed hats, or both. We looked like quintessential pirates. Fortunately, none of us had a peg leg or a hook hand, or an eye patch. We were all able bodied pirates, back then.

Justin would have had one, an eye patch that is, if the bullet had not blown out the back of his head. If the ball just stayed lodged in his eye socket, he might have survived it. He would have lived and seen just fine out of his other eye. But it would never be the same, for him. His vision would be hampered, to be sure.

We were fortunate that we were a company of able bodied pirates who could put up a good fight, if need be. Except for Virginia, of course. Even though she was pregnant, she still looked like a pirate woman; with her colourful sash and hooped ear rings.

As for me, I hadn't gone that far yet. I didn't look quite so piratish as my friends. I guess I was chicken about poking holes in my ears, and had no reason to pierce them yet, either; not having survived any shipwrecks. I hoped I would never be shipwrecked, but vowed, if ever I was, I would then follow the sailor's tradition and pierce my right ear lobe. I did wear a colorful bandana under my hat, though. I thought it made me look a little bit piratical.

Anyway, after the beautiful sails had been unfurled, we sang a loud sea shanty in honour of our glorious company and danced a happy jig on the deck. When it was Virginia's turn to dance, she danced a jig, much to everyone's delight. She called it, 'the fat lady's polka.'

The ship handled the sea well, but was not as swift as the sloop, the merchantman being broader abeam and built more like a tub. I found her quite different to handle but got used to her pretty quickly. We all took turns handling the wheel, it being one of the fun things about sailing.

When we had been at sea for three or four days, somewhere off the coast of Hispaniola, and flying a Dutch flag, which the men had brought back from Port au Prince, we were hailed by another ship flying a Dutch flag. She was a West Indiaman, obviously expanding trade for the mercantile empire of the Dutch.

Fortunately, Frank Buttons could speak some Dutch and invited the crew of the West Indiaman to come on board for a party.

We all shouted, 'Ya, ya, come, come, party, party!'

At first the Dutch were reluctant, but, the captain, being a true Dutchman, liked to drink with some fellow Dutchmen. And besides, our ship fascinated him. He had never seen a ship painted such as ours.

We all repeated, 'Ya, ya, gute, gute,' and hoisted our tankards in salute.

Gradually, the Dutch sailors appeared on deck and waved; all the while smiling at our beautiful women. As it turned out, there were only twelve of them, altogether, including the captain. We couldn't believe our luck. We were not even cruising as pirates, and here we had a perfect opportunity facing us. What could we do but get the Dutchmen drunk and steal them blind?

The Dutch sailors came on board and we partied with them, giving them lots of rum, or ale, or wine, whatever they preferred. The women prepared a sumptuous feast and we all ate and drank and enjoyed a merry company. The fact that only one of us actually spoke Dutch didn't seem to phase them. They were more interested in looking into the lovely cleavages of our gorgeous women, who made sure they got plenty of eyefuls. The captain was particularly interested in Virginia's bosom. I watched his eyes when she poured his wine.

Unbeknownst to the Dutchmen, we were drinking very watered down ales, so as not to get drunk. We were professionals and did not drink when we were working. Being the quintessential pirates that we were, we pretended to get drunk along with the jolly Dutchmen, until they all passed out, including the captain. Then we nonchalantly relieved their ship of its contents.

When we were done, we carried the Dutch sailors back to their ship, and left them lying on their deck. By the time they woke up, we were long gone into the mists of the West Indies.

The swag from the Dutch ship was a very impressive one and gave us a perfect opportunity to celebrate the next day, when the loot was examined on deck.

What we had looted from the West Indiaman was the following, in no particular order, just the one I wrote down at the time we examined the cargo:

Three gold watches, two of silver, a box containing five hundred and sixty silver rijksdaalders and daalders, fifty bags of salt, fifteen bales of cotton, twenty eight bags of sugar, a hundred bales of tobacco, fifty kegs of rum, fifty of ale, twenty barrels of salted herrings, ten hogsheads of wine, twenty five barrels of pickled sea turtles, a chest containing sixty golden Ducats, twelve good charts, twenty books in Dutch, twelve coils of good rope, sixteen sails, thirty sabres, thirteen muskets, ten pistols, with plenty of ammunition, five kegs of powder, a five pounder cannon, with twenty five balls and grapeshot, a box with assorted spices in crystal jars, twenty fine crystal wine goblets, two lace tablecloths, a massive Geneva Bible, a beautiful set of silver flatware, a Dutch naval captain's uniform, and a comfortable mattress from the captain's bed.

It was an impressive haul and we celebrated accordingly.

Lest you think we took everything, let me assure you that we left the Dutchmen with their water and some of their food stuffs, enough to get them back to Holland, we figured. Of course, without charts, they would have to be pretty good star navigators, but I feel we took care to leave them their potatoes, and a keg of herrings, that being pretty much what we figured Dutch men eat, anyway.

We stowed the loot below and found that our merchantman could hold plenty more cargo. So, we decided to continue doing what we had done with the Dutchmen, except this time we flew a French flag, to see if we could lure a French ship in for a party. More of us could speak French, so the ruse would probably work even better.

Painting the ship the way we did, was the best decision ever made in the history of piracy, I'm convinced of that.

Anyway, now that we had plenty of food on board, we cruised up and down the coast of Hispaniola for the following twelve days, enjoying the sunshine and the spacious deck of our new blue ship. Most of us kept a gentle glow in our cheeks with the beverage of our choice. Except Virginia, of course. She contented herself with water and fruit juices.

On the thirteenth day we sighted a slow moving French ship. She was heavy in the water and plowing big waves at her bows. It looked as if she was loaded to the scuppers. We couldn't wait to discover what she was carrying. It seemed all so easy.

When we came close to the French ship, we saw that she was carrying twelve six pounders which were sticking out of ports on both sides of the ship. Obviously, she wanted to scare pirates away with a show of arms. Fortunately, they did not suspect us and hailed us with a friendly, 'Bonjour mes amies! Comment alley vous?' etcetera.

Of course we invited them on board for a party.

And, what a party it was. We had a lot of fun with those Frenchmen. They sure could drink and sing and dance. The fact we had four pretty women for them to dance with, made them all the more susceptible to the charms of our beverages, which this time we spiked with a little extra of Wapoo's fortification, just to make sure the French sailors, who numbered eighteen, including the captain, would pass out and not wake up for days.

This time our haul was significantly larger, requiring some items to be lashed on deck, our hold being totally full of everything our village needed, for years to come, with some exceptions, of course. I will provide one more list, to show you the sorts of things we obtained, eventually requiring a warehouse to store it all.

The French ship was relieved of the following:

Five chests of gold coins, three chests of silver coins, a chest of precious stones; emeralds, rubies, and sapphires, seventeen hogsheads of ale, twenty five of wine, thirty hogsheads of Jamaican rum, nineteen books, two in English, twenty eight bales of fine cotton cloth, fifty barrels of salted fish, five barrels of pickled beef, one hundred sacks of oranges, thirty sacks of pineapples, fifty sacks of cane sugar, fifty crates of fine cigars, six magnificent crystal decanters, sixteen crystal wine glasses, sixteen fine China plates, with the rest of their settings and bearing a fleur de lis in their centers, six bales of good leather, a cobbler's complete kit, a medicine chest full of everything we could possibly need to stock our infirmary, more rope, ten new sails, four kegs of white lead, a carpenter's tool kit and six kegs of nails, twenty pairs of soft leather gloves, five elaborate French wigs, twelve silk overcoats, twelve elaborate, plumed hats, five pairs of good shoes, a silver candelabra for twelve candles, sixteen boxes of tapers, and a case of very fine brandy.

When the French were far behind us, still sleeping off the coast of Hispaniola, we sailed back to our cove, enjoying fine brandy and cigars along the way.

We returned to our cove, five days later, and were greeted with a sorry sight, which immediately sobered us to a new reality. Our cozy pirates' cove had been discovered!

Our tower had been chopped down and our buildings were still smoldering from a ravaging fire.

The *Phoenix* was gone. It was a good thing we did not leave anyone behind. They would have most surely been killed, or worse, taken prisoner.

When we dropped our anchors, we went ashore as rapidly as we could, to look around and assess the damage.

We discovered that our little village had been thoroughly ransacked. All of our stored provisions were gone. The garden was trampled. Blankets, clothes, everything was taken, and the buildings burned. The only thing the raiders did not get was our Mayan gold and silver, which we quickly retrieved from the forest, lest the raiders were to come back.

We decided, then and there, it was time to find a new cove, which we did, forthwith.

The women did their best to rescue what plants they could from the trampled garden; tenderly digging them up and placing their roots and soil in burlap bags, which we carefully set side by side in some old chests.

Fortunately, the wind held and we were able to sail away from our island, feeling totally violated and vulnerable. The sorry state of Heaven's Cove, and how to prevent it in the future, became the main topic for discussion over the next number of days. We were not about to repeat our mistakes.

It took us six days to find another cove, suitable for our purposes. We found it also in the Caicos Islands, however, it was a much better location, because the cove was even more secret than our first home.

Our new cove had an entrance which was between tall, rocky outcroppings. The little island, to which the cove belonged, was about a mile long and about half that wide. The center of the island had a tall hill of about five hundred and fifty to six hundred feet. Flora and fauna abounded. Fish filled the cove with their frolicking; often jumping out of the water to catch some hapless insect. Their splashing was a noticeable sound in the quiet retreat. The water of the cove was carefully sounded before we entered with the merchantman. Fortunately, it was deep enough to float our blue ship in 20 feet of water, not far from shore.

We didn't see any sharks in the crystal clear water, which was not to say they were not there. In tropical waters one should always be careful. Hence, no one swam ashore, all of us patiently waiting until we could be ferried ashore in the boat.

The first order of business, when we were all ashore, was to explore the island, to see if there were any signs of other humans having been there. Virginia and I stayed on the shore of the cove, because she was beginning to bear the burden of carrying a child, whom we figured had to be at least five months old, by now.

When the others returned, they reported the island was clean and there was nothing to worry about. We decided we would build a lookout tower on top of the hill, from which we would be able to see for miles around. From then on we never left our village unattended or unprotected.

The first order of events, as they unfolded, was to clear ground and rebuild our garden, the plants requiring replanting, because many of them were showing signs of trauma, their wilted leaves a testament to their dislike of sea travel.

The second order of business was to begin building a better, fortified village, with a powerful stockade. We again built the houses on stilts. Everyone got their own house, couples theirs, singles theirs. No one elected to stay on board ship, finding sleeping in a hammock, in a thatched hut, with lots of windows, far more comfortable than sleeping in a stuffy wooden ship.

By, what we figured was the end of March, and Virginia and I had been away from Halifax for at least a year, our new village was ready. We had worked hard, but found it was worth it. We felt much more secure.

The next order of business was to build the observation tower on top of our mountain. Because the hill was already quite high, we felt a twenty foot tower would suffice, because it would look sufficiently over the trees, below the crest of the hill, to provide a three hundred and sixty degree view of the ocean and several other small islands nearby.

We took our time building the tower, completing it six weeks later. This time we built a very pleasant, roofed observation platform, on which we could all sit, for an afternoon of sun tanning, drinking, and pleasant conversation. We even built a table with benches around the walls and a cooking area with a brazier and a preparation counter. It became one of our collective favorite places to spend time together, when we weren't working on refining our village, which became ever more elaborate, as the men and women began taking great pleasure in the joy of design and construction of their houses.

Eventually, the topic of women for the single men was raised in earnest. Therefore, a voyage to a port was necessary. However, Virginia suggested that it was highly possible that word, regarding our colorful ship, might be filtering back into the region. Because, unlike most pirates, we didn't kill most of our victims, and therefore, risked easy detection in our colorful ship.

Hence, it was voted that we repaint our ship totally black, with blue railings, and totally blue sails. The repainting was not such a difficult task, and we attended to it in about ten days. Fortunately, we had enough paint left from before, and managed to make the blue paint black with the addition of a lot of charcoal from our bonfires.

We even renamed the ship, *Bon Adventure*, from *PCII*. Of course only we knew what the letters stood for, 'Pirates' Cove Two.' It would keep others guessing.

This time Virginia, the other women, Russell, and I stayed behind. Wendy was happy about that. She never liked it when Russell was gone. We were left with plenty of ammunition and weapons, including a five pounder with balls, fuses, and powder, which we set up to guard the cove's entrance. We waved good bye from the beach.

During the time the others were gone, Virginia gave birth to our baby girl. We were all overjoyed at the new addition to our little pirate family. The other women, especially Marianne, were a big help to Virginia, and certainly relieved me of a lot of stress. I watched little Catherine come into the world. It is the most incredible experience I had ever witnessed. No matter how hard I tried not to, tears poured from my eyes, as I hugged Virginia and our little daughter. It was a truly momentous occasion, which I shall never forget to the day I die.

After nearly two months away, our friends returned with seven new women and three more men to add to our pirate colony, as it was obviously beginning to be.

The new women were paired up as follows: Andrew with Judith, a white skinned redhead with a big grin, Colin with Meira, a tall, elegant brunette, with a flair for the dramatic, Frank with Sarah, a petite blonde, with an infectious laugh, George with Marta, a fiery Spanish woman with thick black hair and a sharp wit, Robert with Susanne, a tall, thin, French blonde with big blue eyes and a sexy voice, and Marvin with Kate, a pleasant, plump girl with a very pretty face and pleasant disposition.

Even Wapoo had found a woman for himself, a fellow native person from an obviously different tribe. Her name was Narkat. She had a ring through the center of her lower lip. She couldn't speak English, only a little French, and of course one of the native languages, which Wapoo spoke.

The three new men were: Jake, a tall, skinny lad with bright red hair, and freckles on his face and arms, Jock, a somber, square framed man with steel gray hair and piercing blue eyes, and Sam, a simple minded fellow, but pleasant and kind.

The new people came from four different locations, Havana, Kingston, San Juan, and Santo Domingo.

Now our colony numbered thirty, which would provide enough people to divide up the labor and make life even better for everybody. It certainly would provide plenty of help for Virginia and our little Catherine.

The first thing we did, after introductions, was to prepare a big welcome feast and bonfire on the beach. While the new people were being shown around the island by Bill and George, the rest of us prepared a feast fit for the kings and queens we were. Roasted fish of various sorts, from our cove, salted pork, salted beef, a big pot of tortoise soup, bowls of cooked onions, leeks, and peppers, fried bananas with nuts, pineapples, and coconut, and lots of fresh bread, baked in the oven we had built. The smell of the baking bread wafted for quite a ways on the gentle breezes, which whisked about the island.

By seven o'clock we were ready to feast.

And feast we did; lubricated liberally with the beverages of our choice, ale, fruit juices, rum, water, or wine, and various mixtures thereof. The meal was accompanied with much laughter and humorous toasts, roasts, and general camaraderie, and of course, many toasts welcoming our baby pirate to the world.

Catherine seemed to like the attention she was getting.

The party lasted well into the night, long after my little family and I had gone to bed. We could hear the men and women laughing and singing jolly songs as we drifted off to sleep, glad to be members of our happy company.

A couple of days later, after everyone had fully recovered from the welcoming party, we began unloading the ship. This time the goods were all bought and paid for. No opportunities for larceny presented themselves, except for the six cannons they had stolen from a Spanish man o' war; in dry dock, having its hull scraped.

When the supplies had all been safely stowed away in our warehouse, we spent the rest of the day relaxing in our various ways, and getting to know the new people, who all turned out to be friendly and happy to be members of our gang.

The next day was devoted to preparing locations to park the new eight pounders. We figured the sooner we defended our cove, the better. There were lots of ships in the West Indies, the chances of being found were always there. This time we were not about to give up our home so easily, as before.

It took five days to set up the cannons properly. They all pointed out to sea and were well hidden in amongst the leaves of plants and amongst the rocks. Anyone firing the cannons was well protected with rocks or trees. Each cannon was provided with five eight pound balls, and enough fuse and powder, wrapped in banana leaves, to fire the balls a goodly distance. We would still have to find more cannon balls, because thirty balls would not be enough in the event of an attack.

The problem pertaining to the cannon balls was solved a month later, after the men decided it was time to go roving again. They were getting bored and needed some excitement. I didn't go with them. Neither did Russell and Wapoo. A few of the women went along; Marta, Meira, Sarah, and Susanne. Those of us who stayed gave them a happy send off.

While the pirates were gone, we continued to work improving our colony. Six new huts had been built in the last month, and an addition had been put on the meeting hall, making it large enough to have an indoor party with all thirty of us, and then some.

The observation platform, by then, had a signaling system installed, involving three coloured flags which could be raised, depending on what we were dealing with. Red for danger, Blue for all clear, and Yellow, our friends are back. We thought yellow an appropriate color, because it symbolized sunshine.

We had also rigged a long rope, so that a person could ride a chair down from the hill, and be at the bottom within less than a minute. The chair could be pulled up the hill with another rope we had rigged for the purpose.

The island, like the other one, had a spring with fresh water, but unlike the other island, this one had a beautiful large pool in which we bathed. Some of the men, who were clever carpenters and engineers, fashioned a bamboo pipeline to bring fresh water to our kitchen. They had fashioned a spigot. From then on we always had fresh, cool, running water in our cooking area. This greatly facilitated our preparations in the culinary arts. They also rigged a number of buckets which could be hauled up to the observation platform, with ropes and pulleys, in order to provide water there, as well.

Near the beach we had built a ten person sauna. This became a very frequent place to sit, in the evenings, before bed. The sauna was a great way to relieve sore muscles, from a day of work on our village.

While the pirates were away, those of us who stayed behind, added a new building which we dubbed, 'The Library.' We stocked it with the books I had brought, and those we had managed to obtain on our earlier adventures. We built a couple of easy chairs, for which Kate and Marianne made comfortable pillows, stuffed with dried grasses. We placed the chairs in the library, making it a comfortable place to sit and read.

When the pirates returned, two weeks later, much to their, and our delight, they had brought twenty new books, in English, which they managed to obtain from an English merchantman. Eight of the books comprised a brand new publication by an Englishman named, Edward Gibbon. The books were published in 1776 and were titled, *A History of the Decline and Fall of the Roman Empire.* These books were eagerly read by Bill and I, over the ensuing months. Several of the other men also took an interest in them. The books were a welcome addition to our growing library.

Two new men had joined our crew. They jumped ship from the merchantman, thinking that our way of life was a better choice. When they beheld our developing, armed colony, they were very impressed and reiterated, numerous times, that they had made the right choice, and had found heaven.

The new men, who were named Bart and Bernard, quickly built

themselves a hut, along the same plans as the rest of the huts. Many of the original members helped them, so that it was done before the end of their fourth day.

Other items brought back from the raiding trip were several bales of magnificent blankets, and three bales of cotton sheets, which we readily shared out, so that everyone had at least five nice new blankets, and a collection of white cotton sheets, with which to cozy up their huts and make their beds more comfortable.

The raid also added another complete set of a dozen silver eating utensils and twelve settings of exquisite bone china, with golden rims, and a hand painted rose design in the centers. The pottery came from the Josiah Wedgewood, Etruria works at Hanley. The tableware was a welcome addition to our table and made dining an ever more elegant affair, complete with our beautiful candelabra in the centre of our long dining table, which had to be lengthened again, to accommodate the new arrivals.

Other wonderful things, which came from the raid, were ten more hogsheads of excellent wine, five of red and five of white, one hundred cases of beautiful ceramic tiles, sixty glass windows in frames, five marvelous paintings, also in frames, by some Dutch artists. I think their names were, Rembrandt, Rubens, and Vermeer. I believe we had two from Rembrandt and two from Rubens. Of course the paintings went into the library, and our dining hall. They also captured; sixty boxes of tea, four hundred pounds of coffee, one thousand pounds of sugar, five barrels of salted beef, twenty boxes of fine English shortbread, a chest with twenty beautiful lace tablecloths, six chests with assorted women's clothing, twenty complete men's outfits, complete with wigs, sixty pairs of assorted shoes, men's and women's, of various sizes, a magnificent floor length mirror, which, the moment it came off the ship, was immediately given by everybody to Virginia, since she was the first to bring a new little pirate into the world. The mirror made a welcome addition to our little house, which already had an other room added on.

Other items were the usual sorts of things; a box of money, silver and gold, the captain's crystal decanters and wine glasses, a beautiful globe on a carved stand, also for the library, and most importantly, twenty brand new muskets, ten kegs of musket balls, twenty kegs of powder, five boxes of fuses, one hundred and fifty, eight pound cannon balls, five boxes of grenades, and ten more eight pounders, still in their crates, which made their movement and installation a simple affair.

The most amazing thing, which came from this raid, was a piano forte and five stringed instruments; two violins, a viola, a cello, a bass viol, and a beautiful brass ship's bell. When everybody beheld the instruments it was decided, then and there, that it was time we built a concert hall.

I don't remember what else came off the ship, that time. There always was so much that it is hard to remember everything. Sure, I kept notes, but not always of every item, like a scribe in ancient Mesopotamia.

Anyway, during the time between that last raid and the next one, we built the concert hall and installed the piano forte. Sam knew about tuning such an instrument and he, with his brothers, Jake and Jock, could play it, and the violins. Andy could play a cello, and surprisingly, Marta could play the viola. They taught Wapoo to play the bass viol. Fortunately, a book of sheet music came with the piano forte, so that by the time the storm season arrived, we were treated to a concert, much to everyone's delight. Later on, the band improvised shanties, jigs, and reels, which they played with much gusto by our nightly beach fire. I remember Catherine clapping her little hands with delight. It is so good to have music in one's life.

Between our raids, the bounty provided by the lagoon, and the island forest, we lived very well and enjoyed our lives. In two of our raids we managed to liberate some farm animals, namely; five adult pigs, one male and four sows, twenty chickens and a rooster, plus two horses, male and female. These creatures became very welcome additions to our island. Soon we had more of their kind.

As we became more self sufficient, we went out raiding, less and less. All the while we refined our buildings and the means to protect us, in case of storms or attacks. Eventually, our island became quite a mighty fortress, which gave us all a great sense of security.

As time went by, we only went out about four times per year; to fetch supplies in San Juan, or to try and find new female recruits in some of the other ports. When cruises came up, we took turns staying home on the island. After a while, some people never wanted to leave, and felt perfectly content to stay there forever. However, for others, a cruise was a welcome change from the island. A change is as good as a rest, they say. And, so it was when Catherine, Virginia and I went on a cruise to Havana in 1779.

It was on that trip when Virginia sent a letter home to Halifax. By this time we figured we had been away over four years. Catherine had already had her second birthday, as far as we could reckon. In the letter Virginia explained herself and our circumstances, without revealing where exactly we were. She told her parents about Catherine and me, and that she missed them, but she was greatly enjoying her new life and that they need not worry about her. She left the letter with a shipping company, which handled the mail. They would ship the letter to London, from whence it would go to Halifax, on the regular packet.

It was also on that trip to Havana, when I made a great leap forward in my development as a pirate. It wasn't something I was particularly looking for, but I had no choice. The advancement was thrust upon me out of the blue. It was a good thing I was carrying a loaded pistol in my sash, as Bill had taught me. I had to use it to kill a man. It was either him or me. I am so glad it was him and not me. I still had way too much living to do and a book to write. He was just a scum bag and needed killing. I felt no remorse.

The circumstances are as follows:

Virginia, Marianne, Marta, William, George, and I had gone out for dinner at a restaurant. We were dressed nicely and enjoying a pleasant evening out. Kate and Meira were looking after Catherine, back on the ship, anchored in the harbour.

As we were dining, a rough looking malcontent in an English navy uniform, who was sitting with two other officers, recognized Bill. They were probably off the English frigate anchored in the middle of the harbour. We noticed her when we came into port.

Anyway, this officer, a commodore, stood up from his table and walked over to us. He addressed Bill in a very rude fashion, in a tone of voice no man should put up with. 'I have good reason to believe that you are, William Bartleby, the notorious pirate,' said the commodore loudly. 'I am placing you under arrest, in the King's name.'

Many faces turned to look at what was going on. People did not generally address others in such a manner, especially not in a genteel eating establishment.

George cautioned the officer to watch the tone of his voice and suggested, in no uncertain terms, that he was mistaken.

The officer persisted and had the temerity to grab Bill's shoulder, something you never do to a pirate such as William Bartleby. 'In the name of His Majesty, King George III, I am placing you under arrest,' said the silly commodore.

I had to admire Bill, because he stayed very calm throughout this entire ordeal. He looked up at the government official and told the man to let go of his shoulder, or it would be the last shoulder he would ever grab, meaning clearly, let go or I will kill you.

The officer did not seem to understand the tenuousness of his situation. There he was, interrupting our dinner and threatening our captain.

Bill stood up and took the man's hand from his shoulder and with one rapid move, broke the man's wrist.

The commodore went down on his knees in pain, as he held his broken wrist with his good hand.

'I warned you,' said Bill.

The scream of pain sent the other officers scurrying over to our table with pistols drawn and pointed at us.

'Shoot them!' shouted the commodore, 'They're pirates!'

We had no choice but to shoot the three of them, right there in the restaurant; bang, bang, bang!

Of course, that spoiled everyone's dinner. So, Bill threw five gold pieces of eight on the table, enough to pay for everyone's meal, and provide a week's income for the restaurant staff. Then we hightailed it out of there, quickly finding another restaurant, some blocks away. This time we made certain to check that no English navy officers were on the premises. When we ascertained that the coast was clear, we sat down and ordered a round of drinks, to settle our beating hearts. When our jovial mood had returned, we ordered another dinner. This time we were able to finish it.

News of the shooting spread like wild fire through Havana, however, since people generally didn't like the English, nobody came forward to identify who the killers were. Hence, we were able to continue our stay in Havana, without further complications.

However, we did feel a certain obligation to blow up the English ship of the line, knowing that England was, by then, engaged in a war with the American colonies, which wanted to be free of oppression from the English Crown, and we were, as you know, vehemently opposed to that English institution.

We were able to buy a keg of gun powder, which we used to make some bombs out of empty wine and rum bottles. Then we made a long fuse; long enough to reach down to the water line of the frigate, through a gun port near the munitions stores, which Bill knew to be amidships.

One night, when all was ready, we found ourselves a couple of drunken English sailors and waylaid them. We stole their uniforms. Then two of us, who the uniforms fit, Gerry and Andy, I think, snuck on board the English ship, carrying the long fuse. They found their way down to the munitions stores and, after overcoming the unsuspecting marine guard, managed to put the fuse into a keg of powder. They ran the fuse out through a gun port and let it down the side of the ship. Gerry made sure the fuse was nicely hidden and then they made their way off the ship, and back to us on the *Abundance*.

At midnight, six of us went out with our long boat and lit the fuse. Then, to distract the English, we threw our bottle bombs on board.

The bombs went off with loud bangs, sending fragments of needle sharp glass in all directions. We're not sure how many English were cut by the flying glass, but judging from the screams, we got at least five, or six of them. Meanwhile, we rowed back to our ship, under cover of the night and sat on the deck, waiting for the spectacle.

We had all just sat down on the deck with a cup of our favorite beverage, when all hell broke loose in the English ship.

First there was a bang, like a clap of thunder. Next we heard a roar and watched as the ship began to vibrate. Then a massive explosion ripped the centre right out of the ship, sending wood, ropes, cannons, balls, bodies, spars, sails, and hundreds more things flying in all directions. Several pieces landed in the water about twenty yards from our ship. Fortunately, the explosion did not damage other ships in the harbour, the English having anchored their ship right in the centre, near the entrance. It did, however, immediately send the frigate to the bottom of said harbour, never to be used against the brave Americans again. We felt badly about the loss of so many good sailors, however, such were the fruits of war.

Of course, we did not cheer. Killing that many innocent people was not something to cheer about. Each one of us stood quietly on deck and watched as pieces of flaming timber floated about on the quiet waters of the harbour. I think many of us had second thoughts about that caper.

Next afternoon we slipped out of port with a ship load of supplies and three new women, who had decided to hitch their fortunes with Jake, Jock, and Sam.

Jake brought Juliette, a tall, sassy girl, with quite large breasts, who had a great sense of humor.

Jock found Samantha, a brown skinned, mulatto woman, with jet black hair down to her waist. She loved to laugh and have fun.

Sam, the youngest of the brothers, found a girl named Sandra, a gentle creature, with long blond hair. She had been abandoned as a small girl, and grew up with her grandparents, who were dead, by then. She had nowhere to go, and took a real shining to Sam. I have no idea how old she was, fourteen or fifteen. Considering that Sam was only eighteen, she seemed appropriate for him. As it turned out, the two of them became excellent friends over the time we traveled back to our island.

When we hove into view, we saw the yellow flag go up on our mountain.

Suddenly, a loud boom reverberated in the air. Someone had set off a cannon, without a ball, as a welcome signal. We thought it was a nice gesture and fired a return salute. When we came close enough, we pulled the long boat alongside and I, with seven others, climbed into it, in order to pull our big ship into the cove, where it was totally hidden from view; so perfect was our hideout.

That night we held a welcoming party for the new women with a bonfire and feast; the perfect ending for a successful cruise to Havana.

Chapter Eleven

Some weeks after our return from Havana and the, 'Big Bang Event,' as we came to call our blowing up of the English ship, a problem arose concerning, Leonard, necessitating the holding of our first real court of justice. Leonard had been accused of countless breaches of the work code. He was judged to be lazy and uncooperative by everybody.

The girls accused him of lechery, having caught him on several occasions watching them, when they were naked, bathing in the pool. Not that they were prudish, or anything. Swimming naked together, in the pool, was normal for us. However, none of us sat in the bushes, secretly watching just the women, bathing. Of course, the women realized Leonard was still single, but they just didn't like him, and felt that he was not a suitable candidate to continue living with us.

Leonard spoke in his defense, but it was to no avail. He was voted off the island by secret ballot.

Next day, fifteen men, me included, took him to Port au Prince and left him there, with his duffel bag, and three gold coins. We left port immediately, not bothering to look back at Leonard, left standing on the dock.

Leonard was not pleased and yelled numerous invectives in our direction, along with threats to get even. Of course we did not listen to, what we thought, were just idle threats, he being essentially, powerless.

On the way back to our cove, it was decided that, since we had not done any roving for a while, it was high time that we did so. Everyone on board was anxious for the chase; anxious to pursue, what we came to regard as, sport.

I couldn't agree more. I was beginning to develop a real taste for the chase, myself.

We decided to sail to Santo Domingo and find out what ships were in port.

After our arrival, we heard about the explosion of His Majesty's ship in Havana. We couldn't help but laugh when we heard the story recounted to us by a couple of sailors off a French ship, that had just come from there. The sailors asked us what was so funny about a war ship exploding.

We just laughed and drank a hearty toast.

The French sailors served on a ship which carried many crates of cigars from Havana. They were in Santo Domingo to pick up a load of dried fish. We asked them if they knew anything about some of the other ships in port, but they had no idea.

We eventually drifted off to another tavern, but found nothing there, either.

In the third pub we visited, we met some more French sailors, one of whom could speak English. These chaps loved to drink, but had very little money. They loved us because we had lots of money, and were not adverse to sharing it.

So, we bought them drinks, and more drinks, and more drinks, each time toasting something or other. The toasts became ever more serious as time went along, and the alcohol seeped into every corpuscle of their bodies. Then, after a little more prodding, the English speaker blurted out what we wanted to know. The French ship was loaded with gold and weapons for the war effort in America.

Since we didn't believe in war, we thought it was better that we took care of the gold and the weapons, and managed to do so in a very clever way.

The sailors told us that the ship had thirty marines on board. They were on duty, while the rest of the crew was given shore leave. The officers were waiting for intelligence, to let them know where the gold was to be landed. English ships were plying the waters off the coast of Florida to Nova Scotia. The French had to be very careful.

We heartily agreed, one could not be too careful in those days.

Since there were only fifteen of us on board, and thirty marines, plus officers guarding the gold and weapons, we needed more men. And, we needed a special plan.

Trying to relieve the French of their gold in port was foolish. The marines would be on guard the whole time. However, at sea, they would most likely spend their time in their mess, playing cards, or whatever. There would be no need for them to be on deck. At sea, with no threats apparent, there would be no need for high security. The marines would follow routines like everyone else, such as sleeping at night, with minimum watches.

Hence, recruitment began in earnest. We sought out suitable candidates in every tavern, along the docks, in warehouses, out on the streets... After many hours of searching, we found ten more good men, who were attracted to the promise of a share in the treasure. We didn't tell them what treasure, just so they would not let the cat out of the bag.

Since we had met the French sailors, we saw them on several other occasions, and eventually found out when they would be sailing.

Hence, we pretended to buy many barrels of goods, actually three hundred empty barrels, which we filled with sea water and stowed in our hold, making the ship sink deeper into the water, as if we were carrying a heavy load, like that on the French ship. Then, when it came time for them to leave, so did we; following them with sails full out, staying two leagues behind them all the time.

Of course, the French thought we were fully laden with cargo and couldn't go any faster, considering we were constantly two leagues behind them, with our sails full out.

After three days sailing, on the third night, when clouds obscured the moon, we made our move and emptied the water from the barrels and dumped the barrels overboard. We prepared our cannons and weapons and snuck up on the French ship by running our blue sails, which were impossible to see in such a dark night.

We reached the French sometime after midnight and managed to climb on board their ship before the watch saw us. When he did, it was, unfortunately too late for him. We had no choice but to knock him on the head and gently set his body down, without making a sound.

Very quietly we completely occupied the deck with armed pirates.

When we were all in position, Bill knocked on the Master's cabin and woke up the captain, to inform him that we were taking command of the ship; a situation to which he did not respond very well.

The captain's righteous indignation was vociferous and loud, waking up the rest of the crew and the marines. Of course, we had the upper hand, and held everyone at bay with our muskets pointing at them from all angles, including the yards. The Frenchmen knew they were defeated and had no choice but to stand down or risk needless blood shed.

When all hands were on deck, six of us proceeded to force the twenty six Frenchmen to unload their ship into ours, including their ten, five pounders and all the ammunition, etcetera, etcetera. Of course, what we were most interested in surprised us by the amount that was there. Enough gold for every member of our gang, plus their descendants, for centuries to come. No wonder the French ship was low in the water.

It was decided that we would only take half of the gold, since there was so much, and it was going to a good cause. We didn't want to deprive the colonies of the means to beat King George.

When we told the captain that we were taking only half of the gold, he felt very relieved and thanked us for our magnanimity. We told him that it was on condition he would not send the authorities after us. Since the captain appeared to be a man of honour, we felt comfortable about releasing those Frenchmen to carry on their task; helping the colonies fight English oppression.

Having taken what we needed, we set course for Kingston, in order to spend some of the gold on presents for our wives and girlfriends. We also needed more supplies, to keep our colony going.

While there, our new men found girlfriends to bring back with them. When we returned, our colony had grown again. It was another time for celebration. The new comers were officially welcomed with one of our incredible bonfires on the beach. Our women received their presents, and the gold was divvied up. It was a very happy party. People sang and danced into the wee hours and the next three days.

Over the following weeks, the new people built huts for themselves, so that our colony actually began to look like a town, which would soon see more children arriving, since, Marianne, Marta, Susanne, Tanya, and my Virginia were all pregnant and showing.

Catherine was growing like a sprout, with a strong resemblance to me, and yet with lots of Virginia, as well. I greatly enjoyed watching her growing and loving our life on the island. She had a little pet monkey who followed her around wherever she went. Virginia and I could not get enough of watching her playing in the sand, or doing whatever. We were the quintessential doting parents, soon to be the parents of two children. Our life couldn't have been more peaceful and blessed.

Then, one day, darkness arrived. We should have known it would come in the way it did. Maybe we should have been more ruthless, but we weren't. Now that mistake had come back to haunt us.

It happened one afternoon when Andy started ringing the bell and flying a red flag on the mountain. A ship was sighted, headed directly towards our island. It was flying a black flag and didn't appear to be friendly.

We had all practiced manning the cannons, and now that we had quite a number of them, we felt impregnable. People quickly ran to take up their positions.

As the ship approached we could make out that it was flying a Jolly Roger. This surprised us, since we had not seen other pirates in our waters.

Suddenly, as the ship came past us, it let off a volley of cannon shots, right at some of our strategic placements, as if they knew exactly where to shoot.

Alas, Kate and Marvin were manning one of the posts that was hit. Neither one of them had a chance as five balls came thundering in their direction.

Then, as the ship came around, it let go another volley of cannon fire, this time hitting one of the new men, who had just joined us on the last trip out. Fortunately, the end came quickly for those who were hit.

When the ship had come a little bit closer, thinking we were not at our guns, we fired and managed to splinter the mizzen mast. It came down like a felled tree.

Suddenly, the ship's cannons roared again and we lost a ten pounder, along with Frank and Sarah. It was uncanny how the attackers knew exactly where to aim.

We fired back with another stout volley, this time punching holes into the hull.

Judging from the way they were positioning themselves, they had no idea regarding our recently acquired cannons, catching them in a cross fire, from which there was no escape.

Eventually, we knocked down the mainmast and punched more holes into the hull. The ship was beginning to list. We could hear screaming and orders shouted, but they were to no avail. The ship was listing so badly, they could no longer shoot their cannons. We let them have another round, splintering the deck and scattering bits and pieces of pirates all over the ravaged boards. A final volley finished them off.

We watched the pirate ship sink, and cheered loudly as the last of her disappeared under the waves, leaving a mess of flotsam floating where the ship had been.

The seventeen survivors were quickly rounded up and brought into our village, where they were tied to posts. One of the attackers looked familiar to me. I asked Bill to take a look at him. Upon closer inspection, the bedraggled pirate turned out to be, Leonard.

After the prisoners had been firmly secured, we set about the burial of our dead. The loss of five good people was a great tragedy for us. We gave them an excellent send off, with a huge funeral pyre. It was a sad day in Heaven's Cove II. Kate, Sarah, Frank, Joachim, and Marvin were caring people, who took a great delight in Catherine, treating her as their own. She was especially heart broken over their deaths.

Next day it rained quite hard, and we all stayed inside, dealing with our grief. The prisoners were left tied outside. We were not overly concerned about their comfort, especially not Leonard's. We tied him up separately from the rest, out in the open, where we all could see him. How to murder him was foremost in everybody's mind. Revenge is what we wanted. It was a very negative emotion which ran through the village, that rainy day.

After the rain had quit, and the ground had dried, we held a war council. What to do with the prisoners was the only item of business. First we would interrogate them and find out, if perhaps they might know something about the burning of our first village. Then we would ask them how they wished to die. There was no question of taking them into the colony. We couldn't trust them.

Colin suggested we troll for sharks with them.

Robert thought we should use them for target practice.

Andrew suggested we drop them off the cliff, on the backside of our mountain.

George thought it might be appropriate to blow them up with cannon balls, just like they blew up our friends.

Sandra suggested we made them walk the plank, in shark infested waters.

Jock had heard about keel hauling, and thought that an appropriate punishment.

Virginia suggested we maroon them on an island. That way they would keep their lives, and be thankful to us for that, as long as they were able to live without rescue. There were so many little islands, that the chances of them being found depended entirely on their own resources. At least it gave them a modicum of a chance.

Bill looked at the prisoners and frowned. 'Well, they certainly have a lot of choices. However, I think we definitely need to kill Leonard. He betrayed us. He committed treason, even though we expelled him, our code forbids an act such as his.' Bill looked at each member of the colony.

Everyone agreed that Leonard should die for his treachery.

Satisfied the sentence was the collective will of the colony, Bill pronounced the death sentence on Leonard.

What happened next I wish I wouldn't have to tell you about. It may make you ill, dear reader, as it certainly did me. However, I watched, just like everybody else. Horrendous as it was, it was fascinating, none the less, to see severe pirate justice carried out by experienced, hardened pirates.

In England, the punishment for treason was drawing and quartering. Fortunately we were spared that grim spectacle, but what was devised for Leonard was, non the less, agonizing and prolonged. It was decided that Leonard would be crucified and exposed to the tide.

Now, dear reader, you may think that is not such a bad punishment as being drawn and quartered; that crucifixion merely entails the tying up of the individual on a cross, with nails through the hands and feet. But, that is not how it was done to Our Lord, and not how it was done in this case, either.

The ship's carpenter, Colin, fashioned a sturdy cross, while several of the other men prepared a place to position it, where it would be able to withstand the tide and crashing waves and not fall over.

When the cross and the footings were ready, three days later, Leonard's ordeal began, as everybody, but Virginia and Catherine, watched.

With the other prisoners watching, Leonard was first tied firmly to the cross so that he could not move. His arms and feet were tightly lashed, effectively cutting the circulation off.

Then the real trial began as George drove a big spike right through Leonard's forearm, between his right radius and ulna. Leonard screamed in pain and begged for forgiveness, as George drove another spike into Leonard's left forearm. The pain must have been immense for Leonard passed out, having to be revived with buckets of cold water. Then, just as was done to Jesus, a large spike was driven through his heel bones, to make certain he would stay firmly attached to the wooden beam.

Leonard had long passed out again, when the cross was picked up and carried down to the water, where it was firmly set in place, facing out towards the sea. A constant reminder that there were consequences for treason.

The lesson was not lost on the other prisoners, who clearly saw that we meant business. We did not tolerate being shot at. We took pride in not killing people, except for the odd English officer, but that doesn't really count, and here we were attacked by fellow pirates.

We decided to take Virginia's advice and took the errant pirates out to various islands, where we left them in groups of four, with a knife, some flints, a barrel of water, and a couple of blankets. The captain we marooned by himself, without a knife.

If they were lucky, they would be rescued. If they were not lucky, justice served them what they deserved.

* * *

After a few more months went by, babies started arriving.

First, Marianne gave birth to a healthy baby boy, whom she and Bill named, Michael. Then came Marta's baby, another boy, whom she named, David. After David, came Tanya's baby girl, whom she named, Jacqueline. Susanne and Virginia gave birth at the same time, the former delivering a baby girl, named Jocelyn, and the latter, my sweet Virginia, gave birth to our son, Joshua.

And so, our colony grew again.

Bill must have felt like some sort of patriarch.

It was a time of celebration.

It was time for a bonfire.

We partied and gave thanks for our healthy new arrivals and deliverance from the attackers.

* * *

Some months later, I went down to where we stuck Leonard, and found very little of him left. What little remained of his arms and feet were still attached to the cross, but the rest of him was long gone. I know it was a harsh punishment, but he was responsible for the deaths of five of us friends. I didn't feel sorry for him. I thought it was a fitting end for a betrayer.

When we sailed back to the islands, a year later, to see if the other pirates had made it, we were able to account for ten of them, finding their bleached bones on their respective islands. We couldn't account for the captain, which we found strange, unless he was rescued, or he tried to swim and was eaten by a shark. We had no way of knowing.

Chapter Twelve

In the summer of 1781, Virginia and I, along with many members of our colony, took another cruise to Havana. Most of the children stayed home on the island, but Virginia and I elected to take our two children, Catherine and baby Joshua with us. It was a fabulous trip, on which none of us had the slightest desire to engage in larceny. We just wanted to enjoy ourselves and not think about working. We had so much money, by this time, that larceny was not necessary anymore.

We generally sailed under a Dutch flag, not wanting to choose sides with regard to the war still raging in the American Colonies. English and French ships were abundant in the region and sometimes they came to blows. We did not want to be caught in the middle. The Dutch were not overly involved in the war, tending, instead, to focus on trade; a much more civilized way to interact with the rest of humanity.

When we arrived in Havana, many of us had letters to send to various people, and did so at the same office where we sent a letter to Virginia's parents. To our great delight and surprise, a letter was there for Virginia, from her parents, whom, by this time, we had not seen for six years.

Virginia was overcome with emotion, as she accepted the thick letter from the clerk at the post office.

Of course she wanted to read it right away.

We walked a little ways and found a place to sit, in a little park, where trees provided adequate shade and Catherine had a place to play with her baby brother.

Virginia opened the letter with trembling fingers.

'Our very dearest, Virginia.'

Virginia started to cry and had to stop reading, lest her tears stained the paper and made the ink run. She was too overcome with emotion that she handed the letter to me and asked if I would read it to her.

I understood, of course, and gladly read the letter, dated, August 27, 1780. I have reproduced it here, verbatim.

'Our very dearest, Virginia,

Thank you so very much for the long letter you sent to us from Havana, dated May 15, 1779. We were overjoyed to hear from you. We didn't know where you were, or if you were still alive, or not. We still don't know, of course. We have no way of knowing if this letter will even get to you. But, we pray it does and will try our best to bring you up to date, regarding us and our life in Halifax.

We miss you so very much, dear Virginia. What ever possessed you to leave us? Yes, I know you wrote things in your letter to us, but it was not enough. We never had a chance to say good bye. It was all so sudden. And then to hear that you are implicated in the escape of a condemned pirate, was all too much for us to bear. To read in your letter that what they say is actually true, that you and that reporter friend of yours, Peter Mann, helped a pirate escape from the gaol, and that you escaped Halifax on Molly Brown's sloop? It sounds all too fantastic to us. How is it possible? Our daughter, whom we raised so well, how could you do such a thing? So many questions.

Life in Halifax has never been the same for us, since you left. Your brother and sisters miss you terribly, just as we do. However, as the years went by, we coped better and better, and for the longest time thought you might have died somewhere along the way, we just did not know. But, now, to have a letter from you and we read that you are alive, makes us all happy to know that you are well and that your life has become so interesting.

However, I can't help express our concerns for your safety. Surely you understand that what you three have done is very serious. The authorities are very upset, as you can well imagine. There is even talk of hanging you. It makes my heart heavy, every time I hear people talk about the gaol break. Even today, years later, we still feel like pariahs. The townsfolk are not quick to forget. They condemn us with their stares, and whispered conversations behind our backs. Your father's firm has suffered from it. However, in his business, ships don't have a lot of choices to obtain their supplies, so we are still doing well enough. Most of the foreign ships don't know anything about your story. That is a blessing.

Apparently, the King is very upset that William Bartleby escaped from under his nose. Your father and I have had to appear before the governor. There were even suggestions that we should be put in gaol. You can imagine the shame and humiliation that put us through. I think your father lost twenty pounds, and his hair went quite gray, not long after that. It is a terrible tragedy, all of this. We can never stop asking, why? Was your life so terrible here? What ever possessed you?

You have always been a head strong girl. Your father and I never had any idea how head strong you are. Oh, well, there is not much we can do about it now. What is done is done. We still love you, just the same.

James, Anna, and Beatrice never gave up, with regard to you, either. They always maintained that your were alive, and were not quite so surprised when we received your letter. It was a real family affair, when your letter arrived, and we sat in the parlor and read it together. We girls had quite a lot of tears during the reading, which was handled by your brother. I sensed that your father was quite moved, as well, which is unusual for him, as you know. It's that Scottish streak in him. Some of them can be so dour. Your father is a lot like your grandfather.

Three days ago, James announced his engagement with Mister and Mrs. Black's daughter, Angelina. She is a lovely girl. James met her on a trip to Lunenburg, on business for the firm. All the time he has lived in Halifax, he never saw her, when she lived here. As you know, her father, Joseph, owns the feed mill.

Angelina was visiting with relatives in Lunenburg, who happened to be the very people with whom James was conducting business. It always amazes me how these things come about. Take you and Peter, for example.

Anna married Paul Marché in May, 1778. She is expecting her first child next month. I hope it comes easily for her. Her pregnancy has not been an easy one. She is not looking her normal self, and appears to be lacking sleep. I try to help her, when I can, but I don't get an opportunity to go and see her more than once a week. She lives in Dartmouth now. Paul's parents own a general store, which he will eventually take over.

Beaty is the same as ever. Happy, and single. There are at least a half a dozen young men who are expressing an interest in her. One is the son of doctor Jansen. He is a fine young man. I hope Beatrice makes a decision soon. She is too old not to be married. She turned twenty three last month. But, then, I should remember, you were twenty five, when you left, and you weren't married. Perhaps we rush into this marriage thing way too soon. I was eighteen when I married your father.

Your sister seems perfectly content living the single life. She has lots of friends, of both sexes, and many are the times when she has friends visiting over here. They sit in the parlour and sing funny songs to each other, and debate interesting issues. Three of her friends are attending university. They are a lively, intelligent bunch. I like it when they are here. Your father usually goes into his study and closes the door. He doesn't understand the younger generation.

Jake died in January, 1777. He was old. I can't remember how long we had him. I think he was a puppy when you were about five. He had terrible arthritis in his joints and could hardly walk anymore. He passed away peacefully in his sleep. We buried him in the garden. There is a beautiful rose bush growing over his grave. We all miss old Jake. He was a good dog.

Your cat, Misty disappeared not long after you left. We have no idea what happened to her.

Your great grandmother will be ninety seven, next month. We can't understand how she is managing to still go on, sprightly as ever. We moved her into your room. We have to help her up the stairs, but otherwise, she gets around just fine. Your father doesn't scare her one whit. It is quite funny to hear her harangue him when she doesn't agree with his politics. As you well know, she is a staunch Jacobite.

The Swansons have moved and now there is a new family from Maine living in the house next door. They are a very nice family. Mister Burton is a barrister. They have three lovely children, aged, nine, seven, and five; two boys and a girl.

As you probably know, the American colonies are at war with England. Apparently, they have an issue with regard to taxation. It is a real sorry mess. English war ships are quite often in the harbour. We have also seen some French ships. It is not a good thing when they are both in port, at the same time. The sailors sometimes come to blows, when they have been drinking, which appears to be their favorite sport when they are here. I imagine your uncle Frank is making a lot of money from his tavern. He renamed it, 'The Stag and Hound'. Your father and I went there, once; since he renovated it. However, I don't suppose we will be going back, since your father had a falling out with his brother. It seems they can't agree on the simplest of things. When the two of them are together, they are always arguing. From what your grandmother has told me, they were at each other's throats almost from birth.

Your uncle Thomas is a different story. He and your father have always gotten along famously. I just don't know why your father is so difficult with his middle brother. It is always a wonder to me, how different your uncles are from your father.

Now I am a grandmother, you tell me in your letter. I actually have a grand daughter named, Catherine Anne. I am very touched you named her after me. However, I am very sad I have no opportunity to see her. She must be four, already. I can imagine her looking a lot like you, probably with brown curls and hazel eyes. Perhaps you will write me a description of her in your next letter. If there is even going to be a next letter. Of course, I have no way of knowing if this will even get to you. I pray it does.

Well, I don't know what more to say, except to give you all of my love and best wishes. Your father sends his best wishes, as well. And, of course, your brother and sisters send their love. Beatrice has asked to write a little something on the bottom, so I will turn this over to her in the hopes this letter finds you well and happy.

All my love and affection
Your loving mother
Anne Spencer

Dear Sis,

I can't believe that you have gone off on an adventure with Peter. I am very envious and wish I was wherever you are, enjoying the sun and fun. Life in Halifax is boring, as always. Please, if you get this, try and make arrangements to rescue me from here. With love from your baby sister,

Beaty.

When I finished reading the letter, Virginia was overcome with emotion. Her tears came in buckets. Catherine came over to comfort her mother and asked her what was wrong. Virginia smiled weakly and told her that she was just a little emotional, at the moment, over a letter from their grandmother in Halifax. Catherine said she understood there was nothing to be concerned about and went back to her play.

I sat with Virginia for a long time until she regained her composure. I made a little joke; about thinking twice before we pick up mail, next time. She smiled through the mist in her eyes and gave me a weak nudge with her elbow.

After Virginia felt more composed, we went for a walk with the children, to stretch our legs and discuss what was in the letter.

The gist of our conversation turned out to be a plan to visit Halifax and introduce her parents to their grandchildren. My parents were dead, so it didn't matter for me, but I could tell it meant a great deal to Virginia. The letter from her mother and sister stirred up a lot of memories. Virginia realized, after all these years, that she missed her family.

It was a difficult task for me to convince her it would be suicide for us to show our faces in Halifax, even after all those years. I told her, that even though her mother did not mention it in her letter, there very likely was a bounty on our heads. Because of that fact, it was likely not only government agents were looking for us. Collecting a bounty was a good way to alleviate poverty, for lots of people.

Virginia insisted we could disguise ourselves. 'We managed disguises, before,' she said. 'If it hadn't been for a disguise, how else would we have gotten Bill out of gaol?'

Disguises might work, I agreed, however, convincing the gang to go to Halifax, would be another issue. Everyone was wanted, as part of William

Bartleby's gang, the old friends, at any rate; George, Robert, Andy, and Colin.

Virginia suggested that we could go with some of the other, unknown crew members. During a time when everybody preferred to stay on our island, anyway, and the ship wouldn't be in use for a couple of months.

When she put it like that, I couldn't help but agree, her plan did have merit. In the summer it made sense, July and August was the perfect time to go to Halifax.

As we discussed these ideas, at some length, Virginia and I came to the conclusion we would propose the idea to the gang. It made her happy that we, at least, were agreed to pursue her desire to visit her family.

At dinner time, as was prearranged, we all met together at a restaurant, not far from where our ship was moored. Gradually, over the space of a half an hour, or so, people arrived in groups, from their various travels and discussed the day's events.

Bill, Marianne, George, and Marta had gone sightseeing in a jungle, not far from the city. Marianne had brought back a magnificent red macaw, which she had bought from a bird catcher. She named him, Sam. The bird was sitting on Marianne's shoulder, when she walked up to our outdoor table in front of Mama Gonzales' Cantina.

Andy, Judith, Robert, and Susanne had gone shopping for some more weapons and managed to return with three muskets, four sabres, a Spanish halberd, and three helmets; one with a horse tail plume. The three women were wearing the helmets as they walked up to the table, carrying the weapons.

'We thought the helmets might be a good idea for people manning the cannons, in case of attack,' said Robert enthusiastically. 'We may be able to get a few more tomorrow,' he added, grinning from ear to ear. Then he delivered, what was music to our ears, 'We have managed to arrange, not only for a few more helmets, but, best of all, we were able to acquire three five pounders, with sixty balls, and enough powder to blow King George's palace to kingdom come, if we wanted to.'

'Why would we want to blow up his palace?' asked Bill. 'That would be a suicide mission.'

Robert grinned and replied he was hyperbolizing. But, then, he slyly added that perhaps we could effect a few more explosions in English navy ships, 'To help the revolution,' he chuckled.

The way he said it was very funny and raised a raucous response from everyone around the table.

When we were all seated, dinner was brought out by five servers, carrying a platter of roasted pork, another of roasted beef, a big tureen of sauce, two huge bowls of rice, one of sweet potatoes, and bowl, after bowl of; soup, corn, assorted fruits, and a plate of cheese. They returned moments later with three baskets of fresh baked bread, butter, and olive oil. It was a meal fit for the kings and queens we were. The splendid meal was consumed along with numerous bottles of wine, and tankards of rum, or ale. Conversation was lively and spiced with much laughter. We were a very merry bunch, indeed.

Gradually, Virginia and I introduced the idea of a trip to Halifax, but after about an hour of discussion, we were over ruled. A trip to Halifax was just too dangerous. The decision made Virginia very sad, and she had to excuse herself from the table. I told the gang not to worry. I assured them that we understood the situation and accepted the verdict. I followed Virginia in order to comfort her and helped her to understand the wisdom of the decision.

The following day, Robert completed arrangements regarding the ammunition, cannons, and helmets, while some of us whiled away the day in idle conversation over drinks in a local cantina.

Bill, Marianne, Pedro, Virginia, the children, and I went to the beach.

That was pretty much the way it was, when we visited Havana, on that trip. Over the three weeks that we spent there, nothing eventful happened to us. We shopped, we spent time on the beach, and ate in good restaurants. It was like a vacation from our vacation, as life on our island pretty much was. Even though everyone had chores, nothing was an onerous task, because everyone pitched in.

Life was a vacation for us. It was a vacation from the demeaning posturing one had to submit to when in the employ of others. Or the lack of joy, which so many people have because they are so busy with their noses to the grindstone, just to pay their taxes, that they have no time to enjoy their children. It was a tragedy we had managed to avoid for the rest of our lives, thanks to William Bartleby.

So, as I said, our life in Havana was a pleasant vacation, with no worries and lots of camaraderie.

We left Havana on July 23rd, 1781, loaded to the scuppers with supplies. Our ship was deep in the water, and every once in a while, a wave would crash over the bows. We were lucky to make about three knots, so our trip was slow going. We decided to fly a Dutch flag, so as not to involve ourselves with the English, or the French. Flying a Dutch flag was definitely a much safer thing to do.

The days were pleasantly warm. A steady breeze kept our ship moving happily along. We spent the time playing with the children in the day, and in pleasant conversation with our friends at night, over a few tankards of our favorite beverage. We took turns keeping the watch, always three people at a time, so they could keep each other awake and watchful.

On the fourth day of our return voyage we were attacked by Red Eric, who nearly sank our ship and caused us much consternation. The story is interesting in itself so I have given it its own chapter. Perhaps it is appropriate the chapter is number thirteen, considering the eventual consequences of what happened on that fateful day, when a dangerous pirate attacked us, thinking we were merchants.

Chapter Thirteen

Four days out of Havana, we noticed a ship on the horizon. It obviously noticed us, as well, because it began to sail towards us, on an intersecting course. Of course, we didn't make too much of it and assumed, since we were flying a Dutch flag, that perhaps the ship might be Dutch. Perhaps they recognized our black ship. We didn't know, and kept a careful watch.

As the ship approached, we could make out that it was a sloop, much like our former ship, *Phoenix*. Eventually, the ship was close enough that we could clearly see it was very much like our former ship, in fact, Bill and I were convinced that it was the *Phoenix*.

As we were thus watching the sloop approaching, we noticed that a flag was being run up the mainmast. It was difficult to tell exactly what the flag was, at first, but, within minutes it was abundantly clear the new flag was a Jolly Roger, with two crossed femurs under a grinning skull. We were being attacked by pirates! And, with our own sloop, at that!

Suddenly, she let fly a three pound ball in front of our bows. It splashed about twenty yards ahead.

Bill immediately shouted for the women and children to go below. Then he ordered us to man the guns. He did not really have to shout that order because many of us had already begun to grab our muskets, others were preparing the three and five pound cannons we had mounted on deck.

The pirates were still far enough away for Bill to make a deft maneuver, by executing an abrupt come around, which the pirates were not suspecting. As we turned, we managed to give them a volley of balls right onto the bows of the sloop, splintering the bowsprit.

As the sloop was headed straight at us, we had time to ready our cannons for another volley, as we came broadside, heading in the opposite direction. Six balls hit the sloop amidships, splintering gunwales, three pirates, and wreaking havoc with some barrels stored on deck.

They let us have it with eight, five pounders, whose balls slammed into our ship, splintering a few planks on our starboard side. Fortunately, we knew it was coming so we all gathered on the opposite side of our ship. Because the sloop was so much lower than us, their balls hit us, square in the side, punching holes in various places, but none hit below the water line, so we were lucky, for the moment.

When we were just past the sloop, Bill spun us around and we were able to blast a volley into the transom of the sloop, rendering their rudder inoperable. It was at that point we knew they were our victims, and not the other way around.

Bill ordered that we start lessening the attackers' numbers by shooting down on them from the yards. George, Robert, and Jake, had already climbed up there and began shooting down onto the sloop.

'I guess they didn't know what they were messing with,' laughed Bill as he maneuvered the big merchantman, so we were able to fire another volley right into the sloop, splintering the mast. 'He thought we were a lightly armed merchantman, manned by merchant sailors,' joked Bill, as he watched the mast come down on top of the pirates gathered on deck.

Meanwhile, the boys in the yards were firing onto the sloop, hitting pirates at random.

The pirates fired another volley into our hull, but being as how we were so much taller, the balls hit us in our sides, but not so as to compromise our ability to float. It was the last volley they were able to fire, because Bill managed to effect a hard come around, which enabled us to fire another volley into the helm and sides, abaft the mast. Judging from the screams, I believe we hit quite a number of errant pirates with that volley.

After a few more minutes, in which we turned around, the pirates lowered their Jolly Roger and hoisted up a white flag of surrender. Of course we all laughed uproariously, yelling at them that, 'You're smuck pirates, not worth a piss in the ocean,' and similar insults like that. The insult which hurt the most was probably that voiced by Bill, calling the pirates, 'Rank amateurs!'

In spite of the white flag, we did not trust the pirates. Especially not since we all determined the sloop was our former ship, now renamed, *Venture II.*

Our sharpshooters stayed in the yards and kept a look out for traitorous actions, as we came along side the sloop, our cannons trained on them, without interruption.

'We want to parlay!' shouted someone through a speaking trumpet.

'Now they want to parlay,' said Bill, laughing. 'We'll parlay with them, alright.' Then he shouted to them to send representatives over. He did not trust going to their ship, in case their desire to parlay was a trap to grab hostages. He told the pirates to leave their weapons on their ship.

Moments later, the pirates pulled their boat alongside their damaged sloop. Six men climbed on board and rowed their boat over to our ship. All the time we had our muskets trained on them. We were not taking any chances with those scoundrels.

When the six pirates had clambered onboard, we easily identified the captain, because he was dressed more splendidly than his colleagues, in a magnificent French wig, white silk scarf, brocade waistcoat, and a beautifully worked red coat of the finest satin. His breeches were of red velvet and his white stockings, likely silk, as well. He wore gold buckles, buttons, and baubles. Gold seemed to be a metal, to which he had a great affinity.

'Red Eric,' said Bill, the moment he beheld the pirate standing on our deck.

'I should have known it was you, Bill, the moment you came around, like that,' said Eric, 'You are one of the only sailors I know, who manages a maneuver like that.'

Bill chuckled. 'Aye, I guess I am pretty good at handling a ship. I've been sailing a long time.'

'So, now that you have beaten us, what do you intend to do with us?' asked Eric.

'Did you burn our village and steal our ship?' asked Bill sternly.

'Burn your village? Steal your ship?' Eric looked genuinely perplexed. 'What are you talking about?'

'That sloop used to belong to us. It was called, *Phoenix*,' said Bill, remaining calm and professional.

'We changed the name, after we bought that sloop in Maracaibo,' said Eric, sincerely surprised to hear the ship had belonged to us. 'We bought her from some buccaneers who claimed to have seized her in a raid.'

'They seized her in a raid, alright,' answered Bill. 'A raid on our village, when we were on a cruise with this ship.'

'Those dirty, rotten scoundrels,' said Eric. 'They told me it was a merchant's luxury sloop. I ask your consideration over this affair, Bill. We honestly thought we were buying an honestly stolen ship. None of us had any idea about its origins.' He looked at his colleagues and added, 'Isn't that right, boys?'

Eric's colleagues agreed they had been hoodwinked.

'What is the name of this gang of, 'buccaneers?' asked Bill.

'I don't know if they have a name for their gang, but their leader is a cutthroat, if ever there was one. His name is, Golden Jim.'

'Golden Jim,' repeated Bill. 'Never heard of him.'

'He is still a young man. I doubt if he is older than twenty five,' replied Red Eric.

'No wonder he did such a rash thing,' mused Bill, as he winked at me. 'Be that as it may, regardless of his age, someday he will pay for his mistake. I promise you, he will pay for his mistake.' Then Bill instantly changed the subject. 'Now, what about you shooting holes in my ship?' he asked. 'I believe you owe me an apology, first of all, and secondly, I demand compensation.'

'We had no idea it was you, Bill. We thought we were attacking a loaded merchant ship. You are flying a Dutch flag, after all. And, you aren't exactly sailing the kind of ships you usually do. This thing is much too slow.' Eric looked over our ship with a cursory glance. 'It's a merchantman.'

'It serves our purposes just fine, Eric,' replied Bill.

'I'm sorry we punched holes in her,' said Eric sincerely. 'If we had known it was you, Bill, we would never have attacked you.'

'I understand, Eric,' said Bill. 'It is an honest mistake. It could have happened to us.' Bill eyed Eric slyly and rubbed his chin. 'So, how are you going to recompense us?'

Eric looked at his men and then at the splintered sloop. 'The sloop is even more damaged than your ship.'

'You fired first,' replied Bill.

'Yes, that's true,' admitted Eric. Then he looked over the starboard gunwale at the damage to our side. When he had looked over the gunwale for a moment, he raised himself and addressed Bill. 'How about if we join forces? My men will repair the ships. I will turn my command over to you and will help you find those scum, who burned your village, and stole that sloop. I think they are based in Maracaibo. It shouldn't be too hard to find them.'

Bill looked at Eric for a long while. 'I will discuss your proposal with my colleagues,' he said at last. Then he signaled, Colin, George, Robert, and I to step into the Master's cabin. It felt good to be included in the inner circle. I was like the first mate. I felt important.

'I don't think we should trust them,' said Colin, right away. 'I mean, how can you trust a pirate?'

Bill reminded Colin that we were pirates, also.

Colin grinned sheepishly, as we all had a good laugh at his expense.

'I think Eric's proposal has merit,' said Bill. 'It was an honest mistake. We do look more like a merchant ship than a pirate ship. We could have made the same mistake, if we were still using the old methods,' he chuckled.

'I for one, would love to find those scum who burned our village,' said George. 'With more men, and two ships, we could teach them a lesson or two.'

We all agreed that Eric's suggestion had great merit. With two experienced captains, two ships, and many more experienced hands, we would become a force to be reckoned with.

Hence, we agreed to accept Eric's proposal. It was a no brainer.

When we stepped out of the cabin, Eric was grinning from ear to ear. I think he already knew what our answer would be. When Bill announced our decision, Eric gave Bill a big hug.

'Thank you, William. Thank you from the bottom of my heart. I promise, I will serve you as your brother.' Eric then gave Bill a kiss on each cheek, after which he shouted to his men to stand down and greet their new brothers in arms.

A great cheer went up from all the men, and the women and children, who had returned on deck. That night we had a great welcoming party on board our ship and new friendships were established.

Twenty six men, including Red Eric, joined us that day. We now numbered, forty three men, fourteen women, and nine children. We were beginning to be a substantial pirate colony, which became abundantly evident over the next two months, as the new men built their quarters in our village and our ships were repaired. Forty-three men and fourteen women, working together for a common cause, is a significant force, which results in a lot of work done. We lent the new people a hand whenever we felt like working. Everyone got along splendidly. I believe Eric's men were very grateful we didn't make them walk the plank, after their defeat.

In October we began planning our trip to Maracaibo, which we would undertake as soon as the storm season had passed. In the meantime, we began work on refitting our ships to take more cannons. On our merchantman, we added two ten pounders, two eight pounders, and on the sloop we added four more three pounders. It was a marvel to see how many of the men were adept carpenters. By the end of November, the cannons were firmly in place and our ships were ready to take on a new adventure.

December we spent in precise planning. We went over and over the details; what the pirates looked like, what their leader was like, where they could possibly be hiding out, how to deal with them, whether to pick them off, one by one, or to capture them altogether, that sort of thing.

Eric, as it turned out, had a prodigious memory and was able to give exact details.

We etched the details into our memories. We were determined to teach those errant pirates a lesson they would never forget.

And, besides, a trip to Maracaibo would be a pleasant cruise, with all manner of possibilities, even if we didn't catch up with the thieves.

Sometime in the first week of January we took a vote, to see who would stay behind, and who would go to Maracaibo. It actually was not a difficult vote because there were lots of people who were quite content to stay home. Life had become so pleasant on our island, that a trip away was not really all that desirable.

Andy and Judith were pregnant, and nearly due. Judith did not want to be at sea, or in Maracaibo, to have her baby. She had her friends on the island to help her. Tanya and Gerry were pregnant again, and were much too busy with Jacqueline, who was going to be two in February. Jake and Juliette stayed because they had become totally engrossed in horticulture and were hard at work extending the garden, along with their friends, Sam and Sandra, with their baby, and their friends, Wapoo and Narkat.

Virginia wanted to go, but she felt it was too much for Joshua, who was going to be two on February twelfth. He was teething, so he was not in the best of moods. Catherine wanted to go, because she loved sailing. However, her place was still with her mother.

As for me, I dearly wanted to go. This trip would be truly something to write in my book about, I was certain of that. Not going was out of the question, as far as I was concerned. To miss out on the adventure of adventures, was inconceivable to me. It was an once in a life time chance to see pirates in action against another pirate's fort.

Virginia did not see things quite the same way I did. However, she eventually agreed. She realized that my book was important to me. Thus, being the generous spirit that she was, let me go. She knew she would be safe with the others.

Bill assigned six more men to stay behind. These six came from the twenty six who had come with Red Eric. The men were disappointed they had to stay behind, but they understood the necessity of enough people to man cannons, in case of attack. Not that we expected anyone to find the island, however, one never knew, considering smoke could be seen to rise from our island, especially when we had bonfires on the beach. Bill cautioned those staying behind, to keep fires small, just for cooking, or for a small fire on the beach. He recommended that no bonfires be held, when so many men would be away from the village.

The night before we left, we held our last bonfire together. We sang songs of victory and funny ribald ditties, which effected raucous laughter from everyone. Much, ale, rum, and wine was imbibed. Hence, we didn't leave until two days later, all of us having to overcome massive hang overs the day after our farewell party. It was a good thing we were not on a very tight schedule.

February seventh is the day we left for Maracaibo. The year was 1782. It was a sunny and warm day. A good steady breeze filled our sails and took us in the direction of Kingston, where we would make port for a couple of days, before crossing the Caribbean Sea. It was good to watch our risen, *Phoenix*, sailing alongside.

Life on board ship had become routine. With forty one people on board the two ships, most of them experienced sailors, working the ships was not a chore for anyone, and therefore, we had fun making the ships work. Even the women took pleasure in climbing about in the rigging; setting and trimming sails.

The repair work was holding up marvelously well. Our carpenters were consummate craftsmen. They had learned the trade well. I inspected the repaired holes myself, and found no leaks of any kind.

I was beginning to miss Virginia and the children, already. Although my friends, on board ship, were pleasant company, and we managed to while away the time, singing songs, dancing jigs on deck, playing cards, or backgammon, I felt lonely. Seeing the other women, on board, made me miss Virginia even more. I wish she had chosen to come with us, to Maracaibo, instead of staying on the island. I should have insisted. However, in retrospect, I am glad I did not insist.

We reached Kingston in twelve days of pleasant sailing. It felt good to get off the ship and walk around Kingston for a couple of hours, by myself; I needed some time, alone, to think about my sweet woman, and my lovely children, on our island, so far away.

I prayed that I would come through the adventure, unscathed. I could never have foreseen the adventures which lay in front of me; they are so fantastic. Thinking about the following chapters of my life, it is a wonder I came through them alive. If Virginia had known what lay in store for me, she would have insisted I stayed home.

Kingston was a pleasant town of English colonial buildings and shanties, dark skinned Africans, and Europeans. The streets were mud. In the downtown area, wooden sidewalks lined the street on both sides. The harbour hosted a dozen ships; there for: okra, rum, sugar, and unfortunately, slaves. Slaves were everywhere present, being used to haul goods, fix things, and work on the plantations.

As I walked toward a small group of slaves, I could smell them from some distance. It was obvious that their overseers didn't bathe them much. I noticed one of the slaves bore some nasty scars on his back. He stared at me, as I walked by. I could feel his eyes piercing right through my skin. He made me feel his pain. There was nothing I could do for him. It made me feel powerless and weak. I hated that vile institution and vowed, if ever I had an opportunity, I would do something about it. The question was, what could I do?

When I felt ready to meet with the gang, I sauntered back to the ships. I noticed Bill and George were standing with a couple of men, whom I had not seen before. One of them was wearing a blue military coat of some kind, with gold buttons, and lots of gold braid. Under his large, Spanish hat, he wore a French wig. The other man wore a red leather hat with a bunch of colorful feathers. He had a huge black beard and was leaning on a crutch. When I looked at his legs, I noticed one of them was made of wood. I shivered involuntarily as I thought of losing one's leg. The pain must have been excruciating.

'I was beginning to wonder if you had been abducted,' said Bill, as I approached.

George chuckled, 'Yeah, our quill pusher doesn't pose much of a threat, does he?'

I pretended to take offense and George corrected himself, 'Sorry, Peter, I forgot, you nearly beat Tanya in wrestling.' Then he laughed even harder. I ignored George, and turned my attention to the two strangers, whom Bill quickly introduced to me.

The man with the military coat went by the name, Alexander the Great. The other man was called, Blackbeard. They were pirates, whom Bill had known for some years. Apparently they had information about Golden Jim and his gang.

Bill invited the men on board the *Bon Adventure,* for a cup of rum, which the two pirates gladly accepted. Rum seemed to lubricate a lot of pirate conversations.

The two pirates liked the taste of our rum. They happily drank more than one cup.

We were quite happy to oblige.

Eventually, the conversation became more detailed regarding Golden Jim and his gang. Apparently, they made their base near Maracaibo, in the jungle. Their large ships were moored in Maracaibo harbour, and were usually guarded by two or three men. The pirates also had some other vessels, which they anchored near the fort. The rest of the gang were usually in their village, drinking, and whoring, that being what they mostly did.

Bill and George found that to be excellent news, because it would be easy to catch the pirates off guard.

'Are you certain it was Golden Jim who torched our village?' asked Bill very seriously. 'I wouldn't want to be making a mistake.'

Alexander and Blackbeard both agreed that they were telling the truth. Since Bill had known them for a few years, he trusted the informants, who also said that there were about sixty five men, all together, plus assorted women and children.

'I say we torch their village,' said George, vehemently. 'That would be justice,' he added, punching his right fist into his left palm so hard that he hurt himself and had to shake his left hand a few times. George tended to do that sometimes.

Bill cautioned George about burning. He thought it a far better plan to blow up their ships, and leave them without sea transportation. Perhaps hostages could be taken and ransomed, he added.

I thought that to be a much better idea, as well. If their village is in the jungle, I reasoned, some distance from Maracaibo, then we would have to go overland to get to it. We would be vulnerable. The best plan was to take the lookouts as hostages and then blow up their ships. In a small place like Maracaibo, the lookouts wouldn't expect us, because it was not as busy as Havana or San Juan. Maracaibo was just a small backwater port.

'We will discuss these ideas with our friends, at supper time,' said Bill. 'Then we'll take a vote and see what is everybody's pleasure. Whether we go into the jungle and burn their village, as they did ours, or we just take hostages and blow up their ships, or, perhaps, we steal their ships and only burn the village.'

As you can see, dear reader, we had lots of options.

When all of our men, women, and children had returned from their shopping and sightseeing in Kingston, everybody came on deck of the *Bon Adventure*, to show what they had bought and to hear about the plans we had formulated, with regard to Golden Jim and his gang.

Our women prepared the evening meal.

The two informants explained, in great detail, what they knew about Golden Jim and his gang. (Blackbeard was already two sheets to the wind by this time).

Everyone listened intently.

Bill presented his point of view; that it would be best to take hostages off their ships, and then blow up the vessels.

George strongly proposed we burn their village. He wanted vengeance.

I proposed that we not blow up the vessels, but that we should steal some, or all of them. I figured that we had enough sailors, that we could easily sail three more ships.

We were discussing these ideas when dinner was brought on deck and set on a beautifully embroidered sheet. The women had prepared a buffet of; cold roasted meats; beef, pork, and chicken. To this was added a huge pot of delicious sauce, fresh bread, butter, onions, beans, and yams. Plenty of beverages accompanied the meal, making it an altogether friendly way to spend a night in Kingston.

By morning, Alexander the Great and Blackbeard had become our friends and decided to accompany us to Maracaibo. When they had recuperated sufficiently enough to wander to their respective homes, they did so, in order to retrieve their duffel bags, with a change of clothes, bedding, their pillows, etcetera. I imagine they probably took some gold or silver, as well. Which is what most pirates tend to do.

Next day we set off for Maracaibo, across the Caribbean Sea to the Golfo del Venezuela. We were a jolly company; not suspecting, for a moment, the hell which would break loose, enroute.

Two days out from Kingston we were hit by a storm. Not just any storm, but a huge storm. A frightening storm. The kind of storm in which ships foundered. A storm which whipped up waves that crashed over our gunwales with a mighty roar, shivering the timbers and groaning the bulkheads, as the ships crashed into the troughs between the seas.

The women and children were huddled down below decks, with those men who were not needed topside. Everyone did their best to comfort the children, and each other, as monstrous waves crashed over the hatches.

Bill, George, Robert, and I manned the helm of the *Bon Adventure*. Red Eric commanded the helm of the *Phoenix II*. Whom he had chosen to accompany him, I have no idea.

The wind howled through the rigging, which was devoid of sails, except for a well reefed top forward trysail, and a storm jib. How our friends managed to trim sails in those winds, I can't imagine. As we learned some time later, the *Phoenix*, lost two men, when a gigantic wave washed them off the deck.

After many hours of crashing up and down, an incredibly huge wave came at us with a mighty roar. Our ship climbed up the water mountain, which eventually broke over us, splintering our mizzen mast and sending it crashing to the deck. A large piece of it came through the rear hatch, which immediately became a huge problem as we began to ship water.

Bill and George ran off to assess the damage and to organize a repair crew, leaving Robert and me on the quarter deck. Robert, being much larger and stronger, handled the wheel, while I did my best to remain standing, as I strained to see through the thick haze of water.

The sound of the storm was something terrifying. I think, at times, the sound was more frightening than the huge waves crashing into us like mobile mountains. The wind howled and shrieked in the rigging and around the helm like a maddened banshee. At times the cacophony was so intense, it hurt my ears and gave me chills up and down my spine. I imagined if hell had sound, what I experienced on that voyage, was that sound.

The wind whipped up the water into such a frenzy, that it was impossible to see more than a few feet in front of the ship. We had no idea where the *Phoenix II* was. The last time we saw her she was about a half a mile off the starboard bow.

After some hours, the repair crew managed to repair the hole in the hatch and stopped the tide of water flowing into the hold. Shortly thereafter, Bill and George reappeared on deck. They were thoroughly drenched, and shivering.

'She's a doozie,' said Bill, straining to see through the spyglass for a sign of our sloop. 'I think this may very well be the worst storm I have ever encountered in the Caribbean.'

Just as he said those words a massive wave hit us broadside, taking the bow sprit with it, as it passed. Our storm jib, now without a bow sprit, flapped helplessly in the wind and eventually tore away from the mast, and flew off into the blackness, ropes and blocks flying after it. Moments later another huge wave tore the long boat loose, sending our boat onto its own journey. Where it eventually ended up is anyone's guess.

Bill became concerned that the loss of the fore stays would compromise the overall stability of the spars. However, as long as the shrouds remained fast, we probably would be alright, he hoped.

I noticed George looked worried.

We were now sailing with bare poles and no fore stays; driven relentlessly before the wind. It was all that we could do to hold on to the wheel and keep the ship into the waves, as she was tossed like a cork on the tumultuous sea.

I asked Bill and George if they knew how the women and children were faring below. Apparently the children were very frightened; seasickness exacerbating their fear. Below decks was beginning to reek of vomit. At least they were dry and relatively safe, compared to those of us topside; cold, wet, and shivering.

We battled the storm for over thirty hours. No one got any rest, as the waves tossed our ship up and down, this way and that, relentlessly before the wind; impossible to see ahead. We didn't have a clue where exactly we were, and how far off course we had been blown. It was a most uncomfortable and fearful situation we were in. However, we remained brave and did the best we could to keep the bows turned into the waves and avoid broadsides. The broadside we received, when the bowsprit was lost, nearly careened the *Bon Adventure*. We wanted to avoid that at all costs.

Albert appeared on deck and struggled to walk towards the ladder, to get up to the quarterdeck. He was coming to relieve me. We watched him climb up the ladder and suddenly he was gone in a massive wave of briny foam. We never even heard him shout. There was no question that Albert had become fish food. We had no way of saving him. It was a very grim reminder of the incredible forces we were battling. It was a life and death struggle we faced during that horrific crossing; far more frightening than ships bearing cannons and ill will.

George grabbed the wheel and Bill told me to go below. He shouted for me to tell Douglas and Gerry to come on deck and take over. It was high time two of us took a break below deck, out of the driving wind and rain.

The climb down the ladder was a harrowing experience, as the ship lunged into a deep trough, distorting my equilibrium. I nearly fell. In that instant I saw my life before my eyes. Thankfully I made it to the hatch and was able to go below, shutting the sliding lid quickly behind me.

I was cold because my trousers were wet. The rain slicker had done a good job keeping my topside dry, but my legs took a lot of rain and sea water, standing at the helm. I was glad to be inside and stood where I had entered, as I adjusted my eyes to the dim light, bracing myself against the port side wall. Inside the cabin, the sound of the storm was only slightly less of a cacophony, but the crying of children filled in the spaces.

I did my best to inform Albert's friends, that he was lost overboard. It is not an easy task to tell people that a loved one has gone to his Maker. I noticed that John became very pale and tears welled in his eyes. I found out later that he and Albert were cousins. I offered my sincerest condolences and then asked John to fetch Douglas and Gerry. Having done my duty, I made my way to my hammock and climbed in with some difficulty. Being bone tired, I drifted to sleep; the ship rocking me like a cradle.

When I woke up, the first thing I noticed was the ship was not moving quite so much as before, and the noise of howling wind was gone. I climbed out of my hammock and, rubbing my eyes, made my way to the head. The going was much easier now. The ship was gently moving up and down, as on a calm sea.

'Is the storm over?' I asked Penté, one of Red Eric's men, who was standing at the end of the short line up, to use the head.

'Ya, tank Got eet ees,' answered Penté, making the sign of the cross. 'Eet vas zum ferry bad vun, dhat shtorm.'

I nodded weakly, and leaned against the bulkhead. I was suddenly feeling queasy in my stomach and realized I had not eaten for a long time. 'Is there food?' I asked.

'Ya, ze vimmen mate zum hot foot unt zey alzo mate hot drinks,' he replied, smiling broadly, as he stepped into the head. He closed the door and moments later I could hear him groaning.

I decided I would go to the other head, in the fo'c's'le of the ship.

On the way I saw few people below decks. I guessed rightly everyone had gone topside to get fresh air. From the reek of vomit, which greeted me, I realized there was a very good reason to go topside. The reek of vomit pervaded the head, to the point where I almost tossed my gastrointestinal juices, there not being any food in my stomach. It was the most uncomfortable time I ever spent on the head and did my business as quickly as possible before I threw up.

The moment I stepped on deck I breathed and breathed, sucking clean air into my lungs and clearing my senses. Then, as my eyes adjusted to the bright sunlight, I beheld the damage. It was not a pretty sight.

Our mizzen mast was snapped off, just below the crows nest. The snapped off piece was sticking out of the rear hatch, at a precarious angle. The carpenters had sealed a plug around it, the spar being much too heavy to lift out of the hole, with out the aid of block and tackle. The bowsprit was snapped right back to the stem. Ropes were swinging from the fore mast. The *Phoenix* was nowhere in sight.

When I stepped on to the quarter deck, Bill greeted me with a cheery hello.

'We're still floating!' he said happily. 'We could easily have foundered, but this fine ship held together, thank God.'

I asked if he knew where we were.

'We're about twelve leagues north of the Lesser Antilles,' he answered.

'I figure we can put in at Otrabanda or Punda. Hopefully we can repair our ship there.'

A number of men were already clearing the deck, trying to bring a sense of order back to our ship. I went over to give them a hand and ended up spending a good part of the day, hard at work. The storm had done a really good job of rearranging everything on deck. Ropes and blocks were lying hither and thither. Large pieces of splintered wood from broken spars lay scattered everywhere. Cannon balls had come off their brass monkeys and were rolling about on deck, proving to be somewhat of a hazard; much like a game of ninepins with human pins. One eight pounder nearly broke my foot, as it rolled past at some velocity.

We managed to round up the loose balls and restacked them on their brass monkeys, restoring order on deck. Next we cleaned the salt water from the cannons, which had sat on deck through the entire ordeal. Only one had come loose and was lying against the opposite gunwale. We needed to rig a block and tackle to restore it to its cradle. As we worked on the cannons, other men were attempting to refasten the forward stays to what was left of the bowsprit. Looking up, I could see, Colin, Meira, Russell, and Wendy in the yards, setting the main sail. Wendy waved to me, when she saw me looking up.

When we finished the work, as best we could, we shared a meal together, after which most of the men, me included, who had been working on the heavy cleanup, went to their hammocks, bone tired from the laborious work. I fell into another deep sleep, dreaming of Virginia and the children.

When I awoke it was morning and we were sailing into the crystal clear waters of Saint Anna Bay. Since Bill was not familiar with the harbour at Otrabanda & Punda, we sent up a signal, requesting a pilot.

An hour later the harbour master and pilot came out in their longboat. From their facial expressions and gesticulations, I could tell that they were impressed to see our crippled ship had made it through the horrendous storm. Two sailors rowed the officials' boat alongside and moments later the two officials climbed on board.

'Ik kan zien dat jullie door een groote storm hebben gezijld,' said one of the gentlemen, thinking we could speak Dutch. When he realized we did not speak Dutch, he attempted to address us in Spanish. Although his Spanish was not very good, we had lots of Spanish speaking people on board, who understood what the official was saying.

However, Bill, not being fluent in Spanish, preferred to talk English and ventured to ask if the gentlemen spoke our language, which so happened to be the case. The Dutchmen spoke fluent English, with thick Dutch accents.

After introductions the harbour master asked us our business. He seemed somewhat suspicious of us, because we obviously did not look like merchant mariners, even though we were sailing a merchantman.

Bill explained that we had to come into port to repair our ship.

Then the harbour master asked point blank if we were pirates.

Bill did not so much as blink and answered straight off that he hired out his ship to pleasure cruisers. He explained that all of the people on board were mostly paying guests, who wanted to cruise in the Caribbean.

The harbour master and pilot looked skeptical, but seeing an opportunity to make some money for Punda, permission was granted to come into the harbour and the docking fees were assessed. Moments later, we pulled up our anchor and following the pilot's instructions, sailed our ship through the channel past Fort Amsterdam, an imposing fortress guarding the harbour entrance.

Fortunately, the ship building yard had a docking station available, so we pulled our ship alongside the pier and made her fast. Bill paid the harbour master fees to cover a month in port, then he paid the pilot his service fee. The two Dutchmen thanked us courteously and then returned to their longboat. We watched as they were rowed back to their office in the Handleskade, the Trading Quay along which a row of colorful, Amsterdam style, merchant's houses, warehouses, and offices stood facing the harbour.

A number of Dutch ships were in port, dropping their cargoes from the Old Country, including tons of roof tiles, used as ballast. In exchange they were filling their holds with salt for curing herring, the Dutchman's favorite fish.

The towns of Otrabanda and Punda stood on opposite sides of the channel leading into a multi bayed lake called the Schottegat, a marvelous creation of nature, with crystal clear waters full of many varieties of fish. It became somewhat of a hobby of mine, during the time we spent in Curacao, to peer into the waters of the lake for fish I had not seen on previous days. It happened quite regularly that I would spot a fish I had not seen before. I wrote a lot of their descriptions in my journal, thinking that I could compile an encyclopedia regarding tropical fish, sometime in the future.

As the days rolled by, we took lots of opportunities to go sightseeing around the cactus covered, wind swept island. One of the interesting places, to which the locals directed us, were the, 'Grotten van Hato', a series of large caves on the other side of the island. The caves were an incredibly marvelous experience full of sculptural stalactites and stalagmites. I revisited the caves on several occasions, and even attempted to draw some of the formations into my journal. Alas, I am not much of an artist, so I have not included my drawings with this text. Perhaps I will hire an artist to interpret my sketches and include them in a revised edition, at some future date.

Repairs to our ship proceeded apace, with the addition of twelve slave laborers, who we were able to hire from a slave trader with an office on the Otrabanda side of Saint Anna bay. As part of the job, we ordered the cutting of oar holes, with shutters; outfitting the merchantman to be able to travel in the event of becalming. We also had oars specially made, which were stored below deck.

As time passed, many of our people came to enjoy working with those hard working black men, and even befriended them. This situation eventually resulted in our resolve to, either buy the slaves, or to simply steal them. Then we would give them the option of joining our colony and helping with the attack on Golden Jim. Or, we could let them go.

When the idea was presented to the slaves, unbeknownst to the dealer, they happily agreed to join us and help fight the rogue pirates at Maracaibo. Hence, the following day, William, George, and I went to the dealer and asked him his price.

Of course, the dealer's price was much too high and we had to do some fierce bargaining, but the old Dutch skinflint wouldn't budge on his price, stating that he earned lots of money renting the slaves to ship owners.

Hence, we resolved to simply steal the slaves, and if the dealer put up a fight, we would remove his life force. We had no use for people who traded in human flesh, anyway.

When the repairs were completed, a week ahead of schedule, we stocked up on supplies, and simply sailed out of the harbour with our new friends, out of sight of the slave dealer in Otrabanda. We set sail for Maracaibo, two hundred and fifty miles, South, South West of Punda at 11 degrees North, by 72 degrees West, all the time wondering if we would meet up with Red Eric again, or if he and his crew were lost at sea.

During our passage to Maracaibo everyone made an effort to get to know our new friends better. Their names were, in alphabetical order: Anton, Bebu, Carl, Donka Petu, Edgar, Famak Kultu, Gaston, Habu, Nickolas, Pabu, Rock, and Tobie. Several of the new men spoke English, others spoke; Dutch, French, Papiamento, or Spanish, plus numerous dialects pertaining to their homes in Africa. We were becoming a multi-lingual colony. I thought that to be a particularly fortuitous circumstance, for the sake of my children. Perhaps they would become multi-lingual, which to my way of thinking, had tremendous benefit. I wished that I was more proficient in other languages. For a journalist, that is really a necessary skill; it gave one access to more people's stories.

One of the former slaves, in particular, took a real shining to me. We became friends on the voyage to Maracaibo. Donka Petu came from a country on the mid west coast of Africa, in the neighbourhood of the Gold Coast. Donka Petu spoke, Dutch, French, his native African tongue, Papiamento, and a little bit of English; just enough for us to communicate. Whenever he couldn't come up with the right words in English, he would speak in his native language to his friend, Famak Kultu, who came from the same tribe as himself.

Famak Kultu was somewhat more proficient in English. Over the time that he served as our interpreter, Famak also became a close friend. The three of us were often seen huddled together on the forward hatch. Me sitting on a keg, with my notebook on my knees, facing the two new friends, who would sit side by side on the hatch cover, as we talked about their former lives in Africa and the rude interruption of same when the slave traders abducted them. Their tale is a harrowing one, which graphically points out the horror of the human flesh trade.

The two men told of their life in Africa. How they lived in a peaceful village, which was in a country capable of providing a rich diet of; wild game, berries, fruits, tubers, and a wide assortment of other wild plants. The two Africans were in their teens when their village was overrun with musket wielding slave traders. Donka Petu's sister was brutally raped and murdered when she put up a fight. Donka and Famak and the other people of the village were made to watch as the traders tied her to a stake and whipped her to death. The effect it had on the people of the village was such that they peacefully submitted to the slave traders, lest any more people would be killed. The villagers had no weapons which could match the power of the guns.

Hence, all the young men and women of the village were rounded up, some torn from their children, and subjected to the humiliation of the slave chain. The thirty five captured villagers were forced to walk for many miles without food or water; the traders riding camels behind which the chained slaves were pulled. Whenever any one stumbled, they were mercilessly struck with a horse whip.

When the villagers finally reached the coast, they were herded onto a beach, filled with hundreds of other villagers from various tribes in the region. Day by day the people were taken by longboat to a ship anchored in the bay. There they were driven into the hold of the ship and forced to lie on their sides, spooned side by side, in row upon row of four tiered bunks, with no padding of any kind, just bare skin on wood. No provision was made for bodily functions in the hold, so unless one was able to pinch one's bladder, or bowels, the people on the lower bunks suffered the privations resulting from a constant trickle of urine and feces. Eventually, the hold reeked of human excrement, concentrated urine, and vomit. Even with the hatches fully open, letting plenty of air into the hold, the smell was overpowering.

To attempt to keep the bodily functions to a minimum, the slaves were fed and watered but very little during their voyage to Jamaica, so that those slaves who lived through the three month voyage from Africa, lost so much weight, that they were skin and bones when finally stepping off that horrible ship. Both men had lost friends on the voyage, whose bodies were used for fish bait; the fish thus caught, served as food for the slaves. They had to eat the fish raw, like the animals the traders thought they were.

Some of the people committed suicide during the Middle Passage. Others attempted to starve themselves, and were subjected to force feeding with a device which opened the mouth. Others were horribly tortured with thumb screws, floggings, or even hangings for showing signs of recalcitrance. It is a wonder any one lived through the ordeal.

In Kingston the people were taken to a fortress, and held there until they were sold to the plantation owners, some of whom were kind, and others who were cruel.

The two friends were sold to the slave dealer in Curacao, and rented out as casual labor to the various ships' owners needing help with cargo and such. Neither man had any idea where his relatives were. They only had each other. They had been friends since they were children.

The Africans generally got along very well together because they realized, as slaves, that their enemy was not the man from an other tribe, but the man who enslaved them. Hence, their desire to be fully involved with us, became ever more clear. They saw an opportunity, just as we did, to get even, somehow, with the oppressive people responsible for their enslavement. They had a particular hatred for the English, because it was English slave traders who brought them to Jamaica.

When Bill heard the Africans' sentiments regarding the English, he couldn't have been happier. 'They're just like us, after all,' he remarked, laughing one morning, as we were standing on the quarter deck. 'Even though their skin is the color of coal, they are just like us, Peter,' he said. 'I think our new black friends will make very good pirates. It makes me feel good that we were able to rescue them.'

Donka Petu overheard Bill say those words, as he was climbing up the starboard ladder to the quarter deck. He was grinning from ear to ear. 'Trust me, Captain, all black men on ship, good men. All feel happy we be free. They all happy give help, even go dead. We owe life to you.' Tears began to well in his eyes. Then Donka gave Bill a huge hug and a kiss on each cheek. He did the same to me and Robert, who was standing beside me. It was an emotional, impromptu moment, which touched me very deeply. The gratitude displayed by our brother, for giving him back, what was his to begin with, moved me. I vowed to write vehement broadsides against the diabolical trade in human beings; a scourge which debases all those who engage in it. I vowed to write such articles and send them by packet to the London newspapers. Indeed, I wrote such an article over the following two days, completing it as we entered the Gulf of Venezuela.

Now we began planning in earnest, involving our new African friends. Bill eagerly sought their input with regard to methods of procedure. We were only one ship, with fifteen less men than we had, when the *Phoenix* was with us. One ship and fifteen less men, made a big difference. We did have twelve new men, however, none of us knew how well we would fight together. At least we knew that Red Eric and his men were experienced pirates. Our African friends were an unknown commodity.

It was decided that we would not sail into Maracaibo, but, instead, anchor the ship some distance north of the town. Bill knew of many little bays along the way, in which we could anchor the ship, and not be seen by passing vessels. Then, some of us would walk to Maracaibo, along the shore, infiltrating the town in small numbers to reconnoiter the situation. Others would row there in the long boat.

We found an excellent little bay, about two miles from the town, and sailed into it. There were no habitations on the shore. We were in a very nice hideaway, not really visible from further out. The anchors were dropped and the next stage of our plan was launched.

The families stayed with the ship. We did not want to risk the women and children, so it was not right to risk the children's fathers, either. We also decided it was best if most of the Africans stayed with the ship. For an already suspicious people, Marabinos would find it very odd to see a large group of black men without white overseers.

Donka Petu and Famak Kultu came with Bill, George, and I; pretending to be our slaves. Of course, we assured them it was for the sake of subterfuge. The two Africans totally understood the ruse and voiced no objections.

'We be slaves of own free will, dis time,' said Donka, smiling. 'It big different.'

We all agreed that, indeed, there was a very big difference, and gave each other a warm hug, just to emphasize that we were brothers on a common path, pursuing a communal goal. We were going to wreak the Lord's vengeance on errant pirates.

I was beginning to see Bill's point of view. I felt like one of God's holy executioners. I was on the side of Truth and Justice. We were engaged in a religious act. We were doing the Lord's work. I felt strong and powerful. I had no fear. The fact that there were quite a number of experienced pirates along, probably helped with my feeling of invincibility.

We set out at different intervals, so as to not show up in town, all at once. Several walked through the jungle, a short ways in from the shore. Bill and I, with our new African friends, and George, traveled in the long boat. I hoped the going was as easy for our friends who were walking. Judging from the denseness of the flora along the shore, I was sure that it was equally dense deeper into the forest. Perhaps they would find a trail, I reckoned.

The shore was lined with a riot of greenery. Every tint and shade of green, which existed on earth, seemed to grow in Venezuela. Exotic birds flew overhead and monkeys chattered in the trees. Huge roots of massive trees tangled around each other along the water's edge. The air was humid and the sky overcast. We expected rain to fall at any time. We had brought our umbrellas, just in case. Not that we would be able to hold them, while rowing the boat, but at least we had them for walking about in town.

Rain began to spatter on the water as we pulled into the harbour of Maracaibo. Naked, aboriginal children were jumping off one of the piers, while others were happily splashing about in the water, below. We rowed past them but they didn't give us much heed. All manner of boats, ships, and people came in and out of Maracaibo on a regular basis. They were used to seeing people in boats. It was a regular occurrence in that part of the world.

The rain was warm, and didn't bother us, either. The rain certainly did not bother the children, who happily continued to jump in the water, just to climb back up, to do it all over again.

After we tied up our long boat, we immediately put up our umbrellas to prevent our clothes from becoming too wet. I remember laughing because it was such a funny sight, the five of us, dressed in our, wet, 'pirate gear,' with umbrellas. I will attempt to describe, as best as I can remember, what we were wearing, to give you, dear reader, some idea of what we looked like, when we went on our espionage mission to Maracaibo.

Bill, who had shoulder length, blond hair and a full beard, at this time, was wearing a Spanish hat of green velvet, with gold braid and a white ostrich feather. For a shirt, he wore the same as George and I; a full sleeved, white cotton chemise with frills, lace collar, and ruffled cuffs. We wore our shirts open at the front. Bill wore several gold chains and a pendant containing a small gold coin from ancient Greece. Over his chemise he wore a green velvet waistcoat trimmed with gold braid. His pantaloons were of green velvet, as well. For a belt he had a wide, dark blue leather strap fixed with a golden buckle. His hose were of white silk, and his brown shoes bore golden buckles, as well. He wore a rapier at his side and had two loaded pistols in holsters under his waistcoat.

George was wearing brown doeskin breeches, with white hose and tall boots with silver buckles. His waistcoat was of the same coloured doeskin as his breeches. He wore a wide brown belt with a silver buckle and a wide belt crossed over his shoulder from which hung his cutlass. George had long brown hair, slightly graying at the temples, and a thick full beard with waxed mustaches. Both of his ears were pierced with gold rings. His hat was of the finest beaver felt, dyed a deep blue, embellished with a magnificent red feather.

Donka Petu and Famak Kultu each wore white cotton, loose fitting trousers tightened around their waists with a colorful sash. Their torsos were naked except for embroidered vests. Around their necks they now wore a gold chain, which Bill had each given them. They also had pierced ears, now embellished with magnificent gold rings, a gift from George and I.

As for me, well, my hair was shoulder length, by this time. I had long ago given up on shaving and sported a fine beard and mustaches. I still had not pierced my ears. My hat was a full brimmed, black beaver, which fit so comfortably, I rarely took it off. I had added a fine silver buckle on a leather band. I tended to prefer silver and all of my buckles were such, my trouser belt, my rapier belt, my boot buckles, all silver. The buckles on my boots I had won in a card game against one of Red Eric's companions. Inside my right boot I carried a dirk with a nine inch blade, which I kept razor sharp. I used it for cutting rope, and various other things which needed to be cut. It worked very well cutting meat of various kinds. I had made a sheath for it, which fit into my boot so nicely, I barely noticed that it was there.

For breeches I tended to prefer the loose cottons of Jamaica, and wore such, stuffed into my boots. I wore a belt and a colorful sash around my waist. And, it being warm, I didn't wear a waistcoat.

So, as I said, there we were, standing on one of the piers of Maracaibo, Venezuela. Nobody paid us much attention as we walked towards an inn, close by.

'We might as well get out of the rain and have a meal and something to drink,' said Bill, as we walked through the door. The place was filled with the succulent aromas of assorted sea foods cooking, frying, baking, roasting… An interesting assortment of sailors, and locals were enjoying their pints and masticating on what was obviously delicious food. My mouth began to water the moment we stepped into the cantina.

'I think we have come to the right place,' observed George, as we sat down at a crowded table with bench seats. To my right sat some Russian sailors and on my left a pair of locals. Lively conversation in a number of languages filled the place and gave it a very special ambiance, which I found quite interesting and entertaining. Looking at so many different people, gathered in that one place, was truly something to behold. The variety of clothing, and assorted languages, gave the place a cosmopolitan feel.

A very pretty serving wench, with long black hair, and dark brown eyes, came over and asked us in Spanish, what we would like to eat and drink.

Bill asked her what was being served.

The girl, whose name was Maria, listed off a menu, from which we each chose something different. We also ordered our favorite drinks for a hot climate. I chose rum in fruit juices.

After we had finished eating the delicious food, we sat back and relaxed with our third round of drinks and began to seriously study the people in the place, for likely looking types who would have information regarding the whereabouts of Golden Jim and his gang. We each lit up a cigar and sat back to enjoy them, all the while eyeing the people coming and going.

Suddenly, two men came through the door, whom we immediately recognized. Julius and Max from Red Eric's gang. Seeing them gave us quite a pleasant surprise.

Bill called the two men over to our table.

Julius and Max grinned from ear to ear and gave us big hugs, pleased to see us in Maracaibo.

We introduced our African friends and then, Julius and Max sat down beside us.

'It is good to see you chaps,' said Bill happily. 'We thought you had drowned.'

'We're lucky to be alive,' answered Max. 'We nearly foundered in that storm.'

'Lost three good men, Albert, Bob, and Parson, added Julius. 'Waves got em.'

We explained that we had not fared well, either. We explained about our time in Curacao repairing the ship. Then we explained how Donka and Famak came to be with us, and how we had split up to come into town.

Julius and Max explained that the sloop had made it through the storm alright, with not overly much damage, except some leaks in the hull. When the storm passed, Red Eric managed to bring the sloop around and caught a wind to take them into Maracaibo. The gang had docked the sloop about half a mile from the harbour in a little bay along the shore. Since they had been in Maracaibo, they already knew about the whereabouts of Golden Jim.

'So where is Eric?' asked George.

'Sleeping,' replied Max. 'He is having his siesta, in his hammock.'

'Where are the other men?' asked Bill.

'Some are with their girlfriends, some are out fishing,' Julius shook his head, 'I don't know, I think Holger, John, and Martin came into town. They might be up at the monastery. Martin befriended a monk. They got into long discussions together. Soon, the other two joined in. Now the three of them have become like a little group of philosophers, discussing whether God is real, or whether the devil exists, that sort of thing.' Julius shrugged his shoulders and smiled. 'To each his own? I just let them be. Not something I'm interested in. We're all different.'

The pretty serving wench returned to the table and took our drink orders. Julius and Max ordered rum in fruit juice; a very tasty drink, I was discovering, much to my later regret. Eventually, the three philosophers gravitated into the same inn and joined us at our table, as well. It became a happy reunion party, as two by two the rest of our scouting party came to be in the same public house, where we stayed and drank, until we were kicked out because the proprietor wanted to get some sleep.

Since the sloop was closer than the *Bon Adventure*, we stumbled to the sloop and managed to find her in the rain, which, by that time, was coming down in buckets and pails; our umbrellas sorely pressed to keep us dry. When we reached the sloop, everyone was asleep, we could hear snoring and grunting coming from below. We tried hard not to make too much noise, giggling and laughing, and stumbling about, until we each found a place to curl up and sleep it off. Before I nodded off I heard a loud fart. Whether it smelled or not, I don't know. I was passed out before the noxious gas reached me.

Next afternoon I woke up with a pounding headache. I decided I had better sleep some more, and did; not waking again until early evening, totally disoriented, and with a crick in my neck from having slept on a coil of rope. It was an altogether unpleasant manner in which I had to suffer through the following three days, until I finally managed to fix the kink in my neck.

Anyway, when I came up on deck, the only people on board were, John and Paul, the rest of the men had gone into town and were having a reunion party at another public house, not far from the monastery. John and Paul were guarding the sloop. They explained how to get to the pub and I set off to find it. Although I vowed I would not touch another drop of rum, as long as I lived, I did not want to miss the party, and vowed I would just drink fruit juices.

When I arrived in the precincts of the said public house, I knew there was a well advanced party in progress. Loud voices and boisterous laughter filled the area with sound. There was obviously much merriment over the reunion of our two parties.

Upon entering the public house, I saw Red Eric and Bill happily sitting together sharing a toast. Both men already had glowing cheeks and were obviously not on their first pints. I ordered a fruit juice from one of the serving wenches, as I walked by her, and then joined Bill and Eric.

Eric gave me a huge hug and a kiss on each cheek. He was so pleased to see me, too. His face nearly split in two with his broad grin. 'Peter, Peter,' he said happily. 'It is so good to see you. Now we are all together again, we can begin to plan what we are going to do with Golden Jim.'

'Aye, Golden Jim,' repeated Bill. 'What will we do with Golden Jim?'

Chapter Fourteen

The question, what to do with Golden Jim, was foremost in everyone's mind. He was the reason we had all come to Maracaibo. Golden Jim was a rogue pirate, who stole from us and destroyed our first village. We were going to even the score. There was no way to stop the inexorable juggernaut we had set in motion. Reason should have dictated a different course, however, such are the affairs of mice and men, sometimes they go aglay, as Robbie Burns was wont to say.

Red Eric had already acquainted himself with most of the information we needed to know. Our own spies, those fellows who traveled through the jungle, instead of with us in the long boat, had also found information from people they spoke with, in three other public houses. They had also spoken at some length with the local padre, who was well informed concerning Golden Jim. Hence, when it came time to hold a war council on the deck of the *Bon Adventure*, we had plenty of intelligence from which to draw out a detailed plan.

Golden Jim apparently terrorized the townsfolk. Red Eric recounted witnessing one of Golden Jim's methods of terror, namely how Golden Jim publicly dealt with a man who had betrayed him, somehow. Golden Jim came into El Torro Rojo, a tavern I had not visited yet, and shot the man's wife and children, point blank through their heads, in front of the man who had fallen out of favour. Then Jim calmly took out an other pistol and put the gun to the man's forehead and pulled the trigger. The pistol was not loaded. Golden Jim laughed and then walked out of the place with his body guard, leaving the man to pick up the pieces of his life, now dead on the floor of the tavern. 'It was all done in a cold and calculated way, without so much as a blink in Golden Jim's eyes,' recounted Red Eric.

When we heard the preceding story, we were even more resolved to wreak the Lord's vengeance upon the errant pirate and his minions. Killing women and children, that is little heard of in the annals of world history. Women and children would be taken for slaves, but the cold blooded killing of women and children has been regarded a crime by most peoples, with few exceptions. The vision of Golden Jim shooting the family in the tavern was utterly revolting, to my way of thinking, and those of my friends. It was certainly something the town's folk had not forgotten. It showed us very clearly what a dastardly fiend Golden Jim was. He was obviously something which had crawled out of a hole, somewhere, and had to be put back into that hole, in quick order.

Little did we know, unfortunately, that powerful forces were at play in Golden Jim's favour. A battle royal was shaping up. Getting even with Golden Jim was going to be a difficult task. A man like him would make certain he had plenty of protection. The local people had attempted attacks on Golden Jim, as recently as seven months previous. However, each time towns folk ended up dead, and Golden Jim did not. Hence, we had no idea what the adventure was going to cost us. Had we known, we would have taken an entirely different course than the one we eventually resolved to follow.

Golden Jim's fort was about six miles south of Maracaibo, in a sheltering bay of the channel between the Gulf of Venezuela and Lago de Maracaibo. Two of his brigantines lay at anchor in the harbour at Maracaibo and three small sloops were anchored in the bay on which his fort was situated. Golden Jim's camp was well protected with a double palisade. Cannons lined the shore, all well hidden amongst the trees. Observation towers were set up on the east and west sides of the camp, with a clear vision of traffic coming and going along the channel.

'Any attempt to sneak up on them would be met with failure,' is how Red Eric described what we were facing.

Hence, it was determined we would attack Golden Jim at night, with a massive bombardment from the cannons on our two ships. Hopefully, we would be able to bombard them with several broadsides before they would have time to man their guns.

Therefore, it was decided that we would move all of our cannons onto our starboard sides, just before reaching the fort. Then we would just park our ships across from their fort and let them have it. If we were lucky, we would take out many of their cannons, and sink their sloops, before they could shoot back.

We decided that we would keep our ships in their present locations until we were ready to sail, so as to prevent any suspicions arising in Golden Jim and his gang. Surely, he must have had spies everywhere. We did not want to take any chances.

'Maybe we should wait until there is a full moon,' suggested Gerry.

Red Eric agreed it was a good idea. 'Otherwise we wouldn't know where the fort is. Under a full moon, surely we will see the first guard tower, above the trees.'

Everyone agreed that it was a good plan, however, the full moon would not be out for another three weeks; just having had a full moon, while sailing to Maracaibo. Very few people were interested in waiting around in Maracaibo for another three weeks. Golden Jim surely had spies, who probably had already reported that there were new people in town.

'There is no guarantee the sky won't be overcast, if there is a full moon,' said George. 'To wait another three weeks for the moon may bring suspicions our way. I say the sooner we do the job, the sooner we get home. Marta misses her friends. I'm sure the others don't want to spend more time here than we have to.'

'If we hadn't lost so much time, because of the storm, we probably could wait it out. We don't want to spend more time than necessary.' Bill looked at each of us. 'I say we wreak the Lord's vengeance on Golden Jim. It is time that the Sword of Michael came down on his neck!'

A chorus of voices supported Bill's call to arms.

I couldn't help but agree. I was missing my family too. I figured the sooner we got on with the project, the sooner we would be home. I was really looking forward to holding Virginia and my children. I dreamt of them nightly. I prayed no harm would befall them while I was gone. I prayed no harm would befall me.

As I was thus thinking about my family, a large raindrop hit me on the end of my nose.

Rain, again. Rain, rain, and more rain. The nearly constant rain was beginning to become bothersome. People wanted to go home. The storm damage cost us a month of down time. We should have been enroute home already, and Golden Jim in his miserable grave.

To make a long story short, we decided, after much discussion, to bombard the fort, as I said, and then let the wind take us south towards the lake. At the earliest opportunity, well beyond the fort, we would drop our sails, and some of us would venture on shore. Then we would sneak up to the camp and pick off the guards and attempt to gain entrance in hopes of capturing Golden Jim, while another group would approach the fort from the road.

So, our fateful plan was put into effect. The juggernaut was launched.

Fortunately, we had the good sense to demand that our women and children be put up at an inn, to guard the gold and silver we had brought with us from our island, for purchases of whatever we required whilst away from home. It was a sizable little treasure, which necessitated leaving the women with some fire power, as well. They each had their own pistols, but we thought it best to leave them with two muskets, which they all knew how to use very effectively. Of course, as a matter of policy, each woman always carried a concealed knife on her person, in case some undesirable came up close, and assumed too much. We had no reason to be concerned about the welfare of our women, children, or gold.

When the cannons were in place, and plenty of balls stacked, and powder, wadding, and fuses were set ready, we launched our venture. I believe it was in the night of April seventh, 1782. Fortunately, at least it had stopped raining when we left on our journey to hell.

Under cover of darkness, we slipped past Maracaibo harbour with the *Bon Adventure*, meeting up with Red Eric and the *Phoenix II*. The air was filled with a thick mist as we rowed in single file. Plenty of lookouts were posted to watch the distance between the two ships, and to take soundings.

We moved slowly, doing our best to keep a safe distance from the shore. The thick mist made it difficult to see more than a few yards ahead. Eventually, after several hours of slow going, the mist began to clear, somewhat.

After, what seemed like more hours, we rounded a point and could make out a small light ahead. As we strained our eyes, we could see what looked like a structure sticking up above the trees, about three hundred yards off our starboard bow. It was the first watch tower. The fort was somewhere further along. As we came around the point, just past the watchtower, we could plainly see the three sloops anchored in a small bay. What we did not see was their long boat, tied to the wharf.

Slowly, silently, we lined up our two ships, trying hard to keep the oars quiet. Our cannons were already loaded and the fuses in place. When the time was right, Bill whistled like a jungle bird; the signal to light the fuses.

Moments later all hell broke loose, as our cannons roared their thunder and launched the first volley into the anchored sloops. The moment the balls flew off to wreak their damage, our men reloaded the cannons. Within a minute we were ready for another volley, which was immediately forthcoming. We could hear much splintering of wood. Moments later one of the sloops leaned over and sank into the harbour. It was a good sign, so we thought at that moment. We let go one more volley, splintering portions of the stockade, and judging from two explosions, we obviously hit a gun emplacement's powder kegs.

Suddenly, just as we were about to light the fuses for another volley, it began to rain again, snuffing them out.

However, for Golden Jim's crew, who had by now scrambled to man their guns, the rain posed no problem. Their gun emplacements were well protected by small canopies built of sturdy poles and leaves, which served a double purpose; to camouflage, and to protect from rain. Fifteen cannons suddenly spewed their iron death directly into our two ships; splintering gunwales, deck planks, people, and punching a huge hole in the side of the *Phoenix II*.

We did our best to try and light fuses, for those cannons we still had left. We managed to fire six more cannons, but the volley was ineffectual, most of the balls landing against the outer wall. The inner wall was not affected.

Bill desperately yelled orders, to man the oars to try and escape.

Just as he yelled the order, another roar of cannon fire warned us a split second before six, eight pound balls slammed into our side and smashed through the Master's cabin.

Nine more balls went directly into our sloop. We heard the sounds of splintering wood and screams of men, reduced to pulp and tattered remnants, in the darkness behind us.

Suddenly, the *Phoenix II* burst into flames, lighting up the area, and revealing us attempting to row away, as clearly as if it had been daylight.

Another roar of cannon sent ten balls in our direction, shattering our rear quarter deck and knocking down the mizzen mast, which crashed down on people, desperately trying to scramble out of the way. The screams of our people was a sound horrible to hear. To this day, I still have troubling dreams over that incident.

Eventually, we managed to row the *Bon Adventure* out of range of the guns.

Alas, the *Phoenix II* was not so lucky. We heard another roar of cannons.

Moments later, our sloop exploded, sending pieces of ship, equipment, and people in all directions, several of which splashed in the water behind us.

Those of us still alive, and not injured on the *Bon Adventure*, did all we could to get our ship to pick up speed, in hope of escaping the remaining sloop, which they might send after us. We had no idea about their long boat, at that time, as I said.

I did my best to comfort the injured. However, there wasn't much I could do for the grisly injuries so many of our good people had suffered. Bart, Jock, and Douglas died of their injuries an hour after the bombardment. Only twenty minutes passed when Gerry died in my arms, with much pain and distress, both of his legs having been blown off. I couldn't help retching, afterwards. The experience was a horror I never imagined would happen to us. I could tell that the other survivors were equally appalled and surprised.

We had rowed for about an hour when we decided we were safely out of reach of Golden Jim and his minions. As we tended to the wounded, the sky became ever more overcast and the rain more intense. The only choice we had was to go below and take refuge from the rain. We huddled in stunned disbelief, regarding the massive hole in the starboard side of the Master's cabin, and the havoc which the balls had wreaked.

Bill and George stared out through the windows, trying with all their might to see through the dark and rain, for a vessel, which may have been sent after us.

As time passed, I gradually fell into a troubled sleep in the captain's bunk, dreaming of the horror and seeing myself blown up by an eight pound ball. Needless to say, my ability to stay asleep was significantly impeded.

I woke up suddenly as loud voices outside penetrated my dream. The sound of many feet on deck reverberated on the planks of the quarter deck above me. I had no idea what was going on, but I suspected trouble.

I rubbed my eyes, to look around the cabin and found that I was the only one there. The noises on deck intensified and I heard much shouting and stomping about. I heard Bill yell something, as musket shots exploded outside.

I immediately jumped out of the bunk and grabbed my cutlass and pistols. I carefully loaded the pistols and then looked about the cabin, to see if a musket might have been left behind. I found one in the gun cabinet and loaded it, as well. Just as I finished, I could hear several boot steps coming down the gangway towards the Great Cabin.

Moments later the door burst open and two men, whom I did not recognize, obviously intent upon plunder, were the surprised recipients of my pistol balls. Said balls I promptly discharged into their yielding bodies, rendering them deceased in an instant. The shots were neatly covered by much noise and commotion on deck, which was fortunate for me.

I dragged the bodies into the cabin and shut the door. I checked them for weapons and whatever else I could use. They were both carrying very nice, loaded French pistols, with ivory inlays in the handles. I stuck these into my sash. I found one of them had a leather bag with seven Spanish doubloons and some English silver. I stuffed the bag into my shoulder bag, which also had my notebook, ink and quills. One of the dead pirates had a pair of large golden hoops through his ears. These I yanked out and threw them into my bag, as well. I grabbed a couple of bottles of rum, and a box of shortbread from a cabinet, where I kept such things, and carefully looked out of the hole in the side of the cabin.

It had stopped raining and the sun was breaking through the clouds. The air was humid and beginning to warm up. The mist was clearing away. I was able to get a good view of what had happened.

Tied to the starboard side lay a thirty foot long boat with eight pairs of oars.

I could hear the sound of many swords smacking against each other. Every once in a while a pistol shot rang out. The sounds on the boards were like thunder under many feet stomping back and forth, as men fought for their lives.

I realized that there wasn't much that I could do, except to escape and watch the proceedings from shore. The only way to get there was by swimming. The problem which immediately came to mind was, how to keep my powder and guns dry.

A solution presented itself quite immediately, as I grabbed a small wooden chest, which easily held my powder, pistols, balls, and shoulder bag. I carefully set the chest on the aft balcony and then, when the cacophony on deck was particularly loud, I let the chest fall into the water. The splash was barely discernible over the noise. I followed the chest into the water, keeping my head down, careful to keep my musket out of the water. I slowly swam to shore, using the chest to assist with my buoyancy.

When I reached the shore, I managed to conceal myself in amongst roots and assorted water plants. I looked back through the leaves to see what was happening on the *Bon Adventure*. I could not hear any more clashing swords or gunshots, and surmised that the fighting was over. I could see men lined up on the deck, but that is all I could make out, my angle of view, amongst the shore plants, preventing a better line of sight.

When I ascertained that it was safe to climb up the bank, I carefully lifted the chest and pushed it in amongst the plants on shore. I hoisted myself up on a root, and as I started to climb up the bank, I almost peed myself as I came face to face with a large snake; an anaconda.

The snake stared directly at me and flicked its tongue. Then it hissed, sending shivers up my spine. It began to stir and moved its huge head closer, enabling its tongue to flick within inches of my right eye.

I remained absolutely still, hoping it would not find me of much interest.

The snake moved closer and stared at me with unblinking eyes; cold and fearless.

I slowly reached for the dirk I kept in my boot.

The snake hissed and flicked its black tongue.

Then, just as the snake came at me, I stabbed it directly through the top of its head. I could feel the blade crunching through the skull as I twisted the dirk with all of my strength.

The snake began to convulse and writhe about, knocking me back into the water and giving me a nasty bruise on my left side, nearly cracking a rib.

Fortunately, I managed to swim free of the convulsing snake, which, as it coiled and uncoiled in its agony, smashed the chest to smithereens and nearly destroyed my notebook. I held my breath for a moment, as I saw what was happening. If the snake had destroyed my notebook, a lot of work would have been wiped out. I was so lucky, that the snake died, shortly thereafter and stopped writhing.

I quickly gathered up my stuff and put it all into my bag. The pistols and powder were not harmed. My musket was dry. The notebook had not opened, so the wet leaves did not affect the ink on the pages. I was very lucky. Actually, it appeared that I really did not have too much to be concerned about, with regard to my personal safety. However, the safety of my friends, was not at all certain.

I peered out at the *Bon Adventure* from behind some large leaves. I could see eight men had climbed down the side of the ship and took up rowing positions in the long boat. Other men were preparing a hawser which they let down to the boat. I watched as the hawser was tied to the stern of the long boat. Several more men climbed into the long boat and readied their oars. I could see that one of the men was, Bill and the other was, George.

When the rowers were in position, they pushed the long boat away from the *Bon Adventure*. The rowers propelled the long boat forward and then made a long arc as they pulled the big ship around and gradually began to tow the merchantman back in the direction of Golden Jim's fort.

So, there I was, left behind in the jungle; a strange, exotic place, full of danger for someone like myself, not accustomed to living off the land. Sure, I had walked through, what one could call, 'jungle,' I suppose, on our islands. However, our islands were nothing like this Venezuelan jungle. It was the first time, for example, that I had seen a huge snake, like the one I had killed. Thinking of that, even now, still gives me a cold chill up my spine. I have never been a big lover of things, reptilian.

When I had sufficiently recovered my wits, I determined to make my way back to Golden Jim's fort, and then try to figure out a course of action. Perhaps, just perhaps, I might be able to effect a rescue. However, what exactly I could do wasn't clear, at that point. All that I could focus on was making my way through the tangled foliage, to attempt finding a path, or an easier course for travel.

Monkeys chattered at me, as I stumbled and crashed about through the bush. Startled birds, with brilliantly coloured plumage, flitted and flapped amongst the branches; some of them screeching insults at me for disturbing their peace.

Eventually, I found an animal trail which ran, more or less, parallel with the water, making my way somewhat easier. However, I still had to climb over huge roots, and push leaves and branches out of my way. Fortunately, because the canopy was very thick, the loss of sunlight somewhat impeded the growth on the forest floor, making my progress not all together impossible.

The entire time that I made my way through the jungle, I was in a constant state of high alert, lest I inadvertently stepped on an other snake, or some other dangerous creature; a biting insect, a spider, perhaps even a jaguar. Although jaguars are nocturnal creatures, they have been known to come out in the day time, because the light in the forest was quite dim in places, it seemed to them to be a lot like night, I suppose.

I have no idea how many hours I worked my way through the forest. I had to stop quite regularly and sit down from my exertions. Covered in sweat, I was a delicious target for all manner of sucking, biting insects in need of salt and moisture; meat and blood. There was nothing to do but try to cope with it, as best I could. My life, and that of my friends, lay in the balance. I had to persevere and stumbled on, ever moving northward.

When night came, I had no choice but to find a place to sleep. I was bone tired and hungry. Looking around for a safe place to curl up, I found the perfect spot in the crook of a tree, about seven feet off the ground. I managed to climb up by utilizing a piece of a fallen tree which I leaned against the trunk and was able to use like a ladder.

The tree was a massive community of trunks which rose a hundred or more feet into the sky. The place where the trunks spread out was large enough for me to, almost, stretch out. I knew it would be a suitable place to sleep.

I set my bag down and climbed back to the forest floor. Then, using my cutlass, I cut a bundle of large leaves, with which I padded the crook, making it a comfortable bed. I took my pistols from the bag and lay them near at hand. Then, putting the bag at my head for a pillow, I closed my eyes and let the sounds of the forest lull me to sleep. However, tired as I was, it took a long time before I drifted off, so many things were going around in my head.

My friends and I were in a sorry predicament. I had no idea how many of my friends were still alive. What would become of our women and children in Maracaibo? How would I ever get back to Virginia and my children? Would I make it out alive? The whirlwind of thoughts kept me wide awake. And, as if that was not enough, the sounds of insects, night crawlers, monkeys; all of the fauna of the world seemed to be present in that jungle, that night.

When morning finally came, and light filtered through the canopy, I opened my eyes and felt something inside my shirt. I froze as I tried to ascertain what it was that was crawling there. Carefully lifting the front of my shirt, I peeked in and nearly died on the spot, as I beheld a scorpion attempting to find a place to sleep.

Now, as you dear reader well know, scorpions are creatures to be avoided. Some scorpions can kill a man with a quick flick of their tail. One can not take chances with those diabolical creatures. Hence, I carefully lifted my shirt, so as not to disturb it and simply waited until it realized it was no longer in a shady place. Moments later it scuttled off and found a new place under the leaves of my bed, which I quickly vacated, leaving the scorpion to enjoy the fruit of my labor.

It took me a few moments to orient myself. I was hungry and thirsty. My thirst being the first of my needs which needed addressing. I thought about where to obtain potable water, as I expelled my tainted waters against the tree in which I slept. Perhaps it could use some of the nutrients still left in the urine, I thought, as I looked around to see if a water source was imminent. When I finished passing water, I fastened my breeches and took a good look at my surroundings.

I found some leaves with little pools of water laying on them. I carefully sipped from the leaves and quenched my thirst, as I reflected on my situation and how the jungle was helping me. It had provided me a place to sleep, and now it gave me water to drink. I knew I would live.

As I sat there, thus pondering the wonders of nature, it began to rain. Fortunately, the canopy kept most of it from falling on the forest floor, so I managed to stay fairly dry. To aid with this, I cut a large leaf and used it like an umbrella, holding it over my head, while I munched on some short bread and drank a little bit of rum.

When I felt ready to move on, I continued my northerly trek, every now and then walking east to get a glimpse of the channel through the trees and vines. By nightfall, on that second day, I saw a light ahead and surmised that it was coming from Golden Jim's fort.

My senses went into heightened alert, for fear that patrols were out. Now that Golden Jim felt vulnerable, and his defenses had been compromised, I realized he would have heightened his security.

As darkness covered the forest like a blanket, all manner of night creature came out, once again, and began to add its particular sound to the overall cacophony which filled the space between every tree and plant; a riotous symphony of discordant instruments directed by a mad man. As I listened to the sounds I wondered how I could have slept through it, the night before.

I tried, as best I could, to make no sounds which would appear out of place within the overall ambiance of the forest. Slowly, step by step, the light became clearer and within a few more hundred yards, I could clearly discern the looming shape of a palisade, in a clearing, ahead. I crept closer and, hiding behind a large plant, observed the fort. I judged the wall to be about twelve feet in height. It consisted of approximately twelve inch diameter, sheared trunks of assorted trees, judging from the variety of colors the pickets presented. It looked to be a very sturdy construction, which would take considerable cannon power to blow through.

I looked around for observation towers. I could plainly see a tower to my left. Trees and leaves prevented me from seeing much to my right. There were no entrances, from what I could see. They must be on the other side, I reasoned. The entire affair looked a formidable place. Golden Jim made certain to protect himself. A lot of labor had gone into making his fort.

Suddenly, I heard voices, faintly at first, but slowly getting louder, as they came closer. I peered into the darkness towards the direction of the voices and could see two figures, walking in the clearing, along the stockade wall. I crept back into the bushes and watched intently.

As the men came closer I could make out what they were talking about. Although their language was Spanish, by now I had heard Spanish often enough to discern the general idea of what was said. The men were talking about my friends and how Golden Jim was going to teach them a lesson. The men were speculating on what it might be; whether my friends would be subjected to immersion in a piranha tank, or with electric eels, or whether they would be boiled alive, or burnt...

Their voices trailed off, as they continued on their way. The last word I could make out was, 'anaconda.'

The word instantly sent me back to my encounter with the snake I killed. I shivered at the vivid recollection of me stabbing the snake through the head. As I visualized the act, it occurred to me that I had left my good dirk in the snake's head.

It was too bad. That dirk was a good knife.

I waited in my hideout for a while longer, to see if anyone else was coming. Not hearing or seeing anyone, I crept out of the bushes and headed in the opposite direction to the way the talking pirates had gone.

Staying close to the edge of the forest, I walked swiftly west, trying very hard to stay in the shadows, lest a guard in the tower would see me.

When I arrived opposite the tower, I crept into the bushes and carefully studied the structure. I could see two men moving about on the covered platform. Fortunately, they had not seen me. How to proceed became the question of the moment. Shooting the guards would be out of the question, because the sound would give away my position. I wanted to avoid capture, at all costs. However, the only way I could possibly help my friends was by getting inside the fort and locating them. How I was going to get into the fort was the obstacle I had to overcome. At the moment, I had not the slightest notion of a solution to the problem.

I decided the best thing to do was to circumnavigate the fort, around the periphery of the clearing, to ascertain the location of a gate, or some other entrance. Fortunately, movement along the edges of the clearing was not difficult. The noise from the jungle covered the sound of my steps beautifully. I had no problem walking past the observation tower and around to the other side of the fort, where there was a large double gate, and a smaller door. The gate opened onto a dirt road, which I assumed led north to Maracaibo. It occurred to me, right at that moment, it was better to return to town and fetch the women. We had left pistols with them, and the gold we had brought with us. Surely I would be able to secure some hired help, and perhaps be able to effect the rescue of our friends, if they were still alive, that is. I had no way of knowing.

The distance to Maracaibo was about six miles, I reckoned. I wasted no time and began my dark walk down that wretched road. However, after walking for about ten minutes, it became nigh on impossible to discern the way any longer. It was pitch black and I had no idea what manner of creature I would encounter, perhaps a jaguar. I was sorely frightened, and decided it was best if I cleared a space on the ground and sat down, leaning against the trunk of a tree. Eventually, I managed to fall asleep, waking up when a big raindrop splashed on my face.

Rain, I should have expected it. Fortunately, I found another large leaf and managed to curl under it, keeping relatively dry, if not comfortable. And so I spent the rest of the night, until day break, curled under my leaf, like some forest creature, bitten by ants, and stung by mosquitos. I imagined my face must have looked like a bleeding pin cushion when I woke up. My neck hurt and I had a crick in my back. It was probably the most uncomfortable night I ever spent, in my life.

Anyway, I gradually managed to straighten my self up and began the rest of the walk to Maracaibo, not meeting any traffic on the way. I reached the town several hours later and went immediately to the inn where Marianne et al were staying. I saw them sitting at a table by the window, as I walked up. They were obviously having lunch. The children were sitting with them.

When Marianne saw me, I heard her say to her friends, 'Oh my God, it's Peter!' as if there was something seriously wrong when she saw me. As she ran over to me, she kept saying, 'Oh my God, oh my God.' As she came up to me, she put her hands to her face and looked most afraid. 'Peter, what happened to you? What has happened to Bill?' She took my hands into her own and stared into my eyes.

The other women also came immediately to me. Judging from their expressions, I must have looked a mess, and gave them reasons to be afraid for their loved ones.

The women quickly sat me down. Susanne went to fetch some cloth and water to wipe the blood off my face. Judging from the blood I saw collecting in the bowl, as she rinsed the cloth, the insects had done a good job on my face and neck, as well as my hands, wrists, and my back, where some creatures had gotten under my shirt. When the blood had been washed off, Marianne put a little bit of rum in a bowl of clean water and gently cleansed the wounds with the alcohol, to prevent infections. The rum stung on every bite; a very uncomfortable feeling, to say the least. While I was being cleaned up, I explained what had happened.

'Oh my God, Bill!' cried Marianne, when she heard the news.

The other women also exclaimed the names of their loved ones, at the same time. When I told them about the men who were lost, Samantha began to cry. It was a difficult task to explain that Jock died quickly, 'He probably didn't know what had hit him,' I told her.

Marianne put her arm around Samantha. The news hit her very hard; it was something none of us were prepared for. We had always been successful in our pirating ventures. This set back came as a hard lesson.

The immediate topic for discussion, after the initial shock had passed, was to figure out how we were going to get our friends and loved ones out of Golden Jim's clutches.

In order to save our friends, we figured we had to act fast. There was no telling what Golden Jim might do. His reputation for ruthlessness was well known in Maracaibo, and he apparently was not much of a procrastinator when it came time for retribution. The people of Maracaibo made certain to appraise us of the pirate's reputation. Their stories made us all fearful for the lives of our friends.

Hence, the first order of business, was to recruit some help. The women had befriended some locals, who were very afraid of Golden Jim, but who were also very adamant that something had to be done about the monster.

The marauding pirate had to be stopped. The only way was for everyone to stand together. We requested that the Marabinos round up as many of their friends and to return to the inn's courtyard, within the hour. There was no time to lose.

An hour later, seventy three people gathered in the court yard and listened to Marianne present an impassioned speech, in good Spanish, requesting the people's help in ridding Maracaibo of Golden Jim. She reiterated Golden Jim's record for cruelty. She spoke of the man in the public house, whose family was killed in front of many townspeople. She made it clear, that unless people acted in unison, they would continue to be oppressed by Golden Jim and his gang of cutthroats.

Each time Marianne made a good point, the people applauded and cheered. Each time they cheered, more people came forward to enlist in the people's army.

Marianne's passionate speech resulted in forty seven able bodied men and sixteen strong women joining the crusade. With over sixty people we were a formidable little force; if utilized appropriately.

I suggested that we should arm ourselves as best we could, and then steal one of the pirate's brigantines out of the harbour. With as many people as we now had gathered, some of whom had sailing experience, it would be an easy job to commandeer a brig. Apparently, they were only guarded by two or three pirates, who were mostly drunk, anyway.

Hence, it was decided that twelve of us would sneak on board each ship and overpower the pirates. Then, we would determine which of the two ships would best serve our purpose.

We pretty much followed the plan, step by step, as I delineated above. Several of the men had long boats, which they used for fishing. So, we simply pretended to be fishermen, rowing out to ply our trade. We were well armed with cutlasses, muskets and pistols.

As we approached the two brigs, we simply drifted below their rope ladders and quietly climbed onboard. The brig I climbed up did not appear to have anyone there. There certainly was no one on deck as far as we could see. Looking up I noticed no one in the crowsnests. Silently we crept over the gunwales and spread out over the ship in groups of three. I stayed to guard access to our long boat and listened with heightened sensitivity for any noises, other than our own, on board the *Navigator*, that being the brigantine I was standing on.

Moments later, three sleepy pirates were pushed on deck, still half drunk from a long, hard night of drinking. Several men tied the pirates to the masts and stuffed gags in their mouths, lest they began to raise a ruckus. I looked over at the other brig and could see that we were successful there, as well

Once we had completed the tying and gagging of the pirates, we roamed the ship to see what we had captured. Our men did the same thing on the other ship. When we had completed the assessments, we met on the deck of the *Navigator* and took stock.

It turned out that the *Navigator* had more cannons, and was better set up as a war ship, with lots of powder, balls, etcetera. Since we had no idea how much time we had, we decided that, given the number of people we had, we took the best armed brig to bombard the fort. However, since I presented detailed information regarding the water battle we fought, I thought it best that we shoot as many volleys as we sailed past, not stopping, in order to prevent return fire from hitting the ship.

Forty men would sail on the ship and twenty seven people would attack the fort from the road. Hence, while the bombardment distracted the pirates to the water, the land force could attempt to gain entry into the fort. Fortunately, seven horses and two wagons were procured, enabling the land force to travel as quickly as possible along the road.

Samantha offered to look after the four children while we were gone, enabling; Marianne, Marta, Meira, Susanne, and Wendy to accompany the land force.

When all was ready, we weighed anchor. A proper breeze began to blow, as we hoisted sails. Within the half hour we were on our way to bring the Lord's vengeance upon Golden Jim.

As we sailed, the cannons were loaded and made ready.

I handled the helm of the *Navigator*. Everything was completely ready when we rounded the point and saw the first observation tower. I looked through the spyglass, which we found in the Master's cabin, but could not see anyone in the tower. It seemed odd that there would not be a watch set, but I reasoned that Golden Jim probably figured he had captured all of us and there was no imminent threat of attack, so soon after a failed attempt.

When we were within shooting distance, we surprised the pirates with our twenty twelve pounders blasting their iron death into the gun emplacements and the first observation tower. Several explosions resulted from powder kegs going off at two of the gun emplacements on shore.

As we continued to sail by, our cannoniers did their utmost to reload and fire as each cannon was ready, and thus a nearly continual bombardment blasted the shore and stockade walls. Another explosion heralded success with the demise of another gun emplacement.

By the time the pirates were able to fire back, we had already sailed out of range, towards the middle of the channel, where we luffed our sails and waited with guns pointed towards Golden Jim' s fort, as we prepared the oars. We could hear gun shots from the shore as we turned the brigs around and then rowed slowly back towards the fort. Unfortunately, the pirates had not abandoned the gun emplacements and began to shoot at us, as we approached. Fortunately, the pirates' cannon balls did not reach us, and in the time it took for them to reload, we were able to swing the brig into position to fire our port side cannons, which neatly rendered the remaining gun emplacements useless, as canopies collapsed, powder exploded, and balls literally tore through flora and fauna, mashing everything in their paths.

When we felt that the shore batteries posed no more of a problem, we decided to risk sending the boats ashore, with fifteen men in each, and plenty of weapons, while the remaining men on board would continue to fire balls into the fort.

As I watched from one of the gun ports, I saw our men beach the long boats and climb ashore. Suddenly, a shot rang out and one of the men went down. The others scrambled hither and thither to take cover. We blasted some more cannon balls in the direction of the gun shot. Moments later screams pierced the air, curdling my blood and shivering my timbers. I had no idea whose screams they were, ours, or theirs.

As we were staring in the direction of the screams, it began to rain again. Moments later, lightning lit the area with a brilliant flash of white blue light. The thunder mimicked our cannons. I could see in the flash of light that our cannons had successfully punched a hole through the inner stockade, as well, making a big enough gap for our men to effect an entry into the compound. Gun shots and the sound of cutlasses and sabres rattling against each other, filled the space. More gun shots rang out. We could clearly hear yelling and cursing.

The sounds continued for about ten minutes, which seemed like hours. I prayed every second of those minutes for our victory. Whether what we achieved was a, 'victory,' or not, that is a relative observation. I shall pick up the thread from the time two of our Marabinos rowed back to the *Navigator* and shouted to us on deck, to come back to shore with them. So, we climbed down the ladder and rowed with them to the shore.

Our cannons had done a good job blasting the pirate's gun emplacements, and indeed had effected some considerable damage to the stockade walls. As I stepped through the brush, I nearly vomited as I began to notice there were pieces of human bodies and blood spattered through the trees and undergrowth. Twisted cannons, bits and pieces of kegs, balls, and the wooden platforms, on which the cannons stood, were scattered all the way to the first stockade wall. It was a very grisly walk into that fort.

What I found there, was even more upsetting and became a pivotal event in my character development.

The fort consisted of seven buildings, two of them barracks, one of them a mess hall. There was a large private dwelling, of quite splendid proportions, and a stable with ten horses. The remaining buildings were warehouses full of swag.

The buildings were grouped around a large central courtyard where a sorry spectacle greeted me. Five stakes were firmly planted in the ground, to which; Anton, Bebu, Donka Petu, Famak Kultu, and Pabu, were tied. All but one man had been garroted. Seeing my friends, dead like that, brought tears to my eyes. I watched for a few minutes, as our people cut the bodies loose.

Facing the dead men was a large chair, much like a throne really, upon which Golden Jim must have sat as he watched our men slowly deprived of their lives. On either side of the chair were a number of benches. It was obvious that our attack had interrupted the proceedings, because Pabu was still alive. Russell and Wendy were untying him as I walked towards a group standing by the meeting hall.

Our men and women had managed to overcome Golden Jim and his thirty followers, who were standing in a sorry, disarmed state, in front of the meeting hall, muskets trained on them from every angle. As I approached I happily spied Bill and George standing next to a man wearing golden clothing from head to foot; golden shoes, golden hose, golden breeches, golden belt, golden shirt, golden waistcoat, golden hat, golden earrings. Even his hair was golden. I surmised he had to be Golden Jim.

As I approached, I noticed that Bill had a black eye.

The moment Bill and George saw me they grinned from ear to ear.

'Peter!' they both shouted.

The moment my name rang out, the entire group started chanting my name, 'Peter, Peter, Peter!', over and over again, as if I was some kind of hero.

'Peter, I am so glad to see you,' said Bill as he gave me a huge hug.

George and Robert also gave me big hugs.

I replied that we had obviously come in the nick of time.

Bill replied that Golden Jim was going to kill everyone of us. If the women and I had not been able to round up help, I would have been the only remaining adult male, who had come to Maracaibo seeking revenge for the destruction of our village.

I asked how many people we had lost in the storming of the fort.

Apparently we lost three Marabinos at the front gate, and one named, Carlos, was killed coming ashore. Six people, including Marianne had suffered cuts and bruises. Two of our African friends were patching them up inside the meeting hall.

'He was going to save the best tortures for us,' spat Bill as he scowled at Golden Jim. 'He was planning to burn us alive. That glowing waste of human flesh was garroting our African friends, because he felt sorry for them. He wanted to put them out of their misery, quickly. He was actually planning to do horrible things to us and then burn us.' Bill cringed. 'You know Peter, we are so fortunate that you were able to escape. We are very lucky that you were able to rescue us.'

I reminded Bill that it was Marianne who had stirred up the Marabinos. I was merely the messenger, I told him. The rescue was effected by the Marabinos, mostly, and because of Marianne.

Bill grinned. 'Aye, my Marianne is quite a woman. I am grateful to have her in my life, thanks to you as well, Peter.'

I asked what the plans were, regarding Golden Jim and his gang.

'We will kill them all,' answered Robert, as he stepped over to me. 'We will simply exterminate them like the rats they are.' Robert spat in the direction of Golden Jim.

'We will not kill them all,' said Bill firmly. 'We may be able to save a few of them. It is wasteful to kill so many human beings, who could work for us.'

'Those scum will never work for us,' replied Robert. 'They are only loyal to that golden piece of dung.' Robert stared at Golden Jim. 'They'll never be loyal to us.'

'He has a point there,' replied George. 'Those pirates are very angry with us, for taking them captive. They thought they were invincible inside this stockade.'

'Aye, but killing thirty human beings, all at once? It is a horrible thing that you are proposing we do. I don't have the stomach for that. Those men are pirates. They were merely following the wrong leader. It is Golden Jim and his lieutenants whom we hang. If we show clemency, I'm sure those men will be indebted to us for their lives. If, at some point in the future, they step out of line, then we kill them.'

Everyone listened very intently to Bill's words. We were not cold blooded killers. What Bill said made a lot of sense to me, and as I looked around at our people, it made sense to them as well. The problem lay with the leaders, the rest of the men were simply followers, who were looking for a family; for a sense of belonging to a group, most of them were probably homeless orphans from the Seven Years War.

'Before we make any hasty decisions,' said Bill, firmly asserting his captaincy, 'I say we tie up these pirates and lock them in one of those barracks over there. We will tie Golden Jim and his three lieutenants to those stakes, and then we will sit down in this hall and figure out what to do.'

Bill's words made sense to everyone, so that the work of tying the gang leaders to the stakes proceeded apace. Tying up the rest of the pirates, was effected quickly by the Africans and Marabinos, who then herded the cutthroats into a building, setting up guards at the two entrances.

At our meeting, everyone helped themselves to Golden Jim's ale, rum, or wine, from hogsheads set in the wall behind the bar. Bill had helped himself to a bottle of fine brandy, and was sipping the amber liquid from a crystal glass, one of Jim's finest.

'I propose we burn Golden Jim, like he was planning to do to us,' began Bernard. 'Golden Jim should taste his own medicine.'

Hearing Bernard speak so vehemently, surprised us because he was a man of few words.

'I agree with Bernard,' said Russell. 'Golden Jim has terrorized the people of Maracaibo for a long time. Burning him serves the cause of justice.' Russell took a long drink of ale and sat down on a bench.

Colin, who rarely took a drink of intoxicating liquors, also a man of few words, stood up and scanned the group slowly. Then, with Meira at his side, he spoke about the loss of his friends, Bart, Douglas, Gerry, and Jock, because of Golden Jim. He talked about the loss of our first village and our sloop. We had to start all over again, he reminded us. Surely the loss of friends, and our homes merited some kind of retribution; justice had to be served. Killing Golden Jim and his lieutenants was the right thing to do.

I watched Bill as he listened carefully to everyone who had an opinion. The African men were in favour of some form of tortuous death for Golden Jim, for the sake of their deceased friends in the court yard.

Pabu thought that Golden Jim and his friends ought to be garroted, the same way his friends met their end, only more slowly.

Pabu's suggestion made sense to me, as it did to a lot of the men. However, I personally did not have the stomach for it. Watching men being slowly deprived of their lives with cords around their necks, was not a spectacle I wanted to partake of. I suggested shooting them was the best option.

When everyone had spoken, Bill stood up and addressed the group in a very serious tone. He reminded everyone that just because Golden Jim was prepared to do tortuous things to us, we really did not want to take the time, or expend the energy to effect such horror. He said that the best thing we could do was to simply shoot Golden Jim and his three lieutenants, as I had suggested. 'Then we take the followers as captives and have them row the brig back to Maracaibo, where they can help us take both brigs out to sea. If any would prove to be recalcitrant, then we would make examples of them and throw them to the sharks. The sooner we shoot Golden Jim and his cronies, the sooner we can go home. I am sick of the rain in Venezuela,' he said, looking at the clouds.

We all agreed, returning to our island was most desirable. We quickly disassembled and set the pirates to work digging graves for the dead. When the graves were ready, we buried our dearly departed with a farewell ceremony involving the pouring out of; ale, rum, and wine over their graves, as I spoke some words of sympathy. Jim's dead were simply tossed into a mass grave and covered over.

When the burial ceremony was over, it was starting to get dark. We herded the pirates back into their barracks, firmly securing the doors with chains and locks. Then we proceeded to have a party in the meeting hall, drinking copious amounts of Golden Jim's libations. We were so happy, to have gained the upper hand on Golden Jim, that we partied well into morning.

We woke up when the day had progressed well into afternoon. I wondered why I had done myself such harm, once again. My head was pounding. I walked, as if on the deck of a tossing ship. The tossing ship image resulted in the immediate onslaught of seasickness, necessitating a hasty stumble outside, in order to evacuate the contents of my stomach, and nearly everything else I carried in my belly; stomach, spleen, pancreas, liver, bladder, intestines… The question, 'Why?' came to my mind, often, as I suffered through the next six hours; sweating profusely, and vomiting the remnants of my celebration in various places throughout the compound. All the while a voice kept telling me that alcohol was the devil's elixir and that I should avoid it at all costs. As the day progressed, I began to feel ever more inclined towards teatotalling.

While I stumbled about, dealing with my stupidity, Bill, Colin, George, Robert, Russell, and our African friends, had organized the pirates into work crews, unloading the warehouses. Others were emptying Golden Jim's house and loading up the Marabinos' wagons. Horses were being led out of the stables, as people argued over who should get them. I noticed a magnificent desk being carried out of the house, just as I had to bend over, to rid my body of some bile, beside a rose bush, next to the grand porch of Golden Jim's house. I could see Jim squirming in his ropes, as he watched his desk being loaded on a wagon.

I ended up sitting on the steps of the porch and watched Golden Jim watching the proceedings, as hour by hour, the contents of his house and warehouses, were loaded up and carted away. Eventually, more wagons arrived from town, as Marabinos eagerly came out to help themselves.

Three days later, we had loaded the last hogshead of ale onto the *Navigator*. Then we assembled everyone, including Golden Jim's gang members, in the court yard and explained to the pirates what our deal was. Either, they came along with us and did our bidding, or they would meet the same fate as their leaders were about to.

Not one of the pirates elected to join Golden Jim and his three lieutenants; Creepy Carl, Hogshead McClinty, and One Eyed Pete.

So, without much further ado, Bill, calm as ice, announced the death sentences on Golden Jim and his colleagues. He asked the pirates if they had anything to say.

One Eyed Pete immediately began to beg for his life and vowed that he would serve us faithfully, claiming he had been duped by Golden Jim's promises.

Jim stared at his colleague and berated him for his disloyalty.

Bill told Jim to shut up and let the man talk.

One Eyed Pete looked at Golden Jim. 'This is all your fault. I told you we shouldn't have burned that village.'

Jim gritted his teeth and scowled at One Eyed Pete.

'That's not true!' shouted Hogshead McClinty. 'I told Jim not to burn the village.'

Creepy Carl looked at Hogshead. 'No you didn't. I told him not to burn the village, and I told him not to steal the sloop, as well.'

One Eyed Pete started yelling, 'Lies, lies!'

By then Bill had heard enough and told the pirates to be quiet. He asked if any of the other pirates could speak in favour of any of their leaders, but none came forward, fearful they would be included in the Lord's vengeance.

'In order to put an end to this gang, you four men are sentenced to death; that being our code. You have trespassed against us. You have caused the deaths of many of our friends. There is no question in my mind, or the minds of all of us assembled here, your deaths are just and necessary.'

Bill stepped forward, cool as a cucumber. He slowly took one of his pistols out of his belt. He calmly stepped up to One Eyed Pete and without blinking an eye, shot the pirate through his right temple. I watched the ball come out of the other side of his head, along with pieces of bone and brain, which landed a few yards away. Pete's body collapsed into the ropes and hung at an odd angle.

'You think this is justice?' shouted Golden Jim. 'This is not justice! This is summary execution without a trial. How can you call this justice?!'

Bill stared at Golden Jim. 'We are your peers.' He indicated with a sweep of his right arm, all of us standing around watching. 'We are pirates, like you. Yet, we do not burn down other people's villages, kill women and children, steal other pirates' ships. indeed, we do not make war on fellow pirates, all of which you have done. Hence, we have judged you to be guilty of these crimes, for which our code demands the death penalty. Our code calls for you, and your entire gang to be exterminated. However, we are not the blood thirsty pirates, you are. It is your style of piracy which gives piracy a bad name. You shall surely meet your maker in hell!'

Bill spat on the ground and then calmly took out his other pistol. He shot Creepy Carl through his left temple. Carl's body slumped forward, a massive hole seeping blood and brains on the right side of his head.

Golden Jim winced as he received a piece of skull and brain on his coat.

'You are disgusting!' shouted Golden Jim, looking aghast at the mess on his coat. 'Look at what you have done to my coat!'

Bill laughed and looked at Golden Jim with some admiration. 'You are about to die and you are worried about your coat?'

Golden Jim stared at Bill, 'I have my pride.' He frowned at the human remains on his precious garment.

'Where you are going, you won't need your coat!' laughed George.

Everyone laughed. It was a funny moment during an otherwise, very grim affair.

Bill calmly walked over to George and took the loaded pistol George handed him. Then he walked over to Hogshead McLinty.

The huge man began to plead for his life in a most pitiable manner.

Golden Jim admonished him to be a man, but McLinty began to cry and slobbered that he would denounce Golden Jim and be our most obedient servant.

'You traitor!' shouted Golden Jim, as he angrily strained against his ropes. 'I trained you. I gave you a home! You traitor! I saved you from the gallows!'

Golden Jim continued to rave, but our captain paid no attention. Calm as a clam, he put the pistol to McLinty's left temple and blew his brains out.

McLinty's body stayed in the same position it was, it being too huge to slump over.

Bill walked over to me and asked if I wanted to finish Golden Jim.

I looked at my friends, one at a time.

They all stared back at me. Nobody said a word.

It was a moment that I shall never forget, as my heart began to race in my chest. I knew this was the moment which, if I seized it, would render me a man of respect amongst my pirate peers, a man who could stand equally next to William Bartleby. If I refused, I would remain merely a quill pusher, writing a book about pirates, with no real hard experience, and a loss of respect from my friends.

After, what must have been a long pause, I nodded and took the pistol from my sash. I slowly cocked the trigger. Then, with trembling knees and a racing heart, I stepped towards Golden Jim.

It began to rain.

Jim must have sensed my fear, because he immediately began shouting at me. 'You don't have the guts to shoot me! You're just a spineless jellyfish! Come on, I dare you to shoot me, you ball less excuse for a pirate!'

A flash of lightning lit the scene with an eerie instant of blue light.

I turned and looked at Bill. He nodded, and gestured to do the job, as a terrible crack of thunder reverberated through the jungle outside the compound.

I looked at Golden Jim staring defiantly at me, rain drops falling from his brow.

He spat in my direction.

I regarded Golden Jim coldly and thought about my African friends. I saw Donka Petu's contorted face and shivered. Then I thought of my other good friends, blown up by Golden Jim's cannons. As I saw their faces before my eyes, my heart hardened. I stared directly into Golden Jim's eyes as I placed the pistol to his forehead. A huge flash of light lit the scene as I calmly, in slow motion, pulled the trigger. Thunder reverberated the air immediately thereafter.

I heard the blast and felt the pistol recoil, but I was not directly conscious, as everything appeared, like in a dream. Golden Jim's body slumped forward, ever so slowly, as I put the pistol back into my sash. A blinding flash of light lit up our world, followed by a heart stopping crack of thunder, which rolled through the thick air like a dragon. I looked down at the deed I had committed. A massive hole in the back of Golden Jim's head was already collecting rain. Jim's blood was drifting away in a trickle of water.

As I stared at the dead pirate, I felt nothing. I had no remorse. I had become pistol proof. I felt I had done the Lord's work.

Walking back to my friends, a mighty cheer filled the air, and my name was shouted, over, and over.

'Peter, Peter, Peter!!!'

I had begun a new chapter in my life as a pirate.

Chapter Fifteen

When the dirty deeds were done, we gathered everyone, who was not riding wagons or horses back to town, and had them go into every building, to see that nothing was forgotten. As each building was searched, others followed and set kegs of gunpowder in strategic locations. Others sprinkled kerosene.

Upon completion of the searches and preparations for conflagrations, we gathered everyone, who was left, into the brigantine. Then we lobbed thirteen cannon balls into the fort and set off several explosions, resulting in instant ignitions inside the dry wooden buildings. The fact that it was raining did not impede the flames. They built up to roaring monsters before the roofs were consumed. Golden Jim's fort became a hellish inferno, instantly drying the rain which fell on the compound, producing a thick cloud of steam, making an eerie, otherworldly spectacle; a true wonder to behold. Bright orange flames devoured the wooden structures like ravenous beasts. Their roar was frightening. Everyone cheered when Golden Jim's house collapsed and fell to the ground.

Satisfied that we had done the Lord's work, as best we could, we unfurled the sails, put out the oars, and had the remainder of Golden Jim's gang, including the six we had tied to the masts, row us back to Maracaibo.

The six miles back to town were slow going for the brig, it being heavy with cargo. However, the pirates were strong men and needed very little coaxing to cooperate with us. They rowed through the night as I slept heavily on the magnificent bed in the Master's cabin of the *Navigator*.

I awoke to the sound of cheering. The sound was loud and enthusiastic. As I regained my consciousness, I sensed that the sound was coming from the port side of the ship. Crawling out of bed, I walked to the windows and opened a shutter. Blinding sunlight filled the cabin. I had to blink a number of times for my dilated pupils to adjust to the brilliant light of a glorious morning. I could see that we were arriving in Maracaibo. The oars were pulled into the ship and the oar ports slammed shut. Then the brig was gently nudged against the dock and made fast with hawsers. All the while a great cheering crowd of Marabinos were chanting, 'Peter, Peter, Peter!!!'

Rubbing my eyes, I looked around to see if there were some decent clothes for me to put on, my own looking considerably worse for wear. My shirt was torn, my breeches had a huge hole in them, and were so filthy, they might as well be burned. As for hose and boots, only my boots were still of any use, but were covered in blood and mud. When I looked at my person, a worse sight greeted me. I was in dire need of a bath and toilette.

The brigantine was a very modern vessel. Thankfully, the Master's cabin had its own head, which I used gratefully. Then, locating the Master's bath tub, which was stowed under the large roomy bed, I pulled it out, intent upon a bath. I opened the door a crack and peeked out to see if anyone was in the gangway. I was surprised by Nickolas, who had been standing outside my door, apparently waiting for me to get up. His skin was so dark, I almost didn't see him, in the dim light of the gangway. He was standing next to an other man, whom I did not recognize; a pirate from Golden Jim's gang. At their feet were four pails of steaming hot water, in the man's hand was a big bar of lye soap.

'This man will be your servant,' said Nickolas. 'William thought you might want a bath and a change of clothes.'

I smiled and thanked the two men for bringing the hot water, which they poured into the bath tub. Before they left, I asked Nickolas to send my compliments to Bill. When the two men were gone, I locked the door and gratefully sank my body into the hot water.

I don't know how long I soaked in that wonderful tub, it felt so good. After all what had happened, I realized that my body had withstood quite a lot of stress and injury. Blood was still tainting the bath water, as I washed off the remains of hundreds of bites, stings, and scrapes. The lye from the soap made the wounds sting and I rinsed as quickly as possible.

When my bath was done, I dried off on a large cotton towel, which had been hanging behind the door of a large closet full of Golden Jim's clothes, not all of it gold in colour; and all of it a perfect fit for me; except for his boots, which were two sizes too large, but suitable enough to wear, in order to make an appropriate appearance on deck, to acknowledge the cheering crowd of Marabinos.

I chose a magnificent white shirt of the finest cotton, with ruffled cuffs, and frills on the chest. For breeches, I chose a pair of soft green doe hide. For hose, I chose silk. The waistcoat was a matching green doe hide, with Celtic designs stitched into the leather. The belt, which I found, after rummaging about in the closet, was a thick brown strip of expensive leather with a golden buckle. My hair being wet, I chose not to wear a hat, although there were several to choose from. From seven pairs of shoes, I chose a pair of brown ones, with golden buckles; stuffing the toes with some cotton, to prevent my feet from sliding.

Before venturing out, I checked my appearance in the full sized mirror on the closet door. I adjusted my hair and then stepped out of the cabin, feeling like a king.

When I stepped on deck, a mighty cheer rang out. I waved to everyone and smiled shyly; not being used to all that adulation, and wondering if I even deserved it. It was Marianne, after all, who stirred the people up with her speech.

When I walked up to Bill, George, and Robert, they each shook my hand and gave me a warm hug, all the while grinning from ear to ear.

'You're the man of the hour, Peter,' said Bill, smiling. 'You saved our lives. You killed Golden Jim. You are now completely pistol proof. It is no accident that you were sleeping in the Master's cabin, because we have decided that the *Navigator*, from now on, will be your ship to command. You have earned it.' Then he looked at the men gathered on deck, watching me. 'Isn't that so, boys? Hasn't Peter earned command of the *Navigator*?'

The men cheered enthusiastically, affirming my mastery of the ship.

I know I was grinning from ear to ear, as I spoke a few words of thanks for their vote of confidence in me. I expressed how honored I felt and vowed I would do my best to be a fair and honest captain. When I was finished speaking, each of the men gave me a warm hug and a firm handshake, confirming their loyalty.

When we had completed unloading the last of the cargo bound for Maracaibo, we took stock of our supplies for the trip back to our island. We realized we needed to address a serious shortage of essential commodities. Hence, we took on ten more hogsheads of fresh water, five for each brig, fresh fruit and vegetables, fifty bags of coffee, and one hundred of sugar, those commodities not being overly abundant in our stores. We also stocked up on fire wood, for the ships' galley fires. For fresh food we acquired two cows, five goats, two sheep, and twenty chickens.

That evening, we said our good byes to the people of Maracaibo with a fantastic party at the inn, where our women and children had stayed. The farewell party lasted for three days. What a farewell party it was. The people of Maracaibo would not soon forget us.

We left the shores of Venezuela some time in the afternoon on April 15th, 1782. I watched the shore line of Venezuela recede from a comfortable chair in the Great Cabin of my new ship. As I sat, contemplating my future as a pirate captain, I sipped a fine brandy from a crystal glass and watched the sunset over a horizon devoid of land in any direction one looked.

Fifteen Marabino men and seven women came back with us, intent on a new life on our island. Half of this group was sailing with William and George on the *Royal Rover*, that being the name of the other brig. Our new friends were named: Anne, Carlos, Charles, Christopher, Cristobal, Edmond, Isaac, James, Jesus, Johan, Johanna, Juan, Karen, Katerine, Kathleen, Maarten, Marguerite, Martin, Paul, Pedro, Phillip, and Tula.

I got to know the new people quite well on the six day voyage to Jamaica. Everyone of them was friendly and willing to fit in with our routines, and with each other. The Marabinos had brought some musical instruments with them, so that we had a lot of fun, sailing side by side, with people playing instruments on both ships; a seafaring symphony of drums, fiddles, and flutes. Many of us joining in with our own improvised instruments; wooden spoons on kegs, a hammer against a cannon ball, two cannon balls against each other, two pot lids, while others danced jigs and reels on the decks.

After six days of pleasant sailing, we made port in Kingston, early afternoon on April 21st. Everybody immediately went ashore, after the ships were secured, in order to go shopping, sightseeing, or just to sit on the beach and soak up some Jamaican rum punch, which Robert had mixed up in a large pot. After six days on board ship, it was nice to go for a walk, which I did with Bill, Marianne, and two year old Michael, an adorable little fellow with curly blond hair, which Marianne had formed into two little braids.

Walking along the main street, we came upon a small group of people intently reading a broadside, pasted on the town notice board. However, it was not the broadside which drew our attention, but the notice next to it; complete with sketches.

The notice proclaimed that our gang, identified as the Bartleby Pirates, were, 'Blood Thirsty Scoundrels of the Very Worst Sort, responsible for a long string of violent captures of merchant ships from many nations.' Our two ships, the *Bon Adventure*, and the *Phoenix* were specifically named. Fortunately for us, those two ships were no longer in our possession. A hefty reward was being offered for us, dead or alive.

Fortunately, the sketches were not very accurate. None of the people, standing around the notice board, recognized us.

Then, as Marianne scanned the notice board she pointed out an old weathered poster demanding the head of Golden Jim. The reward offered would have been a goodly sum, had we brought his head with us. Unfortunately, we had not done so, and just as well. I have no stomach for decapitations. I don't think any of us did.

Reading the poster's descriptions, I saw that Jim's two brigantines were named, along with the three sloops we had destroyed. We never thought to repaint the names, and realized we had better do that, as soon as possible. Without drawing any undue attention to our selves, we just pretended to be curious tourists and moved on, heading directly back to our ships.

The wanted poster gave us very good reason to not spend another hour in Jamaica; a rapid return to our island became our immediate concern. When everyone had returned to the ships, we held a war council and explained the situation, necessitating our quick exit from Kingston. Everyone understood the need for urgency and immediately set about replenishing our fresh supplies, buying some paint, and making absolutely certain to prevent information leaking to the authorities.

Next morning we slipped out of Kingston harbour. Within a short while we had put out a full parade of sails and beat steadily before the wind. We did not bother to make port in either, Cuba, or Hispaniola, as we sailed through the Windward Passage full speed ahead, anxious to be safely home.

I couldn't wait to see Virginia and my children. We had been gone well over two months, I reckoned. The entire trip wasn't to have lasted more than a month, at most. I wondered if Virginia thought something had happened to us. I prayed she was not too anxious over me.

As soon as we were some leagues from Jamaica, several of our men began removing the old names off the brigs, while we thought of new names. Many different names were bandied about; *Phoenix III, Cleopatra, King Solomon, Royal Fortune, the Great Ranger, the King James, Fortune's Dream*, being some of the names I remember from that day of brain storming, over pints of excellent Jamaican rum. The name which we chose for Bill's ship was, *Alpha One*. The name we chose for my ship was, *Omega Two*. We all thought the Greek letters sounded interesting and gave a designation to our two ships, as in Bill's ship was our flag ship, and my ship was our second. Just as I was the second captain of our gang.

Had Red Eric survived the attack on Golden Jim, he would have been the third captain of a triumvirate. As I thought of him, I missed the old rogue. Red Eric was a colorful character, who is probably pulling a fast one on the devil, as I write this.

On the second day out we spied sails on the horizon. At first we were not sure what kind of ship we were seeing, however, as the day progressed, the ship was coming ever closer towards us. Eventually, we could plainly see with our spyglasses, the ship was an English man of war. Fortunately, Golden Jim had equipped the brigs with assorted flags, so we quickly ran up English flags. The new names were freshly painted on the transoms.

By mid afternoon, the man of war was close enough to hail us with a speaking trumpet. 'What ships are ye? Where are ye bound? What is your cargo?' shouted the boatswain through the trumpet.

Colin shouted back, through our speaking trumpet, that we were bound for England, with a cargo of tobacco, sugar, and dried fish. He did not name our ship.

The boatswain then asked about our other ship.

Colin told them that she was our sister ship and was carrying the same cargo, bound for Wapping.

The boatswain shouted back that, when they sailed past Wapping, the Admiralty was hanging three pirates that day. Then he asked if we had seen pirates in the Caribbean.

Of course Colin answered in the negative, as did everyone else on board.

For some reason the officers of the man of war became suspicious of us. I do not think they thought that we were honest Englishmen. Perhaps we were too enthusiastic, regarding not seeing any pirates. I don't know what it was, but the next words which came from the navy speaking trumpet was, 'We are sending over a boarding party to inspect your cargo. Please have your manifests prepared for examination.'

As the boatswain spoke those words, I looked at Bill, standing on the rear quarter deck of his ship, watching proceedings through his spy glass, a hundred yards off my starboard side. I am sure he must have heard the commands from the man of war.

My blood froze, as I raced through my head trying to come up with a plan. Giving the man of war a firm broadside might invite disaster. The navy ship was carrying at least sixty guns, mostly twenty five pounders, which could tear us to shreds if they were unleashed. However, since we were somewhat lower in the water, our guns were perfectly trained to punch holes in the navy ship, with an increased possibility we might punch holes below its water line, if we were lucky. If we were stealthy, we could possibly effect a significant problem for them. Knowing Bill, he would rise to the occasion and I could expect him to be blasting into the monstrous ship, within minutes. My gamble was whether the man of war's guns were manned and ready to be rolled out.

I decided to discuss our options with Colin and Robert.

Colin thought we should wait for the inspectors and then take them hostage.

Robert thought we should just break their necks and sail away, possibly jettisoning cargo to lighten our ships. However, he did like the idea of attempting to sink the English ship.

I thought it a risky venture, however, if we could communicate the idea to Bill, perhaps the two of us would have a chance.

I decided to take a chance and asked two of my men to row across to *Alpha One,* and ask Bill if he would consider sinking the man of war.

Bill's answer was an enthusiastic affirmative. He was already moving his ship into position, as my men returned with the long boat.

In the meantime, the man of war had lowered a boat, manned by six rowers, a boatswain's mate, and two officers. Moments later, they rowed across to my ship and asked permission to come on board.

I gave permission.

The two officers climbed up the ladder and stepped on deck. They introduced each other as, Lieutenant McBeal, and Ensign Raleigh. Then the lieutenant asked to see the manifests.

I told them that they were in the Master's cabin and invited them to come in for a glass of brandy.

The two officers accepted my offer of hospitality and stepped into the cabin; Colin and Robert following. Alas, for the two officers, my cabin was the last thing they saw in the world, as Robert and Colin neatly snapped their necks.

Moments later, Bill had managed to move his ship into position, the navy ship thinking he was merely coming closer to facilitate the inspections. However, the real intent became abundantly clear when Bill ran up his black battle flag and fired thirteen twelve pounders directly into the hull of the man of war.

Frantic orders were sounded from the quarterdeck of the man of war, as sailors scrambled to ready the ship for battle. In the meantime, Bill's men had reloaded their cannons and fired another round into the port side of the navy ship, punching many holes which began to ship water.

Our men had no choice but to shoot the sailors in the long boat, which they did, bang, bang, bang.

The sudden strange turn of events unnerved the officers on the man of war, where confusion reigned. The English officers didn't know who they should attend to first, me or Bill, as I ordered a volley into the man of war's starboard side.

Since Bill was maneuvering into place, all attention went to Bill's ship, enabling my men to fire another round from our twelve pounders directly into the starboard hull, punching numerous more holes, and splintering several guns.

Before the man of war had a chance to fire, we caught the wind, as our gunners quickly reloaded and we sailed ahead, neatly out of range of their starboard guns.

Meantime, Bill had come around the stern of the man of war and let go another barrage directly into the rudder of the navy ship, rendering it a useless pile of splinters.

The man of war shot four twenty pounders out of its transom, but all they did was punch holes in Bill's sails.

Meantime, my men had reloaded our cannons. As we came around in front of the man of war, we let go a volley from our port side guns, directly into her bows, splintering her bowsprit, which brought a pile of rigging and sails down onto the beleaguered ship.

With the loss of her rudder and bowsprit, the navy ship was a lame duck and could not possibly come after us. So, before the man of war could get another shot at us, we merrily sailed away, with fifes and drums playing a happy jig, as we dumped the officers' bodies overboard and set course for home, knowing that we would have to, yet again, change the names of our ships.

A few hours later, the weather started to turn. Dark clouds gathered off the stern and lightning began to flash on the horizon. Soon the wind picked up, driving us ahead at eight knots. Rain began to pelt the deck. I went into my cabin and watched the storm with my friends, Bernard, Colin, Robert, Meira, Russell, Samantha, Susanne, and Wendy. Little

Jasper was sleeping on my bed, and Jocelyn was playing with the buckle of a belt, which she had pulled down from a chair.

As we sat together, watching the storm, we wondered if the *Swallow* could withstand a serious storm with a broken rudder. We all secretly hoped they wouldn't make it, because we knew for certain, if that ship returned to England, our days could be numbered. There would be little doubt a serious hunt for us would ensue, forthwith.

'We should have finished the job,' said Robert. 'We can't rely on a storm to do the work for us. This storm is nothing that ship couldn't handle.'

Just as he had spoken, a brilliant flash of light lit up the cabin, immediately followed by a crack of thunder, which shivered the glass in the windows, and made Jocelyn cry. We could hear the wind had picked up considerably. We could feel the waves crashing against the ship, timbers creaking and groaning. I quickly emptied my glass of wine and put on a rain slicker. I told the women to relax and enjoy the lightning show, while I went on deck to oversee our course.

The other men ran to find slickers for themselves, and joined me on deck, moments later. The storm was becoming a squall. Fortunately, the men who had minded the deck, knew about sailing and had set the appropriate sails, just enough to keep our ship before the wind, and at a reasonable speed. Too fast and we would take too much water over our bows. As it was, the brig was already springing little leaks from the constant pounding against weathered caulking.

Twelve foot seas began washing over the decks, as the wind howled in the rigging. I had to yell loudly for my orders to be heard, the storm roaring like a pack of lions ready for the kill. I couldn't imagine riding out a storm, such as the one which hit us, without a rudder. The waves would push the ship aside until broadsides careened her. I felt sad for the unfortunate sailor men, many of whom were probably pressed into His Majesty's service. However, we were at war with the English, and the man of war was an English ship, which could have spelled a lot of trouble for us, 'The Liberators of Maracaibo.'

By morning the storm had abated and we were none the worse for wear. Our two brigantines rode the storm through, wonderfully. I could see Bill, a half a league off my starboard bow. He had flown a bright green pennant from the top main mast, signaling all was well. I requested that Pabu run up our pennant, which was in the flag locker. Moments later, we too, boasted a long green pennant on our top main mast.

We arrived at our island on the morning of April 27th. Of course, our friends had no way of knowing who we were, our ships not being familiar to them. We could see that the red flag had been run up on the observation platform. Our friends would be running to man the coastal defenses. We had to set their minds at ease. Thus we anchored off shore, flying friendly colours. We lowered our boat and Bill, George, Colin, Robert, Russell, and I rowed our boat ashore, hallelujah!

When our friends realized it was us returning from Maracaibo, great shouts of, 'Hallelujah!' and 'Praise the Lord!' and, 'They're back, they're back!!' came from the shore. Moments later, everyone was jumping up and down on the beach and waving to us, to row faster. The moment I saw my sweet Virginia, with Catherine on her right hand, and Joshua in her left arm, my heart melted. I began to row faster, as did the others, all of us anxious to be reunited with our friends and loved ones.

The moment I touched ground I ran to my little family and grabbed them into my arms and hugged, and hugged, and hugged, and kissed my dearly beloved, long and lingering. I drank her up as my eyes filled with tears of joy at seeing her and my beautiful children, safe and healthy. It was so good to be home.

When our friends on the brigs saw that the coast was clear, they weighed anchors and rowed towards the entrance passage. Long boats were manned and the brigs towed safely through the corral channel, into our crystal clear cove, where the two handsome brigantines presented a very beautiful picture, as they lay at anchor in the calm water.

When everyone was finally on shore, introductions were made, as we all stood in a huge circle, each person saying their name and stating their special skills. It took fully over an hour by the time everyone was finished introducing themselves. Then, those who had been together on the island, showed the new people our town, and helped them get settled in.

Initially, the new people stayed with some of the original members, until they built their own houses, which was not long in coming. But, I am getting ahead of myself.

As was our custom, a massive bonfire was readied on the beach, and a sumptuous feast prepared. Some of the new women quickly added their culinary arts to the development of the feast, while the others became friendly with those members who had stayed on the island, while we went to Maracaibo. Numerous toasts; to the bravery of Red Eric and his gang, to me, to us, to our new friends, and to the devil, King George, helped to oil and smooth the introductions, so that, by the time we all ate together, everyone was in a jolly mood and ready for a party.

Needless to say, as you dear reader already know, when we partied, we partied heartily. The fun was aided by the full moon, and the fact we now had a number of musicians, who struck up a magnificently varied array of jigs, polkas, reels, and assorted other dances, the names of which escape me, because I doubt if there were actually names for the dances we danced around the fire that night.

Our new friends partied heartily along with the rest of us, and many new friendships evolved over the five days that this particular party lasted.

By the time we all sobered up again, we came to the realization we were running out of rum, and our other libations were not going to last much longer, either. The realization of our forthcoming beverage shortage was a further stimulus to sobriety. Running out of the beverages of our choice would mean a significant change to our life style. Something had to be done. We had no choice. With no rum, we had less fun in the sun.

Before we sent the brigs out to go roving, we off loaded the cargo we brought back from Venezuela and packed the goods into our warehouse. While we off loaded, others made certain to change the names of the ships. This time William's ship became, *Divine Retribution*, and my ship became, *The Lord's Vengeance*. We were certain the names would bring good fortune to our upcoming piratical endeavors.

When the names were dry, the ships were loaded with enough supplies for two weeks of roving, with significantly less rum than normal, that being the reason we were going out, in the first place.

Virginia asked if I would stay home this time, and, even though I was captain, I preferred to sit that trip out. I had been away from my sweet lover for much too long. It was almost like I had to get to know her all over again. The exploration was so sweet, she was so yielding. I loved her with all my heart and soul. It was so good to be back on our island, with her and the children, the days just drifted by, almost like in a dream.

Eventually, I began noticing the additions which had accrued in the course of over two months' absence. The garden was now surrounded with a strong fence, to keep the pigs out. The meeting hall had another addition, which served as a game room, where three card tables and fifteen chairs were the predominant furniture. The card tables had come off one of the ships we robbed on a cruise, a year or more previously. A wet bar was built against the far end, complete with tapped hogsheads in the wall. Now we finally had a real place for those huge barrels.

A large underground shelter had been dug out and lined with wooden planks, the entire thing well supported with massive wooden support columns. The builders made it to hold a hundred people, sitting tightly side by side on benches. The centre area contained a table. At one end they had built a private area for a head, with a removable barrel, and a barrel of water, for washing. The latter was ingeniously hung up to provide running water through a pipe, with a spigot. The barrel could be filled from above ground. The former barrel sat in a hollow, and provided a perfect head to sit on. The barrel was fixed with three handles, to which hooks could be attached, in order to hoist the barrel out of the hole and dispose of the contents on our manure pile, down wind from the town. The shelter would serve in the event of severe storms, or as a hideout, in the event of an attack.

The observation platform now sported a closed in head, as well, with a bucket system on a rope, which enabled, who ever drew cleaning duty, to lower the bucket down the hill, in order to dump it in the latrine pit. The pit and the head lined up, so the entire operation was easily facilitated once per week.

The horses had produced another foal.

The chickens had made many more chickens.

Our village was becoming a town.

Perhaps it was time we gave our town a name, I suggested, as Virginia and I were walking, hand in hand, past the houses of our friends, on the way to the beach with our children. Virginia thought it should be called after Bill. 'Williamsville,' she suggested.

I thought it had a very nice ring to it. Of course I told Virginia that Bill would not likely agree to such an honour, he being far too modest for that.

Virginia was not so sure that Bill would decline. She would bring it up at the next council meeting, she said.

'And an other thing we should bring up,' she said quite seriously, all of a sudden, 'Is our trip to Halifax. We have spoken of it so often, over the years. Now that you have your own ship, and we have more people, maybe, just maybe we can go, Peter. It is important that our children know their grandparents.'

I knew it was true. Children should know who their grandparents are, if there is a chance of that. However, in our mixed up crazy world, not everyone gets that opportunity. 'Some of us have no parents, some of us are orphans, we all grow up and manage to live our lives, don't we? To travel to Halifax would be a great risk.' I was not sure if I was prepared to take such a risk. Our lives were still wanted by the English Crown. It does not give up easily when it has been insulted by common folk, such as us. The thought of a noose around Virginia's neck made me shudder. I did not feel the trip was worth the risk.

However, Virginia was adamant and continued to bother me with her ideas for a trip to Nova Scotia. She began withholding her favors from me, which became quite bothersome. It amazes me how a woman can have such control over her sexual urges, that she can easily close her legs and let her man suffer the agony of abstinence; when her scent surrounds his world and excites him to passion.

Eventually, I gave in, and promised to discuss the plan with Bill. The moment I said those words, Virginia suddenly became her passionate self again. She rocked my cradle for a good part of the night, after wards.

Anyway, after an absence of nearly three weeks, our brigantines returned, none the worse for wear, and loaded with libations of many kinds, but mostly rum and wine. They also brought back two chests filled with silver pieces of eight, a chest full of jewelry, four boxes full of fine pewter plate, two chests of fine bone china, twelve bales of excellent leather, twelve bales of cotton, twenty six pigs, forty chickens, sixteen breadfruit plants in pots, a large crucifix, a chest full of books in English, French, and Spanish, five hundred pounds of candles, thirty barrels of dried fish, twenty one barrels of salt, and a dozen fine ladies' dresses. All together it was a good haul.

That night a big bonfire celebrated the return of our rovers. We spread a sail on the ground and dispersed the coins and jewelry from the chests, the bigger shares going to the two captains, Bill and George. Those of us who did not go roving, did not share in the spoils, other than the consumables. The coins and jewels only went to those who actively participated in the piracy. I thought that to be abundantly fair and just. However, one of the Marabinos, a man named Juan, did not think it was fair that he didn't get a share of the coins, just because he stayed behind nursing a sore shoulder.

Bill tried to explain to Juan how our code worked.

Unfortunately, Juan was not interested in listening and became quite vociferous in his demands for a share of the coins. As he continued to consume more and more rum, he became ever more belligerent.

Juan's friends tried to settle him down; one of them even gave him two of his coins, but the irate pirate would not back down. He pushed his friends aside and drew his cutlass, all the while berating Bill and the rest of us for, cheating him out of his share of the swag.

Bill warned the man to put his sword down. 'You have been drinking,' said Bill, trying to stay calm and in control of the situation. 'Right now you are not in your right mind, Juan.'

The drunken Marabino took great offense at the suggestion that he was not in his right mind. As he raised his cutlass, he shouted that he would show Bill, who was not in his right mind.

Bill again asked Juan, calmly, to put his cutlass down, and stop embarrassing himself in front of the company.

Juan stared wildly at Bill and then told us we could all go to hell.

Then, suddenly, without warning, he lunged at Bill, striking our beloved captain on the shoulder with his cutlass.

Bill fell backwards, tripping over the log he had been sitting on. When he landed on his back, his head smashed against a big rock jutting out of the sand. The impact cracked Bill's skull and killed him on the spot.

Juan, not knowing Bill was dead, stumbled after him, but his progress was immediately arrested with a pistol shot through his right knee, administered by George, from twenty yards.

Marianne and I were the first to reach Bill. Marianne saw the blood gushing from her husband's head and screamed, 'Bill, oh no, Dear God!' She sunk down on his chest, sobbing uncontrollably.

Juan lay on the sand screaming in pain; his right knee fractured by the ball from George's pistol. However, no one bothered to attend to Juan, all of us completely stunned by what had just happened.

Juan's screaming cut through our stunned silence.

George stepped over to him and smacked Juan soundly on the skull, with the handle of his pistol.

The screaming stopped and we attended to our fallen captain.

When I felt it was an appropriate time, I gently pulled Marianne away from Bill and sat with her on the log, my arm around her shoulders. Virginia sat on her other side and put an arm around her distraught friend, as well.

Colin, George, and Robert, carefully lifted the body and carried it to the meeting hall, where we could prepare it for a proper burial. Everyone else slowly walked back to their houses, the party having ended on a tragic note.

Russell and I dragged Juan to a post and tied him up with his hands behind his back. We poured some sea water on his wound, to clean it, and then left him to his suffering.

Virginia led Marianne back to our house, where little Michael lay sleeping beside Catherine. Both women were devastated and sobbing uncontrollably.

Me, I was stunned. Losing Bill like that, to a drunken sailor, was not how I foresaw his demise. The entire episode came as a great surprise and a powerful lesson.

Eventually, we all managed to fall asleep in our grief; me dreaming images of our amazing friend, whom we had rescued from the Halifax jail, those seven short years ago. When I mentioned my dreams to Marianne and Virginia, the following morning at breakfast, they said that they had also dreamed of Bill. He was going to be sorely missed.

Everyone in the village was very sad all through that long day, following Bill's passing. Even Juan, now sober and in terrible pain, was remorseful to some degree. However, few took pity on him. Drinking is one thing, but if one becomes irresponsible because of it, there was no excuse for it in our colony. Our leaders, myself included, always set the example, we were always happy drunks. No one ever raised a fist in anger at his brother or sister, on our island, until that fateful night when Bill was killed.

Bill's death gave us all pause to consider the very real need for a set of written rules, which all members had to sign, before becoming a member of our colony. Pirates had written codes in the past, we felt it was imperative we had one too; a constitution in which our rules were spelled out, plain as the text on this paper. Although we would continue to recruit with care and attention, we felt a set of articles, spelling out in writing what we were about, would avoid a confusion such as occurred the night before. Obviously, Juan did not understand, clearly enough, what our rules were.

Andrew, Colin, George, Robert, Russell, and I discussed the issue of written rules, while sitting on our platform later in the afternoon. We talked at great length over cups of rum, all the while enjoying the magnificent view of the ocean and the other little islands, which helped to lift our mood, somewhat.

As we discussed laws for our colony, our women dressed Bill for his wake, to be held that night. In the hot climate it was imperative that we took care of his funeral, as quickly as possible. There was no time to waste in that regard. Bodies decompose quickly in the tropics.

As I discussed a fine point in the wording of an article, I realized that we were all in a very serious mood. Bill's death had pulled a dark shroud of mourning over our colony. However, we persevered, often breaking with anecdotes about our dead friend and former captain. There were moments when we had to look away and deal with the flow of brine from our eyes.

Even though we were a pirate colony, founded on a firm belief in freedom, we six felt ourselves to be the rightful directors of the affairs of our colony, being its original members, and hand picked by the man, whom we came to regard as the founder, William Bartleby. We realized, Bill's death necessitated the writing of the law. We could not risk any future misunderstandings.

Since I was the quill pusher, I wrote suggestions down in my notebook and eventually, some days later, came up with the written code which we proposed to the colony and had everyone sign.

Following are the articles we incorporated for the continued smooth running of our colony:

1.

Every man or woman member of our colony shall have an equal vote in affairs of moment. He or she shall have equal access to all fresh provisions or strong liquors at any time, unless a shortage may make it necessary for the common good to vote a retrenchment.

2.

Every man and woman shall share according to his or her station in the booty gained by participation in a raiding venture. No one has a right to swag who has not participated in its gain, with the exception of food and drink.

3.

Any man or woman who strikes another in anger will be subject to expulsion from the colony. Or, if the case be a mutual argument, the matter will be settled with pistols or swords on the beach. The first to draw blood will be declared the winner.

4.

Any man or woman who defrauds the colony to the value of even one shilling in plate, jewels, or money, shall be marooned.

5.

Any man or woman who steals from a colony member will be marooned.

6.

Every man and woman in the colony will keep their weapons in excellent working order at all times. Failure to do so on the first offense will result in a warning from the master at arms. Failure to maintain weapons a second time will result in disciplinary action at the discretion of the captain, and two other officers.

7.

Any man who seduces another man's woman will be marooned.

8.

Any member of the colony who deserts his or her post in time of battle will be marooned.

9.

Any man or woman who kills a member of the colony will be subject to the death penalty. Method of execution determined by a vote of all colony members.

10.

Any man or woman who shall lose a limb, or in some other way be incapacitated, shall be provided for by the colony at the same level of all other members.

11.

The captain and the quartermaster shall each receive two shares of a prize, the master gunner and boatswain, one and one half shares, all other officers one and one quarter, and private ladies and gentlemen of the colony one share each.

12.

The first member of the colony who sights a prize will receive his or her choice of the finest small arms found on board the said trophy.

13.

Under no circumstances will any member of the colony coerce another to pirate. Any member found to be responsible for coercion will be marooned.

14.

Married members of the colony are under no obligation to pirate and do so entirely of their own free will with the full consent of their spouse.

15.

Gratuitous violence against officers and crew of captured prizes is strictly forbidden. Any member found to have broken this rule will be marooned. The only violence condoned by this colony is that which is justified in case of resistance shown by the prize in question.

Everyone thought that the articles were fair and made good sense. No one refused to sign the articles at the bottom of the large vellum, upon which I had written the words. The signing of the articles was a solemn occasion which we undertook a few days later.

But, dear reader, I am getting ahead of myself. Let's go back to Bill's wake.

As you know, we held the wake the night after he was killed. Marianne, Marta, Virginia, and Wendy prepared Bill's remains with loving attention. They had thoroughly washed his body clean of any blood and then perfumed it with spices and scents rescued from one of our prizes, a year ago. They dressed him in his best outfit; white silk hose, his favorite shoes, with the gold buckles, emerald green brocaded breeches, with a golden sash. His shirt was a fine white silk with ruffles and lace, over which they had put Bill's favorite brocade waistcoat. The women had carefully brushed Bill's beard and hair and topped him off with his favorite Spanish hat, the one with the ostrich feather.

Our African and Marabino friends built a huge bonfire on the beach, while others prepared a magnificent feast, featuring a roasted pig, and many fine preserved meats from our larder. Wapoo and Narkat had cooked a huge pot of salmagundi, and Marguerite, Kathleen, and Tula came up with an incredible salad of mixed vegetables from our garden, which they dressed with copious amounts of fine olive oil and spices. Cristobal, who was a baker by trade, baked a number of special loaves of bread. He was ably assisted by Rock and Tobie.

I remember clearly how everyone pitched in, each in his own way, to make the wake a proper send off for our dear friend. The Marabinos, in particular, made a special effort because, I believe, they were embarrassed it was one of them who had done the dirty deed. I noticed how they avoided looking at Juan, miserably tied to the post by the beach. He seemed to be in great agony, so I directed someone to bring him water. I also asked Habu to have a look at the wound on his knee. When Habu reported that it was becoming gangrenous, I told him to give Juan a hearty cup of rum, and then pour some into the wound. The rum would help to keep the wound somewhat clean, I figured, and possibly lessen his discomfort a little. However, I was under no delusion that anyone would vote to keep Juan in the realm of the living.

When night fell, the moon was still very full and lit the scene with a bright, cool light. Bill was propped up on his favorite chair, in the place of honour. The bonfire was lit and we began a party Bill would have been proud of. Speaker after speaker delivered eulogies, anecdotes, jokes, and numerous toasts to our dearly departed captain. At times, throughout the night there were moments when I had to rub my eyes and take a second look at Bill. It appeared as if he was alive and breathing.

The final words were given for me to deliver, everyone figuring, since I was the writer, I could probably deliver a suitably eloquent speech, which I did, much to Virginia's delight, she told me later. I will not bore you, dear reader, with the entire speech, however, I will give you a few highlights, to give you a general idea about what I said.

I first told the story how Bill and I met in the jail in Halifax and how we escaped and gathered up those of his friends, whom we could find in various places, to form the colony. I tried to keep the history part short and to the point, most of our people already knew that part of the story, anyway.

Then, I spoke at length about Bill, the man. How he was always fair and honest in his dealings with me and everyone else. I emphasized that

Bill had good reasons for becoming a pirate and declaring war on England. I described the scars on his back, when I first saw them. Of course, many of the men in our colony had such scars, so they could all identify with what I described, regarding Bill's treatment at the hands of English navy officials. As I spoke about the scars, I noticed several men examining each other's backs.

I spoke of Bill's generosity and his virtues as a husband and father; and about his unwillingness to support gratuitous violence, which set Bill apart from most pirates who sailed the Seven Seas. He was a man who stood as a colossus in the annals of piracy; a virtual saint of the sweet trade.

In closing I suggested we build a monument commemorating our captain. My closing words resulted in a cacophony of huzzahs. Then we drank a mighty toast to our dearly departed captain, and just continued drinking until most everybody fell into a stupor; some of the people falling asleep where they sat.

Two days later, when everyone had recovered from the wake, we reverentially carried Bill's body to the *Navigator* and towed the brig out to sea. Most of the members of the colony were on board when we gave Bill a proper sailor's funeral, sending his body overboard, wrapped in our battle flag and weighted with two twenty pound cannon balls.

We returned to our island later in the afternoon and spent the rest of the day with our families or friends; everyone under a cloud. Bill's death had cast a veil on our colony, which lasted for several weeks.

Eventually, we came around to discussing Juan's fate. It was decided that we would hold a trial in our meeting house; not one of our mock trials, but a real trial; in which all points of view were examined and a fair verdict rendered. I would serve as court clerk and note the entire proceeding.

George sat as the judge, Robert stood as the prosecutor, Colin served as defense lawyer. Twelve volunteers, selected at random, served as the jury. Everyone else served as an audience of witnesses, who could be called upon to testify. When everything was ready, Wapoo and Tobie fetched the unfortunate Marabino, whose knee by this time, had become a festering mess, surely necessitating the amputation of his leg, if he managed to win his life.

However, as circumstances unfolded, the jury found Juan guilty with regard to the charge of murder. The jury determined that Juan had lunged at Bill, with murderous intent, in spite of Bill's repeated warnings. The fact that Juan was inebriated at the time, was no excuse for his action. Our colony liked its rum, but it did not tolerate irresponsible behavior. Our lives depended on each other. Everyone had to be responsible for their actions, where the colony was concerned. Had Juan not acted as he did, our beloved captain would still be alive. The verdict of the death penalty came as no surprise to anyone, including Juan. The torment of his ruined knee, made the certainty of death, a welcome relief to look forward to.

Knowing that Juan was suffering terribly from his wound, we determined to make his end a quick and relatively painless one. We all reckoned Juan had suffered enough pain and was repentant before God. We would not prolong his agony and immediately after the pronouncing of the sentence, Tobie and Wapoo dragged Juan outside and set him down against the stake, to which he had been tied. Then George took a pistol from his belt, cocked the trigger, and walked calmly and deliberately towards Juan. He asked Juan if he wanted to say any final words.

'I am sorry,' he said. 'Please forgive me, and may God have mercy on my soul.'

Then he bowed his head and closed his eyes.

George looked at Marianne.

Marianne's eyes were filled with tears.

Virginia was also crying, as were many of the women. The entire affair was an emotional time for us. It was, after Leonard, only the second time we performed an execution of one of our members. We did not take life easily. That was the example Bill had set. However, we all knew Juan had stepped over the line and there was no going back.

George looked at Juan and placed the pistol to his right temple. 'Good bye, Juan,' he said calmly, just before pulling the trigger.

An instant later it was over. Juan's body slumped on the ground, bleeding profusely from a massive hole in the left side of its head.

Several volunteers took the body in the long boat and rowed with it past the reef; unceremoniously dumping it in the sea.

Next day we began work on Bill's memorial, a seven foot cairn near our bonfire pit. The cairn was completed a week later and commemorated with a party and another huge bonfire. From its place on the cairn, Bill's sword glinted in the light of the flames. Eventually, the cairn was further graced with an inscribed slab of stone proclaiming, 'To the Memory of William Bartleby, the Greatest Pirate Captain Ever Sailed the Seven Seas.'

Chapter Sixteen

Some months after Bill's glorious wake and funeral, we began to run low on provisions. Our garden, livestock, and the forest, provided enough fresh foods, however; our ale, rum, and wine was coming to a level whereby we had to consider strict rationing again, and, indeed, had to implement same, much to everyone's distress, myself included. I had come to appreciate the constant supply of libations, and did not like the thought of finishing the day without a cup of rum, or wine.

The issue of our dwindling libations was brought up for serious discussion at our weekly meeting on August 10th, 1782. We needed to go roving again. We had no choice. Without the libations of our choice, life would become less pleasant. Minor irritations, amongst the men and women, would become serious business without the smoothing effects of the libations we had grown accustomed to keeping us jolly.

Hence, we decided to set out with my ship, provisioned for a month of sailing. Only the women with children, and their fathers, stayed behind, if they so chose.

Due to the fact I was captain of the *Navigator*, I was duty bound to go, this time.

Virginia said she did not mind too terribly much, because we had a number of wonderful months together. She figured, since we only provisioned for a month, the time would pass by quickly.

Virginia and the children spent a pleasant day with me before we left, playing in the sand, and enjoying our life together as a family. My children were growing up strong and healthy. Virginia was such a good mother to them, my children wanted for nothing. Want was not a condition the colony's children found themselves in. Everyone's children were the colony's children. Each child had a village full of aunts and uncles, who happily helped to care for them.

That night, Virginia and I made love. It was sweet and gentle. We were so deeply in love. As far as I was concerned, the sun rose and set on her. Virginia was my life. The children she gave me were my dream. Our life together was so blessed.

Next morning, flying all the flags and pennants we had, the *Navigator* sailed away on August 15th; many of our sailors standing in the yards and waving to our friends and family on shore; frantically waving back. I watched Virginia and the children through the spy glass. I could see that Virginia was crying.

I made a list of the people who stayed behind, and of those who came with us on that fateful journey. Thus, in order to set the record straight for you, dear reader, I have included the lists here in order to keep you up to date regarding those adults who stayed, and those who came with us on our fateful journey.

Those staying: Bernard, Catherine, Charles, David, Jasper, Johanna, Joshua, Marguerite, Marianne, Marta, Russell, Sam, Samantha, Sandra, Virginia, Wendy, and William.

Those sailing on the *Navigator*, of the original group: Colin, George, Robert, Meira, and I. Of the Africans: Carl, Edgar, Gaston, Habu, Nickolas, Pabu, Rock, and Tobie. Of the Marabinos: Anne, Carlos, Katerine, Christopher, Cristobal, Edmund, James, Jesus, Johan, Karen, Kathleen, Maarten, Martin, Paul, Pedro, Phillip, and Tula. Our crew was further filled out by earlier recruits: Arthur, Cody, Cory, Guy, Joseph, Kevin, Larry, and Murray. A total crew of thirty eight, well armed pirates.

However, the number was not enough, to my way of thinking. Thirty eight pirates was not much of a contending force. So far we had been lucky, however, I had a bad feeling for some reason, and suggested to George that we should put into San Juan and attempt to recruit more volunteers.

George agreed that we would have more success if our numbers were increased, so we discussed the idea with the rest of the crew. We made them understand that putting into San Juan, to recruit, considering our standards, would significantly lengthen our voyage. Fortunately, everyone understood my concerns and readily agreed to sail to Puerto Rico.

Our crossing was uneventful, for the most part. Tobie's, catching of a marlin, was about all the excitement that crossing brought. As we neared the island we hoisted our Spanish flag, to smooth our entrance into port.

We sailed past the massive Spanish fortifications into San Juan's excellent harbour, filled with ships from many nations; Dutch, English, Russian, Spanish, Swedish…loading ginger and sugar, others off loading slaves from Africa, or commodities from Europe. A large English man of war lay at anchor in the middle of the harbour.

We anchored our brig in the lee of a Dutch man of war, guarding three heavily armed merchantmen belonging to the Dutch West India Company. Twelve of us took our boat and rowed ashore. Jesus and Maarten rowed the boat back to pick up ten more men, who soon joined us on shore. Then, Arthur and Larry took a turn rowing the boat, bringing back our six women and four more men, leaving eight on board to guard the ship. All together, we were thirty on shore, a goodly recruiting force to spread out amongst the fifty thousand inhabitants of the city. We arranged to meet at the boat by nightfall.

Colin, George, Robert, Kathleen, Meira, and I chose to travel together. We decided to have a meal at an inn along the roadstead. El Toro Rojo was the name of the establishment we chose, it being quite full of sailors from many countries, it seemed to be the right place to begin. After we had sat down at a table, in the left corner of the room, a black slave came to take our orders. We first ordered drinks and then considered the menu, ordering food after the arrival of our libations.

As we sat there, sipping on our drinks, we started looking around the place to see if any likely candidates for our colony were present in the room. The inn was filled with sailors eating, drinking, smoking, conversing; having a good time in port. The place smelled of rich sauces, assorted meats roasting, tobacco, spilled ale, rum, and wine. The entire place was filled with the din of many voices trying to be heard over all the others. In other words, the place was busy, noisy, and filled with smells.

We invited two English sailors to sit with us and ordered a large meal when the slave returned to take our orders. The sailors were obviously nursing their drinks, a sure indication that they did not have much money. The sailors looked in need of some good food. We reckoned our generosity towards the English sailors might pay off with recruits. Our reasoning, regarding the invitation, is that we realized in attracting English sailors away from their ships, it would be another way to hurt the English Crown. Less sailors made their ships more of a problem to sail, especially a man of war. The English sailors appeared very nervous and constantly looked around, surveying the crowd.

I asked Tom and Franklin, that being their names, why they appeared so nervous. Their reply was, they had deserted their ship and were looking for a means to escape. If they were caught, they would be court marshaled and probably hung from a yardarm.

'If you would care to look at our ship, you will see five bodies hanging in the yardarms. Those poor blokes also tried to escape, but they were caught,' said Tom, his eyes darting from side to side.

Apparently, the two sailors, along with several hundred others on board, were impressed into the navy, and were not at all pleased to be so enslaved.

'They bonk you on the head and drag you out to sea,' said Franklin, angrily. 'The navy feeds you maggot infested biscuits and rotten beef and don't pay you for months and months, and then expect you to put your life on the line over some argument between the King and his subjects in America. I have seen too many of my friends reduced to pieces of bone and bleeding flesh. It is not the life, or death, I want for myself.'

Of course, we couldn't agree more with the two sailors and explained to them who we were, inviting them to join us, an invitation they gladly accepted.

George asked if more English sailors would be interested in joining us.

Both men heartily agreed that most of the ship's company would be interested, but were scared for their lives, because the captain and officers were cruel disciplinarians. Any indication of insubordination was met with the lash or other horrors.

'If only there was some way to rescue those poor blighters,' said Franklin. 'Life on board ship is hell. There is no other way to describe life on board the *Avenger*. Captain Chase is Satan himself.' Franklin's eyes darted from side to side, nervously alert for English marines, out looking for absent sailors.

'I don't ever want to go back to that ship,' said Tom vehemently. 'I'd sooner be hanged and have it done with. I did not come into the world, to be flogged with a cat o nine tails, and treated worse than an animal.'

'And for what?' asked Franklin. 'To be reduced to a bloody cripple, or be blown into a thousand pieces, with no recompense for your poor family back home.' Tom took a long sip from his tankard. 'I hate the navy,' he said, banging his tankard on the table.

As I listened to the two sailors vent their anger, I began to realize what excellent candidates they were for our colony. A vehement hatred for the Royal Navy would easily lead to a general hatred of the English Crown, which would serve us well with Bill's primary objective; to be a thorn in the king's side.

When the food arrived, the two sailors dug in with a gusto I had not seen before. The poor blokes were quite starved. I could not help but feel a profound pity for them. At that moment I vowed that we would rescue every sailor off that horrible ship and said so quietly to George, who heartily agreed we should, and that, indeed, we could do it.

I asked the sailors if there were people on board whom they could trust; who could be relied upon to help with the takeover of the ship.

'Mister Jones, Thomas Jones, he's a midshipman who hates the navy as much as we do. He knows everyone who has expressed a desire to leave that ship, I am certain of that,' said Tom.

'And, there is Cookie, the cook,' added Franklin. 'He stumbles about on a wooden peg, thanks to action off the American coast, two years ago. He was impressed and now he has only one leg, poor bastard. Got hit with a piece of chain, which had torn his friend into a hundred pieces. He told me about it, one day, when I was helping him serve the morning gruel. Apparently, poor Cookie was drenched in his friend's blood, and bits and pieces of flesh and bone. I think it unnerved Cookie, because I don't think he is quite normal in his head. However, if given the opportunity, I think he would slice Captain Chase in twain, at the drop of a hat.' Franklin took a long drink from his tankard.

'Then there's Barton and Brookes, Giles Gilvery, Norman Clark, Nigel, what's his name?' asked Tom, looking at his friend.

'Nigel Sutherland,' answered Franklin, cutting through a thick piece of roasted beef. 'Nigel Sutherland is powerfully strong. Captain Chase has tried to intimidate him several times, with cruel lashings, however, I am convinced, if Nigel were alone with that monster, Captain Chase would be torn asunder.'

'Then, there is Adam Newman, a giant of a man who could break Captain Chase in half, if given the opportunity,' added Tom. 'Adam would be a very good man to involve in a mutiny. Then there is, Martin Martin, and Pewee McAlister, another giant of a man, who got a severe thrashing for supposedly intimidating the first mate.' Tom took a long drink from his tankard and stared off into space for a moment. I saw the tragedy of the ship clearly portrayed in his countenance.

We listened intently as the two sailors talked about the men on board the *Avenger*. They described the men, whom we could likely trust, as a plot began to form in our minds.

When we completed the meal and consumed a few more rounds of drinks, it was the middle of the afternoon. The sun was blazing hot. We sauntered back to our boat. We rowed the two sailors to our ship and introduced them to our friends, who had remained on board to guard our vessel. When the introductions were completed, our guards rowed the boat to shore, in order to also partake in the pleasures of San Juan.

Eventually, everyone returned to our ship, bringing seven more people, who were looking for a better life under our black flag. These seven, three men and four women, were impoverished San Juanians, who had very little to lose.

That evening, we appraised the new people of our rules. We had them add their signatures to our log book. When the introductions were completed, we began serious discussions regarding the new problem we had set for ourselves; namely, how to relieve the Royal Navy of a large number of disgruntled sailors.

We decided that five of us would get ourselves hired on board the *Avenger*. The Royal Navy was always looking for sailors to replace the ones who had died of any of several causes; apyrexies, broadsides, beatings, desertions, fluxes, typhus… Life for sailors was a precarious one, at best. With us, the chances at happiness were so much better. We reckoned our strategy would result in many new recruits, once several of us got on board the man of war.

Franklin and Tom furnished us with detailed descriptions of the men, on whom we could rely. I made a point to write the descriptions into my notebook. Following are the descriptions, as they were related to us by the two English sailors.

Midshipman Jones, apparently, was a man of short stature, with a smiling face and large mutton chops. The cook, was the only man with a wooden leg, on board the man of war, so he would be easy to spot. Barton was easily identified by the red scarf he liked to wear, over his striped sailor's shirt. Apparently, he was slightly cross eyed from a beating he received, many years previously. His friend, Brookes, was a thin man, with dark rimmed eyes, and long, thin, blond hair. Giles Gilvrey, apparently, had a bulbous nose, and very red cheeks. Norman Clark had a squeaky voice, Nigel Sutherland was tall and very strong, with red hair and beard, Adam Newman was a giant of a man, who stood heads above everyone else. Life for him, in the cramped quarters of the man of war, was a hellish time spent smacking his head on bulkheads and walking about below decks, half bent over. Martin Martin was another of the trusted sailors. He had a scar which ran diagonally across his face, the result of a lashing accident. If any of them had a grudge against the navy, it would be him. And, of course, Pewee McAlister was the other one. He actually lost an eye because of the lash. Pewee was not happy with the fact he had only one eye. Pewee could easily be identified because he was also very tall. It was Pewee's job to mend sails, which enabled him to remain seated, most of the work day, he being too portly to do much else on board ship.

'How he manages to remain fat, is everyone's wonder,' said Tom, rubbing his chin. 'Food on board ship is terrible, and not very plentiful, most of the time. He must have access to the officer's food, is my guess.'

'Whatever the case is, it matters not,' added Franklin. 'Pewee is a fine fellow, with an excellent sense of humor. I'm sure he would be a welcome addition to your colony.'

Tom nodded his head and smiled. It was obvious the two sailors liked their corpulent colleague.

Sitting about on the deck of our brig, we spoke of our plans, well into the night. Many people contributed ideas, so that by the time we went to bed, a solid, well thought out plan had been worked out and agreed to. The proposed rescue was an exciting endeavor; I could hardly wait to begin.

Next morning we rose early. Arthur, Colin, George, Robert, and I got dressed in more traditional sailors' clothing, so as to appear like able bodied seamen, instead of the pirates that we were. I put on a pair of loose fitting, white, stove pipe breeches, and a blue and white striped shirt. Around my neck I knotted a bright red bandana. Over my shirt I put on a short, blue woolen jacket. On my feet I placed a pair of sturdy, buckled shoes. On my head I placed a woolen hat, and over the entire ensemble, I wore a long lapped coat. I stuck a sailor's dirk and a marlin spike in my belt.

My friends dressed somewhat similarly, except that George wore petticoat breeches.

The five of us looked like proper sailor men.

When everything was ready, we climbed into the boat with our duffel bags full of loaded pistols. We were accompanied by Carl, Edgar, Habu, and Pabu, who rowed the boat to the *Avenger*, anchored in the harbour, about six hundred yards from our brig.

The *Avenger* was a typical English man of war, three masted and square rigged, with massive fore and rear castles, and a magnificently ornate transom, carved and gilded. The ship's name was emblazoned on a rolled out scroll of oak.

We decided to row around to the port side. As we passed the bows, I looked up at the massive carved ornament. It depicted the archangel Michael, with a massive claymore in his right hand. As we rowed slowly round the port bow of the massive ship, we could plainly see five bodies gently swaying in the yardarms, just as Franklin and Tom had described. Two gulls were perched on the shoulders of one of the eye less corpses, screaming, what, I am sure, were obscenities.

A boatswain's mate peered over the side and demanded our business, in a tone of voice, not at all welcoming.

We shouted up that we were five able bodied seamen, looking for employment.

The immediate response from the boatswain's mate was to pipe us on board.

We tied our boat to the ladder. Then, we climbed up the side of that mountainous pile of timbers, until minutes later, we were standing on a very well scrubbed deck, filled with sailors engaged in assorted chores; polishing brass, fixing ropes and sails, tightening shrouds and stays… Three carpenters were hard at work repairing a broken spar. A cooper was readying the staves of a barrel for banding, nearby. Two officers strode back and forth on the main deck, observing the men working. Looking up I could see a number of sailors in the yards, repairing ropes and sails. In the top mizzen yards sailors were replacing a torn sail with a new one. The new sail stood out in the parade because it was such a different color, it not having been subjected to salt, sun, and wind, as yet. The new sail reminded me how different landlubbers looked from seasoned sailor men; with their dark brown, leathery skins and thickly calloused hands.

A severe looking boatswain and a young lieutenant climbed down from the quarter deck and approached us, momentarily.

The five of us immediately stood to attention and saluted the officers by pulling on our forelocks.

The officers appeared satisfied by the show of respect.

'State your business, or be gone with you,' said the lieutenant, firmly.

'We are five able bodied seamen, looking for gainful employment in His Majesty's Royal Navy,' said George, as sincerely as he could manage.

The lieutenant looked at the boatswain and then back at us. He rubbed his chin and looked us up and down.

'You appear to be able bodied men. We certainly can use all the men we can get. It is not often we get such fine looking volunteers, such as yourselves,' said the lieutenant. 'Isn't that so, Mister Rogers?'

The boatswain nodded. His face screwed up into something resembling a scowl and a smile at the same time. I could sense that he was one of the men who would have to be deprived of his life, at some point in the proceedings.

'I will fetch Captain Chase,' said Mister Rogers.

The lieutenant nodded and the boatswain rushed off to fetch the captain.

As we stood waiting for the captain to grant permission for us to join the ship's company, the lieutenant peppered us with questions regarding other ships we had served on. Fortunately, my friends knew lots of ship's names and were able to cover my ignorance in that regard, not having served in the Royal Navy at anytime in my life.

Some time later, the boatswain returned, followed by a short, stout man in an impeccable uniform covered in gold braid. On his head he wore an expensive peruke with multiple curls and an officer's beaver with white feathers. The man sported waxed mustaches with needle sharp points and a short beard on his chin. His face betrayed a stern, Puritan ethic, which shouted to all who beheld it, 'Ye Do Not Cross This Man!' I couldn't help but feel some trepidation creep into my backbone. The man's face sent shivers up and down my spine and made the hairs on the back of my neck tingle.

Captain Chase came to stand directly in front of us with his hands clasped firmly behind his back. With the eyes of an eagle he looked us up and down and bored into our brains, searching for a hint of something amiss. Men did not often come of their own free will into the Royal Navy. When five come, all at once, suspicions can be easily aroused. However, we five stared blandly back at the captain, looking every inch like the able bodied sailors we were supposed to be. We aroused no hint of concern on the captain's stern countenance.

'Enter their names in the book,' said the captain curtly. 'Mister Rogers will show you to your quarters.' Then he turned on his heel and walked back to the Great Cabin, followed by the young lieutenant.

Our duffel bags were hauled on board with a rope.

We waved good bye to our African friends, who rowed back to the brigantine.

Mister Rogers led us to the fo'c's'le, where he appointed us to hammocks, formerly belonging to the hanged men in the yardarms.

'When you have stowed your belongings, find me on deck and I will sign you into the ship's register.'

'Aye Sir,' we replied, pulling our forelocks.

Mister Rogers nodded before turning on his heels, leaving us to attend to our business.

The crew's quarters was a stifling, smelly place, with extremely poor light. Fortunately, many of the ship's gun ports were open, letting air circulate through the lower decks, otherwise the rotten air would have made me gag, I'm sure of it. Some surely looking sailors were lying in hammocks, attempting to sleep, while others sat on chests, playing cards. No one paid us much attention, as we stowed our duffel bags in the hammocks we were assigned. The fact that the hammocks had belonged to recently deceased sailors did not bother us; death being ever present in our world, we were not affected by it, like some more gentle folk; who would most assuredly have desired the destruction of the said hammocks in cleansing flames. I shrugged my shoulders and tested my hammock, to see if I would be comfortable in it.

When we had completed our business in the fo'c's'le, we climbed the ladders and looked for Mister Rogers on deck. He was standing by a table on which the ship's register lay, waiting for us. He explained that our wages would be one pound four shillings per month. If a prize was taken, we would receive a share, as determined by the prize office in London. Then, he launched into a long list of rules and regulations we were to follow on board. He indicated that breaches of discipline were met with severe penalties, including death. Mister Rogers gestured towards the dangling corpses above our heads.

'Those men tried to desert ship,' he said. 'Captain Chase does not tolerate much, so I warn you, mind your business. If you do as you are told, and perform your duties faithfully, without question, you will do well. Any slip up, and I warn you, there will be repercussions on board His Majesty's ship.'

When the boatswain had completed his instructions to us he had us sign the register. Then, he assigned us to the stations formerly occupied by the dangling cadavers. As soon as our signatures were dry in the register, the boatswain informed us that no shore leave was granted any sailors, because the ship was making ready to leave port in two days.

We told the boatswain we were ready to sail, and did not need to go into San Juan for any reason; our good byes having been said to friends and family.

Satisfied that all was in order, Mister Rogers welcomed us on board and reminded us, once again, to be prompt when our watches were called. Then, he walked off towards the Great Cabin, leaving us standing by the forward hatch.

'Leaving in two days?' asked George. 'We either have to move fast, if we want to effect changes on this ship, or we will have to mutiny at sea.'

'If we had known this ship was scheduled to leave port, so soon, perhaps we should have rethought this entire plan,' said Colin nervously. 'How do we let the others know? I thought we would just entice the crew off the ship, while in port. Going to sea on this man of war, is not what we planned on.'

Robert looked towards our ship lying off to starboard. He shrugged his shoulders, 'I'm sure our friends are keeping an eye on this ship. They'll see the signs, when this ship is readying to leave port. I don't think we have to worry about our friends not following us.' Robert looked at Colin. 'Besides, organizing a mutiny is going to take a bit of time. At sea we can get rid of bodies a whole lot easier.'

Suddenly, Robert stopped talking and indicated with a subtle gesture, we had to change the conversation.

Two sailors walked past, eyeing us suspiciously.

We just nodded in greeting and watched, as they went about their business on the fore deck. Other sailors were busy with blocks and ropes. Still others were cleaning the deck, the railings, the brass work; everything and anything which could be cleaned was being so treated. Captain Chase obviously ran a clean ship. I watched carefully to see if perhaps one of the sailors fit a description given by Franklin and Tom.

Suddenly, George nudged me and pointed towards a large sailor polishing a door knob on the door to the after castle. The sailor fit the description of Nigel Sutherland; the man being a big, strong looking, red head.

'Let's go talk with him,' said George, beginning to saunter towards the sailor.

I looked up to the quarter deck and noticed three officers watching us. 'Perhaps just you go, George,' I said, indicating the quarter deck. 'I think we are being watched.'

George looked at the officers watching us. He nodded and tugged on his forelock. I did the same, as did the others.

Our show of respect seemed to please the officers, who stepped over to the port side of the deck and gazed out towards the assorted vessels anchored in the harbour.

As soon as the officers were no longer watching, George and I approached the red head.

'Are you the new men, who have just come on board?' asked the sailor, as we approached him.

We nodded.

'Nigel Sutherland,' replied the sailor, as he began shaking each of our hands.

George smiled. 'You fit the description your friends provided.'

'Which friends?' asked Nigel, scratching his chin.

'Franklin and Tom,' I said.

Nigel looked surprised. He looked around, to see if an officer was listening anywhere nearby. Satisfied that we were out of earshot of any officers, he asked about his friends.

George assured him that his friends were safe.

'Captain Chase has sent marines out to scour the city. He is determined to find them, before we weigh anchors,' said Nigel fearfully. He advised that we should go below, where we might have some more privacy. 'We'll go down to the first gun deck,' he said conspiratorially. 'Follow me,' he added, as he opened the door and darted inside.

George and I quickly followed Nigel through the door and down a ladder to the gun deck.

As soon as we arrived in the stooped environment of the gun deck, Nigel again asked if his friends were safe.

George reassured him, regarding Franklin and Tom, as I studied the place where I was standing.

The three of us had to stoop over on the covered gun deck, where twenty four, twelve pounders stood silently in their carriages, gun ports open to allow air circulation. Several gunner's mates were fixing a broken carriage wheel, amidship. A powder boy, about ten years of age, was sitting on a cannon, watching the men working.

Since we were out of earshot from the gunner's mates, and other unwelcome ears, we confided in Nigel, who we were and what our purpose was.

The news came as a welcome surprise to Nigel. He assured us we could count on him to help effect a mutiny.

'I'd rather risk a hanging, than to go on another voyage with Captain Chase,' said Nigel sincerely. He added that easily seventy percent of the men on board would be in support. 'However, you must be extremely cautious,' he warned, 'Captain Chase has spies everywhere.'

Just as he said those words, three marines stepped onto the gun deck. They walked past, totally ignoring us, intent on making their appointed arrest. In this case it happened to be the powder boy.

The gunner's mates tried to present an argument in defense of the boy, but it was to no avail. Two marines grabbed the boy and dragged him away, kicking and screaming.

'He probably stole something from the pantry, again,' said Nigel sadly. 'Poor little blighter was probably hungry.' Nigel shook his head. 'He done it before. This time he could be in deep trouble. They're probably taking him to see Captain Chase.'

Nigel stared after the marines. 'They are hated on board ship. Those bastards always follow the captain's orders, without question, no matter how cruel or diabolical.' Nigel spat in the direction the marines had gone. 'Marines are the children of Lucifer.'

Judging from the expressions on the faces of the marines who walked past, I could see that Nigel was telling the truth; the expressions were those of automatons, who would never question the ethics of an officer's orders.

Nigel looked at us very seriously and cautioned us further about the marines. 'Their mess is amidships. I suggest you avoid going there. The less the marines see of you, the better.' Nigel grimaced, 'I suggest you don't get in the faces of the officers, either. You can't trust any. Except Doctor Johnson. He's the only one. All the others are the minions of Captain Chase.' Nigel stared towards the stern of the ship. 'I do so want to rid this ship of those people.'

Nigel spoke the words which sounded like music in our ears. His sincerity was unquestionable. He was genuinely interested in stirring up a mutiny.

We told Nigel in more detail about us, and what our plans were, regarding the liberation of all impressed sailors. We told him about our brigantine, waiting to follow the man of war when she sailed, and how we would have enough men to overpower the officers and take control of the ship.

I can still envision his expression, the moment he heard we were pirates. A sudden light came into his face; the light of hope. I believe that Nigel saw the light of freedom. He saw an end to his enslavement. It made me feel particularly warm, knowing I would be instrumental in his departure from the King's navy.

George asked Nigel if he knew of other men who we could rely on.

Nigel assured us there were plenty of others, and began to name two men, suddenly stopping before completing the second name. He looked at us suspiciously. 'How do I know I can trust you?' Nigel suddenly looked very scared. 'How do I know you're not spies pretending to be pirates?'

It took us by surprise, to be taken for spies. To be thought of as collaborators for the minions of Satan, was an insulting feeling and we said so, in no uncertain terms.

Our vehement sincerity convinced Nigel immediately. From then on our veracity was never questioned again; not by Nigel, or any of his fellow mutineers, to whom we were introduced over the next two days, as time permitted and opportunities arose; all the time striving for utmost secrecy. Under no circumstances could we risk detection.

Later in the afternoon, all hands were called on deck by the shrill whistle of the boatswain's pipe.

Everyone scrambled to obey the call and rushed on deck, quickly standing in ranks facing the quarter deck upon which Captain Chase stood with his officers. Moments later, two marines came forth, dragging a kicking and screaming ten year old boy, whom they quickly tied to the main mast. I recognized the boy to be the young fellow the marines seized from the gun deck.

'The errant creature you see tied to the mast is powder boy, Marcus deWitt!' shouted Captain Chase. 'He has been caught, on three separate occasions, attempting to pilfer food from the galley stores, claiming he was hungry.' Captain Chase paused and stared at us standing on the deck. 'The Royal Navy takes pride in how well it feeds its sailors. There is no excuse for powder boys attempting to steal rations out of the mouths of all of us assembled here!' Captain Chase smacked his hands on the railing in front of him. 'I will not tolerate theft on board my ship! You will all bear witness to my displeasure.' Then without batting an eye he added, in a tone cold as an Arctic wind, 'Twenty strokes, Mister Sweeney, if you please.'

Mister Sweeney smiled as he shook out the cords, in preparation for the first stroke. Then Boatswain's Mate Sweeney swung the cat, with all of his weight behind it, fully onto the naked back of the quivering boy. The poor little chap screamed with pain when the first stroke scarred his little back. I couldn't help wincing.

For the next stroke, Sweeney made certain the strands were untangled and each one available for another assault. The creature wielding the cat took a few steps backward and then laid into the little chap with a run, to give his stroke even more momentum.

Marcus screamed so loudly it brought tears to my eyes. His back was already beginning to bleed. There were to be another eighteen strokes.

After each blow, Sweeney made sure to fully extend and unravel the tortuous cords of his horrible instrument. Putting all of his weight behind another stroke; he tore the boy's flesh into multiple strips of bloody pulp.

By the tenth stroke the little fellow had passed out.

I thought of Bill, at that moment, as a young boy receiving ten strokes. Little Marcus was to receive ten more. More tears came to my eyes, making further observation of the event ever more uncomfortable. I am sure many of the men were feeling the same terrible sadness, as we watched little Marcus slowly reduced to a bleeding mess.

By the time Sweeney was done with him, the little lad was barely alive. Two sailors were told to draw water from the sea, with which they washed Marcus off. When they were done, they sent the little boy to his hammock in the fo'c's'le. He died some days later. His body was unceremoniously dumped overboard; an embarrassment to Captain Chase. I knew, then and there, Chase had to die.

Three days after coming on board the winds became favorable, enabling the man of war to set sail and leave San Juan. I was assigned to the capstan crew and learned what a job it was to pull up a three thousand pound anchor, all the while goaded by the boatswain's mate and midshipman. I tried to get a glimpse of our brig, but was prevented from so doing in the execution of my duty.

Colin and George were sent aloft, while Arthur and Robert were assigned below decks.

I did not get an opportunity to talk with my friends again until the following morning, when we met at breakfast; a meagre meal of gruel and a piece of boiled beef.

'I haven't worked that hard in a long time,' grouched Robert, checking the blisters on his hands. 'Pumping bilges is not exactly my job of choice.'

'Me neither,' said George, rubbing his shoulders. 'I haven't worked the yards for many years. It is definitely a young man's trade.'

I knew exactly what they were talking about. My whole body ached from the workout I had been through. I realized I hated the navy already, and I had only served for three days. I could easily see why people, who had been impressed and forced to serve in a ship such as the *Avenger*, would be easily convinced to give piracy a try.

Robert asked if we had seen the *Navigator*.

We had to answer in the negative. Neither, Colin, George, or I had seen our brig set sail. The information was an uncomfortable revelation. We were not prepared to take on a full compliment of ship's officers, and their minions, without some backup.

'Unless, of course, we can count on a large number of men joining us in the mutiny, then we have nothing to worry about,' said Robert. 'The only issue being, weapons. The officers have marines, with weapons on their side. What have we got? Dirks, marlin spikes, clubs, and a few pistols we managed to bring on board.'

'We need to get access to the armory,' said George, just as Boatswain's Mate Sweeney walked past, apparently overhearing what George had said.

Sweeney stopped and turned around.

'Who needs to get access to the armory?' asked the boatswain's mate, suspiciously.

Watching him, up close, in the cramped quarters of the mess, I could see that Sweeney was a dead ringer for Beelzebub. I determined, right then and there, that I would help the Lord wreak vengeance upon that errant minion of the Devil. I vowed I would effect his removal, at the earliest opportunity.

'Answer me!' demanded Sweeney, 'Who needs to get access to the armory?'

We stared dumbly at Sweeney and did not answer him.

'You men are not planning a mutiny, by chance?' asked the boatswain's mate, standing over us, a sinister smirk on his face. 'Because, if you are, let me warn you right now, you are wasting your time. A mutiny can never work on this ship.' Sweeney cackled a croaky laugh. 'I'll be keeping an eye on you boys, you can be assured of that.'

As I stared into his ugly face, I knew that Sweeney would have to be removed, forthwith, and wasted not another moment.

'I'm planning a mutiny,' I said. 'Perhaps you should take me to Captain Chase, so we can discuss it?' I smiled mischievously, egging Sweeney on.

He took the bait. 'I knew there was something sinister about you, the moment you men came on board,' he said. 'You had better come with me peacefully,' he said, grabbing my left shoulder.

My friends regarded me with concerned expressions.

I winked, to assure them that I was alright and knew what I was doing.

I followed Mister Sweeney towards the stern of the ship, through a gangway to the Great Cabin. When we entered the narrow hallway, we were completely alone. I wasted not a second. From my belt I grabbed the marlin spike and stuck it deep into Sweeney's neck, twisting the metal spike to ensure maximum damage to a carotid artery.

He began to spurt copious amounts of blood.

Sweeney gurgled something, as I pulled the spike from his neck and drove it deep into a kidney. He grunted and began to twitch, as I manhandled him into a storage locker, making sure to keep his mouth firmly covered with my left hand, to prevent discovery.

I had to jab the marlin spike into Sweeney several more times, just to make certain he would bleed from lots of holes. Then, I stepped back and examined the mess. It was an ugly business, doing the Lord's work. I now had a better idea about the sort of things Bill had gone through, in pursuit of the Lord's vengeance. How was I going to explain my self being covered in blood? That was the question of the moment, as I stood hunched over my victim in the storage locker.

Remaining inside the locker until dark, was out of the question. I would be missed on my watch, which was quickly coming up. I had to find clean clothes, or else I would be in big trouble. I had to obtain clean clothes, as soon as possible. The question was, from where?

As I stood there, trying to figure out a plan, I could hear someone coming down the gangway. I held my breath, just as Sweeney groaned loudly. Putting my hand over his mouth and nose, I tried to prevent him from making any more noise, however, it was too late, the door of the locker opened, revealing an able bodied seaman, who found himself immediately pulled into the locker, smashing his face against the bulkhead with the help of my right hand. I smacked the hapless fellow on the back of his neck, sending him crashing to the ground. My sudden ability to commit violence surprised me. I guessed that I was actually becoming a pistol proof pirate. I realized that Bill's mentorship was beginning to pay off.

I quickly grabbed the unconscious sailor, otherwise he would have soiled his clothes with Sweeney's blood forming a pool on the deck. I dragged the sailor away from the blood and quickly undressed him. I stabbed him through the heart. I had no choice. I could not afford to be discovered.

I ripped off my blood spattered clothes, wiping my face and hands with the back of my shirt. I quickly put on the cleaner clothes of the dead sailor. Fortunately, he was almost the same height as me. His clothes fit relatively well and would not appear abnormal. I placed the bloody marlin spike in his clenched fist.

When I was ready, I listened carefully to hear if anyone was coming. Ascertaining that nobody was near, I cracked the door of the storage locker and peeked out. Nobody was in the gangway, so I quickly stepped out of the locker and closed the door; leaving the area as rapidly as I could, returning to the mess where my friends were completing their breakfast.

'What happened?' asked George when I sat down beside him. 'You have blood on your cheek.'

I was suddenly afraid. Someone else might have seen the blood on my cheek. I quickly wiped the blood off with a handkerchief Robert offered.

'Did Sweeney take you to see the old man?' asked George.

I stared at George for a moment, and then smiled wickedly. 'I don't believe Mister Sweeney will be taking anyone to see the old man, ever again.'

'What do you mean?' asked Robert, leaning closer, to hear me better.

I had to keep my voice down, lest someone over heard my words in the crowded mess. 'I believe, Mister Sweeney has gone to his Maker,' I said calmly. 'He is now the late boatswain's mate. I had to wreak the Lord's vengeance upon him for whipping the powder boy. His miserable corpse is bleeding in a storage locker, in the gangway under the quarter deck. I assume someone will find him, before long.'

From the expressions on my friends' faces, they regarded me with a totally new level of respect.

'Boy, oh boy, Peter,' said George happily, 'You have indeed become one of us.'

Smiling he clapped me on the shoulder. 'I guess you are now a true, man of respect.'

My other friends heartily agreed and each gave me a warm handshake.

Being so recognized by my colleagues and friends made me feel good to be alive. To be so respected by one's fellows, gave me a good feeling inside. Too bad I had to kill someone to get that feeling. However, I felt no remorse, as I contemplated Bill's admonition, 'Some people deserve killing.' Sweeney was definitely such a person. I did the world a favour, ridding it of the boatswain's mate. As for the hapless sailor, whose clothes I now wore, he was an unfortunate victim of circumstances. However, I still felt badly for having had to kill him.

When our watch was piped we separated to go to our various tasks, vowing to meet later in the day, by the forward hatch, to discuss our progress on board ship.

Sometime later in the day, we were all piped on deck. Apparently, two dead men had been found, in a storage locker below the quarter deck. Captain Chase sounded quite apoplectic as he demanded to know, who was responsible for the demise of Boatswain's Mate, Sweeney and Able Bodied Seaman, Topaz.

Of course, I volunteered nothing, and kept my mouth shut. My friends, likewise, said nothing.

With nothing to go on, we were dismissed, to resume our various tasks. I kept my satisfied smile, inwardly directed.

When our watches were finally over, my friends and I met for a pipe of tobacco, in the only allowed place on board ship, that being the fore deck, in the lee of the forecastle. A number of other sailors sat or stood there for the same purpose. The aromatic smell of twenty pipes of tobacco, filled the air with a delicious aroma.

As we so stood there, enjoying our pipes, I carefully asked my friends if they had seen our ship.

Neither Colin, nor George had seen anything of her, from the yards.

Their revelation disconcerted me, however, I tried not to let it bother me. Our brig was a fast ship, and could easily out sail the ungainly man of war.

I asked if any of the sailors, whom Franklin and Tom had identified, besides Nigel, had been met up with. As it happened, Colin had managed to speak with Midshipman, Thomas Jones, who had indicated he would attempt to arrange for us to meet several more sailors, on whom we could rely. The meeting was to take place the following evening. We were to meet over a game of dominoes, on the fore deck, after supper, towards dark. We had to be extremely careful, lest the wrong ears or eyes detected our intentions. The Royal Navy did not like mutinies, and did its best to prevent them, by keeping sailors scared to death.

Next day, when the appointed time arrived, we five set up a dominos game on the fore deck. Gradually other sailors, with some spare time to kill, drifted over to watch the game. As I began to study the sailor's faces, I realized the men were those whom Franklin and Tom had described.

Nigel and Midshipman Jones had brought the entire group of conspirators plus a few extra. I met, Cookie, Barton, Brookes, Giles, Norman, Adam, and Pewee McAlister, a giant of a man, even taller than Adam.

How he managed to live on board the cramped quarters of the ship was a wonder to me. Several men lit up pipes, which they covered with small perforated lids. Fire on board was to be avoided at all costs. Considering the captain's sternness, it was a surprise that men were allowed to smoke, at all.

Another sailor, whom I met, that evening, was a grim faced man by the name of, Martin Henry; a man who would affect me in ways I could not possibly have imagined. I wish to this day I had never met him on board that accursed ship.

The dominos game proceeded apace, during which serious talk ensued concerning our plan to rescue the ship's sailors. However, the fact that our brig was still nowhere in sight, made setting of a definite time somewhat difficult. We remained hopeful our brig would catch up with us.

'What if our ship does not catch up with us?' asked Arthur. 'I mean, it's a big ocean out here.'

'Aye, what if'n yer brig don catch us, what den?' asked Cookie, stamping his wooden leg impatiently. 'We can nay take on dem marines by oursefs.'

'I can get the key to the armory, I think,' volunteered Thomas, the midshipman.

'That's good,' said Robert. 'If we can get their guns.'

'There's always a guard,' said Pewee McAlister.

'How many?' asked George.

'Two,' replied Pewee.

'You can take them out by yourself,' chuckled George.

Pewee smiled and nodded his head. He knew that was true.

Suddenly, Colin, who had been watching the main deck, cleared his throat, warning us there was someone coming.

Moments later, Lieutenant Kirby and Boatswain Gordon walked up to the fore deck. The boatswain was carrying a small cat in his right hand. His whistle hung from his belt.

Colin called us to attention. 'Officers on deck!'

We all stood up and saluted the two officers by pulling on our forelocks.

'Playing dominos? At this hour?' asked the lieutenant. 'One can hardly see, it is getting so dark. Or is it that you men are up to something?'

'Up to sometin'?' asked Nigel. 'Why d'you say that? We're juz sittin here smokin our pipes and enjoyin some conversation wit our friends, guvnor.'

The lieutenant looked sternly at Thomas. 'Fraternizing with the lower classes, Mister Jones?' Lieutenant Kirby pursed his lips. 'If Captain Chase knew about your sympathies, he might be less inclined to favour you.'

'He doesn't favour me now,' replied Thomas, not missing a beat.

'It doesn't look good for a midshipman to be fraternizing with common sailors. It is not becoming a navy officer.'

Thomas stared at the two men. 'Is that what you came up here to tell me, lieutenant?' he asked calmly, not taking his eyes off Mister Kirby.

'No, as a matter of fact it isn't,' replied the lieutenant. 'Seeing you gathered up here, I thought I might ask you men if you know anything about the murder of Mister Sweeney and that sailor, what's his name?' The lieutenant turned to the boatswain.

'Marvin Topaz,' replied the boatswain.

'Yes, Marvin Topaz,' repeated the lieutenant. 'Did any of you men know that sailor?'

We all grunted something to the effect, we didn't know the man.

'The man's clothing was stripped from the body. We presume that someone is wearing his clothes, because we found discarded, blood stained clothing, presumably those of the murderer.'

Lieutenant Kirby looked directly at me when he said it.

I tried desperately to remain calm and disinterested. My knees were shaking. I prayed he did not notice.

'What about you?' he asked, staring at me with eyes that could have bored through steel.

'Me?' I asked, trying to keep my voice steady. 'What about me?'

'You're one of the new men, are you not?'

'Aye, that I am,' I replied. 'Signed on in San Juan.'

'State your name,' demanded the lieutenant, coldly.

'Peter Flynn,' I said, using the name I wrote in the ship's register.

'You were seen leaving the sailor's mess with Mister Sweeney, on the day he was murdered.' Mister Kirby raised his chin and stared down his nose at me. 'What do you say to that?'

I stared at the officers and then looked at my friends. My knees were quaking and cold chills were running up my spine. The thought that my friends might betray me, at that moment, crossed my mind. However, I quickly dismissed the negative thought and faced the officers calmly.

'Mister Sweeney came to fetch me on deck. He wanted me to clean up some vomit,' I said calmly. 'I never saw him again, after he showed me what he wanted cleaned up.'

Lieutenant Kirby grunted and then turned his attention on Nigel. 'What about you, Sutherland? There was no love lost between you and Mister Sweeney. You had good reason to murder him.' Mister Kirby leaned towards Nigel. 'You had good reason to murder him, because he flogged the tar out of you a few times, didn't he, Sutherland?'

'It's no reason to murder a man,' said Nigel, as sincerely as he could manage.

Lieutenant Kirby grunted something unintelligible. Then he looked at each one of us in turn. 'The murder investigation is not over yet. We will get to the bottom of this, I can assure you of that. And when we do, you can rest assured that justice will be served and the murderer hanged for his crime.' The lieutenant stared once more at me, then turned on his heels, followed by Mister Gordon.

I sighed a long breath of relief when the two officers were gone. The episode scared the heebie jeebies out of me.

'Don't worry,' said Robert, 'They won't find out who did it.'

'I wouldn't be so sure,' replied Cookie, knowingly. 'Those officers are a relentless group of ruthless bastards! If they wanna find a murderer, they will.' 'Whether the poor bloke actually done it or not, doesn't matter,' added Nigel ruefully. 'Just so's they can hang someone, to set an example for the rest of us.'

'Speaking of, when are they going to take those poor fellows down?' asked Colin, looking at the five bodies, still dangling from the yardarms above our heads.

'I think, Captain Chase intends to leave them until they drop into the sea, of their own accord,' said Pewee sadly. 'It is disgraceful how we are treated.'

'Aye, it is disgraceful,' said Robert vehemently. 'We can't let these men continue commanding this ship.'

We vowed to push our plans forward, regardless of whether our brig was on the scene or not. Therefore, we set the day and time for two days hence, during the morning watch, when Captain Chase would be in his cabin, and most of the marines in their mess. All of us would carefully spread the word amongst the crew.

When we finally completed our, 'dominos game', we sauntered off to our hammocks and slept, full of dreams regarding our dangerous venture.

Next day, we went about our routines, whispering information to sailors whom we trusted, who spread the word amongst their friends, and so on. By the time we went to sleep, the night before our intended mutiny, I was confident that we could count on a large number of oppressed sailors to help us.

Morning saw a glorious sun rise, portending a beautiful day. A slight breeze propelled the massive ship at a comfortable six knots with sails full out. Looking to port I could see islands in the distance. I assumed them to be the Caicos Islands, not far from our island. The timing for the mutiny could not have been better. We could be home before we knew it. I could almost taste Virginia's kisses, she being only miles from where I stood looking out. I breathed deeply and cleared my head. I walked to the bowsprit to evacuate my bowels, a place infinitely better than the cramped, smelly head below decks.

When my watch was piped I went to work swabbing decks, all the while being harangued by the first mate, who shouted from the quarter deck that we were a pack of lazy dogs, and should work harder. As I listened to him, my heart continued to harden. I set my intent on the demise of the arrogant English officers.

Suddenly, a shout rang out from the mizzen crows nest. 'A sail! A sail, ho! Off the port stern!'

I ran towards the quarter deck and looked out to sea, hoping to catch sight of the sail, however I couldn't see it yet, the sail being still too far away for my angle of view. If I had a spy glass, I might have been able to see it. I just hoped that it was our brig.

As the morning progressed, the ship came closer. We could clearly see that the ship behind us had two masts, square rigged with fore and aft sails. There was no doubt the ship was a brigantine. However, there was no telling if it was ours.

When nine bells were sounded, our plan began to unfold, as Robert, leading ten determined sailors, overcame the marines guarding the armory. The officers on deck had no idea what was happening below decks. I eyed them carefully for signs, as I swabbed, just below where they stood on the quarter deck.

Suddenly, a shout rang out from below decks, then a gun shot, instantly alerting the officers on deck. I watched them nervously pull their sabres and pistols out, as the boatswain shouted orders for us to organize in ranks on deck. The first mate shouted an order for one of the officers to go below and ascertain where the shot came from. However, before the officer could descend the ladder, a large group of armed sailors stormed on deck.

The mutiny had begun.

Chapter Seventeen

A shot rang out.

I heard the ball whizz past my head.

Then I heard a groan as the ball smashed into Arthur's shoulder.

I watched as Arthur fell backwards. When I looked up, I saw that the ball had been discharged from Lieutenant Kirby's pistol.

'You scurvy knaves!' he shouted, waving his navy sabre. 'You will never take this ship!'

Of course we had to disagree with him.

Norman Clark, one of Franklin and Tom's friends, raised his musket and pointed it at the lieutenant. In his strangely squeaky voice, he shouted to the lieutenant, to put his weapons down, and for the other officers to do the same.

'Do you think you scum have a chance? Think of it, there are thirty marines on board this ship!' shouted the lieutenant defiantly. 'Don't you suppose they will be on deck, apace, to investigate the gun shots?'

The marines did come up on deck, at that moment, pushed and prodded by numerous sailors brandishing sabres, muskets, or pistols. At their head came, Colin and George.

Suddenly, as the marines were being herded on deck, several marines grabbed George, which instantly provoked the other marines to begin manhandling the sailors, brandishing muskets. The resultant melee gave Lieutenant Kirby, and his colleagues, the opportunity of discharging pistols at our sailors, knocking several down to the deck with ugly wounds. More shots rang out and five marines went down, one of them spilling blood on my arm, as he fell against the gunwale.

Robert tossed me a pistol. 'Come on, let's go fetch Captain Chase. He must be wondering what is going on.'

I smiled and said I would be pleased to assist with informing the captain. Then I called to, Colin and Nigel, fighting nearby, to come with us.

'One moment!' shouted Colin as I watched him toss a marine over the port side of the ship. I heard the man scream just before he splashed into the sea. I suppose he was afraid of sharks.

More gun shots rang out over the clashing of steel and the screams of men, as we rushed into the cabin under the quarter deck, followed by six more assistants; two of whom I recognized, as Barton and Norman Clark. We could plainly hear, from the chaotic clumping of boots on the ceiling, that our men had succeeded in gaining the quarterdeck and had begun to engage the officers there. Captain Chase must have been wondering what was amiss. However, like most martinets, he was a coward who remained in his cabin.

Three officers stood in front of the captain's door with pistols drawn.

I told the officers there was no need to risk their lives for the captain. However, if they did not move out of the way, I told them we would most assuredly send them to hell, in short order.

Without warning, one of the officers fired his pistol directly at me. The ball hit my left wrist, shattering the bones, and rendering my left hand instantly useless, thereby causing me to drop my cutlass. The instant result for me was excruciating pain. The result for the three officers was instant death, as my colleagues discharged at least seven pistols, at point blank range. The smell of burnt powder and smoke filled the cramped space.

The pain rushing up my left arm was incredible. My left wrist was shattered but not bleeding awfully much, considering the wound. The ball had completely passed through. It was a miracle it had not hit my chest. Perhaps my cutlass deflected the ball, somehow. Anyway, there was no time to deal with the wound, at that moment. I told the men to open the door.

It was locked.

I shouted to the captain to open the door and come out, peacefully.

The captain's reply was a challenge, 'You will have to break the door open to get at me! And I warn you, I am well armed!'

Suddenly, a loud blast of a pistol came from behind the door, instantly followed by a crack and splintering of a hole in the door, sending slivers, and a ball directly at a man standing next to me. The ball caught him in the right eye. He fell backwards against the men behind him, screaming with incomprehensible pain. I wasn't certain which one of us was in more pain. I imagine that the loss of an eye is a horrible thing. I think I felt almost lucky, at that moment, it wasn't my eye that got hit.

I shouted once more to the captain, to come out, peacefully. He answered with another gun shot through the door. Fortunately, we had all moved aside, so that the ball and splinters harmed no one.

The reply from the captain was enough for us to realize we were going to have to break the door down. However, with the captain able to shoot through the door, we would be vulnerable.

Colin suggested we try and climb down the transom. 'We can get him through the windows. Just keep him busy, thinking we are all outside the door, while Robert and I climb down to the balcony.'

I agreed it was a good idea and wished my friends well, as they ran off. I noticed the noises outside had subsided and sent one of the men to go see if we had succeeded to take the ship. At that point, I was still not certain.

Moments later, he returned with the good news that we had, indeed, taken the ship. All of the officers were accounted for and assembled on deck. Twelve marines and sixteen sailors were dead.

I shouted to the captain that we had taken the ship and that he should come out of the cabin.

The captain's response was another shot through the door.

'You can't win!' I shouted through the door. 'What can you possibly do, by yourself, against a whole ship full of armed mutineers?'

'You murderous scum!' he shouted from behind the door. 'You think you can best, Captain Montgomery Chase? I am a Royal Navy officer! I do not give in to maggots like you!'

Suddenly, another shot blasted through the door. The ball crashed into a bulkhead with a loud thud.

I shook my head sadly. The captain was putting up an unnecessary fight, endangering more lives, when his was the only one we wanted.

'I am giving you one more chance to change your mind!' I shouted.

Another ball came through the door and crashed into the same bulkhead, as the previous one.

Suddenly, a loud crash and a gun shot rang out from within the cabin. We heard scuffling, shuffling, and muffled voices. Suddenly something heavy hit the floor.

Moments later the door opened and Colin stood there; a big grin on his face.

'Captain Chase will see you now,' he said.

I could see that the captain had sustained a knock to the head. A large blue/green welt was rising on his forehead. He was sitting dazedly in a chair. I told the men to bring the captain up on deck. Then, grabbing a bottle of the captain's own rum, I poured a healthy amount into my gullet, and the rest on my wound. The burning alcohol made me wince, as the pain rose up my left arm, and shattered somewhere in the back of my brain. 'Find Doctor Johnson,' I groaned. 'My wrist needs attention,' I added.

I followed the men, dragging Captain Chase up on deck, where loud huzzahs greeted us. I climbed painfully up onto the quarter deck and addressed the men, standing below, with the captured officers and marines.

As I was climbing up the ladder to the quarter deck, I looked to port and could clearly see a brigantine quickly pulling up behind us, about a mile, or so, away.

'It's the *Navigator*!' shouted George enthusiastically, putting the spy glass down and handing it to Robert.

I managed a smile over my pain. Then, I faced the men standing on the deck below and congratulated them on taking the first step towards the suppression of tyranny. I told them they were brave men, and that they would be welcome additions to our pirate colony, if they chose to join us. However, with the exception of Midshipman Jones and Doctor Johnson, we had no choice but to kill the officers. Allowing them an opportunity to return to England, would most assuredly result in our severe persecution. Stealing one of the King's men of war, was not something King George took lightly.

When I mentioned that we would have to kill the officers, several began pleading with us, to spare them.

I told them to stop whining and asked the sailors if any would vouch for the officers.

Only one man stepped forward and vouched for a petty officer, who had shown him a kindness, some months previously. As a result the sailor had only received forty lashes, instead of a hundred.

I replied that the officer should have prevented the lashes all together. It was not enough of a kindness, as far as I was concerned. The Lord's vengeance would be manifested that day, I said to myself, as I watched some sailors cut their friends down from the forward yards. Watching the poor blokes being lowered, my heart hardened further.

'Clap the captain in irons and lash him to the main mast!' I shouted. 'As for the rest, throw them overboard!'

The jettisoning of officers began immediately, over their vociferous protests.

One by one the officers were sent to the fishes, with boisterous farewells, and gleeful huzzahs.

Captain Chase was clapped in heavy irons and lashed to the main mast, just as our brigantine began to come along our port side.

'Ahoy there!' shouted Meira through the speaking trumpet.

'Ahoy there!' shouted Colin happily. 'It's about time you got here!' he added, laughing. 'The mutiny is over!'

When the crew of the *Navigator* heard that, a mighty cheer went up, quickly joined by all the sailors on board the man of war. Everyone felt they had won a war and desired to celebrate that fact, with as loud a noise as possible. On the *Navigator*, several people were banging on drums and blowing trumpets. The cacophony was deafening.

The brig pulled up along our beam and soon the boat was pulled up to ferry several of our friends to the man of war, in order to see for themselves what we had wrought. They were able to watch as we took care of Lieutenant Kirby.

'You will all rot in hell!' he shouted, as Colin assisted him over the side.

Moments later, the lieutenant landed with a loud splash, still yelling curses at us.

As I looked some distance past the splashing officers, I saw a large, gray dorsal fin, moving lazily in the water. 'It won't be long,' I said, nodding my head. 'Soon they will be inside the fishes.'

George and Robert stared out towards the dorsal fin and smiled happily.

When the last of the officers had been dispatched over the side of the ship, I shouted orders to bring the ships about, in order to immediately head for our island, the winds being favorable. Then, I went to the Great Cabin and lay down on the captain's comfortable bed, while Doctor Johnson attended to my fractured wrist. He gave me something to dull the pain, and I gradually drifted into a deep, dark sleep; a nightmare from which I awoke two days later, with a bandaged stump where my hand had been.

It was not a happy waking.

I grimaced with pain, as I opened my eyes, slowly at first, my pupils being terribly dilated, because of the drug Doctor Johnson had given me. My whole body felt sluggish and my stump burned. As my eyes became accustomed to the light, I could see Doctor Johnson sitting in a chair, reading a book. He must have heard me moan, because he turned around and looked at me with a concerned expression.

'Where is my hand?' I asked, tears beginning to form in my eyes. 'Where is my hand?' I repeated, staring at the blood stained bandage on the end of my left arm.

'I had to amputate,' said Doctor Johnson sympathetically. 'There was no way to save it. Your wrist was too badly shattered.'

'Too badly shattered?' I asked weakly. 'Are you sure it was too badly shattered?' I looked at the stump, 'Are you sure there was nothing you could do? I mean, what will Virginia say?'

'I am sorry, Peter,' said Doctor Johnson. 'I did what I could.'

Choking back tears I nodded to the doctor and pressed my lips together, summoning up my courage to be stoic and bear the pain. Focusing on the fact that lots of men, throughout history, have lost hands, feet, arms, and legs; going on to achieve ever higher levels of glory, I sat up and vowed not to let the loss of my left hand be the end of my writing career. Fortunately, I still had my right hand, and said so to Doctor Johnson.

'That's the spirit, Peter,' he said. 'With that kind of attitude, you will heal quickly.'

I smiled at the doctor and shook his hand warmly. 'Thank you,' I said. 'You probably saved me from something far worse.'

'Gangrene,' answered the doctor.

When I felt ready to get out of bed, a day later, we were approaching our island. I could hear happy shouting on deck and quickly got up and looked out of the windows. My heart immediately gladdened to see the yellow flag waving from the platform on our mountain. Two light cannon shots rang out, indicating two ships arriving. I strained my eyes and could see people on the beach, waving.

Dressing with one hand proved to be something of a problem. No matter how I tried, I could not get into my clothes and had to call for help, which was promptly handled by my new friend, Doctor Johnson.

'Eventually, when your stump has healed,' said Doctor Johnson, 'We'll have a carpenter and blacksmith fashion you a hook. With practice, you will find yourself able to function quite well.'

All I could think of was how would Virginia cope with my lack of a vital body part. I would not be able to give her a good back rub, with only one hand. However, she would have to get used to the change. There was nothing I, nor anyone else could do about it. My hand was gone. I shrugged my shoulders as I stepped into my boots. Then, squaring my shoulders I stepped on deck.

We had to anchor the man of war, off shore, because its draft was too deep to manage the shallow passage into the cove. However, she had sturdy anchors and in the lee of our island, would pose no problem.

It took many hours to ferry all of the men and women on shore. A task I was glad not to have to partake in. As I was being ferried to the beach, I could see Virginia and the children waiting for me.

Doctor Johnson obviously saw the concern on my face because he told me not to worry. 'Virginia is the mother of your two children. Do you think she would cast aside her husband, the leader of a powerful group of men, because he is missing a hand? From all that you have told me about her, I think she will be sympathetic, if anything.'

Doctor Johnson was correct in his assessment of my sweet wife. Fortunately, Virginia was not only beautiful on the outside, she was equally so, on the inside. My dear wife was totally empathetic, as it turned out, and did not give in to pity, but accepted me no differently. She made the homecoming a sweet and blessed affair. I was so fortunate and grateful.

That night, with Captain Chase firmly tied to the post, in the centre of our village, we had a massive welcome home bonfire on the beach, under a glorious full moon, blessing the scene with a beautiful yellow light, which under the influence of a cigar, fashioned by Wapoo, from some plant he found in the forest, I was able to enjoy the evening with absolutely no pain, or a troubling thought about my missing hand. Indeed, as the night progressed, I saw my left hand on the end of my left arm, exactly where it was supposed to be. I am convinced I was holding a bottle with that hand, leaving my right hand free to fondle Virginia, as we kissed from time to time.

Several couples had moved away from the fire and were making love on blankets spread out on the sand. I could hear their gentle moans, off in the dark, as I soared into an incredibly euphoric night of drinking, singing, and fondling my fine woman.

I woke up in my house, several days later. I believe it was August 25th or sixth. My stump was throbbing with a burning pain, however, I could sense it was getting better, already. Later in the day, Wapoo came to see me and gave me some herbs, which helped to kill the pain considerably, still enabling me to function for a good part of the day, which I spent enjoying my family. I was so glad to be home.

The new sailors, who had joined us from the royal man of war, were a sizable number, requiring several hundred new huts, a work they set to accomplish over the next few months. By the time they were done, sometime at the end of November, our town hosted 325 new houses, in addition to the buildings we had put up, previously.

A week after tying Captain Chase to the post, we decided it was time to put the captain out of his misery. We asked the sailors, who sailed under him, what they felt the appropriate method of execution should be. The majority of the men chose, breaking on the wheel; the method of execution favored by many countries in Europe.

I tried to dissuade the men, appealing to their sense of humanity. However, it was to no avail. The sailors wanted revenge. I had to let them have it, or there would have been a problem, with regard to our maintenance of order in the colony. We were over five hundred, now that the company of an entire man of war had come on shore. With that many pirates, things were bound to go wrong, hence it was best to keep a lid on the potentially boiling pot.

The execution was slated for the following afternoon.

Fortunately, or unfortunately for the captain, it rained the next afternoon. We did not want to perform the execution in the rain. It rained again the following day and the next and the next. Finally, after six days and nights of rain, we finally got a beautiful sunny day; a perfect day for an execution.

The blacksmiths had made two, four foot long steel bars, two inches square, with round handles, twelve inches long. Carpenters had fashioned a St. Andrew's cross of heavy oak timbers, with cups under the places where the captain's knees would lie. This massive contraption was set on a base, placing the entire affair at the height of an average man's thighs. The sailors chose to take turns hitting the captain with the steel bars, hence no one man would be responsible for the captain's death.

When the appointed time arrived, Captain Chase was given a chance to say a few last words. He vilified everybody and spat at me, for standing too near. Then, at a signal from me, the first blow was delivered to the captain's right ankle by a tall, skinny sailor. The sound of cracking bone was quite audible over the cheers of the gathered throng, however, the captain's screams went unheeded by the delirious mob; hurling insults at the tortured soul, whose limbs were going to be reduced to pulp.

The next blow was delivered by a large, heavy set man, who addressed the captain, by telling him, the blow he was about to receive, was to make up for the thousands, which the captain had ordered, over the years. The sailor smashed through the captain's left wrist and pulverized the bones with one mighty blow. Again the captain screamed and begged for mercy.

'Like the mercy you showed us, you bastard!' shouted many of the sailors in derision.

Two sailors stepped forward, and each taking a bar, smashed them simultaneously on the captain's lower shins. These blows must have been so excruciating that Captain Chase broke one of the leather straps, firmly holding his left arm.

George and Robert quickly tied him up again, all the while Captain Chase begged for mercy.

When he passed out; we revived him with buckets of cold water.

And so it went on, all afternoon, and well into the night, as bit by bit, every bone in the Captain's arms and legs were pulverized with powerful blows delivered by several hundred sailors bearing the scars of the officer's cruelty.

Eventually, there were no more bones left to pulverize, the captain's appendages having been reduced to strangely twisted, bloody protuberances from a heaving trunk, screaming with intense pain.

'Please shoot me!' cried the captain. 'How can you men be so inhumane? You will all burn in hell for this!'

George looked at me for an indication what we should do.

I suggested we put the captain out of his misery, but the sailors would not hear of it. Instead of killing the broken man, they carried the man, on his cross, down to the beach, on the other side of the island, where we wouldn't hear his screams any longer.

They left the captain there to die on the sand, a fitting end to a tyrant. We held a huge bonfire the night the deed was done, in celebration of the captain's demise. However, I was not in a party mood. The breaking of Captain Chase was not a happy affair, to my way of thinking, and left an uncomfortable feeling in the pit of my stomach.

* * *

Five days later, after everyone had sufficiently recovered from the celebration party, we felt it necessary to send the *Navigator* on a quick cruise for supplies, before winter came. Fortunately, the man of war carried a chest, with an excellent collection of gold coins, which enabled us to send a crew, with the brig, for a quick trip to a near by port in Hispaniola, to purchase a ship full of supplies. Had we taken the man of war, we probably could have brought more supplies back, however, until we repainted her, and changed her name, we thought it best to leave her anchored off shore.

When the winter winds arrived in December, our town was ready to face the worst. Many of our men were superb carpenters, who had built strong houses, and significantly strengthened the stockade, which also served as a wind break.

By the time my stump had sufficiently healed, two of the carpenters fashioned a perfectly fitting wooden cup, to which one of our blacksmiths fashioned a beautiful silver hook. Inside the cup was a soft pad of felt which was very comfortable on the end of my stump. The entire affair was strapped to my arm with wide leather bands. When my friends saw me, for the first time, wearing the new appliance, Robert quipped, that everyone should call me, 'Captain Hook,' from then on.

I laughed and held up my new silver appendage. 'Aaargh!' I growled, pretending to be very threatening, as I pointed my gleaming hook.

My friends jumped back in mock fright and pretended to run away, all of them yelling, 'Oh no, here comes, Captain Hook, the terror of the Seven Seas!'

My friends' silliness made it easy to forget about my missing hand.

* * *

A massive storm hit our island sometime in late December, however our village handled the onslaught fairly well. The man of war lost the top fore mast, but that was all. The problem was a relatively minor one and, when the stormy season passed, the spar was quickly repaired by our capable carpenters.

By February, 1783, it became necessary to make a trip to a large center, in order to fill the man of war and brigantine with supplies, as well as to recruit a large number of women for the single men, who were becoming a problem because of their lack of feminine attentions.

Before the voyage, we changed the name of the man of war to, *William*

Bartleby, in honour of our late captain. We launched the ships on their necessary voyage on February 10 th, 1783. I did not accompany the ships, because I wanted some time for my stump to heal, and to get used to the hook. Besides, it was a routine supply run. I wanted to spend time with my family.

Virginia and the children were content on the island. There was no reason, that they could see, for wanting to spend days and days on a cramped, smelly ship, with a bunch of hungry men. Playing on the beach, sunning, reading, walking, talking, tending the extensive gardens, watching clouds from our observation platform, under the influence of one of Wapoo's concoctions; life on the island was a pleasant one, to say the very least. It was idyllic. The island was our very own utopia.

The island provided everything we needed, excepting the libations of our choice. We had not taken the trouble to build a distillery, in order to make our own rum. It was just too much of a problem, and hardly worth the effort, considering the ready availability of all three of the beverages we chose to imbibe; ale, rum, and wine. Every ship we ever plundered, always carried a supply, except for one Puritan merchantman, on which the officers and crew were teetotalers. They were a rare breed on the Seven Seas.

One day, while Virginia and I were sitting on the beach, watching Catherine and Joshua playing together in the sand, my sweet wife announced that we were pregnant with our third child. I couldn't express enough, how pleased I was to hear the excellent news. I must have kissed her a couple of dozen times, at that moment; I was so grateful for her. I stroked her belly and spoke to our new progeny developing in her womb. We decided to call the baby, William, if it was a boy, and Willemina if it was a girl. It was a more permanent way of remembering our dearly departed friend, whom we both missed considerably.

Sitting on the beach, one afternoon, Virginia and I again discussed a voyage to Halifax with Marianne. This time I was equally enthusiastic, and agreed we would take the brig, in the beginning of June. That way, we could take advantage of summer winds and pleasant weather, enabling us to return before the winter set in. We figured that, it being eight years since we left, we would be safe.

Our ships returned sometime towards the middle of March, fully laden with tons of provisions, and one hundred and twenty five new women, and thirty children, hailing from: Fort de France, Havana, Kingston, Kingstown, Maracaibo, Punda, San Juan, and Saint George's, in Grenada.

Fortunately, some of the men, who had gone on the voyage, had elected to stay in various places the ships stopped. Otherwise we would have felt ourselves getting crowded. Hence, when I took a census, after the new people had settled in, I recorded the following statistics: 363 men, 138 women, 23 children, (10 boys, 13 girls). Sixteen women were pregnant. Alas, we lost seven babies due to various reasons; two died in childbirth, the other five succumbed to various ailments, which Doctor Johnson had no cures for. Not even Narkat and Wapoo's potions could do anything. The babies were buried in a burial ground we were developing on the far side of the island. A large wooded cross stood over the graves of our friends; Frank, Kate, Marvin, Sarah, the seven babies, and 22 sailors, off the Royal Navy ship, who died here and there, in the course of time spent on our island. Some died from fluxes, others from apyrexies, and one died from yellow fever.

Our farm, at the time of my census, consisted of: 53 cats, 15 cows, 35 dogs, 12 horses, 63 pigs, 43 laying hens, 2 roosters, and 34 sheep. Our gardens covered about three hectares of land and grew an assortment of vegetables; assorted beans, carrots, cucumbers, eggplants, leeks, onions, potatoes, squash, tomatoes, turnips, water melons, and yams. On a separate piece of land, we grew sugar cane.

Of fruit trees we had an abundance, throughout the island, plus the ones we cultivated in our gardens; bananas, breadfruit, coconuts, guavases, lemons, limes, mangoes, papa fruit, plantains, plus three little apple trees we had rescued from a ship, two years previously. These three trees were likely going to bear fruit, that coming summer.

Our town consisted of nearly 400 houses, (53 of two stories, 21 of three stories, one of these being my fine house), a meeting hall, which could accommodate over a hundred people, five warehouses, a chapel, for those who wanted to have a formal place to pray, a large underground cold cellar, a three thousand square foot, covered bath house, partly over the pond, not far from the village. We also built a similar establishment jutting into the cove, next to the pier we had built towards the centre of the cove, enabling direct land access to our brig. Two new long boats were tied to the pier, as well.

Some other buildings; a barbers' shop, two tailors' shops, Doctor Johnson's office and infirmary, the blacksmith's shop, three cobblers' shops, the nine hundred and fifty square foot library, which at the time of my census housed 173 volumes of books in seven languages; Danish, Dutch, English, French, German, Spanish, and one in Chinese. We had a Bible in every language except Chinese. However, the Chinese book was likely a Confucian text of some kind.

The newest books were those of Edward Gibbon, published in 1776, about which I told you earlier. Some other volumes were by philosophers, Aristotle, Francis Bacon, René Descartes, Thomas Hobbes, Gottfried Leibnitz, John Locke, Baruch Spinoza, and Plato. I was trying to wend my way through those volumes, but they were hard going, as was Gibbon's history. What I preferred to read, above all the other books were; *Don Quixote* by Miguel de Cervantes, *Robinson Crusoe* by Daniel Dafoe, *Gulliver's Travels*, *The Drapier's Letters*, and *The Battle of the Books* by Jonathan Swift, and a marvelous copy of Roman history by Tacitus. The library was a popular place, but already needed an addition, where more readers could sit during inclement weather.

On the down wind side of the island we built a large latrine facility, with barrels for collecting our dung, which we used to fertilize our gardens. Running water was conducted to this necessary establishment with a bamboo pipe, which collected water from the pond, with an ingenious system of waterwheel and gravity; the pipe being suspended through the trees and gradually sloped down to the latrines. Up wind from the latrines we had dug a channel to allow water from the cove to flow into a beautiful, rock lined bathing pool, a fire pit, for heating stones, was nearby, to service the thirty seat sauna. Proper hygienic standards were strictly enforced in our colony; Doctor Johnson saw to that. We wished to avoid diseases and infections, as best we could, utilizing modern ideas. Good health depended on several things; good air, good drink, good food, and good hygiene.

Some very interesting wooden carvings, some over twelve feet tall, began appearing, here and there, in places throughout our village, as men, who needed to spend their time doing something productive, if they were not working on fixing up their houses, or tending to necessary chores, would carve all manner of things; animals, birds, monsters, people, reptiles, assorted flora, real or fanciful, gradually turning our town into a work of art.

Other folks spent time painting pictures on walls, painting walls different colors, painting the sculptures... Our town was becoming a true wonder and a most incredible place to live; my heart growing ever fonder of our happy home.

Twelve women had set up a knitting and weavers' shop, where they produced some magnificent woolen blankets, scarves, and sweaters from our sheep's' wool.

Two enterprising sailors had started fishing with one of the long boats, and within several months, had built a little fisherman's market stall, by the pier. These two would go out every morning and bring back their catch in the late afternoon. Their catch was eagerly traded for all manner of specie and assorted trade goods.

On a piece of bare rock, jutting into the ocean, we built an abattoir, where we slaughtered and dressed the meat of our pigs, and occasionally one of our bovines. The offal we simply dumped into the sea, where it was quickly consumed by crabs and fish. Sometimes sharks would thrash about under the gutting room as intestines and organs were dropped through the hole, under the hanging carcass. Apparently, one time, when two of our butchers were at work, cleaning a pig, a shark came right up through the hole and grabbed onto one of the pig's front legs, pulling the entire carcass off its hook and into the sea. Neither man attempted to reach in and grab the carcass back. Instead, they modified the hole under the gutting room, preventing future entry by unwanted carnivores.

Five enterprising men, and their wives, had built a wonderful restaurant where Virginia and I often ate. The restaurant was across the street from our concert hall, where we could hear a number of musicians practicing, most everyday, in preparation for one of our many concerts and dances.

As more ships were relieved of cargo, over the years, a marvelous collection of instruments had accrued. At the time of my census we had acquired: a piano forte, two bass viols, a crum horn, three bag pipes, four violas, three violins, six drums, of various sizes, a cithern, a balalaika, two coronets, a trumpet, an oboe, four French horns, a sacbut, an oude, a concertina, three lutes, seven flutes, a piccolo, fourteen block flutes, of various sizes, from alto to bass, and an incredible conch, which, when blown, produced a beautiful rich tone.

Our sheet music collection, which we carefully housed in a weather proof trunk in the concert hall, contained music by; Allegri, Bach, Gabrielli, Monteverdi, William Mundy, Mozart, Palestrina, and Georg Philipp Telemann, the director of music for the German city of Frankfurt am Main. The beauty of the sheet music was that our musicians could read it, regardless of the language in which it was printed. We were so thankful that musical notation had attained some level of standardization.

Near the pool, two couples had established a sort of health spa, where one could receive soothing treatment in one of three large wooden barrels filled with hot water, followed by a massage and skin treatments with oils, which they made from coconuts and olive oils.

Right next door, three women had set up shop as hair dressers, a place Virginia liked to frequent. She always came back glowing from a visit there. Since I was captain of which ever ship I wanted to command, I always received a goodly share of all goods and moneys collected. In other words, Virginia and I were very wealthy, and of the highest status. She could afford to go to the spa.

Marianne, who had found herself a very fine new man, whose name was Donald MacIntyre, was also of high status, and equally rich, having inherited Bill's fortune, it being considerable at the time of his death.

Andy and Judith, Colin and Meira, George and Marta, Robert and Susanne, and several other couples were also considerably wealthy, and being original members, from the times before Bill's death, had very high status in the community. Samantha, who was still single, received a regular pension, on account of Jock's death in our service. Wendy and Russell had separated and were living with other partners. They split the money they had accumulated together, so they were moderately wealthy.

Virginia and I were truly pirate royalty, however, we did not flaunt it overly much. We tried to remain humble.

As time passed, our homes became ever more splendid, as they filled with fine furniture, rugs, paintings, statuettes, silverware, the roofs covered with proper tiles, and the walls plastered like the houses of Europe. Our town was a pleasant place to live, where people minded their own business, and exchanged friendly repartee. We all contributed funds for the general welfare of the members, nobody wanted for anything. Our colony was Paradise. We felt God was on our side. I couldn't have been happier.

Chapter Eighteen

As the time grew closer for us to travel to Halifax, Virginia, Marianne, and I became increasingly anxious to make the trip. We spoke of the upcoming adventure often, and at length, whenever we were together over dinner, lounging on our platform, sitting together in the sauna, wherever. Halifax became an obsession for us and we planned carefully and incessantly, including handpicking those people whom we would invite to accompany us; Colin and Meira, George and Marta, Robert and Susanne, Russell and his new wife, Wendy and her new husband, Samantha, Wapoo and Narkat, and another twenty folks whose company we enjoyed, they being a happy bunch of uninhibited actors, clowns, and musicians. Of course all of our children came with us, as well. None of us were going to leave our precious offspring, for over two months, in the care of others, no matter how loving the care they would have received.

On May first we careened our brig, to make her ready for the voyage to Halifax. We carefully breamed her using burning faggots to heat the abundant growth infesting the bottom of our wonderful ship, making the foul infestation easier to chip off. When all the barnacles, little mussels, seaweed, and assorted marine growth had been burned off, we carefully sealed every crack with pitch. Then we coated the bottom with sulfur to discourage creatures from re-attaching themselves. For a final touch, we used tallow to make the *Navigator* as slippery as possible.

On June the third we began to outfit our brigantine for the voyage, making certain to stow everything carefully in the hold. We wanted to make the trip as comfortable as possible, as was befitting the lifestyle we had grown accustomed to. Hence, by the time we had completed the preparations, including some modifications within the ship itself, providing private quarters for each couple, our ship resembled an armed, luxuriously appointed, passenger ship.

During the months leading up to our departure, Marianne, Virginia, and I, had assembled a chest full of rich presents for family and friends in Halifax. By the time we had filled the chest, it was heavy and had to be carried by four men. We also took along two small chests of gold and silver coins, which we planned to bury in the same place as Bill's Halifax treasure; the treasure which had enabled the genesis of our new lives. The other chest, also filled with gold and silver coins, we planned to bury in Virgineola, hence securing the first two locations for stashing our wealth, in the event we were ever dispersed from our island home.

Favorable winds arrived on June eight. We were ready to take advantage, and with flags flying; drums, bagpipes, flutes, and piccolos providing the appropriate cacophony, twelve men carefully rowed our ship through the channel, as we unfurled her sails. When we were safely through the corral channel, the tow rope was pulled in, our ship positioned, and with a steady breeze filling our sails, our ship began her voyage to Canada. Cannons boomed a parting salute, answered by ten cannons on shore. Those of our friends, who were not manning guns, waved from shore, and from our platform on top of Mount William, that being the name we had given our hill.

When we were well on our way, Virginia and the children joined me in our big cabin over the stern. Virginia had made the place a cozy home, with curtains on the windows, and several potted plants, firmly held in wooden brackets on the sills. Our bed was covered with snow white cotton sheets and multicolored blankets. Our pillows were of the softest down. Our children slept in a bunk bed, built against the starboard bulkhead. The bunks had railings, which prevented the children from tumbling out of their cozy beds when the ship rolled. Their sheets were like ours and their blankets consisted of the same sort of multicolored patterning as our own blankets.

Our cabin furniture consisted of a large oak table with six carved chairs, dressed with the finest silk coverings. We even had a small table and two small chairs made for Catherine and Joshua.

On the walls hung paintings by Sandro Botticelli, Andrea Mantegna, and a strange artist, H. Bosch; the former two being Italian painters, and the latter being a Flemish artist with a strangely original, almost nightmarish vision, showing Christ amongst his accusers. Botticelli's picture was of a Madonna with the baby Jesus on her arm. Mantegna's picture showed a picture of Christ blessing the children. Considering there were a number of young children on board, we felt it was an appropriate picture to take on the journey with us.

A beautiful cabinet against the port bulkhead held some books behind glass doors. Three crystal decanters held two types of Jamaican rum and a red wine from Spain. Twelve magnificent crystal glasses hung upside down from their bases, in holders above the decanters. A mirror reflected the sparkles of light playing in the facets of the glasses. On the floor lay a thick Persian carpet, with an intricate design in rich colors ranging from a deep maroon to a light blue of delicate tone.

Over the table hung a multi candled, brass chandelier of the finest workmanship. It was a prize from a rich merchantman we lightened some years ago. When the twelve candles were lit, the chandelier filled the cabin with a soft, warm light, under which Virginia always looked extra beautiful. At that time she was about six months pregnant, and glowing.

Catherine and Joshua were growing like little sprouts. They played very well together in the cabin or on deck. Catherine was almost seven years old, her birthday being July 12th, and growing into the spitting image of her handsome father, if I may be so bold?

Joshua had turned three in February and presented something of a hand full, at times. He was more curious than a cat, with the energy of a bee; buzzing about here and there, examining everything he could get his hands on.

Little Catherine was a very attentive big sister. She looked after her little brother. They were the best of friends.

The other children got along very well together, the older children gladly keeping an eye on the smaller children, as did everyone else on board. In our colony the children were everyone's children. During the day, there was always someone willing to teach the older children important things like, how to read and write; how to do arithmetic; how to read a sextant and compass. Everyone took a keen interest in educating the children, which was a real blessing. As our colony grew, over the years, our children were all reading and writing by the age of five.

Because the adults all felt responsible for the children, sometimes they would discuss some of the abuses they had suffered, as children; in order to understand why and how abuse can be prevented. Every adult in the colony wanted better for their offspring. The issue of perversions against children, such as beatings, severe chastisements, and even more grotesque, the utilization of children for sexual gratification, was openly discussed, amongst the adults.

Having studied the history of Greece and Rome, we were aware that sort of thing was a normal part of life, back then. Indeed, most of us were well aware of the horrors inflicted on children in the Old Testament of the Bible, many copies of which we had in our library. Indeed, most of us had been so afflicted as children, some of our friends revealed they had been very seriously abused. Their stories were every bit as horrid as those Bill had told me about his childhood. Hence, since we did not want our children to ever suffer, we made it a hard and fast rule; adding it to our original code, 'Anyone suspected of child molestation; beatings, withholding of food, or other privations; including sodomy, or other sexual conduct with children under the age of eighteen years, will be severely dealt with, possibly including capital punishment; the type of punishment to be determined at the discretion of the voting members of the colony.'

Many discussions had revealed that we all preferred the Golden Rule, 'Do unto others as ye would have done to yourselves,' over any other rule. Every member sincerely expressed their desire to mind their own business, and for others to mind their own business. We all agreed that everyone had equal rights; to our lives, our liberty, and our property. We collectively voiced, out loud, why we were pirates, and why we were living on the island in the first place; it was to get away from oppression. We all vowed to strive for the attainment of Paradise on Earth, hence our rules were few and easily understood. Everyone knew and understood the law.

The penalties for subversion of the rules were clearly spelled out and enforced. Fortunately, we did not have to enforce too many of the rules, because everyone agreed with them, with the exception of the errant Marabino, the previous year. Before we had actually written our rules down. However, as I have said before, there was no excuse for Juan attacking Bill. Members of a colony, such as ours, do not naturally attack their brothers or sisters. That fundamental rule should not have to be written down, but carried in everyone's heart.

One afternoon, while I was sitting in my comfortable chair on the quarter deck, contemplating how I was going to write the ideas expressed in the previous paragraph, I looked up and couldn't help but grin from ear to ear, as I watched Joshua attempt to join the older children in a game of hopscotch. Several adults had joined in and the children were having a good time, their laughter filled the space through which our ship traveled, making the journey a most pleasant experience for everyone on board. There is no more wondrous sound than that of children laughing.

In the evenings, after the children were fast asleep, the adults sat about on deck enjoying the beverage of their choice, smoking covered pipes filled with any one of several fragrant plants; cannabis, tobacco, and some unknown plant Wapoo had introduced us to. Everyone was always in such a good humor, that our evenings were always pleasantly spent on deck, telling jokes, laughing about misadventures, things the children said or did, how pleasant our voyage was, up to that point, and so on. We were a very happy company, totally compatible, so I thought, at that time. However, in the real world everything is not always so perfect. Every barrel of apples will contain at least one fruit with a worm in the core. Alas, so it was with our company of friends, as we were to learn some days later, when we stopped in Virgineola.

The voyage from our island to the lovely isle of Virgineola took ten days, during which we had only fair winds and sunshine. It was probably one of the most pleasant cruises I had yet experienced. Perhaps it was because of the addition of the laughing children, or the fact my Virginia was large with child, I don't know. Whatever it was, when we made port, I was over flowing with gratitude and joy. Looking around at my companions, I got the distinct impression the feeling was mutual.

A number of Dutch, English, and Portuguese ships were anchored in the harbour, two of them were frigates belonging to the hated Royal Navy. We made certain to anchor some distance from them, on the lee side of three Dutch West Indiamen. None of us had any desire to draw the attentions of the Royal Navy, who were no doubt wondering where, the *Avenger* had gotten to. A brigantine crewed by people representing assorted ethnicities, wearing colorful scarves, and exotic clothing, including women and children, such as ours, were certain to draw undue attention. We did not look exactly like the average immigrants, or what one would call, 'genteel folk' enjoying a vacation cruise.

When, the *Navigator* had been securely anchored, we ferried ourselves ashore with the long boat.

Three trips brought all but three men, one woman, and an ill child, ashore. Kathleen volunteered to look after Linda, a six year old girl who had fallen ill, two days previously. Her parents, James and Karen, felt it was better if the girl remained sleeping in her bed. Kathleen, being the wife of Pedro, who had drawn the first watch in port, along with Carlos and Martin Henry, decided to stay with her husband. She assured James and Karen their little girl would be safe in her care.

Some time later, while we were enjoying a pleasant meal at an excellent restaurant overlooking the harbour, Carlos proceeded to get himself gloriously drunk on board our ship, while Kathleen and Pedro took the opportunity of enhanced privacy to go off to their cabin, believing Linda to be safely asleep in her bed.

It was sometime in the middle of the afternoon, when Kathleen and Pedro were napping, after their conjugal pleasure, and Carlos was passed out on a coil of rope, when, Martin apparently snuck down to James and Karen's cabin, where Linda lay sleeping; a fever warming her brow.

Of course, exactly how events accrued on board, is mostly conjecture, on my part. I was not there to witness what actually happened. However, I relied on the witness of Linda, who was old enough to understand what Martin had done to her. Of course, Kathleen, who caught Martin on the scene of his crime, heard what she heard, and saw what she saw.

Apparently, Martin snuck into Linda's family cabin, while the girl was sleeping. He managed to lift her bedclothes and availed himself of her private parts with his index finger. Linda, who had received a sleeping potion, to help her sleep off her illness, did not wake up right away. We have no idea how long Martin did what ever he did, however at some point Linda woke up. She managed to scream once, before Martin put his hand on her mouth, attempting to shut her up. However, Martin did not realize that pirate children are not so easily intimidated, even when groggy from a sleeping potion.

Linda bit his hand.

Martin yelled.

Linda screamed.

Kathleen and Pedro heard the noise and rushed to Linda's cabin, discovering Martin attempting to cover Linda's mouth to stop her screaming.

Pedro manhandled Martin away from Linda and threw him against a bulkhead. However, Martin being quite a lot larger than Pedro, over powered him, necessitating Kathleen shooting Martin in the shoulder with her pistol. This stopped Martin just long enough for Pedro to smack him over the head with the water pitcher he found sitting on the sideboard.

Kathleen and Pedro dragged the unconscious child molester out of the cabin and tied him up in the fo'c's'le.

When the rest of us returned to the ship, just before sunset, Kathleen and Pedro pulled, Colin, George, and I aside, and explained what had accrued during our absence.

Linda told her parents what had happened when they looked in on her, immediately after returning to the ship.

The news, thus received, was not good.

Of course James wanted to kill Martin, right then and there.

I can not say I blame James for feeling that way. If the girl had been my daughter, I would certainly have felt the same way. However, because we believed in justice, as was spelled out in our law code, we would have to hold a trial. Our laws were not the plethora of rules posing as mediators of justice, such as the common people lived under. Our laws were a few, easily understood rules, which led, in my way of thinking, towards the practice of real justice in our colony.

Hence, it was only fair that we held an immediate trial, while memories were fresh, and ascertained, without a doubt, whether Martin was guilty. We conducted the trial the very next day.

That night I slept poorly, because I would have to serve as judge, being the captain. Even Virginia's soothing ways could not bring on sleep. I am sure I must have looked a wreck the next morning. I certainly felt it.

When everyone had breakfasted, and felt ready to conduct the trial, Martin was brought out and made to sit in a chair, in the middle of the deck. His wound was a painful reminder of his folly. We did not bother to remove the ball, because we were not sure if Martin would live for very long, if found guilty. So, rather than cause him further distress, by digging in his shoulder with a hot knife, we thought it best to wait until we heard the verdict of the court, who were the assembled members of our company, who either stood, or sat in, what amounted to a horse shoe, with Colin, George, Robert, Wapoo, and I sitting in chairs at the head of the horseshoe.

The trial began by letting Martin tell his side of the story first.

Martin claimed he had gone to see if Linda was alright, considering that Carlos had gotten drunk, and Kathleen and Pedro were enjoying conjugal pleasures in their cabin. He completely denied having touched Linda.

Kathleen was next. She explained that Linda was asleep, and that, since she and Pedro were in the cabin, right next door, they felt it was the perfect opportunity to enjoy each other, since Carlos was sleeping, and as far as they knew, Martin was working on a piece of scrimshaw he was carving. Apparently, Martin had told Kathleen and Pedro he did not mind them leaving him for a while. Kathleen described how she heard commotion and Linda's screams from next door. She had to dress quickly in order to arrive decently attired in Linda's cabin. What Martin had managed to do to Linda, in the mean time, is anybody's guess. However, from the time Kathleen heard the screams, to the time she entered the cabin, she figured was about four minutes. She explained why she felt it necessary to shoot the defendant in the shoulder.

Pedro's testimony corroborated his wife's. He added his involvement with regard to pulling Martin off the girl, but had nothing further to add.

Finally, Linda was brought forward. She explained that Martin was touching her private parts, when she woke up, because she felt something attempting to come into her. Fortunately, she woke up in time and managed to scream, and push Martin away, before he could penetrate her. Linda was proud of herself for biting Martin's hand, and did not seem overly traumatized by the incident.

However, the rest of us were pretty much disgusted with Martin, but, in order to make absolutely certain that we could trust the word of a six year old child, against that of an adult protesting his innocence, it became necessary to use torture. We had no option but to torture Martin in order to find the truth. We were not about to execute an innocent man on the word of a child alone. We needed one more piece of evidence.

Martin knew there was no option, and I am sure, he must have prayed for strength to withstand the pain and not incriminate himself. He was well aware of the consequences, should he admit to having done the deed.

In order to conduct the torture, without the children present, the women, accompanied by six men, took the children sightseeing in the Crystal Caves, a magnificent natural feature of the island. We figured Martin's trial would take a few hours, so we advised the women and children to stay away until nightfall. We reckoned we would have the truth by then.

I will spare you, dear reader, the gruesome details of the torture. However, in order for you to have some understanding, under what sort of conditions a man will confess to a crime, which will surely be punished with death; without going into too much gory detail, I will merely present a few highlights.

The torture was conducted by two impartial men, who had some experience with the process, having been tortured by officials of the Spanish government some years previously.

Martin, who was sweating profusely, continued to proclaim his innocence, as he was firmly tied to the chair he was sitting on. In the meantime, a brazier was set in front of him, in which a small fire was crackling. Eventually, a white hot bed of coals received a pair of carpenter's pincers, a short sword, and a metal prod.

When the aforementioned items were white hot, they were applied in various ways to Martin's torso, causing him to emit grotesque screams, over which he protested his innocence. It was when the pincers were applied to his right nipple and twisted, that he finally gave in. He admitted he had done what Linda had said; he had attempted to penetrate her little vagina with his right index finger.

'Hang him!' shouted Robert.

'Cut him into pieces and throw him to the sharks!' shouted Russell.

'Cut his testicles off!' shouted Colin, as he spat in Martin's direction.

'I say, cut off his offending finger,' said James, calmly. And then, I think we should just continue to cut the rest of his fingers off. He can fend for himself here, in Virgineola without his fingers.'

'What about Kathleen and Pedro?!' shouted Martin angrily. 'And what about Carlos, he got drunk, when he was supposed to be watching Linda?!' Martin stared at Carlos and Pedro, 'Are they not guilty of negligence?'

Of course the three people, whom Martin named, were guilty of negligence. We knew it and they knew it. What exactly their punishment would be, remained to be discussed. In order for Martin to realize we were fair minded, we agreed with his point of view regarding dereliction of duty, which shut him up, as he waited anxiously for us to decide what his punishment should be.

The deliberation took about thirty minutes, as all manner of horrible punishments were discussed; Martin being privy to every suggestion. Eventually, the voices of reasonable punishment prevailed.

James and Karen accepted what we collectively agreed upon.

Martin, of course, protested vociferously, as we cut off his right index finger, and for good measure, cut off his left one, as well. Then we simply castrated Martin and left him, with Carlos, Katherine, and Pedro, in Virgineola, where they would realize the error of their ways, as they sought to survive with nothing but the clothes on their backs. No one could argue with the fairness of our justice.

We left Virgineola on June 20th, gentle winds blowing us north, until we hit foul weather, five days later. We were blown significantly off course, as we battled twenty foot waves, which crashed over our bows with tremendous force, shivering the timbers from stem to stern, as the ship dug into deep valleys between the massive frothing peaks.

As we were tossed this way and that, all manner of objects came loose and began to clatter and crash about here and there throughout the ship, necessitating people rushing about fastening things down, and making sure the hatches were battened as tightly as possible.

Various places began to spring leaks, as the timbers were pounded by the unrelenting waves. Our carpenters did their best to plug the leaks but it was a difficult struggle, trying to keep the ship dry, requiring sixteen men, to constantly work the pumps.

Suddenly, the main top mast splintered, when a massive wave hit us broadside, while we were in a trough. Tons of water crashed on the deck, bringing twisted rigging and sheets down with it. Fortunately, the rest of the spar remained standing, enabling the unfurling of another trysail, at great risk to the sailors who did the work for us.

George, who handled the wheel was hard pressed to keep our nose into the waves. He had to rely on Colin and me to help hold the wheel steady. It was at this time that I came to appreciate my hook, because it helped to hold the wheel in place, when we were hit hard on the port bow, splintering a piece of the forward port railing; shrieking banshee winds scaring the color out of everyone's cheeks.

The storm abated three days later, as all storms eventually do. We each thanked God, in our own way, for our deliverance. Storms, which take spars and rigging, are always a fright, no matter how seasoned the sailors. As soon as the weather returned to glorious sunshine and warmth, the children came back on deck and filled our ears with their happy laughter, equally glad to be delivered from the horrible forces of nature.

George and I ascertained that the storm had blown us considerably off course, in the direction of Connecticut, where a revolution was still brewing; heightening the possibilities of running into American frigates, or English men of war. We decided to play safe and ran up our Dutch tricolor, as we set a course for the whaling station on Nantucket island; not that we wanted to, but we had to repair our broken spar and really did not have too much choice in the matter.

Fortunately, we did not meet up with government ships and were able to find a suitable anchorage on the little island, where we stopped to recuperate from the ravages of the storm. The weather was warm and a light breeze was blowing, enabling us to open all the port holes, to air out our ship, which the women cleaned thoroughly with vinegar, in order to wash the smell of children's' vomit and other disgusting odors away.

The carpenters got to work fixing the broken spar, while others repaired leaks in the hull, the result of the relentless pounding waves. Because I was the captain, I was allowed to sit on the beach, and watch the children playing in the sand. As I watched them dig about, it occurred to me that Virginia and I had forgotten to bury one of our treasure boxes in Virgineola, something we would have to correct on the return voyage.

During the time we spent on Nantucket Island, the women acquired some local cats and let them loose in the ship, quickly scaring the rats away. I watched two brown rats climb down an anchor cable and attempt to swim to shore. Whether they made it or not, I have no idea. However, knowing something about the resourcefulness of rats, I suspected they did make it and were already producing offspring, to ravage the island.

Five days later our ship was ready and the winds favorable, enabling us to continue our voyage to Halifax, arriving there five and a half days later, our stomachs full of butterflies, and our knees slightly wobbly. We had no idea what we would find there and prayed that Virginia's family was still alive and living in the busy town.

Chapter Nineteen

We sailed into the familiar harbour and immediately noticed that Halifax had grown considerably. The roadway had more piers running perpendicularly into the water. A large new warehouse imposed its presence, not far from where we anchored. The harbour was filled with a forest of spars flying flags from many different countries. The shipping appeared twice as numerous, as when we lived there, eight years previously. Obviously Halifax was prospering.

We dropped anchor in a secluded spot, between two Danish ships, waiting for berths along a pier by the lumber mill. We quickly made our ship secure, all of us anxious to go on shore.

Several Danish sailors waved to us, welcoming us between their ships.

We waved back, but, since none of us spoke Danish, we could only shout enthusiastic, 'Ya, ya, gute, gute,' and, 'Velcomen, velcomen!' Our attempts to sound friendly with, what we thought were Danish words, had the desired effect because the Danish sailors were very vociferous in welcoming us, as well. Perhaps the fact our women were standing on deck, waving at them, may also have had something to do with it. We just figured it was a fortuitous situation, because friendly relations with one's neighbors can be of great benefit. It ensured enhanced security.

In order to avoid drawing undue attention to ourselves on shore, we decided to dress in the clothes befitting wealthy patricians. Even the children were dressed as little adults, with waist coats and tricornered hats for the boys and bonnets for the girls. When we stepped foot on shore, no one could have suspected us for pirates; assuming us to be wealthy merchants taking a stroll with our wives and children.

Marianne, Virginia, our three children, and I decided we would go in search of Virginia's family warehouse, to see if the Spencers were still in business. Our friends went into town, shopping and sightseeing.

Marianne's little boy, Michael, was the same age as Joshua. They seemed to get along fairly well, all things considered, seeing as how they were two and a half and needed regular coaching, to share their toys. However, they strolled along, at their own pace, often stopping to examine things they found on the ground.

Catherine, like a little sheep dog, kept a close watch on the two toddlers.

As we approached the location, where the family enterprise was located, we were surprised to see a different sign on the building. The building itself had not changed much, but the sign now proclaimed, 'Abercrombie & Trimtab, General Merchandise.' Peeking in, we could see that the business conducted was still the same, namely supplying general merchandise to the ships in the harbour, however, the people working there were different.

Virginia ventured to ask a clerk, what had happened to her father and her uncle.

The clerk didn't know, but an elderly man, who was writing in a large book, did.

The elderly man looked up from his book and took off his spectacles. Then he explained that Edward Spencer had succumbed in a house fire, in which he and his family had expired, sometime in the winter of 1781. Apparently, Virginia's uncle had sold the business and left Halifax, shortly thereafter, likely returning to England, from whence he came.

The news hit Virginia like a ton of bricks. As soon as she stepped outside, she started to hyperventilate, and moments later, broke down into a gush of tears and self recriminations. Marianne and I did our best to console her, as the three of us sat together on a bench, outside the warehouse. Little Catherine asked what was wrong with her mommy, and Marianne explained that she was just a little upset, at the moment, and that she need not be worried. Just to help take her mind off her mother's dilemma, Marianne took Catherine, and the two toddlers, for a little walk, while I helped Virginia regain her composure.

When Virginia had choked her tears back, she was ready to take a carriage to have a look at her former home.

We loaded up the children, and Marianne, and drove, in an open carriage, to the place where Virginia's family home had stood.

A fine new house stood where the Spencer home had been. The only evidence, that there had been a fire, was the charred trunk of the huge elm, which still stood in the front yard. Fortunately, the fire had not taken the tree. It continued to provide shade for a new family.

A servant must have seen us standing in front of the house because, a few moments later, the butler came out on the verandah and asked us who we were, and what our business was.

We explained that we used to know people who lived at that location.

'Oh, the Spencers,' said the butler. 'Yes, a most unfortunate thing happened, when their house caught fire. It happened in the middle of the night. Arson was suspected, but never proved.'

'Arson?' I asked.

'Yes,' answered the butler. 'Some people were very angry with the Spencers because their daughter apparently helped a dangerous pirate escape from the gaol. It is highly possible the house was torched by anti pirate activists, who had been taunting the Spencers for years. I guess it all came to a head when Mister Spencer shot one of them, after they assaulted him outside of his business.'

Marianne asked if the entire family perished.

The butler answered that three people died in the fire. Mister and Mrs. Spencer and Virginia's sister, Beatrice. The other children had married and were living elsewhere, he said. The man did not know where James and Anna had gone to.

I thanked the man for his information and led my distraught wife back to the carriage, where Marianne sat with her and the children, while I queried the neighbors.

Not any of Virginia's former neighbors lived in the houses next door or across the street. Eight years away and almost everything had changed in Halifax. I assured Virginia we would locate her brother and sister, but

Virginia just sat there, staring wide eyed at her hands. She broke down and resumed her tears.

We rode silently back to our long boat and waited for some of the others to come back, so we could row to the brig, where Virginia immediately shut herself up in our cabin, sobbing uncontrollably.

Marianne volunteered to look after the children, while I returned to shore, accompanied by Colin, and Robert, who came with me for protection, as I conducted further investigations regarding the whereabouts of Virginia's siblings; which, on that first day, produced no results.

When I returned to my cabin, Virginia was sleeping. I quietly closed the door and sought my children, who were sitting with the others, enjoying their evening meal. The children's laughter and happy banter lifted my spirits and I began to feel lighter. I located my cup and poured myself a hearty rum. It had been a trying day.

When it came time to put my children to bed, I helped Marianne prepare Joshua and then brought Catherine and my little son into our cabin. Virginia was awake and looked blankly through blood shot eyes, as the children came to kiss her good night. Virginia reacted, as if she didn't know the children, and pushed them away, which made Joshua cry and startled Catherine and me.

Virginia, realizing what she had just done, pulled Joshua into a hug and assured him she didn't mean it, and was sorry. She said the same thing to Catherine as she embraced our sweet little daughter. 'Mommy is just upset, that is all,' she said gently, and then smothered the children with kisses. Sending them to bed, happy and content that their world was still safe.

When the children were snuggled into their cozy bunks, I went over to sit with my wife and held her in my arms for a long time, the two of us not saying a word, but communicating with our bodies; me sending her all the strength and support I could muster in my firm embrace.

Virginia put her head on my chest and stared vacantly, thinking of her family.

'We should never have gone with Bill,' she said after a long silence. 'If we hadn't rescued him, my family would still be alive,' she stammered. 'My baby sister would still be here.'

'The butler did say there was no proof regarding the arson charge,' I said, reassuringly. 'Maybe it is just hearsay and the house burned because of another reason, which has nothing to do with us,' I told her. Then I assured her I would return to town, the following morning, and continue my investigations. I felt certain that someone would know what happened. My words of comfort helped Virginia out of bed. She was able to eat some food and drink a glass of wine, shortly after which she returned to bed and dropped into a deep sleep, within minutes. I stroked her hair gently and then left the cabin, in order to converse with my friends over another cup of rum.

Next morning, while I was sitting on the quarter deck, enjoying breakfast with my family and friends, two port authorities pulled alongside in their long boat and requested to come on board, in order to assess the anchorage fees.

Wapoo waved them on board.

'We would like to speak with the captain,' said the shorter official, who wore the black clothes of a Puritan.

Wapoo directed the officials to me, by pointing at the quarter deck.

Moments later, the two officials stood before my table and asked which one of us was the captain.

George pointed at me.

The officials bowed slightly and then the short Puritan asked me, point blank, with a suspicious air, where we had come from, and what our business was in Halifax.

I told him that we had come to investigate a business opportunity in the port. I told him that we were an international company of actors and musicians, contemplating the erection of a theatre in Halifax.

The Puritan pursed his lips and looked at his associate. 'Actors and musicians?' The man shook his head. 'We don't need, such as you, in Halifax,' he said. 'Between work and church, the people have no time for frivolous pursuits, like the sort of thing you people are planning to establish here.'

I smiled and winked at my friends, then I told the man we would judge for ourselves, whether Halifax wanted a theatre, or not.

My remark did not sit well with the officious Puritan, however, there was not much he could do, Halifax was a free port.

Then he asked how long we were planning to stay.

I looked at my friends and shrugged my shoulders. I replied we were not exactly certain, however he could charge us for two weeks, and then we would see, after that.

The Puritan sniffed haughtily. Then, with a pompous air of religious superiority, he looked over the railings at our friends, assembled on deck. The Puritan official looked down his nose at our happy friends, enjoying their breakfast; children happily running about. 'Actors,' he snorted. 'Children of the devil.'

'If we are children of the devil, than so be it,' I replied. 'At least we have smiling faces and are happy in each other's company.' I pointed at the man's associate. 'Judging from your dour expressions, I don't expect you are having much joy in your lives,' I laughed.

My breakfast companions thought it a funny response and joined me in a good laugh, at the officials' expense.

The staunch Puritan did not like us laughing and felt it an insult. 'The Lord did not put us on Earth to be frivolous,' said the unhappy man, raising his voice. 'Life is serious business.'

'Aye, it is serious business,' I replied. 'That is why it is so important to make that business a pleasant one, as much as possible. It lessens the load, so to speak.'

The Puritan looked down his nose and wiped it with a handkerchief he kept in his left sleeve. 'I assure ye sir, someday ye will face thy Maker, and ye will be held to account for thy sins.'

'Aye,' replied George, 'That we will. And whatever they be, I will account for them and pay the price. However, wherever I go, after this life, I will go with no regrets and a smile on my face, which yours hasn't seen in a long time, I suspect.'

'I will smile when I see the Gates of Paradise,' replied the Puritan. 'Until then, I am forced to live in the world amongst actors and thieves.'

'You are calling us, thieves?' asked Colin, indignantly rising from his chair and reaching for the pistol in his belt.

'Actors and thieves come from the same class of people,' answered the man knowingly.

If I had not restrained Colin, I think he would have shot the man right there on our quarter deck.

We were beginning to tire of the man's depressing point of view. He was putting a stifling blanket over our morning.

'I would love to sit here and discuss all of this with you, sir,' I said, 'However, we are on a schedule, and are expected ashore, momentarily. Therefore, if you will kindly assess the fee we will pay it. Then you can leave our company, because, quite frankly sir, you are beginning to depress me, and my friends.'

The Puritan snorted and stared at me with the blazing eyes of a man in fear of the Lord. If he had been living in a world of his making, he would have had me killed on the spot, such was his expression.

The official assessed us a fee of five pounds sterling, an exorbitant price, however we paid it immediately, obtaining a receipt from the other official, who never said a word the entire time he stood on our decks; a tall, sullen looking chap of about twenty seven, with thin, wispy hair, and a sad expression on his face. He also wore the black clothes of a Puritan believer, without the hat. I couldn't help but feel sorry for the bloke, for some reason. He had probably been hit hard in the head, with a thick Bible, which had rattled his brains, when he was but a lad.

When the officials had their five pounds of silver firmly established in the official purse, the two men climbed back into their boat. Their slave rowed them to shore and I returned to my breakfast, pondering the Puritan and his unhappy Christian claptrap.

'If we're made in God's image, I'd rather his face be like yours, Peter,' said George, 'and not like one of those, sour pusses. I prefer to think God has a smiling face, not like one of those, there, tight lipped Christians.'

'I'll drink a toast to that,' said Robert, raising his cup.

'Here is to Our Smiling God!' we shouted in unison, as we smacked our cups together and laughed heartily, glad we were not Puritans.

After breakfast, Colin, George, Robert, and I rowed ashore, with eight of our friends, who wanted to get off the ship for a few days to stay at an inn. Virginia and I went ashore to find out what more we could, regarding her family. Of course we could not risk seeking out acquaintances, because people talked, and we knew that the Crown had a memory like a steel trap. If word of our presence in Halifax leaked out to the wrong people, we could be arrested; something we wanted to avoid at all costs.

It occurred to me that the Morning Post would have information regarding the Spencers, they were a prominent family in Halifax. Surely there would be information regarding the fire and the whereabouts of the rest of the family. However, I could not be the one going into the office, just in case someone recognized me. Hence, Colin and Robert volunteered to seek the information I needed to know.

The Morning Post was located some distance from the harbour. It being a beautiful day, we decided to walk, which quickly became a problem, when we began to discover, our legs were not used to the exercise. By the time we had walked about five and a half blocks, our legs were feeling the effort. Fortunately, a public house was close by, where we sat down to discuss our lack of exercise over a pint of cool ale.

'We need to walk more,' said Colin.

'It's the cobblestones,' observed Robert.

'We simply don't walk enough on board ship,' said George, rubbing his left calf muscle. 'We don't climb rigging like we used to, either. Perhaps we should consider implementing an exercise program, when we are on board ship. We could walk up and down the deck, climb the ladders, that sort of thing.'

'We used to do that, when we were sailors,' said Colin, looking towards the sea. 'We have become fat, lazy pirates.'

'Aye, but we're rich pirates, don't forget that,' replied Robert, smiling over a gold doubloon. 'We may be fat and lazy, but we can afford to be. We have done our work.'

'Well, I for one want to be in better condition,' said Colin, emphatically. 'I don't want to grow old and can't walk twelve steps, without having to sit down and breathe.'

We agreed that Colin had a valid point and vowed to get more exercise, beginning with the remaining walk to the Morning Post building.

When we arrived in front of the building, all of us were feeling muscles we had not used much. As we stood in front of the building, I observed that an addition had been attached to the left side. On the right, several new establishments occupied land, which had been empty when I left town. One of these new enterprises was a book store and the other, an apothecary. While Colin and Robert sought out information in the office of the Morning Post, George and I sought out the book store.

As we entered the shop a little bell tinkled above our heads, signaling the book seller there were potential customers in his cluttered shop. I had the distinct impression I was entering a spider's cavern, overflowing with the printer's art, which like a web, stuck me there and had me completely captivated. Books by the hundreds filled shelves, lay on tables, and were stacked on counters. On a large table, in the middle of the room, lay a magnificent portfolio of navigation charts, which immediately attracted George and me. We were standing over the charts when the book seller came into the room.

'Good day, gentlemen,' said the book seller; a small man with a long, thin nose, bearing spectacles. On his head he wore an old peruke, long devoid of powder. His clothes were rumpled and well lived in. 'How can I help you?' he asked in a gentle, croaky voice.

We told him we were interested in some of the charts, and would be pleased to look about for some books, to expand our library on board ship.

'My patrons are primarily gentlemen of the marine trade,' he said, smiling and rubbing his hands together. 'Therefore you will find, gentlemen, that my books and charts are of the finest quality, made to withstand the rigours of a sea voyage.'

As he talked, the book seller picked up a leather bound copy of, *Meditationes de Prima Philosophia*, which we already had in our library. He was impressed when I told him so.

'Perhaps I can interest you in the poems of Ovid? Or perhaps you would prefer a contemporary copy of Danté's, *Comedia*?' The bookseller grabbed a book off the shelf and held it out to me, 'This is an excellent edition of Samuel Johnson's, *Lives of the Poets*. It was published four years ago. I just received five copies, last month.'

I examined Johnson's book while the book seller grabbed another book, a fine edition of Adam Smith's, *An Inquiry into the Nature and Causes of the Wealth of Nations*. 'Published in 1776,' said the book seller, pointing to the colophon.

I remarked that it was the same publishing date as Edward Gibbon's massive work, pertaining to the rise and fall of the Roman Empire.

The book seller looked over his glasses at me, obviously impressed with my observation. 'You know books, do you?' he asked.

I told him that I was a writer, which impressed the book merchant even more. However, I did not pursue the conversation further because George enthusiastically suggested that we purchase the entire portfolio of charts; they obviously being something we could make good use of.

Hearing that we were purchasing the entire portfolio surprised the little man. He carefully ventured to mention that the price, of the entire portfolio, was twenty five pounds stirling.

Without blinking an eye, I told him we would purchase a number of books, as well, and began to pick some volumes off the shelves, setting them on the table next to the charts. I could tell the old book seller was beginning to have a very excellent day.

As George and I were organizing our purchase, Colin and Robert entered the shop, sad expressions on their faces. When I asked them what was wrong, they informed me that Virginia's sister, Anna had died in childbirth, and her husband, Paul Marché, had moved to Montreal.

It was a sad bit of news, but I was not surprised, considering what her mother had said about Anna, in the letter we received in Cuba. Virginia's mother had written that Anna did not look well during her pregnancy. It was one of the tragedies of our times. I knew that Virginia would understand that, and hoped that she not take the news too hard.

Colin continued to talk about what they had found out at the Morning Post. Apparently, James, Virginia's brother, was killed in a mishap, enroute to Lunenburg on company business. A horse, he was riding, bolted and knocked him off the saddle. He apparently struck his head on a rock and died on the spot.

That news was indeed the worst of it, I think. It was very sad, and meant that Virginia was now alone in the world. Her entire family was dead. Her family was gone. All she had left were the children and me.

Virginia and the children is all I had, as well. Perhaps it is why we were so close; so deeply in love with each other. We were all the family we had, and must have known it all along.

I thanked my friends for the information, never thinking that the bookseller had any remote interest in our conversation, however, thinking about it all now, I am certain he overheard every word, as he wrapped the books in paper.

Colin and Robert were also interested in books and began to pick out a few volumes to take back, as well. By the time we were done, we had spent fifty pounds stirling, which made the book seller exceedingly glad. He was even more ecstatic when we paid him with three gold doubloons.

The purchase of reading material for our library, and the charts, necessitated the hiring of a carriage, because we couldn't carry so many books, and a portfolio of charts. Since we had the carriage, anyway, we decided to buy some nice things for our women and children. I knew, if I brought a nice present for Virginia, the news I was bringing her, would not strike quite so hard. However, I could well imagine how a sensitive person, like Virginia, would take to the news that her entire family was dead. I dreaded having to tell her.

We loaded the carriage up with beautiful dresses and jewelry for our women, and toys for the children. Then we happily rode back to our boat. We quickly unloaded the carriage and paid the driver, giving him some extra coins, for which he thanked us profusely. He waved when he left.

Rowing back, a seagull dropped an unwelcome packet, which splattered on one of the packages containing books. I was glad they were wrapped, as I beheld the white, slimy blob oozing on the paper. I did my best to brush it off, without soiling my cuff. I washed my hand in the sea. The water was warm and pleasant to the touch.

I sniffed the air deeply. It was redolent with the smell of fish, kelp, and salt. The cries of the gulls floating above the ships, filled the air with a cacophony of sound. However, I heard little of it, as I focused on Virginia and what I had to tell her. When we arrived alongside our ship, Virginia and the children were waiting for me, happy to see me. We passed the packages up and I handed my purchases to Virginia and the children, who were very happy with their presents.

When our purchases had all been brought on board, another group of friends rowed off to enjoy the evening in town.

Virginia asked me if we had found out any thing pertaining to her family and I nodded. I led her down to our cabin and told her the tragic news. However, instead of breaking down in a paroxysm of sobs, Virginia took the news calmly. I believe she had some prior knowledge of the news and was already prepared for the worst.

I held my wife for a long time and rocked her gently in my arms. I stroked her silken hair and kissed her gently on her cheek. Then, when she requested to spend some time alone, I left the cabin and joined the children and adults on deck, quickly joining in a game of hide and seek.

Two days later, when Virginia was feeling much happier, we decided it was the perfect day to take the children, and our treasure box, to the place by the bend in the road; where Bill's treasure had been buried. Ten of our friends were going into town, so we all gathered in our boat and rowed to shore, where I hired a carriage. We did not take a driver and handled the reins ourselves. I let Catherine handle them, for most of the way outside of town, something she greatly enjoyed, and took very seriously.

Traffic was light, on the road out of town, which enabled us to travel the distance in twenty minutes, or so; stopping the carriage off the road, near the bend, where the oak tree still stood, guarding the flat rock. We set our box of treasure in the hole, under the rock, hiding the key carefully at the base of the tree; twelve paces from the flat rock, just as Bill had done. The entire operation took no more than ten minutes. When we were done, I made certain that Catherine took good note of the location, in case she should have to rely on the treasure, at some point in the future.

Catherine diligently followed me to the tree root and showed me where the brass spike was, hiding the key's location. Then she paced twenty steps, to the flat rock; her steps being shorter than an adult's.

When we felt confident, all was well, we drove the carriage some ways further into the country side, enjoying the sunshine, and the clip clop sounds of the horse's hooves. Eventually, the sky began to cloud over and a cool breeze blew in from the north east. It was time to return to town; arriving there in the mid afternoon, a good time to enjoy a fine meal at a restaurant, before returning to our boat.

We quickly rowed back to our ship; arriving in the nick of time, just as the sky opened up; dropping tons of water on our decks.

Not that we cared, we were warm and dry in our cozy cabin.

It rained all that night, and the following day, preventing anyone from going to town. The wind blew cold, when we celebrated my daughter's birthday. However, the jovial company of our friends made the day a joyous celebration. Catherine received some very nice gifts from our excellent and loving companions.

Catherine showed her appreciation by giving everyone a big hug.

The adults happily participated in making a good party for the children. We all had a marvelous time listening to their happy laughter, as we played hide and seek throughout the ship; the cannon we called, 'The Kicker,' serving as home base. After dinner we told stories until the children's bed time. When the children were sleeping, the adults continued the party, many enjoying the beverages of their choice until the wee hours of the morning. Virginia and I bowed out shortly after midnight, as did the other parents, with young children. None of us had any trouble sleeping. We didn't think there was anything to worry about.

Next morning we woke early when Joshua woke up, and needed to be cleaned up and fed. I felt good, having slept well. Virginia was in a better frame of mind, coming to accept the loss of her family. Losing family members, or entire families, was not an uncommon occurrence. Such was life in the eighteenth century.

I was excited with the prospect of going back to the book seller's shop. My mind was hungry for books. On our voyages, and our time spent on the island, I had all the time in the world, to read, think, and write. In books lay knowledge. In knowledge lay power. The book seller's shop was a gold mine, where I was about to spend a small fortune.

After breakfast, we rowed quickly ashore, all of us anxious to get on with a day in town. Robert wanted to check on our friends, who were staying at the Lonely Boar, an Inn not far from the harbour. Virginia and I wanted to go to the book seller's. Wapoo and Narkat were going to visit with a Mi'kmaq family they had met. The others just wanted to be on shore; to shop, visit, drink rum, and generally enjoy the port.

The roadstead was already alive with activity. Wagons loaded with all manner of goods were offloading at the warehouses along the road. Others were being loaded with goods, to be hauled to ships tied to the piers, jutting out from the roadway. The morning smells of fish and kelp filled the air, which hung like a gossamer sheet over the scene. Gulls were already hard at work, screaming at each other, and at us, as they circled in the air, looking for something to eat.

A patrol of Royal Marines arrived in a long boat, not far from where we had tied our boat. I assumed, at the time, they were looking for absent sailors. I paid them no further attention.

I hired a carriage and driver to take us to the book seller's shop; arriving there just as he was unlocking his front door, readying the store for the day's business.

When the old man saw me, his expression was one of suspicious surprise, which I found odd, at the time. He quickly changed his countenance to one of oily solicitousness and wished us a good morning. 'How can I be of service to you, sir, and madam?'

I told him we had come to purchase some more books.

The little book seller rubbed his hands together and asked if we wanted assistance, or whether we just wanted to pick books, more or less, at random. 'I have copies of *Candide*, by a French writer named, Voltaire. It is quite a humorous tale.' The book seller smiled at the little book in his hand. Setting it down, he reached for a thick book, bound in brown leather. 'Or what about this book by Daniel Dafoe?' The book seller held the book out to me. 'It is about a man, who is shipwrecked and spends years alone on an island.' The old man nodded. 'It is a very good story. I have read it myself.' The book seller eyed me suspiciously as he mentioned that the shipwrecked man was rescued by pirates.

'Pirates,' I sniffed pretentiously, 'The scum of the Seven Seas. Should all be hanged.' I winked at Virginia, as I took the book from the man's hand. I nonchalantly added the book to the pile Virginia was assembling on the table, in the middle of the cluttered room.

'I have a volume by Charles Johnson, *The Lives and Adventures of the Most Famous Highwaymen*. It is an interesting account of some of England's famous rogues. I have heard from people, who read it, that it is very captivating.' The book seller handed the book to Virginia.

I told him to add it to the pile.

By the time we were done, we had purchased twenty six more books at a cost of twelve pounds, six shillings, thropence. I paid with some gold I had in my pocket, which satisfied the book seller immensely. 'I like gold,' he said, as I counted the coins into his sweaty palm.

Transaction completed, the little man carefully wrapped the precious books in paper and tied the packages with string. He helped carry the books to our waiting carriage. Then we drove off to find a nice restaurant in which to have lunch.

When we returned to our boat, later in the afternoon, five Royal Marines were standing on the pier, examining our rowing vessel. None of our people were nearby.

We decided to drive on a ways and stepped from the carriage, some yards distant, all the time carefully observing the marines.

Virginia and the children sat down on a bench, in front of a warehouse, where I joined them, momentarily. We had a clear view of the marines, occasionally obstructed by horses and wagons passing in front of us. After about twenty minutes had passed, Colin, George, Robert, Marta, Meira and Susanne came walking towards us, with their children in tow. Little David was crying.

Robert was carrying a large sword wrapped in cloth. It appeared to be a two hander, of some sort. I found out later that it was a claymore.

Virginia asked what was wrong, as our friends approached us.

Marta explained that David was upset, because he did not get enough sleep. They were bringing him back to the ship, so he could have a nap in his own bunk.

I pointed towards our boat and asked if anyone had an idea why the marines would be standing there, obviously waiting for us.

'Do you think they know something about us?' asked Virginia suspiciously. 'Nobody knows we are here, do they?' Virginia looked at me. 'You didn't contact Stacey and Stuart, did you?'

I assured Virginia, none of us had spoken our names in Halifax. 'Perhaps it is just a routine inspection,' I ventured.

Robert suggested that the Puritan harbour official may have been suspicious of us. 'I mean, how many companies of actors and musicians do you know, who have their own brigantine, and obviously appear to be rich?'

Robert had a point there and we all realized it. We had been very cocky with the Puritan. Perhaps we should have been more circumspect when we addressed him.

'What do we do?' asked Marta, looking worriedly towards the five marines standing by our boat.

We sat there and pondered our predicament for a few minutes when the idea struck me, to simply hire a boat. 'Surely someone has a boat for hire,' I said, looking towards some men, who were standing on the pier across the road. 'Maybe they might know,' I suggested, pointing towards the men.

Robert walked across the road and came back a few minutes later with the news that there was a boat for hire, two piers over. 'A man by the name of Primney takes people out to ships, with a yawl,' he said, smiling broadly.

'That was easy,' I remarked, smiling at Virginia, as I stood and helped her up. Her belly was quite swollen by this time; a little help getting up was always appreciated. She thanked me graciously.

As we walked across the road, happily chattering about not having to row for a change, I noticed that one of the marines was pointing at us. I mentioned this to the others, as I watched the marines all turn to look at us hurrying towards the pier, where the boat lay for hire.

'We had better be quick,' I said, as I watched the marines begin to run along the pier, headed to the roadway along which we were hurrying.

Each of the men grabbed a child and carried him or her, to aid with our rapid escape from the marines, who were obviously chasing us.

Virginia did her best, but being as she was quite advanced with her pregnancy, running was not something she managed very well.

George grabbed her up in his arms and carried her, as we ran along the road, reaching the pier, well ahead of the marines.

A young man was sitting on the deck of the yawl, smoking a pipe, when we came running along the wooden pier. He stood up and greeted us, as we quickly stepped on board.

'Is your name, Primney,' I asked.

The man shook his head. 'No, Mister Primney has gone into town.'

'We need to get to our ship, in a hurry,' I said. 'Can you sail her?'

The young man shook his head. 'I can't take the boat out, without Mister Primney,' he said.

I looked back towards the roadway and saw the marines were getting closer.

'Look,' I said, 'My wife is pregnant. She needs our doctor, who is onboard our ship,' I lied.

Virginia performed some convincing moans, which put a concerned expression on the young man's countenance.

I sensed it was an advantage and pushed the issue, by telling the young man we would pay handsomely for the use of the yawl, and that we could sail her, with no problem.

The young man vacillated, but I could sense he was interested in the handsome reward I suggested.

'I don't know what Mister Primney will say, but if there is a handsome reward, I'm sure he will agree,' he said, smiling and holding out his hand.

Robert handed him a guinea, which made the young man very happy.

The young boatman quickly sprang into action.

We did too.

Robert and I quickly untied the boat and began to push her off, just as the marines came running along the pier.

Colin unfurled the sail and we began to move away from the pier.

'Stop that boat!' shouted one of the marines. 'In the name of King George, I order you to stop that yawl!' he shouted again.

The young man looked worried and asked why the marines were chasing us.

We told him that we had no idea and urged him to continue.

Suddenly, a shot rang out and a ball came whizzing through the air, catching me neatly in my right eye; knocking me flat on my back; my eye gushing blood. The pain was intense. I must have passed out, because I do not remember much, other than hearing several more gun shots, and Virginia frantically screaming my name, before I blacked out.

I woke up two days later with a massive headache. I slowly opened my left eye and realized that my right eye was covered with a huge bandage. As I looked out of my left eye, I began to notice familiar surroundings. I was in my own bed in the Master's Cabin of the *Navigator*. Heaving a sigh of relief, I tried to sit up, but the pain in my head was less hurtful when I remained lying down. I called Virginia, but no one heard me. Hence, I lay in my bed and pondered my fate.

Eventually, after what seemed a long time, Virginia came into the cabin to see how I was faring. She smiled and asked how I was feeling.

I told her about my headache.

Virginia frowned and looked at me sadly.

I asked her what was wrong and she began to cry.

'We should never have come here,' she sobbed. 'We should have stayed on our island. This voyage has become a disaster.' Virginia fell down on the bed, beside me, weeping on my chest.

I had to ask her several times why she was so upset, each time she cried harder. When I asked her a third time, she told me the awful truth.

'You've lost your eye!' she sobbed. 'Your eye is gone.'

They shot my eye out? That was something I had not ever expected. My eye was gone because of a Royal Marine. The revelation was a hard one to bear. I did not relish having to wear an eye patch. I never liked the look of those things. However, wearing a wooden eye in the empty socket, was not something I was interested in, either. Losing an eye was a great inconvenience.

I asked Virginia what had happened to the marines.

'We were able to sail away in the yawl. I don't think the marines saw where we disappeared to, amongst all the ships anchored here,' she said. 'Unless they question that young man, but I don't think he will talk. George gave him some extra money to keep his mouth shut. Robert scared him with death, if he talked. I think the young man understood we meant business.'

Virginia, looked at me with a mournful expression, shaking her head sadly. 'We never should have come. It's all my fault,' she said. 'I am a jinx. I am the reason my parents and sister are dead. I am the reason you lost your eye. I hate this place and want to go home.' Virginia broke down in a torrent of tears.

I told her she should not blame herself. It was not her fault the family house burned down. There was no conclusive evidence the house was torched. And, to blame herself for me getting shot, was ridiculous. I told her it was an accident. The marine was probably trying to scare us into stopping and didn't mean to hit me in the eye.

'He was trying to shoot one of us, for escaping their clutches,' replied Virginia firmly. 'Those people shoot first and ask questions later.'

Everything I knew about marines, from things my father, and Bill had told me, led me to agree with what Virginia had said. I told her I thought all things military were like that. Militaries are specifically organized to kill people.

Suddenly, while we lay side by side, talking about what had happened to us, we heard a commotion developing on deck. We could hear loud voices and the clumping of many feet. Virginia quickly jumped up and looked out of the starboard window. 'There's a long boat, alongside,' she said fearfully. 'It's filled with marines.'

'Fetch the children, quickly,' I said, as I painfully climbed out of bed and quickly dressed. I was fastening my belt when the children, followed by most of the others, came clomping into our cabin, it being the safest place, in case of attack, which is what we were under, it seemed.

A gun shot, and then another, reverberated in the air.

A loud scream followed.

I grabbed three loaded pistols from a drawer and stuffed them into my belt. Then I slung my cutlass belt over my shoulder. 'Stay here,' I commanded the children, as I took the cutlass out of its scabbard and stepped out of the cabin, firmly closing the door behind me.

The sound of more gun shots, more screams, more clumping boots on deck greeted my ears. I heard men yelling, as steel on steel clashed loudly outside.

I made my way carefully forward, towards the door leading to the main deck. Suddenly the door opened. A Royal Marine came into the gangway, not expecting to find someone on the other side of the door. I ran him through with the cutlass, twisting the blade firmly, as the man slumped forward, blood gushing from the wound through his liver. For good measure I stabbed the marine in the neck with my silver hook, opening one of his carotid arteries, drenching my shoulder with hot blood.

I shoved the man backwards and pulled my cutlass from his quivering body, as he sank to the deck.

More gun shots and screams topped the general commotion.

I carefully pushed the door open and peeked out of the crack. A marine was about to attack George, just on the other side of the door. Fortunately, I was able to prevent the marine from hurting my friend.

I quickly dropped my cutlass and grabbed a pistol, which I discharged at close quarters, directly into the back of the marine's head, the ball coming out of the front of his forehead, along with some brains and a gush of blood, which hit George square in the face; a splinter of bone gashing his cheek.

George grinned. 'Thanks!' he shouted, as he quickly turned around to fend off a pike wielding marine, intent on skewering the two of us. Fortunately, we both had more loaded pistols, two of which were discharged into the marine's chest, killing him on the spot.

More gun shots and screams filled the space.

I turned around and noticed Russell and Wendy tossing a marine over the starboard gunwale of the quarter deck. The man landed in the water with a loud splash.

Another gun shot reverberated over the deck. I watched Johan fall straight on his face, blood flowing from a wound on his right temple.

A man fell over the quarter deck railing, his left arm smacking against my right shoulder, knocking me against George, just as a ball smashed into the lintel of the door, directly behind my head, sending splinters flying; several hitting me in the back.

'Look out!' shouted Colin.

I looked up; in the direction of the voice.

Colin was taking aim with a blunderbuss from the main starboard shrouds. The device fired with a loud explosion, shattering the chest of a marine, who was about to slash Tula, bravely defending herself against a burly marine, bearing a sabre. I watched Robert cleave the man in twain, with the claymore he had purchased on shore.

I had never in my life imagined a man cleft in twain. Here it was, immediately in front of my eyes. It was a scene directly from the deepest depths of hell. I shall never forget the sudden massive gush of blood, brains, heart, lungs, as the massive blade sliced right to the man's entrails. The two halves stood for a moment leaning in opposite directions, on legs which began to jiggle. As if in slow motion, the mutilated man fell backwards in a pool of blood.

Robert looked wild eyed at me and yelled a loud battle cry.

A gun shot silenced his cry.

Robert crumpled on top of the man he had sliced in half.

I saw where the shot had come from and aimed my third pistol, however, the smoke and commotion on deck made it impossible to draw a bead on the marine who had shot Robert.

Suddenly, five gun shots blasted, all at once, from behind me on the quarter deck. Instantly, four marines tumbled to the boards, as another one came at George and I, still standing by the door.

George shot the man through his fore head. He fell at my feet.

Several more gun shots added to the cacophony.

Then, suddenly, there was silence.

We had overcome the marines.

I guess they had no idea who they were messing with.

'Toss the marines over board!' I shouted. 'We have to get under way!' I looked frantically towards the navy frigates. 'They surely must have heard the gunshots! We can't risk staying here any longer. I suspect they are on to us.'

People sprang into action. Seven dead marines were immediately tossed overboard. Five, who were still alive, were tossed overboard, as well.

Our sails were unfurled and the anchors weighed. Fortunately, we had some breeze coming from the north west, enabling us to maneuver our ship out of the harbour, leaving the marine's long boat floating in our wake. We sank it with a neatly placed shot from a five pounder mounted on the stern railing.

'If we stay here, we are bound to have more visitors,' I said, anxiously watching the frigates. 'I think someone must have realized that we are pirates. Maybe Virginia and I were suspected. Whatever the case, we have to get out of here.'

My friends realized the wisdom of my words and made every effort to ensure our speedy exit from Halifax harbour.

As we passed the breakwater, I noticed that the frigates were preparing to set sail.

As we desperately tried to catch every little bit of wind, our women tended to the wounded and our dead.

Unfortunately, we had no choice but to give our departed friends a rapid burial, as we raced to open water, the frigates beginning their pursuit.

Dead were; Cody, Gaston, Johan, and Samantha, who had received a blow to the head, with the stock of a marine's musket.

Fortunately, Robert had only received a ball in his left shoulder, which was easily removed, it not having gone in very deeply. Habu had been knocked out by a marine, who was shot by Tula. Kathleen had a nasty gash in her left thigh, which was bleeding profusely, however, Marianne was attending to it. And, Phillip was missing a piece of his left ear.

Our deck was red with blood.

When we were well out to sea, we drew buckets of water and splashed the decks, in an attempt to wash the blood off. However, we could not spend too much time washing decks. We needed every able bodied person to man the sails, if we were going to outrun the navy frigates.

Fortunately, the winds were favorable. We ran out a full parade of sails and began to run close to the wind, picking up speed; quickly reaching eight knots.

Eventually, some seven hours later, we had managed to out sail the frigates. However, it was not a reason to grow complacent. I made certain to double up the watch, that night, before retiring to my cabin, where Virginia and the children were sleeping peacefully. My empty socket was throbbing with excruciating pain. I had no choice but to numb it, as much as possible, with a hearty drink of laudanum and rum, which helped me to pass into a hard night of disturbing dreams.

Over the next eight days, as we continued to sail under a full parade, intent on reaching Virgineola, as quickly as possible, we kept a constant watch off our stern, never trusting, for a moment, that we had successfully outrun the Royal Navy frigates. For all we knew, they could be just over the horizon.

We reached Virgineola on the ninth day after leaving Halifax. My empty eye socket was beginning to heal nicely. I was still troubled by headaches, but they were becoming less intense. Virginia and my friends took good care of me. Laudanum and rum also helping immensely.

Making port, we quickly set about replenishing fresh victuals and water, in order to spend as little time as possible on the island.

Virginia and I found a safe place to hide our second treasure box, unbeknownst to anyone but us. We quickly effected the burial and returned to our brig.

The following morning we left the island and, catching excellent breezes, continued our journey, untroubled by anything but simply ways and means to stay pleasantly occupied. In my case, I began to delve into some of the books we had purchased.

We reached our island home on August fourth, a sadder company than the one which left the island, two months before. By this time I was wearing a black eye patch, which Virginia had sewn for me. Kathleen was limping, Phillip was missing a piece of his ear, and four of our friends were dead. The homecoming was a sober affair this time; none of us was particularly interested in a bonfire, that night, all of us just going to our individual houses, to be with our families and our thoughts.

We held a bonfire the following night, when we were all feeling much better and happy to be home on our safe, and cozy island. The party lasted well into the following morning; many toasts being celebrated in honour of our departed friends.

Chapter Twenty

September, 1783, was another very special month for my little family; the birth of our second son, William. Virginia and I named him after our departed friend, Bill Bartleby. Our second son was born, with a full head of brown hair and large, alert, blue eyes. He was also born with an excellent set of lungs and healthy pipes. His cries could be heard for some distance, sometimes waking our neighbors, as the sound had little trouble piercing the thin walls of our houses.

Virginia's birthing went fairly easy this time. She was in labor for about seven hours, as opposed to the much longer times it took for Catherine and Joshua to come into the world. For midwives she enjoyed the assistance of Marianne and Meira, two of our dearest friends.

September was also a propitious month because, as I learned later, it was the month in which England ceased hostilities with the American colonies. This was a pleasant situation for us, because, without hostilities off the American coast, we were able to take advantage of the incredible increase in shipping, which would result off the coast of Florida and points north. However, we did not find out about this fact until some months later, on the voyages I will describe to you, dear reader, in this chapter, further detailing our incredible adventures.

By September my empty socket no longer ached and I was able to wear the patch without discomfort. I was able to see, well enough, with my remaining eye. Reading, and normal functioning, was not greatly affected. Although I had a little difficulty with the perception of depth, which somewhat hampered my ability to fight effectively with a cutlass, at first. However, with practice I quickly became accustomed to the difference, and actually improved my performance, according to my excellent teachers, Colin and George.

By October, people were getting restless on the island and needed a diversion. Hence, it was decided that we would take our man of war and seek some rich prizes, off the coast of Hispaniola. The big ship had not been breamed for some time, therefore, a crew of twenty men sailed her to a nearby island, where they were able to bring the big ship onto the beach, the approach being deep enough to accommodate the big ship's draft. Of course, we had completely emptied her of every cannon and other weighty objects, so she floated high in the water, and the work proceeded apace. Our men completing the task in just over three weeks.

After the men returned with the *William Bartleby*, we replaced her cannons and provisioned her for a voyage along the coasts of Hispaniola, and the Leeward, and Windward Islands; hoping to find some prizes and worthy swag. We felt invincible in our big war ship.

When the ship was ready, two hundred men climbed on board with their assorted personal weapons. Colin, George, Robert, and Russell also came along, leaving their wives and children on shore.

The winds being favorable, we set sail on October 14th, 1783, intent on no more than a month's absence from our happy island.

The voyage from our island to the coast of Hispaniola took but a day, the winds being fair, and the big ship having been recently smeared with tallow. Keeping the coast about three leagues to starboard, we sailed along the north coast.

During the entire time we sailed, before making port at San Juan, we never saw one sail. We hoped it was not a sign of things to come. No sails meant no swag.

We had to stand off San Juan for two days, the winds not favoring our entrance into the harbour.

In the afternoon of October 18th, we managed to finally put in at San Juan de Puerto Rico, to obtain some firewood, fresh water, and victuals. We continued on our voyage the next day, sailing along the north east coast of the Leeward Islands and the east coasts of the Windward Islands, as far south as Grenada. The voyage taking altogether eight days, during the entire time we saw not one sail, other than some small fishing boats.

We stayed in Grenada for three days, taking on fresh water, and victuals. Then, we headed back towards San Juan, along the coasts of the Lesser Antilles. Arriving back in San Juan de Puerto Rico on the last day of October, under cloudy skies and drizzling rain.

Coming into port, we finally found what we were looking for. A large Spanish convoy was organizing in the harbour. Three men of war, two frigates, and a corvette were anchored near twelve merchantmen, heavy in the water, and obviously carrying what we needed; many tons of swag.

When we had found a suitable place to anchor, we ferried fifty of our men ashore, to spread out, and gather intelligence regarding the convoy forming in the harbour. I stayed on board, not feeling particularly energetic, that first day in port. Perhaps it was something I ate, I was not certain. Maybe I had breathed some foul air in the man of war, which was highly possible, considering the filth which had accumulated in the bowels of the ship; the province of beetles, cockroaches, rats, and worms.

When most of our men returned to the ship, later that evening, they were full of information about the Spanish convoy. They had even managed to identify two ships, which were carrying gold and silver bullion, they being a leased Portuguese ship by the name of, *Nossa Schora do Cabo*, and a Spanish ship named, *Santa Anna*.

Next day, we took our boat and rowed amongst the convoy ships, in hope of specifically identifying the treasure ships. We tried not to draw undue attention to ourselves, as we rowed amongst the Spanish vessels.

The harbour was crowded with barks, long boats, sloops, yawls, and assorted other vessels, servicing the anchored ships with; victuals, cargo, water, etcetera. Gulls soared overhead, adding to the general noise of bustle in the harbour. As we passed the ships, all manner of odors drifted our way; rotting food, excrement, pitch, spices, tar, urine…

The Portuguese ship lay between two Spanish galleons, which had obviously seen many years of service. Reading their names was difficult, the carved, wooden letters lacking paint. Fortunately that was not the case with the Portuguese ship, *Nossa Schora do Cabo*, and the Spanish ship, *Santa Anna*; they were both quite new ships, the paint fresh, and wood, newly varnished. We noted that the treasure ships were lying particularly low in the water, obviously heavily laden with precious cargo.

We also took note of the ships' defenses; the Portuguese ship carrying twelve, eight pounders and a few small swivel guns mounted on the railings. The Spanish ship carried sixteen guns, eight being twenty pounders, and some mounted swivel guns, for shooting grapeshot and nails. Both ships had reasonably formidable defenses, but were no match for the guns of our man of war. We hoped it wouldn't come to that. However, we had no idea how jealously the Spaniards guarded their treasure.

When we had fully reconnoitered our prizes, we returned to our ship and discussed ways and means of relieving the ships of their precious cargoes. It was out of the question to attempt the operation, while the ships lay at anchor in the harbour. Although, we were aware it had been done before. George and Robert had both heard a story about a famous pirate, long dead, who had managed to sail amongst the ships of a convoy, while they were anchored off the coast of Brazil.

This audacious pirate, whose name was John Rackham, managed to relieve the Spaniards of a significant amount of treasure; right under the nose of the Spanish navy. It was an excellent story, but we did not feel the circumstances in San Juan were as favorably inclined towards such a bold venture.

We decided that we would have to overtake the ships in open water, by sailing in amongst the ships of the convoy, pretending to be a converted man of war in the service of commerce. If we were lucky, we would be able to overcome a treasure ship, before the Spanish navy ships would be able to get to us. Everything always depended on the favour of the four winds.

As the days drifted by, we waited patiently, all the time keeping a close eye on the preparations of the convoy. The men, restless as they were, stayed close to the ship, in the event we would have to weigh anchor in a rush to follow the convoy when it sailed out. While we waited, we repainted the name of our ship. We decided to give her a simple Portuguese name. Something easy and quick to paint. *Santa Rosa*, was the shortest name we could come up with. We painted, *Lisbon*, for the port of origin.

On the ninth day of November, the winds became favorable, enabling the convoy to weigh anchors and set sail for a winter voyage to Spain. We were close behind, flying a Portuguese flag, no one in the convoy wise to our purpose, Spain and Portugal being on good terms. We also figured, since a Portuguese ship was already a member of the convoy, a second one would not be suspect.

On the 20th of November we saw the perfect opportunity to come alongside the Portuguese ship. George reckoned that we were about 400 leagues from San Juan at the time we made our move. The Spanish navy ships were at least a half a league distant when we sailed abeam the *Nossa Schora do Cabo*.

Several of our men could speak fluent Portuguese. A man by the name of, Jorge Barroso felt confident enough to hail the treasure ship through the speaking trumpet, asking if they would like to come aboard for a visit. Jorge further greased the invitation with a promise of libations.

Of course, the Portuguese had no idea how many men were on board the *Santa Rosa*; our men being carefully hidden on the gun decks. They also had no idea we were carrying a full complement of sixty guns, our gun ports all firmly shut.

The captain of the Portuguese ship asked us what an English man of war was doing, flying a Portuguese flag.

Our man did not miss a beat and told the captain that the ship was sold by the British navy and been reconditioned for mercantile service by the enterprising Portuguese merchant, Juan Fernando de Sampaio, from Lisbon.

Of course, the captain did not question further who, or what we were. He accepted, as legitimate, the name of the merchant, he obviously not knowing every merchant who plied a market in Portugal; there being many.

Anyway, the Portuguese captain thought it an excellent idea for the officers to come over to our ship, for some camaraderie and libations of their choice; a nice change from the dreary routine of an ocean crossing.

An hour later, five Portuguese officers entered the Grand Cabin, where we received them with generous hospitality, one of our Portuguese men pretending to be our captain. Drinking several toasts to the Portuguese Crown, we made the Portuguese men totally comfortable and relaxed; our three Portuguese speakers doing an admirable job of convincing the visitors that we were, who we said we were. Of course our guests had no idea their drinks were spiked with a strong sleeping potion, a concoction Doctor Johnson had prepared for us.

When the visiting officers were fast asleep in their chairs, we ran up our Jolly Roger and informed the Portuguese sailors that we were holding their officers hostage and they should welcome a boarding party.

The Portuguese sailors, seeing our black flag, decided to take matters into their own hands, thinking we were but lightly manned; and wanting to prove themselves heroes for protecting the rich treasure they were carrying.

Suddenly, a shot rang out and one of our sailors fell down with an ugly wound in his stomach. It was a fatal mistake for the Portuguese sailors, whose lives we wanted to spare, but had now thrown their cards on our deck. Another shot rang out and another one of our men went down.

My response was to call the order to board the treasure ship, instantly resulting in twelve grappling hooks being tossed to the Portuguese ship, seven of them firmly catching hold; enabling us to pull the two ships together, as more of our men stormed on deck.

A loud blast signaled the discharge of cannon balls from the treasure ship; several of which hit our port side; taking out two guns.

My response was to call for a violent retort, as twenty five gun ports were opened and cannons rolled out. Moments later all twenty five cannons blasted holes into the sides, deck, and sails of the treasure ship. Numerous screams were heard coming from our opponent's ship, signaling a successful broadside.

The Portuguese sailors, upon seeing our cannons, and what they were capable of doing, chose to take a safer course of action and surrendered their ship. The fact we outnumbered them by five to one, also directed their decision.

I told Jorge to tell the Portuguese sailors, they were wise to capitulate because it saved them from certain death.

The Portuguese sailors indicated they were thankful we gave them the opportunity to spare themselves and were most accommodating as we boarded them and examined their cargo.

Of course, the cannon shots alerted the Spanish navy vessels, a league, or so away. We knew they would be maneuvering to come our way, necessitating the rapid evacuation of what turned out to be a very rich treasure, indeed. Fortunately, we had lots of hands, so the treasure was quickly brought on board our ship.

As the last chest was being hauled on board, someone on the crow's nest shouted that sails were rapidly bearing down on us.

I shouted orders to bring the Portuguese officers on deck and deposit them in their long boat, an order quickly effected, we not wanting to be burdened with those men. Quickly setting sails, we caught wind and began to pull away from the now, much lighter merchantman, bobbing on the water, her sailors not knowing exactly what to do.

As we sailed away we lowered our Jolly Roger and continued to put out more and more sail. However, now that we were considerably heavier with rich treasure, our ship sailed a whole lot slower, than before, enabling one of the Spanish frigates to catch up with us, after three days of hard sailing. When the navy ship came close enough, she shot two balls from her forward guns. The balls crashed into our transom, but did not hit any vital places.

I ordered a rapid come about, at the same time commanding the running out of our port guns, which, as our ship turned, were discharged into the oncoming Spanish frigate, splintering her port bow and sprit.

Then, just as we passed the ship, the Spaniard let loose a volley from twelve guns and six swivel guns loaded with grapeshot and nails, wreaking great havoc amongst the men on our deck. We managed to loose another broadside as we slid past, significantly splintering the port side of the frigate's hull; rendering seven cannons out of commission.

Our men, being seasoned veterans of our ship, quickly had the cannons rolled out on the starboard side, so that, when we came about, we were ready with another broadside, which we launched into the frigate's beleaguered hull, rendering the rest of her port side cannons out of commission, altogether. Several of our balls had crashed against the frigate's main mast and rendered it suspect of continued service. Another volley in its direction would most assuredly bring the spar down.

The frigate attempted to negotiate a sharp turn to starboard, in order to bring her useable guns to bear on us, however, we were prepared to shoot. We sent another volley directly amidship, igniting the powder magazine; the instant result being a massive explosion, sending pieces of sailors and ship flying in all directions, some of it landing in bloody pools on our deck, and in our rigging.

Within minutes we watched the frigate lean over and disappear below the frothing waves. We managed to rescue thirty five sailors, who we quickly clapped in irons in the fo'c's'le, not trusting their loyalties. They were thankful we saved their lives. We gave them victuals and wine.

When all was ready, we set sail, once again in order to continue the voyage back to our island, no other sails behind us.

On November 28th all hell broke loose as a massive winter storm hit us broadside, only days away from home.

This storm was not like anything I had ever encountered at sea. Most of the experienced jack tars on board expressed the same surprise at the sudden ferocity unleashed against us. A number of our sailors were complaining that perhaps the storm was God's retribution for stealing the Spanish gold.

'Surely a storm, such as this, is God's work!' shouted an English sailor, as he climbed down the port side mizzen shrouds.

With a mighty roar a huge wave crashed over our starboard bow, sending a horrific amount of water crashing onto the decks, shuddering the timbers and sending waves of fear up every man's spine. The wave stopped us dead in the water, as if a gigantic hand had suddenly fastened a vice grip on the hapless ship.

Suddenly, another wave hit us broadside, immediately followed by another one, which cracked the top main mast in twain, just above the crow's nest. Sails, spars and rigging came crashing down, one of the spars, piercing straight through the deck, just aft of the forward hatch, necessitating the instant call to duty of the ship's artists, to repair the hole and prevent us shipping water.

As the carpenters were hard at work, under the most difficult circumstances, a violent wind whipped water into a foaming frenzy, biting our exposed faces like blows from a cat.

Suddenly, a horrific cracking noise heralded the destruction of the rest of our main mast; taken by a forty foot wave, which engulfed the ship in a blanket of water. It washed six of our carpenters over board, others were crushed by the falling spars.

The ship went down by the head, flooding the fo'c's'le, where the Portuguese sailors were clapped in irons. We attempted to send men forward, to undo their fetters, but were prevented from doing so by a powerful rush of water, flooding in from the punctured deck, as wave after wave washed over the bows.

A powerful flash of light lit the eerie scene, followed by an immense crack of thunder, which reverberated throughout the ship. It was a deafening clap, which rendered me momentarily unable to hear clearly.

Another flash of lighting and another mighty clap of thunder rent the air, as ever more of Neptune's anger smashed our ship and tore the rigging asunder.

Bulkheads groaned, as the hull sprang numerous leaks, which quickly became a torrent of water, filling our holds and overpowering our bilge pumps.

The air was dark with torrents of water, whipped by the powerful winds, which pummeled us; making it almost impossible to see further than a few feet in any direction.

When the wind shifted, it pushed us from behind, forcing the ship down by the head, further flooding the fo'c's'le. The shackled sailors were doomed. There was nothing we could do.

Then, the unthinkable happened, as we were pushed into a wave, which held the ship motionless, another wave crashed into us with such force, the rest of our spars disappeared and we were rendered, a helpless hulk.

Suddenly, through the haze I spied a massive rock rising out of the water, half a league to port. It was an island, which would most assuredly have rocky satellites protruding through the waves. However, there was nothing I, or anyone could do, as the ship was relentlessly driven before the wind, directly towards the island; a most distressing situation.

Without warning the ship suddenly stopped, as a mighty sound of splintering timbers crashed around me. A huge wave rolled over us, as we began to tip on our starboard side. More cracking timbers and screams filled the air, as men and women were trapped by falling spars, or crushed by a powerful rush of water, smashing them into bulkheads, cannons, and whatever else arrested their uncontrollable falls, as the ship careened over on her side.

I was thrown overboard, as the ship tilted, totally blind as to where I was and how I landed. Fortunately, I was able to discern a spar floating nearby and managed to grab a hold of it, firmly digging my hook into the wood. It was a good thing I did so, because the next thing that happened was, a wave picked me up, and tossed me, spar and all, through the air. I landed some distance from the crumbling ship.

The wind howled and the water tossed me this way and that, but I was able to hang on, thanks to my hook, firmly imbedded in the spar. The last thing I remember, before I passed out, was George shouting for help.

Chapter Twenty-One

I have no idea how long I was unconscious, or when the storm abated. I only remember opening my eye and observing a small crab, up close, and personal. Its stalk eyes were regarding me curiously. It was seeing me as a potential food thing. I'm sure, if it had lips, it would have been licking them. As it was, the crab was moving its mandibles and clicking its pincers. It scurried away when I moved my hand in order to right myself.

I was lying face down on top of the spar, which was lying on sand., drenched in sunlight. The day was warm and I felt dry. I had obviously been lying there for some time. As my senses began to return, I began to hear the surf breaking on the beach, a short way behind me. I directed my senses to ascertain the state of my body and found that my whole body ached from the ordeal, and I was ravenous with hunger. I was in so much pain that raising my body was something of an onerous task, hampered by the fact that my hook was so firmly imbedded in the spar, I could not pull it out and had to unstrap the appliance from my stump, otherwise I would have been stuck to the spar and eventually eaten by the crabs.

When I had disengaged myself from the spar, I slowly stood up and took note of my surroundings. I was standing on a beach. Behind me was the ocean crashing on the rocks and sand. In front of me was a thick forest of tropical plants and trees filled with the sounds of insects and birds. Looking to the left and the right, to the length of the beach, in each direction, I saw no other human being. I was alone and had no idea where I was.

Looking up, I noticed that the sky was clouding over again, necessitating finding shelter. I did not want to be wet again. I walked painfully to the forest and sought some large leaves I could fashion into an umbrella of sorts, like I had done when I was in Venezuela. Fortunately, I found a banana plant, with a cluster of green bananas. I quickly pulled a number of bananas off the bunch and managed to cover myself with the huge leaves, just before the rain began to fall, hard.

Under my leaves, in the pouring rain, I had quite a time trying to stay completely dry, however I managed as long as I did not move and adjust the position of the leaves, which, whenever I did move, allowed little waterfalls of water to cascade onto my arms or legs.

Lightning lit up the area and a massive clap of thunder followed it immediately after, heightening my fear and misery. Winds began to hit the island, dropping the temperature considerably. I was shivering, as my body gradually stiffened from having to sit crouched under the banana leaves, eating green bananas to stave off the gnawing hunger in my stomach.

After, what seemed like only minutes, I became quite ill, with a massive ache in my stomach from the green bananas; heightening my misery.

Eventually, the rain stopped, and just as quickly as the storm had come, it was gone. The clouds parted and glorious, warm sunshine became the order for the rest of the day.

With great discomfort I disentangled myself from the leafy shelter I had gathered around myself and stumbled to the beach, in order to dry off and warm up. As I stood, thusly enjoying the warming sun, I thought of my hook, still stuck in the spar, lying a hundred yards from where I was standing. I walked to the spar and attempted to pull the hook out of the wood. It was a struggle to get the hook out of the spar, it being very firmly imbedded. It took a few whacks with a piece of drift wood to finally dislodge the silver appliance. It fell to the ground with a small thud.

I picked up my hook, shook the sand out of the cup, and then strapped it to my stump, cinching the belts and tightly buckling them fast. It felt better to have my hook on the end of my stump. It somehow made the loss of my hand something easier to bear. Having become quite adept at using the hook, it was almost like a hand, and a great convenience to me.

Next, I checked over my clothing. My shirt was torn on the left shoulder and my breeches were ripped in sundry places. My hose was virtually non existent, they having been torn to shreds. I had no idea where my shoes were. It was a completely uncomfortable realization that I was marooned and had better get myself organized to find water to drink, my mouth being quite dry, by this time. I elected to return to the forest and walking, as carefully as I could, on feet not used to walking any distance without boots or shoes, I went in search of potable water.

The forest was very similar to that on our island, hence I was confident I would find what I needed. I did not have to go far to find my first drink, which came from a pool of rain water which had collected in the hollow of a leaf, just like the time in Venezuela. Several similar leaves furnished me with enough water to quench my immediate thirst, enabling me to continue with my search for a more permanent source, a spring, a stream, a pool, anything holding fresh water, for without it, I should certainly die, and that I did not desire to do. I wanted to get back to my family.

After walking for some time through the forest, climbing over and under roots, vines, and prickly bushes, I found a pool of clear, potable water, obviously fed by a spring. Clearing away some leaves and algae from the surface, I carefully dipped my hand in the water and drank a mouthful. The water was cool and refreshing. Finding the pool lifted my spirits considerably.

The next things I needed were, food, and shelter.

My stomach still ached from the green bananas, as I stumbled about looking for other things to eat. Luckily, I found another plant with nice small, ripe, red bananas. I broke the bunch from the plant and threw the bananas over my shoulder. Walking back to the pond, where I thought I would attempt to build a shelter, I came across the hoof prints, of what were unmistakably those of a pig.

The place had wild pigs! It was a great relief to see those hoof prints. I knew with meat, I would survive. How to procure it, that was another question. I had nothing with which to kill a pig, nor did I have the means of making a fire to cook the meat. The dilemma posed an interesting problem, which needed to be resolved at the earliest opportunity.

As I stood there for a few moments, contemplating the wild pigs, I realized that the afternoon was quickly waning and night would soon be upon me. I had to make a shelter. It occurred to me that flotsam and jetsam from our ship might have washed up on the beach. Perhaps I might find some sail cloth and spars, I reasoned, or maybe even a barrel of food, or other things I could use to secure my survival.

I could see the ocean through the trees and quickly made my way in a zigzag manner to the beach.

I noticed some objects lying in a heap about two hundred yards distant. I quickly stumbled to the spot and discovered two intact kegs of rum and a sealed box of hard tack. Further along the beach I found what I needed for my shelter; a piece of sail and some rope. With these in hand and hook, I quickly made it back to the pool and deposited them in a clear area between three large trees, on the east bank of the pool, near the path, which was beginning to form where I had walked.

As it was beginning to get dark, I made one more quick trip to the beach to attempt the retrieval of one of the kegs of rum. I managed to return to the canvas and rope by rolling the keg carefully through the bush, further making the path apparent.

Then, when I returned to the place, where my camp was going to be, it was already too dark in the forest to see anything. There was just enough light for me to knock the bung out of the top of the keg, with a rock I had found nearby. The process spilled some rum on the ground, instantly surrounding me in the delicious fragrance of Jamaica's wonder drink.

I laid the canvas on the ground, in such a way, that I could wrap myself in a corner and be perfectly comfortable on the ground. Then I proceeded to avail myself of the rum, attaining a glorious drunk, at some point in the evening, after which I slept like a baby, swaddled in my corner of the sail.

The ground provided a soft pad of plants and leaves which, in my inebriated state, was like the soft feather bed I shared with my wonderful Virginia. Her face appeared to me, time and time again, throughout the night. I am sure I must have slept with a big smile on my face, until something bit me on the cheek, waking me instantly. I almost swatted at the creature with my hook, stopping myself just in time to avoid a gash from the needle sharp point on the end of the silver device.

Moon light glinted through the trees and bathed the place in an eerie light, which became suddenly very unsettling, as the forest noises seemed to increase their intensity. The sound had become a brain splitting cacophony pounding in my head. The noise kept me awake for a long while. So, what else was there to do, but drink more rum. I sat under the stars on the beach and became even more gloriously drunk, until, thankfully, I passed out, not waking again until sometime in the afternoon with the realization, the rum was not a good habit to get into. I would get nothing done to secure my safety and die in the place I was at. Hence, I returned the bung to its hole in the lid of the cask and set the cask in the shade under a plant with large leaves.

When I felt able to walk, I stumbled to the pond and cleared some scum off the water. Then I stuck my face in the pond and drank and drank. I guessed that the rum had dehydrated me, which was another reason not to drink it too much. Dehydration in the tropics is probably not a good thing for the human being.

When I felt better, I ate some red bananas and then set about building a tent with the sail and rope, a relatively simple task. First, I carefully prepared the ground, so that it would be level and provide a comfortable surface on which to lie. Then, I strung rope between two trees and slung the sail cloth over it, pinning the cloth down with rocks, set side by side along the bottom, where the cloth touched the ground, some three feet on each side of the rope. The extra cloth served for a floor. When I was done, I had the beginnings of a tent, however, the ends were open and required some more cloth to close one end and provide a door on the other. I drank some water and then took a walk to the beach, in search of more sail cloth to complete my tent.

As I walked along the beach, close to the tide line, I began to find all manner of flotsam from our ship, which was most heartening. Fortunately for me, a trunk belonging to Colin had washed up on the beach, containing extra clothes, a box of flints, his dirk, a hat, and assorted personal effects, including some rare gold and silver coins from ancient Greece and Rome. The find was both a happy, and sad one, at the same time. I missed Colin. I dragged the trunk well up from the water line, and managed to drag it to my tent.

I also found the remains of seven dead friends, scattered amongst the flotsam; some of them grotesquely disfigured from the explosion. It was a most disheartening experience, especially since the digging of graves would be a major undertaking for me. A hook does not lend itself well, to holding a digging implement. Plus, my body was all aches and pain. I did not feel up to the effort, but on the other hand, leaving the bodies lying on the beach, would result in an odiferously disgusting spectacle. The solution, which I chose, was to build a massive bonfire and cremate the bodies. It was the only way.

Hence, the rest of my day was spent gathering combustible materials, with which I built a massive bonfire. Burning seven bodies would take a lot of combustible material. I did not want the job to be poorly done. Fortunately, I found three kegs of pitch, and a keg of kerosene, which would greatly help to start the conflagration.

The hot sun made the work a laborious chore for the next three days, as the bodies began to reek, necessitating covering my nose with a bandana I found in Colin's trunk. Tying it on was a problem, since I only had one hand; which is a great inconvenience, let me tell you, dear reader. When you try to do what I was attempting, with only a hand and a hook, nothing is easy and everything becomes more time consuming.

Gulls and crabs had already begun to feast on the decaying corpses. The spectacle was not a pretty one, however, I had to accept the fact that when the life force is no longer animating the matter, of which the body is composed, it disintegrates and goes back to the elements from which it was made. That is a fact of life and death. Our brains are made to see the destruction of the body as something sinister and macabre, which it most certainly was to me.

And yet, at the same time, as I neared the completion of the cremation fire, four days after beginning the task, I had some opportunity to examine the bodies from time to time, as I took a break from my labors. I found the disintigrative process of the human body, a fascinating study, which both repelled and attracted my interest, as I began to notice how living creatures were beginning to discover the various ways and means, to gain access to their feasts. Little crabs had crawled into ears and nostrils. Gulls had pecked out eyes and had begun tearing at exposed flesh. Various other birds came and fed. Several bodies had starfish clinging on them.

The consumption of the corpses was a constant irritation to me, as well, in that the gulls were becoming a great nuisance. I tried to scare them away from time to time, but it was all to no avail. I had to accept the fact, I would be burning what remained of the bodies, by the time I was ready.

In order to get the bodies up on the burning platform, I had rigged a spar with a block and tackle. Several hooks were amongst the flotsam, so I was able to use these to fasten to the bodies, in order to pull them up onto the platform. Getting them to the platform entailed carrying and dragging the odiferous, leaking corpses. Hauling the bodies onto the platform took a day and a half. It was such disgusting work I had to frequently wash in the ocean to try and rid my self of the smell. By the time I was done, I threw off my reeking clothes and tossed them on top of the bodies, which I dabbed with the tar.

I climbed down from the pyre and poured the kerosene over the copious kindling I had placed deep inside the pyre. I had left a hole to get to the centre, and by striking two flints together, managed to produce some sparks, instantly igniting the kerosene, singing my eyebrows and lashes, and nearly giving me a very nasty burn on my face, had I not instantly reacted and fallen backwards.

Within moments, the pyre ignited and a massive yellow flame began to consume the combustibles, producing an amazing amount of heat for some significant distance around the pyre. Within ten minutes, the flames began to work on the pitch smeared bodies, sending a black, oily smoke into the sky. As the fats began to drip into the flames, the fire burst into a new explosion of white hot flames, which rose skyward for fifty feet, or more. The entire time, while the funeral fire burned, I sat some distance upwind and watched the spectacle, consuming liberal portions of rum, while contemplating my mortality and predicament.

When the platform collapsed, everything fell into a large burning pile on the sand. Not much remained of the bodies, which were still burning, as the entire mess lay on the sand in front of me. It was at this point that I left and went for a long soak in the fresh water pool, on the opposite side from where I took my drinking water.

I have no idea how long I sat in the pond, but by the time I climbed out, it was getting dark. I dried myself off on some absorbent cotton cloth, which I had found in Colin's trunk. Then I donned clean, dry clothes, which fit reasonably well, albeit somewhat looser than my own, Colin being somewhat taller, and heavier than me. There were also a pair of shoes, which were about two sizes too small. Hence, I resolved to manufacture moccasins, to make walking in the forest easier and more comfortable.

When night came, I was suddenly very tired. I fell into a troubled sleep and dreamed of the awful chore I performed on the beach; the labor for which had taken quite a toll on my body and strength.

I rested the next day, by sitting on the beach, leaning against a log and drinking rum. In spite of my resolution earlier, the rum helped to ease my mind and relax my body. The previous six days had been like a visit to hell. It took me a few days to recompose myself.

When I finally gathered my wits together, I began planning how to bring everything useful from the beach to my camp. Boxes of hard tack, a keg of salted herrings, two kegs of rum, a keg of salted beef, three more trunks with people's clothing and personal effects, a box of tea, a chest from the galley containing; two pots, some cups, utensils, a large knife, and an old pewter plate. I also found more sail cloth and a trunk with blankets, and, to my great joy; my leather bag, containing my notebooks, quills, and a bottle of ink. Miraculously they were saved. I had stored them in a cabinet, under my bunk. I was greatly relieved that my notebooks were not water damaged.

The found items enabled me to make a very comfortable camp for myself.

I cut back the vegetation from the tent and modified its appearance, with the addition of more sail cloth, and a better arrangement of ropes and spars. After a few hours of work, I had made a cozy, covered space of ten square feet, completely enclosed and fairly insect proof. One side contained a slit, which served for a door, over which another sheet could be pulled, in order to keep creatures from climbing through the slit, to visit my exposed flesh for a meal or drink.

The blankets were perfectly suited to make a soft, very comfortable pad, on which to sleep, and to cover my self, as the nights were quite cool; at times actually cold.

Some days later, it occurred to me, that I would eventually lose track of the days, if I did not mark them off, somehow. I solved the problem by carving notches in a stick for every day I was marooned there. Thinking back, I realized I had already been in that forsaken place for fifteen days, and subsequently carved fifteen notches, to start my calendar; a practice I kept up, without fail, every morning I awoke.

On the seventeenth day, I decided I felt completely well, and fit enough to go for a walk, to explore the beach and see if I was, in fact, on an island. I had managed to fashion a pair of moccasins from a piece of sail cloth, which made walking a lot easier. In order to prevent further sunburning of my skin, I fashioned an umbrella from some sticks and a piece of sail. I was able to lash the canopy to a three foot long stick. When my umbrella was ready, I packed my leather bag with some food; bananas, hard tack, and salted herring, which I wrapped in a piece of sail cloth. Three limes, from the tree nearby, and a piece of salted beef completed my picnic lunch. I carried drinking water in one of the pots, for which there was a lid. I carried the umbrella over my left shoulder, and held it in place with my hook, which I had to adjust slightly, in order to get the angle correct. The pot of water I carried in my hand.

Thusly provisioned, I set out to explore my surroundings, heading north, past the charred remains of the funeral pyre, still smoldering on the sand. I paused for a moment, to examine what remained of my friends. Seven charred skulls lay amongst the carbonized bits of unburned wood, and bones; one entire rib cage, some hips, and several leg bones. In one spot lay an unburned hand, which I quickly buried in a hole, I dug with a stick. The rest would have to cool down and then I would dispose of the bones in a decent manner.

I couldn't help the tears, as I reflected on the fine friends I had lost.

When I was finished examining the tragic remains, I continued my walk along the tide line, my mind filled and my heart, heavy. The sand was smooth, cool, and easier to walk on than the dry sand further up, which was hot, and burned the soles of my feet, right through my moccasins.

The beach was about a hundred yards wide and was made of a fine, white sand, which reflected the sun mercilessly back at me. I was glad for the clothing I had on, and the umbrella I had made. Without it, I would have been baked alive.

After walking for about three quarters of an hour, I came upon some more flotsam from our ship. The pleasant discovery was a trunk, containing two dueling pistols in a beautiful carved box, complete with all the tools and materials necessary to keep them in fine working order. The trunk also contained a box, in which; a horn of powder, and a leather bag with twenty six balls, flints and fuses, completed the ensemble necessary for the successful discharge of said pistols. It was a most fortunate discovery, and lifted my spirits considerably.

As I dug further into the trunk, I found a leather bag, with twenty five doubloons, nineteen guineas, twelve rijksdaalders, and ten ducats. I chuckled, as I looked at the little bag of treasure, while pondering the loss of the massive fortune in our shipwreck, after all the trouble we went through to procure it. It was an ironic moment. Here I was, in a place where money was of absolutely no use, holding a bag of money, which would buy me passage to the other side of the world and back; yet, it, like the lost treasure, was of no use to me; not as useful as food, clothing, and water.

I dragged the trunk higher up on the beach and took a pistol, with the powder horn, some balls, fuses, and flints, thinking, I might find something to shoot. Or, maybe I might need it for protection.

Need it for protection? The thought suddenly occurred to me. I really had no reason to suppose I was alone where I was. Just because there was no one else, where I was, did not imply everywhere else was devoid of people.

As I continued my walk, I was on heightened alert.

After walking for another two hours, or so, I came upon a small stream, which was trickling out of the forest, through a channel it had dug in the sand, forming something of a delta. It was a lucky find because it enabled me to refresh my water.

I crossed the stream and continued my walk, eventually coming upon a rocky area, which rose up to a cliff of stone, rising about two hundred feet above the water.

Waves crashed against the rocks and sent spray into my face. I had to be careful to keep my right eyelid pressed shut, to avoid sea water getting into the empty socket, an uncomfortable feeling when it did. The patch, which Virginia had lovingly made, was lost somewhere in the shipwreck.

In order to traverse the rocks, I had to move into the forest and climb over moss covered rocks, reaching the top of the cliff, a half hour later. I sat there for a while, eating some of the food I had brought. As I sat there munching on a piece of hard tack, I thought of my family and wondered how they were faring. I was missing them considerably; their faces a constant presence in my mind. I prayed that Virginia and my children were well and able to bear my absence, for however long that might take.

Looking out from my perch, all I could see was water, right to the hazy horizon; leagues away from where I sat. Where exactly my family was, I had no idea.

When I was finished my repast, I took a long drink of water, and carefully walked along the top of the rocky cliff, eventually reaching the other side, where I climbed down to another sandy beach curving to the south. I was beginning to get the impression that I was indeed, on an island.

Two more hours of walking confirmed my suspicion, as I began to come upon flotsam from our ship, strewn hither and thither; a far more significant pile of stuff, than further north, where my camp was. Amongst the bits and pieces of oak, sails, ropes, spars, broken barrels, kegs, and boxes, I found a ship's compass, in its box, sitting on top of a rock, almost as if someone had placed it there for me to find. It was a most extraordinary feeling when I retrieved the precious instrument from its rocky perch.

A large bag of flour had miraculously washed ashore, nearby. The outer two inches of flour had formed a hard solid cake, while inside the flour was perfectly dry and useable. A keg of salt lay next to it.

I found another trunk, which contained, thank God, some books; including, ironically enough, our colony's copy of Daniel Dafoe's marvelous book, *The Life and Strange Surprising Adventures of Robinson Crusoe of York, mariner delivered by pirates,* etcetera. The title could fill a paragraph. Suffice it to say, the story does justice to the title. I also found, within the trunk, a box of candles, which made my nights so much more pleasant over the next number of weeks, until the candles were all burned up and I had to resort to other means for evening light.

Over the next few weeks I dragged all of the useful trunks and assorted flotsam back to my camp, which began to resemble a storage yard, with seven trunks sitting amongst, spars, ropes, sails, kegs, boxes... By the time a month had passed, my camp was as comfortable as I could make it, providing a pleasant location to sit and read the books I had found, rereading the adventures of Robinson Crusoe, they now resembling my own misfortunes.

When another month had passed, I was beginning to notice that my supplies of meat and fish were dwindling. It was time to consider hunting a wild pig, and doing some fishing. The latter was easier to do than the former, however, over time I managed both. Both of my successes, regarding the procurement of protein, are worth relating, so I shall give you, dear reader, the details, which, Lord forbid, you will never have to put to use, but you never know.

I had observed, since coming to the island, that wild pigs lived there, as I told you. They must have come from a ship wreck, in my opinion, because they were not indigenous animals to islands, such as the one I was on. Anyway, I found that the pigs had made a trail down to the pond, in order to get their water. They usually came twice per day, once in the morning and again, just before night fall. Hence, I determined to dig a pit, directly in the centre of their trail. I would place sharpened sticks in the bottom of the pit, and then cover the hole with branches and leaves. When a pig stepped on the cover, it would fall into the hole, and become impaled on the sharpened sticks. It was an excellent plan, however, as I told you earlier, digging with a hook, for a hand, is not an easy task, especially if one does not have a spade.

Digging the hole, therefore, took me considerable effort, utilizing one of the pots to scoop the sandy soil. Eventually, as I managed to dig down about three feet, the soil became much harder and necessitated the loosening of the dirt with a pointed stick.

When a hole, about four feet deep, had been achieved, after two days of digging, I carved six very sharp stakes, which I placed deep into the soil, at the bottom of the hole. Then I carefully covered the hole with sticks and leaves, over which I sprinkled sand, to make it look absolutely like normal.

Fortunately, one pig thought it was normal. He landed on the stakes just before sunset. I heard the crack of the branches and the sudden, hysterical squeals of the impaled pig. I quickly rushed to the hole with a loaded pistol and put the poor creature out of its misery, with a ball through the head. Then I covered the hole and allowed the pig to bleed into the hole through the night.

Next morning, I slung a block and tackle over a branch, directly over the hole. Then I firmly attached a hook into the pig's rear leg tendons and hoisted the creature off the stakes. I gutted the pig right there, letting the entrails fall into the hole, which I subsequently buried with some of the soil I had removed, a fit meal for the insects and worms. I skinned the pig and stretched the skin out in a sunny spot to dry.

I let the pig hang for a few days, not being able to hang it longer, on account of the insects and the sun. Meat rots quickly in the tropics.

I cut the pig into appropriate sized pieces and smoked some over the fire. Other pieces I dried in the sun. The remainder, I salted, and stored in an empty cask, which I put in a cool pit I developed. Some choice pieces of ham, I roasted for my evening's meal. The smell of roasting pork was such a wonderful aroma, my mouth was watering, well before eating it. The first bite of the roasted pork made the entire time spent, obtaining the pig, well worth the effort. I gave thanks there were wild pigs on the island.

As time drifted by, and an entire keg of rum had been consumed, the island was well into the winter season. Temperatures were considerably cooler at night. The island was hit with wind and rain. It was during those times that I felt so glad I had found blankets, books, and materials to make a weather proof shelter.

Although I had books to read, eventually, being all alone, with only oneself to talk to, becomes very trying, and not at all pleasant. Every day I thought about my family and how I was missing them. I had no idea if they were safe; if they had any idea about me. Considering we were only going for a month, and I had already been gone for over three, my poor family must have been wondering where I was. Their, not knowing, became a great concern for me, and troubled me daily.

Anyway, there was not much I could do, so I made the best of things and tried not to let thoughts of my family bother me, too much.

* * *

I was going to tell you my fishing story, to get back to a more interesting chapter.

So, here then, is how I managed to obtain fresh fish from the ocean.

With great care and attention, I had carved a harpoon out of the fork of a sturdy branch. The ends of the fork I fashioned into very sharp points. By very carefully cutting slits in the prongs, I was able to insert thin, sharp pieces of shell, which I fastened, by wrapping the entire affair with thongs I had made from the pig's skin. The harpoon's handle was about five feet long, and enabled me to thrust it with some force. I tied a strand of rope through a hole in the end of the shaft, and the other end I tied to my belt, so that when I thrust the harpoon, I would be able to retrieve it, if the fish decided to swim away with the weapon.

When my harpoon was ready, I went out into the surf and waded to a tidal pool, not far off shore, where I knew fish lurked. I had to be very careful, because sharks lurked there too.

Anyway, I would stand on the edge of the pool and wait until I saw an appropriately sized fish, into whose body I would thrust the weapon, neatly catching the fish between the prongs. The weapon worked wonderfully well. I was able to eat fresh fish whenever I wanted, from then on.

Other creatures, which I discovered were good to eat, were a type of reddish coloured crab. It was delicious, roasted, poached, fried; cold, hot, with or without vegetables, there were so many ways. Other seafoods which I obtained were: oysters, mussels, shrimp, and two sea turtles.

In the beginning of, what I thought to be, March, I made another circumnavigation of my island, heading in the opposite direction from the previous time. It was during this trek, that I discovered access to the small mountain in the centre. I had not noticed the trail last time, because it was only visible from one location, where there was a gap in the trees, near the cliffs. Hence, I vowed to attempt a climb, the following day.

With my leather bag packed with food and my pot of water in my hand, I slowly made my way through the forest. Vines and creepers of all kinds clung to me, or grabbed at the handle of the water pot, causing me to spill some of the precious liquid.

Branches grabbed at the straps and buckles of the bag. In several places I had to crawl under branches obstructing my progress. However, I persevered and gradually, step, by arduous step, I made my way successfully through the forest, reaching a barren, rocky outcropping. The summit was about a hundred feet above the rocks.

I carefully made my way along a narrow path, between two large, jagged rocks, and managed, by putting my bag and water pot on top of a rock, above me, I was able to climb up after them.

I believe the climb to the summit probably took about three hours from the time I left my camp. It was not an unreasonable amount of time, however, there had to be a better way to get to the top. I hoped to find it by looking from the top down.

The summit was similar to the top of the mountain, on the colony's island, commanding a three hundred and sixty degree view of ocean, ocean, and more ocean. The island was alone, as far as my eye could see. However, given that I only had one good eye, and the horizon was hazy, I must admit, it was highly possible there were other islands some leagues distant, which, if I had a spyglass, I would probably have seen. As far as I could tell, my island was alone. That is the information I would have to go on. Making assumptions is not good science.

As I sat eating my lunch, on top of the mountain, I began to scrutinize the place more closely and noticed there was a path leading down the hill. It must have been made by the pigs, who undoubtedly liked to come up for the view. It would make coming down a whole lot easier, I figured.

When I was done my lunch, I looked towards the west, believing Virginia and my children to be out there, somewhere. I prayed for their safety, and for my rapid delivery from the lonely fate which had befallen me.

I headed back to my camp, utilizing the pigs' path, which made the going considerably easier, than the way I had come, giving me an idea for a method of signaling, what ever shipping might be in the region. Perhaps, by building a permanently smoking fire on top of the mountain, I might attract the attention of a ship.

It was worth a try. The path could make it possible.

Alas, after hauling kindling and wood up the hill for a week, I realized, after it was all burned away, in three days, the labor intensive struggle would only be worthwhile, if I spied sails, and then ran up the hill to light the fire. I could not sustain burning a large fire, continuously.

I solved the problem by building a bonfire ready to be lit. All that I would have to do, if I spied sails, was run up the path and light the fire, using the kerosene I had placed there, to help ignite the conflagration. However, I never saw any sails. I began to think I might spend the rest of my days on the island.

As the weather warmed up in the spring, I began to spend more, and more time, sitting on the beach, under an awning, reading, or carving: wooden statuettes, masks, utensils, puzzles, or rereading the books, yet again. In the case of Robinson Crusoe, for the third time, while watching for sails, which never came.

The preceding is an accurate account of exactly how I spent my time, from when I regained consciousness on the beach, until great fortune befell me sometime at the end of May, about which I will tell you next. My rescue came in a completely unexpected fashion. However, like Robinson Crusoe, my rescue was also effected by pirates.

Chapter Twenty-Two

One day, during another walk around my island, on the same route I had taken the first time, it being a beautiful day towards the end of May, as far as I could reckon from the notches on my counting stick, I made an incredible discovery, which, at first, made my heart stop, but later turned out to be a most fortuitous circumstance.

As I was on my way home, it being later in the afternoon, and my circumnavigation of the island nearing an end, at a place not far from where I found the ship's compass, I discovered two pairs of human foot prints in the sand. The discovery shocked me, because I was not expecting to see them, and not knowing whose prints they were, the idea came to mind, the prints might belong to savages.

Near the water's edge lay a well made raft, with a good straight mast and torn sail. Several kegs and boxes were strapped to the deck. I thought, at first, that two natives had found my island and were wandering about, perhaps having found my camp. I wasted no further time and hastened to my camp, cocking my pistol on the way, as a precaution.

Sneaking through the bush, trying not to make any sounds, I carefully inched my way towards my encampment; all the while listening intently for sounds which would identify the presence of humans in the area. As I came closer, I could hear two male voices, discussing, in English, the circumstances of my camp. Straining my ears, I had the distinct impression the voices were familiar. When I finally reached the pond, I crouched behind the trunk of a large tree. Then, I carefully pushed some leaves aside and peered at my camp across the water.

The sight which greeted me made my heart sing and jump for the greatest joy imaginable. My friends, Colin and George, were sitting outside my tent, gloriously drunk, with one of my kegs sitting between them.

When they saw me, tears streamed from their eyes, as there were tears coming from my eye, as well. We hugged each other for a long time, the three of us standing together, grateful for our mutual deliverance.

When we had collected ourselves, and sat down for a welcome toast, my friends told me their story; every bit as interesting as mine, however, with four hands, instead of one, they were able to achieve a reasonably pleasant circumstance for themselves, in a quicker time than it took me.

My friends were amazed by the camp I had managed to put together, pointing out that I was lucky to receive so much flotsam from our ship. They had no idea why the storm had sent them to a completely different island, five leagues distant from mine, to the south east.

Apparently, my friends had climbed onto a hatch cover, which had blown off the ship. They eventually landed on their uninhabited island. They believed themselves to be the only survivors.

Anyway, Colin and George floated at sea for some days, making shore on the island which harboured them. They stayed there until finally they built the raft and sailed towards my island, after seeing my smoke on the summit.

'We had an idea it might be one of us,' said Colin happily, 'When we saw the smoke, we knew it wasn't the doings of natives and had to be a signal of some kind.'

'It was a smart thing to do, Peter,' said George. 'Now that we are three, we should be able to figure out a way to make it back to our happy cove.'

I told them that I had a compass, which brought big grins to George and Colin's faces. With a compass and a solid raft, filled with supplies, we figured it was possible to rescue ourselves and find our families.

I also showed Colin his trunk and gave him back the ancient coins I had found in there.

Colin was happily surprised, as he rummaged through the trunk and reconnecting with his things. He noticed the shirt I was wearing and remarked how good it looked on me.

I asked him if he wanted it back, but he declined. I told him there were more shirts in the other trunks, noting the shirt he was wearing was in dire need of replacement.

The following day, with our plan firmly in our minds, we set about modifying the raft, in order to accommodate many of the enhancements we could add with the many items of flotsam I had gathered off the beach.

Spars and good ropes enabled us to make a larger raft with a jib and main sail, like that of a sloop. We also fashioned oars, to facilitate handling and movement in the event of becalming. We made a better rudder to enable us to stay on course.

When the raft was done, we loaded her up with trunks of supplies, kegs full of water, and one of rum. Then, when all was ready, we used a block and tackle, fastened to a large rock, some distance past the surf, to pull the heavy raft into the water. She left deep marks in the sand, as the massive raft was pulled slowly into the water and through the light surf.

We waded through the breakers and climbed on board, Colin and George quickly manning the oars, while I disengaged the hook attaching us to the block. When we were free, Colin and George began to work the oars, moving the raft slowly away from the island, which had been my home for over six months.

When we were well clear of the surf, we put up the sails and set a course, in what we thought was the general direction of the Caicos Island chain. Figuring the islands lay to the west, we simply set a course in that direction and hoped for the best. We figured that we would surely hit an island, or Florida, Mexico, or somewhere in South America. All we knew was in the west there was land.

The raft was a slow moving vessel. Even with the sails up, the raft moved at a snail's pace, only attaining a maximum speed of a knot and a half. However, the slow speed was to our advantage, because we couldn't go much faster, anyway. If we did, the shallow draft brought too much water flooding our boards.

In the middle of the ocean, the sun was relentless in its desire to heat up the entire body of water, in as short a time as possible. Fortunately, we had taken the necessary precautions, by rigging an awning under which we happily sat drinking rum and talking about our adventures, or quietly reading a book, several of which we had taken with us. Our trip on the raft was rather a relaxing affair; quite enjoyable, really.

However, one day, we had a frightening encounter which heightened my fear of sharks, a healthy concern, a human being should harbour, regarding those monsters of the deep.

We realized that sharks could easily get onto our raft, if they so desired. We had no freeboard, so the shark could lunge, and land on top of us with no problem. Hence, we always made it a point to post a watch. We took turns, anxiously watching for the dreaded dorsal fins.

The fin we most did not want to see, appeared near the raft one afternoon, when we had been drinking a little bit heavier than normal, and each of us had considerable color in our cheeks. In fact, I believe that Colin, usually not much of a drinker, had managed to put himself in a close hauled position, with all sheets to the wind, causing him to lean precariously. Colin's pronounced lean became a problem when he attempted to urinate, causing him to fall, face first, into the sea.

George and I were moderately plastered under our awning and did not react to the splash. It wasn't until we heard Colin frantically yelling for help, that we stumbled out from under the awning, and beheld Colin struggling for all he was worth, attempting to get back on the raft, as a large gray dorsal fin was bearing down on him.

George and I immediately grabbed the pistols from the trunk under the awning, and rushed to where Colin was pulling himself up.

Just as Colin rolled onto the deck of the raft, a huge mouth, full of razor sharp, triangular teeth, came out of a rush of brine, followed by the streamlined mass of a tiger shark.

Without hesitation, George and I instantly discharged the pistols directly into the shark's head. A sudden gush of red blood spurted over Colin, as he incredibly avoided the horrible mandibles from biting his left leg off.

We quickly helped Colin on his feet and pulled him back, as the shark began to thrash about, smashing one of our trunks containing dried pork and some other food stuffs. George grabbed an oar and began jabbing at the distressed shark, hoping to push it off the raft, before it smashed everything to smithereens. Of course, the fact that we were under the influence of a considerable amount of rum, made the ordeal all the more difficult to deal with. Fortunately, the shark managed to thrash itself back into the water, where it disappeared, leaving a bloody trail behind itself.

Suddenly, without warning, the water began to froth and seethe as about twenty sharks appeared on the scene and devoured their bleeding friend in a matter of seconds; the sea turning blood red as their hapless brother was torn asunder.

We considered our selves fortunate it wasn't one of us being so consumed. The thought of being eaten by a shark made me shiver, requiring another hearty cup of rum to settle my nerves. Needless to say, we did not sleep well that night.

Three days after the shark attack, George spied land far off to starboard. It was vague at first, but eventually, I could see it too, as we drifted closer. Then, to make things even better, we spied sails bearing upon the island, some distance north of us. The fact that a ship was heading for the island meant we were approaching an inhabited place, bringing us the immediate hope of learning where we were, in relation to our village.

By nightfall we could see lights on the island. Seeing those lights was even more of a happy occurrence than seeing the sails. Lights meant habitation. Lights meant a town or village was near, and help would be available to us.

Sometime in the night, our raft washed up on a beach, south of the lights. We had attempted to steer for them, but the current, wind, and design of our craft, did not facilitate very accurate navigation. Hence, we washed up on a beach and decided to stay there through the remainder of the night.

Next morning, we attempted to make ourselves look as presentable, as possible, although our ragged clothing, and long matted hair and beards, made us look like beggars. Fortunately, I had brought the bag of coins, so we were heartened to know, our ragged state would be soon changed to something resembling a more civilized appearance, reasoning that, where there was a town or village, there was a barber and a haberdasher.

A walk of several hours brought us to a town perched above a natural harbour, in which seven ships lay anchored. The noise of hustle and bustle drifted towards us on the wind, as we approached the town from the south. None of us had any idea what town it was; each of us on his guard, and wary of the slightest challenge posed by the inhabitants; who stared at us, as we walked into town.

The first thing we did was ask a friendly looking man where we were.

The man stared at us blankly, not comprehending our English, so we tried asking in French and Spanish. It was the latter tongue which suited the man. He informed us that we were in Port Nelson, on a small island in the Bahamas chain named, Rum Cay. The town was basically a victualing place for ships plying the Bahamas trade route. The main industry was the provision of dried fish and rum, the smells of which were thick in the air.

We asked the man where the local barber plied his trade.

He smiled and pointed us in the direction of the place we desired.

When we stepped into the barber's shop, he grinned from ear to ear. 'Where do you boys come from?' he asked. 'You look like you have been to hell and back.' The barber took a sniff and wrinkled his nose. 'Judging from the odors you track with you, I would say you spent some time in hell.'

We apologized for stinking up his establishment and he suggested that we should avail ourselves of the public baths, which were next door. The man frowned and suggested we visit the clothing store across the street, first, in order to replace the rags we were wearing. 'You don't want to be climbing into those rags, after a nice bath, do you?' asked the barber. Then he paused and frowned. 'Do you have money?' he asked suspiciously.

I jingled the leather bag of coins, which seemed to satisfy the barber. He held the door for us, and pointed to the clothing store. Then, as we walked across the street, I sensed that the barber was swinging his door back and forth, to circulate air through his shop, to clear our stink away.

When we stepped into the clothing store, the proprietor at first suggested he did not do business with criminals and destitute people.

I assured the man we had the means to pay for clothing and jingled the coins in the bag.

The man, seeing that the leather bag held a hefty number of coins, immediately assumed we could manage our account with him and politely asked us where we had come from, and why we were in that state of dishevelment.

We told him that we were shipwrecked sailors, who had managed to make a raft and float to Rum Cay. We did not go into any more detail than that.

The man never asked, how it was that poor sailors had as much money, as we obviously had, when I paid him with three gold doubloons, for the outfits we picked out.

Then, when we had obtained the clothing we required, we walked across the street and enjoyed a glorious hot bath, attended by three beautiful black women, who spoke a little bit of broken English.

I don't know how long we spent in the baths, but I am sure it must have been well over an hour and a half, as we soaked and scrubbed months of grime from our bodies and hair, not having seen soap for over six months.

When we finished with our baths, the girls helped us dry off and assisted me with my dressing, noting I had a little difficulty, because of my hook.

The new clothes felt good on my clean body, putting a spring in my step, as I entered the barber shop first.

The barber smiled and said he would be pleased to attend to my hair and beard, the operation taking about an hour, after which I looked like a proper gentleman, once again.

My friends received the same treatment. Within the space of three hours we were completely transformed, like caterpillars metamorphosed into butterflies. Anyone who had seen us that morning, would no longer recognize anyone of us.

I paid the barber handsomely for his work, for which he profusely thanked us. He waved, as we walked past his front window, on our way to a restaurant down the street, where we satisfied our hunger with a delicious meal of hot food and copious tankards of cool ale, topped with a pint of the local rum.

After dinner, we took rooms at the Goose Head inn and slept in real beds. We had to relearn the joys of comfort, by staying at the inn for ten days, before we even bothered to try and find transportation back to our families and friends, on our happy isle.

The next day, as we sat over a prolonged meal in the afternoon, George asked me if I was planning to have my right ear pierced.

When I asked him why, he explained that it was a custom amongst sailor folk, to have their right ear pierced upon the survival of one's first shipwreck.

George already bore two rings and was planning to have his left ear pierced again, to commemorate his third ship wreck. Colin was having a second piercing performed.

I already knew about the custom, hence, I did not hesitate any longer. I felt I owed it to myself to commemorate my salvation from Neptune's clutches.

After lunch, we found a place that performed piercings. It was in the back of a small shop specializing in beads and baubles, gold, silver, coins, bullion; it even catered to those who wished to mark their skins with tattoos; a practice I did not wish to partake in. Piercing my right ear lobe was enough of a pain, I did not wish to succumb to more, by having my flesh etched with a sharp instrument.

The piercing of my ear lobe was a bizarre operation, which required placing my earlobe on a small anvil. Then, the piercer, a brawny no neck, with tattoos on both of his arms, and the sides of his bald head, punched a hole into my lobe with a nail and hammer. I must say the pain was such that it instantly brought a tremor down my spine, as a lightning bolt of pain shot out in many directions. However, I remained calm and submitted to the ordeal; the man pouring rum over the wound. Then, he inserted the gold ring I had chosen, closing it firmly, so it would never come out. He reminded me to pour some rum on the wound every day to keep it clean. Then, he did something I did not expect. He expressed concern over my lack of an eye patch, to keep dirt and water out of my socket.

I explained that I had an eye patch made by my wife, but it was lost in the shipwreck.

The man, whose name was, Leopold van der Loos, held up his right index finger and, winking, said he would be right back. He returned a moment later with a beautifully made, black velvet patch, with a pair of silk ribbons, to hold it in place. He gave it to me, free of charge, for which I was very thankful. The patch felt nice on my face and presented a dignified appearance, as far as I could tell by looking in the mirror. My friends also thought it looked very dashing, especially with the tricornered hat I had chosen at the haberdashery.

I flinched, as I watched the man punch Colin and George's ear lobes in the same manner, completing the process with similar rings to the ones they already had. When we were done, I paid Leopold with a golden ducat for the piercings, and three doubloons for the rings.

When we were done, we bid good day to the piercing specialist, and walked happily towards the docks, hoping to find transportation back to our island. I had enough money left, with which we purchased a small, 23 foot, ten year old yawl, a barrel of water, and some provisions.

We sailed from Rum Cay in the morning of May 26th, 1784. We had been gone from our families for over seven months. I could hardly wait to get back to see my lovely wife and children. I prayed nothing had happened to them. I missed them terribly.

En route, we stopped along the beach, where our raft still lay, and rescued some of the things we wanted to take home with us, such as the books, and, of course, the compass, the delicious salted pork, and what was left of our rum.

When we finally arrived in the vicinity of our island, three days later, we could clearly see that a red flag was flying from the mast on the platform, indicating someone was keeping watch. Of course, our friends had no way of knowing who we were, so we ran up a white cloth, to indicate we were coming in peace, and presented no threat; not that our yawl presented such, but our islanders were admonished, to not take chances with strange vessels approaching our shores.

We slowly maneuvered the yawl into the channel leading to our cove, making it obvious, to the people on shore, that we knew where we were going. When we came within hailing distance, we shouted to our friends that we had returned.

Our friends and family on shore were a little perplexed, in that we did not look like the people who had set out on an adventure, nearly eight months earlier.

We sailed our boat right up to the pier, to which our brig lay tied. Then, we tied the yawl to a cleat, next to one of our longboats, the one the fishermen used to provide fare for the colony's tables.

A number of our friends had come out on the pier, to see who we were. It took them a few more minutes to recognize us. The moment they realized it, a great shout rang out, as the people rushed forward to embrace us.

As we were walking to shore, I saw people running towards the beach. Within a flash I recognized my wife, carrying little William, followed by Catherine and Joshua. As soon as my feet touched the shore, Virginia flung herself into my arms, and buried her face in my shoulder, tears of joy streaming from her beautiful eyes. Moments later, my two children grabbed my legs and hugged me with all their strength, as they happily shouted, 'Father! Father! We are so happy you are back!'

The homecoming was equally warm and joyous for Colin and George.

Alas, it was not such a pleasant occasion for the families of our friends, who had died in the shipwreck, including our close friends, Andy, Robert and Russell.

The loss of so many good men and women, and our man of war, with the Spanish treasure, was very tragic news, which put the soggy blanket of sorrow over everyone but, Colin, George, and I, who were happily enjoying a return to the arms of our happy wives and children.

That night Virginia and I made love in our wonderful bed. It was so good to be home.

Three days after our return, I resided over a huge bonfire tribute to the friends, who were lost in the attack on the treasure ship and subsequent shipwreck. Many toasts were drunk and eulogies spoken, as everyone, who felt confident to speak, presented anecdotes and reminiscences regarding the friends who were lost.

The commemoration party lasted six days, as copious amounts of alcoholic libations were consumed, necessitating an almost immediate voyage, a week later, as we discovered a serious depletion in supplies of the beverages of our choice.

Fortunately, a hogshead of rum was discovered, stored in the wrong warehouse, enabling us to continue for a few more weeks, however, when no choice remained, either we set up a distillery, or we sailed. Of course, the latter became the order of the day.

The brig was quickly readied and 45 men set sail on June the 15th.

Neither Colin, George, nor I, had much interest in sailing, so soon after our return. Our wives were pleased we chose to stay home. Even though I was now the leading captain, by popular vote, it was not necessary that I attended to every voyage. It was tacitly understood that we, who had suffered a shipwreck and marooning, could choose to do whatever we wanted, for however long we chose.

Hence, I stayed home and enjoyed my family, now including little William. The little fellow was the image of his mother; big blue eyes, and lots of brown hair. At first he was shy of me, because I presented something he was not used to, not having seen me for most of his life. With my black eye patch and silver hook, I did not look like everyone else in the colony. However, it did not take too many days of him observing how his siblings reacted with me, to realize that I was his father.

Joshua was growing up to be a sturdy little boy, who adored his big sister. He would follow her around like a puppy, which Catherine did not seem to mind, she being a very devoted big sister. I was so pleased to see how well the children got along together, it made my heart glad to have such a nice family, with the best of all partners to share them with. I felt blessed and happy to be alive.

One afternoon, as we were sitting together on the beach, watching the children playing in the sand, Virginia mentioned my ear ring. 'I thought you were never going to get your ear pierced.' She examined, the still sensitive wound, where the golden ring punched through the lobe.

'Shipwreck commemoration,' I told her. 'A ring in a sailor's ear means, he survived a wreck at sea.'

Virginia said that it was a very excellent practice. She told me she was blessed to have me back, and that was also to be commemorated with the ring. Then, she kissed me long and passionately, gently holding on to the ring in my ear.

Some weeks later, our brig returned, filled to the scuppers with hogsheads of ale, rum, and wine; the beverages of our choice. The brig also brought back a dozen bread fruit in pots, plus ten trunks of assorted clothing, twenty boxes of women's shoes, thirty boxes of men's shoes, fifteen blunderbusses, twenty three brand new cavalry sabres, nine ten pound cannons, with a supply of two hundred balls and ten kegs of powder, plus a box containing two thousand guineas. It was quickly apparent our men had plundered a ship.

When the swag was sorted out, the families of the men, who had perished in the attack on the treasure ship, or the shipwreck, were recompensed for their loss, with a generous payment from the box of guineas; certainly enough money to keep them in pleasing circumstances for a period of, at least, five years. The rest of the swag was divided up to those who needed the goods the most.

The libations were rolled into our warehouse and dispensed according to our custom, no one denied the libation of their choice, whenever so desired, unless a shortage was apparent.

The successful return of our brig was cause for a bonfire celebration, which, this time, Virginia and I only attended for a couple of hours, choosing instead to go home and make love in our comfortable bed.

Following is a brief account of how I spent my days with Virginia and the children.

The day after the bonfire, we took the children for a visit to the tidal pools, not far from where Leonard was crucified. Catherine asked about the weathered cross, still firmly standing in the tide pool, where our able artists had placed it, so long ago. I never told her about Leonard. Instead, I explained that the cross was a reminder of our Christian values and left it at that. She never asked about the two heel bones, still firmly spiked into the vertical beam. Maybe she never noticed them. I don't know.

* * *

On another day, we took the children for a walk up the mountain, to sit and watch the ocean, which I did for a long while, as the children played and Virginia picked flowers. I pondered the shipwreck and my marooning. I felt that my return was somehow miraculous and gave silent thanks for my deliverance.

Another afternoon was spent swimming in the lagoon The children liked that best of all, because they got to play with a friendly dolphin, who liked to swim in our cove. Catherine named him, *Happy*, because it appeared as if the creature was perpetually smiling.

One day, we took a walk around our island, enjoying a picnic lunch on the other side. The walk reminded me of my lonely treks around my island. The weight of my steps in the sand were much lighter on this occasion.

Each day was as pleasantly spent as the preceding, our life was truly a dream, which I never wanted to end. My life with Virginia and my children was so perfect, I could not imagine it ever ending and indeed, prayed it would always remain so.

Alas, as things turned out, like so much of our lives spent on this beleaguered sphere, perfection lasts but a short while and sometimes comes to an end. Everything falls short of the glory of God. Paradise is a dream; a gossamer veil fringed with gold. As it moves in the winds of change, the veil parts to reveal the hard, cold facts of the real world. And so it was to befall us. The veil parted and paradise disappeared.

Chapter Twenty-Three

Towards the end of July, 1784, the skies began to cloud over and winds were beginning to hit our island, increasing in intensity as time went on. We could see that something untoward was brewing in the east. Everything indicated a storm was heading our way. My stump ached and my empty socket felt odd, somehow, as if air pressure was changing in my skull.

Other members of our colony, with missing limbs, or severe rheumatic aches, also felt pain in their joints. Two other men, with recently missing eyes, also reported an odd sensation in their empty sockets.

Our farm animals seemed strangely restless. The horses were stamping their hooves and running about, as if suddenly spooked. The pigs were all gathered together, and squealing at each other, as if discussing the oncoming event. I noticed the cats had disappeared and the dogs were anxiously looking out to the east, where the sky was beginning to become ever darker and sinister. As the winds picked up, they began to bend the palm trees at their tops.

Everyone in the colony was aware that a massive storm was heading our way, and set about securing their homes, and our communal buildings. The women and children were advised to go into the storm shelter, the moment the first indications of worsening weather revealed themselves.

The shelter was provisioned with food and water for five days, the latter poured with buckets into the funnel leading to the barrel hanging below ground. Overhead spanned a massive beam from which hung a block and tackle over top of the covered hole, through which the barrel for the head was raised. The three hooks on the end of the ropes were swinging precariously in the wind and had to be battened down, before they hit someone.

Several adjustments had to be made to the palisade, which served as a wind deflector. Over time we had not kept up with maintenance on it, not having been bothered by major storms, and having grown complacent about attacks. The work proceeded apace. Fortunately, we managed to complete the work, before the hurricane hit our island with a full broadside on August first, at two o'clock in the afternoon.

The women, children, and the infirm were quickly evacuated from their homes, and the infirmary, to the storm shelter. When the women and children were safely in the shelter, the men moved deeper into the forest, to the lee side of the mountain, where we had dug a cave, large enough to hold a hundred people, as well. It was provisioned with a barrel of water and a trunk of dried foods. There was no head, the forest serving for that purpose.

As the wind increased in intensity, an insane howling pierced the air, frightening the young children, who apparently cried with intense fear, according to Virginia.

On the lee side of our mountain, all that we could see was the bent tops of the trees, waving back and forth. It was the sound which frightened us more so than the wind. Although, had I been on the other side of our mountain, and witnessed what the wind was doing to our village, I would have been equally frightened by it.

We passed the time in our cave by discussing plans for future modifications to our colony's buildings, future adventures, past experiences, the treasure we lost, and the shipwreck we suffered. The family men spoke of their wives and children. Some men played cards, several others played backgammon, watched by others, who contributed advice.

Outside, things went from bad to worse, as the full extent of the hurricane's fury was unleashed on our island, wreaking great havoc with all that we had built. Had any of us been in our houses, we would most assuredly have died.

After, what seemed like seven hours of intense wind and howling, the air became suddenly very still and an eerie silence enveloped us. As we came out of our cave, we could see the sky above us was clear, yet, as we climbed up the mountain, to have a better look, we could see that the sky was a swirling mass of clouds all around us, at some three leagues distance.

We were in the eye of the storm.

The interlude in the eye gave us enough time to check on the women and children, and to take stock of damage to our village. At this stage, our palisade was still holding, but definitely showing signs that it had received a major pounding. Our brig had lost a yard arm; I could see the spar lying by the boards. Seven houses had lost their roofs. A tree had fallen on one of our cows and knocked it senseless. Other than that, we appeared to be faring relatively well. Alas, it was only a prelude to what was to come, when the eye passed us, we were hit with something only Diablo could have fomented.

When the next phase of the storm hit us, we collectively believed Armageddon had arrived. Unbelievable screaming winds pounded our island, necessitating the plugging of ears, lest one became deafened by the sound. All manner of crashing and smashing sounds came from the forest, as tree after tree was blown over or snapped like a toothpick. We, in the cave, could only imagine what was happening on the other side of our mountain.

Suddenly, a mighty cracking noise and a rumbling of things coming down the mountain heralded the end of our platform, as massive pieces of our structure tumbled down in front of our cave entrance, effectively blocking it.

I prayed, as I sat there, that Virginia and the children were not suffering harm in the shelter. I tried to send Virginia my best, positive energies, hoping she would sense them in her heart. I'm sure the other family men were feeling the same anxiety for their families, as the noise worsened and the crashing intensified.

The storm lasted for another two days, before it finally left us, in search of other victims; leaving our island a devastated wreck. Our gardens were demolished, three of our cows, six pigs, one dog, and a cat lay dead. Our houses were essentially ransacked, as the winds had battered through the walls and blown everything inside, hither and thither. Our meeting hall was gone, as were seventy houses, the chapel, and two warehouses; barrels and assorted goods, scattered in broken pieces throughout the trees. The roof of our music hall had collapsed and crushed the bass viol, two cellos, and a violin. Miraculously the other instruments were not harmed.

The barricade was a sorry character of its former self. How wind could twist and bend such a structure, was a remarkable observation.

Some incredible things had been done by the wind, which became a marvel for all those who saw those wonders. A pewter plate had been driven vertically into the trunk of a palm tree. A twenty pounder cannon was lying in the crook of a massive tree, twenty six feet above the ground. The main mast of our brig was imbedded in the east side of our mountain, like a spear tossed by a giant. Not a rope, or yard arm was left on our ship, all of them strewn about, like so many match sticks.

Our women and children emerged from the shelter, somewhat bleary eyed, but otherwise non the worse for wear. One of the infirm people, a sailor from the man of war, had gone to his Maker, but the other infirm people were no worse and able to help themselves out of the shelter. The dead sailor was duly buried in our cemetery, a friend speaking a heartfelt eulogy expressing the virtues of the dead jack tar.

Our platform on top of the mountain was missing everything but the floor. All of our water works were wrecked, and most of the cannons of our defenses had been rearranged, or were covered with fallen trees and debris. Cannon balls lay here and there, throughout the bush. The beach was strewn with all manner of flotsam and jetsam from, who knows where. Bits and pieces of ships and their cargoes; intact kegs of various commodities, a complete sail, lengths of rope, assorted shoes, not any of them paired, three oars, the stem and part of the keel and sideboards of a long boat, one trunk without contents, one trunk with contents, including a pistol, a short sword, a dirk, a marlin spike, a complete change of regular clothing, a lapped coat, two sailor's hats, a pair of shoes, a worn, dog eared Bible, a note book, two quills, a small bottle of ink, and a diary containing the memoirs of a sailor named, William Spavens. The latter I requested be given me, when everything useful had been gathered from the beach and deposited in our square; then completely littered with pieces of our town.

The devastation was heart breaking. Catherine and Joshua were quite bewildered and upset over the destruction of the top two stories of our magnificent house, completely obliterating the children's rooms and scattering their toys and other belongings to the wind. We found most of their things strewn about in the forest behind our house, which greatly helped to cheer them up.

Eventually, everyone took the stoic attitude, that such was life in the world. Storms happened. Unless we built of stone and brick, expecting to withstand a hurricane, with houses made of wood and thatch, or even those of our houses built with clay tile roofs and plastered walls, such as mine, was foolishness. Our houses needed to be made much stronger.

Hence, it was decided in a general meeting, that we would attempt to rebuild our town with brick and stone, in addition to wood and thatch. We determined to re-build the storm wall of stones and bricks. We were not going to succumb to another storm again.

We rebuilt our town over the following seven months. This time we built the first stories of every house out of local stone and imported brick from San Juan, and from a ship we lightened after our brig had been repaired.

Because so many good men had been lost in the attack on the treasure ship, and the subsequent shipwreck, we did not have to build as many houses, as before, which greatly facilitated the rapid rebuilding of our town.

In between the times we worked, Colin, George and I discussed plans for a major adventure, having become bored with our fat lives on our island. It had been well over a year since we had set foot on the decks of our brig. We each desired to go back to sea for a little piracy. Our hearts desired adventure. We were committed to follow through with our heartfelt desires.

'We are pirates,' said George emphatically. 'There is no denying that. Hence, we must do what we must do.'

'Hear, hear,' replied Colin, smiling broadly. 'I can hardly wait.'

When we realized our stores were dwindling, sometime at the end of March, 1785, we decided to take the repaired brig, with a crew of seventy five men, and a full magazine of powder and balls, to commit a considerable act, hopefully netting us more fortune and at least another year's supply of the necessities of life; ale, rum, wine, and fresh clothing, bedding, books, victuals, and sundry other commodities which availed themselves, in the assemblage of swag.

We set sail on April 12th, when favorable winds would take us towards the coast of Brazil, where we had learned a lot of Spanish and Portuguese shipping plied the waters, often times carrying diamonds, gold, silver, and precious woods. One of our plans was to seize a suitable ship, in order to replace our brig; it becoming water logged and infested with teredo worms.

In spite of her age, our brig was still a comfortable, and relatively speedy ship to sail. I had grown quite fond of her and was not relishing the idea of replacing her, however, there was not much choice. 'Wooden sailing vessels gradually rot away, not much different from humans,' I commented wryly, one afternoon when we were sitting on deck discussing our options, en route to Rio de Janeiro.

One of our Portuguese men explained that the name, Rio de Janeiro meant, *January River.* Apparently the city was named that because the site was discovered in January and named *Rio,* because the Portuguese explorers mistook Guanabara Bay for the entrance of a river. It apparently was a wealthy place and could possibly provide us with rich swag and a new ship.

The voyage from our island to Guanabara Bay took forty three days, during which we lost three good men, due to illness. I guessed the men had come down with fluxes, however, George thought they died from rhume, or possibly fever. Whatever it was that killed them, it did a good job, because the men were definitely dead, we made sure of that, before we buried the poor fellows at sea, somewhere at 10 degrees, 3 minutes west by 45 degrees, 6 minutes north, some three hundred leagues off the coast of Venezuela. We gave the chaps an appropriate send off with a wake, the night before we sent them to see Davy Jones' locker. The party continued well into the following day, rendering everyone semi comatose for several days after. It was a lucky thing we did not run into inclement weather, or were faced with a challenge from other pirates. We would have been too inebriated to respond.

We crossed the equator at 33 degrees south longitude on May the third, which was another excellent reason to have a great party, during which all of us, who had never crossed the equator, were summoned before King Neptune and made to atone for our sins, and strongly encouraged to drink copious amounts of rum. My punishment was to be dunked in a tub of water a dozen times, and cursed with all manner of curses so foul and detestable, I shall not repeat them here, lest I insult your gentle sensibilities, dear reader. Suffice it to say, pirates are masters of the art of the curse, and all manner of excretable utterances.

Seventeen of our company were brought before the King of the Seas. The party was great fun, the older, more experienced sailors, making the entire affair a truly theatrical event, complete with all manner of outlandish costuming. It was an event I shall always remember with great fondness, particularly because of the fine friends who made the affair such a success for us.

We rounded Cape Sao Rogue on May 11th and from there on, we pretty much hugged the coast the rest of the way to Rio de Janeiro, arriving in beautiful Guanabara Bay on the twenty fifth, thankful to have made a successful voyage; notwithstanding the loss of three good men to illness.

The bay and the harbour were filled with ships. We had no idea what we would find in the busy port, when we set out from our island, however, judging from the bountiful number of ships we discovered there, we knew that our ships had come in, so to speak. I noticed Colin and George rubbing their hands together, as we floated past a richly gilded, Spanish ship, armed to the teeth with twenty pounders and swivel guns. It was obviously the ship of a rich merchant, who protected his property.

The Spanish ship was a beautiful specimen of commercial success, with gilded ornamentation on the transom, and a magnificent sculpted mermaid, with sensual, erect nipples, which immediately made me think of Virginia, whom I was missing tremendously, having been at sea for forty three days.

'As splendid a ship as that is,' said George, 'It is not the ship for us. It is too easily identified. We need something common; a sturdy, common ship. Hopefully another fine brig, such as this one.'

'Aye,' agreed Colin. 'The *Navigator* has served us well over the last few years. It will be sad to leave her here, however, someone might still be able to get some use out of her, plying local trade.'

'We should sell her,' I suggested. 'Then we will take up lodgings, for a time, and do some serious investigating. We should attempt to pick one or two, maybe three ships out of this collection.' I gestured towards the ships we were gliding past. 'I think we should do some recruiting on shore, and then simply steal as many suitable ships, as we have sailors to sail them. If we plan carefully, we could easily come home with something worth traveling all this way for.'

'Aye, aye,' agreed Colin and George.

Wapoo, who had been listening, nearby, smoking his covered pipe, pointed to a fine looking brigantine lying next to an old Swedish barque. 'There,' he said. 'That is ship we want.' He said it so authoritatively that we all turned to him, and then looked at the ship he was pointing at.

Off to starboard, between a Dutch West India Company trader and a Danish merchantman, lay a marvelous example of American craftsmanship; a beautiful, streamlined ship, with a racing deck, perfectly suited to piratical purposes. Under the main deck ran a gun deck, and storage holds were probably below that. She was of shallow draft, and could run out twelve pairs of oars from the lower deck. Her transom was handsomely shaped. George suspected the ship may have been a navy frigate, which was converted to mercantile service.

As we slid past, I noted the graceful lines of the American ship and could not help but agree with Wapoo, it was indeed a worthy candidate, to replace our aging brig.

We dropped anchor beside a fat tub of a ship, belonging to a Dutch trader named, Willemzoon van Trijn; a jovial man, who immediately welcomed us to the anchorage and invited us on board for a drink of jenever, a potent, clear distillation favored by those hardy folk from the flatlands.

While our men secured the ship, Colin, George, Wapoo, and I rowed to the Dutch ship and clambered on board.

The jolly Dutchman poured us each a cup of the clear distillation and made a toast, welcoming us to the splendid city.

When I tasted my first drop, I had the distinct impression the liquor could be used for volatile purposes such as, explosions. When I had drunk my first cup, I had the feeling the top of my head was about to come off, and declined further involvement with the potent Dutch elixir, gladly accepting a cup of grog, to ease the burn in my stomach.

The jolly Netherlander laughed at my discomfort and told me that I was a green horn, and that he could drink me under the table, an honour I was glad to let him keep.

The Dutchman spoke very fluent English and questioned us regarding our purposes in Rio de Janeiro; observing that we did not exactly look like regular merchants, or traders of some kind.

I told him we were actors and musicians hoping to establish a theatre in Rio.

The Dutchman thought that to be a splendid idea and heartily congratulated us on making such a bold move. 'The world needs more actors and musicians,' said the jolly merchant happily. 'Life is so dreary, most of the time, we need diversions to entertain us and make our days more pleasant,' he said. Then he raised his cup and suggested a toast, 'Here is to actors and musicians!'

We all drank heartily and then thanked the Dutchman for his hospitality, telling him we had things to do, with regard to securing our ship, contacting the harbour master, obtaining food and drink, and most of all, to get off the ship, on which we had spent over forty three days.

The Dutchman heartily agreed it was good to go on shore and suggested we would meet later, at an incredible restaurant, Mama Rosa, not far from the docks.

We agreed to meet the merchant later at the restaurant he suggested and then took our leave of him and returned to our ship to begin the process of ferrying everyone to shore with our long boat.

Colin, George, and I went to pay our respects to the harbour master, while the rest of the men fanned out to explore the fabulous city, happy to be off the ship

The harbour master's office was on the second floor of a large stone building, facing the harbour. We climbed the creaky stairs, in single file, as other sailor men were coming down. The office was obviously busy. Stepping into the office, we had to stand in line, in order to be served. When our turn came, we simply told the officials we had come to obtain precious woods.

The official assessed a fee of twenty five crusadoes per week.

I paid the man a hundred crusadoes, in order to ensure our anchorage for a month. In return, I was given a stamped certificate testifying we had paid the fees.

Formalities done, we decided to take a walk and reconnoiter the incredible city, below the equator. Unfortunately for us, just as we were about to step foot outside the building, it began to rain, which immediately altered our plans and saw us take refuge in a public house, close by.

Stepping through the doors, we quickly realized the place was a popular rendezvous for all manner of sailor folk and their minions. Legitimate, able bodied, and regular seamen, from many countries, were boisterously carousing with every thing from strumpets and tarts, to society women, out looking for an adventure away from their husbands. Noise and commotion filled the place with a lively atmosphere. In the corners, men, with obviously evil intentions, eyed us suspiciously.

As we wove our way through the crowd, I happened to bump fully into a buxom, young serving wench. In the crush of people she was pushed against me, in such a way, that her young, firm breasts pressed into my chest and her pubic mound pushed against my right thigh.

It was all that was necessary for my unruly appendage to rise firmly to the occasion. In the closeness of the contact, the girl obviously felt my salute and giggled, as she looked me directly in the eye, smiling coyly.

I was sorely tested to prevent myself from kissing her and fondling her lovely, ripe breasts. Feeling her pressing against me was an overpowering feeling. I realized how much I loved the sensation of a woman's body against my own. I realized how much I missed Virginia.

The moment passed as quickly as it came about. The girl continued with her work, wending her way through the crowd, holding her serving tray above her head. I watched the girl disappear in the throng and continued to follow my two friends, to a place where we could stand and have a drink.

Against one wall ran a twelve inch wide, polished wooden plank, which served as a place to lean one's elbow and set a drink down. When a different serving wench came by, I ordered a pint of ale, my friends ordered grog, it being too early in the day to drink full bodied rum.

As we waited for our drinks I looked around at the people inhabiting the popular tavern, while Colin and George got into a discussion regarding the merits of drinking grog in the afternoon, as opposed to drinking rum without water, a topic in which I had little interest.

Our drinks arrived, moments later, delivered by the young wench who interested my pocket monster. As she leaned down, to place the drinks on the board, she gave me a marvelous view of her ample cleavage. It was enough to effect another stirring of the beast in my breeches. I was seriously wondering if Virginia would have minded me knowing the girl, however, I did not want to find out. I respected and loved her too much, to risk losing her over a momentary affair. It was not worth it.

The temptation to know the serving wench was most powerful, however. I could not help myself from taking a deep sniff of the girl, luxuriating in her scent; further pumping blood into the beast. I was glad when she left, after paying her a healthy tip. The agitation in my groin was an uncomfortable reminder that I was a randy goat, who took no pleasure in that boring, solitary act. I meditated on the arbitrary shackles we willingly put on, when we marry. The shackles were something I was very tempted to break, as I found my self thinking about the serving wench, naked in my bed; a delicious nipple between my lips...

As I was thusly standing, in a sweet day dream of erotic pleasure, a loud yell rang out, shattering my happy vision. A group of swabs had gotten into an altercation. I watched as one of them smacked a sailor over the head with his ale tankard; the smitten man falling backwards into a group of sailors, sitting at a table behind him. The seated sailors stood up, and began to roll up their sleeves, as the tankarded sailor's friends came to his defense. The sailors stood facing each other; exchanging curses and lewd remarks.

Then, without warning, all hell broke loose, as the sailors went at each other with murderous intent.

An instant later a burly jack tar fell backwards, directly into my right shoulder, causing me to spill my tankard of ale, which I did not appreciate very much. I gave the man a hearty smack on the head with my empty tankard, and pushed him away with my left elbow and forearm.

The jack tar was well into his cups and did not need much persuading to fall in another direction, which happened to be on top of a table full of drinks belonging to five sailors, enjoying an afternoon on shore. The immediate result was that the burly sailor upset the table and tumbled to the floor, table and all.

You can well imagine that sailors do not take well to people knocking their drinks over, hence the five sailors grabbed the fallen jack tar and demanded he pay for their drinks.

The drunken sailor slowly stood up and told the five sailors to take a flying leap.

It was the wrong thing to have said to these particular sailors. They grabbed the errant drunk, and threw him, head first, through the doors, into the street, yelling after him that he be the one to take the flying leap.

The drunk's friends saw what had happened, so they stormed over and another fight broke out right beside us.

We decided it was time to move to another side of the room, from where we could watch the circus, without fear of losing our drinks. Fortunately, a table became available, when four sailors vacated the chairs, in order to rush over and watch the fight close up.

Sitting down, I noticed three sinister looking men staring at us from the corner table, nearby. Colin could not see them, because he was sitting with his back to the men, however, George and I were able to keep an eye on them from our positions at the table. I sensed that the men were practitioners of the sweet trade, but from their scowling countenances, did not encourage me, with regard to the issuance of an invitation to join us at our table, let alone involve them in our plans.

Some minutes went by, when, suddenly, one of the men stepped over to our table. He was a tall, unattractive looking fellow, with a gold ring through his prominent, hooked nose. A small skull was tattooed on his forehead. As he approached our table, I took note, he was obviously not very well to do; his coat being patched, and his cuffs, frayed. The man was carrying a cutlass, which hung from a wide belt over his left shoulder. His eyes were ringed with dark circles, like those of a raccoon. I did not get the impression he was brimming over with robust health.

I surreptitiously cocked my pistol, expecting trouble.

The man stopped beside me and stared at us closely. Then, looking directly at Colin, he asked if we were the pirates, who had defeated Golden Jim in Maracaibo.

'Who is asking?' queried Colin, eyeing the man suspiciously.

'I was a member of his gang, when you were captured,' said the man, changing his expression to one of admiration. 'I fled when you attacked. It was my chance to get away from Golden Jim. He held me and my friends.' The man pointed to his friends in the corner. 'Golden Jim held us captive and forced us to serve him.' The man looked at each one of us separately and then added, 'I understand that you killed him.'

We stared at the man for a few moments, assessing his sincerity. We were not about to admit killing someone to a sinister looking fellow we had never seen before.

'A man never admits murder to a stranger,' said George wisely.

'My name is, Alesandro de Jesus, Moranos,' replied the man with an exaggerated flourish. 'I proclaim my self, the friend of the man who killed Golden Jim.' The man stared directly at me when he said it, his eyes blazing with sincere energy.

With my hand on the pistol in my belt, I stared calmly at the man and asked him why he was so anxious to know if one of us had killed Golden Jim.

'I want nothing more than to join your company,' replied the man anxiously. 'My friends and I have a great respect for anyone who killed that golden monster. As I said, he held us captive and forced us to work for him.'

The man's sincerity eventually won out and I admitted to pulling the trigger on Golden Jim.

The moment Alesandro heard me admit to killing Golden Jim, he pulled a pistol from under his coat and pointed it directly at my chest. 'I knew I recognized you,' he said, a sinister grin on his face.

When Alesandro's friends noticed that he was pointing his pistol at me, they immediately stood up, cutlasses in their hands.

Unfortunately for Alesandro, he had no idea who he was threatening. Had he some inkling, that Colin was a master of the martial arts, he would never have gone to stand beside him, thinking a sitting man could cause him no problem. How sadly he was mistaken, as Colin instantly acted by smashing the pistol from the man's hand, at the same time that I shot him neatly through his forehead, blowing brains out of the back of his head.

Seeing what happened to their friend, Alesandro's companions charged with their cutlasses, ready to slash us to shreds.

Colin, seeing the two men charging, managed to turn his body out of the way at the same time swinging himself out of his chair and taking it with him. Then, he used the chair to good effect, by swinging it, like a weapon, quickly disarming the two attackers; their weapons flying off in the direction of a group of sailors standing on the side, watching the altercation.

In the mean time, George stood up, and without hesitation, smacked a bottle over the head of the errant man to my right.

Colin subdued the other man by smacking his head against the floor. The man groaned.

Colin wiped his hands on the man's back and calmly returned to his chair. He winked at me, as he took a hearty drought of grog.

We resumed our conversation, as if nothing had happened.

'Thank you Colin,' I said. 'I had a feeling we couldn't trust him.'

'He did seem oily in his sincerity,' replied Colin. 'I had an inkling there was something wrong.' Colin made a fist. 'I was ready.'

'We are a formidable team,' laughed George, lifting his tankard for a toast.

Looking at Alesandro, still bleeding on the floor, I reminded my friends we had better be on our guard, from then on. 'If there are three, there will be more,' I said.

My friends agreed, as we toasted our success.

The audience returned to their drinks, leaving the dead and unconscious men where they lay; no one willing to reveal themselves as friends or colleagues of the three attackers, until we were well out of the door. We had managed to instill a healthy respect and fear in the sailors, who had been standing around watching us.

We found another public house not far from the previous one, this one a whole lot more friendly. Within a short while we had seven sailors sitting at our table, enjoying happy banter about our sundry adventures on the Seven Seas. The seven sailors soon became our friends and did not need a whole lot of coaxing to join our adventure.

The Super Seven, as we came to call them; Adam, Carlos, Eduardo, Federiko, Ignatz, Juanito, and Xavier, who came from Switzerland, were all fairly large, strong men, with big grins on their happy faces. The seven men had been friends for a long time. They operated a transportation company whereby they utilized a small fleet of long boats and barges, to ferry supplies to the ships at anchor in the harbour. The Super Seven employed fourteen slaves and twenty free men. The seven friends complained they were losing business to a larger company employing over two hundred slaves, with ten boats, and their own warehouse. Our seven friends were losing business and had come to the tavern to discuss sacking their freedmen.

After we had drunk a number of toasts, we realized five o'clock was approaching; it was time to meet our Dutch friend at Mama Rosa's. We invited our new friends to join us, which they readily did, the ten of us gloriously in our cups by the time we arrived at the restaurant. When we entered the door, Willemzoon happily hailed us from a table already spread with food and drink, in anticipation of our arrival. Our host was also well on the way to a healthy state of inebriation, thus we all fit into the moment very well, indeed. Our jolly Dutchman graciously welcomed our seven new friends, saying that any friends of ours, were friends of his.

The serving staff quickly added another table, chairs, and dishes to

Willemzoon's table, then we all sat together for a welcoming toast proposed by the jolly Dutchman.

The meal was a sumptuous feast fit for the kings we were. Roasted chickens came on a huge platter, surrounded with a great variety of vegetables covered with delicious gravy derived from the roasted birds. Other dishes included fried plantains with red snapper, roasted iguana with green onions, red peppers and goat's cheese, an incredibly thick and creamy seafood chowder, and to top the entire meal off, our host had brought a hearty sampling of delicious Dutch cheeses called Edam and Gouda, after the places where the cheeses originated; they being two places in the United Provinces. The meal was accompanied with a delicious red wine from Portugal.

Our party lasted well into the wee hours of the following morning, after which, unable to venture to our ships, we accepted an invitation to sleep in the houses of our new friends; Colin going with Eduardo, George with Adam, and I gratefully fell into a happy sleep in Xavier's cozy home, next door to Ignatz.

Willemzoon elected to stay at the inn, next door to Mama Rosa's.

Next day, we all met up at Mama Rosa's for breakfast, where we began to discuss our plans for some piratical fun, thinking that we had nothing we needed to hide from our Dutch friend, Willemzoon, who, upon hearing of our plans, thought it a splendid idea, to plunder some ships; easily seeing the potential profit he could realize by allying himself with experienced pirates.

'I vuld zugest ve shteel frum ze Eenglish, zey are zo arrogant zey zink dey own ze vurld,' said Willemzoon banging his tankard on the table. 'Az far az I am conzernt, ze Eenglish are shtill ze enemy of my peeple.'

Of course, we couldn't have been happier to hear our very own philosophy expressed by our friend from the Netherlands.

As we delved deeper into our plans for larceny, we decided that, even though we admired the American brig, it belonged to a country, which also fought the English. We decided not to take Wapoo's advice and chose to pursue a different ship, equally splendid and well suited to our purposes. The ship belonged to the wealthy Company of Gentlemen

Trading in and Around the Hudson's Bay, who by now, owned many ships plying a multifarious trade in sundry commodities.

When we suggested the alternate ship to Wapoo, his face lit up. He explained that his Mi'kmaq friends, in Halifax, had spoken of that company of traders. They had told him that the company did not trade fairly with the people, demanding many more times the value of the commodities they sold. Wapoo related how his friends had told him; the people would have to stack beaver pelts to the height of a musket, in order to purchase the weapon, which would have been easily purchased for the price of one rich pelt in London.

Hearing Wapoo's story determined us even more, with regard to the removal of the aforementioned ship, our Dutch friend heartily agreeing to the plan, and willing to offer what assistance he could.

Over the days that we spent organizing our selves in Rio de Janeiro, we sized up a number of different ships, in addition to the one mentioned above. Other candidates, for removal to our island, revealed themselves over time, as more and more intelligence came in from our friends, who had gone out to seek information regarding the ships in the harbour. Eventually, we decided to board three ships, two belonging to the British West India Company, and the ship belonging to the Company of Gentlemen Traders, a company which I considered to be anything but an organization run by gentlemen; preferring to call them a company of rogues and thieves, instead.

Three weeks after our arrival in Rio de Janeiro, we held a war council on the deck of our ship. Our Super Seven had brought their men, and thirty six more friends, eager for adventure, and hungry for swag. Now that we had a total of one hundred and forty five men willing to take the risk and pirate with us in Guanabara Bay, we felt confident that we could remove the ships right under the noses of the owners living luxuriously on shore, in the local inns.

We decided to split the men into three groups under the direction of Colin, George, and I. We gave each group a name, in order to expedite the organization. My group chose to call ourselves, 'the House of Lords.' Colin's group became, 'the Blue Raiders,' and George's group became known as, 'Sweet Revenge.'

When we had organized our plans, everyone gathered up their things from the brig and took rooms at the local inns, enabling us to sell the emptied brig, with her cannons, to a local ship dealer for the sum of eleven hundred pounds sterling, a price which more than paid for our collective rooms and board. I had remembered to remove our black flag.

Our plan was put in effect on June 22nd, a miserable, dreary day of cold rain blowing in from the south east. The reason we chose such a day was that most everyone would be inside, taking refuge from the precipitation.

The three ships we had selected were easily approached with the Super Seven's boats. The ships were not well guarded, most of the sailors carousing in town.

The inclement weather enabled us to sail the ships out of the harbour, without anyone really taking much notice. The jolly Dutchman followed behind.

Most of the skeleton crews of the three ships elected to join us, believing their fortunes better made with us than with their tightfisted masters. Several officers also decided to join us. Those who refused were given a long boat and supplies, to row themselves back to Rio.

We managed to effect the entire enterprise without one shot fired, or one blade run through a living human being. It was a good feeling to plunder without blood shed. It was a happy voyage we undertook, as our new ships beat their way slowly back to one of our favorite ports, a place where we would be safe to share out the swag we had obtained.

Beating up the coast took much longer than the journey from our island directly to Rio. When we neared the mouth of the great Amazon river, we were driven far to eastward due to the powerful current of the river flowing into the Atlantic Ocean. It was a difficult task to beat north against the strong current wanting to push us away from the continent. When we finally managed to catch a breeze, it enabled us to achieve a westward tack, some days after coming into the Amazon current. We arrived in Maracaibo, nearly two months after leaving Rio, having had to put into port several times along the way, to replenish our firewood and water, which in some places, was worth its weight in gold.

We had to stand off the coast of Venezuela for three days before the winds allowed us entrance into the beautiful Gulf. We dropped our anchors in Maracaibo's harbour on the morning of August 21st. We were received as heroes, the people still thankful for their liberation from Golden Jim. On the night of our arrival, a huge welcoming party was celebrated in the town square, in front of the cathedral; the padre serving as host.

The party was great fun, and a wonderful surprise for our new friends; our jolly Dutchman joining right into the fun, even performing a hilarious dance with one of the local women, a full head taller than her dancing partner, much to the great merriment of his crew.

Our stay in Maracaibo had to be prolonged because of a hurricane off the coast, which brought a whole lot of inclement weather our way. Rain, rain, and more rain; for days and days it rained, keeping everyone indoors, pretty much. It was an excellent opportunity for our single men to spend time in the local taverns, in hopes of meeting some compatible females to bring back to our island.

The hurricane blew itself out some time in the afternoon of August 29th, after which we began preparations for the voyage home; everyone anxious to see their loved ones. We re-victualed the ships and took on lots of fresh water, that commodity being plentiful in Maracaibo. When all was ready, we collectively bid good bye to the townsfolk, many of whom came down to the harbour to watch us leave, every flag and pennant happily flying in the yards. The date was August 31st.

Keeping our four ships closely together, all within hailing distance, we convoyed across the Caribbean Sea to Jamaica under fair winds, making the 200 league journey in seven days. We would have reached Jamaica sooner, if we had not deliberately slowed down the three new ships, in order for our Dutch friend to keep up in his slower moving tub.

Because everyone was anxious to get home, we only took on some fresh victuals and water in Jamaica, leaving again the very next morning, the winds remaining fair all the way back to our home island.

Our arrival caused quite a stir, the bell ringing, and the red flag run up. Our friends had no way of knowing that the ships were ours until I had our Jolly Roger run up the mast.

The moment our people saw our distinctive battle flag, the yellow flag was run up and three cannons were discharged with a welcoming salute.

We dropped our anchors off shore, and ferried ourselves to the beach, where our friends were waiting to greet us.

I looked for Virginia and the children, but did not see them on the beach, which I thought strange. She and the children were always there when I came home.

Marianne approached me, giving me a long warm hug.

When I asked her about Virginia, she informed me that my sweet wife was very ill, and that Meira was caring for my children.

Immediately, after hearing the news, I rushed to my house, to find Virginia with a terrible fever, barely able to move, dripping sweat on our bed. Her beautiful eyes were barely open. She managed a weak smile, when she saw me, but was unable to speak.

I sat by her side and held her hand. It was hot to the touch. Even her hair was hot.

As I was thus sitting with Virginia, holding her hand and stroking her hair, Meira came into the room to welcome me.

'I thought it best if the children stayed playing outside,' she said, as she gave me a big hug. 'Welcome home,' she said.

'It feels good to be home,' I replied. 'Except that I am sad to find Virginia in such a state.'

Meira informed me that my wife had fallen ill, a month after I left. Everything Doctor Johnson tried did not seem to work. The doctor figured the fever would run its course, however, up until then, nothing had changed, and Virginia had remained incapacitated.

Three days later, Virginia died in my arms. The date was forever etched in my mind; September 16, 1785.

The pain of that loss is with me still, to the very day that I write this, dear reader. Losing her filled me with an intense sadness, which I never fully got over, and forever filled me with longing for her. She had been an excellent partner and my best friend. We shared so much joy together. The sun rose and set on my sweet Virginia. She was my universe.

I shed so many tears over her loss, that I thought, my eye would become incapable of expressing that emotion, any longer. Losing Virginia hardened my heart against the injustice I felt I had been served by her loss. It was not a good feeling. I prayed I would get over it.

Virginia's funeral was attended by everyone in the colony; many people speaking eulogies praising her gentle nature, her willingness to help others, the excellent example she set as a mother and a friend... Tears streamed down my cheek throughout the ceremony.

My three children reacted in different ways to their mother's death. Catherine was most distraught and immediately began to miss her mother. However, as Marianne became ever more a presence in our home, she eventually began to regard her as more than an aunt. Eventually, Marianne became a mother figure.

Joshua cried during the funeral, and kept asking why his mother was being put in the ground. It took him a while to understand that she had died and her spirit had gone to Heaven. I told him he could pray and talk to her, but that she would only reply in his heart. He seemed to accept the idea and was quickly adjusted to our new circumstances.

Little William was still a toddler, so he did not have much of an idea, regarding the changes in our circumstances, happily playing with a stick as we stood by the grave.

Some weeks later, when I was starting to feel better, and beginning to cope with my loss, I drew a design for a stone cairn and paid to have one constructed over Virginia's grave; the children and I helping to gather the stones from the beach. We placed mementos of Virginia inside a hollow, in the middle of the cairn; her hair brush and mirror, her favorite gold pin, and the first ring I had given her. We closed the cairn on October 5th.

Marianne's second husband, Donald MacIntyre had succumbed in the shipwreck, hence she was a single mother, with whom I had already a good friendship, on account of our adventures together, right from the beginning of this tale. Eventually, as the months passed, and she and her son Michael spent ever more time with me and my three children, she and I fell in love. I married her on Saturday, the fifth of May, 1787. Our little Christopher arrived ten months later, a happy little tyke, the spitting image of his pretty mother.

As time passed slowly, thoughts of Virginia became less frequent.

Marianne amply filled her new role as my wife and partner. She had a quirky sense of humor, which at first took some getting used to, however, once I caught on, we laughed a lot together. However, there was always something missing, which I could not put my finger on, except to say, Virginia left a permanent mark on my heart.

Some time later, many of the men, me included, were beginning to get restless. We had not practiced our sweet trade for two years, the three ships we stole, having yielded enough stores, which supplemented our own victual production, and kept us amply supplied. Hence, we saw no need to put our lives in jeopardy.

Before our jolly Dutchman left, to return to the Netherlands, he had contributed twelve barrels of salt, and five hogsheads of rum, further contributing to our larder.

Willemzoon also contributed five sacks of cochineal, from which, Marta, Meira, and Susanne made some magnificent red dye, eventually producing a wonderful array of bright red skirts, shirts, scarves, and sheets.

Anyway, as time passed, and we became restless for adventure, many of us began talking about going out to pirate again. Even though we knew that we would be risking our lives, in the process, piracy was in our blood. The desire for adventure and swag was a powerful emotion, which we could not appease any longer, by the time January, 1788 arrived. Hence, on Sunday, the 20th we held a war council.

One suggestion was that we sail across the Atlantic and tempt fate on the Barbary Coast. However, the moment the Barbary Coast was mentioned, someone reminded us it was the home of the Barbary Corsairs, a ruthless breed of murderous brigands who plied the sweet trade off the North Coast of Africa. The man strongly suggested that we should not engage them.

Apparently, the Corsairs were barbaric in their cruelty. Another man, one Alfonso Rodrigo, who came from Malaga, described a Corsair castle, which had large steel, triple tined hooks imbedded in the wall, on either side of the main gate. The bodies of their enemies were impaled there, in various stages of decomposition. He described the horrific scene, with a look of great revulsion on his troubled face. The man mentioned how he witnessed the Corsairs tossing someone off the wall, to become suspended upside down, with a hook through his left thigh.

The scene Alfonso described was not something I wished to personally experience. I shuddered involuntarily and wondered at people's cruelty, including our own. We lived in a cruel world, I reasoned. However, it does not justify such practices. I vowed I would keep our violence to a minimum and never to resort to gratuitous violence, like the Corsairs practiced. Throwing people onto hooks, and letting them rot there, is a disgusting practice. I can't imagine how people dealt with the flies and the smell.

The next suggestion was of a more pleasant nature. However, to make a major journey to the Malabar Coast of India, long fabled for its abundant riches, was immediately shot down, because it would necessitate a journey of well over a year. No one wanted to be away from home, that long.

The third suggestion was for us to attempt some raids in the English Channel, however, when the specter of execution dock was brought up, our sights were quickly set elsewhere.

The fourth suggestion is the one we chose to follow, namely to sail to the Guinea Coast of Africa, some 2000 leagues directly east! It was the coast from whence our African friends had been wrested. We felt it was time to pay some slave traders a visit. We had no idea what sort of success we would meet. Our adventure to Africa was a truly singular experience I shall never forget. The things I saw there were truly remarkable and worthy of their own chapter.

Chapter Twenty-Four

Preparations, for our journey to Africa, began in earnest on February the first, a Friday, when the weather was pleasant. Three work crews sailed our ships to the island, where they could be careened and breamed. The task required a month of steady work, as one of the ships was heavily infested with marine growth, and another was in dire need of re-caulking.

The men returned on leap year day, February 29th, the ships ready for loading, a process which took the next two months, as we worked to make the ships as comfortable as possible, for the long journey to Africa. We also took the precaution of renaming the ships, *Santa Maria*, *Nino*, and *Pinta*, after the ships of Columbus. The ship I chose was, the *Pinta*. It formerly belonged to the Company of Gentlemen Traders and was a most comfortable ship.

We positioned cannons, loaded ammunition, stocked the arsenals, prepared ropes and tackle, checked our sails and yards, and as the time for departure drew closer, we began to victualize the ships and fill the water barrels. All was ready by April 21st. However, we still had to wait nine days, before the winds would take us east to an adventure I will never forget.

Each ship was manned by fifty men, eager for the voyage, even though it would take two months to make the crossing. Sixty days at sea was a long time to spend on a ship. Fortunately, we were able to make the ships quite comfortable, they not being overcrowded, and well stocked with the beverages of our choice.

The weather, for most of the journey, was very cooperative, a steady breeze keeping us on a steady course. I used the time to work on my book, spending many hours alone, writing and rewriting several chapters. When I got to the part about Virginia's funeral, I broke down and cried for a long time, tears staining the paper I was working on, necessitating rewriting the page when I had collected myself.

We only saw three sails during the entire crossing. Staring through the spyglass, I was not able to ascertain whose ships they were, the distance being too great to see anything more than some white sheets on the horizon.

Our ships performed admirably. The fact we had breamed the ships before we left, greatly aided the crossing, as the vessels slid smoothly through the tossing Atlantic waters.

The two months it took to reach the Guinea Coast, was spent in a variety of ways. We played games; from chess to cards, and shuffles, a game Colin and George had invented, whereby flat disks of wood were pushed with a long pole, so that they slid across the deck into a long, narrow grid, chalked on the boards. Each square had a number in it. The object of the game was to get one's disks in the square with the highest number. In order to effect this, it often became necessary to slide one's disk against the opponent's disk to make it slide off the grid, or to a lower number. Our deck was large enough to accommodate two chalked grids, enabling more people to play.

The Inside Passage took its toll on the lives of our companions. However, we were blessed, only losing five men, altogether. One on my ship, three on the *Santa Maria*, and one on the *Nina*. My friends reminded me that it was not uncommon to lose ten percent of the sailors to diseases sea folk were plagued with; ague, apyrexies, fluxes, malaria, rhume, venereal diseases, or yellow fever. The deceased companions were each given a wake and then, with pomp and circumstance, were sent to meet Neptune.

We arrived on the 15th degree south latitude and 23rd degree longitude after forty days at sea. We had reached, Praia, on the Portuguese island of, Sao Tiago. Everyone was anxious to get ashore, to stretch their legs, and relearn walking on land; which was always a funny thing to see, the first hour we came ashore. After walking heaving decks for forty days, one's body doesn't seem to understand that the land doesn't move, except in an earthquake.

The people of Praia comprised an interesting assortment of peoples from many places, who had intermingled and produced a people called, 'Mestico.' The Mesticos speak an unusual language made up of words from many other languages, called 'Crioulo.' I was able to understand bits and pieces of it and was soon able to speak with some of the locals.

Slavery was widely practiced on Sao Tiago, as it was on the other islands, as well. Indeed the trade in humans was one of the reasons the Cape Verde Islands were colonized by Portugal. The islands served as an excellent jumping off place for the Guinea Coast of Africa, where rich supplies of slaves were easily obtained.

While we sojourned in Praia, we learned about two notorious slave forts named, Cape Coast Castle, and Elmina, from whence many poor wretches were being taken off the dark continent. The former was once owned by Swedes and formerly known as Fort Carolusbourg. The English had taken the castle and apparently carried on a barbarous maltreatment of living human beings there. The latter fort belonged to the Portuguese. The information we gathered about the notorious castles, determined us to visit those places and take a look for ourselves.

We obtained the coordinates and an excellent chart of the Guinea Coast from the harbour master in Praia. He was an excellent old Portuguese navigator, who had retired on the island, to live out his life in the service of the town. He admonished us to be careful, because, 'De guvernur ov ze plaze iz a cruel dezput. Dey call him, 'Olt Crackers,' said the man, in his broken English. Apparently, John Leadstone, the governor, liked watching the slaves beaten for no apparent reason, to instill them with fear and constant insecurity; never knowing when they would be next for maltreatment. The navigator owned several slaves, who came from the castle, and had told him about it. From the old navigator's description of the governor of Cape Coast Castle, I developed a great dislike for that slave trader. I saw him ever more as a candidate for rapid liquidation; it becoming a modus operandi for our enterprise on the Guinea Coast.

We set sail for Africa on June 23rd, and rounded Cape Palmas six days later. We stayed about two leagues off the coast and beat our way east, rounding Cape Three Points at 2:23 pm on July 3rd. Cape Three Points was the landmark our old navigator had told us, was a short distance west of the fort we were interested in. Other forts were visible along the coast, but none fit the description of Cape Coast Castle, which supposedly resembled a pleasant colonial hotel, with white washed walls and red tile roofs.

We stood off Cape Three Points for four days, as we readied our ships for possible trouble. Cannon balls were stacked on their brass monkeys, powder and fuses were prepared, and set ready by our cannons. Ropes were tied through the rings of grappling hooks, and boarding axes were placed at intervals along the port gunwales. Blunderbusses and muskets were loaded and placed at the ready in many places on deck, instantly accessible, if needed. We also placed loaded weapons and ammunition in our crowsnests, to facilitate shooting from the yards. On one of our adventures, we had acquired a number of crossbows, which were also placed at the ready, being very effective weapons at closer range, shot from the yards, especially.

Our artists had fashioned special grappling hooks, which were now attached to the tips of the yard arms, in the event we came alongside a ship and needed to hold her fast to us. The hooks would grab on the rigging of the opponent's ship and hold her fast. Of course, close and personal like that was not a tactic we used much. Not even in the days of William Bartleby, generally preferring to overcome ships in a more genteel fashion, without a lot of fighting and bloodshed. William had always said, 'There were more ways to cook a fat pig.'

When all was ready, we ventured to sail further east, noting a number of ships under full sail, obviously weighed down with heavy cargoes, leaving the African coast and heading west. I assumed the ships were slavers heading for the West Indies.

Two days later, we sailed past Fort Elmina, an oppressive looking pile of buildings and towers, sitting on a big rock. The buildings were ugly, and of no interest to us, it being a Portuguese fort.

Within an other hour and a half we could see our destination; the white washed walls of the English fort. Several ships, belonging to the Royal Africa Company, lay at anchor, off shore.

From a position, four hundred yards on the lee of one of the slavers, we dropped our anchor in fifteen fathoms of water.

Taking our spyglasses in hand, we studied the castle, in order to best understand how to approach the place without raising suspicions about us and our true intentions, which at that point, were not very clear, other than to effect a reason for the governor's death certificate.

The castle sat on a bank of shale, which reached into the water. Sandy beaches lay to the east and west. I could discern about fourteen heavy guns pointed out to the bay, from the massive ramparts facing the sea. There appeared to be only one immediate access to the castle, from the beach, lying directly to the east of the red and white fort.

The old harbour master had been correct in his assessment of the place, it being a beautiful fort to look at, more closely resembling a fortified hotel. Looking through the spyglass, I could see the administration buildings facing a courtyard, from which a fine looking stairway rose from east and west to meet at a landing, from which a single set of stairs rose directly into the building's higher level.

Apparently, the dungeons containing the slaves, were built under the ramparts. I could clearly see the small windows used to ventilate the cells. I had no idea what was actually the situation, at that time, not knowing the full extent of the horror, which lay within the formidable walls of the English fort.

Our ships were flying English flags and the pennants of the Gentleman Traders, making it look as if we were planning to conduct business with the castle administration. The castle, shortly after seeing us raise our colors, ran up a welcoming pennant, ensuring us safe passage to shore, in order to pay our respects to the governor.

Colin, George, Wapoo, and I decided to represent, 'The Company' and dressed accordingly, assuming the clothing of gentleman traders; clothes which felt tight and restricting, after having worn loose cottons on the entire voyage across the Atlantic. Even shoes felt restrictive; having gone barefooted, or with sandals, on board ship.

I carefully concealed a dirk behind my back, and placed my two pistols in their holsters, under my coat. My companions armed in a similar fashion.

I gathered up some gifts to present to the martinet of the castle; a fine silver snuff box and a gold watch, taken from the captain of an English ship we plundered, two years previously. I carefully placed the gifts in a small wooden box lined with green felt. I also took a bag of gold and silver coins; a down payment for slaves, in order to effect a ruse, if necessary.

When we were ready to depart, I carefully checked my appearance in the mirror, on the door of my cabin. I stepped on deck, to the admiration of my companions, who whistled and hooted, as 'His Lordship' stepped on deck; 'His Lordship' being the appellation for me, which was bandied about the boards by my bemused friends.

Colin, George, and Wapoo were equally, splendidly dressed, the four of us looking every inch the gentleman traders represented by the pennants we were flying. Ten of our friends volunteered to act as company sailors, and rowed us ashore, a company pennant flying from the transom of the long boat.

Our men deposited us on the beach, where three traders were loading slaves into long boats. The poor wretches were attached to each other by chains, which ran through leg and wrist shackles. One column of thirteen men, were attached to each other with neck rings, which were attached with a long pole running through loops on the rings. The poor Africans were wailing, and putting up a fuss, which resulted in several being viciously whipped. It was a terribly sad affair, which pulled at our hearts, and determined us further in our cause.

We made our way laboriously through the sand to the stairs leading up to the main gate, on the other side. As I climbed the stairs, I counted the heavy guns mounted on the ramparts; a formidable defense, capable of significant damage to ships attempting a bombardment of the castle.

We passed a guard house, where two soldiers were posted. They asked us our business. Of course, we acted every bit, the arrogant English gentlemen traders, which seemed to satisfy the dim witted clods, with their army issue muskets. They allowed us to pass, unhindered, to the main gate. Behind the prison, a town had grown, or perhaps the town was there before the fort was built, I have no idea. At any rate, a substantial number of buildings lined a number of streets spreading out in several directions.

A guard at the main gate also requested our business, which we told him was to buy slaves. He looked suspiciously at Wapoo, who did not look exactly like one of us, being a dark skinned, native South American; albeit his clothes were those of a European gentleman, complete with a beaver tricorner. We explained that our friend was the offspring of the Earl of Wessex, and a member of the House of Lords.

The guard was obviously impressed. He saluted Wapoo most sincerely, as we walked through the gate into the courtyard of the castle, where we saw the first example of the horror we would find at Cape Coast Castle.

A black man was crumpled down at the base of a post, his arms tied around it. His entire back, or what was left of it, was covered with buzzing flies. A guard stood nearby, indifferently watching the buzzing insects depositing their eggs in the man's wounds. Judging from the crusted, brown color of the blood, the man had been there for some days. I could not tell if he was alive or dead. The sight made me shudder involuntarily; the hairs standing up on the back of my neck. I adjusted the pistol under my left arm. I felt like killing an Englishman, right then and there.

We ascended the stairs, previously described, and entered the administration building. Entering the lobby, of the governor's office, I noted the two guards posted at the entrance to the office suite. As we stepped into the large room, we were immediately hailed by a lieutenant, from a desk in front of the door, I assumed correctly, led to the governor's office. The officious young lieutenant reminded me of Corporal McFee, from the jail in Halifax, being the same sort of oily character, who was sired by a devil and borne by a demon. I made a mental note to kill him, as well as the governor.

'The governor has demanded that all who wish to trade here, deposit funds in advance, to establish good faith. You will be given an appropriate receipt for the moneys,' said the oily lieutenant.

I set the bag of coins on his desk, beside the little box, containing the gifts for the governor. I explained what the little box was for.

The man nodded and said he would give it to the governor. Then he lifted the bag and ascertained it was of goodly weight. He opened the bag and examined some of the coins within, letting the gold and silver coins run through his fingers; an act which seemed to please him immeasurably. I had the distinct impression that he was drooling. He placed the bag on a scale and noted the weight in a ledger, after which he wrote a receipt. When he handed the receipt to me, he told us to wait, until he had spoken with the governor. The lieutenant stepped up to the governor's door and knocked twice, in a very deliberate rhythm. I made note of the very specific knock, storing the information for possible use.

Moments later, the lieutenant entered the office, closing the door behind himself. While he was gone, we took the opportunity of examining the lobby to the governor's office, it being splendidly appointed with wooden masks and sculptures from the interior. On one wall hung a magnificent African shield, with two crossed spears behind it. I figured that little ensemble would look good in my study.

The door to the governor's office opened and the oily lieutenant beckoned us to enter the sumptuous room. As soon as we four were standing in the marvelous room, the lieutenant returned to his desk, closing the door behind us. Two other people were sitting in the room, facing the governor, who sat behind his desk. The men were the governor's secretary, and the commander of the fort, Captain Marshall.

The governor was a short, stout man, with the build of a gorilla. He had virtually no neck, on which sat a head, devoid of hair of any kind. I don't think the man had eyebrows, even. I remember clearly his high pitched, almost squeaky voice, which did not suit the man, in any way, the voice being totally different from what one would have expected from a man who was called, 'Old Crackers.'

'So, you want to buy slaves?' asked the governor, with his unusual voice; examining the snuff box I had given him.

The voice so surprised us that it took us a moment to respond. 'Aye, er, yes,' I said, hoping I had not blown our cover.

The governor looked at me strangely. 'We have lots to choose from,' he said. 'The price is 10 pounds sterling for a healthy man, and 8 pounds for a woman. Children are five pounds a head,' he said coldly, as if human beings were no different a commodity than cattle. As I heard him rattle off the prices, I determined to kill the man, in front of the slaves, and not in the privacy of his office.

'Yes,' I replied confidently. 'We are looking to buy about three hundred slaves, one hundred and fifty of each; men and women.'

Hearing there was a goodly profit to come from us, the governor's face lit up greedily, as he looked at his secretary.

'We have sixteen hundred on hand, at the moment,' said the secretary, consulting his ledger. 'There are twelve hundred men and three hundred women. The rest are children.'

The governor looked at us and smiled, as he sat back in his chair, with his hands clasped on his ample belly. 'Of course we can't let you have all of them. Those chaps, in the bay, are still working on some financing, to take another three hundred and fifty, I think.' The governor looked at the secretary. 'We could probably let you have the rest.'

The secretary examined the ledger and nodded; stating that, no outstanding orders were on the books.

I reiterated to the governor, we were only looking to buy three hundred.

'Yes, yes, I understand,' said the governor. 'What I mean to imply is, that you can have the choice. You can pick over the slaves that are left, to get the pick of the litter, so to speak; of the slaves that are left over, after we are done with the transaction presently on the table.' The governor smiled. 'You are in luck, gentlemen,' he said happily. Then, taking a cigar from a wooden box, he asked if we would like to examine the merchandise. 'It's good product that we sell. I'm sure you will be satisfied with what you'll find here,' he added, clipping the end of the cigar with a small pair of scissors. 'You will find that those who are left, are still premium, first rate Africans.'

I told Old Crackers, that we had come to Cape Coast Castle because it had a good reputation for excellent quality slaves.

The governor smiled and signaled to the commander. 'Captain Marshall will take you for a tour of the pits, where we keep them. Then you can see what is there.' The governor cleared his throat gently, then suggested we make sure to take scented handkerchiefs with us. 'The place is quite odiferous,' he said, holding the handkerchief which was hanging from his right sleeve, to his nose. 'Those filthy creatures defecate on the floor where they eat. It is disgusting,' he said. 'I suggest you avail yourself of scented handkerchiefs, from my lieutenant, who has some complimentary ones available at his desk.'

We thanked the governor for his offer, and then, without further ado, we were escorted by the captain for a tour of the slave pens, a sobering experience, to say the very least.

The Africans were divided into two groups, men in one group, and women and children, in the other. They were being kept in large open chambers, 'Sometimes 1500 to a room,' explained the captain without blinking. 'We have to cram them in, when the harvest is particularly bountiful.' The captain stared down through one of the grated openings, into the dark pit, full of black skinned human beings looking up, the whites of their eyes, and their teeth, being the only things visible in that hellish hole. A foul reek emanated from the place, necessitating the placement of a scented handkerchief close to my nose. A terrible wailing of despair sent shivers up my spine and further resolved me, to effect a drastic plan.

While we were thus standing over the pits, looking down on the miserable wretches, moaning below, it was time for them to be fed and watered. A cart was pulled up, with a foul looking pile of rotten vegetables, and pieces of dead animals lying on it. Workers grabbed pitchfork loads full of the assorted vegetables and animal parts, and threw them down the holes. They dispensed the contents of the cart into three of the holes, the others being empty. A terrible commotion erupted from the holes, as the starving people fought over the miserable scraps.

Moments later, another wagon pulled up, on the back of which stood a large hogshead, to which a pipe was attached. When the wagon was pulled up, between the openings, water was poured onto the Africans. If one was lucky, he or she was ready with hands cupped. For the rest, they had to get down on their hands and knees to suck the water off the disgusting floor of their pit.

'We lose about twenty percent down there,' said the captain, casually. 'It's when we are particularly well stocked.' The captain shrugged, 'It's not too bad, to lose twenty percent. We more than make up for that, on the sale of the ones that are left. As you no doubt understand, you are quadrupling your profits, when you deliver those things to market.' The captain smiled and rubbed his hands together. 'Yes, there is a good trade in those creatures. There's plenty more where they came from, as well. A person can get rich here.' The captain smiled greedily, 'I have also managed to make a good profit off them.'

As the captain spoke, and expressed his contempt for his fellow human beings, involuntarily ripped from their homes, and kept in appalling conditions, not even fit for domestic animals, he added himself to the list of people, who would become deceased, in his fort of misery. I would have done it right there, and thrown him into a pit, however, there were too many others watching. I had to be patient. Our plan would have to be effected, with more of our friends, and at night, I reasoned. The sooner the better.

The captain pointed to the beach below the fort. 'The only way they get in and out of there, is by sea. They arrive by sea and they leave by sea.' He pointed to a long, sloping causeway, leading from the beach into the wall below us. 'That is the only way in and out for them. We'll load em out to your ships from there, with our longboats. They're specially fitted to carry slaves. The boats have means for fastening them in place, so we don't risk them upsetting the apple cart, as it were.' The captain laughed at his little joke and then continued, 'Above the door leading out, we have painted, 'Door of No Return.' The captain laughed, 'Not that any of those ignorant savages can read it, but we felt it was appropriate, to give them a sign of what to expect.'

The captain took a silver snuff box from his pocket, and taking a pinch between his right thumb and forefinger, he added, 'Really, what should a black skinned savage, who runs about naked in the forest, expect? God means them to be slaves. After all, they don't have souls, do they?' The captain sniffed the pinch up his nostrils, adjusting the pressure in each, with the back of his left hand. Momentarily, he sneezed.

During the entire time I thought of different ways to wreak the Lord's vengeance on the unfeeling officer.

The captain continued with the tour, leading us along the ramparts, to admire the heavy twenty five pounders directed towards the ships in the bay.

George commented on the excellent arrangement, and positioning of the cannons, which made the captain swell with pride; he taking the comment as a compliment, being proud of his position, as the assistant to the chief military administrator of so obviously, marvelous a fort.

The air drifting up from the slave pits was quite nauseating, prompting Colin to ask whether the dungeons were ever cleaned.

The captain explained that water was thrown into the pits, after each batch had vacated the place. However, no one entered there to scrub out the places in any particularly fastidious fashion, hence the stink; it being the accumulated feces and urine of the people kept there. The idea, that human beings were expected to spend, so much as a second in those places, was a horrible thought. According to the captain, sometimes the people were kept there for several weeks, before being shipped out.

The sight of those miserable people looking up at us, with eyes full of fear, and loathing, was such an affront to every thing we stood for, my heart hardened with regard to the people, who owned, and ran the place, including the slavers in the harbour.

When the tour was completed, I explained to the captain that we would take all the slaves they could sell us; having three ships to carry them. The fact that would entail crowding over five hundred more people on each of our ships, did not trouble the captain, for a moment, the numbers obviously being reasonable, for the size of our ships, which to our way of thinking, were just right for only ten percent of that number. Obviously, slavers must have crowded their black passengers, like herrings in a barrel; another sobering thought.

Upon the completion of our tour, we thanked the captain, and told him we would make the financial arrangements, when we returned on the following day. He assured us he would draw up the sales contract and have it ready for us in the afternoon.

I thanked the captain for the tour and told him, we would return at one o'clock with the money necessary to complete the transaction. The captain told us we would get a ten percent discount for hard money, 'So much better than a promissory note from the Company of Gentlemen

Traders,' he said. 'Not to say your company's credit is not good with us,' the captain made certain to add, 'However, we are short of specie, at the moment, and have wages to pay.'

The captain frowned, as he looked down at the beaten African, lying at the base of the post, in the middle of the courtyard. He prodded the man with the toe of his boot, effecting a soft moan. The captain shook his head. 'It amazes me how strong these wretches are. This one is still alive, after five days like that.' The captain looked at us and smiled ruefully. 'They're a lot stronger than we are, that's for sure. It's a good thing we have guns.'

We couldn't help but agree, it was fortunate the English had guns. If they didn't have them, the blacks would have overrun the fort a long time ago and committed every Englishman to the spit, and every other trader, in human flesh, along the Guinea Coast. Alas, the blacks lacked the technology of the traders, who hailed from every seafaring nation in Europe, and many of those belonging to the Mohammedans, as well.

When our tour was finished, we again thanked the captain, and quickly hastened away from that detestable place.

The moment we were out of ear shot of the guards, all four of us expressed our disgust, at exactly the same time, each of us vowing to effect the escape of the slaves being presently kept there, and to help the grim reaper gather up some more detestable traders, in quick order.

When we stepped on the deck of the *Pinta*, our friends gathered to ask us about the things we had seen at the fort.

After describing what we had seen, their collective desire was to effect the rapid demise of the traders, anchored nearby, and to execute every person involved in the trade, who resided in that monstrous fort.

Everyone was anxious to begin planning right away, so that before Colin and George went back to their own ships, we knew exactly what we were going to do, and wasted no further time readying for action.

Unbeknownst to the slavers anchored nearby, we were carrying a fine collection of assorted cannons on board our three ships. These instruments of destruction were readied to effect broadsides with which to sink the slavers, if they proved belligerent. However, we reasoned, it was better to save the ships and turn them over to the Africans, if they wanted them, hence we only considered the use of our cannons in an emergency.

We wasted no further time and began our adventure, when one hundred of our friends, quietly slipped into the water, that very night; swimming noiselessly towards the two slavers, not so much as making a splash, which greatly impressed me. I watched anxiously from the quarter deck of my ship. I could just barely see men climbing up the side of the ship, which lay closest to mine.

Moments later I heard shouts and then all was quiet.

It was all over ten minutes later, as I watched bodies being dumped over the sides of the ship, correctly assuming they were the carcasses of the despised slave traders. Some time later, several men returned to advise me that the slave ships were secure, and the slaves were being released. When all the shackles had been thrown off, we armed as many of the slaves as we could, constantly admonishing them to keep quiet, lest we alert the castle.

Then, when all was ready, we quietly went ashore, some of us with the long boats, to keep the weapons dry. The sentries on the beach never saw it coming, as a number of stealthy black Africans neatly dispatched them, without a sound. I saw the entire thing, and marveled at the speed and efficiency of the dispatch. I hoped some of the men would be interested in joining our gang. Such black skinned assassins would be useful in future campaigns, I reasoned.

When we arrived at the main gate, we found it closed. There were no sentries in sight, because they had been neatly dispatched; their bodies lying in the bushes, nearby. The problem of the closed gate was quickly solved as well, since we had brought ropes with grappling hooks. These were tossed over the wall, and as soon as they held fast, a number of our new African friends quickly clambered up the wall, followed by several of our own fellows. Some minutes later, one of the gate doors opened and we quietly crept into the castle, dispatching every Englishman we found there, including the entire garrison of forty five soldiers.

Colin, George, and I decided, that we would capture the governor and captain alive. Then, we would turn them over to the Africans, to do with them as they would; thinking they would appreciate to exact revenge and settle the score, at least a little bit.

We found the captain and governor asleep in their beds. They were very indignantly surprised, to be so rudely awakened and taken from their beds in their night clothes. The governor, in particular, railed us with a plethora of invectives and dire warnings, regarding the consequences of our rash act.

I told the governor it did not matter the consequences, because we were already dead men, since we were pirates, and not merely some group of armed abolitionists.

As we led the governor and captain down the stairs of the administration building, into the courtyard, we could hear a mighty cheering coming from below the ramparts, where our men had managed to free the people held captive in the dungeons. We could hear much splashing, as people jumped into the sea, to clean themselves of the stink and filth which had accumulated during their captivity.

'We will put the captain and governor in the dungeon, for the rest of the night. We can decide what to do with them tomorrow,' I said to my fellows, a suggestion to which they readily agreed, much to the chagrin of our two captives.

'Dump the bodies of those guards and soldiers into the pit,' shouted George, a command quickly followed, as body after body was dumped through one of the holes in the ceiling of the dungeon, the Africans had just vacated.

We placed the captain and the governor in the same dungeon as the bodies of their dead garrison.

'You are inhuman swine!' shouted the governor, as we dropped him into the pit, on top of a pile of bodies, quickly followed by the captain, who cursed us to the nine heavens, and beyond. 'You will pay for this crime against civilized men!' raved the governor from the stinking hole.

We ignored his rants and decided to find a comfortable place to sleep, leaving the men to sort out the rest of their night.

I chose to deposit my weary bones in the governor's fabulous bed. George chose the captain's chambers and Colin the lieutenant's. I believe Wapoo slept in the secretary's bed. The secretary, of course, was lying in the heap at the bottom of the dungeon, probably keeping track of affairs in hell.

Next morning, I was awakened by a noisy commotion outside my windows. The raucous noise was coming from the courtyard. I stretched luxuriously in the fine feathered bed. A few moments later, I pulled my self off the comfortable mattress and stepped to a window. Parting a curtain, I looked outside.

Below, in the courtyard, a large throng of Africans was shouting my name, 'Peter!, Peter!' in a rhythmical fashion, my pirate friends standing amongst them, smiling up at my window. When I waved to the people, I felt like a king, as a mighty joyful shout filled the air and filled me with happiness.

I dressed quickly and adjusted my mustaches, which had rearranged themselves during sleep, as per usual. I stroked out my beard and then, giving my appearance a final inspection, in the governor's magnificent standing mirror; a mirror, by the way, which eventually graced my cabin and then my home, I stepped outside onto the landing of the staircase.

The feeling of gratitude was overwhelming as I stepped outside. The entire place was filled with a gladness, which is of such a spiritual nature, one feels totally fulfilled and grateful. To have had a hand in the liberation of those happy people, waving and smiling up at me, filled me with an indescribable joy.

Before I descended the stairs further, however, I made sure Colin, George, and Wapoo were with me, to serve as body guards, not wishing to be crushed by so many adoring new friends, who would most definitely want to touch me, the Africans being a people who like to touch.

When my body guard was suitably assembled, we descended the stairs and came out amongst the people, an experience which, to the very day I write these words, still impresses me with a feeling of intense gratitude and joy, as the people, one by one, gently touched us; our hair, our beards, our hands, our clothes…each person's face filled with a radiant light; the light of freedom. The experience was overwhelming and brought a flood of tears from my eye.

A brilliant sun was rising in the sky, brightening the scene with a glorious light; as if God Himself was looking down on us and thanking us for what we had done. It felt good to have done the Lord's work.

The poor wretch, who had been tied to the post, unfortunately had perished during the night, and never had a chance to enjoy what we had wrought, however, given how God Himself had looked down on us, I am sure the poor fellow was taken at that time, into the bosom of the Father, and blessed for eternity. I am sure he was recompensed for his suffering.

The immediate problem which faced us, as eventually everyone had finished touching us, was how to handle the soldiers, who lived in town. They would most assuredly come to the fort, at any moment. Hence, sentries were posted and eventually, as five soldiers did come from town, we abducted them and extracted the information necessary to locate the others, which was promptly effected.

An hour later, another twenty five soldiers had been rounded up and brought to the castle courtyard, where we had to be firm, in preventing the people from tearing them apart; thinking it more civilized to simply shoot them; they being simple soldiers.

The Africans realized it was a better way and quickly helped to dispatch the men, dumping their bodies into the pit, on top of the rest.

'You foul, murderous pigs!' shouted the governor. 'You will hang for this!'

We paid no attention to the governor's shouts, instead advising the people to leave the place and go back to their homes. 'For surely more white people will come, and they will exact a powerful vengeance, when they learn of what we have done,' I told them. I offered them the slavers ships, but none of the people were seafaring folk; having been brought from villages far from the ocean.

All of the people, but 37, elected to return to their villages on foot; the 37, who stayed, comprised ten couples and seventeen single men. Some of these people could speak one or more of the languages someone in our group spoke; Creole, Danish, Dutch, English, Portuguese, or Spanish, hence communication was not a problem.

The other people understood, there was no time to waste, and left that accursed place, not needing to be told twice that they were free to go. Hopefully, they managed to find their way back to their respective villages. Of course, we gave them all some gold and silver coins from the castle's treasury, with which to purchase things they might need on their treks home. The balance went out to my ship, it still being a sizable sum, I estimated at near sixteen thousand pounds stirling. So much for the captain's assertion they were short of specie.

When the last of the Africans had left the castle, we plundered it at our leisure and then, using the wagons, hauled the swag down to the boats, including those of the slavers, enabling us to take everything back to our ships, including the governor's magnificent bed. I believe it took about five days to effect the entire operation.

While the boats were being loaded, we posted sentries in the uniforms of the castle's soldiers, to prevent people attempting to visit the place, or from being suspicious, while we were busy emptying her out.

On the third day, Colin, George, Wapoo, and I decided to take a walk through the town, to see if we could find a restaurant, in which to obtain a meal.

The town was made of mud and thatch houses, one of which was quite grand, compared to the rest. We found out later it was the house of the local king, whom we thought better not disturb, on account of the fact he was in collusion with the English at the fort and had a large army at his disposal.

The restaurant was a friendly place, which accepted us as merely some more slave traders, who had come to Cape Coast to trade in human flesh. We, of course, never said a word about what we had done and ordered a meal and beverages.

As we sat there, waiting for our food, in the dark room, I noticed two sorry looking men sitting at a nearby table. I pointed the men out to my friends, who turned to look at them and, like me, also thought that one of the men looked familiar, somehow.

The two men also seemed to take an interest in us, I noticed them often looking our way and seemingly discussing us. Eventually, one of the men got up. The moment he stood facing us, we recognized him immediately. It was Robert! Robert had survived the shipwreck!

'Robert!' we all shouted at once. 'What in the blazes are you doing here?!' we shouted happily as we rushed towards each other, each of us giving our long lost friend a happy welcome hug.

We invited Robert and his friend, whose name was, Frank Norman, to sit with us. Then, after drinking several toasts, and sharing happy reunion overtures, Robert related his story.

Apparently, he had floated for days on a piece of the ship's sideboard, eventually being picked up by a slaver, heading back to Africa from the West Indies. The slavers had left him at Elmira castle, but he preferred to be near the English, not speaking Portuguese. He had managed to find a little work at the castle, white washing walls, and fixing some broken wood work inside the buildings. It was a meagre living, but he had managed to survive on the little bit of money he earned, supplemented by handouts.

'It is good to see you again, Robert,' I said clapping him on the shoulder.

Robert was overjoyed to be reunited with us and heartily glad we had done what we had done in the castle, to which we repaired immediately after our meal, taking Frank Norman with us, as well.

When the castle had been sufficiently relieved of its goods, we quickly vacated the unhappy place; our ships loaded with excellent swag from the castle. We never did bother to execute the governor and the captain, preferring to leave them shut up in the pit, with the piles of stinking corpses, a reminder to them of their crimes. I learned some time later, Africans had gone back and, either they burned the governor and his captain, or they hacked them to bits, with axes and swords. There was even a story which I heard years later, the Africans had gone back and had taken the governor and captain back to a village, far from the Cape. What happened to them there is anyone's guess. I am sure they got what they deserved.

We left Cape Coast on the 12th of July, Catherine's birthday. I thought of my lovely daughter, who had attained her champagne birthday when I was not there to celebrate with her. I prayed she was alright and not missing me too much. I wished there was some way I could send her a message and hoped she could feel my positive energies, all that distance away in the West Indies. I hoped we would return to our island, as soon as possible. I was missing my family.

Fair winds enabled us to return to the Cape Verde Islands in short order, with two more ships than we had left there with. It was a successful venture, as far as we were concerned, to that point. We had three ships loaded with swag from the castle, and two empty slave ships crying for cargo. How we filled those ships forms the text of my next chapter.

Chapter Twenty-Five

Our return voyage to the Cape Verdes was a happy affair, during which copious quantities of ale, rum, and wine were consumed on the five ships, these delicious supplies having come from the cellars of the castle; five hogsheads of rum, seven of wine, and twelve of ale. By the time we reached Praia we were all in an advanced state of inebriation, nearly resulting in the collision of the two slave ships with the *Santa Maria*. Fortunately, the accident was averted in the nick of time, requiring the use of drag anchors to slow and turn two of the ships. Unfortunately, the winds were such that we had to stand off the bay and anchor in the lee of a promontory. Two days later, we were able to tack into the bay and dropped anchors on the 22nd of July, the year being 1788.

We did not stay in the Cape Verdes very long, just long enough to gather wood, water and victuals. We also took some time to modify the slavers, to carry some of the swag from the other three ships, making the loads more manageable for the long journey home. We sailed out of Praia on the 26th, everyone anxious to return to our happy isle.

On the 13th of August we spied sails off to starboard. As we kept an eye on them over the next few days, it became apparent there were three ships, heading ever more towards us, on an intersecting course, which would see us abeam, within another three days. I posted lookouts in the crowsnests, to keep a constant vigil, to ascertain whose ships they were, and to shout the information, the moment they could discern a flag.

On the 15th of August, the lookout on the forward crow's nest yelled out that he could discern Spanish flags. He further entertained us with the information that the ships appeared to be heavily laden, prompting me to take my glass and see for myself what was being offered to us by some Spaniards, greedy for New World gold; gold which would better serve us than them.

We hoisted our Spanish flags.

At five in the afternoon of August 16th, we came alongside the Spanish ships. Everyone luffed their sails, in order to enjoy a little bit of socializing on the high seas, the Spanish sailors anxious for a party, just as much as we were. We invited the officers on board my ship and showed them the extent of our joyful hospitality. The Spanish officers, when they were well into their cups, allowed our men to go on board their ships, to meet with their sailors for some camaraderie.

That night, a beautiful full moon lit the scene, as eight ships rode gently swelling seas, and happy men availed themselves of the copious stores of beverages we had available, for which the Spaniards were most grateful. Of course, we spiked their libations with a copious quantity of one of Wapoo's herbal concoctions. The Spaniards had no idea that we were working, we never let on that we were merely drinking very watered down distillations, not capable of intoxicating a flea.

Around two in the morning of the 17th, we proceeded to effect our plan, which was very simple, really; the best plans usually are.

Since most of the Spaniards had passed out, plundering the Spanish ships was a very simple affair, done right under the sleeping noses of the owners and their crews. When everything, worth taking, had been carefully stowed on board our ships, we set sail, leaving the much lightened Spanish ships to ride much higher in the water; the crews having to sleep off the effects of Wapoo's concoction, for several days afterwards.

Fortunately for us, all of our ships carried some considerable weight, to keep our ships stable in the water, which became most necessary, when we ran into foul weather, a day later. However, the weather was nothing any of us needed to be concerned about, it being a regular squall, of no great consequence, other than that it blew several sails from the slavers, they not being very good canvas, somewhat rotten around the grommets.

How the sleeping Spaniards fared in the storm was not known to us, having lost sight of their ships in the swirling water and wind.

On the 25th of August, we lost one of our new African friends, to some strange malady we could not identify. Karte Onak was buried at sea, with the same respect we always showed our friends, whenever they became deceased.

Two days later, we lost three more Africans, Bentu, Korleo, and Mufata, plus one of our Marabino friends, a man named, Adam.

Fortunately, those were the only deaths we accrued over the long voyage home, a testament to the better conditions we provided on our ships.

Our island came into view on the second of September, but the winds being uncooperative, caused us to stand off to westward for five days, until we were favored with a breeze, which enabled us to tack closer to the entrance for our cove.

Our friends, recognizing our ships, flew the yellow flag on the observation platform. As we came closer to the channel, we noticed that it had been widened, enabling us to sail directly into the cove.

People were coming out of the forest to welcome us from the beach. Several cannon blasts furthered the welcoming, as we carefully sailed through the channel, into the beautiful cove, where our anchors were dropped, everyone grateful to have returned safe and sound, with five ships loaded with swag.

That night, we held a huge bonfire, under the glorious harvest moon. The party lasted for nearly seven days, everyone so glad to have come home safe and sound, with such a massive amount of plunder.

Marianne was very pleased, when it came time to divide the spoils. It was another reason for a party, there being so much. Of course, the governor's bed was ceremoniously carried to my house and installed in our bedroom, much to my wife's delight. She showed me later how delighted she was, making sweet love to me on the soft feathers of the expensive mattress.

Everyone came away rich from our adventure to Africa and the accidental swag presented by the Spaniards; twenty two chests of gold and silver ingots, plus bales of cotton, cochineal, okra, salted fish and turtles,

Brazil wood, weapons, clothing, and the usual collection of dinner ware, crystal, and place settings, from the captains' tables. I was glad to see more books come to the library, as well. I was also glad to receive three fine wooden boxes of excellent cigars, out of a crate which contained five dozen boxes. For a time afterwards, cigar smoke drifted over our town, filling the air with its delicious aroma.

The cigars were so well enjoyed by everyone who smoked them, that when we ran out, many folks were quickly ready to effect another voyage, in order to obtain more. Hence, one of the slavers was taken by a small group of forty five sailors, to make a quick trip to San Juan, to buy more cigars for the colony.

I ran out of cigars, while the men were gone, and felt seriously deprived, constantly looking forward to the return of our tobacco ship. Alas, it never did return. What ever happened to it has remained a mystery to the very day that I write these words. Needless to say, I eventually got over my tobacco cravings, and soothed myself with some of Wapoo's herbs, instead, as I spent pleasant days with my children and lovely wife.

During the five months we were gone to Africa, the colony had grown by another batch of children, twelve in all, whose cries could be heard, here and there throughout our town. The number of children in our town determined us, one day, to provide them with a school, where they might learn to read and write, in more formal circumstances; perhaps our artists could teach them about, alchemy, astronomy, biology, physik, ship building and repair, all those things a person of the late 18th century ought to know about. All of us were desirous to have our children become other than pirates, and be able to make their ways successfully in the straight world of, so called, legitimate enterprise. We disliked the thought of our children also having prices over their heads, and risking a hanging, every time they visited a town or city. Although piracy had done alright by us, we did not want that life for our precious offspring.

My book was coming along nicely, the chapters shaping up the way I wanted. I was happy for the opportunity to stay home again, for a while. The swag we acquired enabled us to live even more comfortably. Our fine new bed made our love making ever more pleasurable, it having a nice height, as well as being so wonderfully soft. The governor's bedding, which I made sure to include in my share of the swag including the governor's sheets, which were of the finest silk and cottons. The cover was of velvet and boasted a magnificent coat of arms.

My share of the booty, being one quarter, further made my family very rich; riches of which we had an excess, ready for burial in the next secret location.

The previous two burials were well documented on maps which I had drawn, and safely stored in a strong chest I kept at the foot of my bed. Our third treasure chest was sitting beside it. I always kept two loaded pistols nearby, safely out of reach of the children. Although I had carefully acquainted Catherine and Joshua with pistols, the fact the weapons were loaded, with readied flints and fuses, made them potentially lethal; I wished to avoid accidents, at all costs, especially where my children were concerned, who over the years were growing to be magnificent human beings.

Marianne's son, Michael, whom I had adopted as my own, was Joshua's best friend, the two boys being the same age. They played everywhere together. Even if they were just sitting, looking at books in the library, not saying a word, they were happy in each other's company. It amazed Marianne and I, how much alike they were, even preferring to wear the same clothes, the only difference being, Michael preferred silver, Joshua liked gold.

Catherine was the spitting image of her dad, already a confident young lady at the age of twelve and a half. Looking at her, at times, I thought I was seeing myself as a young woman. Although she was not manly in any way, it was in the shape of her eyes and nose, where she most resembled me.

Catherine's 13th birthday in 1789, was celebrated with a huge party, Marianne and I sponsored, having first traveled to San Juan, in order to purchase libations and a special present; a pair of ivory handled pistols, with silver metal works, and gold filigree embellishments. The pistols came in a highly polished Brazil wood box, complete with a silver powder horn, and two smaller wooden boxes, with silver hinges containing fuses and flints. A third box contained twelve silver balls. Inside the lid of the box was an envelope containing a soft white cotton cloth for polishing.

On the cover of the lid we had her name inscribed on a small silver plaque, affixed with small gold headed nails. Of course, Catherine was very happy to receive such a splendid gift, thanking us copiously with hugs and kisses. She shot the pistols that very same day at our practice range, retrieving the silver balls from the sandbags behind the target at which she aimed.

I celebrated my 40th birthday with another massive party, this time entirely orchestrated by Marianne and my friends, Colin, George, Robert, and Wapoo. I had no idea the party was coming, not really doing much about my birthday, all those years previously, it falling on the day after Christmas, and being considerably less important. However, this time my birthday was celebrated by over a hundred and fifty people, complete with fireworks, and a huge pig roast on the beach.

Entertainments had been prepared, where I was royally treated to marvelously funny dances, skits, re-enactments of our adventures, and an incredible concert of music, entirely written, and directed by Marianne. The music brought a tear to my eye, it was so beautiful. The entire concert was dedicated to me. Marianne handed the score to me, at the end of the concert.

From Colin, I received a copy of a marvelous French book by Jean Baptiste Bourguignon d'Anville, about his travels in Egypt.

George gave me an incredibly beautiful sword, with a silver blade, and golden handle, in the shape of a dragon's head.

Robert presented me with a fine gold coin from ancient Greece, set in a silver ring, affixed to a beautiful long golden chain.

Wapoo and Narkat presented me with a stunning Indian headdress, with hundreds of exotic feathers of multifarious colors.

The list goes on and on.

Suffice it to say, my 40th birthday was a celebration of abundance and grateful friendship. The party lasted a full nine days and nights. It was a great feeling to be so well feted by my family and friends. I truly felt like a beloved king, and wondered why any king would not want to be so regarded. Many kings, by oppressing their subjects, make them hate him. It was one of life's mysteries.

By the middle of January, 1790, I was beginning to grow restless, not having been to sea for over a year. Marianne understood my desire for adventure and heartily agreed it was a good idea for me to take a ship with some of our best men to go roving, once again. Hence, plans were begun to make a journey to the coast of Florida, and then work our way along the shores of the newly formed United States of America, thinking we would most assuredly encounter good swag coming from, or going to the new world, it being safe for us to sail there, so we thought.

The *Pinta* underwent a name change, in the event our ship was implicated in the nasty business at Cape Coast Castle. This time I named my ship after my daughter, Catherine. The ship became, *El Katarina*, to my daughter's immense delight.

My friends, Colin, George, Robert, and Wapoo decided they also wanted some more adventure. In spite of the fact that George was already approaching 49, he was like a young man when it came to adventure. It was as much in his blood as in mine.

Together we hand picked seventy five men to accompany us, all of them exceptionally well armed and capable of effecting serious damage on an enemy. Amongst those going were seven musicians, who brought; two bag pipes, a crumhorn, two trumpets, and a large drum. The instruments would come in handy in the event we chose to effect a cargo extraction with a direct attack on a merchantman at sea. The instruments would be used to vapor the opponent. A loud crashing drum and off key trumpets and bagpipes could easily send chills up the spines of those whom we attacked; fear being a powerful weapon.

April 19th was the date when winds became favorable for our journey. We were ready to take advantage and happily set out on our voyage to purgatory.

Chapter Twenty-Six

We were sailing along the coast of Florida when we spotted sails on the first of May. The ships, to which the sails belonged, were seven in number, flying French flags. We could see through our spy glasses that the ships were heavy with cargo and were accompanied by only one navy vessel, a frigate with thirty guns. We immediately raised our French flag, which enabled us to approach the convoy without belligerence from the navy vessel.

Pretending to be also a loaded cargo ship, by filling empty hogsheads with sea water, we eventually managed to ship alongside, and with our sails fully out, like theirs, we kept pace, and at times were able to mingle amongst the ships, carefully assessing each one for its prize worthiness. By the fourth day we had our ship singled out, a fat merchantman belonging to the French West Indies Company.

Keeping a careful eye on the ship, we stayed about a half league to her starboard, careful to keep up the ruse of being a loaded ship, as well as keeping a careful watch on the frigate, a league behind us. We had no reason to suspect we could not effect a proper attack and steal the ship away, with minimum bloodshed.

The morning of May fifth began in a heavy fog bank, obliterating our view beyond a few feet. It was time for a steady bell, to alert other ships of our position. However, as soon as we ascertained where our prey was, we stopped ringing our bell and carefully maneuvered our ship in the direction of the bell belonging to the vessel, we thought to be, the fat merchantman.

Alas, unbeknownst to us, the navy frigate, having grown suspicious of us for some reason, had managed to catch up to us and had replaced the merchantman, off to port. The night and fog had obscured the frigate's tactics, hence we were caught totally unaware of what was about to befall us.

The frigate, being a navy vessel, practiced a very strict discipline, which resulted in their having many people awake, and alertly watching for any sign from us, indicative of other than peaceful intentions. Hence, when they saw us, inching towards them, without sounding our bell, they knew we were up to something and were prepared to react.

The fog was so thick that none of us had any idea regarding the frigate until it was too late; the grappling hooks in our yards had become entangled in the ropes of the navy vessel, sucking our ships together.

Suddenly, a horrific roar signaled a direct broadside into our port side freeboards, smashing timbers and cannons, and numerous pirates, getting ready to board the ship, we thought to be a lightly armed merchantman. A minute later, another massive broadside shivered the timbers of my ship, as massive beams and oak planks were reduced to lethal splinters.

I yelled orders and directed the men to fire back, however, our guns were not run out. Before we could fire, another broadside smashed into us, rendering all but three guns useless. Firing them had little effect on the frigate, merely knocking some small holes through the hull.

Our pirates, although momentarily stunned by what happened, were quickly rallied to action, pulling the ship closer with their boarding axes. Others were already clambering aboard the French vessel, where they were met with a volley of lethal fire from the muskets of thirty five marines.

I saw seven of our men fall into the sea.

Gun shots began to fill the air, as our men began to fire from the crowsnests and shrouds.

Several marines fell. The others reloaded quickly and fired another round into our friends, six more falling.

Seventeen of our men managed to climb onto the deck of the French ship, with their cutlasses and pistols in hand, however, they were mowed down by grapeshot from two swivel guns on the railing of the frigate's quarter deck.

Screams, gunshots, and curses filled the air, as more of our men swung themselves on board the French ship, barely able to see where they would land, the fog being thick like salmagundi. I could hear the clashing of metal, as men were desperately fighting with swords and axes.

Suddenly, another volley of gunshot rang out and painful screams rent the fog. I had no idea whose screams they were.

A loud cannon shot rang out. Suddenly, the man standing beside me was shredded with links of chain, which had come whipping across from the other ship, splattering me with blood and pieces of the hapless fellow.

Having only one eye hampered my ability to see in the fog, which had enveloped us. I heard George yelling to Colin, and then two loud bangs followed by a screeching howl, of such intense pain, it was as if I could feel the man's torment deep into my own bones.

The fighting continued for more than an hour, and then, all of a sudden, a voice rang out through a speaking trumpet from the French ship advising us to put our arms down. 'Ve haf alrrredie killed feeftie of yur men, do yu want ve kill zem all?'

I looked at Robert and Wapoo.

Robert shrugged his shoulders. 'It could be a trick,' he said softly.

'Look around and see if you can see our men,' I whispered.

Wapoo quietly snuck off and carefully stepped about our decks, looking for our men. He returned some minutes later, shrugging his shoulders.

'I no see many,' he said, frowning.

'Put down your arms!' said the voice again, through the speaking trumpet. 'Ve haf yu outnumbered. Yu don't haf a chance.'

I looked at Robert and Wapoo and was at a loss what to do.

Suddenly French navy men came swinging onto our decks, armed to the teeth with cutlasses and pistols.

Seeing the number of French men suddenly coming onto our ship, made it abundantly clear to us that we had better surrender. Perhaps we might find a way to escape, we reasoned.

As we stood there on the quarter deck, hands in the air, the fog began to dissipate, revealing the carnage wrought on our ships. Nine of our men were lined up on the French deck, muskets pointed at them by the remaining fifteen marines. I was heartened to see we had taken out more than half of them. French sailors littered the decks as well, some lying on top, or under our men. Heaps of dead men, due to a major error, from which I learned a very strong lesson.

The French clapped us in irons, stole my silver hook, and locked us in the fo'c's'le; Colin, George, Robert, Wapoo, plus nine others: Adam, Clyde, Francois, Jan, Jean, Jose, Nabu, and Peka, one of the Africans we had rescued from Whydah, that being the name he preferred to call Cape Coast Castle. The word is pidgin for, 'Why there?' I think. I never asked him about it.

Thirteen men, shackled and crowded into a small, unlit, stuffy cell, in the bows of the ship, was a singularly unpleasant experience. It gave me some idea what it would have been like for those black wretches we rescued on the Guinea Coast.

The French let us up on deck for air and exercise for two hours every day, rain or shine. After a particularly miserable, rainy day, we were returned to our cell, soaking wet. I have never been so cold and miserable, as I was during that fateful passage to Marseilles. I had no idea that I would be facing a far worse scenario.

The food they fed us, were the leftovers from the sailors' mess, which was never very much, leading to slow starvation, as we traveled to Marseilles. I am willing to bet that I lost nearly twenty pounds in that month.

Eventually, Adam met his Maker. He died in his sleep, about half way to Marseilles. The cramped quarters, and poor food, exacerbated a cough he had developed, shortly after coming on board the French ship. The cough got worse and worse. He was a good man.

Adam's death was quickly followed by Jean, and then Nabu. Each time it happened, the French unshackled the man and dumped the body overboard, without ceremony; pirates obviously not deserving a decent burial; a situation no different with the English. We don't deserve decent burials, because we don't go along with the program; even if that program is a lie and a gigantic fraud.

The journey to Marseilles gave us lots of time to think things over. To pass the time we engaged in conversations, which often times went deep and probed into the realm of philosophy and natural sciences.

One afternoon, after our exercise on deck, I was engaged in a wonderful conversation with Colin and Francois about the implications of Matthew 23, and how the words of Jesus Christ have been ignored all these centuries, under supposed, Christian kings and queens.

'Our Lord said, 'Let no man call you master, not even the Messiah. Ye have but one master, who is God, your Father in Heaven.' Francois was well versed in the Bible, having come from a very Christian family in Cuba. 'He also said that we are not to call any one, *Father*. Only God. Only God is Our Father. Hence, the whole idea of kings and queens above us; any person assuming to have power over us, is a fraud. Jesus told us we have no one above us but, God.'

'We are being held under false pretenses,' quipped Colin. 'However, what can we do about it?'

'We can try advising the captain,' laughed Robert. 'Maybe he will let us go, when we show him that he is engaging in a most un Christian business.'

'Think about it,' said Jan, 'The king kills and steals, using goons like these navy fellows, or armies...'

'Or with privateers, under their letters of marque,' added George. 'We musn't forget that. Some times kings and queens steal with a piece of paper, which some people believe, gives them the right to kill and steal.'

'That is true,' agreed Jan. 'The king steals and kills with pieces of paper upon which he has fixed his signature. It is just paper and ink, yet thousands of other people, who profess to be Christians, follow the king's orders and commit atrocities.'

'None of those Christians have obviously read Matthew 23,' said Francois. 'Although Jesus says we are to render unto Caesar what is Caesar's. Everyone seems to have interpreted that to mean that we actually have to render something to Caesar. What Jesus meant is, we owe Caesar nothing. So render nothing unto Caesar. He cleverly worded the phrase, so those who are too blind to see, continue to render their lives unto Caesar. I really don't think Christians really understand what their Bible actually teaches them.'

'Or, if they have read it, they have not understood it and taken it to heart,' added Robert.

I remarked that the Bible could be used in so many ways. 'It justifies horror as well as exemplifies true love.'

'Just look at what happened in the Inquisition,' said Colin. 'Torturing people for differences of belief, is completely un Christian, considering the words of Our Lord in Matthew 23. He is telling us that we are sovereigns.'

'Yes, not only there, but also where it says that we are created in God's image,' said Francois. 'If we are made in God's image, how can we be anything less than sovereigns?'

'We should definitely bring this up with the captain,' laughed Robert. 'We are being held in un Christian circumstances.'

We laughed at Robert's little joke. The idea was a good one, however, we were under no delusions that the captain would listen to us. He would laugh, just as Robert was laughing at the top of his lungs. Tears were welling in his eyes, as his whole body shook with merriment. 'We are being held in un Christian circumstances.' As he said it, Robert burst into more laughter.

Robert's laughter was so infectious, he soon had us all laughing at the top of our lungs, until our bellies hurt.

The world was mad, and we knew it. We might as well laugh. What better way to spend time in our sorry surroundings?

Moments later, the door of our prison opened and a burly marine came into the filthy hold to tell us to stop laughing. 'Zere is nuting to laff about,' he told us. 'Yu ave nuting to be appy about. Only peepel viz ope are appy. Yu ave no ope, an zerefore yu shud stop laffing.' He rattled the door of our cage.

Colin growled at him.

Then, suddenly, we all began to growl, and otherwise make menacing animal sounds, as we collectively lunged at the bars of our cage.

The guard jumped back. Then he snarled a warning that we would all be guillotined in Marseilles, and instead of laughing, we should be contemplating our sins, and making peace with God.

We laughed even louder.

The guard sneered at us and stumbled out of the reeking place, back to his more comfortable station behind the massive door to our prison.

The world was truly mad.

By the time we reached Marseilles, having been clapped in irons, in that disgustingly cramped prison, for forty seven days, we emerged gaunt and wasted, barely able to walk the gang plank onto the roadway. We were made to stand in a row and kept waiting for an hour, before the arrival of a group of jail guards and some pompous looking gentlemen, one of whom was a military officer. The pompous men were officials of the jail, come to inspect the captured pirates.

When the officials learned that I was Peter Mann, 'Ze famous, Scourge of ze West Indies,' they decided right then and there, to send me to Paris, leaving my friends behind, to face the French legal system in Marseilles. Obviously, I had gotten a reputation, which on the one hand, was a great compliment, but on the other hand, was a sure road to that horrid method of execution the French preferred, breaking on the wheel. I shuddered at the thought of having all of the bones in my arms and legs broken with steel bars.

When I mentioned the wheel to one of my jailers, he laughed, and assured me that France had caught up with the modern world, and was utilizing something called a 'guillotine,' named after a benevolent doctor, who wanted to eradicate the suffering of condemned people. The marine on the ship had mentioned the device, but he never described it. When the man described how the death machine worked, I cringed and involuntarily grabbed my neck with my right hand.

The jailer laughed and assured me, we would all face the instrument, in short order; the French courts not generally lingering very long over, obviously guilty pirates, such as ourselves.

Our prospects did not look good.

The jailers shackled my friends together and marched them off to the Marseilles prison.

'Good luck!' shouted Colin, as he was being led away. 'Take heart, Peter. We'll see each other in Heaven!'

'Yeah, good luck!' repeated George. 'We'll meet again. Don't you worry! Stay strong, my brother!'

'Good bye,' said Wapoo sadly; all too aware of what he was facing, as a guard rudely tugged at the chain.

I nodded ruefully, tears streaming down my cheek. I waved to my friends and told them not to lose heart. I told them to stay positive; 'A way out will present itself,' I said, hopeful it would come true.

Robert assured me he would break out of jail, at the first opportunity. 'They'll never hang me!' he shouted defiantly, tugging on the chain and receiving a blow across his shoulder, with the flat side of a sword blade; the wielder a powerful looking monster with a blue steel helmet on his massive head. Robert spat at him. The monster threatened to cut him in half. The guard was restrained from doing so by the military officer.

'Be patient, Montreux, he vill get ze chop soon enuff,' laughed the officer diabolically.

I watched as my friends were marched along the roadway and up an inclined street, where they disappeared around the corner of a building, overlooking the harbour. It was the last time I saw them.

Moments later, a coach approached us. Two soldiers sat on the driver's seat, and two soldiers rode on the back. When the coach stopped, the door was opened by one of the soldiers and I was prodded to get in, and promptly shackled to a ring in the wall of the conveyance. A surly looking soldier climbed in and sat down on the seat opposite me, armed with a loaded musket.

The door was closed.

The other soldier returned to the back of the coach and shouted to the driver, 'Allé!'

The whip cracked.

The coach lurched.

I was off to Paris, just like that.

Clank! Clank! Clank!

* * *

The trip to Paris was a bumpy affair, not at all pleasant in the military issue coach, sparse like a Spartan's toilet. The guard was an illiterate boor, who had nothing to say, hence the trip was quite boring, as well as uncomfortable. I passed the time looking out of the window and thinking about my family on our beautiful island, so many thousands of miles away.

France was going through a revolution at the time of my capture, which made everything extremely uncertain for me, as well as lots of other folks. Signs of the turmoil were evident everywhere along the roads we traveled; burned buildings and dead animals littered the countryside. Here and there a body was hanging from a tree, or a head appeared on the end of a pike, near a roadside Catholic shrine. It was all very gruesome and worrisome for me.

We arrived in Paris thirteen days later, my muscles cramped and my stomach empty, the soldiers not feeding me very much along the way. I had a powerful thirst, but was not given water until some hours later, when I was deposited in a cell, deep in the bowels of the Bastille, a notorious prison and armory in the eastern part of the city. Apparently, it had been successfully stormed by a mob, some years earlier. Looking at the dreadful building, I couldn't imagine a mob breaking into that formidable pile of stone, but apparently they did it at the beginning of the revolution, now tearing the country apart.

I was left to rot in a small, dank room, a trickle of foul water creeping along a corner where several rats were drinking. The only light came from a tiny grated window, high up in the wall, through which rain dripped in.

A drain in the middle of the room carried fluids to hell, which I am convinced, was directly under the floor of my cell, judging from the screams and moans which came from there. A thin, filthy blanket lay on a wooden rack, posing as a bed. There was no mattress, only the rough planks forming the platform of that wretched piece of furniture. In the corner stood a dented bucket and a small bowl. The former functioning as the head, and the latter, as a container for my food. There was no spoon. I noted that the place was distinctly worse than Bill's cell in the Halifax jail.

A few hours later, I heard footsteps coming into the cell block. Momentarily, the heavy wooden door of my cell opened and a severe looking citizen, with wild eyes, stepped into the room, as I stood up from the cot.

'Yu are, Peter Mann?' he asked insinuatingly. 'Yu are ze famous, Scourge of ze West Indies?'

I agreed that I was, Peter Mann, however, being called the, '*Scourge* of the West Indies', was a bit much. I explained that I never saw myself as a scourge, merely a person who helped to balance world economics, by spreading its wealth out a bit more.

The wild eyed citizen did not quite see things my way, although he did agree there was a definite economic imbalance in the world. The fact that I was a famous pirate, was enough for him. 'Yu vill suffer our hospitalitee until such time zat a judge vill hear yur case an determine yur sentence,' he said. 'In ze mean time, I zujest yu make yursef at ome.' The man laughed; emitting a cruel sound, which grated on my ears. 'Enjoy yur stay.' The man continued to laugh, as he stepped out of the room. A second later, he was back and instantly ripped the gold ring out of my ear lobe, tearing the flesh. Blood spurted on to my cheek and neck. 'To help yu balance ze economics of ze vurld, I zujest ve begin by redistributing zis gold.' The monster laughed his ghoulish cackle and perfunctorily stepped out of the room.

The guards slammed the door shut. The sound of bolts and chains shivered my timbers and worried my soul. My torn ear was burning with pain and bleeding like a stuck pig. I had to tear a piece off my shirt to attempt to stem the flow of blood, holding the cloth over the wound and pinching the torn lobe until the blood clotted.

Next morning, after eating a hunk of dried, crusty bread, and some kind of thin, soupy gruel, in which I found a dead fly, I was taken from my cell by two soldiers. They took me to another room, one flight down from the cell block. The room where they took me had no windows and was lit by three torches, casting an eerie light in the otherwise dark chamber. I had the distinct impression the room was directly under my cell block.

As my eyes adjusted to the changed light, I could see four other men standing in the room. A fifth man was sitting in a chair, facing a sort of bed. Beside him stood a table, on which an assortment of strange looking instruments were lying. A brazier was softly glowing, nearby.

'Zo, zis is ze famous pirate?' asked the seated man, his voice like ice. 'Velcome to my special chamber. I am sure yu vill remember yur visit, monsieur. I try to make ze experience memorable for our veesitors.' The man smiled, revealing several gold teeth. 'Put him on ze rack,' he hissed, gesturing with a nod of his head.

The soldiers roughly executed the request, basically throwing me on the hard wooden planks. My arms were rudely pulled over my head and my wrists and ankles were shackled. Moments later, two of the men, working on either end of the rack, turned two wheels, as ratchets clicked on cogs. My arms and legs were stretched to their full extent, putting a severe strain on my joints and causing me much discomfort. A large belt was cinched over my hips. My shirt was ripped open and my shoes were pulled off. By that time, there was nothing left of my hose. Sweat was dripping from every pore of my body. I am sure my eye must have been bulging out, as the man casually picked up a long, thin, steel needle.

'Let's see how teecklish yu are,' said the man, handing the needle to one of the men standing to the side. 'Hans vill ascertain vether yu ave teeklish spots, von't yu Hans?'

Hans grinned with a mouth full of black and broken teeth. Perhaps one of the guests had kicked him in the mouth during an interrogation session.

I told the man that I was very ticklish, and that it wasn't necessary for him to test me.

'I vant to know exactly vhere yu are teeklish, monsieur,' replied the man, a twisted grin on his countenance.

Again I assured him, I was very ticklish, everywhere on my body. 'I assure you sir,' I said, sweating like a pig, 'You don't need to test me. Really, I am very ticklish everywhere.'

'I don't believe yu,' said the man. 'Ve vill zee for ourseves.'

Hans smiled and grunted, what a pleasure it would be to find my ticklish spots. He took the needle to the brazier, setting the pointed end into the white hot coals. Then he obtained a glove, and moments later, brought the white hot needle to bear directly into the ball of my right foot.

Instantly messages to my brain told of an extreme pain existing in most of my right leg and my lower torso, eliciting an intense scream I didn't know I was capable of. The sound shocked me as much as the intensely powerful jolt of excruciating pain coursing through my body, and convulsing all my muscles.

'I zee yu are teeklish, yu Eengleesh pirate peeg,' laughed the man, gesturing to Hans to test my other foot.

I told the man it wasn't necessary to test the other foot, assuring him it was ticklish, also.

The man thought me terribly funny and he, and the others, laughed uproariously, as Hans placed the needle in the brazier.

'Ve vill try eet once more,' said the man, when the needle was white hot.

To try and determine which of the two needles hurt more, the first one, or the second one, would be an exercise in futility. The pain was every bit as intense, and nauseating, as the first needle. In fact, having received the treatment on both feet presented such an overpowering sensation of intense pain, that I passed out, having screamed out all of my breath.

I have no idea how long I was unconscious, but I woke up with water splashed on my face.

Then the beating started.

A wide leather strap was used by another of the, 'specialists,' to beat the soles of my feet mercilessly, until they swelled up to three times their normal size. When the man had exhausted himself, the third man began to beat my chest with the same belt, rendering my torso, a black and blue nightmare. When I passed out the second time, they were done with me.

'Drag heem back to is ole,' said the man coldly.

Through the pounding in my ears I heard the man say, 'Next?'

As I was being dragged down the hall, another hapless victim was being led to the *Special Chamber*, this one obviously knew what was waiting for him. I got the distinct impression, from his struggles and constant requests for mercy, that he had been tested for his, 'teeklish' spots, before. I noticed that the man was missing some fingers, as he was dragged past me.

When we returned to my cell, I was dumped on the cot, breaking one of the boards and smashing my left elbow, rendering it useless for three weeks, as it healed from a massive bruise, which only disappeared two months later.

With my feet in the state they were, I couldn't walk, which made the execution of my bodily functions an extremely painful affair for weeks, as I hobbled about, barely able to stand for more than a few seconds. It was a most miserable circumstance.

So my life began in the Bastille, kept alone in my cell, twenty three hours per day, without so much as a piece of paper to write on, for the first year. For one hour, every day, the guards allowed me to walk outside, by myself, as they watched. I used the time to exercise, and keep my body fit. In spite of the garbage they fed me, I was maintaining my weight fairly well, supplementing my diet with insects and an occasional rat, which I managed to trap under my bowl, with a little piece of dubious meat I sometimes found in the gruel, on a better day. Eventually, the guards showed some pity and would skin the rat for me. They would let me roast it on a brazier, which made eating the thing much more palatable. Eating a rat, raw, never became a meal I looked forward to.

I was tortured twice more, during my stay in that accursed place. The following two times were on the anniversaries of my imprisonment, July 10th, two days before Catherine's birthday. Each time, I was taken to see the man, in the *Special Chamber*. Each time, he had a totally different regimen of pain inflictors. Needless to say, it took me a full two and a half months to recuperate from the first visit. The second visit required about the same amount of time to recuperate, and the last time, a little bit less. Every time the torture was something different, equally unpleasant. The last torture resulted in a long scar on my left cheek, where they sliced me, to serve as a constant reminder of their hospitality. Each time they tortured me, I vowed to kill the man, and his minions, which made them all laugh.

The food they served, I classified into three categories; bad, worse, and disgusting, each time writing a review in my head, rating the productions coming from Diablo's kitchen. Over time, I began to notice, that every so often the food would be worse, almost on a schedule, and then there would be several days in a row when the food was so disgusting, I had serious trouble eating it; the insect supplements tasting better than what came from hell's kitchen.

When the first winter came, I was given another, equally thin blanket, the jailers thinking, with two blankets, I should be warm enough, most prisoners having only one. The fact the larger cells had braziers in the halls, to warm the guards, did not impress upon the guards, that I required more than two thread bare pieces of cloth, to guard against the winter's cold. My complaints had no effect. I froze that first winter, and caught a massive cold, which lasted for months. The second winter I received another blanket, this one a little thicker and warmer, but infested with lice.

In the spring, my cell was generally wet from the rain, as it was in the fall. Water would pour in through the grate, which served for an air duct, more than a window. The water would run down the wall, making a small river along the floor to the drain. Each time the rain stopped, I noticed the little river had carved a channel through the filth on the floor of the cell.

During the summer, the smells were overpowering, as things rotted inside and out, the smells drifting through my cell, like a thick, invisible ooze. One time, someone urinated directly into the window hole, the urine splashing into my cell. I guessed the man didn't know there was someone in a cell, below. Or, just perhaps, it was a deliberate act, I don't know. By then I was so used to indignities, the event bothered me not at all. I was much more concerned about other matters.

The good thing about summer, was that it brought lots of insects into my cell; ants, bees, beetles, cockroaches, (in greater numbers than the other seasons), crickets, grasshoppers, ladybugs, and, of course, fleas, lots of fleas, I ate those too. The plethora of insects provided me with extra protein, usually mixing them in the morning's gruel. I discovered, some insects actually taste better than others. Bees tasted good, and I liked the taste of crickets. Cockroaches were my least favorite, however, they were the most plentiful, unfortunately.

And so I lingered, without a trial, in abject squalor for three years under those unimaginable conditions, overseen by a cruel tyrant, who ordered my yearly torture. It is a wonder I lived through my ordeal in the Bastille. During those revolutionary times, cruelty and death were the only certainties, all the rest was uncertain chaos.

As time progressed, I began to wonder why I was still alive and still enjoying the hospitality of the Bastille. It occurred to me, the Frenchies were too busy executing everyone else, that they simply forgot about me.

Or, they thought that incarcerating me, in the bowels of the Bastille, was punishment enough, an ordeal not many lived through, anyway; it being a slow lingering death, rather than the rapid slice of a falling blade on one's neck; death then arriving in about two minutes. The guillotine was indeed a much quicker end, than what was practiced before. I suppose, in a macabre sort of way, Doctor Guillotine was, indeed, a humane man.

I gained my freedom, when some bizarre change occurred in the administration of the prison. Without explanation, I was set free on April 15th, 1793; unceremoniously dumped in to the streets of Paris, without a sous to my name, and looking like a destitute beggar, stinking to high heaven.

Being dressed down, at that time, was probably a good thing, judging from the finely dressed victims being daily marched up to the vile chopper. I got the distinct impression that I was better off, not dressing up for the occasion, lest I be thought a man, who needed to have his body separated from his head.

With my long matted hair and beard, dressed in filth, I looked like all the rest of the beggars, who tried to eke a living in that revolutionary city. It was not an easy thing to find my way and means in those cruel times. However, I managed by stealing a chicken here, a duck there, always on my guard. Eventually, I regained my vigor, and managed to find my way out of the city where, after walking for some miles, I found a pond, far removed from any sort of habitation. The pond lay along a road heading south, away from Paris.

Looking around and seeing that the coast was clear, I stripped off, what was left of my clothing, and dipped my aching body into the cool water. I had not immersed my body in water for the entire time I was kept in that horrible building. I lay in the water for a long time, just looking up at the clouds, listening to the birds twittering in the trees, and wondering what was to become of me.

As I lay there, luxuriating in the cool water, the sound of horses' hooves came clomping along the road, behind which I could hear the crunching sound of wheels. There was obviously a carriage coming along the road.

I quickly scrambled behind the rushes and watched, as the carriage stopped beside the pond, in order to let the horses have a drink. Moments later, the carriage door opened, and a lovely young woman climbed out, assisted by one of the coachmen. She stretched her arms and yawned.

'On ne peux pas rester ici,' she said, with the most charming French accent. 'C'est trop dangereux. C'est un probleme pour ma famille et moi. C'est un situation de la vie ou de la mort,' she added.

'Oui, mademoiselle,' replied the coachman. 'Nous sommes bien sédulé. Ill faut donner de l'eau au cheveax avant de continuer.'

'Oui, moi aussi. J'ai soiffe,' she said, reaching for the glass of wine offered by the coachman.

Suddenly, as I stood there gawking, I lost my balance, due to the slippery nature of the pond bottom. I fell backwards with a loud splash.

'Qu' est ce qui ce passe?' I heard the girl ask, startled by the sound and fearing a problem.

'Nous allons voire,' said the coachman, as he and the driver rushed to where I lay in the water, trying to remain calm.

Unfortunately, the pale nature of my skin was difficult to disguise amongst the greenery. The men saw me and quickly obtained a pistol, which the coachman pointed at me, advising me to come out of the rushes, or else he would shoot.

I guessed everyone was a bit nervous in France, at that time, so I understood the concern they expressed, especially since the young lady had said, there was an issue of life and death at stake.

Grabbing some leaves, with which to cover my private parts, I slowly stepped out of the rushes and stood, naked and shivering, in front of the two coachmen and the surprised young woman, who appeared shocked at first, and then assumed a most charming countenance, graced with a shy smile of such a delicate nature, my heart melted at the sight of her.

'Excuse me, miss,' I said in English, slightly bowing at the waist. 'I did not mean to startle you. I was having a swim.'

'Along a public road?' she asked, responding in perfect English.

'It is a beautiful day,' I replied, surprised by her command of my native tongue. 'There is not much traffic on this road. I thought I was alone.'

The young woman giggled, thinking it a funny situation. 'Where are your clothes?' she asked, looking around.

'Someone must have stolen them,' I lied.

'These are terrible times,' she said, shaking her head. 'Nothing is sacred any longer.'

I couldn't help but agree with her.

She told me, I looked like someone she knew, from a long time ago. An uncle who had lost his hand, in service of the French Crown. He apparently had been an officer in the hussars, who saw service in the American colonies, before the Revolutionary War.

'The amazing thing is, he also had a scar on his face. He told me it came from a sabre cut,' she observed, studying me closer. Then, the words which changed the entire direction of my life, sang like an angelic host in my ears. 'We are on our way to Orléons. Perhaps we can help you,' she suggested, smiling so charmingly, I thought I saw cherubs winging about her person.

'Help?' I asked innocently, totally captivated and charmed by the beautiful young woman.

'You have no clothes, obviously you need help,' she said, it being the most obvious thing in the world. 'Besides, it is the Christian thing to do, to help our fellow creatures, in these revolutionary times,' she said sincerely. 'I guess this is your lucky day,' she added giggling. Then she asked me where I was going.

I replied I was going to Orléons.

'Well, I suppose you can ride with us,' she said smiling. 'However, you are naked,' she added, looking directly at the leaves in front of my stirring monster. 'We will have to do something about that.' She signaled the coachman, 'Gaston, une couverte, s'il vous plait.'

'Oui, mademoiselle,' replied the coachman.

He returned a moment later with a blanket; handing it to me, as if he were giving it to a dangerous animal.

I dried off with the blanket, as I wrapped myself in it, and then stepped closer to the finely scented angel. She stepped back involuntarily, my body odors being still somewhat strong, in spite of the pond.

'Perhaps you should ride outside,' she said. 'When we get to Orléons, you can have a bath with soap. Perhaps we can see about that hair and beard, as well,' she added, smiling. Then, with no further ado, the horses having finished their drink, she ordered the commencement of their journey, with me sitting on the luggage rack, at the back of the coach, grateful for the blessing which had come my way.

The trip to Orléons passed uneventfully, with the exception of three road blocks, where we were thoroughly examined by citizens, each time giving them the story, I had fallen in a cess pond, and my clothes were ruined. The fact my hair and beard, and overall appearance, signaled extreme neglect, did not phase the citizen guards, who accepted it as somehow, normal.

We arrived at the girl's family home, sometime in the late afternoon. It was a magnificent chateau on the outskirts of the city, so beloved of Jean d'Arc. The grounds were protected with a massive wrought iron gate, which was opened by a porter. Moments later, we pulled up to a beautifully appointed porch. The young woman's parents, two maids, and a butler came out of the house to welcome her. No one paid me the slightest attention, as the coachmen drove the conveyance around the side of the house into a courtyard, where a stableman stood waiting to receive the horses.

The coachman came around to the back of the coach and told me to enter a building, nearby. It was a bath house, where soon I was able to enjoy a tub of hot water and a bar of good, scented soap.

The hot water felt like no water I had ever sat in before. It was incredible how my body craved the heat and the soap. I felt myself gradually relaxing and drifting into a deep sleep, as I lay there in the tub, soaking up the heat, as my thoughts whirled through the past four years, and attempted to bring some sort of order to the progression of events.

I drifted into a troubled dream regarding my family in the West Indies, who by then, must have thought me dead. I wondered if Marianne had remarried, and what my children were facing. Over top of the images of my family, I saw men dangling from ropes, their tongues horribly blue, and sticking out of their mouths. As the images came closer, I saw my own face, horribly twisted, my tongue blue and sticking out of my mouth.

I was awakened by a man standing beside the tub. He startled me and I reacted accordingly. It is a good thing for him I did not have a pistol in my hand, I would surely have shot him; the dream had made me very anxious, indeed.

The man turned out to be the barber, whom the young woman had sent to return my hair to some semblance of civilized appearance.

The choice we made, was to cut the hair off, as close to my skull as possible, ridding me of the fleas, and other creatures, residing in that hirsute mess. I could tell that the barber was not looking forward to the task.

Cutting my hair took almost an hour, the beard somewhat less. All the while, the barber never said a word, and concentrated on the operation; the disgusting, matted hair falling to the floor, various creatures scurrying away in fear; having lost their homes. When the man was done, he rinsed his scissors off in the bath and then advised me to wash my head well, with strong soap and hot water, which I did forthwith.

Then, as I was standing admiring my new hair cut in the mirror on the wall, a servant entered the bathroom. I immediately grabbed the towel and placed it in front of me, however, judging from the girl's countenance, she had seen more than she should have.

The girl apologized, as she handed me a bundle of clothes. 'Eere,' she said. 'My meestress tol me to geeve zeeze to yu.'

I thanked the girl, as I accepted the bundle from her.

She curtsied before she left, leaving me to dress in a reasonably good set of clothes, obviously well worn, but still very serviceable. The fact the clothes had belonged to a larger man, made them fit loose, and comfortably. My angel had even included a new eye patch of black velvet with silk ribbons. It was a surprising find. I wondered if someone in the family was also missing an eye.

When I was suitably attired, I located a broom and swept up the hair, which I disposed on the trash heap, near the stable, returning to the bath house to wash my hand and finish up.

While I was thus cleaning up, an other servant came to tell me that I could find something to eat in the kitchen. She pointed to the back of the house. Then she set about emptying the tub, leaving me to find my own way to the food.

It wasn't difficult to find the kitchen, because my nose easily followed the delicious aromas coming from the back of the house, where the kitchen was located. When I arrived at the back of the house, my young friend was standing there, waiting for me beside a table, set on the flagstones, beside the door leading into the house.

'Well, now,' she said smiling, 'you look a whole lot better.'

'I feel a whole lot better,' I replied gratefully.

'You are probably hungry,' she said.

I nodded. My stomach was empty and gnawing. The delicious aromas wafting from the kitchen was having an effect on my mucous glands, because my mouth was dripping.

My hostess indicated a chair. 'Please sit down,' she said.

'Thank you,' I replied, trying not to drool.

I sat down and continued to regard the girl.

'I still don't understand why are you helping me like this?' I asked. 'I don't even know your name.'

The young woman regarded me for a moment and then replied that her name was, Juliette Cocteau. She rescued me because, I reminded her of her uncle, someone who was very dear to her. He was guillotined, the year previous.

'These are dangerous times,' she said. 'We have to get out of this place, before they come for us. I found out in Paris that my family is on a list. It is why I was in a hurry to get here. We have to find a ship and escape to America. We have family in New Orléons.'

When she mentioned a ship, lights came on in my head. I told her more about who I was, and that I had lots of experience with ships, suggesting I would be able to help her, in return for what she had done for me. I never mentioned to her then, that I was the famous pirate, Peter Mann, just merely telling her that I had been a master on a ship, before my incarceration, which prompted the question, why I was incarcerated in the first place.

'Who knows? These days one can be arrested in France for any reason.'

My answer was obviously the right one because Juliette agreed heartily.

'That is why we have to leave Orléons, at the first opportune moment,' she said. 'My family is not safe here, any longer.' Juliette looked pleadingly at me, 'Perhaps you can suggest where we should go, to seek a ship?'

I thought about her question for a moment and then ventured to suggest, Marseilles, assuming that the west coast ports would be much too busy, with traffic to England. Then, in a flash of brilliant clarity, it came to me to suggest, I take Juliette and her family to my island home, in the Caicos Islands.

My suggestion was met with an enthusiastic response. Juliette thought it a brilliant idea and ran off to suggest it to her parents, leaving me to enjoy a pleasant meal by myself, seated at the table outside the kitchen door. I remember feeling exceptionally good at that time, as I clearly saw my way home, where I hoped Marianne and my children were waiting.

Some minutes later, Juliette returned with her parents and introduced us by saying, 'This is the man I told you about.'

I introduced myself and shook Monsieur Cocteau's hand. He was a big man, with a portly stomach. He had a kind face, with jowls; the jowls gave him the appearance of an old blood hound.

I kissed Madam's hand and then gestured for them to sit down at the table, Juliette sitting beside me, on my right.

'Peter thinks he can get us a boat,' said Juliette enthusiastically.

I corrected Juliette by telling her, it would take more than a boat to get us to my island; that it would require, a ship.

Juliette smiled and corrected herself, telling her parents I would help them with, a ship.

I smiled, as I explained that I was a seasoned captain, whose home was in the West Indies, and that I was jailed for some odd customs foul up in Marseilles. Then, I spoke of my island home, not letting on, for a moment, that our town was anything other than a legitimate port in the West Indies. I told my hosts that I would be able to help them sail away from France.

'Perhaps it will only be for a short while,' I suggested. 'The madness will blow over,' I continued, trying to sound hopeful and encouraging.

'Yes, perhaps,' said Juliette's father sadly. 'However, in ze meantime, ve haf been put on a leest, apparently. Zat leest also had names vich are scheduled for execution. Ve believe, it is only a matter of time, ven our names vill be moved to ze execution leest. My grandparents haff a minor connection to ze Crown. Ve understand ze aristocracy is being liquidated, not to zujest zat ve are aristocrats, but my family does haff connections, and vell, as yu understand, monsieur, times are very uncertain and chaotic in France, today.' Mister Cocteau looked pleadingly at me. 'If yu can elp us, monsieur, ve vud be forever in yur debt. Name yur price.'

'Name my price? 'I assure you, sir, the price has already been paid by your daughter,' I said chivalrously. 'She helped me. Now I will help you.'

The Cocteaus thanked me profusely, Madame and Juliette each giving me a kiss on each cheek. Monsieur Cocteau shook my hand even more warmly. I felt very good to be so hospitably taken in, by such a fine family. I thanked God for my good fortune.

That night, I slept in a soft feather bed, which very quickly became uncomfortable, it being too soft, necessitating me throwing the bed cover on the floor and sleeping there, on a much harder surface.

Juliette found me, curled up on the floor, the next morning, when she came into my room with a breakfast tray, and a big smile on her face.

'Oh, you poor man,' she said, standing over me. 'Your body can't handle a soft bed, anymore?' Juliette shook her pretty head and smiled sympathetically, as I opened my eye and blinked, blinded by her beauty.

I croaked, 'good morning,' which made her giggle.

'I think you need a drink of water,' she said, happily pouring a glass of water from the pitcher on the tray. She handed me the glass and I took a long drink, being quite dehydrated.

'I had the kitchen cook you some eggs. There is coffee and bread, and cheese, and some delicious preserves, made by my aunt,' enthused the angel, as she set about rearranging things on the tray.

Standing up, I thanked Juliette, and then, as she was about to walk away, she brushed against me, bringing me a delicious scent of honey blossoms and vanilla; that being her perfume. Her lovely aroma filled my nostrils and sent me momentarily on a spiraling flight, straight to Heaven. I had to restrain myself from embracing her and smothering her with kisses, not quite understanding my exact place, with regards to her universe.

When Juliette had left the room, I ate the breakfast ravenously, being exceedingly hungry. It was the best food I had ever tasted. It was so many millions of times more wonderful than the best gruel served by the kitchens of the Bastille. The eggs were so full of flavor. I couldn't remember when I had tasted eggs as good as those, which Juliette had brought me. I savored that breakfast; taking an hour, or more to eat, tasting each bite and deriving maximum flavor, by masticating slowly and deliberately.

Breakfast over, I was surprised to find a much nicer set of clothes laid out for me, on a chair beside the dressing table. The clothes were those of a proper French gentleman, and fit me like a glove. Dressed, I presented a fine figure; a far cry from my appearance, the day before. I again wondered about Divine Intervention and thanked God for my good fortune, truly believing Juliette to be a real angel.

When I felt ready, I joined the family in the parlor, where we began to plan in earnest, the utmost haste being required, since the arrival of a message, that morning, from friends in Paris. The plan called for immediate action, so we set to work in earnest, getting the family ready to travel.

Monsieur Cocteau rounded up every gold and silver coin, and other valuable asset, which could be easily converted into a ship, or passage on a ship, and assembled them in a sturdy wooden chest. He gave me some of the coins, in order to purchase a new hook, managing to obtain an excellent pewter model from the prosthetics dealer in Orléons, the following morning.

Madame and Juliette packed some clothing and assorted personal things in two trunks, which were brought out to the wagon. Eventually, the wagon was loaded with trunks, and two very comfortable, reading chairs. The family coach would transport us.

Mister Cocteau had closed his business, and settled his affairs in Orléons. Fortunately, he was still left with some money, which he happily added to his trunk of valuables.

When all was ready, three servants accompanied us, along with the coach driver, two livery men, and the drivers for the wagon. We pulled out from the chateau, sometime in the mid afternoon of April the 28th, storm clouds gathering in the sky.

An hour later, we were pelted with a driving rain, which turned the roads to mud, greatly hampering our passage. However, we persevered, reaching Gien, some time later, where we took shelter from the rain at the

Hotel Louis Plantagenet, renamed, Hotel d'Liberty. Fortunately, it was not very busy. We were able to obtain a fine meal in the fire warmed dining room.

That night we stayed at the hotel.

The rain continued through the night, turning the roads to mush. However, we had no choice, but to attempt travel the next day. It was still raining, however, considering how events were continuing to unfold in France, we felt we had no time to waste.

Eventually, the sun came breaking through the clouds. I commented, that the weather seemed to be an appropriate symbolic representation of what the family was going through; leaving their home in Orléons and heading for a new adventure, which hopefully would result in continued sunshine. The family appreciated my hopeful encouragement.

As we traveled, ever south, every now and then, examples of the revolutionary madness presented themselves; time consuming road blocks, burnt houses, cadavers, and hungry people, begging along the roads, for anything of value, even a kernel of corn. It was very depressing. I couldn't wait to get home.

Arriving in Marseilles, twelve days after we began our journey, we were subjected to a very thorough examination, as ignorant bumpkins searched our coach for anything they could use, to bring more people to the advocates. Fortunately, they were amenable to graft. Ten francs sent the bumpkins scurrying for another coach to fleece.

We checked in at a fine hotel, not far from the harbour. The Hotel Marie was still providing excellent service, considering the times. However, now the hotel played host to crazy eyed citizen leaders of local murder tribunals, and other revolutionary types, who felt it was their place, to bring their boorish peasant manners into a genteel place of refined living. Watching the revolutionaries order waiters around in the dining room made me want to teach the men some lessons in manners. Alas, given our circumstances, it was best not to draw attention to ourselves and I let it be, making it a point, to be extra nice to the servers.

Next day, we began the search for a vessel, to take us to the happy isle, finding a suitable little sloop for sale, seven days later. She was a fifty foot harbour vessel, used for carrying passengers, and small cargoes, to and fro in the harbour. She had a high stem and transom, making her more than suitable to ride the waves of the Atlantic. Her sails, rigging, and spars, were all in excellent condition, the vessel having been refitted, just prior to being put up for sale.

Monsieur Cocteau bought the sloop for eight hundred Louis d'ors, and victualed and watered her for another twenty. Seafaring clothing came to twenty seven Louis d'ors, outfitting, Monsieur and Madame, Juliette, Gaston, the butler, and his wife, Madame Gautier, an excellent cook I was to find out, Ben, the wagon driver, who was also their gardener, Chantelle the upstairs maid, Clarissa, the downstairs maid, and their horse master, Marc-Andre.

I decided, it would be expedient, if we hired five professional sailors, to come along, as well, the crossing being what it was, potentially hazardous at that time of year, it being early May.

Hence, while the ladies made our vessel habitable, Monsieur Cocteau and I set out, to find suitable sailors in the local taverns, where they liked to spend their time; until another captain hired them. Monsieur Cocteau had never been in sailor bars; it being quite an experience for him.

'Sailors are not like landlubbers,' I told him. 'They are human beings, who know how to party; spending their money freely, recklessly pursuing the pleasures of the bottle and the flesh.'

I could tell, Monsieur Cocteau was shocked, to see a licentious couple fornicating in a corner, while the sailor doing the riding, was squeezing another woman's right breast with one hand, while holding onto his tankard of rum with the other. Such sights were not exactly commonplace in Monsieur Cocteau's world. It wasn't my cup of tea, either. Such acts were better left for private moments, in the right places; not in a public house, in front of other customers. However, such was the world of sailor men in the early nineteenth century. Their pubs tended to be a significant departure from the status quo.

The orchestra, which consisted of two screeching fiddles, a concertina, a tambourine, a bagpipe, and a drum, was making such a racket, it was difficult to hear one's own words, let alone those of another. Monsieur Cocteau and I had to shout to be heard.

To the left of the bar, a group of sailors were watching two muscular colleagues arm wrestling over a small table. Nearby, two lusty people were groping each other, as their friends were laughing, and encouraging a more dramatic show of human affection. The words they used, to encourage the sailor, were of a rather crude nature, which we did not tend to use much in our colony; talk like that being an indication one has no self respect, in our opinion. Not to suggest that none of us ever used expletives, which we all certainly did, from time to time, in moments of stress. We just happened to believe, there is a time and a place for everything, a public house is not a place to have one's pants down, for example, and one's snake in the air. I believe Monsieur Cocteau felt the same way, judging from his reddened cheeks.

I took Monsieur Cocteau to sit at a vacant table, some distance from the copulators, and ordered drinks, all the while carefully watching the crowd for suitable candidates. After about an hour and a half, I had managed to attract two able looking seamen to our table and explained what I was looking for, and where we were going. When I mentioned the West Indies, both men were very happy to sign on for a reasonable wage. Lucky for us, the two sailors had three friends, who were also looking for work; we happily providing it.

The next day, I went shopping for charts and flags, a sextant, a clock, a reliable compass, two new pistols, and some other weapons, five cutlasses, three muskets, and a blunderbuss. I explained to Monsieur Cocteau that the expense of good weapons, and navigation tools, was well worth the price we were paying for them, that being thirty nine Louis d'or for the tools and weapons, and twelve for the charts. Monsieur Cocteau never complained about the expenditures. I guess he figured his family's life was worth the money. I would have done the same, if the tables were turned. We also bought five books, without which the trip would be a great chore for me, and the Cocteaus, they also having a penchant for books.

As soon as the winds allowed, we set sail on May 12th, 1793, three years and seven days from my disaster in the fog. It was a great feeling to be going home. I could hardly wait to embrace my wonderful family.

Regarding the five sailors we hired; three were French: Georges, Jacques, and Pierre. The other two were Swedes; Olaf and Pedersen. They immediately proved their worth, quickly taking responsibility from me and handling the sloop, much to my satisfaction, enabling me to become more acquainted with the Cocteaus and their lovely daughter, for whom I was developing a great fondness. However, I resisted the temptations she presented, being a married man with principles and an abiding sense of loyalty to my spouse.

The book I had chosen to read, was a marvelous account of the lives of pirates, by that master story teller, Daniel Dafoe. Many times I had to laugh, as episodes in the lives of Dafoe's pirates, mirrored my own life, and those of my friends and colleagues. My laughter attracted the attention of Monsieur Cocteau, who asked me, one day, what I found so funny about Dafoe's book.

I figured I owed it to that fine man, to tell him the entire truth about myself. So, I came clean and told him I was a pirate, who had been thrown into the Bastille, because I was known as, 'The Scourge of the West Indies.'

Juliette, who had been listening, immediately said words, which were music to my ears, 'You're no scourge, Peter,' she said sweetly. 'If anything, you are a kind, and decent man,' she added.

I must have blushed ten tints of red, hearing her expression of obvious affection. I was getting the distinct impression that Juliette had grown fond of me, as well. The realization made me warm all over.

Monsieur Cocteau smiled at his wife, who was sitting behind us, sunning in her marvelous chair. I think he suspected there might be something developing with his daughter and I. To redirect the attention, he steered me back to my admission of piracy, admitting, he was impressed to hear, who I actually was, having heard of me from a merchant friend of his.

'Looking at you, now, I don't see you as much of a scourge, either,' said Monsieur Cocteau, shaking his head.

I had to remind him that I had been in prison for three years. That was bound to take some of the scourginess off a person. 'Wait until you see me back to my full weight,' I said, trying, for some strange reason, to defend my title. Thinking of it now, that I write these words, I have to laugh. It was so preposterous. 'Scourge of the West Indies', indeed.

We made port at Mahon, four days later. We stocked up on some fresh victuals, from a woman, who rowed out to our sloop, with a boat load of fresh fruit and vegetables. We also made sure to top up our water barrels and obtain some more fire wood, while we were there.

The weather was so magnificent, that a walk along the beach, and a picnic, became the order of the day.

Our circumstances in Menorca were so pleasant, right from the beginning, that we spent a very wonderful fortnight, waiting for another wind, to take us further south, towards the Strait of Gibraltar, and the Atlantic Ocean. We stopped at Ibiza for another fortnight, life being so pleasant there, as well.

Our sojourns on the islands gave Juliette and I a lot of time to spend together, which I readily sought out, much enjoying her company, and just watching her; her expressive face, her sparkling, intelligent eyes, her hair, her graceful arms, her beautiful hands, her feet... Juliette eventually became an obsession. I couldn't get enough of her, and obviously she not of me, either; spending as much time as possible with me, without giving away too much to her parents and the household staff. But, a person would have had to be blind not to see our infatuation with each other.

I explained to Juliette, that I was married, and under vows of fidelity, which she found even more attractive about me, saying so one night, as we sat together in the sand, watching the moon reflecting on the water. 'We will see what happens, when you get home,' she said. 'You will have been away for three and a half years, by the time you get back to your island. Perhaps things have changed there.' I could sense a hint of hope in her voice, as if she wished for things to be different.

To be so sought after, by that fine young woman, was a great compliment to my manhood, and provided me plenty of reason for erotic dreams of her and I. It was all I could do to keep my hands from fondling her young breasts.

We left Ibiza on June 17th, reaching Gibraltar a week later. I had never seen that bizarre rock before and found it to be quite an incredible anomaly, stuck right there in the bay, across from Algeciras. Where that rock had come from was a mystery no one had an answer to. I wondered if it had fallen from the sky.

Gibraltar was overrun with Englishmen. Hence, I chose to visit there, but one day, preferring instead to begin the journey west, hoping to reach our island sometime towards the middle of August, preferably not during a hurricane.

The long passage across the Atlantic took its toll on several members of our group, not that it killed them, but for some days, Madame Cocteau, and Juliette, were very ill with sea sickness, the waves of the Atlantic tossing our vessel somewhat more than they were used to. Chantelle also became quite ill, and asked several times, to be put out of her misery, her suffering being so terrible.

Eventually, the illnesses passed and everyone happily continued with their various past times. The sloop practically sailed itself; Georges having rigged up a device for keeping the tiller set for the proper course, enabling us all to lounge on deck, when the weather was nice, which it was for most of the passage, experiencing only six days of inclement weather; rain and strong winds.

I sighted our island on August 14th, it appearing out of a bank of fog, three leagues off our starboard bow. I congratulated myself on my fine navigating, glad to have taken the lessons from Bill and George, those many years ago.

Unfortunately, the wind did not allow us to make the island, instead we had to stand off an island, to the lee of our own, for a day, before we managed to catch a breeze, taking us within hailing distance of our beach, sometime in the afternoon of the 17th.

I found it strange that no flag had gone up on the platform, which was clearly visible. No persons came running to the beach, no cannons sounded. The place appeared deserted.

Since the sloop was a much smaller vessel than our brigs or merchantmen, we had no trouble sailing into the cove, totally perplexed at the lack of people. We could clearly see houses through the trees, but judging from the dilapidated state of the pier, our island was no longer inhabited.

Because we had no boat, it became incumbent to swim for the shore, which Pierre happily undertook, pulling a painter behind him, in order to pull our vessel closer to shore. We dropped anchor in three fathoms, a mere twenty feet from the shore. Then, one by one, everyone jumped into the water and made their way to the sandy beach where I was standing, wondering what had happened to the colony; and most importantly, what had happened to my family.

When Juliette stepped on shore, I asked if she wanted to see my house. Everyone else wanted to see it, as well. So, we all marched into the village, to find most of the houses in a sorry, dilapidated state, totally devoid of any household goods, except for the odd torn blanket or broken pots.

The roof of my house had collapsed, but most of it was still standing, however, everything was gone, the bed, the mirror, our box of treasure, my maps...

As we were thus looking through my house, Juliette found a letter, pinned to a post, in what used to be my bedroom. The letter was placed in such a way that rain would not have affected it. The letter was from Marianne. The envelope was dated February 21, 1792. It was addressed to me.

I opened the letter with trembling hands.

Juliette came to stand beside me and put her arm around my waist, as we read the letter together.

> 'Dear Peter,
>
> You have been gone for almost two years. Without your leadership, and that of Colin, George, Robert, and Wapoo, the colony has fallen apart. Many people have already left, as I write this. Most of the people fear that you are all dead, the victims of another wreck, or other circumstances. I do not know if you are dead, or not, however, I am taking this chance to write you, in the event you find your way back here.
>
> First of all, I want you to know, those of us who have remained, waiting for you to return, took a vote, two weeks ago, and determined that you have perished.'

I noticed at that point, the ink had run in several places, Marianne obviously crying when she wrote those words. I pointed it out to Juliette, who squeezed me tighter for support.

Anyway, the letter continued,

> 'Taking that position, I have to advise you, if you find this letter, I am going to remarry. The children need a father. A good man has offered to step in your place. His name is, Marcus Silvanus. He gets along very well with the children, and they all seem to like him, most of the time, except William. However, I am sure with time, he will come to love Marcus, like a father. Marcus is an excellent carpenter.
>
> We have one ship left, the *Santa Maria*, which we renamed, *New Venture*. We finished loading the ship two days ago. It looks like we will have favorable winds soon, so we could leave any day.
>
> I left you some of the money, from the big chest, your notebooks, and your maps, and put them in a water proof chest, in the secret hiding place, you know where I mean. I won't write it out, because you know where it is, if the person reading this letter is, Peter Mann. Otherwise, the maps and money will just stay where they are, until I retrieve them sometime in the future.'

I looked at Juliette and smiled.

Her eyes were radiant. Obviously the words of the letter were agreeing with her. I sensed she was snuggling into me, indicating where her intentions lay. Of course, it was no surprise to me. Julliette's affections made me exceedingly happy as I continued to read the letter.

> 'We are going to San Juan, having made friends there, and it not being too far from here. Because we have lots of money, our lives will be comfortable, so you need not worry about us. Of course, if you read this, you will find us in San Juan. However, Peter, please don't be too hurt. By the time you read this I will be remarried. I have no way of knowing if you are dead or alive, and, like I said, the children need a father.

Catherine, Joshua, and Michael miss you terribly. Little William was still too young, to have much of a memory of you, although we all remind him of you, most days, telling him that his father is the greatest pirate who ever sailed the Seven Seas.'

I had to smile when I read those lines. I reminded Juliette that I had only sailed the Atlantic and the Caribbean. 'There are many more seas to see,' I said smiling broadly.

Juliette told me she would love to sail the Seven Seas with me.

It was at that moment we kissed for the first time, a long, deep, warm kiss, full of love and affection. Every pore of my body tingled, as she probed with her tongue, and pressed herself against me. The sensations were overwhelming. It was most unfortunate that her parents were elsewhere in the house, exploring my former circumstances and assessing my worthiness for their daughter, otherwise, I am sure we would have made love, right then and there.

When Madame Cocteau called to see where we were, Juliette and I broke off our kiss and quickly joined her parents downstairs.

'Theese ees a nice ouse,' said Madame Cocteau enthusiastically. 'I don't theenk eet weel take very long to feex eet up, no?'

I looked at the dilapidated state of the house and reckoned, it would take us a month to fix it. If we had a crew, then it would take a lot less. I reminded the Cocteaus that we had well over 500 people living there, at the height of our piracy. They understood, 500 people make a big difference, in how quickly a town or village develops.

I advised the Cocteaus, and their friends, to make a climb up the mountain, while I took Juliette with me, excusing ourselves from the others, to take a walk along a trail, leading to the other side of our mountain, where deep in the cave, at the far end, Virginia and I had made a hole in the rock, over which a slab of stone had been fitted. The slab was covered with the same dirt as the rest of the cave floor, and was not discernible to anyone, but someone knowing where to look.

Lying along the opposite wall was a five foot metal bar, which appeared to be an object, which had broken off something else. In fact, it was a pry bar, to lift the slab off the secret stash.

Juliette helped me lever the slab off the hole, and then, eagerly looked within. Much to her delight, a heavy box sat in the hole, requiring both of us to lift it out. When she tried to open the lid, she found that it was locked.

'It's locked,' she said, disappointed.

I smiled and stepped over to the wall behind her. I reached high above my head, to a small ledge, on top of which lay the key. I handed the key to Juliette and then asked her if she would marry me.

Juliette enthusiastically threw herself into my arms and smothered me with kisses.

I presumed that meant, 'Yes!'

My heart jumped for joy.

I had been loyal to Marianne, there was nothing I needed to be ashamed of. Marianne had remarried. I was free to love Juliette, and I did, for the rest of my life.

We carried the heavy box between us, having to take frequent rests along the way, it being very heavy. Eventually, Juliette could not carry it any more, so we recruited the two Swedes, Olaf and Pedersen, to carry it to the shore, ready to take on board the sloop. We did not tell them what was in the box, and kept it locked.

During the time of our visit on the island, I showed my new friends around the place, pointing out the many amenities we had designed and built. I showed them our platform, and explained how water was brought up to the wet bar. We walked through the gardens and found the skeletal remains of a goat and a cow, long ago devoured by the creatures of the island. I was surprised there were still pigs. Their hoof prints were clearly visible in the soft soil.

The bath house and concert hall had fallen down. The warehouses were still in an excellent state of repair. To our lucky surprise, there was still rum in one of the hogsheads. Our sailor friends were particularly pleased, there being still a goodly supply, which we transferred to two empty kegs, we had on board.

Madame Cocteau was happily surprised to hear that we had a concert hall. 'I luf ze concert. Moozeek eez zo good for ze soul. N'est pas, Hugo?'

Monsieur Cocteau agreed whole heartedly, as did Juliette, who admitted she played the piano forte, and the violin.

We were all saddened to see that the library's roof had caved in and that it had been abandoned. Many fine volumes were left, to grow moldy on the water logged shelves. Fortunately, my fine copy of Daniel Dafoe's story, about Robinson Crusoe, was gone, but my volumes of Gibbon's fine work, pertaining to the fall of the Roman Empire, were completely infested with mold and spider webs. I couldn't help but shake my head at the tragic loss.

In our wanderings, I was surprised to find two cannons still sitting in the bush, guarding the entrance to the cove; surprised that they were left to grow rusty. They appeared to be in good shape, otherwise. I did not see any cracks in the barrels. Perhaps the ships were overloaded and couldn't carry any more.

Seeing all that we had built over the years, greatly impressed everyone; all of them expressing a desire for similar circumstances, seeing the potential for a pleasant life on the beautiful island.

Fortunately, the pond was still filled with fresh water, and fruit trees abounded. We even found some melons, onions, and sweet potatoes, which had continued to grow in our gardens. The fresh food was a welcome addition to our table, obviously supplemented with an abundance of sea food, readily available from the cove.

After spending a few days on the island, I was beginning to get the idea, the Cocteaus and their friends were beginning to like the place. I could tell they were already seeing themselves as inhabitants. Hence, I was not surprised, when later in the day, serious discussions began over supper, regarding a resurrection of the colony; not for the purposes of piracy, but for the purposes of developing a beautiful place to live.

'Wiz plenty of money ve can buy vatever ve need to supplement vat ze island already provides. If ze issue is to live, an do it well, an all needs are provided, vy must vun lif in a crowded, smelly ceetie?' asked Madame Cocteau, with her charming French accent, gesturing towards the dilapidated town.

Madame Cocteau expressed the question of the day. Even our five hired sailors thought the idea a good one, but for one condition. They would stay, as long as we brought more women to the island.

The idea of resurrecting the colony was a good one, to my way of thinking. The island was my home, not San Juan. A goodly part of the village infrastructure was still in place; the stone foundations of the houses, and portions of our storm wall was still as solid, as the day we built it. Bits and pieces of our water conveyances were repairable, and the entire storm cellar was intact. Rebuilding would not take a great amount of time with the right crews.

Living on our island was very pleasant and enabled one to do pretty much what one wanted. I found it a great place, to read and write; it being such a peaceful island paradise. Hence, after some consideration, I agreed to put my support behind the plan, vowing to help with recruitment of suitable candidates.

'Ve vill found ze colony on ze principles of, Life, Liberty, an Property,' said Monsieur Cocteau enthusiastically. 'Ve can name our main street after, Voltaire.' Monsieur grinned from ear to ear, as he held up his cup, and proposed a toast to that great French intellectual; a writer whose works I was not familiar with. I hoped to correct that as soon as possible, with a visit to the book seller in San Juan.

When all were agreed on the plan, we drank a toast, pledging each other's total support for the idea. It was a happy group that vowed to live together in harmony; having done it well on a small vessel for over three months. I knew, if I found more excellent people, like my present company, the island would again be, Paradise.

Chapter Twenty-Seven

September sixth we set sail for San Juan, the winds being fair. We had revictualed with; fish, fruit, and vegetables from the garden. We filled our water barrels from the pond. We would eat well on the short voyage to San Juan de Puerto Rico, sailing along the beautiful north coast of Hispaniola; a voyage I always enjoyed, it being such a beautiful trip.

The Caribbean sea was a delightful play on blue, manifesting itself in everything from a deep, dark blue gray, to magnificent blue green. If I had been a painter, the marvelous blues would have inspired me to grab brushes and paints, to capture the marvelous colours on canvas. Whether I would have been able to replicate the incredible varieties of the azure hue, is debatable. To describe the colors of the Caribbean with words, can only give you, dear reader, a mere wisp of an idea, but that is all. You may see some blues in your mind, but it can only be a mirage; an interpretation of my words, but not really what I was actually seeing on those glorious days. Regarding the colors of the Caribbean, I would have to say, a picture is truly worth a thousand words.

Nearing land, we were pleased to see quite a variety of tropical sea birds. I didn't have a book identifying them, so I have no idea what they were. Suffice it to say, they were a welcome sight, as they soared over us, or skimmed over the waves, looking for fish. However, there was one bird we all identified, as nothing other than a sea gull, of which there were as many, as anywhere else along the shores of the world.

Flying fish is a creature the Cocteaus had never heard of. They were amazed to find a number of them, every morning, still struggling for breath, as they flopped about on our decks. If they were still breathing, we always tossed them over board, to allow them an opportunity to live another day and frolic in the waves. The dead ones we used for bait.

Another amazing fish was the needle fish, which one had to be careful about, they being sharp little projectiles, which shot out of a wave, landing on deck, sometimes stuck in a rope, or sail. If they stuck in a person, the needle sharp prick was quite irritating.

Everyone was most particularly pleased when porpoises accompanied us for a time, gracefully swimming ahead of our bows, and jumping through the waves, as if to show us humans that they could out swim, and out maneuver our ship; they being in their element, and we, merely landlubbers. From their chatter, I had the distinct impression they were laughing at us.

We reached San Juan in five days of pleasant sailing, the winds being fair to moderate. I must have seemed anxious, because Juliette asked me if I was looking forward to seeing my family. Of course, I had to admit I was anxious. My daughter would be a strapping young woman of 17, by then. My sons, and step son, Michael, would be 13. I wondered if they still remembered me. Joshua and Michael certainly would, but not William. He was just a little tyke when I left.

Juliette came to stand beside me and put her arm around my waist. I smiled at her and gave her a kiss on her cheek. I snuggled her closer, as we slid into the harbour, finding anchorage in the lee of a beautiful American frigate, proudly flying the colors of the newly founded, United States of America. Everything about the ship displayed modern confidence and an adventuresome spirit. Over the days that the American ship lay beside us, I admired her magnificent lines, and often commented on it, thinking such a ship would be perfect for our service; a touch of piratical larceny creeping back into my blood. I didn't mention any of this to Juliette. Not at that time, anyway.

When our vessel was secure, we hailed a long boat passing by, seeing there were seats available, enabling all of us, but Gaston and Madame Gautier, to go ashore. The butler and the cook were willing to guard the ship. I think they actually wanted the privacy, so they could engage in a little, in / out, if you get my meaning. I'm sure if anyone were watching, at some point later in the day, our sloop was probably bobbing on calm waters. I wasn't surprised they stayed behind, because I saw how they were at breakfast, like a young couple, frisky and cute.

The ride to shore, for all of us, cost a shilling, which Monsieur Cocteau gladly paid. I could tell that he and the missus, the maids, Ben, Marc-André, Juliette, and our sailors, were totally awestruck by the city which had grown up on the other side of the world. San Juanians would have them picked out as tourists right away, as they gawked, eyes wide and mouths open in awe.

As we were thus standing, admiring the busy port and harbour, an evil looking man approached us. I sensed something sinister, in the way the man came to stand next to Georges and Pierre. He leaned closer to them, so as to be discreet, and said something which I could not quite hear. I noticed that the two sailors began to smile, as the man spoke. Moments later they beckoned Jacques and the Swedes to come and listen. I had a good idea what was being spoken of. I believe Monsieur and Madame did, as well; discreetly clearing their throats and looking the other way.

'What are they talking about over there?' asked Juliette, naively.

I explained that the man was probably a pimp, obtaining work for a brothel. He seemed the type; darting eyes, fine clothes, uncalloused hands, rings…

Georges came over to tell us they would spend the night in town, and not to worry about them. He sported a lascivious grin on his countenance; poor sex starved creature. Being a young man, his life force needed to express itself. He had been too many days at sea, watching three beautiful young women on a small sloop, without being able to touch them. I could well identify with their desire to get laid.

I told Georges and his mates to enjoy themselves, admonishing them to be careful, as I eyed the pimp, who was busy explaining services and prices.

Georges smiled and happily joined his fellows, as they followed the pimp, to whatever heaven they were promised.

I suggested to my companions that we find a place to enjoy a coffee, it being readily available in San Juan.

My companions, being French, loved coffee, so they heartily agreed, it was a splendid idea.

Thus, we strolled off to find a café, finding one two blocks away from the docks. It was exactly what we were looking for. Judging from the number of persons also enjoying the delicious elixir, we had come to the right place.

Gratefully sitting around a table, on the outdoor terrace overlooking the street, savoring the aromas of roasted coffee beans wafting over us, we felt content and relaxed. I believe we all realized that San Juan was a very nice place to be.

A waiter came to the table and obtained an order for eight coffees, with cakes and biscuits. He quickly returned with a wooden tray on which eight cups of steaming coffee, a small pitcher of rich cream, a small bowl of sugar, and eight silver spoons, were neatly arranged around a dish of delicate biscuits and cakes.

'Yu vill not find anyzing better in Paree,' observed Madame Cocteau, happily pouring cream into her coffee. 'Zis ees a very vonderful place. I could see myself leeving ere.' She looked at her husband, smiling. 'Vat do yu zeenk, Hugo?'

Mister Cocteau nodded and agreed, on the surface, San Juan seemed a civilized place. 'Zis café certainly gives one ze impression zis place ees civilized,' he said, picking up his cup of coffee and luxuriously inhaling the delicious aromas.

Marc-André smiled at Chantelle, as she bit into a cake, crumbs falling on her ample bosom. 'Zis ees juust ze right place for Chantelle, ees eet not, ma petite chou?' Marc-André chuckled as he looked lovingly at his fiancée dropping crumbs on her cleavage. He reminded us how much Chantelle liked to eat cake.

Judging from the way, Madame, Juliette, Clarissa, and Ben attacked the delicious pastries, they too were cake lovers. Eventually, we ordered another plate of delicious pastry creations.

As we sipped the dark beverage, our conversation turned to my children and how I was going to locate them, the city being quite large.

'Zee cheeldren cood be anyvere,' said Madame Cocteau sympathetically. 'Eet eez a beeg ceety, no? I zink it weel take quite a vile to find zem.'

I agreed, finding my children could pose a problem. I did not know where to start.

'Perhaps you can put an advertisement in the newspaper?' suggested Juliette.

'Eef your cheeldren are ere, zere muther mite reed ze paper,' added Chantelle.

I agreed that the suggestion was sound.

When our waiter returned, I asked him where the newspaper office was.

The man gave me directions to a building, not far from the café. We followed his directions, soon after finishing our coffees. I figured, the sooner the advertisement was placed, the sooner I would see my children, and Marianne too, of course.

Juliette, Clarissa, and I went to the newspaper office, while Monsieur and Madame Cocteau chose to go for a walk, to examine the beautiful Spanish built cathedral. Ben, Chantelle, and Marc-André remained at the café.

The newspaper office was not much different from that of the Morning Post. I guess the industry determined that the lobby requires a counter, at which people could stand to discuss their orders. Behind the counter, an office with six desks was occupied by busy scribblers, hard at work preparing the following day's material.

A pleasantly plump woman, with graying hair, came to the counter and asked what she could do for us.

I explained in the best Spanish I could, that I wanted to place an English worded advertisement, and that I wanted people to be able to bring information to the newspaper office, where I could retrieve it. I offered the lady some money and she readily agreed there would be no problem with our arrangement. The woman handed me a piece of paper, a quill, and a small pot of ink.

I thanked her and then proceeded to compose the message, I hoped would reach my family.

"Desperately seeking; Marianne Bartoldi and the children; Catherine, Joshua, and William Mann, and Michael Bartleby. Reward offered for information leading to their discovery. Please reply to, El Journal de Dia.

When I was done, I sprinkled the paper with powder, and rolled a blotter over it to dry the ink. Then I handed the advertisement to the woman and told her to run it for two weeks, starting the next day.

Job done, we walked to the harbour master's office, to pay our respects and settle our anchorage fees. I thought that perhaps he might have information concerning our ships, especially, the *New Venture*.

The office of the harbour master was busy with captains, mates, and other ship's officers paying their respects and settling their fees. When we stepped through the door, all the men's eyes immediately feasted on the two young women, who had accompanied me into the room. The men's admiration was a powerful testament to the women's beauty, and the fact, the men had been at sea for too long.

When my turn came at the counter, I explained to the clerk that I was the captain of the sloop, *Nancy*, and that we had come to San Juan in search of Marianne Bartoldi and my children. I also asked if he had any knowledge of a ship named, *New Venture*, which would have come into port in late February, or early March, 1792.

The clerk excused himself and returned, moments later, with a book; the registry for the previous year. He opened the book and turned to the pages, eventually locating the name, *New Venture*. It had come into port on March 11th and left again, three months later, no destination given.

He asked us how long we were planning to stay in port. I told him two weeks He assessed the fee. I don't remember exactly how much it was, but, whatever it was, I paid it and we left the office.

'Ze sheep left ze port,' said Clarissa, thoughtfully. 'Ze question eez, did Marianne an ze cheeldren go wiz zat sheep.'

'We will find out in two weeks, or less,' I said, pondering Clarissa's question and hoping it was not what she suggested. 'If Marianne is in town, she will hear about the advertisement. This place is not that big. It's not Paris.'

'It is not Paris,' agreed Juliette looking at the harbour where over a hundred ships lay at anchor. 'Paris has no harbour,' she chuckled.

Leaving the harbour master's office, we walked to a restaurant and sumptious meal. We sat at a table, looking out on the street, which kept me distracted the entire time. As I stared at the people in the street, I hoped to catch a glimpse of my children walking by. The girls happily chattered in French and giggled over observations they made about the local inhabitants, who walked by. Apparently fashions were somewhat out of date in San Juan.

As I sat there, absent mindedly eating my meal, I noticed our sailors walking past. They saw me looking out of the window and waved happily. Then, seeing the door, decided to come in and say hello, hoping I would buy them a drink.

When the five sailors were happily sitting at our table, enjoying the drinks I bought for them, they began to talk about their adventures in a local brothel.

The women, being French, perked up their ears upon hearing discussions of things, amorous, and giggled, as the uninhibited sailors recounted their experiences. In the process of the telling, one of them happened to mention that he was shown a girl, about seventeen or eighteen years old, who had a strong resemblance to me. He said that he couldn't accept the girl, because he felt like he would have been doing it with his captain; not something to his taste, he said. The sailors laughed uproariously, as they looked at me, knowing that I was a good sport.

Upon hearing of the girl in the brothel, I immediately cut through their laughter and demanded to know where the brothel was.

The sailor, I think it was Jacques, said he would lead me there, as soon as they finished their drinks; something they did forthwith, at my insistence, anxious to find the girl who fit the description of my precious daughter.

As we rushed to the place, a seedy, run down group of buildings in a narrow alley, not far from the docks, we came to, *Senora Madrid*, the brothel in question.

I ordered the three French sailors to guard the women, outside, while the two Swedes and I entered the place.

The moment I stepped through the door, an old crone stopped us and demanded money, before she would parade the girls. She squinted and regarded the two Swedes. Then she laughed; a loud cackle of a laugh, which grated on my ears. 'So, you two are back, already? Couldn't get enough, eh?' She cackled her croaky laugh. 'So typical of you men. You are so weak.' She held out her bony hand and demanded payment, once again.

I gave the woman a ducat.

The old crone was plastered with white powder and rouge; making her appear like something which should have been dead a long time ago, but was somehow re-animated with life energy. Unfortunately, it had not quite gotten to her head. She was a singularly unattractive example of the female human being; some uncharitable souls would have said, she was downright ugly. I found it difficult to look at her, being so blessed with beautiful faces to look at.

Immediately, after receiving the ducat, the old woman bit it, to see if the coin was gold. Satisfied it was, she clapped her veiny hands.

A moment later, seven women stepped into the room, dressed in undergarments. One of the women was wearing no upper garments, her ample breasts crowned by a pair of large, pink nipples, erect and hard, ready for action.

She smiled provocatively at me, hoping I would be her lunch and dinner that day. Or, even possibly, her living for the next few days.

None of the seven women was my daughter. I must have looked disappointed because the woman croaked, 'What's the matter? They are not good enough for the likes of you?'

I asked the woman about the girl who looked like me.

The old crone laughed, 'If I had a girl, who looked like you, I would be out of business!' She croaked louder, even making the Swedes chuckle, as they looked at me and nodded their heads.

I did not think it was funny and remained sober faced.

The old woman apologized and looked closely at me. She agreed that, indeed, 'Catherine looks somewhat like you.'

The moment she mentioned my daughter's name, I grabbed her roughly, and demanded to know where she was.

The old woman told me that she was with a client.

It was all that I needed to hear. I rushed through the curtain, separating the lobby from the back of the establishment, where a number of curtained cubicles contained the tools of the strumpet's trade; a bed and wash stand. As I rushed past each of the cubicles, I ripped open the curtain, to see if my sweet daughter was there.

I found her in the fifth, dirty cubicle, just readying herself, to receive an inebriated sailor with his breeches down.

The man only lived for a few seconds longer, as I mistakenly grabbed him with my left hand, forgetting my hook, which sliced through his neck, opening a jugular vein, instantly spurting blood against the wall, beside my shocked daughter; her sunken eyes filling with tears.

'Daddy!' she cried, as I tossed the bleeding sailor aside and rushed to my sweet daughter, sitting on the bed. 'Oh, daddy!' she repeated as she flung herself into my arms. 'Oh, daddy, daddy, we thought you were dead.'

Catherine's eyes were flowing tears, as my eye was also; our tears mingling, years of sorrow and suffering dripping on the bed and staining the sheets.

As we sat there, the two burly Swedes dragged the bleeding man out of the cubicle, leaving a trail of blood, on the floor, from there to the back door. The sailors disposed of the unfortunate victim in the back lane, where he would be found by his friends.

When Catherine had somewhat recovered, she dressed herself, embarrassed to be found naked by her father.

I assured her it was alright, there was nothing for her to be ashamed of. I told her that I loved her, no matter what, and that I was blessed to have found her again. Then, as she was getting into her clothes, through sobs, she explained what had happened.

Not long after their arrival in San Juan, Marianne was murdered by her new husband and the children sent out in the street, to fend for themselves. Catherine had to prostitute herself to provide a living for her siblings; living in a squalid room, not far from the brothel. Apparently, the murderer, Marcus Silvanus, took the treasure and the ships, and had gone off to pirate out of some other port, eventually returning to San Juan, very rich. Catherine explained that she only got to keep a very small part of the money she was paid for her services, the old crone taking most of it. 'I had no choice, daddy,' she cried. 'Please forgive me.'

I held Catherine for a long time, as she cried and cried.

As I held my daughter, and felt her pain, with each sob, I realized I had no choice but to kill the old bitch in the front lobby.

As Catherine collected herself, I told her to get dressed, while I took care of a little matter. Then I calmly walked to the lobby and shot the old bitch straight through her forehead, leaving her a crumpled mess, ready to go back to where she should have stayed in the first place.

Of course the girls, who were still standing about in the lobby, screamed as the sailors, to whom they were showing their wares, ran off to find a safer brothel.

I explained to the girls, when they had settled down, that I would be paying them the money the old woman had taken from them, and that they could now run the place as they saw fit, without that old tyrant sucking their life blood.

'She keeps the money in her room, in a chest under her bed,' volunteered one of the girls, showing me where to find the old lady's room.

My two Swedish friends neatly broke the door off its hinges for me, and then helped to locate the chest the girls had spoken of. The lock required a key, but I did not want to have to ransack the room to find it, so I simply shot the lock off the box with my other pistol.

I was happily surprised to find a considerable pile of coins and some exquisite gold chains in the box; which is all that I kept for my trouble. The Swedes, I gave each ten gold pieces, worth easily a year's wages, then, dispensed the rest amongst the girls of the brothel.

Box emptied, I collected Catherine and stepped into the street, where Juliette and the others were waiting.

I introduced Juliette as my fiancée.

At first, Catherine was taken aback, but very quickly embraced Juliette, congratulating her on winning my heart. The fact that Juliette was only about five years older than Catherine helped them to become friends very quickly. Catherine came to regard Juliette, and the two maids, Chantelle and Clarissa, as new older sisters.

Introductions done, we ran off to find my sons, who were waiting for their big sister in a horribly decrepit tenement, which should have been torn down ages ago. I guessed it had been there from early in the colonial days of the city.

The stairs creaked menacingly as Catherine and I climbed two flights to the third floor. I noticed some boards were missing from the wainscoting, as we walked down the hall to her room, number 307. When Catherine opened the door, several cockroaches scurried into a crack in the floor.

'Catherine!' shouted Joshua, William, and little Christopher in unison, as they beheld their big sister standing in the door way. The moment they saw me they halted, somewhat fearful to see a tall man, with a patch on his eye and a hook for a left hand.

It didn't take Joshua long to put two and two together. He recognized me and immediately yelled, 'Father!' as he flung himself into my arms. 'Oh, Father, we thought you were dead,' he cried.

Christopher also came over to me and gave me a hug, a happy expression on his face.

William, who was but a toddler when I left, looked on, bewildered.

Catherine explained to the little man that I was his father, but William had no reason to react. He didn't know me. However, as time progressed, he came to be a very affectionate son.

It dawned on me to ask about Marianne's son, Michael.

Catherine explained that Marcus had taken Michael with him.

Marcus had left my three children; in abject poverty, to die, for all he cared. I foresaw the man's demise at my hand, in the mists of his future. Leaving my sweet daughter to prostitute herself to support her younger siblings, was inexcusable. I could not think of any other form of justice, than that he be killed, the sooner the better.

I assured my children everything would be well for them, from then on. I took them from that horrible place, bringing them back to the sloop, where Monsieur and Madame helped Gaston and Madame Gautier prepare a sumptuous meal for my dear children, overjoyed to be eating a decent meal, once again.

Our five sailors stayed in San Juan and continued to spend their money, happily enjoying the life of jack tars on shore leave. I wasn't certain if we could expect to find them again, if we decided to return to the island. However, there were plenty of sailors in San Juan, if ours were gone, there would be others. Such was the life of seamen. Fortunately, however, the two Swedes decided to stay in our employ and returned some days later.

That night, my children slept comfortably in soft beds, Juliette and I made for them, with piles of blankets for a mattress. We bought the blankets from a native woman, who sold them out of her canoe, with which she visited all the ships, one by one, until all of the blankets were gone. It was a mixed blessing for her when we bought all of the blankets, leaving her with nothing to do for the rest of the day. For my children, it was worth it.

Over the following days, Catherine filled me in on Marcus Silvanus; what he looked like, where he might have gone, who some of the men were that had gone with him, anything she could remember, which might help me to locate the culprit. As it turned out, Catherine's memory was prodigious. She was able to furnish me with lots of details, which I later transcribed into my note book, for future reference. The one thing she did not know, was that Silvanus was nearby.

Next morning, over breakfast, we began discussing our return to the island. Monsieur Cocteau suggested we purchase a ship load of, bricks, roof tiles, timber, and everything else necessary to build proper houses, plus men to build them. He and his wife had apparently been discussing a more permanent, and comfortable situation on the island. They figured that suitable brick and stone houses would be weather proof, and provide cool, safe lodgings of a more permanent nature; less subject to collapse, as our houses had done.

I explained that, if we hired a ship to bring building materials, we would risk revealing to other people, the location of our secret isle. The only option would be to recruit people, who wanted to get away from San Juan and live the life of rovers. I explained that, the only way people would be attracted to our island was if they were allowed to gather swag. Without swag, there would be no attraction to coming to our island, because there was no gainful industry. No ships docked there. It was alone, amongst other small, uninhabited islands; the only island with people living the good life of peace and calm, the only industry being their own. We didn't know many rich people who could buy such a life.

As we spoke of these things, I thought back to the days, when we helped Bill round up the members of his crew, after escaping from Halifax. Bill had crew members he could round up. Mine were all gone.

I believed that I had to begin from scratch, to round up a crew. Likely crew members would not all be in San Juan, and to get back to our former glory, we needed a much larger ship to transport them in. The logistics were significant, however, like they say, where there is a will, there is a way. When you throw a little bit of luck into the equation, generally the way out will eventually show itself.

Chapter Twenty-Eight

Some days later, we were having dinner in a restaurant near the cathedral. We chose that particular restaurant because it was a sufficient distance from the docks. I figured, for my daughter's sake, eating in a public restaurant would be more comfortable if we chose one, some distance from the docks. I did not want to risk the presence of sailors, who might have recognized Catherine from the brothel. Having killed two people in San Juan, was enough. I did not want to risk having to shoot some sailor, because he happened to have been with my daughter.

Catherine preferred to put the past far behind her and get on with life; a good attitude, in my opinion. She did the best she could, under the circumstances. I did not want any more reminders of her sordid time in San Juan, thrust in her, or my face. It was another reason I was beginning to get anxious to leave the city and sail to another place.

While we were thus seated for dinner, and enjoying a pleasant conversation about modifications to the island, I noticed that Catherine kept staring at a man, who was having dinner with a woman, at a table nearby. When I asked her what her interest in the man was all about, she told me that the man looked familiar, since he was a close friend of Marcus Silvanus.

'When we first came here, we lived in a building with six apartments,' she said. 'We lived in an apartment across the hall from him. Marcus and he used to play cards together, quite a lot. Marcus never spent much time with Marianne.' Catherine frowned, 'He didn't love her. He only pretended to love her, so he could get the ship, and your money. He murdered her. I know he did it. I am willing to bet that man probably helped him do it.' Catherine's eyes filled with tears. 'They found her body floating in the harbour. They had cut her throat.' Catherine had to pause, because she was beginning to cry. 'I think Senior Carambas knows a lot more about all of this.' Catherine pointed discreetly. 'That's him, with the mustaches.'

I turned my head, ever so gently, and glanced at the man who would have to be questioned, before the night was done.

Fortunately, Carambas had not seen Catherine. In order to ensure things remained that way, I had her change seats with me, enabling me to study the man, as we ate our dinner.

While I was about to take a bite of food, I noticed Carambas was getting up. Obviously he was excusing himself to go to the lavatory. Moments later, I excused myself and walked nonchalantly to the lavatory, where I found Senior Carambas standing at the urinal trough.

There was no one else in the room.

'I understand you are a friend of Marcus Silvanus,' I said from behind his back.

'That depends on who wants to know,' replied Carambas.

I told him that I was an old friend, recently arrived, and wanted to see him. I told Carambas I had his friend's money.

Carambas finished his business and looked at me insolently. 'I haven't seen Silvanus, for months,' he replied.

I asked him where he thought Silvanus might be found.

Carambas eyed me steadily and asked how much money was involved.

I told him twenty thousand Spanish doubloons.

That piqued his interest.

Carambas stroked his left mustache and in an oily voice assured me he would gladly give the money to Silvanus for me.

I asked Carambas what kind of fool he took me for. I told him, if he took me to Silvanus, I would give him ten percent of the money.

The thought of making a quick two thousand doubloons interested Carambas immensely. His mustaches quivered and his eyes darted, as he rubbed his sanguine hands together. 'Two thousand doubloons, you say?'

Carambas eyed me from the corners of his eyes. 'How do I know I can trust you?' he asked.

I handed Carambas three gold doubloons. 'There are one thousand nine hundred and ninety seven more, if you want them. All you have to do is take me to Silvanus.'

Carambas took the coins and examined them. Satisfied they were *gold* doubloons, he glared at me with a greedy countenance. 'You say you will pay me another nineteen hundred, plus?'

I nodded.

Carambas felt the coins in his hand, as he thought about whether he could trust me, or not. His avarice got the better of his caution. He agreed to take me to Silvanus.

I asked him if that would be in San Juan, and he assured me that Silvanus was not only in San Juan, he owned a massive house just on the outskirts, on a marvelous piece of land overlooking a natural harbour.

'Is that why I didn't see his ship, the *New Venture*, in San Juan?' I asked.

'Yes, that is right. Silvanus has his own small harbour where he keeps three ships.' Carambas thought for a moment and then told me the names of the other two ships. 'I believe the other two were called, the *Nina*, and, the *Pinta*, after the ships of Columbus.'

Carambas further told me that Silvanus had bought the house, with treasure he had stolen from some dead pirate, by the name of, Peter Mann. 'Of course we had to kill the pirate's wife to get the money, but we did it. He shared some of that money with me and set me up. That's why I can afford to eat in this place,' he enthused.

I congratulated him on his luck, then I asked him, in a man to man sort of way, how they killed the wife of the pirate.

'Slit her throat,' he said, trusting me completely now, and seeing me as a fellow conspirator, since I had money for his friend and benefactor. It being a sizable sum, indicated to Carambas, that I had to be some fairly significant friend of Silvanus. 'Yeah, we slit her throat, and then dumped her in the harbour. She was found some time later.' Carambas shook his head. 'A real mess she was. Sharks been feeding on her.' He paused for a moment and then asked me if I had ever seen a body that's been eaten by sharks.

I told him I was not interested in hearing his description, having to leave the lavatory in short order, lest I threw up and then killed Carambas, right there, in the lavatory, and stuffed his head down a toilet. In as polite, and controlled a fashion as I could muster, I told him to meet me in front of the harbour master's office, at ten o'clock in the morning. He could take me to Silvanus, then.

Carambas agreed and I stepped out of the room, returning to my table, seething and fingering the handle of the pistol, under my left arm. Unfortunately, my little talk with Senior Carambas completely spoiled my appetite, leaving me unable to finish my dinner. It didn't go to waste, my sons gladly finishing it for me, after they were done with their plates. I felt better, as I watched my beautiful sons eating with good appetites. They would grow up to be good, strong boys, I reckoned.

After dinner we quickly left the restaurant and walked back to the docks. I needed to clear my head; so many things were roaring around in there. My little visit with Senior Carambas had quite upset me. Hearing him talk so callously of that dear woman, with whom I shared so many beautiful days, caused me tremendous grief. However, I tried my best to keep it to myself. My companions did not need to hear the details revealed by that villain. The details were so revolting that I was determined to bring the Lord's vengeance to bear on Carambas and Silvanus, before another day slipped past.

Back on board the sloop, after the children had gone to sleep, Juliette helped me to prepare a chest of lead ballast, over which we placed about three thousand doubloons, making it appear to be a chest full of the shiny Spanish coins. She also helped to clean one of my pistols, while I cleaned the other, in preparation for their work the following day.

Of course, I explained to Juliette's parents, and the other members of our company, what I was about to do. I told them there was nothing to be concerned about, since I was an old hand at doing the Lord's work. However, in spite of my many assurances, most of them expressed concern for me, and tried to actually change my mind, Chantelle remarking that I could easily be the one getting killed. However, since they knew Catherine's story, they understood Carambas and Silvanus had it coming.

Just to reassure everyone, I took Jacques and the two Swedes with me, all of us well armed with hidden weapons; dirks in our boots, pistols under our arms and dressed as gentlemen. However, just to be extra sure of success, we hid five loaded pistols under the lead ballast, raising the level of the contents, and making the treasure appear even more abundant. When we were ready, we hailed a boat to take us ashore with the treasure box.

We met Senior Carambas in front of the harbour master's house, where he was waiting for us, a coach hired to take us to the mansion.

En route, Carambas had to be reassured there was gold in the box.

When I lifted the lid, and let him have a look at the beautiful coins, glinting on top of the lead ballast, he was very impressed, indeed. Seeing what appeared to be a box full of gold doubloons satisfied Carambas immensely; a big grin on his face.

The road to the mansion climbed up a hill, lined with beautiful trees. The air was filled with the sound of exotic birds, twittering and peeping; a marvelous orchestra of avian musicians accompanying us on the Lord's mission. Eventually, the road made its way to a massive wrought iron gate set in a high stone wall surrounding a very large area; the grounds of the Silvanus mansion, purchased from the proceeds of Marianne's treasure. Trees had been cleared back for about five hundred yards of the wall, enabling the observers a clear view of anyone attempting to attack the compound. Silvanus had essentially built himself a castle on a promontory overlooking a small natural harbour.

As we pulled up to the gate, I could see several men, whom I thought I recognized from the island, standing guard; muskets loaded and ready for action. I noticed the wall at each corner sported towers of five stories height. I could see men watching us intently from there, as well. Obviously Marcus Silvanus felt insecure.

A tall, sinister looking fellow, wearing a long leather coat and a weathered tricorner, approached the carriage and demanded our business.

Carambas recognized the fellow and addressed him by his familiar name, telling the man that we had come, 'To pay our respects to his excellency.'

When I heard Carambas say the word, 'Excellency,' I nearly choked on some spittle.

He continued to tell the man, we had come to bring a box of treasure owed to Silvanus.

'Show me,' demanded the man, suspiciously eyeing me.

I opened the box and the man looked, his eyes bulging at the sight of the beautiful golden disks.

The man was about to reach into the box. I slammed the lid shut before he could do so, maintaining my poise and command of the situation.

'These coins are for Marcus Silvanus, not the likes of you,' I said haughtily. 'Now, I suggest you let us pass, or I will tell him you were insolent to his best friend.'

I glared at the man.

The man backed off, hesitant and suddenly insecure. Then he made a quick gesture to the men handling the gate.

The men immediately opened the massive wrought iron contraption, enabling us to pass.

We had to pass several more guards, as we drove along the winding road leading to the massive house, overlooking a beautiful, natural harbour in which my three ships were anchored, colorful pennants flying from the masts. I noticed the *Pinta* had received a new coat of paint, the ship's sideboards painted a deep red, and the railings painted yellow. It was an altogether different look, and very appealing. I was already beginning to look forward to sailing her again.

Arriving at the front doors of the four story house, I admired its beauty, and thought it an appropriate place for me to live, when I was in San Juan. The house was built in the neo classic style, with a beautiful Greek porch, sporting eight Ionic columns.

The doors were approached by a flight of twelve steps.

As we stepped from the coach, two men dressed in impeccable silks and brocades came through the open front doors. They stood at the top of the stairs, watching us unload the heavy box, which the two Swedes carried between them, as they followed, Jacques and I. Upon reaching the landing, one of the men asked us who we were, and what our business was.

'I am an old friend of Marcus Silvanus,' I said calmly. 'I have come to surprise him with the repayment of a loan.'

'What is your name?' demanded the man.

Glaring at the man, I told him that I wanted to surprise Silvanus. 'We are old friends,' I repeated. 'There are over twenty thousand gold doubloons in that box,' I said, pointing to the chest.

'Show me,' demanded the man, insolently.

Pedersen opened the box, enabling the man to see the gleaming coins.

Satisfied we were telling the truth, the man told us we would have to be frisked for weapons.

I told the man it was not necessary to frisk us, handing him one of the pistols from under my arms. I told my companions to do the same, as they also gave up a pistol, not admitting to having others.

The man, seeing that we were very expensively dressed gentlemen, obviously accepted that men, such as ourselves, probably only carried one pistol, for protection from highwaymen and the like. We did not appear to be an armed band of cutthroats, my hook, torn ear, and scar not withstanding.

Satisfied that we were disarmed, the men led us inside the magnificent lobby of the mansion; a room I saw myself welcoming my guests in; the gentry of San Juan, in the near future.

We were told to stay in the lobby, one of the men remaining with us, while the other climbed up the magnificently curved staircase with Carambas, to inform their master we were waiting for him, below.

The moment the first man had disappeared up the stairs, we sprang into action.

Jacques cupped his right hand over the second man's mouth, as he neatly snapped the man's neck, then quickly dragged him into another room, stuffing him behind a couch.

The rest of us quickly retrieved the loaded pistols from the chest and quietly rushed upstairs to locate Marianne's murderers.

At the top of the landing, I signaled for us to split up in twos, Jacques accompanying me into the left wing and the two Swedes, heading in the other direction.

As Jacques and I moved along the corridor, we heard voices coming from a room, at the end of the hall, the door being open. Coming closer, I could hear Carambas explaining to his boss that there were twenty thousand doubloons waiting for him downstairs.

'Nobody owes me twenty thousand doubloons,' said a voice, which I surmised, was that of Silvanus.

I signaled Jacques, to quickly fetch the Swedes, as I stepped into an adjoining room, keeping the door open a little bit, in order to continue listening to the conversation from the other room.

'But, I saw them, myself,' I heard Carambas say. 'There is a box full of doubloons downstairs.'

'Yeah boss, there's a heavy box downstairs,' said the other man.

As I was thus listening to the conversation, Jacques returned with the Swedes.

I signaled them to be ready, whispering, in the event the murderers reached for their weapons, to shoot everyone in the room, but not Silvanus. I had other plans for him.

When we were ready, I gave a signal. We rushed into the room, surprising five men, each of them reaching for a pistol, which they never managed to shoot, one of them receiving a ball in the shoulder, from one of Jacque's pistols, the others, including Carambas, receiving a smack in the head, with the handle of a pistol, knocking them unconscious.

Silvanus tried desperately to grab a pistol from the drawer of the desk he was sitting behind, however, he never had a chance to shoot it, Pedersen managing to shoot the pistol from his hand.

'What is the meaning of this outrage?!' demanded Silvanus, the veins in his neck bulging

Before answering, I told Jacques to close the doors and to be vigilant, because others would be coming shortly, having heard the shots. To prevent unwanted entry into the office, we took the precaution of propping chairs against the doors.

Satisfied that we were securely barricaded in the room, I faced Marianne's murderer and introduced myself.

The moment Silvanus heard my name, his visage lost all color and he began to tremble.

'I understand that you killed my wife and stole our treasure,' I said calmly.

'It's a lie! I did no such thing,' he said defiantly.

'You forced my daughter into harlotry,' I hissed, wanting to smash his face in.

'Your daughter?' spat Silvanus, 'A spoiled brat of a child. It probably taught her some humility.'

'Where is Michael?' I asked, remarkably calm.

'Michael?' Silvanus looked at me. A cold, icy stare came into his eyes; a smirk formed on his lips. 'Don't you know? I let him follow his mother. I guess we weighted his body more appropriately.'

Restraining my self no longer, I smacked Silvanus across the head with the handle of my pistol, knocking him out of his chair. I was about to shoot the villain when noises outside the room heralded the arrival of guards coming to investigate the shooting.

I signaled Olaf to grab Silvanus and put him back in his chair. Then we propped the others up, as if they were sitting normally.

A loud knock on the door signaled that the guards were outside, expecting to be let in by their boss, and informed about the gun shots.

We removed the chairs from the doors, quietly, not letting the guards know something was amiss within. Then Olaf and Pedersen stood to the side of the doors. I stood beside Silvanus, my pistol to his head, and Jacques stood by the windows, two loaded pistols ready. When we were standing firmly in place, I told Silvanus to tell the men to come in.

The doors opened and three guards rushed into the room, instantly freezing in their tracks, the moment they saw me with a pistol pointed at their leader's head.

'Drop your weapons,' I demanded.

The three guards did as they were told and then, looking around the room, they noticed there were unconscious men, sitting in the ornate, Louis XIV chairs. The observation intensely added to their fear.

When the men were sufficiently filled with appropriate fear of the Lord, I informed them of their master's crimes. When I got to the part where Catherine became a prostitute, in order to support her two brothers, the guards, obviously being family men themselves, were suddenly moved to deny Silvanus and swear allegiance to me. Fear for their lives obviously had something to do with their sudden shift of allegiance, as well.

A groan from Carambas signaled that he was recovering from the bump on his head. Moments later, he looked about with bleary eyes, wondering what had hit him.

Of the other three men, only two recovered from the blows to their head. Alas, Olaf had put a bit too much Viking power behind his blow and had caved the third man's head in.

'I am reclaiming what is rightfully mine,' I said to the men. 'Silvanus and Carambas murdered my wife and threw her body to the sharks. They forced my daughter into harlotry!' I glared at each of the men assembled in the room, as I collected my self, so as to remain calm and dispassionate. 'According to our rules, Carambas and Marcus Silvanus deserve to die for their crimes. Execution will commence within the half hour, in the front yard.'

Then I told the murderer's minions to round up their colleagues and assemble in front of the house. Failure to do so would result in that person being rounded up and shot, as well, I told them firmly. Then, to put a little extra fear into them, I told the men, a gang of sixty pirates were on their way, along the road, and that another hundred would be arriving on the first wind, with a heavy brig capable of destroying every ship in the harbour. Of course I did not know, at that time, that there were twenty heavy guns pointing at the harbour, from the prominence behind the house, a formidable defense.

We let two of the guards rush off, to tell their colleagues, to lay down their weapons and to gather in the court yard in front of the mansion.

Meanwhile, pointing our pistols at the men, we ushered them out of the room, using the guards to transport the dead man, admonishing them to be careful not to let the corpse bleed on the carpets.

The guards accepted my handkerchief to place over the wound, and then lifted the dead man. They carried him in front of me, as I followed behind, a pistol in my hand.

Arriving on the porch, I had the guards lay the dead man on the third step and then ordered them to go with Jacques, to fetch the other dead guard and lay him on another step. Presently two dead men lay on the steps at my feet.

Meanwhile, men were beginning to gather in the courtyard.

I commanded Silvanus to tell his men to put their weapons down, which they did, reluctantly.

When all the men were gathered in the courtyard, I counted 27, not a large number. Silvanus thought himself safe and protected in his fort; there not being any other pirates in the area, to challenge him, anyway. Silvanus thought that twenty seven was all he needed. Even if he had two hundred, it wouldn't have mattered. We had Silvanus.

My men, assisted by the three guards, rounded up the weapons and set them in a pile, far to the side.

I commanded the pirates to sit on the ground. When everyone was seated, I ordered that a chair be brought out for me; it was brought forthwith and set down, facing the courtyard. Carambas and Silvanus, were made to sit on the steps, below the bodies of the dead guards. Three of my men stood beside my chair, the two Swedes on the left and Jacques on my right.

When all was ready, I addressed the men seated on the ground before me.

'I have come to take back what is rightfully mine,' I said firmly. 'These men,' I pointed to the culprits, 'murdered my wife and stepson, and stole my treasure.'

'How do ye know this?' shouted one of the men seated on the ground.

'By his own words. Senior Carambas, admitted to the crime. I also have the word of my daughter, whom that villain caused to be thrown into harlotry, in order to save her three young siblings,' I replied firmly.

'Ye can't believe everything children tell ye!' shouted another man from the crowd.

'My daughter's word is enough for me!' I shouted back.

'She's a girl!' shouted another man, a small, ugly little fellow, with a fat belly, and thin, stringy hair. 'Ye can't trust the words of girls, they're all witches, as far as I'm concerned!'

'Si, si!!' shouted several others.

'You men are mistaken!' I shouted back. 'My associates, gathered here with me, heard Silvanus say that she deserved it,' I continued. 'These villains,' I gestured towards Carambas and Silvanus, 'slit my wife's delicate throat and threw her precious body into the harbour. Sharks ate of her flesh!' My eye began to water, and my voice started to break. 'These villains impoverished my children and stole their inheritance!' I had to pause for a moment, to collect myself, as visions of my poor daughter, in that cubicle with the sailor, flooded into my brain. It was all I could do to keep myself from shooting Carambas and Silvanus right there, as they sat at my feet. Fortunately, I was able to restrain myself and continued. 'Hence, in light of what I have told you, I pronounce that these men, Senior Carambas and Marcus Silvanus have broken the code we live by. They deserve death. Sentence to be carried out, forthwith.'

I looked down at Carambas and Silvanus. 'Do you have anything to say for yourselves?'

'These men are lying!' shouted Silvanus. 'Don't believe them!'

Carambas and Silvanus shouted the same thing over again, but the men knew what the truth was, and what the code was. Indeed, some of them had been on our island, and well understood the justice of my sentence. Hence, no one resisted us further and we were able to carry out the sentences with no more provocation. I had made note of the girl hater and was contemplating, including him in the proceedings, as well. Men, such as he, can be quite dangerous to girls and women.

Carambas and Silvanus were quickly dragged, struggling and protesting, down the steps and made to kneel on the ground. Then, calmly taking a loaded pistol from Jacques, which I stuffed in my belt, and an other from Olaf, I descended the stairs, calmly and collectedly.

The two kneeling men looked up at me and began to plead for their lives.

'Forgive me,' cried Silvanus.

'Oy madre de dios,' prayed Carambas.

'I will make it up to you,' blubbered Silvanus.

'Please, senior....,' were the last words, Carambas spoke, as I placed a ball directly into the top of his skull, blowing his brains out of the bottom.

The senior's remains crumpled to the ground.

'I have decided I will have you tortured, first, Silvanus,' I said. 'To extract revenge for Marianne and Michael and for my daughter. For all the time my sweet daughter had to prostitute herself. Each day she was dying inside, because of you.'

I began to hyperventilate and had to stop, for a moment, to collect myself.' Tears were flowing, as I continued, 'Now, I want you to feel like you are dying, slowly. Everything I will have done to you, you richly deserve.'

I looked at the assembled members of the villain's gang and pointed at them with my hook. I told them what I expected of them, if they wanted to escape from the Lord's vengeance. 'Each of you men will express your loyalty to me, by taking an active part in the torture and execution of your former leader!'

'Torture?!' Silvanus began to tremble. 'Please don't,' he pleaded. 'Can't you just shoot me, and get it over with? I beg of you, please have mercy on me.'

'Like the mercy you showed my wife and children?' I asked. I shook my head and ordered that Silvanus be tied to the big tree, in the centre of the courtyard, where, judging from the holes in the trunk, lead balls of a firing squad had plunged into the bark. The tree had been used before, to execute someone.

Olaf ripped the murderer's shirt off, before he and Pedersen firmly tied Silvanus to the tree, his arms wrapped around the trunk and his legs spread apart.

I ordered that his breeches be pulled down, as well, exposing more flesh.

With Silvanus thus firmly fixed, naked to the tree, I demanded that a cat be made from an unwound rope, the crude instrument to be made with plenty of knots. When the cat was ready, I ordered that every man give Silvanus three strokes with the instrument; any man sparing in his administration of the whip, to receive a flogging, as well.

Hence, every man put his back into the strokes, rendering Silvanus an unconscious, bleeding mess.

By mid afternoon, we had grown hungry and thirsty, so we all took a break and enjoyed a fine lunch, prepared by the cook and her helpers. We had to admit, Silvanus hired a superb cook and stocked an excellent larder. The good food improved my mood considerably.

After lunch, and several glasses of fine wine, I resumed my work with Silvanus, having him revived with buckets of cold sea water.

Silvanus moaned and asked for forgiveness, but my heart was hardened. I had to carry on the punishment, not only for the sake of wreaking the Lord's vengeance on Silvanus, but I also had to instill a healthy fear into his followers.

The next step was to have Sylvanus turned around, with his back to the tree. He was again tied firmly and not blindfolded. I told everyone to pick some non lethal spot on Silvanus and to place a pistol ball there, at twenty paces, firmly admonishing the men to avoid placing a ball into his head or anywhere near vital organs, at the risk of being killed, also.

Hence, the men dutifully did as I commanded.

Each time a ball shattered a bone, Silvanus screamed, indicating he was still alive and enjoying our justice.

Within an hour, the murderer's limbs were completely shattered by the balls we shot at him. The pain had sent the culprit into the depths of unconsciousness, from which we dragged him, with several more buckets of cold water, an hour later.

Silvanus moaned softly as I approached him, ready to finish him off; thinking he had suffered enough. He looked up at me, trembling with pain, his eyes bulging.

'Shoot me!' he said pleadingly. 'Please, shoot me,' he asked. 'Please, please don't leave me like this.'

'The Lord's vengeance has come to visit you, Silvanus,' I said, as I pulled the trigger; placing a ball through his head, and sending his soul to hell.

It was a sobering moment, watching the body of my enemy slump into a large puddle of blood at the base of the tree.

The ordeal over, I whispered to Olaf, to single out the misogynist; (who we drowned, sometime later, thinking him to be a potential menace to San Juan). I ordered the men to swear allegiance to me, which they all did, forthwith, afraid for their lives. I dismissed them and told them to go back to San Juan, and tell others, that I, Peter Mann, was the new master of the house.

The men's silence was deafening.

I further told them, that if they and their friends were looking for employment as sailors, I would be pleased to consider them. When my speech was finished, the men left the compound, leaving their weapons behind.

The next order of business was to fetch everyone from the sloop.

Olaf and Pedersen rode off with the coach, returning with my astonished friends and family, three hours later.

In the meantime, we set about removing all signs of blood and struggle in the house, however, we left Silvanus and Carambas lying by the tree, just so Catherine could see that her tormentors, and Marianne's murderers, were brought to justice.

The sight shocked and disgusted Catherine, but she was satisfied, the men deserved what they got, not fully comprehending what exactly Silvanus had gotten.

The bodies were removed shortly after Catherine's arrival, they being unceremoniously dumped into the little harbour, where the fishes would take care of them in short order; leaving the bones to settle into the sand and become part of the marine environment.

Thus, it came about that we moved into the large house and settled in San Juan, essentially putting all thought of our island aside, for some time to come.

Juliette and I took over the master's bedroom, after thoroughly cleaning the room of any vestige pertaining to the former occupant. The Cocteaus moved into rooms in the opposite wing. The rest of our staff found delightful rooms for themselves, many with views of the ocean.

Some days later, we sailed our sloop into our harbour, bringing the total of our fleet to four, a goodly number for all manner of marine enterprises, which we undertook, not long after retrieving my treasure from Virgineola, a voyage we undertook two weeks later, returning within the following month.

With lots of capital to invest, Monsieur Cocteau and I developed a trading system, utilizing the four ships, with hired crews, to buy and sell goods around the Caribbean, as far north as Florida.

Eventually, within the space of five years, we had developed an enterprise, which saw us with fifteen ships, and one hundred seventy five thousand pounds sterling, in profits, per year. The profits we realized was a sizable sum for those days, making us pillars of the San Juan community, and important members of the traders' guild, a far cry from my pirating days, about which no one had the slightest idea, except for my close friends and family. However, that was all to change in the seventh year, when catastrophe befell us, not long after my 50th birthday, a story I shall relate to you, dear reader, in the following chapter.

Chapter Twenty-Nine

Our company, Cocteau & Mann, became a major enterprise in the Caribbean. Eventually, we were able to send out four convoys of vessels, one of five ships, two of four ships, and one of three ships, which we armed, over time, with; swivel guns, eight, ten, twelve, and twenty pound deck guns, plus hand weapons; boarding axes, cutlasses, muskets, and pikes, for the sailors to protect themselves, in the event of an attack by pirates. Now that we had become a legitimate company of traders, members of the sweet trade began to cast covetous eyes on our ventures. We made certain to protect our goods and men; training every sailor in offensive and defensive combat. Having been a pirate, I knew how to protect myself from pirates, so I thought.

In order to man our ships, we employed a total of three hundred sailors and stevedores, plus another seventy people were employed by the five trading offices we had established; San Juan, of course, Havana, Maracaibo, to handle the exotic wood trade, Port Royal, and the fifth at, Santo Domingo. We had memberships in every trade guild where we established offices. Excellent managers oversaw buying and selling, some even taking initiatives, with regard to expanding the company's portfolio, by purchasing production facilities in their towns, when they came up for sale and a profit was possible.

The enterprising manager of our facilities in Maracaibo, for example, managed to purchase a lumber mill, which over time, produced a healthy profit for that office. Of course, the manager and his staff received a healthy bonus, the year the mill turned its first profit for Cocteau & Mann.

Our manager in Havana bought a cigar factory, which produced the finest hand rolled cigars, which came packaged in beautiful wooden boxes bearing the trading mark of Cocteau & Mann. Indeed, C & M cigars became highly prized in Europe, as more of our product was shipped there, by others, as well.

Cocteau & Mann traded in everything from cochineal to tubers, no load was unsuitable for us, with the exception of slaves and manure. However, eventually, manure also became a commodity in which we traded, there being plenty of manure to be disposed of.

As for slaves, we rather set them free than trade them. Eventually, it became the policy of the company to purchase three slaves, every year, at each of our trading offices, and then set them free, so they could become employees, with a decent wage. The company was well served by our African workers, as a result.

Garbage became another item we hauled out to sea with barges, from each of the places we had a trading office. The idea to haul the garbage far out to sea, was an idea one of our managers in Santo Domingo tried out. In time, the venture became, indeed, a very profitable one, as we obtained contracts from the other towns. A few years later, hauling garbage brought the company over a hundred thousand pounds stirling profit, per annum. There was a lot of money in garbage.

My favorite trade items were fine rums, wines, and cigars, plus books, of course. The library in the mansion had grown to house a thousand volumes, in many languages, mostly English. It was one of my favorite rooms in the big house. It was where I had a desk and worked on my book.

Family life with Juliette was a blessing in my middle age. She was a sweet, gentle girl, whose laugh always filled the house and brought sunshine to my heart. Eventually, we had children together; a boy and a girl, whom we named, Hugo and Nicole, after Juliette's parents; the boy arriving August 5th, 1794, and Nicole arriving on April 16th, 1796.

My other children were growing healthy and strong, Catherine and Joshua already taking a keen interest in the family business; indeed

Catherine managed the San Juan office, and Joshua oversaw the stevedores. William and Christopher were still little boys, who we let content themselves with play on the spacious grounds of our home.

In 1795, June the first to be exact, Juliette and I hired a tutor for the children, requiring them to spend three hours every day learning, arithmetic, astronomy, geography, history, logic, natural history, reading, and writing. For their musical education we exposed our children to the many musicians, who comprised our ships' companies; many of them spending their days at the mansion, during time in port. We had a second house built, to accommodate the many guests, who enjoyed our generous hospitality; they being the members of our staff and their families.

The ships' artists taught my boys many of the necessary skills required of sea faring men, making able sailors of them; each of them acquiring the talents so desired in captains for our ships.

As our company grew, we began to purchase housing for our staff members, in the various places we had established our trading offices. Our purchase of the housing enabled us to provide affordable rents to our employees, which greatly assisted them to get ahead, and make happier lives for their families.

With hundreds of very loyal and happy employees, our company grew by leaps and bounds every year. On my 50th birthday, Cocteau & Mann announced a profit exceeding three hundred and seventy five thousand pounds sterling! The announcement was greeted with a great cheer from all our staff members, whom we had brought from all the trading offices, our entire fleet of twenty five ships anchored in our harbour.

Every member of our staff received a healthy bonus that day, a share of the profits we made together, following the traditions of the sweet trade, when we shared out swag to each according to his station. The total sharing out amounted to just over half of the total profits that year; one hundred and ninety two thousand pounds, doubling everyone's wages. Seeing all those smiling faces gave me a warm feeling all over. Juliette remarked I was literally glowing, as was her father.

I just attributed it to the copious toasts we drank throughout the night, and the next ten days, as we also celebrated the new century.

Eighteen hundred is the year when things took on a bit of a different color, when several catastrophes accrued, one after another, making that year the single most unlucky year of my life. By the time my 51st birthday came, a year later, I had aged ten years and my business partner was dead. If you bear with me, dear reader, I will fill you in on the details.

January 15th, 1800, Cocteau & Mann resumed services out of our San Juan office. Our fleets took the employees of the other offices back to their respective trade centers, so that, by the end of January, we were up to full operating levels, once again; moving precious woods from Brazil, tobacco from Cuba, coffee and sugar from Columbia, and so on. We shipped everything that was available, advising our captains to always be on the lookout for deals on every commodity traded, in every place we went, fully expecting every convoy to bring us profits, by buying cheap and selling high; such things as; bricks, stone, tiles, nails and lumber, salted fish, pickled turtles, fresh produce, seeds, farm animals, you name it, we hauled it; except, as I said before, we did not haul manure, until some time later.

Cocteau & Mann opened its first bank in San Juan on February 3rd, 1800. Since we had so much gold and silver coinage, we realized that the lending of specie would generate a healthy profit, as well, by charging five percent on the principal and not participating in the usurious practices of the banker down the street. Eventually, we took a good part of his business away, our loans being more reasonable; people only being charged from five to ten percent on the principal, depending on the type of loan and the risk involved.

Our first tragedy struck on April 18th, two days after Nicole's fourth birthday, when a rope snapped.

A crew, under the supervision of my son, Joshua, lost control of a heavy load of cotton bales, when a sudden gust of wind caused the rope to break, sending several tons of cotton, falling from thirty feet, on top of Joshua and three crew members, killing all but one, a man named Marvin McLaren, who lost a leg.

The loss of my son was a great sadness for me, because he was deeply loved and showed so much promise. His gentle spirit, and quick, alert mind, helped him guide himself in such a way, that he learned fast, and took rapid control of situations. All the men who worked under him, considered Joshua a born leader of men; a friend whom they admired and looked up to.

Thinking back, I clearly see when he was born, images of him growing up as a baby, a toddler, a youth, and his becoming a young man. My first son; lost to a cruel accident. It was not how I foresaw his future. His death was a terrible blow.

Joshua's death hit Catherine the hardest, I think; she having spent so much time with her younger brother. The two were inseparable friends, always together, involved in one thing or another; whether it was play as children, or involved with their hobbies, collecting and cataloging the flora and fauna of the area, when they were older. The flora they pressed and preserved in special drawers we had built for them, in their common room. The drawers are still there, as I write this; but the children have long gone.

William was also very sad to lose his big brother. Watching him crying at the funeral, broke my heart. Joshua had always been good to little William, a bond, which had become strong over the time of their abandonment in San Juan. I held his hand and tried to comfort him.

The funeral for Joshua was a family affair, attended by a few close friends, the mayor and his family, and several other dignitaries. He was buried in a small meadow surrounded by trees, where he and Catherine liked to spend time, reading and talking about the many things that went through their minds. Afterwards, Juliette and I hosted a reception in the house, where we went through the ordeal of having to accept everyone's condolences for a loss, which would always remain, thus.

The second tragedy struck a little over a month later, May 28th. Monsieur Cocteau had been feeling uncomfortably for some days prior, complaining of a pain in his chest. A massive heart attack killed him at breakfast, when he suddenly convulsed and dropped dead, right there in front of the entire family. It was a great shock to everyone, as you can well imagine. The little children found it particularly strange, one minute grandpa was there and the next he was gone. It was their first direct experience with death.

Grandpa was buried in his favorite place, a spot overlooking our harbour. He and Madame Cocteau liked to walk there and quite often would sit at that spot, under a glorious stand of palm trees. We erected a beautiful cairn of local stone over his grave with an engraved plaque which read, 'Here lies, Hugo Cocteau, 1734 - 1800. Husband, Father, Grandfather, & Excellent Friend. May you rest in peace.'

* * *

In July we received word through our network of informers and spies, that one of our convoys had been struck by pirates belonging to a gang calling themselves, 'The Red Avengers,' who allegedly stole our ships and our goods, killing all of our men, somewhere off the Cuban coast, near Havana. Our company lost a total of one hundred and seventeen able bodied sailors and capable officers. It was a senseless slaughter of excellent men, who apparently fought bravely to the last, some of them subjected to horrific cruelties at the hands of those sea scum.

The cost to the company, for support of the families of the deceased, became something of a burden, however, we bore it gladly. I personally wrote a letter of condolences to each of the families, who lost a loved one, in several cases more than one. We held a memorial service several weeks later on the front lawn of our mansion.

The loss of the goods totaled, seventy six thousand pounds stirling. It was a significant loss for the company, and not something to be trifled with. I took it as a serious call to arms. Thus, at a board meeting, on July 14th, I set the plans in motion, which resulted in the fourth tragedy.

I ordered seven ships outfitted for a voyage to Havana, hoping to find out where we might locate the Red Avengers. Three of the ships we equipped with as many heavy guns as we could carry, with enough cannon balls to blow kingdom come to smithereens. The other ships we outfitted for quick speed and maneuverability, carrying mostly swivel guns on the gunwales and some twelve pounders in the bows, the stern, and along the deck. These ships carried the most men, all of them armed to the teeth, and well trained in the use of weapons; a great variety of which I had obtained over the years, totally aware, a day, such as the one that was coming, would eventually reach us.

When the ships were victualed and watered, we set out when the first winds allowed, that being August the first. We sailed out of our harbour, with flags and pennants flying. We fired a fifteen gun salute, answered by the battery of cannons overlooking the harbour. The latter came somewhat slowly and ponderously, there only being five of our men, plus the household staff, available to fire them.

I had left orders with Catherine to hire twenty guards, to replace the men we had taken with us on board our ships. Those men had not arrived yet, when we set sail.

The voyage to Havana was passed with constant drills in hand to hand combat with the assorted weapons I was able to assemble, over the years. Weapons required dealers to sell them, and they did not always have what I was looking for. The weapons, I did manage to assemble were: battle axes, blunderbusses, boarding axes, clubs, cutlasses, halberds, muskets, pikes, sabres, scimitars, tridents, seven katanas, and two massive claymores, which I had found in an antique dealer's shop and refinished. As you have already learned, those weapons could cleave a man in twain, if handled by the right persons. In this case the swords definitely were handled by the right people; our claymore specialists being men, who weighed nearly three hundred pounds of solid muscle on six foot, six inch frames.

All the weapons were carefully sharpened and oiled, cleaned and inspected, nothing was left to chance.

When we arrived off the north west coast of Cuba, we were able to tack into the harbour, where we dropped our anchors under the flags of our company, Cocteau & Mann. Since we had a trading office in Havana, our company flags were well known and respected.

After paying my regards to the harbour master, I took twelve of my best men and made the rounds of the local taverns, seeking information regarding my enemies, the Red Avengers, who, as it turned out, were quite well known by the locals and many jack tars we spoke to. We learned that the gang members felt so confident, they walked about freely, with their colors showing; a red bandana they wore on their heads or around their necks.

Most of the locals and the sailors, who had run-ins with the gang, were afraid of them and, although not afraid to talk in general about them, they did not go into specifics, such as the locations of their ships and hideout. That information we had to extract from a gang member, sometime later.

Around nine o'clock in the evening of our third day in port, three gang members strutted into a restaurant where I was having dinner with the harbour master and his wife. My first mate, Pedro Maxis, and second mate, Johanus van Bussum, a tall Dutchman, with a mop of blond hair and piercing blue eyes, had accompanied me.

I immediately recognized the three men as gang members, because they made a great show of their bright red bandanas. They sat down at a table, several tables to my left, and insolently called for service, disrupting the ambiance.

When the waiter arrived, one of the men berated the man for taking too long to come to their table. When the waiter protested that he was busy and came as soon as he was able, the man grabbed the waiter by the front of his apron and pulled him down to the table, all the while berating the man, and telling him he had better improve his service, or else he and his friends would teach him a lesson in waitering.

The man let go of the waiter's apron.

The waiter straightened himself up; a fearful expression on his countenance.

As I watched the spectacle, I noticed that people were nervously looking sideways at the obnoxious pirates, afraid to say something, lest they draw the wrong attention from the rogues.

The three pirates did not realize they had drawn the wrong attention to themselves, which would so tragically result in the events that followed.

When one of the pirates left his table and headed in the direction of the lavatory, I made my move, excusing myself to do the same. The harbour master and his wife had no idea, regarding the pistols under my arms, or the various knives I carried in sundry places. My pewter hook had long been replaced with another silver one, sharp as a needle. Come to think of it, as I write this now, I was a formidable walking arsenal. I liked to err on the side of caution.

When I stepped into the lavatory, three men were standing at the trough, relieving themselves. The gang member was not among them; he was groaning in a cubicle.

Taking up a position by the door, I waited.

A few minutes later the three men left the lavatory; one, two, three, leaving me alone with the groaner. When someone else tried to enter the lavatory, I told the man to come back later, because the place was being cleaned.

When the pirate stepped out of the cubicle, adjusting his belt buckle, I grabbed him by the red bandana around his neck and pushed him against the wall, mindful of his knees and hands, my hook menacingly close to his face.

I told the man that I was Peter Mann, come to revenge the loss of my men and ships. If he would not divulge the identity of his leader and his whereabouts, I would kill him on the spot.

The man knew I meant it, he having obviously heard of my reputation from my younger days, when I was known as the, 'Scourge of the Caribbean.' Thinking of it, I have to laugh, to think people actually called me that.

Anyway, the man, who was about five inches shorter than me, and not as strong, knew he didn't have much of a chance. However, he did try to wiggle out of my hold, causing my hook to scratch his cheek, which immediately spurted blood, making the man pause in his attempt to flee.

I pushed him against the wall and warned him again.

The man held his bleeding cheek and complained that I cut him.

I told him that it was only a scratch and it would heal.

I reminded the pirate, I was not in the mood to play games, and again demanded the name of his leader.

'It's no secret,' said the man insolently. 'His name is, Martin Henry.'

'Martin Henry?' I asked. 'Does he have missing index fingers?'

The man nodded. 'We all think so, because those fingers don't appear real on his hand. We all believe he is wearing prosthetic fingers.'

It was the first time I had ever heard about prosthetic fingers. 'It certainly would make pointing, a whole lot easier for Martin,' I chuckled.

The name Martin Henry had stuck in my head, all those years. He was the only man we ever castrated, and whose index fingers were cut off, for molesting a little girl. We left him on Virgineola, many years ago.

So, there he was, Martin Henry, all those years later; an eunuch who made good, in a bad way. Henry had made the mistake of becoming a blood thirsty pirate. If he had merely taken my cargo, and set my men free, then, perhaps, I could have been convinced to forget my venture. However, he killed over a hundred of my men, leaving families without husbands and fathers. For that I had to kill him. I had no choice in the matter. It was a Divine obligation for me.

'Where can I find Martin Henry?' I asked.

The man shook his head and refused to say.

As we were standing there, at an impasse, a man came into the lavatory.

I told the man he would have to go outside, because we were in the process of cleaning.

The man nodded and without saying a word, turned around and walked out.

I pushed my hook harder against the pirate's cheek, and again demanded to know where Martin Henry was. Before the man would answer, I had to scratch a deep scar into his cheek, emitting copious amounts of blood.

The man tried to scream, but I put my right hand hard against his mouth, as I pressed him into the wall with my body.

The pirate attempted to knee me in the groin, which, because he was shorter than me, failed in the attempt; giving me time to reciprocate.

Unlike him, I connected.

I told the pirate, as he crumpled to the floor, holding his groin, if he did not tell me where Martin Henry was, I would kill him right there, and get the information from his dinner companions.

The man snickered insolently. 'You won't get any more information out of them, than you will get out of me,' he said, thinking I wouldn't kill him and was only bluffing.

Unfortunately for him, my patience had run out. He quickly learned I was not bluffing. I dragged the pirate's body into a cubicle and left him there, closing the door on another piece of dung, which should have stayed in the colon, from whence it came.

I noticed there was blood on my waistcoat and the ruffles on my chest. I tried to wipe it off, but couldn't do much about it. Therefore, since the blood consisted of only a few drops; when asked about it, by the harbour master's wife, I told her I had a nose bleed and accidentally dripped on my clothes.

When the next pirate left his table, to use the lavatory, or to see what was taking his friend so long, I had to repeat the process all over again, excusing myself on the pretext that I was expecting another nose bleed coming on. This time I used a pistol and merely pointed it at the second pirate, demanding where Martin Henry was. When he refused to tell me, I simply shot him, figuring with only one pirate left, the three of us would have no problem overpowering the remaining red pirate and extracting the information, in a more persuasive fashion, on board ship, thus leaving the remaining cubicle for a guest of the restaurant.

The remaining pirate, after sitting alone for a while, got up to go and see what happened to his friends in the lavatory.

It was at that point that I prompted my companions, to help me with my nose bleed, as I rushed to the washroom, followed by Pedro and Johanus.

We caught the pirate in the act of discovering his deceased friends when we grabbed him and rushed him outside, through a back door, next to the lavatory.

Johanus had the man in a vice grip, from which he could not escape, as I held a pistol to his head. I asked Pedro to offer my apologies to the harbour master and his wife. I told Pedro to tell them it was because my nose bleed had gotten much worse, I had to rush back to my ship.

While Pedro went inside the restaurant, I hailed a coach.

When Pedro returned, a coach pulled up, I climbed in first, and then Johanus pushed the pirate inside. Then he, and Pedro climbed on board.

We told the coach driver to take us to the roadway, where we took a boat to my ship and clapped the pirate in irons in the fo'c's'le.

Next day, after a leisurely breakfast, we brought the pirate on deck and asked him again to reveal where Martin Henry was.

The man again, would not say.

I gave him one more chance to tell me

'You'll never get me to tell,' he said defiantly.

Without going into the details, dear reader, you can well imagine what we had to do, in order for such a hardened pirate to tell us what we wanted to know.

After telling us, where we could find Martin Henry, the man begged me to spare his life. 'Please don't kill me,' he begged. 'I told you what you wanted to know.'

I hoped he told me what I wanted to know. You never knew with pirates, if they were telling the truth. I was not sure I could trust the man.

I told him, that if I found out his information was false, I would most certainly kill him. I asked him, point blank, if he was involved in the piracy of my ships and the murder of my men.

The pirate nodded, a slight smile on his lips, as he thought of the event. Then he asked me again if we were going to kill him.

I told him we wouldn't kill him, unless his information was false.

The pirate heaved a sigh of relief. 'Then I know I will live,' he said. 'Gracias, senior.'

The pirate appeared entirely sincere, which gave me cause to be optimistic of success, having heard about the location of the Red Avenger's harbour, the number of ships he had, types of armament; indeed everything we needed to know, in order to effect a positive result in wreaking the Lord's vengeance.

The man asked again, if we were going to kill him, and I again I told him, I had given my word we wouldn't kill him, if his words proved true.

The pirate looked at me and at my friends gathered on deck. He smiled happily, in spite of the pain we had subjected him to. 'So, what happens to me, after you have destroyed Martin Henry?' he asked. 'Do I find employment with you?'

I laughed. 'Employment with me? After helping to kill my men?' I shook my head. 'No,' I said, 'I don't think so. I think you will have to fend for yourself, for as long as you live.'

'If any of Martin's men find out I told you, I will be dead,' he said. 'They will surely kill me.'

'We won't tell them it was you,' I replied, smiling.

Then I gave a signal to the two Swedes, to grab the pirate and throw him overboard.

As the pirate was being dragged to the starboard gunwale, he yelled, 'I can't swim! I can't swim! You said you weren't going to kill me!'

I laughed and replied that we were not killing him, the sharks would do it for us, instead.

Then with a nod of my head, the Swedes threw the pirate overboard.

I heard his splash a few seconds later.

With the pirate disposed of, we began making our plans for the raid on Martin Henry's fort, in the cays to the north east of Havana.

Apparently, his pirates used small, light weight sloops, carrying twelve pounders, very able to hit near the water lines of merchantmen. The sloops were generally sent out in groups of three or five, each carrying from thirty to fifty men, depending on the size of convoy they were plundering. The slow moving merchantmen were no match for the swiftly maneuvering sloops, who would, according to the pirate we interviewed, 'Float like butterflies and sting like hornets.'

The plan we devised, was to pretend to be a convoy of heavily laden ships, simply flying my company's pennants and flags. The appearance of heavy lading would be obtained by dragging hogsheads of water behind our ships, the ropes easily cut to free us from the loads, a similar trick we tried in the early days of my training.

Hence, to that end we bought every empty hogshead and barrel to be gotten in Havana. We rigged nets, in which to drag them behind the ships attached to two cable's length of rope. We would load the vessels with water, when we were out to sea, and then sail by the cays, certain the Red Avengers had look outs watching for convoys of heavily laden ships, slow under full sail, heading north east through the Florida Straits.

When we were about three leagues from Havana, we began preparing our guns for quick roll out. We stocked every nook and cranny on the deck with loaded weapons, ready to grab and fire, as well as readying boarding axes, halberds, and pikes. All cannons were loaded and ready to fire. What ever Martin Henry would send after us, if we managed to attract him, was no match for my ships. The unsuspecting pirates did not have a clue they would be messing with a much smarter and experienced pirate, Peter Mann, 'the Scourge of the Caribbean.'

Our lookouts spotted the cays, four leagues to our starboard, at six twenty six in the morning, a day after leaving Havana. I recorded the time in my log, in order to keep a close track of events, as I hoped they would accrue. I was curious to see how quickly we were sighted and pursued.

We did not have to wait long, for within two hours we sighted five sails coming from the cays, bearing directly upon us. At ten o'clock the five sloops were less than a league to starboard. It was time to begin our preparations. I ordered that all haste be made to get ready.

Hence, each crow's nest was manned with two men, each crow's nest holding five loaded muskets, and enough balls and powder, to enable one man to load while the other fired a constant volley. Our gunners had all hidden themselves below, on the gun decks of our various ships, which comprised a converted man of war, two brigantines, a schooner, and three converted West Indiamen.

When the five sloops were within half a league of us, they hoisted their battle flags, a red rectangle, on which white femurs were crossed like an X, under a grinning skull. Beside the skull and crossed bones they had stitched the figure of an hour glass, 'Signifying that *their* time was limited,' I quipped wryly, just before I ordered the ropes cut, freeing us of the heavy loads of water filled hogsheads and barrels; suddenly changing the handling and speed of our ships.

The sudden change in our ships' speed and maneuverability must have greatly surprised the attackers, who had no idea who, or what they were messing with. Their surprise was heightened, when we suddenly came about, and in so doing, were able to unleash the fire power of seventy five cannons directly at them, many balls crashing into the stems and fore decks of the oncoming sloops.

The startled pirates tried to come about, in order to attempt flight, when they realized we were not what they thought we were.

In the meantime, we reloaded our starboard guns and managed to catch up to the sloops, unleashing another massive amount of fire power into their port sides, smashing timbers and spars; pieces of pirates and their weapons, blasted to kingdom come.

The pirates fired back, unleashing at least fifty, eight pound balls into our sides, killing seven men, and injuring another twenty three, with various sized splinters, in sundry parts of their bodies.

When the wind shifted, our ships were pushed towards the sloops, enabling us to foresee a boarding party. We adjusted our sails accordingly and beat closer to the sloops, who were desperately trying to get away.

The pirates fired another round of balls at us, but being eight pound balls, did not have too much effect on us, other than in relatively minor ways, unlike the hell we unleashed upon the sloops.

Two of my ships, the schooner, *Prosperity Always*, and the brigantine, *William Three*, managed to come alongside a rudderless sloop and quickly boarded it, capturing the pirates, who gave up with out much of a fight.

The three West Indiamen, gave chase and caught one more sloop, managing to shoot into her stern with the bow guns, rendering another rudder, a useless mess of splinters. Another round knocked her mast down. The sloop was quickly boarded and the pirates captured.

As I was standing on the deck, watching the unfolding scenario, I had lost track of one of the sloops, which, in the billowing smoke of the guns, had managed to come about and tacked directly at my ship, the converted man of war, *Catherine One*. I was standing on the rear quarter deck, watching the action off the port bow, when the sloop managed to come alongside and loose her cannons into the starboard hull, abaft of the midship bulkheads, exactly where our powder stores were located, resulting in my fourth and fifth tragedies.

By some freak accident, some balls managed to find their way into that heavily fortified room, setting off an explosion, which ripped through the centre of my ship and out through the main deck, abaft of the mast; massive splinters of wood flying in all directions, tearing through my friends, like knives through soft butter. One massive splinter managed to find me, slicing through my right leg, just under the knee.

The next thing I remember was hearing another massive explosion, which deafened me considerably, as a brilliant flash of light lit up the scene; my ship coming apart around me and throwing me into the sea.

I think the Lord must have been watching out for his servant because, just like the last time I was shipwrecked, I found a large enough piece of my ship to latch my hook into, thus saving my life, as I watched the battle quickly finish; the *Juliette*, and the *Marianne*, blowing the sloop out of the water and ending the battle.

I was rescued shortly, thereafter, when a boat with six of my men came looking for survivors. I do not remember much else, until I woke up some hours later, the lower part of my right leg, a shattered mess, and causing me extreme discomfort. There was only one cure for the pain I was suffering. It was laudanum. I consumed enough to knock me out for twenty four hours.

When I woke up, my men brought me a report, assessing our damages and successes. In spite of my pain, it heartened me to learn that we had destroyed two sloops, and captured two others, which were repairable. One sloop had managed to flee. We lost thirty five men, with another seventy wounded in various places, two of whom lost limbs. The pirates lost near a hundred men, and many more were injured. We captured sixty three pirates, none of whom was Martin Henry, the six fingered eunuch.

We decided to stay in the area, for a while longer, hoping Martin would send out some larger ships to do battle with us, but he never came out. Hence, we had to resort to more drastic measures, to obtain the location of his fort, in order to bring the battle to his home base.

The drastic measure we undertook was to extract information from the captured pirates, which actually proved to be easier than I had thought. We only needed to torture one pirate, in front of the others, which quickly got us the information we needed; none of the men believing their loyalty to Martin Henry was worth having their limbs mutilated.

The pirates were given the option of joining us, under threat of death should they betray us. To a man they pledged their loyalty to me, which to my way of thinking wasn't worth a hapenny, but I could use the extra man power, considering our losses and injuries. Pirates, like those, have no real loyalties, except to those who kept their bellies filled and their pockets full. I don't trust most pirates.

My injury, after four days, was beginning to become a festering mess. In the opinion of the ship's doctor, the leg would have to come off; the bones having been shattered to such an extent, there was nothing he, or anyone could do to fix the thing. Hence, the fifth tragedy came upon me on, Tuesday, August 26th, 1800, at nine o'clock in the morning.

Twenty minutes before the operation, I drank a hearty dose of laudanum and rum. Then I lay down on the doctor's table and he, and the ship's carpenter, a man named Dan Downey, strapped my arms, and my left ankle, while another strap was placed over my thighs and buckled down. When I was nearly unconscious from the laudanum and rum, Doctor Smith put a hard, one inch thick spindle in my mouth, to keep me from biting my tongue as he applied the tourniquet. The doctor made some incisions in the skin of my lower leg, in order to have skin with which to wrap the bottom of my stump. The pain, of the knife cutting into my skin, overcame the pain that was already there from the damage.

When the doctor had finished, the carpenter began to saw off my right leg, just below the knee, leaving the knee intact, and removing everything else below that. The entire procedure taking about two hours, under such an intense pain, in spite of the laudanum and rum, that I passed out, having nearly bitten through the spindle.

When I woke up, some hours later, an intense pain filled every cavity of my body, the like of which far exceeded anything else I had ever experienced. Losing my leg had to be the most incredible pain I have ever suffered, not even laudanum or rum could assuage. All that I could do was to stay in my bed and live through the suffering, while we continued to conduct our war with the Red Avengers.

I ordered a chair and a support for my leg to be brought up on deck, so that I could sit there and conduct our affairs. The chair, and the support for my severed limb, were nailed to the deck, so they would not move, as the ship rolled on the waves.

We had managed to find a suitable anchorage, off the lee of a small island, finding a good sandy bottom at six fathoms. A number of the men went ashore to look for fresh water, fruits, and hopefully, a wild boar. I would have loved to have gone with them, but that was now out of the question. Whether I would ever be able to walk again, was a question which went through my mind quite a lot during the time it took for my bloody stump to heal.

Since I did not have very detailed charts of the cays, I sent the schooner, with some of the pirates, to reconnoiter the western islands. I sent a brig, with some of the other pirates, to see what they could find in the eastern islands, instructions being simply to look for any sign of the

Avengers and to draw charts, with soundings, so that we could plan our strategy.

Two of my men, who had also lost limbs, one an arm and the other his leg, midway up his calf, came to sit with me on the quarter deck of my new ship, that being the *Juliette*. On my orders, special chairs were also rigged for them, in such a way that we would not be in the way of the helmsman and my mates. During the time we waited for our reconnaissance ships to return, the three of us discussed the bizarre experience of losing a limb.

It being my second, I had some experience regarding a phenomenon, the two men related to me, that being the sensation that their limbs were, in fact, intact; as if a ghostly remnant of the limb had replaced the severed part. I assured the men, whose names were, Tomas Eakins and Wayne Surton, the experience was normal and would go away, more or less.

While we were thus sitting on deck, four afternoons later, enjoying a glorious sunny day, a lookout on the *Marianne,* announced there were sails heading in our direction. Immediately, everyone jumped to their battle stations, to wait until we knew exactly what ships they were. An hour later we realized the sails were our ships, the schooner and the brig, come to report on their findings, we thought.

As I watched the ships approaching, I began to notice that something was not quite right about the way the ships were sailing, abeam of each other, close hauled like they were. The way the ships were being handled gave me the distinct impression they were not captained by my men, whose sailing habits I was very familiar with. I mentioned this fact to Pedro and Johanus, who concurred there was something amiss, as we watched the sails bearing down on us, from the south east.

Suddenly, the watch called out there were sails coming around the island, behind us. When I turned to look, I nearly fell out of my chair, as I beheld five ships, each flying the Avengers' flag.

Immediately, upon realizing what was about to befall us, I ordered anchors weighed, sails unfurled, and guns loaded and run out. The boatswain whistled the orders, which were quickly repeated on each of my ships.

Fortunately, all of my men and captains were very well trained in combat and hence, were an excellent match for the ships coming for us, I hoped.

Three of my ships managed to catch a breeze and sailed from the anchorage, enabling them to maneuver around the oncoming ships, leaving my ship sitting, like a duck, with the island to starboard and our port side facing the oncoming ships.

Fortunately, we were not exactly lame ducks, with twenty five heavy guns run out of our port sides, and all the swivel guns mounted on the port railings.

When the five pirate ships rounded the island, we were quite ready for them, as my captains, manning the three ships, which had left the anchorage, came on them, guns ready.

The first volley came as a defensive ploy from the pirates, most of their balls splashing harmlessly in the sea, or punching minor holes in the fore decks, not very serious damage, easily repaired.

The second volley came from the forward guns of my ships, which managed to strike home in three places, shattering some deck planks.

The five pirate ships began to split up from their formation, at the same time that our brig and schooner came within half a league of the *Virginia*, bearing upon her with great speed, guns run out and ready for battle.

It was a tragic thing to see my own ships being used against me by a group of cutthroats. I hated to lose the ships, but if I did, such was the price we had to pay to rid the earth of Martin Henry and his minions. I mentally tallied up the costs, and realized that the city of Havana would probably reimburse me for my loses.

Suddenly, our cannons were fired at the first ship to come within range, sending a lethal barrage of twenty pound balls, and grapeshot through the ship's bows and forecastle, shattering her bowsprit and ornament. Judging from the screams, I got the impression we hit some pirates, as well.

Our gunners were very adept and had our cannons reloaded within less than a minute, sending another barrage into the lead ship, shattering her port side and essentially rendering most of her gun deck inoperable, necessitating a come around, in order to use her starboard guns.

In their hurry to come about, the pirates misjudged the distance of two ships, immediately behind them, causing the outside ship to ram into the stern of the ship coming about. The resultant collision tangled the ships together, rendering them immobile and an easy target for my three ships bearing down on them.

As the third ship came past the tangle, we were able to unleash another massive broadside into it, also severely damaging the bow and fore deck, splintering the base of the foremast and several pirates, who were preparing to fire two forward swivel guns.

Meanwhile, the schooner and brig came behind the three ships, which we had managed to send off. The schooner let fly a volley into the stern of *Joshua One*, which knocked some holes into the Master's cabin, and damaged the stern post.

Fortunately, *Joshua One* was able to come around and fired her starboard guns, destroying the mizzen of the schooner, the spar crashing to the boards, on top of the helmsman, causing the schooner to veer off to port, enabling the *Virginia* to let go a volley, which neatly finished the transom of the schooner, utterly destroying her rudder, and creating a significant leak at her water line.

Our brig, *William Three*, fired her forward guns and splintered the poop deck railings of the *Virginia*, just as she managed to fire a broadside into the fourth pirate ship, which had come around from behind the island.

Powder smoke filled the air, as more guns blazed, filling the space with fire and thunder.

Moments later, one of the pirate ships exploded with a loud roar, sending pieces of ship and occupants flying in all directions, several pieces of bloody flesh landing on my quarter deck, right beside the chair I was sitting in.

As the guns blazed, and the air became thick with smoke, it became ever harder to see clearly, what was happening.

Suddenly, the timbers of my ship shivered, as one of the pirate ships crashed into our port side, sending grappling hooks over our gunwales and pulling the two ships together. Before the distance was completely closed, seven of my guns were able to fire another volley into the pirate ship, splintering her port side and sending several more pirates to hell.

My men were ready to receive the boarding party, with pikes and halberds, pistols, muskets, and cutlasses. Screams, shouts, gunshots, and clashing metal filled my ears, making it difficult to shout orders and be heard.

Moments later a crazed looking pirate came rushing at the three of us sitting on the quarter deck, our bloody stumps bleeding through our bandages. The pirate lived for another twelve seconds, as we three shot him at the same time, sending three heavy caliber balls through his head, effectively removing it from his shoulders.

Another pirate, hell bent on gaining the quarter deck, came up the ladder.

Fortunately, Tomas had another loaded pistol, which he discharged into the pirate's chest, causing him to fall backwards. I think he may have fallen on a colleague, judging from the shouts I heard coming from that direction.

More cannons sounded and more lethal splinters ripped through yielding bodies, emitting intense screams of pain, further adding to the cacophony of the battle, raging like a dragon for, what seemed like an hour, until suddenly; a heavy stillness came down on us, like a black velvet curtain.

The sudden stillness was an eerie moment, which I shall always remember. It lasted for at least two minutes, before the quiet was broken by a voice through a speaking trumpet. The voice I recognized as belonging to Martin Henry, admitting defeat and requesting terms.

I looked at Pedro and Johanus, who shrugged their shoulders, not certain whether to trust the pirate's declaration.

'Maybe it's a trap,' suggested Pedro.

The voice sounded, once more, again admitting defeat and requesting we cease firing.

As the smoke cleared, I could see that the pirate ships were badly damaged. Two were tangled up, due to the collision. Three had severe damage from our twenty pounders, no match for their eight pounders, and our schooner had been retaken by our men, who had boarded her from the *Virginia*.

Our brig, *William Three*, had also been retaken by our men. The pirates had brought them along for a cruel purpose, I was to find out about, later, the mere contemplation of which, merited the quick demise of the person harbouring such thoughts; he being, Martin Henry.

Winning the battle was a mixed blessing. Certainly, it gave me great satisfaction to achieve our objective, ridding the Caribbean of Martin Henry and the Red Avengers, but the loss of my leg was a heavy price to pay for that victory. It pained me for many years, afterwards; a constant reminder of that tragic year.

The remaining pirates, numbering two hundred and sixteen men, were shackled and tied in every fo'c's'le, on every ship, including the three still serviceable pirate ships.

The other ships were run aground on the little island. We punched holes in their hulls, the Red Avenger's pennants left flying in their masts; a reminder to local shipping that the Red Avengers had been defeated.

The only pirate we did not stuff into a fo'c's'le was the six fingered eunuch, Martin Henry, for whom we had a different plan in mind, after he had shown me where his fort was; pointing it out on the chart we found on board his ship; a sleek little schooner of shallow draft, perfectly suited to the local waters.

Martin Henry's fort was located about three leagues from the scene of the battle, on a cay, which he had named, Dead Man's Cay, a beautiful location, not easily found and reminiscent of my island in the Caicos, although it was quite a lot smaller.

Unfortunately, because of my injury, I preferred not to be carted about, sightseeing on Martin's island, and in his splendid house. I contented myself with sitting on the quarter deck of my ship, as I watched men carrying tons of swag out of the buildings of the fort. I could see clearly through the spy glass, as a cornucopia of magnificent art treasures, furniture, rugs and, thankfully, a library full of books, and treasure chests, full of gold and silver coins, precious stones, and jewelry, were carted from that place and safely stowed in the holds of our ships. The haul clearly indicated that Martin Henry had done alright for himself, since the time we left him in Virgineola; when we should have killed him in the first place. I knew back then there was reason to be concerned about, Martin Henry.

It took a full three days to empty out Martin's place, utilizing the forced labor of the captured pirates, who received a swift lashing if they did not cooperate. When the last keg was removed from the warehouses and not a thing left in the houses, worthy of our attention, we conflagrated the place in front of the defeated pirates; letting them clearly see that their gang was no more. The Red Avengers would avenge no longer. I noticed tears in Martin's eyes, as he watched his house erupt in an explosion of flames.

We watched the burning of the pirate's compound with great satisfaction, toasting each new eruption of flame with Martin's rum. The fire lasted for a day and a half, burning out when it began to rain, necessitating my removal to the Master's cabin, after issuing the orders; to tie Martin to the foremast, and to clap all of the others back in the fo'c's'les, where we kept them confined for the entire voyage back to Havana, a trip of three days.

Unfortunately, seven pirates died, en route, which we thought not a great pity, since we would be paid for each head, anyway. Hence, when we made port, we handed over all of the pirates, plus their dead colleagues, with the exception of Martin Henry, for whom I had something different in mind.

The Havana authorities were overjoyed to receive so many Red Avengers, clearly indicating the gang was at an end. Many of the captives were already up on charges, so it was a double fortune for Havana, to have so many criminals apprehended. The authorities had no problem with my request to keep Martin Henry, essentially telling me that he was a present, still paying me the thousand pounds, offered for the eunuch. For each of the other pirates, I received twenty pounds, for a total of fifty three hundred pounds, not a large sum, considering how much Martin had cost me.

However, since the goods and treasure, taken from the pirate's compound, were mine, as were the three pirate ships we captured, my company was more than compensated for our losses. When the inventories were completed, twenty five days later, in San Juan, our swag amounted to five hundred and sixty three thousand pounds, sixteen shillings and a thropence. I think the accountant put in the thropence to show me how thorough he was. I paid him handsomely for his services.

Since the company had lost a significant sum, half the swag was kept by the company, and the rest was distributed amongst the sailors who participated in the battle against Martin Henry and his minions. The families of those sailors, who were lost in the battle, received extra compensation, two years' wages, to help them adjust to the loss of their sailors. The sailors, who were injured, were also compensated extra, the amount depending on the severity of the injuries.

My return, without my leg, was a terrible surprise for my family, who had great sympathy for me, and helped me to convalesce quickly. Juliette and her mother nursed me very well, so that within the space of four months, I was able to be fitted with a wooden leg and a comfortable crutch, necessitating relearning how to walk.

I heard some years later, on my next visit to Havana, to inspect the company's trade office, that the Red Avengers, whom we had delivered to the authorities, were given trials. Seventy three were hanged, and the remainder thrown in jail for various lengths of time, some for as much as twenty years.

As for Martin Henry, we made an example of him, by having him strapped to a St. Andrew's cross, and leaving him exposed to the tide, at the entrance to our harbour; his banner flying above his head.

Five weeks later, to commemorate my two shipwrecks, I re-pierced my right ear lobe and added a second ring in my left lobe. Two shipwrecks; two rings.

Looking in the mirror, afterwards, a completely different Peter Mann stared back at me; a man of fifty, with two earrings, a patch on his right eye, and a long scar down his left cheek, from eye to chin. Looking at my changed countenance, I was suddenly thankful for Juliette and my children, that they still could love such a blood soaked, disfigured old pirate, such as myself.

Standing there, in front of that mirror, was a moving experience for me. I could not hold back tears any longer, they flowing copiously from my eye and dripped on the carpet, under my wooden peg. For once in my life, I suddenly felt very sad for myself, and what I had become, a cripple with a hook and a peg, a patch on his eye, a scar on his face, and rings in his ears.

Fortunately, I have never been prone to self pity, so my negativity lasted but a short while, after which I felt cleansed and grateful to be alive. I never again felt sorry for myself and carried on with my business, growing the company and fathering my children, until that fateful day in 1815, the year Napoleon was defeated at Waterloo when my world crashed to pieces, a story which I shall relate to you presently, after first giving you an accounting of some of the highlights which accrued, in the years between, Martin's execution, and the year above mentioned.

Chapter Thirty

As Cocteau & Mann's fortunes became ever more bountiful, I was able to extend our trading empire along the northern coast of South America, the East coasts of Central America, Mexico, up to Miami, Florida; establishing trading offices in Cartagena, Portobelo, Limon, Belize, Veracruz, Tampico, Corpus Christi, Galveston, St. Petersburg, and Miami. Our splendid company owned a fleet of forty two West Indiamen, perfectly fitted for trade along the coasts I mentioned, plus ten barges for hauling lumber, six coal haulers, five brigantines, two American style frigates, a Dutch built East Indiaman, and a fine yacht, on which I took my family and friends for outings and trips to our island. We also operated numerous garbage and manure barges in all the towns and cities, where we had offices.

In 1802 I had amassed enough surplus revenue to spend on Madame Cocteau's dream, that of a resort on the island. She had often spoken of going there, after we moved into the San Juan mansion, however, with the way we were working the family business, we only went there once, or twice, to spend a week relaxing on the beaches, but we never did go back and live there. Hence, the discussions we engaged in, concerning the island, saw a plan to build a hotel and some cabins in amongst the trees, all of which could be rented to people seeking a vacation.

We spoke of developing a tiled patio on the cove, with tables and chairs, served by a restaurant, under the direction of Madame Gautier and her husband, Gaston. There would be gardens, as before, to provide fresh produce, to supplement that which we shipped with our own vessels, from our own warehouses in San Juan. In 1802 we brought about the beginnings of the development, which eventually became the resort we had dreamed of. We opened the resort on December 3rd, 1806, and right from the beginning it started making money, which by 1810, amounted to a profit of 75,000 pounds stirling per annum.

Our resort attracted people from North and South America, plus many places in Europe. The guest list included famous actors and actresses, authors, composers, scientists, and just plain, old, wealthy people, who wanted to get away from their crowded cities, for some clean air and water, rest, and relaxation. Some of the names I remember reading off the guest list included; the British actor, Edmund Kean, the German composer, with the seemingly Dutch name, Ludwig van Beethoven, who apparently had come to concentrate on revisions to an opera he had been developing. The historian, Henry Hallam spent a week, as did the English composer, John Field, and the Italian composer, Nicolo Paganini played his violin for our guests in 1808. Of French painters, we saw Jean Dominique Ingres, and Francois-Marius Granet, and of English painters, a wonderful landscape artist by the name of John Constable paid us a visit. Our manager had the foresight to buy some of Mister Constable's pictures. The French painters did not paint, while they were on the island, merely sketching and relaxing, apparently.

May First, 1803, four days before Christopher's 16th birthday, was a momentous day in our lives, when my daughter, Catherine married, Salvador Meléndez, an ambitious young man, with a great interest in business, finance, and the study of history, philosophy, and politics. I quite liked my new son in law, he and I having spent many evenings together, discussing his interests, long before I gave him permission to marry my precious daughter.

The wedding was a huge affair, for which we required San Juan Cathedral. Many of the country's finest people were there, including some dignitaries and friends from Havana, and Maracaibo. The governor, Field Marshall Ramon De Castroy Gutiérrez and his family were there, as was Toribo Montes, who became governor the following year, and his family, plus many business associates, and the extensive family of my son in law, made the wedding one of the most splendid weddings San Juan had seen. The reception was held on the lawns of our mansion on the hill. The party was an event to remember, as many of my officers and sailors, who were in port, were also invited to enjoy our abundant hospitality.

Fortunately, Salvador's home was San Juan, he not wanting to live anywhere else but, Puerto Rico. It was fortunate for the company, because Catherine was able to continue her management of the trade office, which had grown to be a sizable operation in itself, with five warehouses to keep filled and emptied. I was also fortunate, because I loved my daughter's company, and did not want to have to sail across the world to enjoy her.

Salvador became governor of the island in 1809, eventually serving for nineteen years in that capacity. He and Catherine lived a happy life together, bringing me my first grandchild in 1805, a bright little boy whom Catherine named after me. I must have popped some buttons, I was so greatly honored by that. It was a great blessing for me to be able to see the little chap on a regular basis.

In 1806, on a beautiful August, a Sunday afternoon, at two o'clock, before another large crowd of people, my son William married, Maria, Isabella De Castroy y Gutiérrez, the daughter of the former governor of Puerto Rico. The ceremony was officiated by Father Menedez. The reception was again, a wonderful party, well attended by many fine people.

Christmas in 1807 was a memorable family affair. Madame Cocteau had come from the island to spend a few weeks with us, leaving again on the seventh of January, 1808. On the 27th we received word from the island that she had passed away, peacefully in her sleep. Because of the climate, she was buried on the island in a ceremony attended by many of the guests of the resort.

Juliette and the children and I held a private memorial service at home.

In 1809 our company suffered another pirate attack on a convoy of ships sailing out of Miami. Fortunately, my men were able to repel the rovers, my ships being well armed, and my men well trained. However, we did lose two ships, carrying lucrative cargo, and all the gold we had left over, after buying more cargo with the proceeds of the sale of goods we shipped there. It was apparently a sizable sum. In addition to the loss of the ships, the company lost twelve good men.

Fortunately, I had taken the precautions of insuring the vessels and their cargoes, so the loss of the material goods did not matter too much, however, the loss of twelve good sailors, who bravely defended the company's property, was not something I took lightly. When my captains reported to me what had happened, I made a point of carefully remembering everything they said about the pirates and their ships. After they were gone, I drew up a carefully worded description of the culprits and had copies made, to be circulated to all of my captains, with instructions to fire first and make all effort to sink the offending vessels.

I was glad that the company had made it a policy, right from the beginning, because of my experience with piracy, to train all persons running our ships, in the art of combat with assorted weapons, including practice in firing cannons, and maneuvering ships for battle. After the attack, training was stepped up, and armaments improved on all ships plying the Florida trade route.

In 1810, I received word that my ships, a convoy of ten, had managed to surprise some pirates, as my ships were heading south for Havana. Three pirate ships were sunk, and the others severely damaged. It was a good feeling to know that our company policy was beginning to pay off. I was certain that word would get around to any other pirates in the area; my company ships were not to be trifled with.

June 10th, 1810 saw Christopher marry a lovely young woman, the daughter of Jose Ramon Becerra y de Garate. As with the other family weddings; this too was a major social event.

Juliette began ailing in 1814. For some strange reason her breathing became labored. A few days later, she began to cough up blood. Of course, I spared no expense for the best doctors, but there seemed little they could do. By December of that year, she was totally bed ridden. I spent many hours by Juliette's bedside, reading to her from her favorite books; Don Quixote, Robinson Crusoe, and the Adventures of Gulliver in Lilliputt, by that wonderful story teller, Jonathan Swift.

My sweet angel from Orléons passed away on a Thursday morning, May 11th, 1815. She was forty one years of age. We buried her on the grounds of the mansion, near her father's grave, overlooking the harbour, a place she also liked to sit and read.

Hugo and Nicole were devastated by the loss of their mother; as I was too. The three of us grieved together, for a long time; each day seeming an eternity without her. We missed her voice, her smile, her beautiful face, her gentle manner, her smell... For months I lost all interest in the company, leaving more and more up to Catherine, Christopher, and William.

Many days were spent, just idly sitting near her grave, looking out over our harbour, where my beautiful yacht lay anchored. I would quite often fall asleep there, on a warm afternoon, waking up thinking Juliette was in my arms. When I found she was not there, my eye filled with tears. Losing her was one of the greatest tragedies of my life. I mourned her loss for years, afterwards, not many days going by when I did not think of her, and wish she was still with me.

Eventually, like all the events of a person's life, my grief passed, as my children and I began to focus, ever more on the good fortune we had, to have experienced Juliette Cocteau in our lives. When Hugo and Nicole felt better, they began to take an active part in the family business, ably assisting their older brothers and sister, leaving me with more free time to work on this book.

Unfortunately, all of that happy bliss came to an end in 1819, two months before my 70 th birthday, a story I shall relate to you, dear reader, in the following chapter.

Chapter Thirty-One

In the year 1817, two years after Juliette's passing, I had become attracted to a very fine woman by the name of, Pauliana Salvatore, a tall, fiery Italian, with a beautiful black mass of hair, which reached to the small of her back. Thinking of her now, that I write these words, imagining her splendid appearance, brings me great happiness, as my three wives did also. I was always very grateful for the women in my life, who were all very beautiful, which was certainly reflected in my children and grand children, of which I had seven, by then.

Pauliana accompanied me on my last voyage to Halifax. It was in May of the year mentioned. I decided to finally make a return to Halifax, in order to retrieve the treasure I had buried there, 34 years earlier, with Virginia at my side. I hoped the chest was still there in the ground, and not under some construction, such as a farm building, or perhaps tree roots. Maybe the road was altered? I had no way of knowing what I would find upon my return.

Our yacht, *Golden Prosperity*, was outfitted with a special deck chair, in which I could put my leg up and relax on deck. The crew was specially handpicked for friendliness, intelligence, loyalty, skill, and strength. My mates, Johanus and Pedro served as my officers.

Golden Prosperity was a beautiful, American style frigate, of 110 feet length and 450 ton capacity. She was light weight and fast, beautifully finished in exotic woods, highly polished, reflecting the shiny brass fittings. The deck planks were of teak. Because it was our company yacht, the interior was fitted with ten roomy cabins, and comfortable quarters for the crew. Our galley was first class, and our meals fit for the kings and queens we were. Never believing in the separation of sailors from officers, we all ate together, when possible, usually in two sittings. Our sailors were happy, healthy men, with whom I never had an issue regarding discipline.

En route from San Juan, we stopped at our island resort, and visited there for two weeks, relaxing by the sea. My joints ached by this time, and the sun and relaxation did me much good.

Our resort had become a popular destination. We had acquired half a dozen yawls, which were used to transport guests to the other little islands, where they could 'really get away' for a few days, pretending to be marooned. Of course, the resort set it up, in such a way, that the guests would find provisions on the shore, like flotsam, including the beverages of their choice. The five islands we employed for the fantasy vacations, had pleasant little cabins, hidden in amongst the trees. Every island was equipped with a hogshead of fresh water, which was replenished, as required.

When the winds allowed, we continued our voyage, reaching Virgineola on June 5th. By then Virgineola had become known as, Bermuda, and was a proper English colony. However, it did not matter to me what they called the island, it would always be Virgineola, to me; memories of Virginia flooding my heart, as we approached the harbour.

We visited the British colony for a very pleasant three weeks, the guests of the former governor, Sir James Cockburn and his wife, Laura, two fine English people, with whom I had many refined conversations, concerning a multiplicity of topics.

During our stay in Bermuda, I showed Pauliana where Virginia and I had buried a treasure. I explained how it was the treasure, which enabled Monsieur Cocteau and I, to build our business, enabling us both, to become exceedingly wealthy. I further explained to Pauliana, that the treasure in Halifax, if it was still there, contained as much, if not more than the Bermuda chest. I couldn't remember exactly, at the time, there having been an interval of 34 years. However, as I described the treasure, as best I could remember it, I grew excited to find it, there being some very interesting items of jewelry, which I knew would look good on my Italian lady.

Bermuda was becoming populated, it having grown to be a well supported colony of Great Britain. Hence, the island was over run with English people. Fortunately, over the years, my attitudes, regarding the English, had softened. In fact, I found them to be a friendly, fair minded people, so that my stay amongst them was pleasantly spent, drinking tea, and watching cricket with the new governor, William Smith.

When the winds favored the furtherance of our voyage north, we said good bye to our hosts, James and Laura, and set sail for Halifax, re-victualed and watered, on July the first.

The passage from Bermuda to Halifax became a bit of an issue for Pauliana, due to the weather growing inclement and tossing us about in ten foot seas, for three days. When the storm passed, my friend recovered her normal fire and vigor. Judging from the way she made love to me, two nights after the storm, I knew she had fully regained her strength, as she happily wore me out. I slept with a big grin on my face, I am sure.

Sable Island came into view, late in the afternoon of July the eighth. The little island appeared out of the mist, off the starboard bow, approximately four leagues distant.

Halifax was not much further away.

As I stood on deck, balancing with my sturdy crutch, I was growing increasingly excited to visit the bustling city and find my treasure.

Unfortunately, the winds did not favour a direct entrance into Halifax harbour, requiring us to stand off the coast for 37 hours; me growing increasingly impatient to step ashore. We were able to tack into port on Tuesday, July 13th, 1819; lucky to find a suitable anchorage alongside a merchant ship from Bremen. Unfortunately, none of us spoke German, hence we did not have much contact with our neighbors.

As soon as the yacht was secure, we put out the yawl and went ashore, not suspecting that there was any reason to be concerned. Alas, I was to find out differently within a short while after my arrival.

The city of Halifax had grown immensely, in the time that I had been away. Her increased commercial importance was reflected in the incredible number of ships in the harbour. It occurred to me, Cocteau &

Mann should consider establishing a trading office in the bustling city. A trading office in Halifax, and one in Boston, I reasoned, would help open up our trade into the north, and to England. The treasure, which hopefully was still available to me, would be more than enough to purchase the necessary buildings, and hire the appropriate people. Possibly there was even enough treasure to purchase a merchant ship, or two. I just had no idea.

Pauliana and I took up lodgings in a very comfortable new hotel, choosing rooms overlooking the harbour. We made certain to test the bed, with a pleasant interlude, before having a superb luncheon at a table outside. Our time in Halifax quickly became a very pleasant, romantic, get away.

The next morning, we woke up to a glorious sun rise, heralding a magnificent summer day; the perfect day to go treasure hunting. Hence, to that end, we hired a private carriage, with a gentle horse; and with a picnic lunch packed, Pauliana and I set off to find the road, first of all, and then the bend, where the oak stood guard over the flat slab of stone. I had taken the precaution of securing a prying bar from the hotel keeper, to facilitate the removal of said slab.

It took me a while to remember how to get to the road leading out of town, so much having changed, and my memories being weakened by my advancing years, they being 69, then. Eventually, we found the road and twenty minutes later, were stopped at the bend, which was still there, the road not having changed much. The only real difference was, the city had crept out on the road, somewhat further. Where we were stopped, however, was still rural, and essentially uninhabited, except for a new farm, which had developed across the road, in the opposite direction from the treasure box.

When traffic had passed, and we were once more alone, Pauliana, expertly guided the horse across the road and onto the land, towards the oak tree, which was still standing there, patiently guarding its patch of ground, and hopefully, my treasure chest. I directed Pauliana where to stop the carriage, our horse, quite content to stand there, since the grass was plentiful and obviously delicious. Pauliana helped me out of the carriage and I hobbled to where the stone still lay, serenely covering the treasure, I hoped.

My heart nearly sank, when we pried the stone aside, as I didn't see a chest, at first. Fortunately, it was only the darkness and my eye's inability to adjust to the light change. As my eye finally adjusted itself, to my great relief, the treasure box sat there smiling at me.

Within another minute, the chest was sitting on the ground beside us. I pointed to the tree and told Pauliana where to find the key.

My beautiful Italian lady promptly retrieved the key, it still being, exactly, where Catherine and I placed it, all those years before. I let Pauliana unlock something, she had never seen before; a pirate's treasure!

And what a treasure it was! It was everything I had remembered, and more; easily surpassing Bill's treasure by half, at least. And, yes, it did contain the silver jewelry I wanted for my Roman princess; a silver chain from which a magnificent ruby pendant hung, surrounded by diamonds. There were matching ear rings, making an altogether exquisite ensemble, which looked sensational on Pauliana.

Her gratitude was generous and warm, as we made love, right there in the field, behind the oak tree, not bothering about the traffic we could hear crunching on the road, on the other side of the willows and shrubbery.

The air was warm, enabling us to lie there, for several hours, basking in each other's arms, dozing in the sun, and loving life. It was an altogether delicious experience, which warmed my old bones, and made me feel like a young man again.

I have no idea how long we stayed there, in that field, the treasure box beside us, coins glinting in the sun. However, I do know we arrived back in Halifax, deeper in love, and even more fabulously wealthy. We retired early to our hotel room, with a bottle of fine French champagne, and more joyous love making, in that wonderful bed.

Around midnight, a loud knocking on the door interrupted a perfectly timed orgasm, which did not amuse Pauliana, nor me. I dismounted; my monster still quite firm and wondering what had happened. Donning my sleeping robe, I walked out of the bedroom and through the parlor, to the front door, and demanded to know who was disturbing my rest.

'We have reason to believe that Peter Mann resides in this room,' said an obnoxious voice. 'We have a warrant for his arrest.'

The words hit me like a ton of bricks. A warrant for my arrest? After all those years?

The man banged again.

I rushed back to the bedroom and retrieved my pistol.

Pauliana looked at me with a concerned expression and asked me what we should do.

I advised her to get dressed, as I quickly did the same.

Meanwhile the banging on the door continued.

'Open this door, in the name of the King!' shouted the voice.

I took my time dressing, not wanting to appear other than a worthy gentleman trader, such as I was; my piracy days being long behind me. It never occurred to me the Royal Thugs would break down the door of a hotel room.

I was mistaken, because the door came crashing in, four burly soldiers, suddenly standing in our parlour, followed by a tall, slim man, totally dressed in black; a long, black leather coat, reaching to his ankles. He wore two pistols in his belt. The man's countenance was a face I will always remember; it being a cold, cruel face, with piercing blue eyes, and a smirk on its lips.

The soldiers stood respectfully aside, as the man stepped into the room and unfolded a piece of paper. He read, in an insulting tone of voice, 'Wanted for crimes against the British Crown, Peter Mann, a pirate. Reward offered by His Majesty, King George III, King of England and Ireland, King of Hanover, Duke of Cornwall etcetera, etcetera, the sum of ten thousand pounds sterling, Dead or Alive.'

The man looked up from the paper and glared at the pistol in my hand. He smiled, as he spoke in American English, 'What are you planning to do with that? Shoot the five of us?' The man laughed and signaled to the soldiers. 'Arrest him,' he hissed.

'No, no!,' shouted Pauliana, rushing at the soldiers.

'I would advise, you madam,' said the man coldly, 'Not to interfere, or you may end up in gaol with him.'

Pauliana stared at the man and put her hands on her hips, as she regarded him defiantly. 'Eet would be bedder, I go to a gaol wid a heem, den stay ere alone widout heem.'

The man and soldiers laughed.

'You will be in separate quarters, believe me madam,' sneered the man. 'Your husband won't have access to you.'

Then the man said something so rude, I had no choice but to react. 'Your husband won't have access to you, but we will,' he said, a lascivious grin on his reptilian countenance.

I reacted by shooting my pistol, but in the heat of the moment, I was not able to aim it very well, hitting a soldier, who was standing behind the man. I think I unwittingly killed him, intending the ball for the man in black.

The next thing that happened was, a scuffle broke out, as I lunged at the man, attempting to slice his throat with my hook.

Unfortunately, the soldiers reacted before I could kill the man, smacking me squarely on the back with the stocks of their muskets.

I passed out, hearing Pauliana begging them not to hurt me.

* * *

I woke up in the Halifax jail.

As I regained my senses, I looked around myself and noted the irony of my imprisonment. I was lying in the very same cell in which William Bartleby had been kept, fifty years earlier. It was a strange feeling for me, so long accustomed to luxury and splendor, to wake up in that filthy hole, even more disgusting than it was when Bill lay there, while I interviewed him from the other side of the bars.

Thinking about that Halifax cell, in which I was kept for nearly a year, I can't say whether it was better or worse than the cell in the Bastille, they being equally wretched, in my opinion; places I highly recommend, you avoid, dear reader.

Anyway, when I awoke, the cell block was empty, but for me. My head and back ached with tremendous pain, leading me to suspect, right away, that two of my ribs were cracked.

I called for help, but no one came.

In fact, no one came, until two days later, when I was hungry and parched from not having been given food or water. Imagine that, dear reader. There I was, an old man of sixty nine years, being subjected to such abuse from younger men. It was a tragic reminder that nothing was sacred anymore. A man's age did not warrant respect, in those hard times.

In a fog I heard the door open at the far end of the cell block. Moments later, voices entered the space. I recognized one of them as that of my sweet Venus, come to save me, I hoped.

Pauliana had tears in her beautiful eyes, as she looked at me, lying wretchedly in that filthy cell. 'Oooh my darleeng,' she cried, 'What haf a dey done to you?'

I moaned that my ribs were broken, and that I needed help.

Pauliana turned to the man, who had accompanied her, and demanded a doctor be sent, to look at me.

The man smiled and assured Pauliana a doctor would be sent for.

Then, my dear Italian friend introduced the man, as the superintendent of the jail, Captain McTeer

'He can not stay in zat cell,' said Pauliana forcefully. 'He must haf a bedder accommodations,' she said. 'He must zee a doctor. We weel a pay for zem, eef necessary.'

The superintendent smiled greedily, as he rubbed his hands together, well aware of my wealth and standing. 'We can provide better accommodations,' he said, with his oily voice. 'We will have him moved this afternoon,' he assured her.

'And he must haf fresh water and goode food,' she further demanded, a little gentler.

The superintendent assured Pauliana that everything would be, as she demanded, as soon as the room was made ready, in the upper levels of the prison, near the administration offices.

Pauliana gave the man a gold coin, for which he thanked her, and again assured her that all would be as she asked. The man left the cell block, leaving my Pauliana alone with me.

I groaned, as I gradually pulled my self up, and slowly raised myself to hobble to the bars, to touch my friend's hands.

We kissed and tried to touch foreheads together, however the bars did not allow for much contact. Better facilities were definitely worth paying for, I told her.

Then I told Pauliana that she had to get me out of the jail, at the first opportunity, it being no place for the patriarch of Cocteau & Mann. I told Pauliana to hire advocates and barristers, to plead my case, as soon as possible, since I did not want to spend another winter in a prison, the Bastille having soured me on that experience.

Pauliana agreed that she would do what she could.

She left me an hour later, and apparently, attempted to return with baskets of food and bottles of water and wine, but was refused entrance to the jail and told to come back the next day. Fortunately, she was smart enough to realize not to leave the food with the guards. Pauliana was not born yesterday, either.

The following morning, I was painfully escorted by two guards to a very nice suite of rooms, down the hall from the administration centre. The rooms were well appointed, if a bit shabby, with worn furniture, and a lumpy bed. However, there was a small library of some interesting material, including a copy of, *Harris's List of Covent Garden Ladies*, However, before I had an opportunity to peruse the spicy material, much more spicy material arrived, in the person of my fine Italian friend, Pauliana, coming to bring me hampers of food and good drink, over which we could discuss plans to get me out of jail.

My sweet friend stayed with me for the entire day, bandaging my rib cage, which ached like hell. She stayed until visiting hours were over and she was told to leave by one of the guards, who had been standing outside the doors of the suite.

After a long kiss and hug, Pauliana returned to the hotel, and I was returned to the dungeon; a cruel trick, for which I did not forgive the superintendent, who came to tell me personally, the next morning, that if I wanted to continue using the suite, to entertain Pauliana, I had better not say anything about sleeping in the dungeon, or the suite would stop and her visits forbidden.

I had no choice but to agree to the ruse, as Pauliana paid handsomely from the treasure, in order to keep me in the suite, so she thought.

The barrister and solicitor, who came to see me, five days after my incarceration, were two gentlemen, supposedly learned in the law, who, because of their immense learning, were also digging into my treasure with both hands, in order to prepare my defense against the Crown; which as you well know, dear reader, could spare all expenses to prosecute me, and see me hanged.

The charges, which were brought against me, were no surprise, except for the fact, it was so many years later. I had no idea old King George had such a long memory. He still had me on charges, for helping Bill escape. He also had me up on charges for the piracy of seventeen English ships, only thirteen of which I was involved with. Where the other four ships came from, I had no idea. There were other pirates in the world besides, Bill and I. Of course, I pleaded ignorance, because I couldn't remember the names of the ships; there were so many, over the years, so long ago. I could tell that the defense was going to be expensive and the process drawn out.

Meanwhile, every day I was brought up to the suite, but never allowed to bathe, hence, at a certain point, two or three weeks after my imprisonment, Pauliana asked me why I was becoming so odiferous, given there was a tub in the bed room. It is then when I whispered to her, what actually was going on.

When Pauliana heard what the superintendent was doing, I had to cup my hand over her mouth, to keep her from alerting the guards, so vociferous was her anger. If the superintendent had been in the room, I am sure she would have attacked him, and torn him to pieces. She vowed, at that point, that we would take matters more into our own hands. 'Leaf it to a me Peeter,' she said, 'I haf a plan. Don't a you worry. I weel get a you out of here.'

Pauliana was so sincere I had no choice but to believe her. If she said, she was going to get me out, I was beginning to look forward to my freedom, however, it meant that Pauliana had to go back to San Juan, and would not return for some months. We had to hope that the lawyers would be able to keep me alive, in the meantime. Considering the amount we were paying them, they should have been able to keep Lazarus alive, indefinitely, I figured.

My fine black haired friend left Halifax on September 20th, 1819. It was a sad day, because it heralded the end of my suite days. The real ordeal began in the Halifax jail, that winter, which was much colder than the winters in Paris, and not a time, during which Pauliana could sail back from San Juan, the northern Atlantic not at all friendly to the sons of Neptune in winter.

Hence, I froze, and starved, not even cock roaches coming out, on the coldest days.

The first snow fell in the middle of October and never stopped for days, some of it filtering down, through the window hole.

At the end of October there was a thaw, which saw water trickling down the wall, which would freeze at night.

By November, the winter had come to stay, clamping his cold fingers on Halifax, and pissing pure ice down my back, which my threadbare blanket did little to assuage.

When my seventieth birthday came and went, I had a massive cold; my nose running constantly, as my body shivered like ship's timbers in a storm. When I complained to my lawyers, they told me to be patient. They were doing the best they could.

The cold affected my severed limbs, tremendously, as well as my broken ribs, which made sleeping painful on the hard wooden cot. However, no matter how often I complained to my lawyers, they always told me the same thing and nothing changed.

When spring finally arrived, I rapidly put on weight, as the insect population increased in my cell. It actually occurred to me, as I began supplementing the swill, which the jail pretended was food, with assorted insects; the insects of Halifax actually tasted better than the insects in Paris. I reasoned that it was because Halifax was by the ocean and the air was cleaner. The insects of Halifax were not so clogged up with city filth. I remember a type of beetle, which tasted particularly good, but those beetles were rare visitors, the smells of the cell probably scared them away.

Spring brought vaporous humors, giving me grief in my lungs, causing me to further hurt my damaged rib cage, as I coughed and coughed up copious quantities of slimy fluid. By the time June rolled around, I was beginning to fear for my life; not because of hanging, but because of my ill health, due to my wretched confinement in that dark, dank place.

Sometime in the first week of June, I received word, from one of my guards, that there was trouble brewing in the harbour. Apparently, thirty well armed ships, flying the colors of the Spanish island of Puerto Rico, and company pennants belonging to Cocteau & Mann, were anchored at the entrance to the harbour, effectively blockading all shipping.

Apparently, one Danish ship tried to go past the blockade and was severely damaged by cannon fire. According to the guard, the ship had to return to port.

The news was music to my ears.

Three days later, the superintendent came into the cell block and stormed down the hall, confronting me with the news regarding the blockade, and an apparent demand for my release.

'I will release you over my dead body!' shouted the superintendent, angrily. The sudden rise in blood pressure caused Captain McTeer's face to become quite purple. 'You are one of the most notorious pirates of this century! You will not go free, you will hang, most assuredly, as soon as those damn lawyers are finished tying up the proceedings!' When he was done yelling at me, he stormed out of the cell block, leaving me to ponder my upcoming release.

A few days later, the captain came to see me again, and demanded that I sign a paper, ordering my ships to stop the blockade. Of course, I refused to sign the paper and the superintendent threatened me with torture, if I did not sign.

As I thought of his threat for a moment, I realized there was no way he could hurt me worse than I had already suffered at his hands, rotting in that filthy cell. Hence, I told him to go and take a flying leap off the ramparts, which did not sit well with the superintendent. His response was to have me flogged thirty strokes, in the courtyard of the jail.

Now, dear reader, lest you think I was some sort of super man, let me assure you, there were far worse punishments inflicted on hapless prisoners than thirty strokes. However, I was seventy years old, my body not being too overly endowed with flesh, due to my meagre diet, plus, being old, my body had begun to shrink, somewhat. The pain I endured was unbelievable, and nearly killed me. It was the reason the superintendent became the ex superintendent, some weeks later, about which I will tell you, presently.

I lingered near death for several more weeks, as the results of the blockade were beginning to be felt in Halifax. Eventually, the civic authorities began to waver in their resolve, to keep me until the trial.

By the middle of July, the city had enough of the blockade, and attempted to send out several armed navy ships, to do battle with my company ships. The navy probably thought, that armed navy ships would be able to overcome the challenge from a mercantile enterprise, which they mistakenly believed to be merely, 'a sheep in wolf's clothing.'

It was an unfortunate mistake on the part of the British navy officers, because they returned to port, thoroughly humiliated, their main masts lying by the boards of both ships and their hulls full of holes. They did not realize that our company sailors were trained in combat tactics and maneuverings. It was a costly error for the navy and the city of Halifax.

During July, Captain McTeer tried to get me to sign the paper, several more times. He reasoned that, since a flogging did not break my will, other, more extreme measures were necessary. However, what ever he did to me, none of it worked, because I knew help was on the way, and I would be free very soon. I prayed that my body would hold out long enough, before the superintendent killed me with his attempts to force my signature.

On the eighth day of August, the city had enough of the blockade and demanded that I be set free, in order to meet the company's demands.

Thus, sometime in the middle of the afternoon, of the ninth of August, I was roughly pulled from my cot by two guards, and dragged up the stairs to the courtyard, where they dumped me, like a sack of potatoes, on the ground, in front of Pauliana, Johanus, and Pedro, plus twenty armed sailors, and several city dignitaries, including the mayor.

The moment Pauliana saw me, tears streamed down her cheeks, as she saw what condition I was in. Her vociferous complaints filled the courtyard, as she berated the superintendent in a most eloquent fashion, filled with colorful expletives. She threatened the captain with dire legal actions, which I could tell, the superintendent merely scoffed at, thinking us powerless, with regard to the legal system there.

Captain McTeer was sorely mistaken, because we paid handsomely for his dismissal, and reduction in rank to that of corporal; a severe drop in his pay and status; which he would never rise above, we made certain of that.

The process to effect a deal with the military, and the city officials took several weeks, during which I convalesced on board my yacht, rapidly regaining weight, as my cook fed me every delicious meal he could think of, and Pauliana nursed me back to health.

In September we returned to San Juan, where I resumed my role as patriarch of a fine family and director of a massive commercial enterprise. By the time my 71st birthday arrived, I was back to my full vigor, only occasionally bothered with pains in my ribs.

As the years passed, I became less and less interested in running the business, leaving it all up to my children; Catherine, Christopher, William, Nicole and Hugo, by then also involved in managerial capacities, according to their strengths and interests. By the time we held our annual company picnic, on the grounds of the mansion in 1825, we owned one hundred and thirty assorted vessels, and twenty six trading offices throughout the region. Nicole and Hugo had become very interested in resort development, and due to their natural cleverness and business sense, they developed two more island retreats, one in Trinidad, and the other in St. Martinique, both of which generated significant profits right from the day they opened to receive guests.

Pauliana died the following year, in May; May the tenth, to be exact. My fiery Italian treasure breathed her last at one o'clock in the afternoon; having succumbed to yellow fever. It was a very sad loss for me. I would be alone in bed for the rest of my days, afterwards, not really having time available for romance, anyway. I was too busy getting my book in order, and organizing notes for others I planned to write during my retirement.

In 1830, I celebrated my 80th birthday, with a huge party attended by most of San Juan and my company's employees, who were able to attend. The celebration lasted a week, during which I gave away presents to all who attended; a silver medallion, with my face in relief, and my dates, and on the other side, a beautiful relief of a sailing ship, flying the company pennant and the flag of Puerto Rico, on a sea of money.

My health began to decline in 1832, and gradually, day by day, I began to feel weaker and weaker. Of course, I knew it was old age, and did the best I could, to make certain I continued to eat well, but the desire for food diminished, and I spent more and more time, just lying about in my easy chair, thinking about the past and, when my grandchildren came to visit, telling them stories of my days as a pirate; 'The Scourge of the West Indies'.

I became bedridden in 1833, essentially remaining there from then on; often visited by my children and many grandchildren, who by then numbered 14; a continual blessing for me, making the process of leaving this world, a pleasant one, surrounded by my family and friends.

As I lay in my comfortable bed, I often thought about my past and what my future would bring. I was not afraid to die, and knew that I had done the Lord's work, ridding the world of some really bad people. I did not think I would be judged too harshly and slept contentedly at night; not plagued with nightmares, or visions of damnation. I believe I slept with a smile on my face.

Chapter Thirty-Two
Epilogue

Peter Mann, the Morning Post reporter, turned pirate, became the respected patriarch of Cocteau & Mann, an international company, with offices in 30 nations, died peacefully in his sleep on January 1st, 1836, having reached his 85th year.

Peter was buried in San Juan Cathedral, after a Requiem Mass attended by many dignitaries, from all the countries of the Caribbean, and of course, every company employee, and his loving children and grandchildren, who continued to speak of their father and grandfather, for many years afterwards.

The epitaph over his grave was inscribed in bronze letters,

> Peter Mann was a titan amongst men.
> He is missed by all who knew him.
> 'The Scourge of the West Indies'
> The quintessential pirate.
> A
> man's man.

The End

Bibliography

Botting, Douglas, The Pirates, Time Life Books, Alexandria, Virginia, 1978

Cordingly, David, ed., Pirates, Terror on the High Seas From the Caribbean to the South China Sea, JG Press, Inc., North Dighton, MA, 1998

Cordingly, David, Women Sailors & Sailors' Women, an Untold Maritime History, Random House, N.Y. 2001

Crystal, David, The Cambridge Biographical Encyclopedia, Cambridge University Press, 1995

Grunn, Bernard, The Timetables of History, Simon & Schuster, N.Y. 1991

Gruppe, Henry E., The Frigates, Time Life Books, Alexandria, Virginia,1979

Lenman, Bruce P. ed., Dictionary of World History, Chambers Harrap, N.Y., 2000

Spavens, William, Memoirs of a Seafaring Life, Folio Books, London, first published in 1796

Williams, Glyndwr, Captain Cook's Voyages, 1768-1779, The Folio Society, London, 1997

The World Wide Web

Some selected sites:

Haiti Archives: www.hartford-hwp.com

Mark Rosenstein's Sailing Page: www.apparent-wind.com

Monthly Calendar and Phases of the Moon:

http://einstein.stcloudstate.edu/Dome/moonPhases.html

The Kings & Queens of England: www.frhes.freeserve.co.uk

RIPPLES IN OUR LIVES

by Nancy and David Brundage

David Brundage experiences three near-death experiences and out-of-body experiences while in the hospital! During the first surgery, his heart stops as soon as the incision is made in his abdomen. The second surgery is done after the doctors check his heart out, which completes the original surgery. The third is after he gets an infection and eviscerates, requiring emergency surgery and a colostomy bag. And the fourth is to reverse the colostomy.

David develops "ripples" in his fingernails after each near-death experience. While the ripples are present in his fingernails, he has a connection to the spirit world and the paranormal. Take a walk in David's shoes as he sees spirit guides, angels, ghosts, dark shadows and entities. Read about the physical and emotional horror he and his family go through while experiencing surgeries, infections, hallucinations, depressions and so much more.

Paperback, 247 pages
6" x 9"
ISBN 1-4137-5683-2

About the author:

David and Nancy Brundage have been married for over twenty-four years. They have three adult children, Susie Angel, John Angel, and Jacqueline Brundage. Over the years, they faced many challenges, but this one brought the family closer to together. They live in Austin, Texas. Please visit our website at www.ripplesinourlives.com.

THE PAPER CANVAS
A BOOK OF POEMS

by Bret Anderson

The Paper Canvas is a book of poems that discusses prospects of influencing positive change for the world. Among these written works are the proposition of global nuclear disarmament and poetic statements of activism, love and peace.

Paperback, 59 pages
6" x 9"
ISBN 1-60474-471-5

About the author:

Born in 1984 in San Diego, California, Bret B. Anderson is a member of the Soka Gakkai International, and is dedicated to the philosophy of Nichiren Daishonin's Buddhism.

011909c